G000153548

JORDAN ORLANDO was born in 1966. He attended the Dalton School and the University of Chicago. He lives in New York City.

the object lesson

JORDAN ORLANDO

A TOUCHSTONE BOOK
Published by Simon & Schuster
New York London Toronto Sydney Tokyo Singapore

First published in Great Britain by Simon & Schuster Ltd, 1993
First published in Great Britain by Touchstone, 1994
An imprint of Simon & Schuster Ltd
A Paramount Communications Company

Simon & Schuster Ltd
West Garden Place
Kendal Street
London W2 2AQ

Simon & Schuster of Australia Pty Ltd
Sydney

A CIP catalogue record for this book is available from the British Library

ISBN 0-671-71848-7

This book is a work of fiction. Names, characters, places and incidents are either products of the author's imagination or are used fictitiously.
Any resemblance to actual events or locales or persons, living or dead, is entirely coincidental.

Printed and bound in Great Britain by
HarperCollins*Manufacturing*, Glasgow

the author wishes to express his gratitude to

Eadie Adamson / Wayne Adamson / Robert Asahina
Julia Hodges Bovey / Gordon Miller Buehrig / William M. Dince Ph.D.
Melinda Eades / David Feige / Andrew Gottlieb / Paul Gottlieb
Tom Huber / Paul Lerner / Dan Lissit / John McMillan
Katie McMillan / Jed Miller / Arthur Morin / Josh Olesker
Eleanor Orlando / Logan Orlando / Miriam Rabkin / Emily Rapp
Jonathan Rapp / Tom Rapp / Jonathan Rose / Barbara Schiller
Hillel Schiller / Hellyn Sher / Charles Simon / Louis J. Slovinsky
Lauren Tillinghast / David Trubatch / Janett Trubatch
Sam Turich / Kay Voss / Hamza Walker / Eric Warshaw
Alexander Keats Weinstein / Kimberly Witherspoon
Lars Wulf / Laura Yorke

For My Mother and Father

An index of the object's preponderance is the impotence of the mind—in all its judgements as well as, to this day, in the organization of reality. The negative fact that the mind, failing in identification, has also failed in reconcilement, that its supremacy has miscarried, becomes the motor of its disenchantment.

THEODOR ADORNO

book I

chapter 1

I remember the night that Nick Blanchard called me for the first time in five years and we went to the hospital. Right around then the young collegiate woman who had been working as a summer intern put in her last day and returned to New England and I realized that for her, years began and ended at odd times and were barely recognizable as years—I had sat across the newsroom talking on the phone to a city commissioner while she cleared out her desk, and as she came across a paper hat from the Fourth of July the time that had passed was visible, like the shadow that follows a searchlight. She said goodbye to me along with the others, giving me a casual handshake, and I got the message, reminded of what I'd almost done, so when the phone rang that night, just as I arrived home, I answered quickly, hoping it was her, but it was Nick, amazed at having reached me.

"I'm still here," I said. "It's been a long time, Nick."

"Listen," said the quiet, sandy voice I remembered well. "We've got a disaster here— Are you all right, buddy? You sound terrible."

"I just came in the door," I said, winded by the walk and by the narrow flights of stairs. "What do you mean, a disaster?"

"I mean an accident," said Nick. "You remember Douglas Taft? This neighbor of his called me right after he'd been picked up by the, you know, the ambulance, and she says they're—that the guy said—they're on their way to St. Mark's Hospital, you know, East Sixty-eighth, so I'm heading up there."

"I don't understand," I said, catching my breath, dropping the mail to the floor—I heard Manhattan traffic beyond Nick's voice as

I groped for a lamp, irritated at being disturbed, flattered that he had called. "Did she say what happened?"

"She doesn't— Mike, this is some hysterical woman, she's barely talking, she's saying there's blood everywhere and he's barely alive— I've been wasting time calling everyone and nobody's home. Look, are you going to meet me? I mean otherwise, you know, I'll explain later."

"Jesus Christ," I said. "Is he all—"

"I don't know," Nick interrupted. "I tried the emergency room and they haven't arrived yet, so— Look, you'd better take a cab if you've got the money. I'm leaving now—you can meet me outside and we'll go in together."

"But what happened to him?" I asked, reaching into the closet—I had a battered brown corduroy jacket that I'd worn in the evenings all through the summer, and I wore it for the last time that night.

"I don't *know,* damn it," said Nick. "Something violent. Michael, just get up there."

By the time I left the subway and emerged onto a dim Manhattan street corner it was seven-thirty and the air was washed in traces of grey but storefronts were glowing all around and the streets shone with reflections of headlights. The dark limestone walls of the hospital's Gothic façade were punctured by grimed windows bunkered shut with their backlit curtains drawn, the sawtooth battlements scissoring the sky, the cement ramps up to the gates of the emergency room blazing with halogen floodlamps, and Nick stood backlit in his overcoat near a stationary ambulance, occupying the ramp area as if it were a theatrical stage, wearing sunglasses and khaki pants and a black overcoat, his camera as always slung under his arm, drinking a bottle of beer. He was characteristically unshaven and his face had the geometry that I remembered well, but as he turned toward me with a relieved, resigned smile, I could see the effects of the passing years, the way his hair had thinned and receded, the ways in which the lines on his face had, as far as I could tell, become more pronounced. I put out my hand but Nick came forward and hugged me, his camera swinging painfully into my ribs, and before I could react I was hugging him back and there was a moment where I was looking across the back of his head at the shining surface of the ambulance—I remember this clearly—before we released each other.

"Nick, you bum," I said, out of breath.

"Michael," said Nick. "I don't believe it."

"Waiting long?"

"Just got here. He's not— I've been inside," Nick said dazedly, pointing over his shoulder as he lit a cigarette. "I asked at the, you know, the guy at the desk, and he told me to talk to the, um, some damn nurse in there, but"—Nick put the beer bottle down on the oil-stained cement, swaying toward the darkened doors—"but she's behind a curtain and the guard won't let me through. Let's go."

We walked down a wide, clean corridor and I heard blurred voices and metallic sounds, the voices mounting as we passed through wide metal barriers—the emergency room was cold and bright and saturated with the smells of alcohol, vomit, and coffee, broken by rows of dirty orange chairs and presided over by several hospital guards, and in the chairs, various people sat alone or in groups with their coats and hats on, ignoring the uniformed police officers whose belt radios blasted static and garbled voices. A middle-aged woman appeared to have fallen asleep, or passed out, with her tennis shoes removed, one alarmingly swollen and discolored foot splayed across an orange cushion that had been taken from the adjoining row of chairs, where two men dressed in brown uniforms like park rangers sat hunched over a single clipboard, using two pens to complete a printed form. As we entered, another door crashed open and a moaning Hispanic man on a steel stretcher covered by a white sheet stained with vomit was quickly wheeled through the room and pulled out through another door.

"I hate hospitals," Nick said, guiding us toward a glassed-in alcove with a drawn white curtain, where a woman with a white plastic badge identifying her as A. BALDWIN R. N. stood poring over a sheaf of papers. I could see Nick clearly as he leaned to get the nurse's attention and I noticed that he still looked older than me, his stylish appearance out of place against the hospital walls—I kept waiting for him to take off his sunglasses but he left them on almost that entire night. "Excuse me—you're the lookout?"

"I'm the triage nurse," Baldwin said, pointing at Nick's cigarette—she had flat dark hair and large glasses and looked to be in her twenties. "You'll have to put that out, sir."

"Sorry," said Nick, nodding, dropping the cigarette on the linoleum and stepping it out. "I'm looking for Douglas Taft," he said, gesturing with his hands. "Little white guy, your age— An ambulance just—"

"Douglas *Taft*," Baldwin said, squinting at her forms. "Nobody knew his last name."

"You saw him?" Nick asked, chin darting forward. "Is he— Is he all right?"

"I have no idea," Baldwin said, looking past us as if caged. "Dr. McCord took charge of him right after I completed the initial classification—I'm just waiting for the EMS report and then I'm done with him. Are you family?"

"We're friends," I said, stepping forward. "I'm sorry—what does that mean, 'initial classification?' "

"It's a trauma case," said Baldwin impatiently, "so he's classed as 'emergent'— It's just a categorical determination for emergency room patients. If you'll have a seat, I'm sure that any—"

"Excuse me," said an accented voice behind us, making me jump. The park rangers had walked over and the taller one—Martinez, according to his plastic name card—was holding out the clipboard. "Here's the form for that John Doe."

"Thank you," Baldwin said brightly, reaching past Nick's shoulder and taking the clipboard. "These are his friends—his last name is Taft," she murmured, looking over the form and glancing at Nick and myself, compelling us to step out of the way. "You should have called in the vitals."

"We were busy with the on-the-spot stabilization," said Martinez. "Ringer's Lactate—it's all there."

"Good," said Baldwin, tapping the clipboard with her fingernails. "This is it? I can send it through with the entry form and you're finished?"

"Yeah," said Martinez, pointing with his thumb at the door. "Simple stab wound, Sturgis started the line"—he indicated the other paramedic—"and we brought him in. Look, there's another call—we're just waiting for the stretcher."

"Stab wound?" said Nick, looking at me and at Sturgis. "Stab wound? What happened to him?"

"We don't know," said Sturgis in a heavy Brooklyn accent. "We got the call, we show up, here's the kid lying in the, what, the vestibule, top of the stairs, this screaming woman in my face— Signs of a *struggle,* torn wallpaper, lock's broken on the door—"

"No it wasn't," said Martinez, confused.

"Broken lock," interrupted Sturgis, nodding emphatically. "You never notice anything— But heavy bleeding, the kid looks pretty shocky, she says it's been half an hour, so we brought him in."

"Okay, boys," said Baldwin, nodding at the clipboard.

"Here's the stretcher," said Martinez, pointing. "Let's shake a tail feather."

"Look, the two of you could do me a favor," Baldwin told us as the paramedics hurried away. "You're friends of his—do you know if he's covered by Blue Cross or Blue Shield?"

"He must have insurance, damn it," Nick said angrily. "I wish you'd just let us—"

"If you could find his wallet," Baldwin said quietly, pointing at a green plastic bag on the floor, "I could get his Social Security number for our records. That stuff should be with him anyway, if you could take it along."

I knelt on the cold floor and began hunting through the bag, which contained Douglas' clothes, damp and bloodstained and evidently torn off of him—on top was a white Brooks Brothers shirt on which the streaks of blood hadn't dried, and the bottom half of the shirt, where the paramedics had torn it open, was almost entirely scarlet. I swallowed and moved the slippery shirt aside, reaching deeper into the bag and finding a pair of hand-tailored grey trousers, similarly torn and wet. I patted the wet pockets of the trousers and then fished in the left front pocket for Douglas' wallet, shoving papers and a cigarette pack and other detritus aside—a clear plastic box containing a microcassette dropped onto the floor, and I absently put this in one of my jacket pockets—and stood up with the calfskin wallet, thumbing through the neatly arranged credit cards and the billfold, seeing an old Harvard student ID and eighty dollars in twenties. I handed Douglas' Social Security card to Nurse Baldwin and then stood there in a strange posture, arms out, wondering how to get the blood off my hands.

"Thank you," Baldwin said, handing me some towel paper while looking at the card. "I think you can go through," she said, pointing at the doorway where the guards were stationed—as she spoke, another stretcher was being wheeled into the room by two more paramedics, and I realized that we had already lost her attention.

Nick and I went through the guarded door into a darker area, where more patients on stretchers had been placed along the walls near curtained alcoves. The moment that I'd picked up the bag of bloody clothes I'd realized that there was something heavy in it, something long and hard made of metal hanging in the bottom of the bag, and I carried it carefully as we hurried toward one of the alcoves—Douglas was behind the half-shut curtain, smaller and paler than I remembered, stripped to his underwear and draped in a blood-soaked white sheet, convulsing violently, pinned down against a stretcher by a white-knuckled nurse and a large, black-bearded man wearing a white coat and a stethoscope. "No, no, leave me alone," Douglas was moaning, eyes tightly shut and watering, face flushed as his head thrashed back and forth, his pale body gleaming with sweat.

"He's going to shake the IV loose, Doctor," the nurse said, struggling with Douglas' thin bare trembling arms.

"I think we can spare him another shot," the man ordered another nurse, who began unwrapping a fresh syringe and swabbing a forked juncture in the shaking IV lead.

"Leave me *alone,*" Douglas cried out, bucking against the nurse's grip as his entire body arched like a mainsail, his face twisted in agony.

"Douglas, you're safe," the bearded man was yelling down at him. "Listen to my voice—you're in a hospital and you're safe."

"I'm falling," Douglas screamed as one of the nurses lost her grip on his sweat-greased arms and his hands fluttered up to his throat, wet cheeks flashing as he screamed again, a bolt of pain, wordless and pure.

"Damn it, hurry up," the bearded man was shouting at the nurse while managing to regain his grip on Douglas' wildly thrashing arms, their struggle having tossed the bloody sheet aside to reveal a large blood-soaked cotton bandage round Douglas' abdomen. "Listen to my voice," the bearded man said. "Listen to my voice."

"Oh, fuck, oh fuck, it hurts, it hurts," Douglas was panting. "Oh, fuck, I'm falling—" The nurse had managed to get the syringe into the IV lead and was carefully injecting a small amount of clear fluid into Douglas' blood.

"Douglas, can you hear me?" the bearded man intoned, bending over Douglas' shivering body, pulling the sheet back up and gesturing toward one of the nurses for a blanket. "I'm Dr. McCord. Can you tell me your name?"

"Douglas Taft," Douglas whispered, his panic-breathing having relaxed into a quiet panting. "Make it go away, make it go away," he whispered rhythmically, a penitent whisper, closing his eyes as Dr. McCord draped the green blanket over him.

"Can you tell me where you live?" McCord said more quietly, adjusting the blanket and stretching his cramped arms.

"No," Douglas whispered, tears rolling sideways off the corners of his eyes. "I go to Thorndike High School."

"We're his friends," Nick said, stepping forward, pointing at Douglas.

"Just a minute," the man snapped, glancing at us sharply and then turning back to the cot. "Douglas, I need some information from you."

"Yes," Douglas whispered, eyes still clenched shut, still breathing rapidly.

"I need your permission for surgery."

"What?" Douglas whispered sharply. "Oh, Jesus—"

"Shh," McCord said. "Don't be scared— To make the pain go away we need to perform a small operation."

"Okay," Douglas whispered, still breathing heavily.

"Good. Get ready to move him," McCord told the two nurses as he stood up and reached for another clipboard. "Douglas, I need you to answer some questions for the anesthesiologist— When did you last eat?"

"What?" Douglas had opened his brown eyes and was squinting vaguely at McCord.

"Do you remember when you last ate?"

"Um—" Douglas closed his eyes. "No."

"Try to remember," said McCord, writing on the clipboard.

"I had lunch," Douglas whispered. "A long time ago."

"Barker's got it," said a young black man, another resident, walking past us into the alcove and making us jump. "Room seven. She's scrubbing now."

"Good," said McCord, handing the clipboard to one of the nurses and walking over to us. "I'm sorry. I'm Dr. McCord," he said, his kind eyes moving rhythmically back and forth between us. "Your friend is very frightened but he's stable—I've administered a codeine-based painkilling medication, which accounts for most of the disorientation you're seeing."

"You're operating on him?" I said, clearing my throat.

"He's suffered an abdominal puncture wound involving massive blood loss," McCord told us, rubbing his eyes, "as well as the danger that one or more large vessels has been damaged, so we need to perform exploratory surgery." As he spoke, McCord was pushing us out of the way of another resident, who was wheeling in an empty stretcher, and one of the nurses reached to move the curtain so as to let the stretcher pass. "We'll be moving him to the ready room upstairs in a minute—you two can't be much help up there."

"Can we come anyway?" I said. "If we don't get in the way."

"Barker's a very good surgeon," McCord said—the nurses had begun shifting Douglas onto the stretcher, taking the green blanket and the bloodstained sheet as well. "Your friend has nothing to worry about."

"Don't give me that shit," said Nick. "His blood's all over the room."

"But he got here in time—we've reversed the hemorrhage. Look"—McCord was lowering his voice and leaning toward us—"It's none of my business, but you might want to call the police."

"Nobody did it?" I asked.

"You call the police if there's a bullet. That's the rule," said McCord. "In this case I'm not sure what procedure is—I think you might want to wait until he's cogent."

"Nick," Douglas panted. We looked over and realized that Douglas had turned his head and had fixed his unfocused eyes on us, shivering as the nurses adjusted his position and began wheeling the stretcher out of the curtained room. "Don't tell anyone. Don't tell anyone I fell."

"Douglas, you're going to be fine," said Nick, his voice rough and broken. "We'll be talking to you soon."

"Take me home," Douglas whispered, his eyes closing again.

"Today's the fifteenth, isn't it?" McCord said, fishing in his pocket and producing a square pad of hospital visitor's passes, quickly scrawling the date on two before tearing them off and giving them to us. "I *think* it's the fifteenth. Here—just put these on. Go through that door and turn left and you'll get to the stairs, and the waiting room is on your left one flight up. You can't miss it."

"It's the sixteenth," I said, gluing the pass to my lapel. "Thank you, Doctor."

We turned to follow McCord's directions out into another corridor and had gotten a few feet before Nick stopped, pointing through a doorway at a window that commanded a dim view of the hospital's dark air shaft, and spent a moment photographing the dark limestone walls outside—it didn't look to me like there was enough light but as I remembered there was ample proof that he knew what he was doing. "Listen," he told me as we continued toward the staircase, "I'm sorry I was so bad on the phone—it's just, by then, I was starting to think, you know, that I wasn't going to be able to *reach* anyone—I called Max *Gantry,* Tina Foster, even Jack *Winfield,* and, you know, nothing but a lot of answering machines. Shit, this is depressing—"

"You tried Douglas' family?"

"I think they're out of town," Nick said as I held the stairwell door for him. "The, um, the neighbor, you know, that woman, she doesn't know Douglas at all, she had no idea how to, you know, how to reach them, but when I called I got a message with something about getting back next month. Mike—I just noticed your glasses are gone."

"I've got lenses now," I explained. "How about Annabelle?"

"Yeah—same deal," said Nick, shaking his head. "Her machine doesn't have a message, just some jazz. She's probably out for the evening. I didn't say anything."

"How'd she get *you?*" I asked as we mounted the stairs. "The neighbor, I mean."

"I wondered too," said Nick, his voice echoing harshly against the stairwell's cinderblock walls. "After they took Douglas away, she found my number in Douglas', you know, in his apartment. She was so relieved that I was actually a friend."

"Jesus— Douglas shouldn't be here," I said, squinting in the stairwell's dim light.

"Sure he should," said Nick, frowning in dismissive confusion as we topped the stairs and moved toward a large steel door. "I'm sure this was the closest—"

"No—it just seems so *wrong,*" I explained.

"I know what you mean," said Nick, holding the door for me. "It shook me up, too. Seeing him—I mean that's the *worst,* man, not being safe in your fucking home. I should get some new locks."

We'd entered a small, otherwise-unoccupied waiting room and I put the plastic bag down on the worn carpet while Nick closed the metal door against the cloying smell of alcohol, and we sat awkwardly facing each other on couches, Nick looking at me kindly, his eyebrows protruding above his sunglasses.

"No one's seen you in ages," Nick said.

"I'm still here."

"It would seem so." Nick fiddled uncomfortably with his camera as he looked at me. "What are you up to, anyway? Do you always work so *late?*"

"I've been at a newspaper for a while," I said, taking my jacket off and laying it on the couch, "but the past few months I've been working for this, um, this Suburban Supplement they've got, and the, um, the hours are funny sometimes."

"Did you have a good summer?"

"It was brutal," I said, remembering how I would leave the television on while I sat and read books in the other room, with no air conditioner, the windows open, not wanting to think about why I left the television on, which was for the sound of nearby voices, and that I would pretend my bed was a bed in a hotel, somewhere far away, which somehow made it easier to sleep. I remembered the afternoon with the collegiate woman, the brush of the hot wind late in the day at the river's edge where we had leaned on the wooden guardrail, the ineptly ordered drinks we'd had later, after putting our sweaters on, and then the shine of her front steps as she turned to ask, keys in hand, if I would make it home all right—the door swung shut and it wasn't long before the days that ended the summer, cleaning out our accounts and polluting our blood. "How'd you track me down, anyway?"

"I've been meaning to call you for a while, actually," Nick said. "It finally occurred to me to check the Brooklyn listings— What are you, living alone?" Nick grinned at me. "You got some babe stashed away over there?"

"I found this cheap place in Carrol Gardens," I said, remembering how to avoid Nick's gibes. "I have to, um, have to get back and forth every day but it's a beautiful neighborhood."

"Yeah, it's supposed to be nice," said Nick, lighting a cigarette with a nightclub matchbook and then looking around fruitlessly for an ashtray. "A newspaper, huh? Does it pay well?"

"Ehh," I said, grimacing. "You know. I get by. How about you, Nick—what are you doing now? Are you still living downtown?"

"Same as it ever was," Nick said, leaning back on the couch, a cloud of fragrant smoke spreading out around him. "I'm logging hours for the carpet company part-time— You remember the carpet company?" I nodded. "I'm *working* a lot, though—I sold some stuff a ways back, this little gallery, a couple stints here and there, but that's a tough market, so what I've been doing, I've been trying for a *while,* the last couple years, to get commercial work. My portfolio's good, but landing a magazine's *always* been tricky, you know, with all these funky connections you're supposed to have." Nick inhaled on the cigarette, stubbled cheeks sucking inward. "Living downtown—yeah, same damn place for six years. I'd move in a *second*, you know, but it's rent-controlled and right now I'm pretty cash-poor."

We sat quietly for a moment, Nick tapping ashes on the carpet.

"I think he's all right, don't you?" Nick said, leaning forward and scratching his face. "I mean he's scared shitless, but that guy seemed calm, right? The doctor."

"I don't know," I said, shaking my head. "I'll feel better when they're done with him—I couldn't believe it when he said Thorndike."

"That was scary," Nick agreed, looking at his watch. "Listen, you know what just occurred to me? Maybe Annabelle got home from wherever the hell she is. You think we should try to reach her?"

"Well, um, we wouldn't want to shake her up too much," I said, concerned.

"Shake her up?" Nick was chuckling disdainfully, the corners of his mouth pulled down as he reared back on the couch, rolling his shoulders, dropping the cigarette and smashing it out against the carpet with his foot. "Man, *try* to shake her up. You *can't* shake her up, buddy—she's got it *made.*"

"I just meant," I said, "that we could wait until we got some word on his, you know, on the surgery, on his condition. There's— You really want to tell her that her brother's in surgery?"

"You're right," said Nick. "Why don't you do it?"

"Oh, give me a break, Nick," I said, pained.

"No, I'm serious," said Nick, fishing a black leather address book from his back pocket. "I've called *enough* answering machines tonight. Come on, buddy—here's your big chance to call Annabelle."

"Nick," I argued, "I haven't seen her since high school. I don't even *know* her. I mean, I've, you know, I've seen her in *magazines*, but—" Nick grinned privately as he thumbed through the address book. "You— You're friends with her, right?"

"I'm in *touch* with her. Mike"—he held out the opened book—"You're a professional type, you know her deal, all I'm asking you to do is make one of these damn calls for me—I've been on the phone all night." I stood up and accepted the address book, stowing it under my arm and absently picking up the green bag of bloody clothes as I started for the door. "I don't know why you're carrying that around," Nick said. "I mean, the Tafts eat new clothes for breakfast."

"The doctor mentioned the police—"

"What do you think they'll do—try to lift *prints* off that shit?" Nick lit another cigarette. "Cold trail, man."

I wandered down the brightly buffed corridor floor toward a nearby men's room, and after almost dropping Nick's address book into a urinal, I rolled up a sleeve and sank my arm into the cold mass of torn and bloody clothes, feeling around at the bottom and finally extracting what seemed to be a pair of gold-plated barber's scissors—I held the long scissors up to the bright bathroom light, hearing the pattering drops of dried blood tapping the tile floor, and then carefully rinsed and dried them, rolled my sleeves back down, and discarded the bag of clothes in a chrome litter basket. I was still holding the gold scissors, carrying them like Kipling's doomed king as I dropped a quarter into a public phone and resignedly punched Annabelle's number, listening to her line ringing several times before she answered, the faint sound of some clear modern jazz drifting behind her voice, which I realized I remembered very well—as she said hello I imagined I could discern the effects of the passing years.

"Annabelle Taft, please?" I said hesitantly.

"Speaking."

"This is Michael Cadenhead."

"Michael!" said Annabelle after a moment. "This is a surprise."

"Annabelle, I'm"—I cleared my throat—"I'm at St. Mark's Hospital, um, with Nick Blanchard. We're here because— We're here because your brother's been in an accident."

"Wait—" Annabelle sounded more confused than alarmed. "I'm sorry—what do you mean, an accident? What sort of accident?"

"We don't know yet," I said, my perspiring fingers slipping on the scissors as I covered my ear against the sound of a doctor being paged. "He was— It looks like he was attacked. Um— He's got some kind of, some kind of stab wound— They gave him a painkilling drug and took him—"

"Stab— Did you say *stab wound?* Is he all right?" Annabelle asked anxiously. "I mean is he badly hurt? Is he going to be all right?"

"Yes," I said, pushing my hand through my hair. "I think so."

"What do you *mean,* you *think* so?" Annabelle's voice was climbing into a higher register of anxiety, and I heard the music shut off.

"Why did you say 'accident'? I don't underst— What *happened* to him?"

"All I know is that his neighbor called Nick," I explained, "and he— And Nick tried to call you *then,* but he couldn't reach anyone except me. Douglas is in stable condition—I think he had a bad scare but there doesn't seem to be any question he'll pull through."

"All right," said Annabelle, sighing, calming down a bit. "All right. Christ, you scared me to death, Michael." I could hear her breathing as she tried to compose herself. "Our parents are overseas. Damn it— Wait, you said Nick *contacted* you? He's there with you now?"

"He's in the waiting room in case there's news. He told me to call you," I continued, awkwardly filling the pause, "and he said I was, um, a professional, that I knew your deal."

"I don't believe it," Annabelle said weakly, and as I waited for her to go on the scissors slipped from my dampening hand and clattered loudly to the floor, just missing my foot. "What was that sound?" Annabelle asked sharply.

"I dropped a pair of scissors," I said. "Look, if you come up here now, we might be able to get in to see him—we're waiting for details, but I think he'll be able to—"

"I can't," Annabelle said. "I can't come up there. Listen, what do you do for a living, Michael?"

"I'm a journalist. I don't understand," I said. "Couldn't you just take a cab or something? You're in *Manhattan*—you're not that far away. There's nobody else here, and we'll be—"

"I can't," Annabelle said quickly. "I'm sorry, I can't— Douglas will understand. I've got to go, Michael. I'm sorry." There was a clattering sound and the line went dead, and I hung up the receiver, bent to retrieve the scissors, and headed back toward the waiting room.

"Mike! Get over here," Nick called out as soon as he saw me round the corner. He was standing in the corridor holding our coats and talking to a diminutive woman in her thirties dressed in surgical clothes, her shoes wrapped in plastic, a tight-fitting surgical cap concealing her hair, a mask hanging round her neck. "They're all done," Nick told me as I arrived. "This is Dr. Barker— Tell him what you just told me," he said to the young woman.

"Yes, Doctor?" I said, returning Nick's address book and accepting my jacket, stowing the scissors in its vest pocket. "How is he?"

"Mr. Taft has suffered only mild intestinal abrasions," Barker told me in a bland, pleasant voice. "The principal damage was confined to muscle tissue, which should heal quite nicely."

"Thank God, right?" Nick said, staring at me.

"Could we—" I stopped to clear my throat. "Would it, um, would it be all right for us to see him?"

Barker was shaking her head. "It shouldn't be a problem, but I'd recommend against discussing the injury," she said, beginning to lead us away. "He's left the recovery room—you can just follow me."

"Will he be, um, staying at the hospital?" I asked as we began walking.

"I think just tonight—he's groggy from the codeine, but he only required a local anesthetic so his convalescence should be relatively brief," Barker said, leading us through swinging steel doors into a harshly lit corridor, past bright, clean rooms filled with complex equipment. "I don't know how fully Dr. McCord explained things to you, but in cases like these surgery is essentially a precautionary measure."

"I talked to Annabelle," I told Nick.

"Good for you," Nick said, not looking at me. "Listen, Doctor, 'precautionary'—what does that mean?"

"Necessary only so as to ascertain the extent of the internal damage," Barker recited smoothly, looking at us. "Are you all he's got?"

"I'm sorry?" I said, my voice blurred by fatigue and strain.

"He doesn't have a family?" asked Barker. "Your friend."

"They're traveling," I said. "They're wealthy people. He's alone."

"That's a shame," said Barker, turning so as to include Nick in her commentary. "You must be good friends of his then—I should have come right out when you got here."

"You had better things to do," I said. "Please don't worry about it."

"Well, procedural considerations still can blind us. Look, nobody can lay bets on the results of even a mild abdominal wound," Barker said. "As it is, your friend was very lucky—he had a frightening experience, but Dr. Gonzalez and I had a simple procedure to perform and the operation was absolutely uneventful. Are you all right?"

She had brought us to a well-made wooden door, and as we stood in a rough circle I realized that she was looking at me critically. "What— Me?" I asked, startled.

"You look awful." Dr. Barker raised her eyebrows at me as she scratched her forehead along the furled elastic edge of her surgical cap, and Nick gazed at us expressionlessly, his sunglasses reflecting square images of the overhead lights. "Don't strain him too hard—he's very sleepy," she told us, smiling as she gestured toward the door and moved to leave. "If you could keep it to just a few minutes, I'm sure he'd be grateful."

"Thank you," Nick said hoarsely, returning her smile.

"Look— Here's my extension number," Barker said suddenly, fishing in a cluttered breast pocket for a business card. "If there's anything I can help you with, feel free to call—I can be reached late into the night."

We slowly stepped into a small, warm, windowless room, lit only by a dim fluorescent tube mounted behind a recessed wall panel, and as my eyes adjusted to the darkness I made out two complicated hospital beds, each flanked by a padded chair. Douglas lay sleeping in the front bed, his soft hospital-issue cotton pajamas unbuttoned to reveal the thick white edge of a large, clean bandage. He still had the particular seersucker look that I remembered, his pretty face tanned and smooth and his hair across his forehead—in a hospital bed he conveyed wounded wealth more than anything else. Nick and I looked at each other and stepped forward, and as Nick finally removed his sunglasses and then carried the other bed's chair over and we sat down side by side, our chairs scraping on the polished floor, Douglas stirred, opening his eyes slightly and then turning his head, looking at us for a moment and then beginning to smile.

"You're really here, Nick," Douglas said, his voice quiet and soft, his breathing regular. "I thought that was a dream."

"I'm here," Nick said quietly, stowing his sunglasses in his overcoat pocket, smiling at Douglas, putting a hand on his shoulder.

"Michael?" Douglas murmured, looking at me, his head moving with profound fatigue, eyes slowly focusing. "Michael, is that *you?* It's been— It's been a long time."

"Hello, Douglas," I said. "It's good to see you."

"I can't believe you're here. I didn't"—his breathing hitched and he winced, closing his eyes, before continuing—"I didn't think anyone was coming."

"Of course we're here," Nick said.

"How do you feel?" I asked.

"Tired," Douglas said. "A little bit nauseous." He opened his eyes. "I've got such a stomachache," he said more quietly, eyes drifting back to us.

"You've got a new bracelet," I said, pointing.

"Yeah," Douglas whispered, keeping his movements to a minimum, his breathing regular but slow. "But they took everything else. I think they sold my watch, but it's been"—his voice hitched again—"falling apart since graduation anyway."

"Your watch is here," Nick said, pointing down at the bedside cabinet, where a Cartier tank watch had been placed on edge, its bracelet and onyx-inlaid crown reflecting the dim light, and as I glanced at the wristwatch I noticed that its crystal was broken by a long vertical crack. "All your stuff's safe—nobody ripped you off."

"Nick, you bum," whispered Douglas, beginning to cry gently. "I can't believe you're here—I didn't think anyone was going to come. I don't even know— I don't even know how long I've been here." He cried without tightening his face, tears gently rolling across his cheekbones, brown eyes closing, and Nick put his hand back on Douglas' shoulder.

"Of course we're here," I said.

"I thought I was all alone," Douglas whispered, brimming eyes closed. "I didn't know where I was and I dreamed about falling." He sniffed and then moved his arm to wipe his eyes. "I dreamed I was dying."

"Take it easy, Doug," said Nick after a moment. "Take it easy."

"I'm okay," Douglas whispered, sniffing again, rubbing his nose with the back of his wrist, sluggishly turning his head back toward us. "Mike, it's good to see you," he said, smiling. "What are you doing these days? How'd you— How'd you know to come?"

"I'm writing for a newspaper," I said. "Nick tracked me down."

"A newspaper. That's good," said Douglas softly. "That's good."

"Is there anything you want?" I asked. "Anyone you want us to call?"

Douglas looked at me, still wiping the tears from his face. "No," he said. "It doesn't matter."

"Should we call the police?" Nick asked.

"Oh, no, that's— Please, please don't do that," Douglas said. "Please don't talk."

"Are you sure?" I said, frowning. "We could contact Annabelle."

"No, don't bother her," said Douglas, settling back and staring up at the ceiling, tired eyes drifting closed again, voice falling toward sleep. "Do me one favor—call where I work. It's the Lineage Institute, you can just call the WATS line"—he gave a phone number—"and tell them I won't be in for a while. Say I'm taking some, um, sick leave."

"I'll do that," said Nick, producing his address book and a ballpoint pen. "Any particular person?"

"Carol Casey." Douglas breathed heavily, in and out, his bandaged waist rising and falling. "Sweet Carol. Don't forget, Nick."

"I'm writing it down," said Nick, doing so. "How about Max Gantry?"

"I haven't seen Max in a long time," Douglas whispered, his eyes closed. "He's building an airplane, right?"

"What?" I said, glancing at Nick.

"That didn't make sense, did it?" Douglas whispered, his hand drifting over to the bandage around his stomach. "I'm sorry. It must be the codeine."

"You probably ought to leave that alone," said Nick. "You're sure you're feeling all right?"

"Yeah. I mentioned the stomachache," Douglas said, chuckling mildly and wincing, pushing air through his chapped lips like a failing athlete. "The doctor explained about the sutures."

"She told us you're going to be fine," Nick said in a scratched voice. "You just need some rest now."

"Okay," whispered Douglas. "Just rest."

Douglas seemed to be falling back asleep, and Nick and I looked at each other, agreeing by a glance that we should leave. "Sleep well, buddy," Nick said, smiling and patting Douglas lightly on the cheek with the fingers of his open hand. We stood as quietly as possible, Nick unfolding his sunglasses as I put my corduroy jacket on.

"Mike," Douglas whispered, almost asleep.

"Yeah?" I said, bending down to hear him.

"I'm sorry," Douglas whispered. "I'm sorry about this."

"Don't worry about it," I said, patting his shoulder awkwardly.

"This goddamned job. I wish I could—"

"Try to sleep, Douglas."

"—tell somebody what those fuckers did to me. I'm not afraid," Douglas whispered, eyes peacefully closed. "I'll remember you came."

We made to leave, but at the door Nick stopped and turned back, raising his camera and taking a picture of Douglas sleeping, the curtained bed behind him, the empty chairs facing him. When he was finished I reached to turn out the light and we left the room, finding our way back along the bright corridors, and soon we were stepping through glass doors to where the street was dark and cool and filled with the sounds of city nights.

"Jesus," I said eventually.

"Some night, huh?" said Nick.

"It's funny that he mentioned graduation," I said, hunching against the wind as we walked. "I think that might have been the last time I saw you, Nick."

"You may be right," said Nick, looking at me, pulling his cigarettes from his coat.

"You remember when we had those drinks at the hotel that day?" I asked, swerving around a passerby as we walked, feeling the cold evening wind beneath my jacket.

"Yeah," said Nick distantly, nodding as he remembered. "That was one hell of a weekend." As the gusting wind furled against my jacket I felt something cold brush my chest and remembered the gold scissors. "You still come up in conversation, you know," Nick said. "I was talking to Tina Foster a while back, and she said, you know, I wonder what Mike's doing."

"Really?" I said, smiling.

We stood near the hospital hunched in our coats, our voices broken by the rising night wind.

"The summer's over," said Nick.

"Yeah."

"It's going to be a cold autumn," he added, taillights shining in his sunglasses like campfire sparks. "I'm in the Manhattan book—call me sometime, you know, and we can go do something."

"You taking the subway?" I asked.

"I'm cabbing it," said Nick, already a few steps away, eyes already scanning the empty street.

"All right," I said. "I've missed you, Nick."

Nick smiled. "It was good to see you, buddy."

"Well, good night," I said, waving and turning away into the wind.

A year has now passed since that September but I remember how the collegiate woman had said goodbye to me at the newspaper, and how I hadn't told her that as we'd stood on her sublet doorstep by the flat edge of Brooklyn Heights with the towers of Manhattan shining across the river on that clear summer night there had been something crucial for me to say, something imperative, and I could keep from speaking only in the panicked knowledge that after her there was no one else. I still remember everything that happened the night of the hospital visit—a woman in a drab winter coat sat next to me on the empty subway, skimming a fashion magazine, and when I got home my possessions looked like nothing at all—the typewriter and baled newspapers were cheap acquaintances, fragile wreckage draped over the hard edges of Nick's voice and Douglas' blood and the lovely stare that Annabelle reserved for the camera lens.

chapter 2

When I was a boy I understood things in a purposeless and inconsecutive way, but as I got older, and awakened into desire, I came to believe that passions moved the world. This knowledge made me restless and afraid, and in my fear I began to suspect that there were people without passions—I had begun to envy these people, dreading that they had discovered some hidden impossibility of life, before I learned otherwise. A short while ago, a matter of years, I discovered that passion tends to be another name that people give to their movement through the world, a hopeful name intended to flatter people's struggles, intended to drape people's satisfactions in the guise of nobility or sacrifice and give them the semblance of heroism. I knew then how frail a life built of desires could be, how my own endurance of fulfilled longing could guide me toward lifelessness, but only when my desires had been so cannibalized did I learn that the world contains a margin of fire, a quiet deadness beyond the maintenance and failure of one's appetites, and that only there, in that calm place, can the possibility of life be regained.

When I enrolled in the journalism program at school I had been told, by faculty and friends, that for several years most of my decisions would be made for me, and true to form I found that the parochial guild-system routines I'd learned in college had followed me around, diminishing from job to job, since I'd taken my degree and returned to New York. The newspaper's Suburban Weekly Supplement, where I worked, would finally be canceled that December, around the time that Oliver North's secret testimony began, and by September the signs of defeat were already clear and people were facing the facts, leaving for higher ground. When the warnings were unmistakable, late that odd summer, I'd quietly begun hunting for a position on the main paper, where I had always believed my life of internship would end.

On the Friday following the night at the hospital I was informed that I'd been accepted for a new job at the Metropolitan Section, starting on the first of October. The only immediate effect of this was that the Supplement editor, without a word being spoken by either of us about it, spent the morning redistributing my assignments, evidently on the belief that I had betrayed a personal trust. Irritated, I took a long lunch, heading up to Columbus Circle alone and walking at the park's edge, where a woman in a pink coat and yellow gloves was standing by the low granite wall and slowly throwing crumbs to the unseen pigeons, and when I returned my doomed editor, in a fit of compassion, took me into his office and spoke to me in a tone I hadn't heard him use before, speaking kind, vague words about his life in newspapers. He had written me a good letter—it seemed at the time a quaint gesture, a farewell salute to my origins in internship—so I thanked him for that, and as he wished me luck, I expressed my regret that the department was faring badly, and he seemed—I can't be sure—to read this as a signal that he should console me, that he should speak kindly so as to ease the ersatz pain of my departure. Confident that we would part on good terms, which seemed somehow necessary, and bereft of work to do, which was fitting, I took a train home to Brooklyn and stared forward into the weekend, wondering, as everyone does, how soon I would know if my life had changed.

A short series of unseasonably cold days had begun, and I felt the cold wind as I left the subway, loosening my tie and anticipating my apartment's dark interior, the barren kitchen, the long flights of stairs, and as my legs failed to muster the stamina I wandered through the neighborhood, delaying my return home. The Brooklyn blocks behind my building were unfamiliar and I turned my jacket collar against the unseasonable breeze, looking down at the deserted afternoon sidewalk, where the faded chalk outlines of a long-dead hopscotch game were still visible and in my memory I heard the faded ghosts of summer sounds. A block from home a white-haired man in moth-punctured flannel clothes sat curled round a wooden cane on the steps of a laundromat, motionless hands holding the cane like a fishing boat's rudder, head bowed, cracked lips pressed against his thumbs, a hatful of pocket change at his feet. The wind brushed past me as I stood locked in the man's half-gaze and right then it was any kind of day you could name, but soon a woman with red hair and lathe-turned legs skirted the street on roller skates and I was back in the land of desire, back among the fears and pains of the age, so as the cold wind dispersed I turned toward home.

AFTER SWITCHING ON lamps and shutting windows I straightened the apartment, gathering together all the Supplement's back issues and feeling the first mild evening hunger as I stacked them on the kitchen table, leafing through their yellowing pages a final time and remembering the Collegiate Woman before binding the papers with twine and taking them out with the other garbage. I walked toward the telephone several times after that, considering ways to get in touch with her, and by nightfall, after I'd made and eaten two sandwiches and diligently cleaned my contact lenses, I found I was restless enough to be glancing at the phone from moment to moment, so I hunted down a Manhattan phone book and dialed Nick's number.

"Nick? It's Michael," I told him.

"Hey, buddy!" Nick sounded pleased. "How you been?"

"I'm all right."

"I was just out the door," Nick said quickly. "Listen, what can I do for you? I mean, anything specific?"

"What? No," I said. "I just thought I'd say hello—I've been busy at the paper this week so I haven't kept in touch. I got a new job today."

"Really? What are you, a detective now?"

"No, just— I'll be working at the Metro Section. I was wondering if you wanted to get together."

"Sounds good," said Nick. "I'd love to but I'm busy tonight."

"It doesn't have to be tonight."

"Well, it's just an inconvenient time," Nick said. "I'm leaving in a couple days, I'm going out West, out to Montana for a few weeks, and I'm pretty occupied with that, so there's—"

"You going on vacation?"

"No, it's work," said Nick. "The big sellout. I've signed to do a series of magazine ads. It's a brand-new deal—this clothing company's starting a new print campaign. I was going to call and tell you," he added.

"Clothing company? Which one?" I asked.

"They're called Octane Fashion Industries—you know, they make those, um, funny high-water jeans that suburban chicks like to wear."

"Sure, I've heard of them," I said, impressed. "You must be raking it in."

"Not bad, huh? We're shooting in this place called Granite Peak—I *think* it's Granite Peak—somewhere near Billings, anyway. There's this incredible national park we'll be shooting at."

"Well, congratulations," I said. "I mean, on getting this job."

"Thanks. Yeah, I've never done anything like this—I just got the gig last week and we've been running all over the goddamned city getting ready. I've got a couple of assistants for this thing, but still, you wouldn't *believe* how complicated this is, Mike— I mean every time I turn around there's some problem, you know, the power requirements for the *lights* or the models' plane tickets or something. I've got to go early since the train takes so long." I remembered that Nick doesn't like to fly.

"I'm glad I caught you before you left," I said, gazing out the window at the darkening sky. "I guess I'll see you when you get back."

"Actually, Mike," Nick said, "if you wouldn't mind going to a bad neighborhood, I'm going out tonight with a friend of mine, taking a break, some drinks, maybe shoot some pool—you want to join us? Annabelle might show up."

"Yeah, I guess that's why I called," I said. "To see you, I mean."

"All right," said Nick. "What time is it now? Seven? I'm meeting Hector uptown in an hour when he gets off work. Did you eat yet, or what?"

"Yeah," I said. My stomach was tightening and I was regretting the sandwiches. "It doesn't matter, though. Just tell me where to go."

"How fast can you get to Times Square?" Nick asked.

"Damn it, I figured you'd drag me into Manhattan again," I said.

Half an hour later I was walking down the crowded east edge of Seventh Avenue past store windows jammed with pseudo-Oriental carpets and pornographic videocassettes, dwarfed by the blinding neon Times Square advertisements, when I spotted two men silhouetted by a bright movie marquis—*Top Gun* was just letting out—standing side by side in identical wary poses. One of them was Nick, looking just as he'd looked the previous week. The man next to him was thin, almost scrawny, with a hawklike face, dark sunken unshaven cheeks, a drooping mustache, and flat, dusty dark hair, wearing steel-framed glasses, a tight black T-shirt, a battered denim jacket, jeans, and steel-toed boots and carrying an orange motorcycle helmet in the crook of his arm. He looked to be at least thirty years old.

"*Here* he is," said Nick, pointing me out to the other man, stepping forward and smiling. "Hey, buddy—Mike, this is Hector Costanza. Hector—Mike Cadenhead." We all had to shout to be heard over the Times Square crowds.

"How you doing?" said Hector in a heavy Bronx accent, more pleasant than otherwise, tipping his chin at me, not removing his hands from his pockets.

"Hello," I said. "Were you waiting long?"

"Just got here," rasped Nick, grinning with his lips pressed together, slapping me on the back. "Come on—we're going down to Tom Allen's."

"Well, good," said Hector, nodding. "That's more like it."

"Who's Tom Allen?" I asked.

"Tom Allen is everybody's friend," said Nick. "No. It's just a name. It's a bar."

"He's probably a real guy," I argued. "How should we get down there?"

"Let's get a cab," said Nick, beginning to wander out into the street. "Hector, you coming?"

"Nah, I've got my bike," Hector said, hooking his thumb toward a Harley-Davidson parked near the curb some distance away. "You guys go ahead—I'll meet you down there."

"Let's go, Mike," Nick called. I looked over and saw that he'd stopped a battered blue gypsy cab—the driver was leaning out the window, wearing a feathered cowboy hat, looking up at Nick hopefully.

"Don't you want to find a regular cab?" I said, frowning.

"This is the same thing," said Nick, gesturing me into the disreputable-looking car ahead of himself.

"If you say so," I said as he slammed the door, peering forward to search in vain for a meter.

"I've got so much to tell you about," said Nick, settling back against the fake-leather cab seat as we pulled out into the downtown traffic. "Everything's changed. I had no idea this kind of commercial work was so *lucrative.*"

"So you can buy lots of new lenses, right?" I said.

"Fuck lenses—I'm buying a *Harley,*" said Nick, turning to look out at the bright signs of the passing stores and restaurants. "Mike, did you eat? I'm starving."

"I had some sandwiches."

"I hope they were good," said Nick, drumming his fingers against his camera. "I can't believe I'm leaving tomorrow—I'm going to be on that damn train all night, crossing the grasslands, and then under the mountains in the afternoon. At least on a chopper you can *touch* things—this way the world's behind safety glass. Hey, too bad you weren't around this summer, Mike—what'd you do for the Fourth of July?"

"Nothing," I said, remembering the Collegiate Woman again. "I went, um, to the thing by the pier with some of the people from the paper."

"Oh yeah?" said Nick, leaning back, looking at me. "Maybe we should give them a call."

"No," I said. "I thought about keeping in touch with them, but with the new job it's going to be difficult," I explained.

"New job?"

"I'm moving to the Metro Section next month," I told him again.

"Really? I'm impressed." Nick looked at his watch. "Damn it—I don't have *time* for this, is the thing—the train's tomorrow afternoon, and I've got to figure out if I should take the—"

Suddenly the car lurched violently and there was a loud, dull crashing noise as the car slammed to a halt and Nick and I were tossed forward, our knees hitting the rubber floor mats, our faces knocking against the Plexiglas partition. "What the *fuck*—" Nick said loudly, recovering before me, sitting back up and brushing himself off, while I got up off the floor, dazed but unhurt. "Mike, you all right?" Nick said, looking around, picking his sunglasses off the floor and putting them back on and then inspecting his camera for signs of damage.

"Yeah," I said, shaken, looking through the partition. In front of us was nothing but a deserted, block-long section of Seventh Avenue, but I could see that the hood of the car had folded neatly backward, blocking the bottom half of the windshield, where a single vertical crack caught the streetlight's glow like a forest cobweb. The driver's side door was open, cold evening air blowing back onto us, but the driver seemed to have vanished.

"What'd we *hit?*" Nick said, peering forward. "Where the hell did the guy go?"

"There he is," I said, pointing out the driver, who had circled round the front of the smashed hood. Several cars had accumulated behind us, honking angrily, and they were just beginning to pull forward round the motionless gypsy cab.

"*Jesus,*" said Nick, opening his own door. "Come on, Mike." I followed Nick out onto the street, traffic rushing past us as we hurried round to the front of the cab, which was utterly destroyed—the fenders and hood had accordioned, the radiator sprayed steam and the asphalt beneath us shone with spilled oil and glittering broken glass. The driver stood motionless, shoulders slumped, his cowboy hat lying unnoticed near his sneakers, staring at the wrecked car with a tragic look of uncomprehending desolation frozen on his face.

"Taxi! Taxi!" called Nick, waving his arms. A cab screeched to a halt near us, nearly causing another accident, and Nick pulled one of the doors open—he had already given the address as I arrived and we sped forward as soon as I had shut the door.

"Jesus," I said, twisting to look out the new cab's back window. As we rushed farther downtown I could see a receding view of the smashed gypsy cab—the driver, who I realized hadn't said a single word in our presence, was still standing with his head bowed in front of the wreck, and cars were continuing to flow forward around him. "I don't understand what we hit," I said, shaking my head in confusion.

"We hit *something,*" said Nick, starting to laugh. "Hector missed a hell of a ride."

"That poor guy," I said.

"Ah, he's been in accidents before," said Nick, aiming his camera out the window. "He rides that crazy *bike*— I mean this was *nothing* compared to—"

"I meant the driver."

For the next ten minutes we sat silently and sped downtown and then the cab abruptly pulled up to a deserted street corner. "I'll take this," muttered Nick, paying the driver as I got out of the car, realizing that we were somewhere on the Lower East Side. Nick lit a cigarette and then led me down a residential street past boarded-up buildings and over to where Hector was standing in front of a small bar with neon beer signs in the window, its green awning inscribed TOM ALLEN—he had locked his motorcycle to a post and was leaning against the green brick wall, arms crossed impatiently.

"Where the hell were you?" said Hector, seeing us and coming forward.

"We had an accident," I said, looking into the bar as an old man in a windbreaker came out, the open oak door revealing a dark interior and the sound of early-seventies funk.

"An accident?" said Hector, squinting skeptically.

"Nothing happened," said Nick, bouncing impatiently on his toes. "We destroyed an illegal passenger vehicle. Come on."

We entered a long, low quiet room with cedar paneling where a crowd of mostly middle-aged Irish men were sitting at the long oak bar, and several women, more blonde than otherwise, were seated at various places around the room. We passed a pair of unoccupied pool tables and arrived at the back of the room, near a window with iron bars and an opened door that led directly into an outdoor alley filled with empty steel garbage cans. Nick and Hector slid some chairs along the tiled floor and we sat around a table covered in empty glasses and wet napkins, and soon a sour-looking red-haired bartender with a pockmarked face came over and began clearing the glasses. "Are you new here? What's your name?" Nick asked the bartender, putting his camera on the table as soon as a corner was dry.

"Barry," said the bartender, not looking up as he wiped the table.

"Never trust anyone named Barry," Nick said mysteriously after we had ordered three domestic beers. "So how'd it go today?" he asked Hector.

"How do you think it went?" Hector said, putting his helmet down on the floor. "Sheila's climbing the walls."

"Hector works for Sheila," Nick explained to me.

"I'm the liaison between everybody and Sheila," Hector told me, taking one of Nick's cigarettes. "I'm the assistant. I can type forty-five words a minute."

"Who's Sheila?" I asked, taking off my sweater.

"We'll get to that," Hector said, grinning belligerently at me. "So today, you know, we're working late, her light bulbs went out, I got up on a table to change them, she starts crying."

"You sound pissed at her," said Nick.

"Pissed? Nah," said Hector, grimacing around the cigarette. "I mean I'm fine. I mean I can't deal with these fucking women who *cry* all the time. I was a kid, I remember—crying is a certain thing, you know? So these women who would as soon *cry* as, you know, put gloves on or anything else."

"Yes," Nick said. Barry came back with our beers and we all fished for our wallets and paid him.

"I spend all my money on vinyl and beer," said Hector, standing up a few inches and returning his wallet to his back pocket. "And the thing is the cavalier attitude? Matter of fact—they say, I was there, I was having a bad day, I felt like just, you know, crying all day, but then it stopped raining. Or some damn thing. *Cavalier,* you know? It's like they're saying of course you know what I mean about the crying, and I want to say, listen, darling, I really don't know what you mean, you're going to have to, next time, you're going to have to explain. I want there to be a Blake Edwards movie starring me and Sheila."

"Don't you?" Nick asked after a moment.

"Don't I what?" Hector asked, looking confused as he wiped a drop of beer from the edge of his mustache with the back of his hand.

"Know what they mean. Sometimes."

"No," Hector said, sipping his beer. "No, I mean, I thought about it. I know what tears mean. I know life, right? So no."

"Neither do I," Nick said.

"I try to be sympathetic. It's just that there's work to be done and I lose my patience. Something happens and she says, don't worry, I'll handle it, I'll handle everything, and I'm like, darling, you couldn't handle a lawn mower."

"Mike, still want to know who Sheila is?" Nick asked me, the green light reflecting in his sunglasses.

"I'm not sure," I said, smiling politely.

"I'm sorry, Mike," Hector told me, raising his eyebrows. "Nick's been listening to this shit for weeks— What I'm talking about, what I do is, I work for this company that distributes cosmetics wholesale—there's a department that deals with promotional material, you know, all the brochures and crap, and just that one department, where I am, Sheila runs *that,* if you can believe it."

"Cosmetics?" I asked. "What kind of, um—"

"Well, our main client is Claude Naget. You've heard of them?"

"Sure," I said, nodding. "I've heard of Naget. Everybody has."

"Oh, you'd be surprised," Hector said, grinning. "The people we *deal* with trying to sell the shit— You'd *think* it'd be easy, with, you know, the most famous cosmetics name in the *world*, prestigious, you'd think it'd be *easy* selling their perfume to all the wealthy New York chicks, but vendors are so *stupid*—those idiots at Naget *finally* realized they've got a market problem, thank God for miracles, they're starting to take steps, a new ad campaign, but Sheila and I are still dealing with these vendors who haven't heard of them."

"You guys want another beer?" said Nick, standing up. Hector and I nodded. "I'm going to go get some more beers," he told us, walking toward the bar.

Hector and I sat quietly for a moment, glancing at each other, each frowning so as to reduce the other's unease. "So you've known Nick a long time?" Hector asked.

"We went to the same high school," I said, "but not much beyond that."

"Right, the school," said Hector, nodding knowingly. "Yeah, what was it like going to that damn school, anyway?"

"I try not to think about it too much," I said. "I mean, it's over and done with."

"Yeah, you'd think so, but Nick's always seeing those people," Hector said, leaning back in his chair. "All casual friends. Kathy always complains that Nick's a guy trying to be casual about things."

"Kathy?"

"Don't you know Kathy?" Hector absently scratched the soft stubble around his mustache. "Kathy's Nick's girlfriend. Not his girlfriend—she's his whatever the hell she is. Yeah, Kathy Schall, she's a high school girl, if you can believe it."

"What's she like?" I asked.

"She's totally beautiful," said Hector, "if you like these unminted coins. I mean, like a Raphael Madonna, really, which is funny 'cause last summer she dragged him to the Virgin Tour. No, Kathy's this nice quiet tiny little high school girl— She's always over at his place and she sits around with the magazines, only talks on the phone, never to the people in the room, and she's always trying to get us to go to Coney Island. Every day, she's saying, Coney Island, and I'm like, darling, could you maybe get a new line there, 'cause there's more to life than amusement, or else go back to the Upper West Side and the delicatessens and the left-wing parents 'cause it's not her fault she's so young. She's sweet, though. As far as I'm concerned, if I get to hear the high school lines— She always says to me, Hector, when Nick and I break up and divide the friends I want you."

"That's funny," I said. "I don't know any of Nick's friends. This is practically the first time I've seen him in five years."

"Yeah, I wanted to meet you," Hector said. "Nick was talking about you."

"Really?"

"Yeah." Hector squinted. "So I wondered what you were like. I mean, I don't like most of the Thorndike people, you know, and they're *everywhere.* Nick wants to make sure I meet everyone. But you know Nick—that kind of guy, you know, he goes and buys all the cameras, and then he goes and buys all the *carrying cases* for the cameras. *Thorough,* you know. So thorough that everything seems half-assed."

"What does Nick say about me? I'm just curious."

Hector finished his beer thoughtfully. "About your being a reporter, mostly. I mean, you may not realize this, but that's something to talk about. For me, even. I don't know any journalists. Listen, how'd you decide to become a reporter? You *decided,* didn't you?"

"Pretty much," I said. "I liked stories when I was a kid—writing them—but I didn't really have anyone to show them to except my father. I didn't get interested in journalism until college."

"Your father? What's he do?"

"He's an ophthalmologist," I said. "Why do you ask?"

Hector shrugged, turning the corners of his mouth down, Brando-style. "You're just supposed to ask, I guess. In California they ask how many miles your dad runs every day. Anyway, why stop?"

"Writing stories? I'm not sure," I said. "They didn't affect anything. And I was so bad at it."

"So what?" said Hector, squinting adamantly. "Fuck that, Mike. So it's bad, but what's the difference? I mean fucking get on with things, I think, is what's hard for people. You want to write other things, go ahead."

"So you're good friends with Nick?"

"What? Yeah," said Hector, brightening, leaning back and stretching, his chair scraping the floor tiles. "Nick and I go way back. We met at—you're not going to believe this—we met in a basement."

"Really?"

"Yeah, a few years ago, a guy I knew named Sugar Man, this guy involved in narcotics, if you can believe it, I mean *trading* in narcotics, is the way to put it, he had this basement of this place on Avenue B and some of the crowds from Orpheum—you know that club?—would head over there, you know, on foot. This was, what, '83. Nick came by on the back of some other guy's bike and we were all milling around in this basement with purple light bulbs, you know, with, like, the Ramones or something going real loud, and all these chicks from the club, party girls, some lawyers, I think, huddling around wondering where their dates had taken them, and all these neighborhood guys, and I see there's this little guy in sunglasses taking pictures of everything. Me, I was in no state to meet anyone, on the account of I was completely fucked in the blood by then, with all the coke moving around this little purple basement, and Nick came up to me and was like, There's not enough light. So I go, Not enough light for what? And he goes, Pictures, asshole. And he goes—he's looking at me—he goes, Nothing important happens when it's bright. And I'm standing there and I say, So how come you wear sunglasses? And that was *it*, you know, we booked out of there on that guy's motorcycle and went and got some fried clams. So we've been buddies for a while, we hang around, and there's these people on the Lower East Side who think we're queers and that it started the night we ran out of the basement. Nobody goes to Sugar Man's anymore."

"Oh, you're telling the story," said Nick, smiling privately behind his sunglasses as he distributed three new beers. "Hey, Hector—who's going to be taking these new Naget pictures, anyway?" Nick asked. "They'll be making so much money."

"I don't think it's set yet," said Hector. "Probably Phillipe Girard."

"Girard?" said Nick with distaste. "But he's terrible."

"He did the swimsuit issue, remember?" said Hector. "He's on the A-list now. Look, Nick"—Hector leaned forward—"you *know* I get accurate information, right? I mean he'll be around *years* after your little Montana deal is over. So don't start getting, you know, don't start *dreaming.*"

"All right, I'm sorry," Nick said quietly, hunching forward over the table and rubbing the back of his neck. I drank from the new, untouched bottle of beer before me, feeling a slight buzz, while Nick and Hector sat looking uncomfortable. "You guys want to shoot some pool?" Nick asked.

"I thought Annabelle was showing up," I said, remembering as I stood.

"Nah," said Nick. "I tried to call her and couldn't get her."

"I'm never going to meet this chick," Hector said, shaking his head sadly.

"I can never reach her," Nick said.

"Man, you lose your shit over a chick and she gives you an ice cube sandwich," Hector said. "All right, rack them up."

"You go ahead and start," I said, heading toward the bathroom. "I'll be right back." When I returned a moment later Nick and Hector had brought our beers and jackets and Hector's helmet over to one of the pool tables and had started a game.

"Look, Nick, there's a lot of hardworking girls out there," Hector was saying as he leaned to line up a shot. "She's in her own little world, and I can't believe— I'm just saying I don't think a girl like *that,* a girl who's got it made in the shade as things *stand,* is going to risk something so *shady* from a, from a legal standpoint—that she'd take the chance of throwing away everything she's *got,* you know, risking, you know, risking it all just for money." Hector's shot was successful and he moved round the table and lined up another.

"She could clear *six million* in two years if this works," said Nick quietly. "She's being fucking ruthless."

"Everyone's trying to make a killing in this town and you want me to keep my mouth shut about this," Hector said, watching his shot fail, speaking over the loud clicking of the pool balls. "But that's a lot of lens caps, Nick, and some new pencils for your friend here." Hector pointed at me.

"She's in her own little world but she knows what money is," said Nick, taking off his sunglasses and leaning over the pool table.

"Six million dollars?" I said, trying to keep my hand in the conversation but wishing for another beer, not wanting to offer to buy. "Who are you talking about?"

"Mike wakes up," said Nick, loudly sinking two balls. "Look, Hector"—Nick pointed at him with the hand holding the cue—"What I'm saying is just that if she wants the money she's going to take the money and if they try to stop her she'll figure out a way to take it anyway. That's *if* she wants the money, and what I'm telling you, I *know* her, right, I'm telling you that she wants the money. I'm telling you these people don't scare her."

"Wait— Nick," I said, laughing, picking up my beer and moving it out of the way of Nick's next shot, "Nick, what the hell are you talking about? You sound like a racetrack man." Nick's shot had too much screwback and he handed his cue to me, and I awkwardly leaned to line up a simple one-ball shot at a corner pocket—I hadn't played pool since college and I was never good at it.

"Is Annabelle Taft her real name?" Hector asked.

"Whose real name?" said Nick, smiling.

"Nick," I said, walking round the corner of the pool table for a better angle, "it's none of my business, but, um, do you know anything more about what happened last week? I mean, with Douglas being in the hospital?"

"What are you talking about?" Hector said, mystified.

"Annabelle's brother," said Nick. "Anna's from this wealthy Manhattan family." I made the shot but sank the cue ball, and Hector stepped forward for his next turn.

"Oh, that's right," said Hector, nodding. "Someone else from that fucking school."

"You didn't call the police, did you, Nick?" I asked casually, tapping my fingers on the felt. "Because—"

"Of *course* not," said Nick in disgust as he ostentatiously chalked his cue. "What— Did *you?* He said he didn't want it, Mike."

"No," I said, sipping from my beer. "That's what I— I got the sense that his, that the attack had something to do with his— With that *job* of his, and I— And I think he was saying that he was afraid police involvement would mess him up at work somehow. I mean I don't know— Did *you* get that impression? Or is it just me?"

"What the hell are you talking about?" Hector muttered distractedly as he leaned to make another loud shot. "Nick, you've got to leave that fucking school behind."

"Yeah, don't remind me," Nick told Hector, patiently ignoring me as he squinted and moved his hands like a surveyor, elbows out, evidently calculating the billiard table's geometry. "It keeps catching up to me. Hey, Hector, remember when we ran into that asshole Ralph DiGrassi? The famous lawyer's son?"

"Wait," said Hector, squinting at Nick. "Oh, sure, that little ugly guy."

"Right," said Nick, smiling back at me. "I *never* could stand that asshole, man. I practically broke his *jaw* that summer, you remember, Mike?" I nodded dutifully, vaguely remembering Ralph, with whom

I'd never been friends. "No, I haven't heard from Douglas, Mike," Nick continued. "I was going to call him the next day, but right then the Octane deal came through, you know, the Montana deal, and I had to deal with *that*, so after I'd called that babe at his office I had to let the thing drop. The hospital, I *still* don't know what the fuck that was about. I mean, could *you* make sense of his talking, with the, with the drug and everything?"

"He didn't really say anything," I said. "He seemed the same as I remember, though—I was wondering what could go *wrong* in his life."

"He misses a belt loop sometimes," said Nick. "He's still as clueless as ever."

"Well," I said, "I guess Annabelle has her own life, you know, so she's not all that, um, informative."

"She's very smart," warned Nick. "She knows what she's doing when she talks to people."

"Oh, for— Let me tell you guys something," said Hector, standing up after a successful shot. "The thing about models is that they're all so *boring*. They're just these dull nineteen-year-old girls who never went to school and don't know anything at all. They have— I mean, I've *talked* to them, and they don't have any personality whatsoever—they come out with these painfully stupid comments and everyone pretends they didn't hear. So sometimes some accidental wit, right, but we've all got *that*, just ordinarily nobody's listening and, you know, writing it down. But they're just *nulls*, each and every one of them, make no mistake."

"Yeah, but, if you know so much about models," said Nick, eyebrows arching over the sunglasses, "how come every time I see you, which is, what, maybe twice a week, three times a week, not counting weekend evenings, every time, I come in and you're in a conversation with one of them?"

" 'Cause they're *down to earth*," said Hector, leaning on the pool cue. "I get *tired* of intelligent interesting people. Anyone want some nuts?"

"I've got a message for you," Nick told me, fiddling with his cue as Hector moved toward the bar. "I almost forgot. From Annabelle."

"A message?"

"Yeah," said Nick. "She just wanted me to tell you that she's sorry about how she was on the phone last week."

"Well, it was an awkward call," I said. "I hope I handled it properly."

"Oh, I'm sure you did fine," said Nick. "But she said, um, she said she was sorry, and not to, you know, trouble yourself too much—not to blame her for not coming to the hospital—to understand that she was too shaken up. Just that she's sorry and you shouldn't be concerned."

"I see," I said.

"I'm sorry too," said Nick with vast difficulty. "I mean, I'm glad we're back in touch and all but I feel like I did something stupid bringing you along. I was just so panicked," he added, his voice roughening with sincerity, "and I decided to call you up. It was a rough night, but it's, you know, it's over, and I don't want to leave town thinking that I caused some problem in your life."

"Don't worry, Nick," I said, smiling. "It's all right."

"I guess the game's over," said Nick as Hector returned with a handful of beer nuts, and we began collecting the pool balls and the cues and returning them to their racks.

"Nick," Hector said reflectively as we retrieved our coats, "you'd better be careful out West."

"What?" said Nick. "What do you mean, careful?"

"I mean you're taking pictures of *cowboys,* which are supposed to appeal to these, you know, bohemians with lots of money who buy jeans, you know? And I say, Oh brother, 'cause bohemians, what, a lot of Jewish people acting like Italians, and when you talk the American West, they can't hear you."

"So they act like Italians," Nick said, using his thumbnail to peel the label off his bottle. "Italians *understand* the West, buddy. You think Clint Eastwood just—"

"Go out and do the shoot, Nick," said Hector, "but if you don't do it *correctly,* the *bohemians* won't know the difference, and you'll still get the damn money, but people all over the *world* see the shit we do in this town and for *them,* Nick, not for the jerks you know, but for *them,* you got to get it right, 'cause what they know is *important,* and you'll never see them but if you don't—if you don't do it right they'll tear you down."

"I'll do it right," said Nick.

"You got a sweet deal—don't let it go to your head. It's late," Hector said, looking around the bar, which, I realized, was emptier than it had been when we came in.

"Yeah, I guess we should take off," said Nick. "I can't wait to get home—I can finally get something to eat."

We put our coats on and Nick swung the oak door open against the cool night air, and I saw the bartender nod at us. "Good night, Barry," I said, closing the door.

"You going to catch the subway back?" Nick asked me.

"Yeah, I'll head over to Canal Street," I said. "It's a short ride back to Brooklyn from down here. You guys heading off together?"

"Yeah," said Hector. "We live the same direction—I'll drop him off."

There was a damp wind without rain and the three of us stood under the TOM ALLEN awning, eyes adjusting to the streetlit dark. "This autumn's going to kill me," I said.

"You just need to get out more," said Nick.

"I'm glad we met, Mike," Hector said, slapping me on the shoulder. "Nick and I, when we break up and divide the friends, I want you."

"Well, have a good trip, Nick," I said, realizing that I would miss him. "How long'll you be gone, anyway?"

"Oh, about six weeks," Nick said. "Give or take. Thanks for joining us."

"Thanks for calling me," I said. "Both times."

"It did the trick," Nick said.

Hector had wheeled the motorcycle out into the street and was starting the engine, and Nick climbed on behind him, waving to me, and soon they had driven out of sight and then the roar of the motorcycle engine, and all its echoes along the dark deserted street, had faded away.

chapter 3

With the move to the Metropolitan Section the last vestiges of internship fell away from my life, and I remember that I spent the first two weeks of October 1986 mired in frantic fatigue as I tried to pick up the subtle, necessary routines of the new, far more complex job. One Tuesday afternoon, roughly a month after Nick's departure for the West, I was sitting ashamed and angry at my desk, burdened by the results of a mild mistake I'd made. I'd written a small bylined story about a city councilman named Tommy Hopkins, who had made a brief statement from the steps of a downtown police station defending controversial changes he'd proposed in the capital spending plan, changes that involved partial privatization of municipal services. "Every day New York is becoming a more dangerous and a more expensive city," Hopkins' statement read, "and publicly funded institutions such as this precinct house will continue to suffer into the next fiscal year until the taxpayers' money is properly allocated." While reporting my story, which ended up on the section's third page, I'd conducted a phone interview with a spokesman from Hopkins' office, who denied that Hopkins' statement was prompted by his fear that his budget proposals, which had received some negative press, had compromised his reëlection campaign. The spokesman also refused to comment on the fact that Hopkins was personally accompanied during his appearance by William Huxley, the editor-in-chief and publisher of a national magazine called *Absolution Journal,* and by the attorney Frank DiGrassi—I'd known of DiGrassi for a while, of course, since his son Ralph had attended Thorndike, but I'd needed the help of a nearby *Evening News* cameraman in order to identify him conclusively. I'd finished my story with several out-of-context quotations from Hopkins and his spokesman and some clipped speculation concerning the possible implications of a professional relationship between Hopkins and DiGrassi, a successful lawyer best remembered from recent mob trials. The editorial staff had had a rough weekend—twenty-one people had been killed in a Manhattan apartment-building fire on Friday, and twenty-two people had been killed by a Staten Island gas-main explosion on Saturday—so due to various circumstances these sentences had survived into the paper, prompting some angry phone calls from Hopkins' campaign office to my new editor, Wilson Pick, who had launched into a tirade about how inconvenient a time I'd chosen for this inaugural foray into the ordinarily acceptable practice of harassing public officials.

"What do you want from this, Michael?" Rachel Geisler asked me later. I had been sitting at my desk at the paper looking over the morning edition when Rachel, a senior reporter who constantly bothered me, had come over and perched on the edge of my desk in the angular sunlight. The paper had been out a few hours and the office was quiet—the front window's fans were stirring strands of ceiling dust and I could hear the hum of the computers' air conditioners as I looked through the Mussolini-scaled front window at two interns taking a cigarette break on the fire escape, silhouetted against the bleached gridwork of facing buildings. "I've been watching you for, what is it, now, a week, you've been here? And you've gotten maybe two hours of sleep, total? And I can't see what you're so worried about—I mean everyone gets to screw up every so often. So what is it you're after?"

"I want to get into high-level journalism," I said, leaning back and smiling foolishly at Rachel, who was fiddling with a red proofing pen. "I mean, Rachel, come on— That's everyone's angle around here, right? At the Supplement they were—"

"This *isn't the Supplement,*" insisted Rachel. "You've got to cut that out, Michael. Look, you've got to remember that I've been doing this for— Well, never mind how long, right, but suffice it to say there were manual typewriters when I had your job. This is a whole new thing for you here, not any kind of cozy—"

"I *do* want to get into high-level journalism," I said.

"Well, who do you know?" Rachel asked simply.

"Nobody," I said. "I know *you.*"

"And you know Wilson, right? You know what Wilson says about high-level journalism?" Rachel was tapping the red pen against her earring.

"What does Wilson say?" I asked, looking around for him instinctively, since none of us in the area was getting anything done.

"Wilson says that high-level journalism is bullshit," Rachel said. "I mean everyone knows it's just a question of rewriting the press releases. All the big boys, Stone, Hersh, everyone knows. In '72 those kids showed up and we all had to start working for a living. That's what Wilson says."

"Rachel," I said, rubbing my eyes, which were aching in the dry air, "I'm just talking, you know, about the eventual thing here. I've only written a couple of things, and Wilson *already* doesn't like me, so, you know, I don't think you have to worry about me getting some—"

"That's not too difficult, dealing with Wilson. So you pissed him off this morning—just keep your head down, and if I were you I'd stick around tonight, you know, showing trust and good faith."

"Yeah, I could do that," I said with dismay, resuming my scrutiny of the column. "There could be— Excuse me." My phone had rung, and I picked it up. "Michael Cadenhead."

"Douglas Taft on line six," the receptionist said.

"Okay, thank you, Margot," I said, surprised, punching the button, looking at Rachel. "It's a friend of mine, so—"

"All right," said Rachel, sliding off the desk, slapping me on the shoulder and wandering off. The lunch-hour quiet was about to end, I knew—already several of the city reporters were filing back into the newsroom, and I could see Wilson sauntering in, talking to one of the sports writers.

"Hello, Douglas," I said, ashamed that I hadn't tried to contact him since his accident. "Are you— Have you recovered?"

"Yeah, I'm all right, I guess," said Douglas, speaking against a background of muted office sounds. "The bandages came off a few weeks ago. You're hard to track down, Michael—I didn't know which newspaper until I came across some piece you wrote today. Listen, I'm sorry to bother you at work—I guess I'm just calling to thank you for coming to see me at the hospital. I was very, um, I was touched that you came in."

"Well, I was happy to be there, Douglas," I said, wedging the phone between shoulder and ear, dropping the morning edition on my desk.

"And that's why I, um, since I felt I was in your debt, I was calling because, it turns out I'm going to something tonight and I was wondering, if you weren't busy, if you wanted to come with me."

"That's nice of you," I said in what I hoped was a grateful tone of voice. "What sort of thing are you talking about?"

"Annabelle's having a party at her house," said Douglas. "Some, um, you know, some high-octane get-together—gentlemen, start your engines. I think you might enjoy it."

"Really? It sounds nice but I can't, Douglas. Some other—"

"Look, it'd be really good if you showed up. Come on, you've got to get back into things, Mike. And I haven't seen you since last month."

"I've got to work tomorrow, Douglas."

"So what? So does everybody." Outside the Mussolini windows a flock of birds circled, their wings grey and black against the bright afternoon sky. "Please come, Michael."

"Well, am I invited?" I asked, chuckling politely. "I mean, I don't want to—"

"What's the difference? It's not that kind of thing," said Douglas. "Listen, do you know how I can get a hold of Nick? I've been calling all over the place, but—"

"He's out of town," I explained. "He's working out in Montana, in the mountains, if you can believe it— Douglas, this just isn't a good night. I'm sorry, but I can't just—"

"Mike, listen to me," Douglas said suddenly. "I think I need someone to talk to."

"Really?"

"I'm sorry," he went on. "I don't want to be any kind of, any kind of imposition. I'm just— I was just so *grateful* to you for taking the time to see me when I got hurt. I've let all this *time* pass, and then I read your article this morning and I thought— Actually, I thought it was *great,* Mike, what you wrote, it was— It actually gave me the idea of talking to you. See, I think"—I was closing my eyes as I listened—"I think I just want to, you know, just want to see someone and *talk,* to talk, strictly on the qt 'cause there's reasons I can't talk to the people at work about what— About what happened to me that night."

"All right— When is this thing tonight? Around what time?" I asked finally.

"Oh, good," said Douglas happily. "You know, the usual. Around ten."

"Okay, I might be able to make it. What's the address?"

"Yeah, hang on," Douglas said. "*That* was a fucking struggle, let me tell you. The school wouldn't give it to me, her *agency* wouldn't give it to me—I almost had to call fucking *Harvard* before I remembered Dad's office. It's somewhere downtown. Just a minute"—I heard him shuffling around—"here it is." Douglas read me off an address and I scratched it in ballpoint onto a newspaper margin. "This'll be good, Mike," he added.

"What's the building look like?"

"I'm not sure, I think it's a brownstone," said Douglas. "It's that neighborhood where— Hang on. *Just a second, Carol!*" Douglas screamed, making me wince, and I could hear a sudden, distant sound of other voices echoing in whatever room he was in. "Mike, I've got to get off the phone," Douglas said. "I'm calling from the Institute, you know, so I'm back on the chain gang. The *real* chain gang, I mean. I've been—"

"I'm sorry—it's the Lineage Institute, right?" I asked.

"That's right. Tell you what, I'll meet you at that, you know, on the corner of Greenwich and Eighth, there's that bar—I'll meet you there at ten. If you can't make it, no problem, I'll have a drink and head over myself. Look, you're going to show up, right?"

I looked around at the slowly moving office. "Well, we'll see how my day goes," I said warily. "I just might."

"Michael," Douglas said suddenly as I was about to hang up, "you've got the scissors, haven't you?"

"Yes."

"Good," said Douglas.

I hung up that phone and sat rubbing my eyes for a moment and then went over and leaned into Wilson's office, where he was sitting as if asleep, the computer on, a sports-trivia book opened in front of him. "Wilson, can I ask you a question?" I asked.

"I suppose so," said Wilson, yawning, looking up at me. Wilson is a large, balding man who favors yellow shirts and brown ties that look like socks. "Listen, Cadenhead, that business this morning— I shouldn't have been— It's been a tight weekend, you understand, with the double-header, all those poor bastards with their buildings blowing up, so the board's a bit tense. What's your question?"

"Can you tell me about the Lineage Institute?" I asked, wandering farther into Wilson's office and leaning on his sooty radiator.

"Sure," said Wilson grandly, leaning back in his swivel chair. "What do you want to know?"

"Just the general idea."

"You don't know *anything* about them?" Wilson shook his head sadly and closed the trivia book. "What we've got here is a Washington think tank, formed about twenty years ago, and back then Lineage was nothing but a Beltway fringe group with an academic orientation and fine folk like you and me didn't have to worry about them except when they went around trying to raise money. With me so far?" I nodded. "Then in, um, 1969, I think, thereabouts, one of these questionable-ethics companies, some Western *brewery,* you know, starts sinking major funding into the Institute, and once they've got their corporate sponsorship the whole picture changes—now we're talking about ties to the major universities, um, I think forty permanent fellows and about a hundred, hundred and fifty outside consultants, and by the early seventies they're involved in a school-textbook campaign, a thing about federal support of day-care centers, welfare, national health insurance, and tactical studies for the State Department, because as you may or may not know we were engaged in a war back then."

"Wilson," I said, "Can't you just—"

"Soon they've put out this thousand-page book called *Principles of Supremacy,* which all these policymakers immediately start using as a bible—there's a copy down in research. What are you doing?"

"I thought I'd take some notes," I said, having produced my back-pocket notebook and pen.

"You should *know* this," Wilson lamented. "So five years ago Lineage opens a New York office and the city contracts them for urban analysis and research, and now things get interesting, because we're talking about upwards of twenty million dollars' worth of business with the New York Police Department, the Department of Corrections, the Mayor's Criminal Justice Coordinating Council—The city's debts to the Institute got so complicated, I remember one time the comptroller started yelling conflict of interest, you know, calling for an investigation of the mayor's finances, and Lineage had to hire Frank DiGrassi and threaten to sue the city for breach of contract before their consulting fees got paid. You knew DiGrassi was involved with Lineage, didn't you?"

"No."

"DiGrassi, as I'm sure you know, is the big-gun partner at Reed Gardner Grant, which is maybe the most expensive boutique law firm in *town,* and Reed Gardner happen to be the experts at keeping Lineage clients away from criminal charges." Wilson was looking at me oddly. "That's why you came in here, right? Because of Hopkins?"

"I don't understand," I said. "I'm sorry."

"Where've you *been?*" Wilson said forlornly. "Tommy Hopkins got into trouble trying to turn our municipal services over to private contractors, right? That's your thing from before."

"Right," I said, nodding.

"So you must have known about how all these local corporations funded a Lineage Institute study on how this would shave the city budget without affecting service to the taxpayer. So we've got kickbacks that could go anywhere, and if Hopkins went and engaged DiGrassi we have to think there's some grease—I mean nobody's ever *proven* that DiGrassi's found clean profit pathways for anyone, mind you, but he's certainly in the right place with the right friends, and it's all the same money in this town. See, what was wrong with your piece"—Wilson was studiously brushing some imaginary lint off of his double-knit trousers—"is that you *speculated* about Hopkins' ties to DiGrassi without understanding what you were talking about—you just sort of mentioned that Hopkins was endorsed by Huxley and was tied to DiGrassi and intimated that that was somehow, um, notable. Now, Huxley's an easy mark, you know, with the *sailing books,* politicians love him because he's the doorway to the Fifth Avenue money, but DiGrassi's someone you've got to watch what you say about. I mean, I don't mind being your daddy when the misquote phone calls arrive, but you know what Charnley said."

"Who?"

"Mitchell Charnley. Look him up," said Wilson, adjusting his tie, yawning. "You keep telling me that you're being responsible because you're being faithful to your sources."

"That's right," I said, stowing my notebook and pen in my back pocket.

"That's not enough," Wilson said, flipping the pages of the trivia book as if shuffling cards. "You've got to be *more accurate* than your sources. With attribution or background, releases, anything, it doesn't matter. Charnley pointed out"— Wilson yawned— "Excuse me. Charnley pointed out that in every journalistic exchange the defining characteristic of what the source states about an event is the fact that the statement is a matter of *record,* and therefore a question of the source's best interest."

"Well," I said, rubbing my burning eyes, "sometimes, yes, that's true, but—"

"It's *always* true. You follow Geisler around, right? Ask her—she's an old pro, she knows, she's learned over time that the source is *always* distorted. You've got to see beyond what you're being told and retrieve the *event.*"

"But the sources are all you've got—"

"Just start doing it right," Wilson said. "So why do you come to me on this day, Michael? Asking me about Lineage"—Wilson was gesturing, vaguely fanning his fingers toward me—"as if Lineage had some bearing on this marvelous recent work of yours, but now it seems you don't quite know what you're asking." Wilson lowered his eyelids. "Or do you?"

"That's right," I said suddenly. "That's right—I came in because of my story. Because I may have a lead. Wilson, listen— I have this, um, I have a friend who works for the Lineage Institute. A— A school friend. Right? And he just— This friend of mine was in the hospital, last month, he was— He got *attacked,* injured, some kind of violent event—but he said something that night to imply that it related— Related to his job. This morning the— Wilson, my point is that he called to tell me that he read my Hopkins piece, um, and to tell me that after reading it he wants to talk to me about what got done to him."

"No kidding," said Wilson, yawning. "So what's your question?"

"Nothing, I guess," I said, noticing the bumper stickers with amusing slogans that Wilson had glued to the wall. "Just that I had intended to stick around tonight, but—"

"But now you've got this thing, which means you can't be here for bedtime, and— You're getting too much sleep," said Wilson suddenly. "That's got to change."

"Too much sleep?" I said incredulously. "I'm not getting *any.*"

"Be like me," said Wilson. "Sleep starts to turn around. Look, Michael, I don't know how to put this, but— You want my trust, right? After this thing today? You're putting me in a tricky position, with these mistakes you're making—I realize you're new here, but it's been almost a couple weeks, you know, and the business with the mistakes, and now you're giving me this song and dance about your evenings. I mean, come on, let's get ourselves straight with things, huh?"

"I'm sorry. I was just asking a question," I said, leaving Wilson's office and returning to my desk.

AT ELEVEN THAT evening I emerged from the subway and walked through an unfamiliar downtown neighborhood in a regulation drab jacket and tie, peering at the torn newspaper margin with Annabelle's address by the light from a beer sign in a bar window. I was wandering toward the row-house staircases at the edge of Annabelle's side street when I felt a tapping on my shoulder and when I turned around Douglas was standing behind me, smiling, hands in his pockets, characteristically dressed in a grey seersucker jacket over a T-shirt and khaki pants under a long black coat, his dirty-blond hair grown a bit long, over his collar, his smoothly shaven face set in its usual altar-boy pattern.

"Douglas!" I said, looking around everywhere and back at him, Blanchard-style.

"I thought you'd never show up," said Douglas. He looked a great deal less haggard than he had in the hospital, his voice and appearance back in elegant order. "What took you so long?"

"I had a rough day."

"Really? Listen, I thought you'd never show up. Come on, let's do this." A limousine emerged from the depths of Annabelle's side street and hummed past us, quickly turning the corner, the boomerang TV antenna on its trunk lid shining yellow in the glare of a streetlight. Douglas pointed forward at the row of brownstones, indicating a façade with overbright windows that emitted a faint, distant drumbeat, before abruptly lurching forward, arm on my sleeve, striding toward the house.

"You've been waiting for me?" I said, following.

"What?" Douglas gave me a distracted look as we walked, his smooth hair falling against his eyebrows. "Yeah, I had a couple of drinks, you know, just sort of getting in the frame of mind for this. This has *got* to be the right one—"

"You haven't been here before?" I said, looking at the addresses through a haze of post-subway adrenaline.

"She's moved," Douglas said. As we watched, another limousine pulled up in front of the brownstone and a man in a tuxedo and a woman in a gown got out and vaulted casually up Annabelle's stairs, and I scanned their faces automatically.

"Douglas," I said suddenly, "this is *Tuesday night.* If you're getting me into a big mess—"

"Let's get this show on the road," said Douglas, leading me up a flight of steps to the green front door, pausing to light a cigarette and going through four matches in the breeze. "Christ, the wind is like the Surgeon General," he said, laughing nervously, smiling in a way that reminded me of Annabelle's smile, smooth cheekbones protruding above the shine of his teeth, getting the cigarette lit and then hitting the brass doorbell.

"Hang on," came a woman's faint voice from deep inside the building, and I glanced at Douglas and saw that he was taking a deep breath with his eyes closed, stubbing out the just-lit cigarette on the stone banister, his hand trembling.

"Who's going to be here?" I asked him, rocking on my feet.

"We'll see," Douglas said, and as I turned and looked at him I saw that he was wincing and bending forward, one hand pressed against his stomach, vaguely positioning himself behind me as he straightened his posture. "I'm sorry—it still pulls a bit," he said apologetically. Right then the door clicked and swung inward and Annabelle was standing there, dressed in a black sleeveless turtleneck dress and gold earrings, her black hair having grown very long, various paraphernalia on one wrist, fluted wineglass in the other hand, and I smiled at her, feeling the warmth of seeing her after so long.

"Michael?" Annabelle said, flaring her eyes with the scandalous smile I remembered very well. "Michael *Cadenhead?* Is that really you?"

"It's really me," I said. "Hello, Annabelle."

"My God." Annabelle stepped forward to kiss my cheek, hugging me—I felt the cold rim of her wineglass against my neck, caught the brush of her lips and the smell of the perfume she wore, which had some effect, so that I suddenly felt a surprising vertigo, felt the brief phenomenon of two structures of memory sideswiping each other, high school against the magazines and billboards of my recent solitary years, and I experienced that trick where it seemed that she complemented me perfectly, that drunken story from Aristophanes all over again, if only for a moment. "Michael Cadenhead. I can't believe it," she was saying.

"It's good to see you, Annabelle."

"I'm so glad you came, Michael," Annabelle said, offering to take my coat as I glanced past her and saw an elegant front room with a large staircase, a few well-dressed people standing round it, mostly elbows and trouser cuffs from my vantage point. "Something's different. Your face looks different. You just—"

"Glasses are gone," I explained mechanically. "I've got contacts."

"You look very good," Annabelle said conclusively. "Well, come on in, Michael, don't—" She trailed off suddenly, and I saw that she was staring past my shoulder. "Douglas," she said quietly, beginning to walk, almost to drift forward, and I slid out of her way, turning to see Douglas still standing deliberately half behind me on the stone landing with his hands plunged in his pockets like weights.

"Hi," said Douglas.

"Douglas, you shouldn't be here," Annabelle said quietly.

"Sure I should," Douglas said, smiling softly as Annabelle stepped toward him. The door was starting to swing shut, so I caught it and opened it again, stepping into Annabelle's foyer and putting my coat down on a chair, while outside the doorway Douglas and Annabelle slowly approached each other and performed a slow, stagnant hug. A tall, tanned man had quickly arrived beside me, holding another fluted wineglass, wearing a boneless suit and a shirt so bright that it looked like it had been freshly dipped in white paint.

"Well, well," the man said in a cultured voice. "I don't think we've met."

"Michael Cadenhead," I said, conscious of my desk-job clothes as I shook his smooth, brown hand.

"Henry Catton," the man said, sipping his wine and gazing out the green door at Annabelle. "How do you do. I'm in arbitrage," he added. "Cadenhead—that's a familiar name. What's your line of work?"

"I'm a journalist," I said, glancing marginally at Douglas and Annabelle still tightly hugging each other outside the door.

"She should do this more often, don't you think?" said Henry Catton, his smile deepening the dimples which framed his mouth like shaving nicks. I nodded and looked outside and saw that Douglas and Annabelle had released each other and were standing very close, speaking to each other in low voices, Annabelle lighting a pair of cigarettes that Douglas had produced from inside his coat. "I thought she had quit," Henry Catton said.

"What?" I said, realizing that he was addressing me.

"I thought she'd quit smoking."

"Difficult thing to do," I said, putting my hands in my pockets and turning to him. "Listen, do you know where I can get a drink?"

"Sure," Catton said, putting his hand lightly on my shoulder and waving vaguely past the ornate staircase toward the back of the house. "The bar's set up in the living room."

"Thanks," I said, wandering into the party, glancing back a final time to see that Annabelle and Douglas were still talking quietly outside the front door. I had to squeeze between several people standing between the staircase and the wall, murmuring my apologies while trying to place them—nobody looked familiar—and as I passed a stack of black portfolios leaning against a closet, I caught myself absurdly glancing backward to see if my shoes were leaving tracks on the whitewashed oak floor. Peering through a doorway into a kitchen, I got a glimpse of copper pans and several cluttered butcherblock surfaces and five or six strangers standing around in there, leaning on the counters talking loudly, interrupting each other in a way that old friends do, performing the evening ballet that they brought from house to house, not noticing me. One of Annabelle's pictures was hanging framed in the hallway, in which she stood soaking wet against a gray background, arched in a convex pose and glaring confrontationally at the camera, her tousled head releasing wild primeval beauty, all the smooth muscles of her body exposed by a minuscule navy-blue one-piece swimsuit with leg-holes that reached above her waist. As far as I could tell the picture had been taken with a large negative, since the detail was amazingly sharp—I could see the crisp edges of every water droplet on Annabelle's curving thighs. As I stood there, Henry Catton wandered by, stopped next to me, and looked at the picture, his cheeks dimpling again.

"Not bad, huh?" Catton said.

"What? Oh— Yeah," I answered stupidly, as if just noticing what I was looking at.

"That's some high-priced merchandise," Catton said appreciatively, leaning to look at the picture. "She cleared about ten grand on this picture alone. Look"—he tapped the glass over the curve of Annabelle's hip, the glass reflecting his protruding finger—"this left pelvic bone, that's probably twenty thousand bucks right there, over a span of, what, maybe three more years, she'll be around. You're the journalist, right?"

"That's me."

"Well, take it easy," said Catton, moving off toward the kitchen.

I continued through the apartment and got to the living room, which was larger than I had expected—there were mattress-sized windows in the back wall showing nothing but reflections from the lamps in the room, and big black speakers that looked to be at least the size of street-corner mailboxes were quietly filling the room with Bill Evans' piano music. One wall was a bookcase and there were various pieces of restrained furniture, a dark grey marble coffee table with a jade ashtray and oversized art books, beige and white walls, a shining black baby-grand piano, and about thirty people of varying ages dressed to varying degrees of formality tightly crowded into the room, the women's clothes standing out against the men's drove-like suits. Once I'd gotten my bearings, I wandered to the bar and poured myself a vodka tonic, waiting to take the vodka bottle from a tall, severe-looking thin man with glossy black hair, dressed in a well-tailored grey suit, who, surprisingly, I recognized from the previous day's Hopkins press conference—it was Frank DiGrassi, and as I accepted the bottle he noticed my glance and nodded politely, obviously not recognizing me. While I was adding a lime to my drink I heard a familiar voice and turned around and saw that Jack Winfield, somebody else from high school, was standing by the piano. I had to deal with five years of changes in his appearance—I remembered his pleasant, freckled face, his faultless manners, his fondness for "beach" clothing—and here he was in a flat grey business suit, short hair combed back, holding a carbonated drink and talking to a woman I'd seen in a movie or on television.

"Jack," I said.

Jack turned and stared at me for a moment, as did the woman, and then he broke into a smile and clasped my hand by the base of the thumb the way he had always done before—my hand snapped into the rhythm by itself. "Michael Cadenhead! How's it going? I *am* sorry"—squinting, shaking his head. "That was so strange—I just turned around and there you are. I'm sorry, this is Mike Cadenhead from my high school," Jack said, interrupting himself, introducing me to the woman he'd been talking to. When I heard her name I placed her as a film actress—one of Hollywood's mid-twenties high-school students.

"Pleased to meet you," I said.

"What do you do, Michael?" the actress asked me.

"Mike Cadenhead, I don't believe my eyes," Jack was saying, still shaking his head.

"I'm a journalist," I told her.

"No kidding," said the actress. "Are you a good journalist or a bad journalist?"

"I beg your pardon?"

"What's your line of attack?"

"I'm just—"

"Mike does *film reviews,*" said Douglas, appearing behind me, hands on my shoulders, startling me. "Sorry to ditch you like that, Mike."

"Douglas, when'd *you* get here?" said Jack. "Have you met Douglas Taft? Annabelle's brother," he told the actress.

"I can see the resemblance," said the actress, nodding. "Pleased to meet you."

"Don't worry about it," I said to Douglas, my unease finally fading.

"Does Anna play the piano?" the actress asked Douglas.

"So Mike, how the hell have you been?" said Jack, speaking with his remembered blend of sweetness and severity. "It's so good to see you."

"I should hope so," Douglas told the actress. "She fought hard enough for it when our parents' apartment got redone. She used to practice all the time, it would drive me nuts—this one Ravel piece, she'd have an epileptic fit playing it. Some damn piece that used the *lowest note on the piano.* She'd keep stopping in the middle and saying, 'Did you guys hear that? *The lowest note on the piano.*' "

"I've been all right," I told Jack. "I live in Brooklyn, um, and I've been working as a journalist. I just moved to the city desk this month." I named the newspaper.

"What's the big deal about the lowest note?" asked the actress.

"Good to be back in touch?" Jack said to me. "You've been totally out of touch, man. I mean, you were even— You were at our graduation thing in Dover, weren't you?"

"There *is* no big deal about the lowest note, it's just another note on the keyboard," said Douglas. "The idea is that Ravel got down there harmonically."

"I certainly was," I told Jack, sipping my drink and smiling at him. "Nobody missed that party of yours, Jack."

"So you're an actress, huh?" Douglas was asking the woman. "I've got a friend who's on a soap, but I don't know which one."

"Oh, yeah?" said the actress.

"What about you, Jack?" I asked. "What are you up to?"

"I mean which *friend,*" Douglas said, cracking himself up, confusing the actress. "I'm kidding."

"I'm at Morgan Stanley," said Jack. "You know, running with the bulls."

"This is a pretty good scene," Douglas said to me, looking around, smiling as the actress got Jack's attention again. "Nice and *restrained.* Where's the bar?"

"Follow me," I said, threading my way between other guests over toward the wall while the Bill Evans disc ended.

"Living here wouldn't be so bad, you think?" Douglas said, his altar-boy voice pleasantly cracking a bit, taking my empty glass and another for himself.

"You're telling me," I said quietly, raising my eyebrows at him, still painfully conscious of my haircut and clothes. Across the room I saw an extremely short actor in spats whose name I couldn't remember, and I sipped my drink as I looked at him, my fingers holding the damp paper napkin glued against the bottom of my glass.

"Mike," murmured Douglas, leaning toward me while picking chunks of lime off a plate and dropping them into our glasses, "does she seem *happy* to you?"

"What?" I said, wiping diluted vodka from my thumb. Douglas looked at me and then yanked the napkin away exasperatedly and I almost spilled the drink.

"Does she seem happy? Annabelle?"

"I guess," I said. "I mean, *I* can't tell. What—"

"Could I get in there?" said Annabelle, from behind us, walking up and pointing at the bar, and we separated and let her through. "Michael, I'm sorry I abandoned you like that, I was being a bad hostess."

"The music stopped," said Douglas, looking away.

"Oh, please," I said, smiling. "Don't worry about it, Annabelle. It was great, I got to meet Henry Catton."

"Hank. Well," Annabelle said with dismay, beginning to construct a dry martini in a brass shaker. "He's always pulling cigarettes out of my mouth."

"That guy Hank Catton, I've seen him before, he's from Cleveland," said Douglas. "He always asks me what I do, every time I run into him. He can never remember. I always want to tell him that I work for him." Douglas laughed. "That would be so *funny.* 'Hello Douglas, what line of work are you in?' 'Hank, don't you remember? I work for *you.*' " Douglas had cracked himself up again. "Nobody ever likes my jokes, damn it."

"Douglas," said Annabelle, shaking her head with affection, putting her arm briefly around Douglas' shoulder, "find another fool to love you."

"So, um—" I said, "how are you these days, Annabelle? It's been a while."

"Is this what I think it is?" said Douglas, pointing at the ceiling, his face set in a constricted expression as Frank Sinatra began to sing.

"I'm all right," Annabelle said, looking at me, which was again startling—she looked small and delicate compared to her imposing photographic likeness. "I've been keeping busy."

I didn't know what time it was— Then I met you— Sinatra sang with his usual delayed phrasing. *Oh, what a lovely time it was— How sublime it was too—*

"So this job's working out?" I asked.

"I know this song," Douglas said, sipping his drink, squinting into the distance, hands in pockets, hair flopping over his smooth forehead.

"It's working out," said Annabelle. "I can't really complain—everybody had a good year."

"This song is so familiar," Douglas was saying. "It sounds so familiar—I remember all those times in Dover when—"

"Come on, you know this," said Annabelle. "*Pal Joey.* Frank Sinatra, Rita Hayworth, Kim Novak."

"Kim Novak is a man," said Douglas, cracking himself up again.

"*What?*" said Annabelle.

"Well, it's what I heard," said Douglas apologetically. "See, Mike, our parents met in 1957—we grew up with the record album."

"Hey, girl in black," said another woman in her twenties, advancing on the three of us at the bar, dressed in a peach silk shirt and a black skirt and high heels.

"Tina, how are you," Annabelle said, glancing up at the droll, flattened sound of the woman's voice, pouring out her martini and smiling as Tina kissed her cheek. "Tina, you remember Michael Cadenhead?"

"Mike! Hello," said Tina Foster, taking my hand, her appearance suddenly snapping into shape as she spoke—the same rounded dark face and pretty eyes and unimpressed expression and voice that had been pounded flat by mallets, all filtered through five years of whatever had happened to her since Thorndike—and before I could stop myself I leaned and kissed her cheek.

"Tina, how are you," I said, smiling awkwardly. "I didn't recognize you."

"Excuse me," said a deep male voice, emerging from the crowd and mercifully drawing everyone's attention away from me. Frank DiGrassi was standing deferentially behind Annabelle, fingers to his face, holding a slim, expensive-looking leather attaché case. "Annabelle, whenever you're ready, I'll just need a few minutes of your time."

"Of course," Annabelle said, swallowing her drink and nodding as she touched DiGrassi's lapel. "I'm sorry, I didn't realize the hour—I'm still a bit nervous about this."

"Douglas! My God," Tina was saying. "Don't go away without talking to me—we've got to catch up."

"Oh, it's not late at all," DiGrassi told Annabelle, politely tapping his attaché case. "You needn't be nervous." There was something indefinably crass about DiGrassi's mannerisms despite the sheath of civility faultlessly expressed by his clothing and demeanor. "There's just a few things to go over. Hello, Douglas." DiGrassi sounded surprised, his thick eyebrows rising as he turned away from Annabelle. "I wasn't expecting to see *you* here. How's life at the Institute? I heard you had some trouble."

"Hey, Frank. Rolling along," said Douglas, tossing his hair off his forehead, reaching around Tina to shake DiGrassi's hand, so that I caught a glimpse of the tank watch with the cracked crystal. "Yeah, there was some nasty business last month but I think I'm all right. How've *you* been?" Meanwhile Tina and I caught each other politely waiting and smiled back and forth.

"I'm just fine," DiGrassi said, putting a hand on Annabelle's bare shoulder. "I'm just hoping this lady can fit me in tonight."

"Frank, you've met Tina Foster—this is Michael Cadenhead," Annabelle said, indicating me. "Michael—Frank DiGrassi."

I was accepting DiGrassi's hand as his expression changed and I felt his grip tighten. "Cadenhead," he said, beaming at me, the smile not affecting his gleaming eyes. "After this morning I knew it was a matter of time before we met."

"How do you do," I said nervously, returning my hand to my pocket, noticing the confused looks on Annabelle's and Douglas' faces.

"So you're friends," DiGrassi said, looking at the three of us. "You know your pal here is a shark. It's true"—he was looking at Annabelle and pointing at me, nodding—"I don't know what he's after, but you'd better believe he's a man you watch what you say around."

"What do you mean?" Annabelle was giving DiGrassi a beautiful startled look. "Michael's good people—take it from me, here's a man you can trust."

"Thank you," I said, flattered. Douglas was looking away, as if his mind was wandering, but Tina gave me a deadpan look from behind everyone, eyelids at half-mast.

"All right, Frank—come on upstairs and we can talk business. I'll be good," said Annabelle, taking the man's arm and beginning to lead him away. "When you get to the dollars and cents I'll take notes."

"Oh, Anna," said Tina suddenly, pointing at her distractedly. "Phillipe's in the kitchen with Hank—he wants to say hello."

"Oh, that's right, *he's* here"—Annabelle flared her eyes—"Frank, I'm sorry, this is business. I'll just take a moment," she told him earnestly, her remarkable face projecting unintended drama.

"I'll just wait in the corridor," DiGrassi said curtly, gesturing Annabelle past himself and then following her out of the room.

"Did you meet Hank? *Definitely* not my thing," Tina said, looking directly at me. "But at least he's not in the *arts*—I mean, I just talked to that guy Girard for four seconds and I think he's the real danger."

"Who?"

Tina shrugged, accepting a cigarette from Douglas. "This photographer Phillipe Girard, as if that's any kind of real name—he's got about five guys in there asking him about the *swimsuit issue*"—her voice dripped contempt—"and he's telling these stories about which girls are good to work with and which aren't."

"Don't call them girls," said Douglas, snapping his lighter shut. "They're women."

"Well, *he's* calling them girls," said Tina, looking around for an ashtray. "I call them, um, my friends complain but I say girl sometimes. Sometimes I say woman."

"How do you refer to yourself?" I asked.

"I want to look like a woman but be a girl," said Tina.

"Listen, I'll be back in a second," I told her, rubbing my left eye, which had been inflamed by the smoke-filled air. "Tina, you know where the, um, where the bathroom is?"

"Yeah," said Tina, pointing languidly out a doorway. "Just go down over there."

"Thanks," I said, still blinking the grit out of my eyes. "I always feel like an idiot."

"In general?" asked Tina.

"That's right," I said, smiling and beginning to navigate away through the living room. *I'm wise and I know what time it is now,* sang Sinatra, finishing the song with his voice nestled between Nelson Riddle's horns like a diamond ring in one of those plush boxes that you're supposed to be able to produce from behind your back and snap open, with the thumb and fingers of one hand, at the appropriate moment.

I DUCKED INTO a pastel bathroom, not bothering to close the door, and searched the medicine cabinet, finding some Bausch and Lomb solution and fixing the problem with my left contact. While I was standing there half-blind, rubbing the wet lens in my palm, I heard a rhythmic tapping sound, and when I turned and squinted to my right I saw an orange plastic bucket sitting on the tiles by the wall, filled with crumpled, sodden sheets of newspaper. "Everything all right?" asked Annabelle, leaning in the bathroom door, concerned, Tina standing next to her, DiGrassi barely visible in the dark corridor behind them.

"Fine, thanks," I said, putting my lens back in, pointing at the sodden bucket. "These damn contacts. What's with the newspaper?"

"There's a leak," said Annabelle, pointing upward. "I should have some boyfriend who knows how to caulk it."

"Oh, you've never had a boyfriend in your life, Anna," said Tina, poking her in the shoulder.

"A leak, huh?" I said, grinning.

"Watch yourself, Tina," said Annabelle, poking Tina back. "All right, Frank, I'm sorry," she said, leaving the bathroom and accompanying DiGrassi toward the staircase.

"You got lens trouble?" said Tina, smiling, the bathroom light catching her flat, coppery hair. "What are you doing now, Mike?"

"Writing for a newspaper," I said, blinking the lens into place and leaving the bathroom. "She's *never* had a boyfriend?"

"Never," Tina said, smiling at me. "Why—you want to get on line?"

"Come on—that's not what I meant," I said, embarrassed. "I just think it's strange. I mean she could have her pick."

"I don't think she *wants* her pick," said Tina. We'd been wandering down the corridor away from the bathroom's horizontal white light, unconsciously following Annabelle, and when we slowed to a stop and faced each other we found that we'd arrived in front of her framed calendar-shot. "Hey, Mike, did you hook up with Blanchard recently?" Tina asked, looking up at me and then over at the picture. "What was *that* like? I mean—"

"It was all right," I said. "I've only seen him a couple times."

"That's the way to do it. Nick's fine in small doses, but—"

"Come on—you can't be *that* tired of him," I said, embarrassed by my association with a person held in such low regard. "He said he'd seen you just recently."

"That's right," said Tina flatly, glancing back toward the framed photograph. "Boy, was that fun."

"Was it that bad?"

"Well—" Tina managed to look bored with her own dismay. "You know—he always does something to make it nice. We only hooked up once during the summer—he'd just had some kind of rough night, he was dodging his jailbait or something—he dropped by, he bought me a nice dinner, nothing happened. Nick always exaggerates. This is some picture, huh?"

"I suppose it's all right," I said, smiling as I followed her dull gaze back toward the framed photograph. "Would you do that for ten thousand dollars, Tina?"

"No." Tina squinted at the picture. "I can understand not wanting your friends to see you this way, I guess. Ten *grand?*"

"Where've *you* been?" I said, beginning to feel the effects of the drinks I'd had. "Come on—there must be college students in *Kansas,* you know, pasting this on the walls of their—"

"Wait," said Tina suddenly, grabbing my wrist. "Did you hear something?"

I strained to hear past the music and voices of the living room, watching Tina squint in concentration. "No," I said. "What did you hear?"

"There it is again," insisted Tina, nodding, and this time I had heard something—a faint, muffled knocking. "I think somebody's at the door."

"You think we should go answer it?" I asked, glancing through the living room door at the other guests. "Annabelle's busy upstairs, right?"

"Yeah, I guess so," Tina said, leading me past the staircase toward the green front door.

"You have good ears, Tina," I said.

"I'm a musician," Tina said, turning the brass knob and opening the door, and Ralph DiGrassi was standing on the stone steps outside, his shoulders stooped, one large hand raised to pound the door again. I was so surprised that I blinked to make sure it was really him, but Ralph's unfortunate appearance made him as eternally unmistakable as Annabelle—he stood staring at us as if caged, a large, ungainly person whom nobody had ever liked, burdened by colorless greasy hair and a hawk-like nose and obtrusive teeth, bad complexion still marring his features. His wide-hipped body was awkwardly draped in stiff-looking wide-waled corduroy slacks and large canvas tennis shoes and he nervously fingered the nylon drawstrings of his crimson windbreaker, face flushed, breath hitching as he stood on the dark, cool steps.

"Ralph," Tina said, clearly startled.

"My father's here," Ralph said, his blurred, sibilant voice immediately reminding me of the years of juvenile ridicule I'd seen him endure. "Am I right that my father's here?"

"Yes," I said. Neither Tina nor I had moved from our side-by-side positions, and I could hear the nervous tapping of Tina's high heels on Annabelle's marble floor.

"One more time. I go to"—Ralph sniffed loudly—"I go to her house and there's a particular person, I tell myself they're not with her, and I'm always wrong. Everyone at Annabelle's house. What are *you* doing here, Cadenhead? What are you, moth to flame, you're back for more grief from these people? Didn't get enough the first time?"

"What?" I said, confused.

"What?" Ralph repeated, eyes widening incredulously as he stepped forward and stared at me, arms moving awkwardly as he clumsily advanced. "What? What? You heard me, Michael *Cadenhead,* now that you're dressed in a tie and you're making the rounds you can still hear when somebody—"

"Ralph, what's *wrong?*" said Tina intently, stepping forward in a way that made Ralph step backward. "What's the— Why are you here?"

"Why am I here?" Ralph said. "Why am I here?"

"Your father's upstairs," I said, voice constricted, standing motionless in the mild wind that stroked us through the opened door, staring at Ralph's face—behind us, within Annabelle's house, I could still hear the sounds of the remaining guests, their voices and laughter drifting distantly forward from the living room's soft envelope of music and smoke.

"I want to tell them both. I am a new man," said Ralph. "I am not the person I was. I can travel anywhere now that I'm free."

"Ralph, you've got to go," Tina told him, glancing sharply at me for support.

"I'm sorry," Ralph said, shaking his head and swaying, shoulders shining in the streetlights. "I've got to see her."

Right then I heard the clattering footsteps of Annabelle and Frank DiGrassi descending the staircase, talking quietly between themselves. "New York is an out-of-pocket state," Frank was saying, "so in the event of a lawsuit they would show damages proximately caused by the breach of contract, claiming restoration or restitution of lost profit." Tina heard also, and together we pulled the door fully open and stepped to either side. Annabelle and Frank both looked down the staircase at exactly the same time, and it was almost comical, in retrospect, seeing their faces change in the same way, simultaneously, DiGrassi in his grey pinstripe suit and Annabelle in her black dress freezing together on the steps and staring, and then I saw Frank's face tighten, his mouth compressed in anger as he sped down the stairs toward the door, not looking at me as he passed. "*What* are you doing here?" he hissed at Ralph, teeth clenched.

"I know what's going on here, Dad," Ralph said tremulously. "I know what you're doing—I want to, I *know* you're putting her in danger, and I want to just, I want to *talk* to you about it, and I want"—Ralph finally broke his father's smoldering gaze and looked penetratingly past me at Annabelle—"I want to talk to *her.*"

"I want you to leave," Frank DiGrassi said slowly, leaning toward Ralph, so that from my vantage point his grey flannel shoulders passed across my view of Tina's alarmed face and bore down toward Ralph. "I want you to go home now. You can't follow me here—this is professional."

"Dad, please," said Ralph, face twisting. "I'm in bad trouble, and I only want—"

"Get out," Frank said in a flat quiet voice, pointing his index finger past his son's shoulder. "I'm with a client. You can't do this. Go home."

"Jesus," I heard Tina murmur quietly, and as I stood worrying that Frank had heard her I saw Ralph suddenly bow his head, and when he raised his face his eyes were brimming—he avoided his father's motionless gaze, looking at me and at Tina and finally past us all at Annabelle where she still stood transfixed on the staircase, and as Ralph turned away Frank reached to pull the heavy green door around and push it shut. I turned with Tina, Frank between us, and we watched Annabelle descending the staircase to meet us, heels tapping the marble.

"Did we see that coming?" Annabelle asked calmly.

"No," said Frank. "I'm very sorry."

"You told me there was no chance it would happen," said Annabelle, having arrived before us, making a fourth corner. "Look, Frank, I'm still apprehensive about all this. I'm not sure it makes sense to—" She broke off and glanced at Tina and myself.

"No need to be." DiGrassi was shaking his head soothingly. "This could all be yours. You'll be doing very well as long as nobody starts talking"—he looked over at me, suddenly, his eyes locking with mine for a moment before he continued—"and soon the contracts will be signed."

The phone rang somewhere. "Damn it," Annabelle said. "Frank, I'll call you tomorrow?"

"So I should proceed?" DiGrassi asked, taking a black raincoat from the coat rack and reaching past me for the brass doorknob.

"Yes," said Annabelle. "Go ahead. I've got to take that call."

"I enjoyed seeing you both," DiGrassi told us, tipping his chin at us and opening the door against the dark night air, and as Annabelle darted off toward the kitchen Tina and I looked at each other.

"You want to go get another drink?" Tina asked.

"All right," I said. I noticed again, after five years, how Tina had an erotic stare that she held in reserve—she could look at you and for a moment she seemed to be gauging you as a potential naked man on top of her, and then her expression would flatten out again and the moment would be gone—I remembered that I had seen her do it many times, but years ago such a thing would never have happened to me.

"What was Frank DiGrassi doing here?" I asked, as we reëntered the crowded living room, dodging round more unfamiliar people, a few of whom Tina recognized and nodded at.

"She won't tell me," said Tina. "She gets a certain way when she's up to something."

"What do you think she's up to?"

"Something risky. I'm so glad you guys *came,*" Tina said, looking up at me. "I haven't seen you guys in *years.*"

"Not even Douglas?"

"Nope. Here," said Tina, dropping limes into the glasses, handing one to me, and we found a vacant spot on the green couch. "So, you know, I remember you writing those things all the time, and now you're a *journalist.* That sounds exciting."

"Not really," I said, leaning back against the softness of the couch and realizing that I was tired despite the soft glow of the drinks I'd had. "I'm just a fact gatherer. It's not doing anything."

"Hmm," said Tina, brushing her thin hair from her smooth forehead, sipping her drink as she crossed her legs. "Why'd you kiss me?"

"I never know when to kiss people," I said, remembering Annabelle's welcoming embrace. "Tina, come on— *Nobody's* still doing the thing they did in high school, right?"

"*I* am. Looks like Ralph is. What's wrong, Anna?" said Tina, suddenly looking up. I turned my head and saw Annabelle standing in front of us, a dazed, frightened look on her face.

"What? Nothing," Annabelle said distractedly, sitting down next to us on the couch.

"Was that Dennis on the phone?" asked Tina. "I told Dennis I was here and he said he'd call."

"No," said Annabelle. "It was just— The person just hung up."

"Who's Dennis?" I asked.

"A boy," said Tina. "Wait—did they *say* anything?"

"No. I think it was that guy again," said Annabelle, closing her eyes, leaning her elbows on her knees and ducking her head, looking momentarily frail.

"I thought that *stopped,*" said Tina, looking concerned, reaching over and rubbing Annabelle's back, her thumb brushing Annabelle's collarbone. "I keep *telling* you you've got to be careful about this stuff. There's always—"

"Excuse me. Annabelle, we're leaving," said a suntanned, prematurely balding man with a yellow tie who was approaching the couch, a clump of people in overcoats loitering behind him.

"Oh—" said Annabelle, eyebrows up, leaning forward on the couch to kiss the man's cheek as he bent over her. "So soon? Well—I enjoyed meeting you," she added, frowning vaguely at the departing guests before squinting covertly at Tina. "Did you even *talk* to them?" she murmured.

"No," said Tina, getting up, moving between my knees and the coffee table. "I'm getting you some water."

"I'm *fine,* Tina," Annabelle said, irritated, as Tina threaded her way between the few remaining conversational crowds and out of view. I looked over at Annabelle—she was leaning back on the couch, fingers on her forehead, apparently still unnerved.

"Has this happened before?" I asked finally.

"Hmm?" said Annabelle, turning to me as if just noticing that I was there. "Well— Yeah, it was going on for a little while, the phone would ring and someone would hang up, you know, and then I started— There were a couple of times that there was this pause, you know, and one time I heard this man's voice whisper 'hi,' you know, really softly, and then hang up. When you called, Michael, that night last month, that's why I was so flustered. Christ, why does everything have to happen at once?"

"Annabelle," I asked, "what's going on?"

"It has to do with graduation weekend," she told me, leaning back on the green couch, gold watch flashing. "See, I— I made a bad mistake back then, something very stupid that I did, and now it's catching up to me. I can't explain more than that. Just that I'm a nervous wreck."

"I'm sorry—I shouldn't have asked," I said awkwardly.

"Michael"—Annabelle looked at me suddenly—"are you here to investigate something? For your newspaper or magazine or whatever it is? I want you to tell me."

"No," I said after a moment.

"You're not here because of Nick?"

"What?" I said, confused. "Not at all. What—"

"That's good," said Annabelle. "Because if you were I'd be— I wouldn't be sure how to take that, Michael. Thanks, Tina." Tina had reappeared with a glass of water and Annabelle took a sip.

"Listen, Annabelle, I think you ought to change your phone number," Tina said.

"It's unlisted," said Annabelle, sipping the water.

"I *know,*" said Tina, "but someone's calling you. Come on, you've got to be more careful. And I would change the locks, too. I mean anything can happen."

"I think it's been Ralph calling me," said Annabelle, running a hand through her hair—a shaded floor lamp shone through the glass as a pale cloud of milky steam faded upward and out of the tap water, and there was something about the way that it looked that gave me the distinct impression, for a moment, that I'd seen exactly the same thing, years before. Looking again, I was sure—something had happened, something violent, and someone had handed Annabelle a glass of water when she was weak, not Tina, but someone else, some man, at a moment years in the past. I remembered Annabelle in her famous cocktail dress, a younger Annabelle sitting somewhere weakly drinking warm tap water, somewhere dark with country sounds, and I seemed to remember that there had been some sort of fight, an actual fistfight that we'd all seen, but I couldn't remember anything else. "Thanks, Tina," Annabelle said, holding out the glass, and suddenly my memory focused a bit more.

"You *fainted,* didn't you?" I asked Annabelle.

"What?" said Annabelle, confused. "Michael, what are you—"

"I'm sorry," I said. "During graduation weekend—I just remembered. You— In the middle of everything, when we were all upstairs, there was some kind of fight, and then you fainted. Right? Tina, you remember? And somebody handed you a glass of water, just like she just did, is what reminded me."

"I don't remember," said Annabelle, shaking her head. "I'm sorry."

"Oh, come on," I said, smiling, rubbing my burning eyes. "You had— I remember this. You had a piece of a willow-tree branch tied around your head. Right? Or, no—I guess that was later on, that you had the branch around your head."

"You have an amazing memory," said Annabelle.

"Yeah, you *did* have leaves in your hair," said Tina, poking Annabelle in the shoulder, sparing me an electric glance and turning back to Annabelle. "Mike's right."

"I'm going to see if I can find Douglas," I said, standing up. "Tina, you said he went upstairs? Annabelle? You mind if I poke around and look for him?"

"What? No," said Annabelle. "Just don't steal anything, Michael."

I FINALLY FOUND Douglas when I cautiously pushed open a door at the end of the dim upstairs hallway, which gave into a tiny room with a single window lit only by a streetlight shining against the ceiling, the rippled window glass casting waving shadows as cars murmured past outside. There was nothing in the room but a television and several stacks of boxes and magazines, and another large framed fashion photograph of Annabelle hung on one wall—just her head and shoulders against a grey background, her hair suspended about her face by a high shutter speed. Douglas sat leaning against the windowsill, holding an open vodka bottle by the neck, looking at the floor, his face obscured by shadow—and at the sound of my entrance he looked up, startled, and then smiled.

"Michael!" Douglas said. "Come on in."

"Are you all right?" I asked. "What are you doing up here?"

"What? Oh, yeah, I'm fine," Douglas said as I sat cross-legged on the dark carpet, facing him, accepting the bottle as he held it out. "I'm doing *just* fine. Is anybody still here?"

"A few people," I said, rubbing my burning eyes. "I can't believe this house."

"I know," said Douglas, squinting in disbelief. "I knew she was raking it in, but this is just incredible. Annabelle looks pretty tonight, doesn't she?"

"She's very beautiful."

"I'm sorry—I thought there'd be more people here that you knew," Douglas said, handing me the bottle. "I guess this is sort of outside your purview."

"It's all right," I said, taking a sip and handing the bottle back. The dark and empty room was somehow reminding me of the Brooklyn summer, of the heat of July—I remembered the crowds watching the fireworks around the restored statue, remembered the boats and the wind—it was passed time, and I was sad, because nobody could hold on to evidence of these things and soon they would pass away. "Douglas, I want you to tell me what's going on. I want you to start at the hospital and tell me the whole thing."

Douglas tapped the back of his head against the window glass. "I remember that night," he said finally. "The night I messed with something dangerous—it's like a dream but I remember it, being at the Hopkins fund-raiser, then the hospital, you and Nick showed up, and you both were"—Douglas laughed and leaned forward, fist round the neck of the bottle, interrupting himself—"Hey, Mike, isn't it so *funny* that Nick Blanchard isn't here? He's going to have a fit when he finds out he missed this. I just think it's so *funny.* First thing that ran through my mind— Where's that Blanchard asshole. I remember in high school I used to always think he was such an asshole."

"Everybody did," I said. "So you went to the Hopkins function a month ago, and then something happened, something that put you in the emergency room and almost killed you, and"—I was rubbing my eyes, feeling my fatigue—"and Nick Blanchard invited me down, and, and when we *saw* you, you didn't want us to call the *police,* and you didn't want me to talk to *Annabelle,* and when I *talked* to Annabelle she refused, she *refused* to come down, she asked if I was a reporter and then hung *up* on me, and then *you* told me that it had to do with your job, the, you know, the Institute, and you said you wanted to explain." I was looking at Douglas' silhouette and reaching for the vodka bottle and as I spoke an image passed across my eyes, a ghost image of something that had happened at the hospital, some small, fleeting event that was worth remembering, and then it was gone. "Then when you called me today you, you mentioned the *piece* I wrote, so did you *know* Frank DiGrassi was going to be here?" I asked. "Is that what you meant about your job? Nick told me Annabelle's doing something legally questionable that's going to bring her six million dollars. Did you have some kind of meeting with them up here? Were you planning on telling me that Annabelle is Frank DiGrassi's client?"

"I didn't know you'd called Annabelle," Douglas said quietly. "What—"

"And then, while you've been sitting up here Ralph DiGrassi showed up. He came to see them both, his father and Annabelle, to *intercede,* he said, and his father threw him out."

"Fuck," said Douglas weakly. "*Ralph* was here. Oh, fuck. That's— Look, Mike, I *heard* Annabelle and Frank come upstairs when I was in here, but I didn't *see* them—I just heard them go into the bedroom. Did she tell you—"

"Graduation weekend," I said. "That's what she told me when I asked."

Douglas stared at me incredulously. "She said that?" he whispered finally, his voice displaying mild fear and deep drunkenness. "She actually *said* that?"

"She said she made a bad mistake graduation weekend and now she's paying for it," I said. "And someone's been calling her, frightening her, and she doesn't know who it is. So now it's time for you to explain."

Douglas gazed at the photograph of Annabelle, clearly groping for words, and I waited. "You know, it makes *sense* to me that you're a reporter, Michael," he said finally. "It makes sense because of the way you *talk.*" Douglas took another swig from the bottle and looked up at Annabelle's picture. "Mike, does anyone know we're up here? I mean, does anyone know I'm talking to you? Did Ralph *say* anything to you?"

"He sounded incoherent," I said. "But his father and Annabelle didn't seem surprised that he was here."

"Jesus, coming to this thing may just be the stupidest thing I ever did, Mike," Douglas said quietly. "I mean, you have— I'm sorry, I've had a bit too much to drink— You have no *idea* how strange this is for me. That's why I called you, Mike"—he took a swig of vodka from the bottle and then handed it to me and I followed suit before he continued talking—"That's why I called. There's something going on, Michael, something important, but it's *hidden.* It's secret."

Douglas," I said, "you wanted me to come. Can't you—"

"No," said Douglas. "No— I'm fine, is what I'm saying. I can't talk about it— I mean you came to the hospital, not like the rest of these assholes, you actually gave a shit and came down, so I thought

I'd be nice and invite you to this thing tonight. I understand about Ralph." Douglas drank again from the clear bottle, his eyes, remarkably like Annabelle's, glittering in the darkness. "Life goes in strange directions when you're alone."

"Can you tell me one thing?" I asked Douglas. "Please— Can you tell me what all of this has to do with Hopkins?"

"What?" Douglas said, startled. "No, *nothing* to do with *him*, Mike. That's— Listen, that much I'm *sure* of. Look, you want to watch out for *both* DiGrassis, the fucking Institute, *Nick*, I mean don't trust *any* of them, but Hopkins is, I mean, he's *nothing*. Believe me, Michael, I can't explain yet. I'm sorry." Douglas leaned his head back against the wall, the pale streetlight catching his hair as it moved, seersuckered forearms on knees. "I just can't *believe* she told you graduation. You know, everything was such a big deal back then—we were, what, seventeen, eighteen, when all that stuff happened?"

"It was a long time ago," I said, leaning back against a cardboard box and looking at Annabelle's photograph.

"We didn't really know each other that well in high school," Douglas said. "I'm so sorry about that, Mike."

"We knew each other," I said, standing up, feeling lightheaded for a moment. "Are you coming downstairs?"

"I'll be down in a second," said Douglas, looking up at me. "Michael— I'm glad you came to talk to me. Will you—"

"Yeah?" I asked, hand on the door.

"Can you just— Will you just be my friend? I mean"—Douglas picked up the nearly empty bottle and then put it back down—"I mean, that's all I'm saying, really."

"Yes," I said awkwardly. "I can do that."

"Take care, Michael," Douglas said softly.

SOON I WAS putting my overcoat on, standing in a huddle of shivering people in coats beside the opened front door, where Annabelle was saying goodnight to her last departing guests, and eventually I interrupted her. "Annabelle," I said, trying to get her attention. "Annabelle, Annabelle."

"Michael?" she said brightly, arms crossed as she finally turned to me.

"I'm leaving. Thanks for having me."

"Thanks for coming, Michael," Annabelle said, leaning to kiss my cheek, hugging me again, which in my drunken state felt a bit like accidentally brushing an electrical cable.

"Goodnight, Tina," I said, as Tina walked up, leaning to kiss me as well.

"See you later, Mike," said Tina in her bored voice. "Give me a call sometime—we can have dinner or something."

"Yeah, okay," I said, waving vaguely at the few remaining guests, none of whom I'd met, and turning to go, when Annabelle suddenly caught my arm.

"A lot of time's gone by," she said, her words fogging in the cold as she touched my shoulder, a look on her face that I pretended was only for me. "It's so hard to stay together in the city. I'm glad you came."

It was past two in the morning—too late for the subway—so I caught a cab, and as we crossed the Brooklyn Bridge I leaned my face against the glass and looked out past the ancient, flickering cables at the clear night sky and the moonlit river. As I lay drunkenly in bed that night the darkness moved with images of everything I'd seen at Annabelle's house, and at around five-thirty in the morning I awoke with a start, staring at a haze of bright green light that eventually focused to the digital numbers on my alarm clock, convinced that something had just happened, but soon falling back into uneasy sleep.

chapter 4

The next day was a Wednesday in October and the sky was cold and white and autumn was underway, unavoidably, the quiet October wind and hushed voices of passersby acknowledging the common defeat as the summer's hopes moved on and the work of the equinox, the task of passing time, gamely began. It was the day that the minted air of winter first arrived and the scent of autumn deepened, the day that the aromatic river wind blew down the avenues and the parks were orange and green with the wet October leaves and the trampled grass. It got colder in the afternoon, raining suddenly as the business-suited crowds migrated, shivering in the sudden chill, and after the rain the dispersing clouds shone gold above the dim streets, casting long shadows down the avenues—the late sun gilded the steel of the rooftop water towers as the grids of midtown ignited, the sky darkened, the evening crowds arrived and the neon lights burned as the street's fresh water reflected the false dawn of the storm's end.

I had awakened that morning to a distant male voice, a voice from another building, and as I struggled from the depths of sleep the voice had haunted me in my half-conscious state because of its resemblance to the sound of my father speaking. I arose to the morning's cold crisp air as it blew through the bedroom window's cracked glass, noticing that I'd overslept, and realizing, as I sniffed the overcast ozone in the wind, that I had dreamed about Annabelle, but remembering nothing from the dream but the slight spur that her name prompted in my head. I was very late arriving at the paper and I sat gingerly at my desk and looked over my assignments, my head aching with humid fatigue, the ATEX screen blurring as my contact lenses burned my eyes, and I'd been trying to do this for half an hour when Wilson wandered up to my desk, grinning, wearing a necktie made of newspaper. "Well, Cadenhead," he said, looking down at me and running his hand through his thinning reddish hair, "how was the thing last night? The big Hopkins lead?"

"It wasn't a Hopkins lead, Wilson," I said, rubbing my eyes. The morning crowd was thin, the office dark, the Mussolini windows drenched with dust. "I think I misinterpreted what my friend said. Jesus, I've *got* to get some new contacts—"

"Oh, well," sang Wilson merrily. "So much for that business before. I talked to Hopkins' office for you so I don't think we'll have to retract. Michael"—he frowned at me, adjusting the stained collar of his yellow shirt, pulling it from the reddish hairs on his reddish neck—"Michael, look, I don't mean to be a big shot or anything, but you remember what I was saying yesterday? About people's motivations in talking to journalists?"

"Oh, give me a break, Wilson," I said, staring incredulously at his tie. "I thought I was on to something, is all." Wilson was already waving his hand in a papal gesture, frowning magnanimously, and I looked around at the quiet newsroom crowd, wondering if he thought he was being watched by someone intriguing.

"You heard what you were told," Wilson said. "A man can tell a thousand lies. I shouldn't have been so hard on you yesterday—it was just"—he yawned magnificently—"excuse me. It was just that the board's still concerned about our coverage of the Rehnquist business. By the way"—he leaned forward—"what do you think of my tie?"

"It's something," I said, fishing in my desk drawer, searching in vain for an aspirin bottle. "Wilson, should I—"

"It's a beauty, isn't it?" Wilson said, fingering the tie lovingly. "Rachel gave it to me this morning."

"Oh, you're wearing it!" said Rachel, bobbing up on the other side of the shoulder-height bulletin-board partition, carrying a stack of printouts from the wire service computer, ballpoint pen clamped in her teeth. "Not bad, Pick, not bad at all."

"I've got to make some calls," said Wilson shyly, in a way that was almost charming, sauntering away, tapping random desktops.

"Rachel," I said, "what's with the tie?"

"You know what's wrong with you?" Rachel said, turning her ATEX terminal on without looking, flipping through the printouts with her other hand, voice still distorted by the pen in her mouth. Today she was wearing a necklace made of injection-molded plastic barnyard animals over a purple smock-like garment. "You never read the news wires. Did you go to some fast-track thing last night? Some downtown party?"

"Yeah, I did, Rachel," I said. "Why do you think I'm two hours late?"

"I think you're getting too much sleep," said Rachel, grinning so as to show off a gold tooth. "That's got to change. Did you have fun?"

"It was a waste of time," I said casually, "except for meeting Frank DiGrassi."

"That big-dick lawyer? You *met* him? What was he like?"

"That's right," I said. "He seemed, um, to be a man you wouldn't want to anger."

"Yeah, *you* angered him, didn't you?" said Rachel, having picked out a single torn sheet and begun reading it intently. "Wilson was talking."

"Oh, Jesus," I said, head throbbing. "All right, I made another mistake. What—"

"Nothing happened last night?" said Rachel, finally looking up at me, holding the scrap of paper.

"I didn't say that," I said. "I just said it wasn't a Hopkins lead like I had—"

"So then you didn't know anything about this," said Rachel, handing me the printout. The lead slug read DEATH NOTICE UPDATES / 10.22.86 / 10:00 EST, and as I stared down at the blurred thermal type it seemed that all the newsroom sounds faded away save for a low humming of my own breath. According to the wire-service database Ralph DiGrassi had died at approximately five-thirty that morning at St. Mark's Hospital—the cause of death was not given.

"Jesus Christ," I said, swallowing weakly, looking up at Rachel. "I saw him last night."

"The big-dick lawyer?"

"No, not the— I mean, him *too,* but his son, Ralph"—I held up the news wire—"the guy who died this morning. I just— He was standing right in *front* of me less than, um, just a few hours ago. Jesus Christ—"

"All right, take it easy," Rachel said, looking around the newsroom, touching my shoulder. "Take it easy. Was he a friend of yours? I'm sorry, I just thought—"

"No," I said, breathing heavily. "I mean, no, not a friend, just a guy I knew in high school. I just— I just happened to run into him last night, when he— Rachel, *thank you,*" I said, looking up at her, contacts blurring my eyes. "I really might have missed this. I might never have seen it until it broke."

"Do you want me to talk to Wilson?" Rachel said, fingering the plastic barnyard animals. "Do you want me to do that?"

"God, Rachel," I said, feeling light-headed as I handed the slip of shiny paper back to her. "If you wouldn't mind, I'd be grateful. I'd do it myself—"

"I understand," said Rachel. "Don't worry—I know how to handle him. But you better be right about there being a lead here."

"This time I know I'm right," I said.

"Good," said Rachel, taking the squib. "I'll take this in to him on my way out. I'm going downstairs—you want anything?"

"Um, could you pick me up, you know, one of those little boxes of aspirin?" I said, fishing out a twenty and handing it to her.

"You're turning into one of those guys," said Rachel, swatting me on the forehead with the twenty and heading off toward Wilson's office, where she stood talking through the doorway, holding out the wire, and then stepped inside and shut the door, casting an animate shadow on the door's pebbled-glass window. I waited nervously, tapping my fingers, looking at the windows—a cracked pane near the AP map had been taped over with newpapers that flapped in the breeze through the broken glass. After a moment I hunted through the phone book and called the Lineage Institute WATS line, staring up at the blackened Edwardian pressed tin of the distant ceiling.

"Lineage Institute," a subdued receptionist told me after a moment.

"Douglas Taft, please."

"May I ask who's calling?"

"Michael Cadenhead," I said, nervously staring toward Wilson's door and seeing Rachel emerge, not looking at me, but no longer holding the wire as she headed through the newsroom's large double doors toward the bank of elevators.

"From where?"

"Um—" I was taken aback, so I named the newspaper.

"Just a moment, please, Mr. Cadenhead," the receptionist said.

I waited through several minutes of excruciating piped-in switchboard music and then the phone clicked loudly, making me jump, and a woman spoke to me in a rich, scuffed voice, notably free of any accent. "Is this the party calling for Mr. Taft?"

"That's right."

"Well, he hasn't come in today," the woman said. "I'm not sure he's working here anymore."

"I beg your pardon?" I said, reaching for a pen and shuffling through the garbage on my desk in search of a notepad.

"Well, I think he may have quit," the woman said. "If you wouldn't mind stating the nature of your business with the Institute, I'd be glad to—"

"It's a personal call," I said. "My name is Michael Cadenhead—I'm a friend of his. I don't understand—did he quit or didn't he?"

"Not in so many words, but it's understood that you can't simply not come in."

"I see," I said, scribbling notes. "You wouldn't happen to have his home phone number, would you?"

"Actually, I've tried to reach him there, but there's no answer," the woman said after reading off a number. "Look, I don't understand this either—I'm a friend of Douglas' as well as a, you know, we work together, we've been working together here, so I tried him at home. He's been going through something, but I don't know—"

"Is this Carol Casey?" I asked suddenly. "Sweet Carol?"

"Yes," the woman answered, startled. "What—"

"Miss Casey," I said, wedging the phone between my head and shoulder, rubbing my aching eyes, "I understand that the Lineage Institute has involved Douglas in some business with the attorney Frank DiGrassi. Could you tell me what that's all about?"

There was a long pause, during which I could see Rachel coming in through the big doors at the end of the newsroom, holding a paper bag from the deli downstairs. "That's— I'm sorry, would you mind telling me what this is in regard to?"

"I'm a newspaper reporter," I said, naming the paper, tapping my fingers on the cracked edge of the desk, "and I'm trying to locate Douglas because there's been a mysterious death and I believe Douglas is somehow involved. Listen"—I was looking at my desk calendar—"on the night of September sixteenth Douglas was almost killed, he almost died of a stab wound. Do you know anything about that?"

"I'm sorry, but I'm really not sure I can answer any more of these questions," Carol said, hanging up.

"All right—thanks for all your help," I said to the dead line, since Rachel was standing right in front of me. "Hey, Rachel," I said, taking the proffered plastic pillbox. "Thank you."

"Who hung up on you?" asked Rachel, frowning, holding out nineteen singles.

"What the hell?" I asked, taking the change.

"The guy only had singles," Rachel said, taking the rest of her purchases over to her desk. I dry-swallowed two aspirin and closed my burning eyes, and as I was opening them and staring at the ATEX terminal a shadow passed over the desk and I looked up to see that Wilson was standing next to me, carrying a crumpled brown paper bag the size of a paperback.

"Mike," Wilson said, sitting on the edge of my desk, inadvertently showing me the white skin of his kneecap through the stretched, fraying fabric of his trousers, "Have you got a minute?"

"Yes, Wilson?" I said, reading the time upside-down off his wristwatch.

"You know that Frank DiGrassi's son died?"

"In the hospital, yeah," I said, leaning back. "I saw the squib."

"Mike," said Wilson, nodding at me critically, "you're from New York, right?"

"I'm sorry, Wilson— What?" I had lunged forward to correct a grammatical error I'd spotted on the screen.

"You grew up in New York, am I right? So where'd you go to high school?"

"Thorndike," I said resignedly, turning toward Wilson as he adjusted his newspaper tie and nodded, his face set in the glazed glare of a man concentrating on something very far away.

"That's what I thought," Wilson said. "Class of '81, am I right? Reason I ask— I saw the thing on the news wire and— Mike, I'm sorry, is this a bad time? Are you—" Wilson waved vaguely at the keyboard, as if barely awake.

"No, I'm sorry, Wilson," I said, leaning back and looking at him. "This is for tomorrow. What can I do for you?"

"Well"—Wilson stifled a yawn—"look, you know there's going to be a slug on the death no matter what, but I just happened to notice that the DiGrassi son—the dead guy— I just happened to notice that he was Thorndike '81, so I was wondering—"

"Oh," I said, vaulting out of the chair and reaching toward my filing cabinet. "You want the *yearbook*, Wilson?"

"Oh, sit down," said Wilson, grimacing with fatigue. "I don't know why you young types are always jumping around all the time. Where you get the *energy*. Me, I get too much sleep. You know how that is, when you get too much sleep? Getting thirsty all the time? That business? I should go out at night and *drink* or something." Wilson squinted at my bulletin board, which I'd left bare save for a torn-out advertisement from our Sunday magazine—a picture of Annabelle standing in front of a bright yellow background wearing a white jacket and a pearl necklace and white polka-dotted gloves. "I wasn't looking for the yearbook."

"Good," I said, sitting back down. "Good, because I'm getting tired of dealing with my high school friends. I'm not— I don't think I like them very much."

"I'm sorry," said Wilson. "You *are* busy."

"No," I said. "No. But do this right, Wilson. If you want to talk to me about Ralph DiGrassi's death, don't tell me Thorndike—talk to me like I was following something and not because I went to that damn school. Talk to me like I'm a reporter."

"I had two friends in high school," Wilson said, still squinting at the picture. "One of them's some sort of activist—one of them *was* some sort of activist—at Berkeley—and then ended up in the tile business. The other's a marketing executive at General Foods. Who *is* this girl?"

"A model. Look, you said there's at least a slug here," I said. "Who's doing the story?"

"We'll see. I mean, I hate to waste your time, Mike"—Wilson seemed about to pat me on the shoulder until I realized that he was stretching—"except that last night you were out with a friend from Lineage, am I right? What's so funny?"

"Nothing," I said, rubbing my eyes. "The ball's really on the other foot now, isn't it? Look, Wilson, what's the question here, exactly?"

"Michael," Wilson said slowly, admiring the startled pout that Annabelle was giving the camera, "do you have reason to believe that there is a pattern of circumstantial evidence connecting the death of Frank DiGrassi's son to other potentially newsworthy events?"

"Yes," I said.

Wilson reached into the paper bag and pulled out a battery-powered microcassette recorder with a special jack that hooked into the newsroom's phone extensions.

"Go," said Wilson, handing over the heavy machine. "Move."

I connected the phone tap as Wilson wandered away from my desk, moving around a pillar and out of view, and then I tried the number that Carol had given me for Douglas. After fifteen rings I hung up and began hunting through the dog-eared phone directory, dialing and then waiting through the rings, gazing blankly at the glass of the ATEX screen. "Reed Gardner Grant," said a woman with a smooth, remarkably lovely voice.

"Um," I said nervously, "Frank DiGrassi, please."

"I'm afraid he's unavailable," said the siren. "If you'd care to leave a message, I can—"

"I'm a journalist," I said, naming the newspaper.

"I'll connect you to Mr. Martins," the siren said.

I waited and after a moment I was transferred to a man with a restrained, quiet voice. "This is Holly Martins—I'm the firm's press secretary. How may I help you?"

"I'm wondering if Mr. DiGrassi would care to comment about his son's death."

"He's given me a press statement," said Martins. "I can try to answer your questions."

"If you have no objections, I'd like to record this conversation."

"That would be acceptable," Martins said smoothly, and I reached to turn on the phone tap. "Funeral arrangements haven't been set, I'm afraid—Mr. DiGrassi has spoken to trustees of the Thorndike School concerning a memorial scholarship fund. If you wish I can give you the address."

"That's not necessary. Do you know where Ralph went to college?"

"Ralph DiGrassi graduated from Princeton University in 1985," Martins read as the phone tap beeped. "He received a Phi Beta Kappa degree in economics."

"Can you tell me what he's been doing since college?"

"He had been living at home with his parents," Martins said.

"Can you give me their full names and ages?" I asked. Martins did so, interrupted by another beep of the phone tap. "Mr. Martins— How did he die?" I asked finally.

"Complications."

"You can't explain what that means?"

"Ralph DiGrassi died at 5:20 this morning of complications."

"All right, Mr. Martins, thank you," I said, thumbing the phone's receiver cradle while flopping the Manhattan phone book open across the desk. I had found Frank DiGrassi's home number, somewhere on Central Park West, and I sat with my finger poised above the dial, frightened, and then changed my mind and found the number for the Thorndike School. I called and asked to speak to the alumni office, identifying myself both as a reporter from the paper and as a Thorndike graduate, and after some mercifully silent time on hold I was connected to an alumni office secretary, and I identified myself all over again and then rehooked the phone tap and turned it back on. "I'm calling in regard to Ralph DiGrassi's death," I said.

"I'm sorry," said the secretary, "but I can't answer any questions."

"Can you tell me about the scholarship fund?"

"We were only just informed of Mr. DiGrassi's plans concerning the fund," the secretary said as the phone tap beeped. "Could you hold? I think I'm getting another call."

"No, that's at my end," I said. "Listen, is the school planning any kind of memorial itself? I mean, I'd like to know just because I'm in—I was in Ralph's class—I'm Thorndike '81."

"We haven't been told," the secretary said.

"All right— All right—" I said, and something occurred to me. "Thanks for your help. Listen, as long as I've got you on the phone, can I ask you something? I was wondering if you could give me the phone number of a Thorndike alum—this is a guy who only went to Thorndike through eighth grade, a guy named Max Gantry. And if you can't find him there's another classmate I'm trying to reach."

"Max Gantry—I'll see if he's in the book," the woman said dubiously, and I waited for a few moments while she audibly turned pages. "Yes! I've got a work number for him," she discovered, reading off a Manhattan number.

"Thank you," I said, scribbling. "I'm sorry, now I need the number of a classmate of mine—graduating class of 1981."

"What's the name?"

"Annabelle Taft," I enunciated.

"Oh—" the secretary said, her voice shifting. "I'm sorry, I've been— I can't give out that number."

"But you've got it," I said, rubbing my eyes.

"Of course we *have* it, I just can't give it out. The family's request— Miss Taft's had some trouble with people calling her, as I'm sure you can understand, so—"

"Look," I said, slapping the desk's edge, "I'm a friend of hers—I was at her *house* last night. I went to the goddamned school for *years.* Can't you just—"

"It's our policy not to give out that number."

"Oh, for— All right. Thank you for your help," I said, hanging up, shutting off the phone tap, leaning back and putting a foot on the edge of the desk. After a moment I dialed the number that the alumni secretary had given me.

"Gantry," said Max, immediately picking up, his familiar firm voice warped by pain and stress.

"Hello," I said, flustered. "This is Michael Cadenhead."

"Mike! Holy shit," Max said bitterly. "What kind of day *is* this, anyway?"

"Max," I said gently, "I don't know if you've heard this, but, um, but Ralph DiGrassi—"

"I know," said Max, cutting me off. "I just found out."

"Well, do you— What happened to him? Do you have any idea?"

"No," Max snapped, cutting me off again. "I don't know anything. I know he died, but that's it. I've been trying to get through on the phone over there and I keep hitting the busy signals, so I guess—"

"Who called you?" I asked.

"What? They've got a cleaning woman," said Max. "I can't believe it's you, Mike, after, what is it, four years, five years? Son of a bitch— But a cleaning woman, you know, a maid—she's been with the family since we were kids, and I was always friendly with her. You know that family's all fucked up—Ralph's been seeing that shrink, right, some psychoanalyst, for *years*— She called me this morning, God only knows how she found me, but she called me in tears—I'm surprised she even knew my last name, she used to just call me the 'little professor'— She reached me somehow, and things sounded lethal, I heard plates breaking, she didn't know what it was, but she told me he was dead."

"Max, I'm calling as a reporter," I said. "The death just came over the wire, and they won't tell me anything except 'complications,' but I've, um, I've got reasons to believe it was something worth looking into. Look, I'm sorry to bother you at a time like this, but, um, I was just wondering if you could help me out."

"Help you out?" Max asked in a wary tone. "What do you mean, help you out? Since when are you a reporter?"

"A short while," I said. "Max, I know this is funny—"

"You're telling me it's funny," Max said. "Why is this newsworthy? Are you at a paper or TV?"

"Print," I said. "I might be doing an investigative piece. I mean, it would be newsworthy in any case because of, you know, because of the family, if it was clearly an isolated incident, but there seems to be more to it than that." Max didn't answer and I continued. "There's been other recent events, um, involving a lot of money and both of the Tafts."

Max sighed heavily. "I don't understand what you're telling me," he said after a moment. "The Tafts, huh? The *other* big family—you know, Ralph used to say he always thought he would have been better off as a Taft. Fuck," Max said with great feeling. "I grew *up* with that boy, Mike—I knew him a lot better than the rest of you ever did, and now he's gone and there isn't even time to react, nothing to make it a particular thing beyond, beyond death. No"—Max coughed—"I'm sorry, I just mean it's bizarre protocol, like you say. You son of a bitch," he added in a grimly bemused voice devoid of anger. "I just realized what you're up to—you know Frank won't take a call from the press so you're having me do it."

"That's right," I said, my heart tightening.

I heard Max breathe in and out. "All right, Mike," he said calmly. "I'm just going to keep trying to get through, trying to reach them, and I'll see if I can find anything out for you—who knows, maybe they even want someone to *talk* to. Give me your number and I'll call you back when I can."

"Thank you, Max," I said with great relief, reciting my telephone extension number.

"Hey, we aim to please," said Max, hanging up.

A moment later I knocked on the backlit pebbled glass of Wilson's door—I heard him grunt noncommittally and opened the door to a view of Wilson sitting with his feet on the desk, holding a bag of potato chips and shoveling a handful of potato chips into his mouth as he raised his thin, reddish eyebrows at me. "Um," I said, "I've got someone calling DiGrassi now. I'm ready to do the notice today, if that's what you want."

"Wait a minute," said Wilson, swallowing the mouthful of potato chips. "I don't understand. If anyone's calling— Why aren't *you* calling him?"

"Well, I'm not sure it's wise," I said, noticing several dark oval potato chip grease stains on the surface of Wilson's newspaper tie. "I mean, he made a caustic comment to me, um, last night, and now his son's dead and he's probably—"

Wilson frowned at me and waved a hand that shone with a dim film of potato chip grease, speaking around another mouthful of potato chips. "If you don't want to call him, why have someone *else* call him? What are you, scared?"

"Yes," I said, leaning a hand on the door. "Wilson, I can do the squib like I said, but if I take this all the way and it leads somewhere, what happens next?"

"First things first," said Wilson, looking at me suddenly. "If it leads somewhere, anything— Even if it leads nowhere, but I want to know where it leads." Wilson chewed thoughtfully, calmly squinting at me as he spoke. "I'm losing my patience with you, Cadenhead."

"What?" I said, hearing, as if for the first time, the clamor of the newsroom outside Wilson's office.

"Listen," he said calmly, "everyone has to go off on some toot sometime. Me, you, everybody. So that's how that is. But I think this is something else." Wilson put the potato chip bag down on his desk and squeaked his chair back around to me, and behind his head, in the overcast air outside, a black piece of plastic, a garbage bag, no doubt, fluttered lazily past Wilson's window like a crow's wing. "I think this is you believing that you're on top of some kind of privileged knowledge here. Call it knowledge or call it high school, I don't care, so you don't have to yell at me again, but you tell me about this appetite you've got and now you're feeding me five hundred yards of phony squirrel tail. I mean, I don't mind your making mistakes now and then, as I've said, and I don't mind your coming in late occasionally, but the next time you ask me some question just because you have some *friend* who works somewhere, you know, Michael, I'm going to get mad."

"Wilson," I began, "What's the—"

"Michael?" Rachel called, from the other end of the newsroom.

"Just a second, Wilson. Yeah?" I yelled, leaning out the door—Rachel was standing at her desk, holding her phone receiver cupped in her hand.

"Carol Casey on line six," she called.

"Thank you," I called back—various people were looking up from their desks, annoyed. "Wilson, um, if you could just—"

"Take your goddamned call," said Wilson, picking up the bag of potato chips.

I dashed over and picked up the phone, punching the line button. "Miss Casey?"

"Um," Carol said nervously. "Listen—Mr. Cadenhead—you said that you were a friend of Douglas'?"

"Yes I am. A high school friend," I said. "Miss Casey, I'm going to record this telephone call with a machine that'll make a tone every ninety seconds to indicate that it's running, according to FCC regulations. Do you have any objections?"

"Who's the *source?*" Rachel was yelling at someone on the phone. "Who's the damn *source?*"

"No, I guess not—" Carol said, sounding confused, and Rachel saw me grin as I punched the buttons on the phone tap.

"Miss Casey, when we last spoke we were talking about a mutual friend, Douglas Taft. You recall that conversation?"

"Of course I remember," said Carol. "Listen, have you"—the phone tap beeped—"Did you get through to Douglas?"

"What? I can't get any answer," I said. "Has he— Did he come in to work since we spoke?"

"No," said Carol, in a somewhat agitated voice. "I don't know where he is. I can't get him at home, and he hasn't come in, and I don't— I just don't know where he is. And I— We spent— He's been working here a while, and everything was— We spent a lot of time together, and there was no indication that— I just haven't known what to *do,* you know? I'm not *used* to this kind of thing, when you get to know someone and then"—the phone tap beeped—"suddenly there's all this *nonsense.* I mean, he was in the hospital, and then he gets back, no explanation at all, and then he just *vanished,* you know, and"—Carol took a breath—"and I haven't lived in the city *that* long, but I thought I knew how things stood with people."

"I understand," I said, watching the miniature tape hubs spin. "I understand."

"Mr. Cadenhead?" The phone tap beeped again. "Listen, before I keep talking, I'm not getting myself in trouble here, am I? I mean, you're a reporter, and—"

"This is personal," I said. "Douglas is my friend. I visited him at the hospital. It's about my friend."

"But you're taping me," Carol said. "You've got that machine going."

"It's personal," I said.

After a moment Carol spoke again, and right then the clouds must have shifted in the sky because the narrow canyon of midtown street beyond the windows brightened, the whitewashed façade of the opposite building shining in the sudden sun. "Douglas was with me the previous night," she said. "The night of the, um, September fifteenth. I mean he was at my house, until pretty late, actually. Several people went— There was the fund-raising party, a bunch of us from the office went to the Hopkins dinner at this hotel, and then several people came over to my house afterwards. You knew Douglas was in therapy, right? I'm trying to remember how he would talk about it— He was going to a therapist named, ah, some German name—*Pershing,* I think. That's right, I remember he'd make this Pershing Missile joke. He'd just gone that afternoon—I remember that he'd headed over there after work and then he came back to meet us at the hotel. Douglas knew Frank DiGrassi would be there, and Senator Rollins, and his father knows all of the— Mr. Taft was overseas, you know, whatever his name is, Douglas' father, but he knows William Huxley and some of the other Lineage people, so we all decided to go."

"I see," I said. "You mentioned that Frank DiGrassi was at the fund-raiser. Do you know if his son Ralph was there?"

"I barely know DiGrassi," said Carol, "so I didn't notice anything except that he left early—I didn't see anyone with him, but of course I don't know his son, so I wouldn't have recognized him."

"Miss Casey," I asked, "do you know why Douglas was in the hospital?"

"No. He wouldn't tell me."

"Have you met Douglas' sister?"

"Sister? I didn't know he had a sister," Carol said as the phone tap beeped again.

"You didn't— He never told you about Annabelle? She's sort of well known—she's a supermodel. I'm surprised that he never—"

"Annabelle *Taft,*" said Carol. "I know *exactly* who she is. My God— *That's* Douglas' *sister?* I guess that makes sense, but— I'm *surprised,* is all. I mean, I'm surprised I never made the connection. That's not the kind of thing that you don't know."

"All right— All right— I just have a couple more questions, Miss Casey. I'm sorry, you're being very patient with me."

"I want to know what to do to help him," said Carol. "Douglas, I mean. If you're a friend of his, you understand— I mean, when I last saw him everything seemed all right, and then the next thing I knew he'd missed work and that guy, um, what, Nick, that guy Nick was calling me, and"—Carol paused and blew her nose, and the phone tap beeped again—"see, he was— Douglas had been scared about something, he was afraid something was going to happen, but he wouldn't explain, and I kept telling him not to worry. Little did I know."

"I see," I said, and again my vision was clouded by a memory of the hospital, of a particular thing that had happened that night, something important—I saw myself crouching on the floor in bright light, my hands moving—but despite my concentration I couldn't think what it was. "Thanks for talking, Miss Casey. If you hear from Douglas, would you call me?" I gave my extension number at the paper as I unhooked the phone tap and shut it off.

"Mr. Cadenhead?" Carol said suddenly.

"Yes?" I said, rewinding the tape.

"What's your first name?"

"Michael."

"Pleased to meet you, Michael," said Carol absurdly, making me smile. "I'm Carol."

"I know," I said. "Take care, Carol."

I hung up the phone, leaning back and rubbing my eyes, and then noticed that Rachel was leaning on the edge of my desk, looking down at me critically.

"How goes it?" Rachel asked.

"I don't know," I said, shaking my head. "It seems to lead all over the place and there's six million dollars floating around here somewhere." I looked up at her face, framed by the ceiling fans. "Listen, thank you again for talking to, um, to Wilson, Rachel. I'm beholden."

"Relax," said Rachel, reaching to finger my tie. "Let me give you some advice."

"Yeah?"

"Get some new clothes," said Rachel. "You look terrible. Get a new tie in particular—if you're investigating something you need a nice tie and maybe a nice suit."

"New clothes?" I said, smiling and reaching past her for more aspirin, knocking the steel microcassette recorder with my fingers.

"Half the battle," said Rachel, slapping my shoulder and walking away.

A DARK AND FADING evening hour of light had ushered in a dim October dusk as I arrived home, realizing bitterly that my open windows had admitted the brief rain as I placed a small table on the sodden floor by the front room's window and hunted down a steno notebook, remembering the night at the hospital and beginning to write down a rough account of what had happened. I began by recounting what my last days at the Supplement had been like, describing my memory of the Collegiate Woman's departure, and as I wrote, the evening that Nick had called me became as sharp and clear in my memory as the view through a train's safety glass, the view that can never hurt you despite its darkness and drama—I was looking through the window at the hospital bed and the IV line and Nick's sunglasses and Annabelle in the magazine and everything was in front of me behind the glass. For at least an hour I labored over the notebook, determined that I could remind myself of the odd detail that I'd known for a while and had foolishly forgotten, and then, as my scribbling brought Nick and myself to Douglas' bedside, I suddenly dropped the pen and stared straight ahead and something happened and I got the shakes—I felt a cold wave across my body and the tight feeling I'd had in my abdomen for hours without recognizing took over and I found it hard to breathe, and I pushed my chair away from the desk and clutched my arms around myself and leaned over, curling into a fetal curve, short of breath, my vision dimming out and fading back in, smoothly, and I felt an embarrassing but acute sensation that right at that moment I needed to talk to someone or I would die, just like that, and it was such a practical thought that the practical half of me started to search my memory, old and new, for someone I could call, but there wasn't anyone to call, and then as quickly as the sensation arrived it faded away and it was as if nothing untoward had happened.

"Blood on my hands," I said out loud, holding my arms out gently in front of me, hands spread as if in supplication, eyes closed as I remembered. "There is blood on my hands."

My eyes were burning with fatigue as I opened my coat closet and hunted through the hanging rows of garments until I found the battered brown corduroy jacket that I'd worn to the hospital, hunting through its pockets for the small plastic box, about the size and weight of a pack of matches, that I'd taken from Douglas' bag of bloody clothing—the box that contained a microcassette. I shuffled through the contents of my desk drawers and found an old Dictaphone that I'd taken from the Supplement office and never returned, and a few minutes later I was lying on my secondhand couch with an old pair of earphones clamped on my head, staring at the circles of amber ambient lamplight that flooded the cracked plaster ceiling and listening to the tape, which contained a low-fidelity recording of a conversation between two men. The first voice on the tape was angular and accented, conjuring an image of a stout, middle-aged man of German or possibly Austrian extraction, and I immediately recognized the second voice on the tape, despite its lower volume and the blurring effects of its greater distance from the microphone.

"Today is Monday, September fifteenth, 1986," said the man with the guttural, accented voice. "I am speaking with Douglas Taft."

"That's me," said Douglas, further in the background. "I don't understand why you're taping this."

"This is work," said the unidentified man. "The basic precept is memory. I want to avoid the problem of your not remembering what you have said to me so I have decided to make a recording you can keep. It is not all that unusual. This is absolutely confidential."

"My father had an old reel-to-reel tape recorder," Douglas said. "A—*Revox,* was the name. Twenty years ago. There was this tape of Mom playing 'Moonlight' on the piano, that's the only thing she could play, but you can hear it, and you can hear me, in the background, like, gurgling while she plays the piano. That's from, like, the mid-sixties."

"I saw a photograph of your father in the newspaper," said the unidentified man.

"Yeah? Oh, right, that thing in the financial section," said Douglas. "Someone in my building showed me— There's this woman across the landing, you know, this nice woman I always see when I'm going out, or when I'm coming in, right, and she seems to think I'm some kind of fucking prince in exile because I keep getting these checks in company envelopes."

"Checks?" said the unidentified man.

"Money," said Douglas. "Finally, after all this time, you know, he just started sending me checks, and to hell with— Dad, I mean, started sending them, and to hell with the pretense."

"Does this bother you?" asked the unidentified man.

"I'm not proud," said Douglas, coughing. "I think Annabelle strong-armed him. He's my father, I can't argue."

"You look quite a bit like him. I assume he has brown hair?"

"Yeah, he has sort of blond hair, actually, but he's completely grey now. If he takes his glasses off, you know, he looks just like me sometimes."

"I was picturing him a certain way after having seen your sister."

"Well, we don't look like"—Douglas coughed again before continuing—"we don't look like brother and sister. Annabelle, she's that one-in-a-million synthesis, right? The whole greater than the sum of the—sum of the parts, but with me the blood's diluted and you can't see who I am."

"You are not paid to be looked at," the unidentified man argued.

"You don't understand her at all," said Douglas. "Listen, what is this, Dr. Pershing? What kind of conversation is this, anyway?"

"I forget how much you wish to avoid discussing her," said Pershing. "Did you have a good day? How is the Institute?"

"It's the same as always," said Douglas. "You know what I did last week? I went to— So I'm not on the ball these days— What else is new— But I was at a pay phone and I misdialed, right, and then I got the operator saying there was no station with that number. So, you know, I asked to be reimbursed so I could try again. I didn't have any change left. I got reimbursed with a check for twenty-five cents."

"So?" asked Pershing.

"So it costs thirty-five cents to cash a check."

"And?"

"And that's what I like. If I go to the bank, and wait on line, I could— I mean I just want to hand them the check, and a *dime,* and say, you know, 'See you later,' and walk away. I mean, what could they *do?*"

"I understand."

"I mean it's that or *keep* the check. But when I don't want to keep it anymore, there's just one way out."

"Throw the check away."

"Are you kidding?" said Douglas, sounding as if he was smiling. "Throw a *check* away? What kind of advice is that?"

"I'm sorry. Do you feel in need of advice?"

"I think things are breaking," said Douglas. "Breaking down."

"What do you mean?"

"You know how glass breaks?" Douglas asked. "Big noise, big deal, all that. The thing is, fine glass, like, I don't know, Steuben glass, it's tough, like window glass, not quite as tough but it's strong. And you drop it and think during that moment it's in the air, you think, shit, I broke it, but it lands and it's okay. You think glass either breaks or it doesn't. But glass weakens, gets fault lines, seams you can't see, so after enough times of you nudging it, dropping it with nothing going wrong, one day you touch it and it shatters." Douglas coughed violently, as if the words were clogging his throat. "Can I get a glass of water?" Dr. Pershing apparently left the room for two and a quarter minutes while Douglas hummed a melody that I eventually identified as the chorus from "Fortress Around Your Heart," and then Pershing returned and I could hear Douglas taking a loud sip of something and the sound of a glass being set on a table. "This is good water. Does this— Do you buy it in bottles?"

"No. It is tap water. It has been standing in the fridge."

"I think *you've* been standing in the fridge."

"Douglas," said Pershing, "Did you remember to bring your notebook diary?"

"Damn. I'm sorry I keep forgetting—I've been *writing* in it, though. I've been working on it. Listen, did you, um, did you ask Annabelle to do a diary?"

"I cannot discuss that with you," said Pershing. "Can you describe your diary's progress?"

"Well, I'm not sure where to start, so, um— So where would you like me to start?"

"Start anywhere you like," said Pershing. "You are not being introspective enough."

"I don't want to hear about that. I don't want to hear about introspection. All the no-handlebars talking. Go ahead and call me a prima donna. I mean that's the one thing about psychoanalysis I'll never get used to."

"I am not a psychoanalyst. I am a Jungian psychotherapist. It is a question of libido."

"Could you explain that?"

"Libido is general psychic energy that serves to regulate the psyche," Pershing explained, "but surfeit libido provides for interaction with the individual's surroundings by means of what we may call the 'object of instinctive interest'—an external stimulus which may in turn provide insights into the overbalance of the libido—but this transference of interest remains an intuitive revelation rather than an act of will. There was a moment"—a chair creaked loudly, the sound distorted by the low-quality recording—"there was a moment in the past, Douglas, a day long ago, a moment which bears upon this intuitive revelation."

For twenty seconds the microphone recorded nothing but a distant car horn. "No," said Douglas finally. "That was years and years ago and it's all over and forgotten and the thing is that everyone was fooled, you know? For some reason everyone was tricked into believing that a certain thing had happened, but the evidence was gone, there were just these stupid traces in our heads, after we woke up and before everything—before everything *kicked in* there was nothing, there was no day."

"The evidence was not gone," said Pershing.

"There was— There was— There was—"

"The evidence was not gone."

"Jesus," said Douglas, "let's talk about something else."

"You say that you had another violent dream, last night, or a few nights ago, so I am wondering what happens in the violent dream."

"I don't remember," Douglas said.

"Everyone has a memory," said Pershing. "Everyone has a past they remember—people that they have known, things that they have done."

"I have no past. I didn't do anything."

"Everyone has—"

"I didn't *do* anything," said Douglas. "I didn't do anything *wrong*, is my point."

"This is reactive denial. There is a certain thing that you did."

"I didn't do anything wrong," said Douglas. "On the weekend of graduation I learned from my father how to do it—how to protect what was important."

"Five years ago," said Pershing, "there was a particular event."

"All right," said Douglas, quietly, after a long pause. "I— I actually see it, when I'm asleep, sometimes, I can dream it, I was dreaming it for a long time, and I would see it in front of me like it was happening."

"And what do you see?"

"I see"—Douglas took a breath—"I see a dark wall, a dark smooth wall, and I'm— I'm standing— I just climbed a flight of stairs. I'm standing at the top of these stairs, feeling sick, feeling weak, and I'm soaking wet. I'm standing there at the top of this dark flight of stairs, I can hear the wind outside, I'm exhausted and soaking wet and cold, my ears are ringing, there's a wall in front of me, and then I see that in the middle of the wall, there's a doorway." Douglas breathed in a constricted manner, sniffed, and after a moment spoke again, his voice difficult to hear. "You're so damn smug, having a box of tissues right here all the time, you know that? So damn smug—"

"Take your time," Pershing said.

"There's— There's a half-open door, a door that's been opened a crack, facing me, right in front of me, and through the crack in the door, past the edge, is nothing but darkness."

"And that is what you see."

"That's it."

"Well, how does it make you feel?"

"It's not a question of how I *feel,*" Douglas said, suddenly, fiercely. "It's not a question. There's things that happened in the past. I *feel* fine."

"Do you actually feel fine?"

"You don't feel anything," said Douglas. "You go through each day, you go around and people are there around you and you try to find some sign, some small sign of life somewhere, keep looking, and— And you complain and they tell you to buy clothes or go to restaurants and you know, hunt for beauty. I already know about beauty but I know it's rare. I don't cry when I can't find it, for God's sake— People say we're sad when we're not on the make—I mean they *put it* nicely, say educated things, but— They're just *dead,* Karl. All the people in this city, walking every day, all these people with all their happy clever party problems and nobody can escape this terrible crushing loneliness that's breaking our hearts, that's killing us all."

"Go on."

"Nothing. That's it. Five years ago I learned something about tears. I had it all. I don't want these people fucking with me."

"What is it, the thing that you did, the thing in the past?"

"Yeah, what is it that I did," said Douglas, apparently blowing his nose. "And you ask, you keep, you asked last time, Dr. Pershing, you, and then I remember one time last month, the air conditioner going and you're, you're asking me again, you've got the— Come on, now. Come on, damn it, it's as if, all the time, here we are talking as if it was *my* idea, damn it, but it was *not my idea* and I'm not, I'm not even *paying* for it, and I don't see why I have to, you know, why I have to say anything at *all* to you, why I should fucking— I mean you can go *fuck* yourself, with your 'It's simple to just say.' Why I should *talk*— After the, after the, after all the *time,* I mean, is that supposed to *help,* with the, just *say* it, with this *recommendation* that I talk? That's, that's supposed to *help?*" There was a pause. "Look at me, goddamn it."

"This is from *An Approach to Psychotherapeutic Technique,* by Edward L. Barnes," said Pershing, shuffling the pages of a book and then reading aloud. " 'The therapist must not reveal his disapproval of the subject's narrative impediments. Evasive tactics may even be encouraged, for it is by means of the resulting associative discourse that the therapist may begin to denote, if not the full rewards of a linear narrative, than at the very least an accumulation of confessional allusions which may ultimately be interpolated into an objective testimonial.' "

"And that's what you're angling for," said Douglas. "What are you— Are you going to tell me this is oedipal?"

"It is not necessarily oedipal," said Pershing, loudly slamming the book.

"Not— You mean there's a *possibility* it's oedipal? Jesus wept. Look"—Douglas' voice had calmed down—"please don't. Don't do it. Don't make me feel the rage. If you get me upset things will happen that I'm afraid of. Please don't frighten me."

"I am sorry."

"So I'm going to this thing tonight."

"Is that wise?"

"Yeah, 'cause— I feel this hope that there's, like, still beauty in the world."

The tape revealed the sound of Dr. Pershing groaning with the effort of standing up and stretching and sitting back down.

"What do you mean?" Pershing asked.

"I mean that beauty is a— As time goes by things are lost, you know, and beauty is a replacement for what's lost during the passage of time. I mean, this job I've got, you know, all my life has been this certain sort of thing. I mean, there were questions I never asked, you know? I mean it sounds pretty fucking stupid, but, you know, I went to college, and I got that first job I had, you know, immediately, that first—"

"Senator Rollins."

"—thing, right, that bullshit with Senator Rollins. I mean, it wasn't my *fault* how things turned out. Working for the Institute, I mean, at least I'm *doing* something, right? There may be some controversy about the *ethics,* right, people can *talk,* but at least I'm doing something. I wanted to get this job, is all I'm saying. I thought it would be a good thing to do—I mean, you know, and it's just more of the office bullshit, but recently it's been changing, and there's beauty in the world, you know?"

"Go on."

"Do you understand what I'm talking about?"

"It would help if I knew more about what this affair tonight is."

"What? It's a fund-raiser," said Douglas. "I'm sorry, I thought I explained. It'll be this big party at this hotel, you know, and I just thought—I just thought it would be fun, because, like, all these people from the office, my friend Carol, all the crew, they're all going, and I think it would be good."

"Do you think it is wise?"

"What do you mean?"

"I mean do you think it is wise? You are aware of the danger you're in."

"I'm fine," said Douglas. "I'm not in any danger."

"It is almost time to close," said Pershing—I could hear the furniture loudly creaking as he stood and moved around. "Douglas, next time, please remember to bring the notebook diary with you when you come."

"Yeah, yeah," said Douglas. "I'm not that into showing it to you, you know."

"Annabelle said the same thing," said Pershing, loudly moving around as Douglas stood up—the tape even captured the hiss of his cigarette dropping into the water glass. "Each time that the notebook was mentioned, Annabelle would—"

"I thought that was out of bounds to talk about."

"—complain about the idea, and then she finally returned it to me. Look, Douglas." There was, after a pause, the sound of shuffling paper.

"Jesus Christ," said Douglas. "She really did a number on it, didn't she?"

"She gave it back to me like this. Please at least try to write it all down. Now I'm sorry, Douglas, but I have someone waiting," said Pershing as they moved around. "Next week we will— What is wrong?"

The tape was silent for a five-second interval here—silent, except that at full volume my Dictaphone faintly reproduced a thin, metallic sound, a clicking of metal against wood.

"I forgot, Douglas—I am sorry."

"I don't— All right," said Douglas quietly. "All right. But I wish you'd remember these things."

"It slipped my mind," said Pershing. "It's part of my desk stationery, so it didn't occur to me to—"

"All right," said Douglas "Jesus, you know I actually feel cold—"

"Are you—"

"I'm fine," said Douglas. "I'm all right. Be more— Jesus, Dr. Pershing, remember these things."

"It is time to close," said Pershing. "Do not forget the tape. There should be a—" Right here, after a loud series of Dictaphone clicks, the recording ended.

I LISTENED TO the tape several times and when I had finished it had grown dark, and I put on my overcoat and went to wander around Carrol Gardens, hearing muted music from the night spots as right after twilight the white shone whiter than white from crushed cups in the gutters and the sky stood still, stained by pale remnants of the petrochemical sunset beyond the New Jersey shore. Returning upstairs, I turned out the lights and collapsed into an aluminum kitchen chair, watching streetlit passersby, random people walking, imagining Nick Blanchard standing somewhere in Montana, light meter round his neck, squinting in the hot Western sun, and I felt a vague longing for the Supplement crowd, whom I missed, wondering how the Collegiate Woman was doing back in New England, or wherever she was, hoping she was happy and realizing, finally, that I would never see her again.

chapter 5

Next came a day of rain, sheets of cold rain that slowed everything down, hammering and whispering outside all the places I spent time that day, pattering the windows of Annabelle's house, smearing the ink and dirt of Grand Central Station early that evening, when the sky was the color of carbon paper held to the light, and softening finally to the fast shimmer of mist outside my cracked windows as I sat between yellow lamps late at night. Early that day—Thursday, October twenty-third—Rachel Geisler and I were loitering in the newsroom, trying to relax because the morning edition was finally asleep. I had been trying to find a file I'd lost in the computer when Rachel had sat on the edge of my desk, handing me coffee, and soon she was talking about her college-student daughter, who had just worked as a summer intern at a small tabloid—I heard stories about her ambitions and boyfriends and habits, stories that the daughter probably wouldn't want anyone to hear. The little guy from downstairs made his rounds, slapping fresh copies of the paper onto every desk, and as he got to us we broke off our conversation and began flipping through the new papers. I turned to the obituary page and began nervously looking over the death notice I'd written, checking for mistakes although it was too late:

DiGrassi—Ralph Emerson, 23, on Wednesday, October 22, 1986, of complications following hospitalization. DiGrassi graduated from Thorndike, a private Manhattan day school, in 1981, and from Princeton University in 1985, and had been living at home for several months. DiGrassi is survived by his parents, Frank DiGrassi, 51, a prominent New York attorney, and Amelia DiGrassi, 42. No announcement has been made at press time concerning memorial services, but the family has requested that any donations be contributed toward a planned scholarship fund at the Thorndike School, 512 East 80th Street, New York, N. Y. 10021.

"I don't understand," Rachel called over from her desk, where she sat with her feet up. "Where's your big piece?"

"I'm still working on it," I explained. "Wilson and I decided to go ahead and run the notice, so that in case the—"

"He's hedging his bet," Rachel said, interrupting me without looking, studiously turning pages. "Don't kid yourself."

"I'll be, um, I'm planning on reminding you of all these things you said, you know, later on, Rachel. There might be a—" My phone rang, and I broke off, picking up and identifying myself.

"It's Max. I'm sorry it took so long for me to get back to you."

"That's all right."

"I spoke to Amelia," Max told me. "She's lost her fucking mind, as you can imagine, but I found out what the deal was. I don't think it's going to be much help, Mike."

"I'm listening," I said, turning on the phone tap.

"She heard screams," said Max. "At four in the morning, and she and Frank woke up, right, and she went into Ralph's room. She said Ralph was— Well, the thing is, I couldn't get her to tell me what she saw in the room."

"What do you mean?" I asked as the phone tap beeped.

"I mean Amelia won't tell me what she saw," Max repeated, irritated. "She won't explain what killed him. She told me Ralph's face was scarlet, and that there were, um, that his veins were standing out, that Ralph was trying desperately to breathe, right, and it looked like he was having a heart attack."

"Jesus," I said, swallowing coffee.

"Right. So they called an ambulance, rushed him to the emergency room, over on York Avenue, and that's all I could get from Amelia—Ralph died, um"—Max was starting to lose his composure and I could hear his voice cracking—"he died in the emergency room corridor, that's one thing she would tell me at the end, right in the goddamned corridor, and isn't that a fucking beautiful way to die, Mike, staring at a fucking Styrofoam ceiling?"

I was tapping my hands on the desk as I listened. "Max, thank you for calling me with this."

"Are you going to put what I said in the paper?" Max asked.

"Amelia wouldn't say anything about what she saw in the room?"

"She said—she said the window was open. She said there were these little green candies all over the floor, you know, like M&Ms." Max was crying. "She wouldn't say what she *saw,* but she just said, she just said that she'll never forget walking into Ralph's bedroom, that it was the most horrible thing she'd ever seen, whatever it was, and, like, the most terrifying moment of her life, with the green M&Ms everywhere. Mike, I've got to get off the phone," Max said, his breath catching painfully. "Are you printing this?"

"Printing it? Your words in the paper? No," I said, sighing. "Goodbye, Max."

After a moment I tried Douglas' home number again, fruitlessly, and then hunted through the business directory, finding a number for the Madison Avenue office of Karl Pershing, Ph.D. After several rings Pershing answered, his voice not much clearer on the phone than it had been on the tape recording I'd listened to the previous evening. "Dr. Pershing, my name is Michael Cadenhead," I told him, switching the phone tap back on.

"I am in a conference right now," said Pershing in a soft voice that I could barely hear. "I cannot talk right now." Several people wandered up to the desk on the other side of the bulletin-board partition in front of me, holding cups of coffee, talking loudly.

"I'm sorry to bother you but it's extremely urgent," I said. "I'm calling about a patient of yours, a young man named Douglas Taft."

"I am in a conference," Pershing repeated. "Douglas Taft is no longer a patient of mine."

"Really," I said. "Listen, I know that Douglas saw you during the afternoon of the fifteenth of September, and that something happened to him that evening, something that I have reason to believe you know something about, and now I can't manage to get in touch— "

"Whoever you are," Pershing grunted, his voice maddeningly blurred by the bad connection, "I cannot discuss my privileged knowledge of my patients' lives with you."

"I'm his best friend," I said, checking that the phone tap was running, closing my eyes against my burning lenses, covering my other ear. "He almost died that night and now I can't find him."

"Our session of the fifteenth was our last," Pershing told me. "I am not at liberty to talk to him or to continue to see him. It is a legal question." One of the loud arrivals in front of me turned on a radio on the desk.

"I'm sorry? By 'legal question,' do you mean— Could you hang on a second, sir?" I covered the receiver and yelled, "Could you guys *shut up?*" at the crowd in front of me, louder than I had intended, drawing startled glances from various people in the newsroom. The arrivals in front of me looked annoyed but turned the radio off and wandered away. "I'm sorry, Dr. Pershing—I'll only take up another moment of your time. You're saying you severed your relationship with Douglas after that night because you were afraid of involving yourself in something illegal?" The phone tap beeped.

"That is exactly what I am saying. What is that sound?"

"I'm taping you," I told him, "but it's still confidential. Dr. Pershing, I'm a journalist and I'd like very much for you to tell me what you know about any illegal events. Perhaps at one time a professional discretion applied but things have changed, you understand, and I'm very concerned about Douglas' safety. I'd be willing to meet you at any time anywhere and I can guarantee that you'd be on background—that your complete anonymity would be preserved. If you can't bring yourself to do that, perhaps you could tell me who else to go to, but I need to talk to somebody soon."

"I am dubious—"

"Don't be dubious," I said hoarsely. "Don't be dubious because you can *trust* me."

The phone tap beeped again as Wilson arrived at my desk.

"I cannot discuss Douglas' case," said Pershing finally. "Do not mistake my tone—I am very concerned by what you are telling me. It is a matter of law. If you cannot reach Douglas perhaps you may be able to talk to his sister Annabelle."

"All right," I said quietly. "All right. Thank you, sir. Once again, I'm sorry for disturbing you." We both hung up and I leaned to shut off the phone tap.

"That's quite a technique you've got there," said Wilson, yawning, rubbing his thinning red hair. "Quite an interview style. What do you call that, anyway, Cadenhead, *Nuremberg* technique?"

"I'm on to something, Wilson," I said, standing up and looking at him. "I really think I'm on to something."

• • •

ON MY WAY downtown, an hour later, wading through the cold rain, I realized that I'd forgotten to pick up a notebook when I left the paper, so I stopped in the depths of midtown and found a stationery store. Folding my sodden umbrella, I tracked filthy rainwater across the sodden carpet, past the exhaustive collection of greeting cards and the lurid wrapping paper, and picked through their collection of "steno" notebooks, and while I was doing this, a teenage kid with a fluorescent orange bookbag wearing a green poncho, a vague-looking young boy with a smooth face and flat wet hair and rain-beaded eyeglasses, was critically examining the store's poster collection a few feet from me. As I looked over the various blank notebooks, the kid solemnly flipped the big poster-display boards, turning them slowly like tabernacle doors so that their aluminum frames clicked together, and in my peripheral vision I could see rock and roll stars, past and present, and "fantasy" airbrush paintings of unicorns and dragons, and then the kid flipped another board and there was Annabelle. This was a slightly racier swimsuit picture than the one I'd seen at her house two evenings before—this time she stood arched like a dancer in a tiny gold foil bikini and a black leather bomber jacket that had slipped from her dropped shoulders, wet black hair tangled round her upraised pouting face and falling in shadowed strands across her neck. The glossy paper brought out the grey background and the sharp detail, the shadows of the jacket's flaps and zippers across her abdomen, the calm, smoldering heat of her gaze, and the poster had a baroque signature across its bottom corner—*Lots of love XOXO Annabelle*—contrived to give the impression that Annabelle had taken a pen to the poster itself. As I watched, the kid hunted through the rolled posters under the display rack, found Annabelle's picture by means of a letter code, and shambled toward the register, and I found a suitable blank notebook and followed. The kid, who was at least a foot shorter than me, purchased Annabelle's likeness in a furtive manner, accepting the change from the oblivious cashier and darting out through the glass door into the rain, the poster sticking up like a car antenna from his orange bookbag.

When I emerged from the subway twenty minutes later the rain had abated and I wandered around the non-perpendicular downtown streets, trying to retrace my steps from two days previous, which daylight made more difficult than I'd expected. Eventually I got my bearings and found Annabelle's street, deserted at this time of day, and soon I was standing atop her front steps, just like the last time, ringing the brass doorbell and waiting until she opened the door, wearing jeans and a black T-shirt and a pair of round-framed tortoise-shell glasses—she was barefoot and looked surprised. "Michael? Hello."

"Hi, Annabelle. Um," I began, hunched into my raincoat, gesturing. "I was— I'm sorry to bother you. I was going to call, but I— I couldn't get your number, no one would give me your number, so I just— I decided just to show up. I wanted to talk to you about a couple of things. It's— It's for my job," I finished lamely.

"Well— Come on in," Annabelle said, standing aside, and I made an elaborate show of brushing rainwater off my shoes before stepping into the foyer. "Let me take your coat. Tina's here—you want some coffee?"

"Well— If you're having some," I said nervously, rubbing the wet chill from my hands and brushing water off my tie and jacket collar, my eyes adjusting to the quiet darkness of the house. I followed Annabelle down between the staircase and the wall, my memory of the party focusing as we passed the framed calendar picture and the bathroom, where the orange bucket of newspaper was still placed under the leak. The living room looked the same as it had two nights before except that it was quiet and empty, backlit by the wet windows, and Tina Foster sat on the green couch in parachute pants and a white T-shirt and running shoes, empty wineglasses filling the table before her, drinking coffee—she glanced up at our entrance, giving me a look that was more bemusement than surprise.

"Michael?" Tina said in her flat voice as I wandered into the room. "Are you here to clean the house?"

"*Tina,*" said Annabelle in mock alarm as she moved off toward the kitchen.

"Hi, Tina," I said. "I just— I came down to ask Annabelle some questions, actually, for a story."

"How do you take it?" Annabelle called from the kitchen. "Hey, Tina, you want to put another disc in?" Tina got up and went over to the stereo.

"Yeah? I'm listening," Tina said, an arm pressing her flat, coppery hair into the top of her head as she faced away from me, her back arching under the T-shirt as she scanned her eyes down the racked spines of Annabelle's hundreds of compact discs.

"Just milk, Annabelle," I called back, moving to sit down. "Um, you heard that Ralph DiGrassi died, right?"

"Yeah," said Tina dully, not turning around. "We just found out. Frank called this morning while we were watching cartoons—he had to cancel an appointment with the babe." Tina pointed lazily toward the kitchen.

Annabelle came in with a small bag of M&Ms under her elbow, carrying two bone cups of coffee, keeping the black one for herself and handing me the creamed one, which I thanked her for. "I don't have that much time, Mike—I've got to go to work," Annabelle said, sitting cross-legged on the couch, pushing her glasses back with a finger, their frames casting shadows on her perfect wide cheekbones.

"Yeah, I've to take off soon myself," said Tina, looking at her plastic watch. "We were talking about Ralph dying."

Annabelle nodded slowly. "I see," she said, glaring at me the way she'd glared at the boy in the stationery store uptown—it was like watching a well-known artist toss off something on a paper place mat that was instantly recognizable.

"Were you— You weren't ever friends with him, were you, Annabelle?" I asked.

"God no," said Annabelle. "You know, it's funny, but I— You know, back at Thorndike—you remember how *odd* Ralph was, right? But back at Thorndike I always used to get the sense that he was following me around."

"It's no secret he was following you around," Tina said.

"All right," said Annabelle impatiently, her gold watch flashing as she settled on the couch, her fingers crumpling the M&M bag as she reached into it, "but recently I was— There were times over the summer when I was sure I'd seen him."

"No kidding," I said.

"Yeah, that stuff lingers with you," said Annabelle, slowly fingering M&Ms into her mouth, slipping them between her slackened lips one by one. "That fear, you know— A man followed me, once, and I thought maybe it was Ralph, you know, but I checked myself, because of course it wasn't, but after the party I thought maybe it was. One afternoon, a few weeks ago, I was walking and I saw this—I saw a man watching me."

"Jesus," I said.

"Where was this?" Tina asked. "You didn't tell me this."

"Union Square," said Annabelle, swallowing coffee. "I was— I had just finished working and it must have been around— I was working late, this goddamned Revlon thing, it took forever, and I was going home, crossing the square—" Annabelle trailed off, staring into space.

"Yeah?" said Tina.

"Sorry," said Annabelle. "I was crossing the square, and there was the farmers' market going on at the end of the, you know, where the fences are—you know—but I was looking at some plants they had, and I looked up and over by the north corner there was a man in a black overcoat, standing in a doorway—I just happened to glance over and I saw him."

"Had this guy been watching you long?" Tina asked. "I mean, had he been following you?"

"I don't know. No," said Annabelle. "At least I don't think so."

"Did he look familiar?" I asked.

"I didn't see his face," said Annabelle. "I glanced away 'cause I was frightened. I couldn't *clearly* see anything except that he was unshaven and that he had dark hair, but I think he saw me looking at him, and then he started moving and I looked away, and when I looked back he was gone."

"You said there was that guy calling you," I said. "That you were sure it was Ralph. Is that— Is that a, you know, a serious problem? People calling you? I mean I'm beginning to understand why I had such trouble getting your number."

"Yeah. Did the school give you a hard time? Well"—Annabelle shrugged—"that's the way we've got to do it. It looks like Ralph was homing in on me, doesn't it? You know—calling and then showing up—"

"Look, Anna," said Tina, "did you think that maybe it's just Raymond calling you?"

"Oh, *Tina,*" said Annabelle, glaring at Tina with resigned dismay. "You *had* to put *that* into my head—"

"Who's Raymond?" I asked.

"A man. No, it *must* have been Ralph calling me," Annabelle said, nodding. "Now I'm sure."

"I'm leaving," said Tina, standing up, looking at her watch again, and I got up as well, feeling archaic but doing it anyway, as Tina kissed Annabelle on the cheek. "See you later, Anna," she said.

"Mmm. 'Bye, Foster girl," Annabelle said, kissing back.

" 'Bye, Mike," Tina told me. "Sorry I can't stick around—give me a call some time, we'll get together."

"Sure," I said, nodding.

"If you do clean the place up, I'm sure she'll be grateful," Tina added as she left the room, and after a moment the front door slammed and Annabelle and I were alone.

"What brings you down here, Michael? I'm sorry," said Annabelle, holding out the crumpled bag of M&Ms. "You want some of these?"

"No thank you," I said, watching as she took several more M&Ms for herself, fishing out what looked to be about six green ones and one orange one. "I'm investigating Ralph's death."

"Investigating it?" said Annabelle. "For your magazine?"

"Newspaper," I said. I was noticing that she almost always had a hand near her head, brushing her chin, rubbing her temples, stroking her hair.

"They're all green ones today," said Annabelle, looking down at the bag of M&Ms. "You remember about green M&Ms? Back when we were kids? They were some sort of big deal—they were supposed to mean sex."

"I don't remember that," I said. "Hey, I saw a poster of you today—some kid was buying it."

"Really?" said Annabelle politely. "Which one?"

"Um," I said, gesturing, "with the— Um— A leather jacket, and—"

"Sure," said Annabelle, nodding. "I'm the Italian biker chick."

"Listen," I said, smiling, "I was wondering—is that really your signature?"

"No. Are you kidding?" said Annabelle. "*Nobody* writes like that—there's an artist at the company that does those. I don't go in for that 'XOXO' business."

"That's funny," I said. "Look, I realize you're busy, Annabelle, but I need your help—the paper's doing a thing about Ralph's death and there's just a few things I'd like to ask you about, if you wouldn't mind. I take it that when you saw Ralph last night it was the first time since school?"

"That's right," Annabelle said, taking another sip of coffee and abandoning the bag of M&Ms. "Unless you count that it was him with all the phone calls. There's—"

The phone rang and Annabelle climbed off the couch, moving with distracted grace as she headed out to the kitchen, where I heard her answering.

"Nick!" she said after a moment. "Hello."

"That's good," she said.

"That won't happen for a while," she said.

"Right, Nick," she said. "Listen, could you call back a bit later on? Michael Cadenhead's here."

"That's right," she said.

"Don't worry," she said. "What?"

Annabelle leaned into the living room, curling luxuriously around the doorjamb. "It's Nick Blanchard," she told me, smiling sardonically. "He wants to talk to you."

I went to take the phone from Annabelle's hand, again noticing how tall she was without shoes. "Hello, Nick," I said.

"Hey, buddy!" said Nick through a fog of long-distance static. "How you doing. Guess what, Mike—I'm coming home tonight."

"Really?" I said, straining to hear him. "I thought it was supposed to be eight weeks— Where're you calling from? I can't hear you at all."

"I'm at the station in Cleveland," Nick said through another blast of static. "I'm taking a couple of weeks off, and then we'll finish up with the Octane Spring Collection in December. Listen, buddy—some guy's waiting for the phone and the train's leaving in a minute so I've got to book but I'm arriving at Grand Central at seven—can you meet me?"

"Um," I said, "yeah, I guess so." Annabelle had left the kitchen and I peered at the phone's base, below the touch-tone buttons.

"Mike," Nick continued in a furtive voice, "what the hell are you doing at Anna's house? What are you, managing to *seduce* her, you bastard?"

"No. I'm putting you on the speakerphone," I said, glancing through the doorway at Annabelle.

"All right, fuck you," said Nick. "I'll get in to Grand Central at seven-twenty—I'll see you then. Take it easy, buddy—and no kidding, good luck with the goddess."

I got off the phone and re-joined Annabelle around the coffee table. "I'm sorry, Michael," she told me. "I'm happy to talk, but I'm expecting a call, and when it comes I've got to go."

"Annabelle," I said, producing my new notebook and a pen, "do you know more about Ralph's death than you're telling me?"

"What?" said Annabelle, looking down at the notebook.

"Um, I mean, all the stuff he said two nights ago about being in trouble, about knowing what his father was doing here, and— Annabelle, what's your involvement with Frank DiGrassi?"

"It's"—Annabelle was shaking her head—"I can't talk about that."

"Well, can you explain your brother being in the hospital? Or about— Or that business about graduation weekend? The thing you said about something on graduation weekend, the thing that Douglas reacted to so strongly, or about whatever's going on with the Lineage Inst—"

"You *told* him that?" Annabelle said, glaring at me, speaking with great anger and alarm. "You went and *said* that? How could you—"

"Nick was up to something," I said, hearing my voice sharpen. "The night that Douglas got hurt he called me up after *five years* and brought me to the hospital and I'm suddenly starting to wonder if he was trying to— He *wanted* me to call you," I remembered suddenly. "And at the party you mentioned him, and you said graduation, and— Can you tell me what Nick was doing? Or what made Douglas—"

"It's none of your *business* what Nick was doing."

"—tell Karl Pershing how badly frightened he was, how the— Right before he got hurt, he talked about five years ago and Pershing said he was in danger, so I'm really wondering what—"

"No," said Annabelle, breathing sharply, shaking her head as she slowly stood up, her lovely face vivid with quiet fury. "No. This is not right. I should have realized this wasn't right, that it was a mistake letting you come in here—pretending we have any knowledge of each other, trying to, trying to make you think I could be *open* to your— Do you know what you *did,* telling that to Douglas? Do you understand the *harm* you did? How dare you—"

"Annabelle—"

"—come into my *house,* into my *family,* my *business* concerns, with the, with the most intimate details of my brother's *life,* right while I've got that *psychopath* calling me on the *phone,* in the middle of a crisis, what— How *dare* you?"

"I am a *journalist,*" I said angrily, standing also to face her from a foot away. "I'm following a *story*— Jesus, Annabelle, do you think"—I realized that my voice was catching and that there was no way to prevent it—"do you think I'm doing this on *purpose?* I'm trying to be a good journalist, trying to do it right, and it's, it's *difficult,* Annabelle— Do you think I *wanted* to spend all this time on my high school dirt? Do you think that's what I *care* about?"

"It's not what *any* of us care about," said Annabelle as we stood face to face. "It's what we're trying to *escape,* and no one's managed to *do* it but Ralph—it's too bad he's dead but I am *sorry*"—she was shaking her head again—"that I can't be all that overcome with grief." The phone rang. "*Jesus,*" Annabelle muttered, trying to move past me toward the doorway.

"I'm sorry," I said, getting out of her way.

"Hello?" said Annabelle, picking up the phone. "Hello?" A few silent seconds went by and I leaned to watch her through the doorway and saw her as she squinted, looking at the phone receiver and then suddenly hanging up, facing motionlessly away from me.

"Annabelle?" I said, alarmed. "Are you all right?"

"It was him again," said Annabelle quietly. "It was him again. Damn it. Oh, Jesus—"

"Take it easy, Annabelle," I said, standing up, walking around the coffee table and over into the kitchen. "It could have just been a wrong—"

"He *said* something," said Annabelle, frightened, looking at me through her reading glasses as I arrived. "He *said* something before he hung up, he *said* something, so this is the—" Annabelle looked terrified.

"Shh," I said awkwardly, alarmed. "Shh. Take it—"

"But if it's not— If it's not *Ralph* then who is it?" Annabelle looked heartbreakingly lost. "Who *is* it, Michael?"

"What did he say?"

"He said 'I dreamed your face.'"

I faced her powerlessly and she turned away, heading slowly back to the couch—she sat down and then immediately stood, moving toward the kitchen, where I could hear her opening the refrigerator, and then opening a cabinet, and while I was writing down the number I'd read on the kitchen phone I heard the loud shattering of a dropped glass. When I arrived in the kitchen Annabelle was standing in its center holding a vodka bottle, her other hand pressed to her face, the glass she'd dropped scattered in wet shards on the black tiles at her bare feet.

"Annabelle, um," I said, "take it easy. Just— You're going to change your number, right? Do you want me to call the police?"

"I'm sorry," Annabelle said. "Jesus, it's just a drinking glass. There's not— This thing's really shaking me up."

"Is that all he said?"

"No," said Annabelle after a moment, looking at me. "He said— He said 'Ralph is dead.' "

"You didn't— You're sure you didn't recognize the voice?"

"I'm sure."

We stood there in the kitchen awkwardly for a moment, on opposite sides of the broken glass, and after a moment I said, "Annabelle, um, do you— How many phones have you got?"

"What?" Annabelle looked at me.

"I mean do you only have that one phone over there, or—"

"There's one upstairs. In the bedroom."

"Would you mind if I used it?" I asked. "I have to make this private call, and—"

"No—go ahead." Annabelle looked at me and smiled bravely. "Don't worry about me, I'm fine. I just have to change the number, that's all." As she stepped gingerly around the broken glass, I went over and went up the stairway, again, and after opening a couple of smooth doors which gave into underused-looking rooms, I found Annabelle's bedroom and walked in. The room was large and dark and there were rain-streaked windows at the back end, directly over the living room windows, affording the same washed-out view of the brownstone garden and the brick walls beyond. There was a large bed covered with a thick white cotton comforter, and an Oriental carpet underfoot, and stacks of books and magazines everywhere. I found the telephone on the floor near the bed, next to a pair of canvas tennis shoes, and I dialed the downstairs number and got a busy signal. So both extensions were on one line—the phone call during her party hadn't come from this bedroom phone. After a moment I dialed the paper.

"City Desk," said Wilson, answering after a moment. "Pick."

"Wilson? Michael," I said quietly.

"Hello, Michael," said Wilson in a fatigued voice. "I remember the day when you would spend your afternoons here at our beautiful office—that was a fine old time. How's your manhunt going?"

"I'm not sure," I said.

"Cadenhead," Wilson said, "you're giving me more squirrel tail."

"I can't help it," I said. "I'm trying to pull it together."

"Well, all right, but keep me informed is all," Wilson said kindly. "You don't *have* to do a piece, Michael."

"I understand," I said hopelessly.

"I'm glad you called, actually—someone's on their way here to see you."

"What? Who is it?"

"Geisler took the call. Some woman named Casey."

"If she shows up," I said, "tell her I'll be right there."

When I got back downstairs Annabelle had cleaned up the broken glass and was sitting on the couch with a glass of vodka, her hands in her lap. "Michael," she said quietly.

"Yes?" I said.

"Do you know what you're doing?"

"I'm sorry?"

"Do you know what you're looking for? Do you know what you want?"

I stood there watching her look thoughtfully up at me.

"No."

"I don't know how Ralph died," Annabelle told me calmly. "I don't know the things you're looking for as a journalist."

"Do you know what happened to your brother?"

"Yes," Annabelle said after a moment, restlessly recrossing her legs and then shaking her head as she looked at her watch. "You've got to go, Michael."

"So that isn't all of it," I said. "Journalist or not."

"That's not all of it," Annabelle said, gazing at me intently. "Really, Michael, you've got to go." She had stood up and was walking forward, compelling me to turn toward the hallway and the green front door. "I'm sorry I got angry. There's not— I'm sorry. It's not you."

"I'm sorry I intruded," I said as we headed down the dark corridor together.

"I don't think this is over," Annabelle said, holding out my sodden raincoat, and I forgave her the photogenic look. "We'll be in touch. And Michael—"

"Yes?"

"You've got a mean streak," Annabelle told me. "Watch your step."

I WENT BACK to the newspaper after leaving Annabelle's house, slogging uptown through the sooty rain—the day had darkened early and the office was quiet, the ceiling lights on, the rain still beating against the windows, and Wilson and Rachel were both off somewhere. Carol Casey hadn't arrived yet, if she was coming at all, so I sat down at my desk and fished through my wallet, eventually finding the small business card that Dr. Barker had given me at the hospital and dialing her number.

"Barker," she said, picking up eventually.

"Hello," I began nervously. "Um, my name is— You may not remember me, but we met a few weeks ago. My name is Michael Cadenhead and I came in with another man to see my friend Douglas Taft, when he—"

"I remember you," said Barker pleasantly. "How's our friend doing?"

"He's fully recovered. Look, I was wondering if you could help me out with something. Do you have access to— I need to find out some information about a patient who died there early yesterday morning, um, a guy who died in the emergency room."

"Well," said Barker, her voice having grown more precise, "there's rules about things like that—I don't think I can help you."

"It's very important," I said. "It's a good friend of mine, Ralph DiGrassi—all I'm asking you to do is find out what the cause of death was. See, he was— Ralph was a high school friend, actually, we went to school together, and I can't seem to find out what happened to him, and— You were so kind when we met, I thought you might be willing to—"

"No," Barker said flatly. "I can't. Don't you understand that you're asking me to break the law? I respect what you're saying about your friend, but the fact that—"

"Terrible things are happening and nobody has anything to say. This morning," I wearily explained, my voice barely disguising my hopelessness, "I talked to Douglas' therapist about the night someone stabbed him, um, and the therapist diffidently explained to me that there were legal reasons for him not talking to me."

"They're good reasons," said Barker.

"There're good reasons for not stabbing people."

"Don't pretend to be a child," said Barker mildly. "This is a hospital. I spent twenty minutes giving Douglas Taft a spinal X-ray because I can't afford to be involved in a lawsuit. You can't expect—"

"I understand that," I interrupted. "Look, that night— Dr. Barker, what was it you told me about being, about being blinded by procedural considerations?"

"You have a good memory," Barker said after a moment.

"I know," I said absently, noticing that one of the white buttons on my phone had started blinking. "Damn it— I'm sorry, Dr. Barker, I've got another call. Could you—"

"Go ahead, take it," said Barker, sighing calmly. "I can wait."

"Thank you. Michael Cadenhead," I said after reaching to punch the blinking white button.

"Mike? It's Tina."

"I'm on the other line, Tina," I said impatiently. "It's— I'm sorry, I'm very busy right now."

"You haven't called me."

"What do you mean?"

"We were supposed to have dinner."

"Is this about Annabelle?" I asked, gazing at the phone's blinking white light.

"I love her," said Tina. "I've known her a long time—I know how peculiar she is. I've made my mistakes. People get bored with betrayal—maybe the best thing for you to do is back away and leave her alone." Tina's voice was soaked in its customary calm and I could barely hear her through the phone's dead static. "Look, Michael, I'm not saying any one thing—I'm concerned, I'm just *calling* you."

"You made that joke," I said, remembering. "That I should clean her house. Why all these warnings?"

"Look, she's trying to play this thing straight. She needs help."

"I've got to go. I'm sorry, Tina," I said, drumming my fingers on the desk.

"All right." Tina spoke with mild dismay. "Just be careful."

I hit the other button, switching lines again. "Dr. Barker?" I said anxiously. "Listen, maybe I shouldn't have—"

"It'll take me a couple of moments for me to find the file you're looking for," Barker said. "Now I'll have to put *you* on hold."

This time I actually found a way to enjoy the terrible music, tapping my feet along with the absurd xylophone melody and gazing at the rain, so that I was startled when Dr. Barker came back onto the phone. "All right," she said in a somewhat hushed voice, over the sound of shuffling papers. "DiGrassi, Ralph— Cause of death— Well, it was a heart attack."

"A heart attack? Jesus," I said. "Well, um, what brought it on?"

"A massive overdose of Toldran-M."

"I'm sorry? What's the—"

"It's a commonly prescribed antidepressant," Barker told me. "It's designed to correct a chemical imbalance in the brain, related to lowered levels of norepinephrine and other neurotransmitters—a doctor would prescribe them for someone who's seriously impeded by their brain chemistry, someone who, you know, can't get out of bed, or loses control of himself in stressful situations."

"And DiGrassi *overdosed* on this stuff? I don't understand."

"Neither do I," Barker said. "I mean, Toldran-M's designed to be very difficult to mess around with. I've come across it many times— they're these little green candy-coated pills, and depending on symptoms the patient just takes a few of them, two or four, but you can take a significant number with no ill effect, except several minor side effects—dry mouth, dizziness, like that—and the need to monitor your blood pressure more often than you would usually. Anyway, when they brought DiGrassi in, his heart was about to go—they shot him full of Librium but it was too late. Time of death was 5:20 Wednesday morning."

"All right," I said, sighing. "Was there any—"

I broke off as I saw a young woman approaching my desk—a diminutive woman who nonetheless gave an impression of stature. "I'm sorry, Dr. Barker, but I've got to go," I said, listening for Barker's acknowledgement and then hanging up and rising. The woman in front of me looked to be in her mid-twenties, although her bearing made her seem marginally older, and she had bright blue eyes and straight black hair, the color of Annabelle's hair, but coarser, her profession, of course, bearing on her appearance far differently than Annabelle's did. She wore a well-tailored, conservative grey pinstripe skirt and jacket over a collarless silk shirt, and no jewelry save a scalloped gold Egyptian-looking necklace.

"Mr. Cadenhead? I'm Carol," the woman said, holding out her hand—as I'd noticed on the phone, Carol had a remarkable voice, soft and smooth but without attempted effects, as if she heard, and took to heart, the languor that her voice draped onto her thoughts.

"How do you do," I said, rolling up my sleeves and gesturing toward a chair I'd pulled over from another desk. "I'm sorry I wasn't here when you called."

"It's all right," Carol said as we both sat down. "They told me you'd be back soon, so I just decided to head over after work."

"I'm glad you came," I said, brushing rainwater out of my hair. "I'm, um, I'm a bit confused, but I'm glad you came."

"I realize it's odd," Carol said, leaning her elbow on my desk, "but after we spoke yesterday I had some regrets about how abrupt I was—I realized that you were just as frightened as I was. It's still hard to gauge the way people *talk* in New York."

"How'd you end up here?" I asked.

"It wasn't all that complicated—I'd heard about the Lineage Institute when I was still in business school," Carol said, "and I thought it might—at the time I thought that it might be an interesting place to work, but my only qualm was that I'd never been to New York and I wasn't sure I'd be—that I'd be able to live here. Of course they keep a low profile, Lineage, they don't do a lot of recruiting, but I knew someone who knew some of their personnel managers, someone who set up an interview, and it went well—when I'd taken my degree they hired me to do financial management, so I took the job and moved to New York and I've been here almost a year now."

"How do you like it?"

"I guess it's been all right," Carol said. "It can be difficult, it's difficult getting used to the way people *think.* It's all finance here."

"I can imagine," I said. As we talked the rain continued, pattering against the black surface of the windows. "What sort of work is the Institute doing now?"

"Fires," said Carol. "Buildings on fire."

"I beg your pardon?"

"It's *amazing,*" said Carol, shaking her head in near-disbelief, her blue eyes wide. "I'm just involved in the financial end of the business, but as far as I understand what they're doing I think it's just remarkable. See, urban fires are accidents, so for all practical purposes they're commonly understood as being absolutely random, unpredictable events."

"I'm with you so far."

"Well, the point of the Institute is that any event can be *under-*

stood provided that some interested party's got a pragmatic reason for investigating it, and also provided that they've got the means to finance a proper study—the fire project's large enough to involve some laboratories out at Cal Tech and a lot of Harvard math people. What we've done is take the city's records from something like a *million and a half* fire alarms and fed them into a series of computers that use all these, I don't know, mathematical algorithms, taking into account the condition of the building, the weather, population, the economics of the area, projecting all these data across a calendar and a city map, and just waiting for the patterns to emerge."

"Patterns? I don't understand—what sort of patterns?"

"Just patterns," said Carol. "It's a common principle—you don't have to understand what's *happening,* you just have to find the pattern, which is simple enough as long as you've got the data going far enough back into the past. We've kept a low profile with this project but soon we'll be able to know exactly where and when the next fire will be."

"My God."

"There's more," said Carol. "Already that would save the city *millions,* which is why they hired us in the first place, but we've also come across twenty years' worth of hard data connecting occurrences of fires to a number of socioeconomic factors—housing deterioration, juvenile delinquency, neighborhood migration, violent crime, and on and on— You understand?"

"This all sounds pretty farfetched," I said. "I mean, someone's serious with this?"

"Very serious. What do you mean, farfetched? It's *working.* Nobody else believed we could do it either, but the results are beginning to come in. When we're finished, when the city can accurately predict every fire, that'll provide them with a precise index of community decay. I'm sorry, this is dull."

"Those two big fires last weekend," I asked. "Did the Institute see them coming?"

"Yes," said Carol. "I think somebody did, probably one of the statisticians, but I don't think it made any difference in terms of the city's actions. No matter what you know it's hard to change things." Carol had been looking around the dark, sparsely populated newsroom as she spoke, and her gaze settled on the photograph of Annabelle on the bulletin board. "Oh, there she is," Carol said, pointing.

"You've never met Annabelle?" I asked.

"No," said Carol, shaking her head, still gazing at the photograph.

"When we spoke on the phone, you said you knew exactly who she was."

"Well, that's"—Carol looked embarrassed—"I never *bought* fashion magazines, you understand, I thought they were horrible, but I used to read them when I was imagining coming to New York, flipping through them at the doctor's office or somewhere. They never name the models in those spreads but she did a Cover Girl ad and then I knew her name, and I always noticed her, because she's so gorgeous, but also because I thought"—Carol looked more embarrassed—"I thought she looked a little bit like me. Much prettier, obviously, but the type."

"You do look a bit like her," I said.

"Thank you," said Carol, smiling. "At Lineage they have this sort of unspoken code about how you should dress, unspoken but actually very strict, so I would keep my eyes open for Annabelle Taft in the magazines and see what they dressed her in, the colors, and sort of take my cues from her. Nine times out of ten, of course, she'd be wearing something nobody could ever afford, except *her*, maybe."

"You sound jealous," I said, smiling.

"Of *course* I'm jealous," said Carol, smirking resignedly at me. "We're avoiding the subject."

"All right," I said, pulling my notebook from my sodden raincoat but dropping it unopened on the desk. "Um, I guess you haven't been able to reach Douglas."

"I keep trying, and there's no answer, so I'm really starting to get worried. You mentioned that you were investigating a death?"

"That's right," I said, rubbing my eyes. "Frank DiGrassi, from Reed Gardner—"

"*Frank DiGrassi* died?" said Carol, alarmed. "I didn't—"

"His son," I said. "Ralph. He's just this guy my age that Douglas and I went to school with, and I was sure it had to do with Douglas' accident. Look, why don't you start by telling me about what happened last month—the night of the Hopkins dinner—and we'll see if we can put this together."

"Well, *after* the fund-raiser, a group of people came over to my house, people from the office, and— I already told you this, right?" Carol said. "I'm sorry—but a bunch of people came over, and then—Douglas stayed late, he was the last to leave, but he didn't just stay late. He was— We became—" Carol turned her bright blue eyes on me, staring through our mutual embarrassment. "Douglas and I, we'd been spending quite a bit of time together, and— I'm not sure how to put this."

"I think I'm getting your drift."

"Eventually we became— That night, we became intimate."

"I see. Miss Casey—"

"Carol."

"Carol, how did you first find out what had happened to Douglas?"

"That photographer called me the next morning," said Carol. "Wednesday. He called the office and asked for me, and told me that Douglas couldn't get to the phone but that he had to take a couple of days off because of sickness."

"Did you wonder what he'd come down with?"

"Yes," said Carol. "Look, I didn't know what the situation was. I was frightened—I'd *been* with him just a few hours before, and whatever happened to him later that afternoon, whatever awful thing put him in the hospital, it happened after I said goodbye to him. I mean I want to make that clear, so that there's no—"

"Carol," I said softly. "Carol, you're not putting yourself at any risk. This isn't any sort of investigation."

Carol looked at me, her face framed by the dark windows and the falling rain. "Then what is it?"

"I don't know," I said, rubbing my eyes. "All right, so Douglas left your house in the morning, and that was the last you saw him, and then Nick Blanchard called you the *next* morning, saying he was— This was the first time you'd ever spoken to Nick, right?"

"Actually, no. He'd called once before."

"Really?" I said. "Can you—"

"Let me see if I can remember," said Carol, leaning back and closing her eyes. "It was a long time ago, sometime in June, I guess, but I can't remember exactly when. He didn't call me specifically, he just— He did what you did yesterday—he called the Institute one night when we were working late and I picked up like I usually do. He said he was an old high school friend of Douglas' and he wondered how to get in touch with him."

"He didn't ask for him? Right then? If he could come to the phone?"

"Oh, he did," said Carol. "But Douglas had already gone home. Nick said he didn't want to bother Douglas—he'd just been thinking over old times and he wanted his home number. I *think* that's what he said—I remember I could barely hear him with all the guitar music in the background, but I asked him if he was sure he didn't want to leave a message and he gave me his name and number." Carol scratched her cheekbone with one fingernail. "He gave me a *couple* of phone numbers, actually—he said he wasn't at home, he was at a friend's house, and he gave that number too in case Douglas showed up in the next hour."

"Can you remember the name?" I asked. "The friend?"

"No," said Carol, squinting. "It was a short name. Two syllables, like—"

"Hector?" I asked. "Kathy?"

"*Kathy,*" Carol said, nodding and pointing at me. "It was a woman's name."

"So, um— Did you tell Douglas he'd called?"

"No. I forgot to. It just slipped my mind."

"You never mentioned it?"

"No. I might have eventually given him the note from the message pad, but I don't remember ever talking about it."

"I'm never going to figure this out," I said, rubbing my eyes. "So Nick called you that Wednesday morning and told you Douglas was taking some time off—that was *Douglas'* idea, by the way, not to alarm you—and then he returned to work a few weeks later?"

"Right. He called me that weekend—a few days later, you know, after he'd been released from the hospital, he called to apologize and reassure me. You know how sweet and polite he is."

"What else did he say?"

"He said that he had had a big problem in his life but that he thought it was over. He said that night he made a mistake and he paid for it. He wouldn't say anything else, and when he came back to work he seemed all right. Quieter, but all right, really. Well—he seemed to be avoiding me. It's only been, um—"

"Five weeks."

"Five weeks, but he's been—*distant,* I guess you could say. It could just be my imagination. He never brought the hospital up and it was clear somehow that it wouldn't be a good idea to mention it."

"And now he's vanished again," I said.

"That's right," said Carol, shifting in the chair, the chair legs scraping the smooth floor against the continuing sound of the rain. "After you called me yesterday I thought of trying his sister"—Carol glanced at Annabelle's picture again—"but I couldn't find a way to—"

"That goddamned unlisted number again," I said. "And here we are."

"I'm sorry I'm not being of greater assistance," said Carol, smiling sweetly.

"No," I said, leaning back and loudly exhaling. "You've cleared things up a great deal—you've narrowed the, um, I'm not sure but I think you've narrowed the field of inquiry. Carol, thank you so much for taking the time to—"

"Come on," said Carol, smiling dismissively, standing up, and I stood also. "People are supposed to help each other out."

"I appreciate it," I said.

"What are you going to do?" asked Carol.

"Last night I began writing it down," I said. "I wrote about my experience at the hospital."

"Why?"

"So that I could remember."

"Thank you for seeing me," said Carol, smiling, her blue eyes flashing.

"It was a pleasure," I said, waiting for her to don her raincoat and then reaching to shake her hand. "If I get a hold of Douglas or if I, um, if I get any closer to understanding what happened to him, I'll let you know."

After Carol and I had exchanged phone numbers and she had left, I opened my desk drawer and found the gold-plated scissors that Douglas had given me at the hospital, steel barber's scissors that you can't bring on an airplane, ten inches long, perfectly made. I was sitting lost in thought fiddling with the gold scissors when I suddenly looked at my watch and realized that it was almost time to go meet Nick, so I turned out my desk lamp and went out into the wet, cool night air, catching the subway with the last of the rush-hour crowds.

NICK'S TRAIN WAS delayed and I ended up spending twenty minutes in Grand Central Station's Main Concourse waiting for him to arrive, standing near the center of that gold and cavernous room, surrounded by the tides of travelers that stormed across the marble floor and looking up at the vast, curved picture of the celestial sky a hundred feet above, the sidereal longitude lines, the Zodiac's classical figures, the electrical stars and the clockwork of the universe. Nick eventually emerged from the rapid crowds, stalking toward me, grinning in the dim amber light of the vast waiting room, the huge, bright advertisements reflecting on his black sunglasses—he was suntanned, his hair bleached by the Montana sun, and he wore a new pair of cowboy boots and an embroidered cowboy belt with a large buckle that glinted from under the flapping edges of his customary dark overcoat.

"Hey, buddy!" Nick said hoarsely, clapping me on the shoulder—his camera was slung under his arm and he was carrying two large leather shoulder bags, one of which he handed to me as soon as he arrived at my side. "No kidding, thanks for coming, man. Were you just working? You look terrible."

"It wasn't any trouble," I said, taking the heavy leather bag. "Welcome back."

"Thanks," said Nick, gesturing us toward the rubber-ribbed ramps that led toward the baroque Forty-second Street doors. "Of course I can't be seen traveling with you."

"So, um— How's Montana?" I asked, struggling to keep up with him.

"Oh my God," said Nick, shaking his head, smiling as he looked away from me. "It's phenomenal. There's so much we have to talk about. Listen"—he was pointing toward a row of phone booths along a nearby wall—"can you spot me a quarter? I've got to call Kathy."

I handed him a quarter and then kept a discreet distance while he talked into one of the phones, and after he had hung up I walked over.

"Hey," said Nick, leaning against the perforated aluminum edge of the phone booth, greeting me again, as if having forgotten I was there. "Hey, Mike, listen—can I come over to your house? I mean it's not even eight yet," he continued, turning his foot and admiring his cowboy boots, "and I would stay with Kathy, you know, but that never works out—she's got school tomorrow and her asshole brother's around and her parents will kill her if I show up over there."

"Why can't you just go home?" I said, irritated.

"I can," said Nick, guiding us away from the phones. "I was just trying to come up with a better plan. So how about it—could Kathy and I come out to your house? She's got this Brooklyn thing. I wish I could tell you about Kathy," said Nick, his voice shifting, as it were, to a finer grade of sandpaper. "We've got this new generation—all the shit these kids do is so bizarre. I can see it in her eyes sometimes, in the evenings sometimes. Can I come over to your house, Mike?"

We were lugging Nick's bags up one of the ramped hallways, our feet clattering with the crowd on the yellow marble, smeared with muddy footprints and echoing with the sounds of the rain outside. "I'm tired, Nick," I said. "I've been very busy—I would've explained on the phone, but—"

"So you've been getting in good with Annabelle, huh?" said Nick, smiling gently and tipping his chin toward me suddenly.

"Well, not really. She had a party a couple nights ago."

"She invited *you?*" said Nick, frowning at a new gold-inlaid watch. "So what do you think of that place of hers?"

"It's very nice. We were just talking when you called."

Nick grinned at me. "What is this, Mike, you nut—I leave for a while and suddenly you're moving in with the crowd, living it up. I mean I don't know."

"Nick, listen," I said. "Ralph DiGrassi died yesterday morning."

"Ralph DiGrassi *died?* Jesus," said Nick, heaving his slipping camera back onto his shoulder with a shrug. "Wait— First things first. How'd you get into Annabelle's house, anyway?"

"I'm already sorry I mentioned it to you," I said as we left the station. "It's a newspaper story."

"I can't believe I'm back in New York," said Nick, looking the other direction, gazing through the misted rain at the bright Forty-second Street headlights and at the dark granite of the curving Park Avenue bridge.

"It started at the hospital, Nick. You decided to—"

"Oh, shit," said Nick tersely. "Nothing *happened,* damn it— We had to go see Douglas 'cause he got hurt. Why do you always make such a big—"

"Nick," I said, listening to the click of his camera photographing the street as we walked, "why don't you care that Ralph died?"

"Why are you *pretending* to care?" Nick said angrily. "You hated him as much as I did and you know it. This isn't about Ralph, this is about you thinking you're mister hot-shit professional man moving into the big-time nightlife territory, you know, hanging out with *models.*"

"Nick—"

"What— I'm *wrong?*" Nick raised his eyebrows above the rain-beaded sunglasses. "Don't tell *me* about, you know, about the shit that runs through a man's head when some *model* shows up. I mean, doesn't matter, right, doesn't matter *who* you are, you get snagged and then comes the, comes the *rationale.* And you don't even know what the fuck you're onto here, believe me. It's not your— You don't have— There are some things you can't just go *ask* people about."

"I don't understand," I said, alarmed. "What— What did I do?"

"You shouldn't be fucking around with this," said Nick. "Believe me—this isn't some bullshit you cooked up. This is something *real.* It's none of your business, is all I'm saying."

"What are you talking about? *What's* none of my business?"

"Look, do me one favor and answer a simple, straightforward question," said Nick quietly. "Mike, do you know what you're doing here? I mean, do you really know what you're—what you're getting after here?"

"Well, can *you* explain it to me, Nick?" I said tightly. " 'Cause I think you can."

Nick didn't say anything and we stood facing each other, pedestrians brushing past us. "You know, I thought over the years you'd changed," Nick said quietly, stepping forward. "I thought, you know, seeing you recently, watching you talk to Hector, I thought maybe you'd—"

"Yeah?"

"—learned to— You always used to be so *stubborn.* I thought maybe you'd learned to change your mind."

"*You're* not changing my mind," I said, abruptly handing the strap of Nick's bag out to him, which he absently took. "I don't want to hear you lecturing me about—lecturing me about *propriety* when you're still taking those goddamned *pictures.*"

"That's a stupid argument," said Nick, looking away.

"It's *not* a stupid argument, Nick."

"Yes it is," said Nick, shaking his head with conclusive anger. "Yes it is. You're dwelling on all this high school crap. Look"—he turned toward me—"I'm sorry I bothered you today, all right? I'm sorry I wasted your time." A cab cruised up and Nick suddenly flagged it down.

"Nick—"

"No— Fuck you," said Nick, walking toward the rain-speckled cab that he'd hailed. "You've got to learn some *decorum,* Mike—you can't do whatever comes into your head just because, you know, just because you think you're seeing some kind of *truth.* As far as I'm concerned you and your goddamned newspaper can go fuck yourselves." Nick dropped his cigarette and stepped it out as he entered the cab and slammed the door and then the cab pulled away and I was left standing on the sidewalk in the cold rain.

chapter 6

At nine-thirty the next morning I had just arrived at work and was rubbing my cold hands and squinting painfully at the ATEX screen when I heard Wilson calling my name across the newsroom—when I looked up I saw him standing in his open doorway, wearing another yellow shirt and another sock-like brown tie, beckoning me into his office. It was a freezing Friday morning, bleak and beautiful—the fresh October air had thinned and the sky was clear, and I'd felt a mild, minted breeze as I walked through midtown, stepping through the fading gloss of yesterday's rain and through shadowed pockets of near-painful chill and back into the sun, where my shoulders felt a feeble winter warmth that called to mind the baking heat of the abandoned summer. I had already informed Wilson that I had to take some of the morning off—I had an appointment at the ophthalmologist scheduled—but I dutifully entered his office and closed the door, sitting in the worn chair that he waved me into.

"All right," Wilson said, sipping from a Styrofoam cup of tea. "Let's talk."

"Good morning, Wilson," I said bleakly. "I know I've been a bit late for, um, a few too many days in a row, but this time there was a subway delay that kept me from—"

"You've spent two days on the DiGrassi death," Wilson said, leaning back and stroking his hands through his thinning red hair. "What have you got?"

"He died of a heart attack," I said, wiping my forehead clear of a thin film of perspiration. "The coronary attack was brought on by an overdose of an antidepressant drug, according to the hospital's report. DiGrassi's mother saw something, um, something in his room, when she heard him screaming and came into the room—something frightening that she won't describe. The night before he died he, um, he told his father that he was in some sort of trouble, and, um—" Wilson was immobile in his chair, staring at me impassively. "Wilson, I've got more details on the hospital report, if you'd like me to go get my notes. The point is that there's a strong chain of evidence connecting the death to a near-fatal accident suffered by my friend who works at the Lineage—".

"Did you talk to DiGrassi's mother?" Wilson asked.

"—Institute. What? She's on background."

"You didn't answer my question," said Wilson, sipping his tea. "Did you talk to the mother?"

"No," I said, leaning weakly back against the wooden chair. "It's thirdhand."

"Who's on the record in this story, Cadenhead?" Wilson asked, staring at me, his voice calm and fatigued.

"I've interviewed several people and I've made—"

"You got a statement from DiGrassi's flack," Wilson said, "and you turned it into an obituary slug, which was a passable bit of work, but since that seems to be the extent of your quotable source material, I'm just politely asking—who's on the record in this story?"

Wilson waited several seconds while I sat without breathing, hearing all the surrounding newsroom sounds, and then he abruptly dropped his hands onto the surface of the desk, startling me into a slight flinch and causing his Styrofoam cup to tremble, spilling several ounces of tea onto a floppy disk.

"All right," Wilson said calmly, rolling his head and looking at me. "All right, that's enough. You don't have a story, Michael. Try as I may, I can't see myself running a piece of squirrel tail claiming that a mob lawyer's son has died under some bizarre circumstances without a great deal more meat, a great deal more *text*, background or not, than what you've got—I can't see myself running that piece and standing up to DiGrassi's inevitable complaints of impropriety and I certainly can't see you ending up in any kind of advantageous position in Metro news with that sort of unfounded speculative piece painted on your airplane wing." Wilson leaned to scratch his ankle. "You now have an opportunity to correct my ill-informed assessment of your position."

"I may not have a straight newspaper story," I said, sighing in defeat as I rubbed my irritated eyes, "but, damn it, Wilson, I'm telling you that there's something here."

"I want you to put this *aside,*" Wilson said sharply. "Damn it, I'm telling you *directly*—I'm doing you the courtesy of letting you know where you *stand* with me. You've *just* arrived at Metro and you have no past actions to guarantee your security here. As far as I'm concerned you've got a great deal of"— Wilson yawned luxuriously—"Excuse me. You've got a *great* deal of ground to reclaim before you've won my good graces again. I think you may have it in you to be a good journalist, Michael," he went on, fishing for a Kleenex and grimacing as he mopped up his spilled tea, "and believe me, I know what it's like to feel that hunger, but I don't think this is your ship coming in."

"All right," I said heavily. "But it's too bad."

"Michael?" Rachel Geisler called across the newsroom.

"Just a moment, Wilson, I'm sorry," I said, rising to open the door and seeing Rachel standing by my desk, holding my phone receiver cradled in her hand. "Yeah, Rachel?" I called.

"Annabelle Taft on line six," Rachel said.

As I crossed the newsroom I circled round several grinning journalists who were looking at me oddly, and I heard them whispering Annabelle's name after I'd passed. "Annabelle?" I said distantly, having taken the phone from Rachel. "Hello?"

"Hello, Michael," said Annabelle, her voice cool and uninflected. "I'm sorry to bother you at work."

"It's no bother," I said, sitting down wearily.

"Michael, I'd like—" I heard Annabelle catch her breath. "I'd like to meet and talk with you."

"Oh really?" I said flatly.

"I'm in some trouble, Michael," Annabelle said.

I had let my head drift back and was gazing up at the pressed tin ceiling. "I can't help you," I said.

"It's a question of investigation," said Annabelle.

"Investigation?" I said, glancing suddenly at the wall clock and remembering the ophthalmologist. "I don't know how to do it. I've got to go, Annabelle—I've got an appointment."

"Yes, but you *do* know," said Annabelle. "So please talk to me."

"I can't talk now, Annabelle. I'm sorry. I'm no longer investigating anything."

"Have you been out today?" Annabelle asked.

"Not really," I said, glancing out the bright filthy windows.

"You should see this day. It's so pretty it sparkles," said Annabelle. "I've got some business uptown today—I was wondering if you wanted to walk south with me when I'm done. Could you meet me at my parents' house at five-thirty this afternoon? Fifth Avenue and Ninety-third." Rachel was performing a silent mime, pointing at the photograph of Annabelle on my bulletin board, and I nodded impatiently.

"Just to talk," Annabelle added.

"Sure," I said finally. "I'll come up after work. Where are we headed?"

"Nowhere," said Annabelle. "Except I've got to make it to the agency by seven—that's across from Tiffany's."

"All right. Ninety-third to Fifty-seventh?" I said. "It isn't a short walk."

"No walk is short," said Annabelle.

ALMOST AN HOUR later I was walking east through the cold morning's furtive pedestrian traffic, passing crowds of schoolchildren as I crossed the bright, wide expanse of Fifty-ninth Street, inhaling the air that had been permanently tainted by the fragrance of the horses that completed the archaic illusion of a European boulevard. When I got to the doctor's office, near Grand Army Plaza, the waiting room was empty save for the receptionist—an odd-looking woman with hair that resembled disproportionately cut shanks of sun-dried wheat who sat behind a large desk. "Excuse me—I've got a ten-thirty appointment?" I told her. "I hope I'm not too late."

"Yes sir," the bizarre, straw-haired woman told me, looking down at a datebook. "An appointment with whom?"

"Dr. Cadenhead."

Just then one of the examination room doors opened and my father stood framed in its jamb, looking at me, and I realized that I hadn't had any sort of clear conception of what he currently looked like—I saw a balding, white-haired middle-aged man with thick bifocaled horn-rimmed glasses and large shoes, a man barely shorter than I was, and I wondered if I could see our resemblance to each other.

"You're late," my father told me in his muffled, grumbling voice.

"Hello, Dad," I said, glancing at the receptionist. "I'm sorry—I'm coming from the office."

"So I understand," my father said, stepping forward and shaking my hand formally. "Daphne, this is my son."

"Well—!" said Daphne, immediately beaming at me. "Well—! He's quite a handsome young man, Dr. Cadenhead."

"No, he's not," I said, smiling.

"No, he's not," my father corroborated. "Daphne, call Mrs. Hempstone about her twelve-thirty and try to reschedule for—"

"That's not necessary, Dad," I said, looking around at the Styrofoam ceiling, the worn industrial burnt-orange carpeting, the chairs, the absurd pictures on the walls. "The place looks good," I told him. "You've been fixing it up?"

"I let Daphne do everything," my father said, gesturing me toward his doorway. "It's *her* waiting room."

I entered my father's examination room and was slowly entranced by the memories the room evoked, the ways in which I could remember having seen it from different, younger vantage points closer to the floor—I remembered visits during which I was not permitted to touch the large, heavy diopter wheel or the hand lenses or any of my father's glittering, well-cared-for optical equipment, at a time when I had barely learned to recognize the diminishing letters on the large standard wall chart. "You used to have a wall chart, didn't you, Dad?" I asked.

"Have a seat," my father mumbled, adjusting his tray of equipment. "Take your lenses out. I use this contraption now," he said, moving to lower the shades and then switching on a piercing, bright beam of projector light. "Why don't you ever call?" he asked, looming over me as I settled down into the padded chair.

"I don't know," I said helplessly.

"Just dropping a note once in a while so we have an idea how you are," my father said in the darkness, fiddling clumsily with several sheets of transparent acetate, threading them through the projector while I steered the steel diopter wheel onto my face. "Read top to bottom, left to right."

"I'm always afraid you'll think I want something," I said, peering at the blurred letters.

"Do you want something today?" my father grumbled resignedly. "Next row."

"Yes," I said, after reading off the letters. "My eyes are killing me."

"Of course they are," my father said, and I could tell by the sounds of his hands that he was critically examining the lenses I'd just taken out. "These are not good. Where'd you get them?"

"A place in midtown."

"You have to watch out for those con men," my father instructed me gravely. "Why didn't you come to me?"

"You're too expensive," I said, watching the next group of letters slide into view.

"I wouldn't charge you," my father told me, twirling the diopter-increment lens before my left eye. "Which is better—one or two?"

"Two," I said. "I don't want to take things I can't afford."

"I can't see the wisdom of living in Brooklyn," my father told me. "Why don't you find a place in Manhattan?"

"I can't afford it."

"You could find a friend to share the burden," my father said.

"I can't think of anyone I could live with."

"You could come home," he said. "Which is better—one or two?"

"Dad," I protested. "One."

"Your eyes have gotten worse," my father mumbled. "I'm so sorry to hear about your classmate having passed away."

"What did— How did *you* know about that?" I asked, bumping my nose against the rubber guards on the diopter wheel.

"I'm sure you're not surprised," my father grumbled, "to learn that we still communicate with other Thorndike parents from time to time." As he spoke my father clumsily positioned a pair of green plastic filters into the projector's stage. "Would you like me to send some sort of contribution?"

"Only if you want to."

"Do you feel that you owe them? The school?"

"I don't know," I said.

"Was he a friend of yours?"

"No."

"Close your left eye," my father said. "How's work?"

"I'm at the Metropolitan Section now," I told him, pulling my head away from the diopter wheel and looking up at him through the green light that filled the room. My father gazed down at me, his greying eyebrows peaking slowly upward, the soft aging folds of flesh around his mouth cracking as he beamed at me.

"The Metropolitan Section," he repeated. "I'm proud of you."

"Thank you," I said. "I haven't done much writing yet."

"I used to help you write," my father said across the dark room's quiet green light.

"What do you mean?"

"When you were a small boy," my father told me. "Don't you remember? You wanted the toys that they advertised on cereal boxes. Your mother and I would help you make the postcards that you would send in to get the toys. They tell you to send—"

"They tell you to send the box top," I remembered. "For proof—"

"—proof of purchase," my father said, smiling. "If you didn't have the box top you could—"

"You could take a piece of blank white paper and write—"

"—write the name of the cereal in block—"

"—block letters on the paper and send that instead," I said, smiling at my father. "You showed me how to write, how to make the letters with a pencil."

"Pen," said my father. "You had to use a pen. Come on"—he had gestured my face back against the steel wheels of the diopter machine—"tell me what you see."

When I emerged from the examination room after another twenty minutes I was squinting—my father had dismayed me by telling me that the examination required the use of the special eye-drops that dilate your pupils. "Just wear these," he had told me, grinning as he handed over a cheap plastic pair of sunglasses, and by the time I was retrieving my coat the eyedrops had already taken effect and the fluorescent bulbs in the ceiling of the waiting room were brighter than the sun seen head on.

"Thanks," I said, gratefully donning the absurd eyewear. "There's something else I need, Dad," I told him, remembering. "With this new job, um, they've been giving me a hard— There've been some complaints about my clothes. Could you recommend—"

"You need a suit?" my father mumbled sharply.

"Well—yes," I said, glancing at Daphne, embarrassed.

"I have one you can borrow," my father said, turning to open the small coat closet and pull out a beautiful soft grey double-breasted pinstriped suit wrapped in plastic. "Just an old, superfluous—"

"But Dr. Cadenhead," Daphne said, her eyes widening, "you're making a mistake—that's the new one fresh from the cleaners'."

"Hush, Daphne," my father mumbled, handing over the suit,

which I slung over my shoulder, the plastic wrinkles shimmering with shining fire. "For an old man I should have more sense. I'll have your lenses on order by the end of the day," he continued, stepping awkwardly toward me. "I'll give you a buzz on the horn when they arrive. May I—"

"Yes?" I said, struggling with my overcoat, still holding my father's suit.

"—May I have your phone number? If you'd rather I didn't have it, I can just tell you that your lenses will take about a week, and you can contact me after the—"

"Here, Dad," I said, pulling out my notebook and pen and writing down my home and work numbers, squinting through the cheap sunglasses.

"Thank you," my father said, handing the scrap of paper across the vinyl-laminated desk. "Daphne, here's where you should send the bill. I'll walk you to the elevator, Michael— Would you like to have lunch? There's a delicatessen around—"

"I should get back to work," I said as we left the office, wincing in advance at the corridor's blinding light. "I've been busy the past few days, so—"

"What are you investigating?" my father asked as we approached the elevator, and despite the sunglasses and my inflamed eyes I could see him accurately, see his age, his small size, his bright eyes and weak mouth, see the detail of him in a way that called to mind everything I knew, the harsh realities of his appearance bearing out my clouded memory.

"My past," I said.

"You can start with me," my father said, smiling at what he seemed to assume was an attempt at a shared joke. "I named you Michael."

"Some people call me Mike," I said, thumbing the elevator button, the upward-pointing arrow shedding emerald light. "Like microphone."

"Well, I can't think of anything else," my father told me, sighing conclusively, glancing back at his pebbled-glass office door. "Are they treating you well? Your employers?"

"I can't complain," I said, turning toward him.

"Well, that's unusual," my father said dubiously.

"Of course I can complain," I said, looking down. "Even without the job."

"The job's difficult?"

"And I don't have— There aren't many people for me. I want to go home, Dad."

"You don't have to say that," my father said, glancing away.

"I *want* to," I said, nodding. "It's just, um, it's just that I can't. It's too late."

"Yes," my father said as the elevator door opened before me. "Yes, I suppose it is."

I TRIED TO look nonchalant in the elevator behind the absurd eyewear, but it was impossible, and when I arrived on the sidewalk it was like walking onto the surface of the sun—bumpers of passing cars shone like floodlamps as I stepped into the street, eyes streaming, my father's suit slung over my shoulder. I hailed a taxi, in defeat, cowering in the backseat against the dazzling light that assaulted me from all directions, and as I emerged in front of the newspaper I found to my dismay that the few remaining clouds had cleared from the western horizon and it looked as if the entire state of New Jersey were blazing in an apocalyptic petrochemical inferno. By the time I'd returned to the newsroom my eyes seemed to have been wrenched into a permanent squint, and I stumbled around the white pillars and managed to make it over to Rachel's desk, pushing the cheap sunglasses as close to my face as possible and sitting on the edge of her filing cabinet.

"You're back," Rachel said colorlessly, staring at her ATEX terminal as she typed. "A package came for you."

"A package?" I said, peering ineffectually at the dark shadow of my desk.

"FedEx—I signed the guy's form. What's the matter with you, anyway?" Rachel demanded, her fingers still popping on the computer keyboard.

"My eyes are messed up," I said, cautiously approaching my desk and draping the plastic-wrapped suit across my chair. The Federal Express box had been addressed to me care of the newspaper, and the return-address portion of the label was inscribed DOUGLAS TAFT, followed by a downtown residential street address and phone number. "I need a dark place," I told Rachel.

"Try the second conference room," she advised, pointing with her chin without interrupting the sentence she was rapidly typing, maddeningly unperturbed by her screen's blaze. "Nobody should disturb you in there."

I hefted the heavy box under my arm and shuffled in my desk drawer with my other hand, fishing out the old pair of eyeglasses that I hadn't worn since high school and the gold barber's scissors. The empty conference room faced the street—I immediately pulled the shades on both of the windows and turned out all the overhead lamps, but the window shades were rimmed with white fire and I still couldn't remove the cheap-looking sunglasses except for the moment that it took me to put the old eyeglasses on beneath them, which marginally clarified my blinding vision. Sitting down in the darkest corner of the room, I cut the duct tape and then opened the box, carefully removing each object and examining them one by one before placing them in a row on the teakwood surface of the conference table. On top was a manila envelope containing a brown leatherette notebook, which revealed itself, upon opening, to be Douglas' "Pershing Diary," and underneath the diary I found a small hardcover volume, old and frayed and covered with dust, its ripped and repaired jacket imprinted with a somewhat gaudy painting of Venice's Piazza San Marco and overlaid with white letters that spelled the title *The Story of Jake Hackett,* above the author's name, Giuseppe Bonomi. Confused, I thumbed through the book, sliding my thumbnail along the red deckle-edge and watching the cracking corners of the brittle pages flaking off until the book opened around a red, check-sized envelope containing four torn slips of pasteboard, printed tickets for *The Thorndike School Class of 1981 Graduation Ceremonies—June 15—12:00 PM,* and a ring-stained paper place mat folded in quarters and emblazoned with an eighteenth-century lithographed engraving of a New England building—LAWRENCE HOTEL, the copperplate caption read, and beneath that, DOVER, CONNECTICUT—ESTABLISHED 1767. On the box's cardboard floor I found a TDK audiocassette in a crushed and scratched plastic box, the graphic design of which revealed the tape to be several years old, with a paper label upon which a young girl, as far as I could tell, had listed the names of the tape's songs with a red Flair pen—*Maybe I'm Amazed, Naked Eye, America, Tempted, Someday Never Comes, Wish You Were Here, Don't Stand So Close to Me, Let My Love Open the Door, Baby You're a Rich Man, Time, I'll Be Your Mirror, Moonlight Mile*—and an old, unopened and probably stale pack of Camel Filter cigarettes with a white abstract-looking label that has since been redesigned, Connecticut tax stamps on its foil edge. Next to the cigarettes I found an expensively made glossy black matchbox, archaically embossed with pseudo-gold-leaf script letters spelling the word *Anthesteria,* and beneath, *June 13th, 1981.*

"White Camels," I said out loud, turning the cigarette pack in my hands. The first cigarette I'd ever smoked had been a White Camel lit with an Anthesteria match, I remembered as I opened the cigarette pack, extracted a White Camel and lit it with an Anthesteria match. I choked on the stale, unfamiliar smoke, my head reeling drunkenly with the toxic tobacco as I sat tapping ashes into the empty box, peering at the notebook through two pairs of eyeglasses, the cigarette coal shining like a demon's eye as I squinted at the windows—along the edges of the shades the sky was brilliant burnished platinum and I realized with alarm that the brightest hours of the day were yet to come.

Pershing Diary *Douglas A. Taft*
June 12 1986

Let's face facts Dr. Pershing we're talking about Cardinal Sin but even so the Even with Cardinal Sin Im not sure quite what you want me to write. Of course I know exactly what you want me to write here but I think I have to start from back years ago and end up where you know I'm going The I can talk about any [*illegible*] when you're not right here facing me with that damn look on your face. People ask me what we talk about but of course we talk about Nothing. The I also Maybe this is working. Back when I got the Lineage job I believed I'd be doing a lot of writing but I ended up on the phone all the time and I've stopped writing letters. When I turned 23 I had a moment of sadness when I looked back over the cards I got and realized the people I've fallen out of touch with. So many names from five years ago. Nick Blanchard, Ralph DiGrassi, Jack Winfield, Amy MacIntyre, Tina Foster, Bill Coleman who's probably working for the Pentagon, Steve Leonard, Wally Patterson, always with the wrestling, Louise Delany. Jill Brooks with the blonde hair all the time and the gymnastic muscles. I was sad on my birthday because one day I had to go past Thorndike and it was like a big bullet had hit me in the stomach remembering it all and sometimes I think all we can do All of us, all we can do is to ignore what was done to us there and I don't want We The I think that's it for tonight

June 14

Ralph DiGrassi of all people keeps coming into the office and giving me a hard time. All my life I've had to put up with that guy and I remember he was actually around during during graduation weekend and that was his Big Major Sin the one that I suppose destroyed it all for him and despite my pity I wish he could leave me alone. I remember he always used to stare at Annabelle I mean not the usual typical staring thing about Annabelle but something different, something else, and these days he's got to ask me about her and he doesn't get the hint, he doesn't He actually hasn't caught on to the fact that I'm telling the truth and I really genuinely am out of touch with Out of touch with Out of touch with her. The last thing Thorndike gave me At the end At The last The last thing was that weekend and after that weekend I thought that nothing, I knew absolutely that nothing could get the taste out of my mouth no sleep travel smoke vodka memory nothing could even get the taste out of my mouth. So on my birthday walking by the Thorn and even considering Actually considering going to the Café DeGaulle for afternoon breakfast was was I think Bonomi had this one passage in *Jake Hackett* that conveyed it. I'm in Riverside Park right now on a bench with no one around and with my legs crossed with this notebook on my lap. I'm not moving until I fill the damn notebook. I'm that committed. I'm sorry I mentioned *Jake Hackett* but my Father would be proud if There's a point where any book makes sense. I am an expert witness. When I get to the end I'll The Well so much for persistence because it's starting to rain

June 15

Today was a good day At work I've met a woman named Carol and for the first time The I don't know her last name yet And for the first time there's something happening to me that I For the first time in years and years I can feel a certain happiness that involves dread and excitement and I think that I can keep from misjudging and feel that theres still beauty in the world. Carol is from outside the city and she's practically just arrived and she is so excited to be here, so excited, and she asks me these questions about being here, she gets scared but she manages to come up with questions that I can answer and when shes scared I feel I can comfort her which is something of a new thing for me, and I'm actually beginning to think in terms of this thing of the two of us meeting coming to an end Dr. Pershing. Carol and I went uptown during our lunch hour today and went to the museum, and it was We got back really late and had to make up some story to tell the others because we'd been gone about three hours. I find that I'm beginning to think The time that I've spent recently with Carol is beginning to Is actually beginning to put the Other business out of my mind, which is incredible. Carol is such a wonderful person. This morning I got out of the shower and for once the view out my airshaft window seemed suspended outside the previous days and the morning was suddenly the end of a line of mornings that stretched back through my life. So Carol and I go off and do these various things and the office thing affects the thing with the two of us and the thing with the two of us seems to affect the office thing because suddenly the light's dawning for some of these people at the office and suddenly Skip and Martin and the other men are all sort of admitting that they all have a thing for her too— The jokes come up and then Skip actually tries to defend me in this joking way— Can you blame the man, he says in this Dartmouth Gruff Voice, and one time Sam and Ben were there and they made the big show of giving me the evil knowing look. Jesus my hand is killing me. I'll try to get this diary back on back on back on track soon but for now you're just going to have to wait because I'm beginning to actually enjoy the For the first time since starting the job it's beginning to make sense

June 17

All day I sit around at the office gulping coffee and sucking back cigarettes trying to stare unobtrusively at various people who come by, the law people and Senator Rollins and that idiot Tom Hopkins and once William Huxley. I thought I was getting away from the motherfucking Brethren. Max Gantry used to call them the Brethren but I think he was just copying something his mother said. The problem is that whatever the hell I think I'm trying to do with this job I keep getting sucked into all the damn office friendships. Sunglasses you can buy off a blanket in the street. Skip is this Dartmouth bright boy who thinks he's taking me on as a protégé and thinks that he should get a Nobel Prize for having endured a couple of years of law school and therefore having the job that he has. I should have realized I was in trouble. The months go by and the fear comes as it tends to come. When I met Carol I couldn't help giving in. So I have this routine. Carol has style. We've been through all that shit. I don't think [*illegible*] I don't I know what Look I'm trying to get at this. Carol told me about the roof where Carol keeps saying what my whole problem is but I know what my whole problem is. She talks about this rooftop in the building where she lives somewhere in SoHo or some damn place. Never been there. She talks about what the view is like from there in the early morning and I know what she's getting at. Carol especially says that says that she has this thing, she can't wait for the end of the summer, she's looking forward to the Autumn when the leaves are everywhere and the coldness comes. She talks about how how there's a window in her Window in her bedroom where she can see the morning light and when she gets up early she watches the birds fly around the water towers, how she can see the silent view and believe that it's good to have come to the city and understand that she can be content and the world can make sense. I mean so she says this stuff all the time and looks at me and I think I'm catching the drift here and its somewhat strange but it makes me understand her and feel happy. The roof though reminds me of Max and Ralph stuff from fifteen years. Airplanes or birds being thrown off a rooftop and somehow again again like choking it led to made me realize everything else and soon Dr. Pershing soon I will write it all down here, not now but soon.

June 20

It's nice here in the park because I hate going straight home after seeing you. Anyway I'm so fucking tired of making fun of myself. I guess I never realize how I talk and how patient you are with me but of course that's your job and Annabelle's and Annabelle's money. Shes a millionaire so hell. It isn't a matter of individual events individual sounds and feelings but a clear sort of object, an entire way of life for years A huge sadness. The park is hushed and still now. The thing is that I can't believe how fucked up things seem to have gotten in my head. If we start imagining we never stop. I'm going to do this properly starting tomorrow. You should rip out these first few pages. You should probably rip out the whole notebook but never mind. I promise if it Kills me I'll get it out. Stay tuned

June 21

I remember the old West End Avenue apartment was so small, it seemed large when I was a little boy but I guess it was too small and as we walked around it we hunched our shoulders and took little top-heavy steps from room to room. Jane was forced to recognize the consequences of her actions because whenever she pawed open a door and padded into a room the door would swing around and bang the wall and freeze her in her tracks and scare her out of the room but it was impossible to keep all the doors closed and all the rooms had doors on both ends so no room was a dead end. It is Sunday and everybody is there, Mom, Dad, me, Anna, Lisa Sparrow—remember her she was

Annabelle's favorite ghost—hunched in different places as morning advanced to afternoon and radios blared and sunlight made squares on the floor and footsteps rattling the brittle woodwork and twisting the throw rugs. Omelettes and chipped glasses and banging refrigerator doors dropping ceramic fruit magnets and whistling teakettles and all the talking heads or grainy films on the television and Anna washing her hair in the sink while my tea was sitting to cool between the newspapers and pencils and saltshakers and Jane sleeping on a table next to the lamp made from a bottle. Boredom making me leave into the sunlight and nowhere to go but the closed stores and no bus pass and this is the second day before school starts again. Banks are closed bagels and coffee in blue Greek paper mugs and back home music all the music, the music battles on all day and the home melody loses to ghostly repeated piano practice. We hit the kitchen for toasted bread or slashed fruit from the top of the refrigerator and the splashed milk of evening cereal bringing on florid towel paper which disappeared sodden into the brown rubber wastebasket that was there all my life. Into the night bathroom pipes making ghost noises, headphones and spiced tea and typewriters for school and the sound reminded me that others were awake. We Would Watch until the creaking floorboards were danger with fear of waking others Duty soon resumed but here a day of rest between the sunglasses and bus rides and the offbeat drumming and the late sleep and sticky eyes lamplight and the book lying upside down on an open page and the ache in my shoulder from holding the phone and the memory of the summer days when all of time had the silent stillness of this moment as the lights are turned out and the alarm clock set for seven and the room is dark while music plays before sleep for years as far back as I can go.

June 23

Graduation weekend was The weekend started I remember The weekend began with Max—I told you all about the F-111 with Max Gantry and how we were going to build this airplane and all that—But that was the earliest weekend with Max that I can remember. The last weekend with Max Gantry was the weekend he saved my life The end of everything was Graduation Weekend and oh Jesus Fucking God it hurts my heart so painfully to think about To remember To think about what happened, about the thing that I will Never my entire life escape being trapped forever by the dark we uncovered that night. Of course I remember how it happened. Of course I remember how it began I remember that I'd been up until five writing my last paper for Chablis.

I remember that Annabelle was standing around in her bedroom with the door closed listening to the Velvet Underground and biding her time and she didn't come with me to Thorndike that morning but that was the day that Max Gantry and I went to the Café—I remember perfectly waking up with Jane curled up at the foot of the bed hearing Annabelle's clock radio taking a shower while my Dad left for downtown and about ten billion people called for my mother. I remember all about how

HAVING READ THAT far I stretched my aching neck and began flipping randomly forward through the notebook, squinting through the sunglasses as I stretched my neck and realizing, as the ink-clotted pages blurred past, that my vision had nearly returned to normal. The notebook had been completely filled with writing and I turned to the last left-hand page, which was bare save for a single block of text, block-letter words carved into the cheap paper with a ballpoint pen as if with a chisel or a plow:

> *NAMES WILL NEVER HURT ME BUT THESE WORDS WORDS WORDS WILL NEVER SAVE ME I WILL NOT CURSE THE DARKNESS I WILL NOT MOVE OR TALK I WILL TOUCH NOTHING I WILL FINISH SOON I WILL ACT ALONE I HAVE GIVEN THE SCISSORS AWAY AND I WILL WAIT WHILE THE WORLD IS DARK*

The following page—the last page in the notebook—had been roughly torn out, shorn from the binding in a jagged vertical slash. As I reread the book's penultimate inscription I heard a clicking sound and turned toward the door, removing the sunglasses and closing the notebook—Wilson Pick stood framed in the corridor light looking down at me, his red-haired hand on the steel doorknob.

"I didn't know where you were," Wilson said, stifling a yawn. "These are supposed to be office hours—what's with the memorabilia?"

"I'm sorry," I said.

"It's *dark* in here," Wilson said, looking at his watch. "Listen—I just heard a rumor that Hopkins may be announcing his withdrawal from the election. Something about 'purported criminal ties'—I told Rachel to fish around and she needs your notes."

"You're kidding," I said, standing as I began to place all the objects back into the white Federal Express box.

"There's supposed to be a press conference in a couple weeks," Wilson went on. "The board said something about those crazy lawyers of his and I suddenly remembered you. Just filling you in," he continued blandly, stretching as he leaned against the door frame. "In the meantime I think it might be a good idea for you to take some time off, Michael. I don't necessarily have any interest in your affairs, but listen—why don't you just clear off the premises for a few days? Maternity leave or something. I won't tell."

"That— *Why,* Wilson?" I said awkwardly, closing the cardboard flaps.

"Because you're useless to me like this," Wilson said as he reached to swing the door shut, "and I love reunions."

IT WAS FIVE-THIRTY in the afternoon and Annabelle and I were slowly walking south along Fifth Avenue, passing prewar apartment fortresses and Victorian mansions, the bright, clear October air moving in cold eddies that nudged the shedding trees at the low brownstone wall that barricaded Central Park. Through my old eyeglasses I could see a great distance, all the way down to where the sparkling towers of midtown shone against the clear blue sky, and I turned to look at Annabelle as she talked to me, her voice calm and quiet, gazing forward along the tremendous avenue. She had emerged from her parents' apartment building a few minutes after I'd shown up, nodding at the brass-band doorman and smiling easily at me, as if there was a great familiarity between us, taking my arm for the moment it took her to guide us around so that we were facing downtown—she was wearing a sable coat over an embroidered green floral dress that I could see flashes of as she walked, black high-heeled shoes and a round-brimmed black hat that emphasized the curves of her cheekbones and the color of her eyes and lashes, and I walked with one hand in the pocket of my father's double-breasted suit, my wrist brushing its soft, thick grey flannel under my own overcoat, my other hand holding the briefcase in which I'd stowed Douglas' notebook and scissors and my own clothing from earlier that day. "It started this past June," Annabelle began. "It must have been June, some night, sometime in the early evening, and I was meeting a friend for dinner."

"Tina?"

"No, this was a man I know," said Annabelle. "Just a businessman—the kind of shy, lonely man who's starting to worry about building a family."

"Not a young man, then?" I asked, watching several taxicabs cruise by.

"In his forties," Annabelle said. "You know—he was trim, he played racquetball, went sailing—I remember that from the start I thought he was a sweet man, and he had a charming way of asking me if I would mind meeting him, and I guess he was wondering if I knew he wasn't married. He's chairman of the board of an aerospace corporation, and I found out much later that he's one of the company's youngest major stockholders. He would explain that he wasn't in New York all the time, he lived in North Carolina, summers on the Vineyard, and he came into the city for when the stockholders met, when the board met, and when the Pentagon, or whoever it is, had their meetings with the contractors and the manufacturers, and he went to Washington, he'd come here too, because he always liked it, and I'd see him when he was in town. Usually we just went to quiet places to eat, when we met, the Palm, Lutèce, you know, the Pierre, one of the places you're taken when it's understood that it'd be a relief to not discuss business, and for me that means no photographers, no agents, no somebody calling your name from another table. So that's what I was expecting that June night, but instead we decided to go to the Upper West Side, where he said there was this tiny Italian restaurant that he loved."

"How did you meet him?"

"At a dinner," Annabelle said. "It was a benefit at the museum last year, I think. His company had given money to whoever it was we were there for—that's when we were first introduced, but we didn't actually get to know each other until later."

"I'm sorry," I said. "You were saying about the Italian restaurant."

"Right. It wasn't bad—his car picked me up and then dropped us off a few blocks away on Columbus because these were warm clear nights and we usually felt like walking. What I didn't know was that Raymond, the businessman, my date, wasn't the only person I knew who liked this restaurant—but I found out the minute we'd ordered salads, when I looked over— We were talking about something, talking about Europe, he was edging into business talk by accident and I was steering him away, and I was just telling myself to relax, that a man asking you about your investments could just be curious—we were talking and drinking red wine and I looked over and Nick was at another table, by himself, just his camera and a plate of pesto linguine and some book—I wasn't sure if he'd seen me, because the waiter was blocking my view, but when I looked up again he smiled and nodded, and I tried to keep my movements subtle because Raymond was very shy and I didn't want to have to contend with Blanchard coming over. I didn't have to worry, though, because Nick left us alone until we were leaving, when he said hello, pretending he hadn't seen me until just then. He got my number, and said it was good to see me, and after Raymond had taken me home and I was getting ready for bed, I realized, Nick Blanchard's back in your life. Because once he's arrived he's not going anywhere, you know, when you see him you can pretend it's done with, but somehow it never happens that way."

"I know what you're talking about."

"I'm not doing this right," Annabelle said, looking at me from under her hat. "I've got to start with the contract. Michael, did you know how my career began? I mean, did you know at the time?"

"No," I said, switching my briefcase to my other hand. "I remember Nick talking in high school, but that was just high school talk. I remember that sometime during graduation weekend everyone was talking about how you were about to be famous."

"Really?"

"Yeah—I'd ridden up to Dover for the weekend, and I saw you and Max and Douglas at that hotel that afternoon, and Nick was talking about some pictures." We had walked a few blocks, crossing the streets and stepping underneath the bright building awnings.

"Right," said Annabelle, nodding. "God, I remember."

"I ran into you right there," I said, pointing—there was nothing but sidewalk and the featureless granite corner of an apartment building. "The last day of school."

"I don't remember."

"Right there," I said, looking at the street corner. "You and Douglas. You were on your way home, in the afternoon, and we talked about the big weekend for a few—"

"That's *right,*" said Annabelle, turning to look at me, taking my arm again. "You'd given me something to read. I do remember that."

"I wish you'd forgotten that part," I said. "That's not worth remembering."

"Does it get to you, being so close to school?" Annabelle asked.

"I don't think about it."

"We had a cat named Jane in those days. So long ago. The cat died that weekend. It was very sad. Douglas killed the cat, you could say."

"With his curiosity?"

"That's right," said Annabelle. "With his curiosity."

We had progressed another block, passing the smooth, stately curves of the Guggenheim Museum, where a group of young tourists emerged from the glass doors, clutching their cameras as they squinted in the sun.

"So five years ago I signed my first contract with Flash," Annabelle continued, "out of the blue that weekend, because of Nick. Nick *knew* people, back then, is what you have to understand, and I didn't really know anything—I didn't know any better, is what I'm saying, I was nineteen, and here it was, so I just signed. Now what I'd done was sign a three-year binding agreement."

"Uh-huh," I said.

"There wasn't anything wrong with it until I started getting certain kinds of work. I left college in '83 for modeling—you have to begin in Europe, but then I came home and started getting on the runways, editorial work, and soon I began to realize that I wasn't in a very advantageous position with the agency. That first contract was *insidious,* you know—you couldn't immediately see what was wrong with it, if you were a young woman just entering the business, because you'd never think to imagine that you'd be *doing* all the things they mention—television, calendars, like that. I mean that's how they get you, is that you're so starstruck you don't realize it's *your* face that *they* need. Eventually I got a sweet offer from someone else and I had to tell them I was bound to Flash, and I finally decided to act, so, that Christmas, when I was talking to my father about money, and he and I were setting up my trust, I mentioned that I was beginning to think I should get a lawyer, and because of his experience with Lineage my father recommended DiGrassi."

"Did he really," I said.

"Dad did some financial work for the Institute a long time ago, and of course he knew DiGrassi through school, so he told me that he was the man to get. When I went down to Reed Gardner Grant the first time, the Wall Street office, I had this odd fear—I was afraid I'd run into Ralph. See, I forgot he was away at college—I figured his father's office, he'd come *in,* or that he'd mention me at home, so I was actually sitting there looking at all the doors while I waited, and when the receptionist asked me how I wanted my coffee I jumped. But Frank told me— We were in the conference room, and he'd just introduced his staff to me—I ended up telling him very diffidently that if it was all the same to him I could do without running into his son. And he was, you know, he was absolutely adamant that I didn't have anything to worry about. He said, you know, We're building a professional relationship—he said he had an investment in my career and he wasn't going to allow anything to disturb his relationship with his client. So when my contract ran out Frank and I met with Flash and renegotiated upwards, and he managed to get rid of the worst parts of the deal, but there was a limit to his *bargaining* power two years ago—I'd just done my first cover but I hadn't done the *posters*, the calendar, the swimsuit issue, I wasn't a *name* yet. So we had to leave in some of the original rider clauses, like, for example, several pages about exclusive subcontracts, but on the whole Frank did very well, and a few months later I had a fresh new contract, and that was when I bought my house."

"It's a beautiful house," I said. "You must have been happy."

"Yeah—I remember when the broker called me and said, I think we've found your place, and I knew even before I'd toured it that I wanted it. Dad covered the first few payments, 'cause he knew I'd be doing well—you know how parents are, he said, This is a loan, you know, very stern, but we both knew what kind of loan it was. So I've worked hard for the past couple of years, paying off the house, trying to keep things *even*, and life is almost as calm as I want it, and now we get back to Nick."

"Running into you in a restaurant three months ago."

"That's right." Annabelle had produced a cigarette pack and a matchbook from an overcoat pocket and we both stopped for a moment as I helped her shield the flame against the wind. "With every cigarette there's that moment when you taste the match," Annabelle said, smoke drifting from her mouth as we continued walking. "Once I'd *seen* him, I knew Nick would call me—it was just a question of *when*. By then Raymond had proposed, and *that* was a tricky few days, and maybe it was sad, but at the time I was just concerned that nobody would get hurt—I think I believed that I wanted to be friends with Raymond no matter—you know, regardless, but of course things like that never go the way you plan. So it was a tricky time, and when Nick called me, and told me that just seeing me had him thinking over old times and he wanted to get together, eventually I agreed, and we went to the Village or something, Sweet Basil, and that was how we really got back in touch, and"—Annabelle paused reflectively—"it was *all right,* seeing him, somehow—I'd missed the things he would say, and I missed the—I don't know how to describe it, but the not caring, you know, just the talking as if nothing mattered and we could just have fun."

"You spent some time with him, then," I said. "I mean, over the past summer you saw him."

"A few times. Before he began to bother me—I mean, I just wanted someone with a brain who I could *talk* to, I just wanted a friend, but when he came over to my house he'd look around like an appraiser, and it was only a matter of time before he asked me who I was with that night at the restaurant, and *that*"—Annabelle was nodding absently—"I had to tell him that that was none of his business. He wanted me to bring him to the things I get invited to—he was always trying to meet people I'd had enough of—and one night I took him to a party and we met the advertising director for Octane Fashion Industries."

"I think I'm starting to understand this."

"So after that Nick was sort of gently trying to persuade me to put in a good word for him, and I would try to be polite, I would tell him that I didn't have any sway with ad agencies about which photographer they used, but he knew better. I couldn't lie to him about this stupid little jeans company and how they'd love to have Annabelle Taft do an ad, and Nick kept whining that it would be so simple for me, just one day of work."

"Did you get angry?"

"I was *furious,*" Annabelle said. "I was saying, Who do you think you're talking to? I'm not a high school girl anymore. Also, I pointed out that I hardly thought this low-rent company could afford my rate. Nick said, It's just a day's work, couldn't I do him a favor, for old times' sake, for back when he helped me that weekend, smooth-talked the Flash people into seeing my pictures, and then he had the nerve to say it was a Thorndike thing, that I owed him because of *school*—the school he, you know, complains about every day, having had to go there. So by last month I was starting to avoid him, but then, suddenly, everything changed—something happened I'd been nervous about for years, and the worst part of it, the absolute *worst,* was that it put me in Nick's debt."

"And what was that?"

"The new Naget campaign," said Annabelle. "Claude Naget, the cosmetics giant—they're launching a worldwide ad campaign. Going after the lucrative younger market."

"Oh, Jesus," I said.

"You remember that guy Hank Catton from my party?" Annabelle said, smiling distantly at me as she spoke. "*He'd* heard rumors about it, he'd seen something in *AdWeek,* but last summer everyone thought it was just hearsay. But they're about to spend millions changing their image, and they're going to find"—Annabelle looked away and then back, her voice having slowed—"they're going to find a new face."

"A modeling contract," I said, gazing toward the park, where I could begin to see the green copper roofs of the zoo buildings between the skeletal trees. "I can't believe this is about a modeling contract."

"A very *big* modeling contract," said Annabelle. "Nick called me and told me that he had to see me that night, something he couldn't discuss on the phone, but it wasn't what I expected. He was very serious—he had something to tell me. He had big news. It was *infuriating,* you know, because just when I was beginning to realize that he actually *had* something he got quiet and I had to start *asking* him, you know, playing a game where he could see me curious, see me wanting something. He hadn't *changed,* you understand, hadn't changed since Thorndike, and I'd forgotten about how when you don't flirt with him you're left with nothing to say and he's still there. Finally Nick told me he had a friend that did business with Naget, and—"

"Hector," I said. "His friend's name is Hector."

"You've met him?" Annabelle's cheeks pulled inward prettily as she sucked on the cigarette, her eyes turned toward me under arched expectant eyebrows.

"Yeah."

"Is he on the— I mean, is he a responsible person you can trust?"

"I don't know," I said. "I think so, but don't take it from me."

"All right," said Annabelle. "So—Hector?—Hector had just accidentally found out that Naget wanted *me* for the exclusive contract for their campaign. Now what you've got to understand is that this is a secret—I mean, right now *nobody* knows this except the promotional department at Naget. They're secretive at the conventions, but Nick's friend found a memo by accident, a letter from Victor Naget in Paris approving my name and approving the budget for me, and once I saw the memo I realized this was for real."

"I'm not sure I understand," I said. "Could you— Would you mind explaining what's meant by an exclusive contract?"

"Just what it says," says Annabelle. "It's the most lucrative thing there is. It means you're their face. It means you're the idea they're trying to sell. It means any time they do *anything* they have to use you. I guess you don't know that most models would *kill* for a cosmetics exclusive—it's like *tenure.* Usually it involves a saturation print campaign, you know, not just women's magazines but the magazine section of the Sunday paper, airline magazines, like that. You understand, the exclusivity pertains to *them,* not you, so you can by and large go about your business. The details are tricky but with Naget we'd be talking about quite a bit of money arranged over several years."

"Six million dollars," I said. "I'm sorry. Nick told me."

"Did he really," Annabelle said tightly. "So that night Nick and I had our big fight. This was about six weeks ago, and I haven't seen him since, but I'll never forget how he sat on my couch with this look on his face, after giving me the Naget news, and brought up the Octane jeans ad business again. You see, Michael, he thought since I owed him a favor there was no reason for me not to just get on the phone and hire myself out at a tenth my hourly rate for that damn jean company and, you know, just sort of get him the Montana job. And we both *knew* I could do it, and we sat there, and I was really angry—I said if he thought that I'd do a *jeans ad* just to get him a job, he was crazy, and that as far as the tip about Naget, I was grateful, but if he'd done it just to get some leverage, all he'd done was hurt me, and we were shouting at each other, and right here was when I made my big mistake."

"Leverage, huh?" I said, nodding.

"See, Michael, the *minute* he showed me the memo I realized I had a serious problem."

"Your contract with Flash."

"Damn right," Annabelle said. "I've got a year left on the thing, and it's still got that damn rider clause—Naget can make the offer and I can accept, but no matter *how* lucrative a deal we make, Flash has the right of attorney and they can keep 85 percent of the profits. I told you how Frank DiGrassi had reassured me when I re-signed, because back three years ago I wasn't even in that *market*—nobody realized that a giant like Naget would want me front and center. So that night I could barely *think* straight because suddenly there was this six-million-dollar deal in front of me and I couldn't *have* it. I practically called Frank that *night*, thinking that with his help there was a *chance* that I could renegotiate with Flash before my offer came to them from Naget."

"Because— I just want to make sure I've got this straight—once Flash knows you have a six-million-dollar offer from Naget, they'll hold you to your standing contract?"

"They'd *never* let me out of it," said Annabelle. "I showed the memo to Frank the next day and asked him what he could do and he explained it to me—as things stand, if I terminated with Flash this *week*, and *then* signed with Naget, Flash could claim breach of contract and sue me. Meanwhile Nick was *shouting* at me about how he wanted this Octane job, calling me ungrateful, calling me various names and saying that I owed my career to him because of what he'd done for me graduation weekend, so I got angry and said that it was *his fault* that I was in the awful contractual mess I was in—and right after I said that I realized what a big mistake I'd just made."

"I'm definitely beginning to understand this."

"Good. Nick's pretty cunning, and the minute I said that, he realized that I could only mean a problem with Flash about Naget, so he just told me that I shouldn't make him angry, because he knew people in newspapers who wrote business columns, people who would be happy to publish his friend's leak about who the new Naget model would be. You, Michael." Annabelle had slowed to a strolling pace, barely moving, and she pulled one slim manicured hand from her overcoat pocket and pointed at me. "You. I remember when he finally mentioned you by name."

"I can't believe it," I said. "I just keep— I can't believe it."

"When you called me from the hospital, you said Nick had told you that you knew my deal. That was the phrase you used on the phone—you said you 'knew my deal.' I couldn't help but think you and Nick were definitely telling me something."

"And you made sure I was a reporter, because you didn't trust Nick that far."

"Right. So I called him up the next day and I said, What the *fuck* was that with Michael calling me from the hospital—are you trying to give me a heart attack? Once I knew Douglas was all right I calmed down, and realized that Nick was serious, that he really would tell you about Naget and that would be the end of my deal."

"I worked for the Supplement then!"

"Nick told me you could do it."

"He lied," I said, smiling weakly at her. "I'm powerless, Annabelle."

Annabelle squinted past the growing traffic toward the approaching white mass of the Plaza Hotel before continuing. "So later that day I had my agent call Octane and offer me for a jeans ad next year, provided that they'd hire Nick Blanchard for their Montana series. Nick was good about that part—once Octane had hired him, he called me and thanked me and told me he'd leave me alone." Annabelle nodded reflectively. "I said fine, but I told him to make fucking *sure* that Michael Cadenhead is convinced that there's nothing newsworthy going on. I arranged an emergency meeting with the staff who handle me at Reed Gardner the day after that, and a few minutes after I showed up at the firm Ralph DiGrassi walked in."

"Just out of the blue?"

"We'll never know," said Annabelle. "He might have heard his father mentioning a meeting with me. He didn't say anything, he just stood in the corridor, out by the elevators, and looked at me through the glass with, with no *lust,* really, but this sort of sad surprise that I was there, and by then I was sure it was him calling me and I mentioned it to Frank when he got inside—Frank was furious and promised he'd deal with the problem."

"Then you had your party," I said.

"Right. Frank came to tell me he'd opened negotiations with Flash—he'd given them a list of proposed changes, hiding the exclusivity rider so they wouldn't realize what he was doing. That's the part you overheard, was Frank being a shark. He's going to pull this off—I'm sure Flash'll sign his version, if we get it to them before the damn offer leaks."

"So you'll get a better percentage?"

"I'll get all the profit," said Annabelle. "Ninety-five percent, and control of the subcontract. So Frank had good news—but when I saw *you* it scared the hell out of me. The last I heard Nick was assuring me I had nothing to worry about and then there you were at my front door." Annabelle was shaking her head reflectively, her gaze far away down Fifth Avenue. "And I could just *see* it happening, the whole Naget package coming together and then losing it because of *Nick* and never getting it back. It's nothing about *you,* Michael. Please, just understand that—it was never personal, that part of it."

"I understand," I said. "Annabelle, I'm sorry—I'm so sorry that I helped Nick take advantage of you."

"Don't say that," said Annabelle, looking at me. "He took advantage of both of us. I'm telling you that I'm not angry at you, that I understand what happened."

We had walked the thirty blocks and were standing near the edge of Grand Army Plaza, and as we waited for the light in front of the Sherry-Netherland, I looked across the gigantic plaza at the gilt statue and at the hotel, stepping into the street as the light changed, retracing steps I'd taken that morning. "Your feet must be killing you," I said.

"I've done so much walking in heels," Annabelle said. "For work. I'm used to it."

"I'm a bit confused still," I said as we crossed the street and continued toward Tiffany's.

"How so?"

"Well— I realize that DiGrassi's a shrewd lawyer, but how'll he manage to arrange a deal that's so completely to your agency's disadvantage?"

"They know I'll be cutting back on modeling soon."

"Really?"

"I just want to be left alone," Annabelle said, looking farther down the tall, crowded avenue. "I want to stop having to deal with people. With the Naget deal I'd be set for life and I could just stay *home*— I'd get the money and it would be *simple,* without taking up my time, I'd go in with Phillipe every so often and that would be *it.* I want to do this last deal and become wealthy all at once and then start to disappear."

"You're wealthy already," I pointed out.

"Not really. There's some investments, but I don't own my house and I have to work constantly. I mean, I'm *liquid* but a lot of that's my family."

"It bothers Douglas too," I said, remembering the Pershing tape.

"It would," said Annabelle. "You always knew my family was odd, Michael. Archaic, somehow, right? When I was a little girl I would watch those families on TV."

"We all did," I said. "How was your parents' marriage?"

"Mysterious," said Annabelle. "As far as I know. You were always a good student, weren't you, Michael?"

"Yeah, straight through," I said, glancing over at the crowds of children in front of the big toy store. "They can't take that away from me."

"They wouldn't bother." Annabelle smiled. "I was a grind, too, for a while."

"That's somehow good to know," I said. "There were people I knew in college, my senior year, who always had your posters up—I never said anything to them but I remember one guy kept his calendar on your month because he liked you so much."

"March," said Annabelle. "What's your point?"

"Just that they were grinds."

"News from the front. I get letters from people like that sometimes—lonely boys all over the country. Has Tina bothered you?" Annabelle calmly interrupted herself.

"She called," I said, shrugging fractionally. "It wasn't any bother."

"I figured she might have." Annabelle was nodding. "I don't know whether she means well or not—whether she's virtuous or whether it's just penance."

"Is it *strange* doing pinups?" I asked randomly.

"Not anymore," Annabelle said. "Part of it is that I can't see."

"I'm sorry?"

"I can't see because I take my lenses out," said Annabelle, smiling at me. "I wear contacts, too." We had arrived in front of Tiffany's and I could see our reflections within the store's smooth glittering windows as we looked at each other, realizing that we would soon go our separate ways.

"You know, I could still marry Raymond," Annabelle said suddenly.

"What?" I said, closing my overcoat against the late-afternoon chill.

"I really could." She gazed beautifully past me. "I hold on to that, and sometimes I come close—some evenings I imagine calling him, I imagine saying hello, and saying, all right, let's do it—give me a few months to foreclose on everything, and then a quiet secret wedding and we'd be *gone*, out in the country, and no one would ever find us."

"Douglas sent me his, um, his notebook from Pershing," I said gently. "I haven't read it yet."

Annabelle took a deep breath, looking away as she answered, and I felt the afternoon sun waning as we stood in front of the store's massive stone façade. "I think I need you," she said, eyes flashing as she looked at me. "I don't want to have secrets. I don't want to be in debt. Whatever privacy is, it's not this."

"I've tried to—"

"Read it, Michael," Annabelle said, reaching into her breast pocket for her matchbook and squinting as she scratched an eyebrow pencil against its inside flap before handing it over. "Here's my new number."

THE NEXT EVENING I sat cross-legged on Max Gantry's roof sharing a bottle of wine with Max and Jack Winfield. The sky glowed bronze with advancing nightfall and we listened to the traffic and occasional airplanes and shouts from the street, dwarfed by surrounding buildings, the latticework of the Brooklyn Bridge behind us, the glowing shoeboxes of the World Trade Center looming farther downtown. Max was leaning against the parapet, wearing a black turtleneck and boots, his coarse black hair tied back, his gentle, pointed face unshaven, dialing his wineglass around with his wrist so that his plastic digital watch rubbed against a small hole in his jeans.

"How was last night?" Jack asked.

Max rubbed his chin. "Lots of guys with their sideburns shaved up too high and lots of pretty girls in ugly glasses." He leaned his head back on the stone and looked up at the sky's dim zenith. "You like my place, Michael?"

"Yeah," I said, glancing round the roof. "Why do you ask?"

"Beats me," Max said, shrugging, his shoulders scratching the cold tar paper. "I've been subletting here for months and it's all illegal, so I figure before I get kicked out by the cops I should at least have someone like it. I know I should see people more, you know, hit the town, eat blackened fish, but—" Max trailed off, looking vaguely around. "I always love being on this rooftop," he added. "This is one of the city's great rooftops."

"Are you serious?" said Jack, leaning back, wearing another Wall Street suit.

"No, it is," said Max, waving toward the building across the street, and once again I noticed and remembered his strange hands—missing little finger on the left, truncated ring finger on the right. "All the buildings around have water towers, you know, and during the summer the pigeons flock around the water towers. They cling to the chicken wire in the oak scaffolding. You know there are building codes about the types of wood that have to be used for the scaffolding of the water towers? The city hires these ornithologists."

"Really?" said Jack. "I didn't know that."

"I'm not kidding," said Max. "Actually, you know, Jack, your family's place in Dover, there are sparrows living under the eaves."

"Didn't know that either," said Jack, running a hand through his crew cut, his gold wristwatch shining, and I turned to watch cars stream along the segment of Avenue C that I could see from the roof.

"Yeah, I can see all these birds shitting on the guests during the big spring banquet"— Max snapped his fingers—"there's that Greek word you use—"

"Anthesteria," I said, sipping my own glass of wine and feeling the rough tar paper under me.

"Very good," said Jack, surprised, nodding at me.

"So I had this sketching teacher in college," said Max. "She used to have me drawing birds all the time—it would drive me nuts, they would *move* so fast. Ralph pointed out the sparrows in the Winfield house to me. During you guys' graduation party."

"He wasn't invited," said Jack. "That was awkward."

"He was always sorry he showed up," Max said, looking at Jack.

"I guess I didn't know that either," Jack said.

"Man, you don't know much at all, do you?" Max murmured, leaning his head back and grinning up at the sky.

"Max," I asked after a moment, "did you see a lot of Ralph, um, before—"

"Just a few times since college," said Max. "Now that there was no one to stop us, you know—I would get these letters from Princeton and I could tell he wanted me to come down, but I never did. I can't believe he's gone," Max said quietly. "It doesn't even— It doesn't make *sense* to me, Mike. That damn family—"

"Things looked to be very difficult between Ralph and Frank," I said. "The previous evening, I mean."

"Yeah," said Max, squinting distractedly, "but I'm saying it doesn't make *sense,* you know? There's got to be more *to* it. I mean we know what sort of person Frank is, really, what he's involved in, but I still can't see him putting his son in that kind of danger unless— So there was something *else,* obviously, something that, something that could *kill* him. Michael, I watched that man wound his only son for *years,* I watched Ralph weather the storm, so things must have changed a whole hell of a lot for them to have— Ah, fuck it. You want some more wine, Michael? There's a little left."

"This *is* a beautiful roof," I said, accepting the wine.

"You're telling me," said Max. "You know, I'll never forget the day after you guys had your big weekend. The Tafts dropped me off and I went back to the crappy building where my mother lives and hit the roof, and it was really *warm*—this was what, June, early summer—and I kept thinking that Ralph had this thing about pigeons—you know, he and I would hang out back, what, fifteen years ago, I'm not sure, back when I was at Thorndike— But I was standing on the roof thinking about my crazy uncle."

"Crazy uncle?" Jack asked.

"Yeah, he was brain damaged. Uncle Bill invented the scissors on his deathbed—two razor blades, you drill a hole, get a nail, and there you are. Fucking Einstein moment for him." Max looked uncomfortable, which was an achievement for him, brushing his Mohican hair away from his face. "You know, I kept thinking about how she looked during graduation weekend. How Annabelle looked—I spent *months* trying to forget that damn weekend. Jack, you got a cigarette?"

"Yeah. I should get home," said Jack, producing a pack of Marlboros and waving it sequentially before each of us as he stood. "Max, I'm sorry about Ralph."

"That's all right," Max said, leaning to accept a light. "Can you find your way out?"

"Sure," said Jack, opening the trapdoor. "Take it easy," he told us both before disappearing from view.

"You were saying?" I said gently, a few moments after the trapdoor had closed.

"I'm sorry," said Max, wiping his eyes. "You're asking me to remember—I remember one time I went over to the DiGrassis' house, during this one summer, long ago, just to hang out, maybe go up on the roof, look at the birds—it must have been around '76, the Bicentennial Summer, and Ralph's roof had a pretty good view of the tall ships, so we went up there to the roof, where it was just so bright and warm, out of the darkness of the DiGrassi place. It always smelled like wood down there, I remember, 'cause Frank and Amelia—they insisted I call them Frank and Amelia but I don't think Frank really liked me calling him Frank, since I had such weird hands"—Max waved his fingers like a pianist, a gesture that had outlived its sarcastic origins—"and I wasn't the— I had to keep it straight, 'cause the other half of the time I was over at Douglas' house and it was 'Mr. Taft' no matter *what* happened, take it from me. But Frank hired some workmen to come glue all this mahogany wood all over the apartment, do this whole fake thing of his, so all through that whole damned summer the place smelled of wood and glue. Ralph tried to help the workmen put up some of the mahogany panels one afternoon and he spilled wood glue on the carpet and Frank hit him, but when Ralph got upset—we were thirteen but younger when we cried—after Ralph cried Frank had the workmen show Ralph how to do it right and sort of beamed at him while Ralph put up all the rest of the mahogany panels. I was there that day, too, I remember—Frank took all the workmen out for dinner and let Ralph and me come and we all ate tons of fried chicken and I kept on calling him Frank. On the Fourth of July Ralph and I stood on the roof and watched the beautiful square-rigged ships sailing in the harbor, everything glittered, the wind blew and I realized that all of Ralph's clothes smelled of that mahogany glue, and when Ralph started crying I hugged him and I could smell the glue rubbing off on my fingers. I'm asking him what's wrong and Ralph said that his father wanted to take him out of Thorndike and send him away to boarding school. What? Why? Because he's not sure, Ralph says, Frank's not sure that it's having a good influence on him. On Ralph—it's making him weak, it's frightening him too much, it's making him not believe in his own strengths. Remember that I left a year later, not that Frank had a *point* or anything, but I wasn't the best person to marshal Ralph's resolve against his father, who couldn't quite remember whatever fucking *reasons* he had for sending his kid to that goddamned school—Where was I, Mike? I'm sorry."

"The roof."

"—Right, Ralph's crying, he says My father only wants me to be strong and he never cares about me being happy and now he's going to send me away. So I'm hugging Ralph and the smell of the mahogany glue is choking me and right then there's this embarrassing thing, which is that while Ralph is shaking in my arms, talking, I can't help but start to notice Ralph's getting an erection. So I pretend I can't feel it and I say, Your father'll listen if you tell him that you're happy at Thorndike, and Ralph looks over my shoulder at the tall ships—I remember back then I'd built models of all those funky ships—Ralph looks over and shouts into my ear that he's *not* happy at Thorndike but he doesn't want to leave, he *never* wants to leave, he wants to fucking outlast everyone, stay right through to the end."

"That's what he did," I said. "All of us did, except you, Max. When it ended he was there."

"So was I." Max leaned back against the parapet again, his hair brushing the brownstone. "You know, what I don't understand is why Nick didn't call me that night."

"Which night?" I asked.

"When Douglas got hurt. I mean, it was just some Tuesday evening, right? I remember—I was home, I wasn't doing anything. I mean we're not exactly friends but I wish he'd thought to call me. Shit, this is big and bad, Mike, and I guess I only know half of it."

"I don't know what you know," I said, "but I know the other half."

"Listen," Max said, turning toward me. "I wanted to ask you one thing."

"Yeah?"

"Michael," Max said finally, "look, I'll do it, I'll tell the story, but I want to know how you *are.* Does your life make sense?"

"Not yet," I said. "I think we're still too young."

Max smiled, watching an airplane etch a silver contrail across the sky's dim edge. "Sometimes it seems like the tide's rising and there's nowhere to go," he said. "Years go by and the tide rises. Don't be afraid."

LATER THAT EVENING I faced Douglas across the floor of his small, nondescript, barely furnished apartment, lit by a low-wattage lamp that shone on the rough floorboards, Douglas looking pale and thin, the opened cotton cloth of his hospital-furnished pajamas revealing the long, curved, mottled scar across his abdomen. "I've spoken with Carol Casey," I told him. "She's concerned—she's wondering when you're coming back in."

"I don't give a shit," Douglas said, looking at me through the warm living room light. "I mean, before, you know, I was *embarrassed,* keeping up appearances, saying I was sick, but now I don't fucking care about anything."

"Well— I saw Max today," I said, reaching into my pocket. "It's too bad you've—"

"I don't want to talk about Max."

"But is it true you haven't seen him? Haven't seen him at all?"

"But so what?" said Douglas angrily. "I haven't seen you *either,* I haven't seen *Carol,* I haven't been— So I haven't *seen* people, why's there all this fucking pressure to *see* people? What's supposed to *happen?* What's the thing people want to have happen when you see them that's supposed to be so fucking *worthwhile?* It's the most overrated thing there is, Mike, and everyone knows it in their hearts but goes on pretending that they *need* the stupid shit their friends do to them. I mean what does everyone *want* from me? I'm not asking for anything—why don't they all leave me alone?"

"Annabelle thinks that way."

"No she doesn't," said Douglas. "Don't make the mistake about her. Attention is Annabelle's life. Attention from *strangers.* Or why do you think she's suddenly talking to you?" Douglas leaned his head back against the wall, the pale lamplight catching his hair. "And lovely Max Gantry? Mr. Emotion? You know, who *saved my life,* that weekend, *literally,* and who I seem to have dissed and dismissed? God, I'm tired."

"Can you tell me about this?" I asked, holding up the Pershing microcassette that I'd pulled from my pocket.

Douglas saw the tape and smiled gently. "Yeah— Karl Pershing, the mind doctor. I really developed a hatred for that particular gentleman, you know? It was like dealing with the crew from Thorndike all over again, and that"—he pointed at the tape—"was our last dance. He knew," Douglas said quietly. "The bastard knew I was in trouble."

"Do you want it back?" I asked.

"No, it's for you, Mike," Douglas said. "Oh, yeah— There's this thing on the tape that's unclear, right—this thing about this pair of scissors he has on his desk. Listen to the tape, you can hear them spinning on the blotter, on the little screw-point. I'm glad I remembered to tell you that." As he spoke Douglas was allowing his head to sink, like a reefed and scuttled boat retreating slowly toward the sea, until his eyes were hidden from me by his hanging strands of dirty hair. "Carol, you know—that was so sad. I mean if I'm falling for someone why can't I actually be falling for someone? Why do I have to be falling for this threadbare bullshit? I'm just so tired of people whose wristwatches are worth more than their souls. Annabelle never faced what I've faced," he said in a quiet cracked voice. "Her friends help her hide from the truth."

"You're all speaking from strength," I realized suddenly. "You're all blind."

"What are you saying?"

"That I can see where you stand," I told him. "I'm saying this is the only way."

"Then I shouldn't be scared?" Douglas smiled cheaply. "I'm sorry—I didn't want to involve you in this, Michael."

"Oh, nobody did," I agreed sharply. "Listen, the notebook's difficult to read. Especially the last few pages. There's—"

"You came for information?" Douglas asked in a tired, surprised voice. "You've been talking to Max and Annabelle, right? What could— What do they need from *me?* They've got everything all wisely figured *out,* am I right? Nothing to tell them."

"No," I said impatiently. "You won't have to worry about them. I'll get the— I'll do all the interviews separately, get the background separately. I'm just having trouble with your *handwriting.*"

"Oh," said Douglas, smiling in distant recognition. "Sorry— Because I'm dying. Didn't you know? When you die your handwriting dies. Tell them that."

"Dying?" I asked.

"My heart's dying. I can *feel* it," said Douglas, touching his scarred abdomen, his eyes glittering in the lamplight. "I can feel it."

"Are you safe?" I asked, looking toward Douglas' damaged front door, remembering the vestibule's torn scabs of wallpaper hanging like shadowed vines against the wall, the splintered banister, the door's demolished lock. "You're going to be all right?"

"Yeah," said Douglas, glancing at the dim half-open door, his hands on opposite shoulders, shivering as if besieged. "Yeah, I've been laying low, you know. I'll be just fine."

ON THE NIGHT that I was finally ready to start writing—I'd bought a box of film ribbons for my secondhand Selectric typewriter and stolen a ream of accordion-fold paper from the newspaper's supply office, and had just spent several hours indexing and marking the reel-to-reel interview tapes that I'd made over the past three days—I was interrupted by the doorbell, and when I peered through the spyhole I saw Nick Blanchard, camera over his shoulder on its frayed strap, portfolio under his arm. "Hey, buddy," Nick said as I opened the door, looking at me strangely as he entered. "I've got some of the proof prints from the Octane pictures, the Montana pictures—I thought you might like to see them."

"Hello, Nick," I said wearily, following him into my narrow, dimly lit apartment and wincing in advance as he flipped on the living room's harsh overhead light. "Come on in."

"So this is your place," Nick said, looking around blankly, new boots tapping the worn floorboards, lamplight shining on his sunglasses as he began unzipping the portfolio. "Not bad. That *subway* ride, though—I don't know how you do that shit every day."

"This isn't a good time, Nick," I said hopelessly, collapsing on the couch. "Damn it, I've lived here for *months,* and tonight you finally—"

"Check it out," Nick said, handing over a stack of Cibachrome prints, which I mechanically flipped through—they were brooding, high-contrast black-and-white images of remarkably charismatic but somewhat cheap-looking young men and women posed against breathtaking Western landscapes, modeling jeans and chaps and hats and other items of Octane clothing.

"These are *good,* Nick," I said, surprised—I had some trouble distinguishing the advertised objects from their atmospheric background. "They're very good. You're on your way. I think you should dedicate them to me."

"That's why I came," Nick said hoarsely. "That's why I'm here. Look, Michael"—he had taken his sunglasses off—"I talked to Annabelle on the phone."

"So?" I said, pushing my glasses up on my nose. "You had me right in front of you the other night and you walked away."

"I needed this," Nick said, speaking in his darkest sandpaper voice as he reached to retrieve the photographs. "Don't you understand that I'm in the *game* now? That finally people are letting me do the thing properly, helping me do it right? Don't you understand? All right, you've got a new job, you sit at the typewriter, you show off, but this is *difficult,* what I'm doing out there, I finally understand that it's an *art.* I wish you could *see* what it's like out there in the mountains with the—"

"I saw the pictures."

"—details of the dirt and trees, I know, the pictures, you saw, but if you could *be* there— I'm doing something that it was always clear I was going to do and finally doing it is something I can't expect you to understand. I mean don't get me angry with this talk about where my life goes and what I do, I've been living down there with my work for so many years dealing with people saying things you can't pin them down on. I needed this."

"Is that what you told Annabelle?"

"I know her *better* than you do, all right, Mike?" Nick whispered, ducking to lean intently toward me, his Montana-bleached hair tossing forward. "All right, you've seen her recently, but— Look, take it from me, man, the best thing anyone can do for her is just stay out of her *way.* You think you're so *special,* as if nobody else had good intentions? I haven't seen her in *months* and I know better than that—I know the only thing she wants is to be left *alone,* and instead she's got people *calling* her, there's actually some—"

"I know who's been calling her," I told him.

"Well— *Who?*" said Nick, glaring at me and then immediately breaking our eye contact. "Don't play games."

"So you came to stop me," I said, glancing at the tapes and typewriter. "Tonight."

"From acting like a crazy man? *Sure*—I mean, come on, you're *really* going to write a fucking *detailed account* of that fucking weekend five *years* ago? Christ, Mike," said Nick, his hands frozen around his photographs, "you'll want to interview *me,* next, right? That awful night? What it was like in that boat with her? With the candles—"

"Keep your voice down."

"—and the gin flask, you can make a nice typed page out of how that felt. Or what about you falling on your ass by the swimming pool? Or Buzzman's ladder?"

"Look at you," I said bitterly. "You're so offended."

"I mean, Jesus Christ, Mike"—Nick turned away as I stood, the yellow lamp casting his blurred shadow across the dark plaster wall—"I never dreamed it would come to this."

"Damn it, Nick," I said loudly, rubbing my eyes, cutting him off,

"I didn't ask for *any* of this. Before you called me I was *fine.* Before the hospital— I was minding my own business without *any* of you."

"You were a mess," said Nick.

"I was *fine,*" I insisted. "Everything in my life was *set*—I was by myself and it was dull but I didn't have to deal with any of this *shit.*" Nick stepped backward toward the corridor as I took an uncertain breath. "I was fine," I said more quietly.

"Look, buddy—give me a call when you're done and I'll come over and read it."

"You want to know the secret," I said, following him to the door. "What happened. You're not so different. Give me a few days to go at it— Go visit Kathy or something."

"Right," said Nick, tapping me in the collarbone with the tips of his blunt fingers, grinning as he pushed me back. "Give me a few to go at it."

"You're pretty funny," I said, holding the door for him.

"Mike," said Nick, turning back to me suddenly, with a pleading look on his face that I'd never seen before, "Don't do it. I'm serious—you want to back off? Last Exit Before Toll."

"It's too late," I said.

"Goodbye then," said Nick, putting on his sunglasses as he turned to go.

I BELIEVE THAT it is possible to have a clear vision, to wonder, perhaps in passing, perhaps in one moment or perhaps through daylight into the night, to ask if the things before you and around you, the pieces of life in your hands, are what you are meant for, your creation intended for, and to understand hopelessly and beautifully that they are. One summer night long ago I walked between the quiet canyons of midtown Manhattan and saw a Sixth Avenue street vendor, an abandoned remnant of the business day, wearing an improbably hopeful expression on his face and selling, of all things, small brightly colored orange-and-green puppets contrived to squeal when their mouths were operated. The vendor in his stocking cap had seen me, and smiled, and had made his puppet speak to me, and to each occasional Sixth Avenue passerby, and nobody had bought his puppets, and I had turned away, sick with a sense of loss, wincing at the footsteps of potential buyers because every squeak was piercing and pure as a dentist's lamp, but the puppets' comical sound persisted and prevailed and soon my heart was filled with hope, because my fear was very small beside the puppet vendor's courage. Nick brought me to the hospital on the night that summer ended, and when he left my apartment with his photographs under his arm I went to walk the cold deserted streets, smoking a White Camel while shivering on a bench, watching the traffic lights change green to orange, signaling for nobody, and while walking home I imagined that I could see the invisible solidarity of everything I passed, the union of individuals after dark, see the surroundings pull together in a way that reminded me of school, of the cinderblock corridors of childhood, the dread at the departure of casual friends, and of college, the sidewalks and bars, the fictional small-town society we carried with us, and the people I'd known—the sculptured athletes from other states, the guitar-playing, leather-clad math majors who enjoyed being ugly, the quiet wayfarers alone together, along for the ride until the end. When I got back home I cranked the first sheet of paper into the typewriter and by the time the deepest slope of the night was underway and the noises from the building and the street had abated I was still there, headphones on, typing as I stared through safety glass.

book II

chapter 7

At seven-thirty on a Friday morning in early June of 1981 a nineteen-year-old girl named Annabelle Taft—by her own account—stood soaking wet wrapped in a small white towel looking at herself in her bathroom door's full-length mirror and listening to the buzzing sound made by a Velvet Underground tape that was rewinding in the stereo. She stood in a way that people stand when they're not being watched or heard, feeling but not minding the warm breeze from the opened window, enjoying the brilliance of the morning sunlight that flooded the bedroom like a box turned on its side, and were anyone watching, they could probably infer more about her by the objects dealt out around her than by her actual presence—there was a blending of high-school and young-woman's paraphernalia that was a bit too deliberately casual, that deliberately obscured the facts at hand, but the story was there in the shining flatness of magazines and records and the snowfall of earrings and tapes on the tables and chairs and the bright horizontal light, not a cold light at all, but a warm light, a crisp light of approaching summer. Annabelle stood in conspicuous solitude, arrested by the view of herself in the steamed mirror, curving body draped in white terry cloth, one leg edging out from the slipping hem, the hard skin of her thigh visibly prickling in the barely audible window breeze and shedding drops of fragrant water as minutes ticked away on the desk clock.

While she posed the tape finished rewinding with a click, breaking the trance, and Annabelle snapped into guilty motion, crossing to start the music and retrieve the cup of cappuccino she'd left on the desk's only bare spot, between a stack of letters and a Zippo lighter and a purple invitation card from a club called "Orpheum" atop a stack of other, obsolete invitations from Orpheum and from other discos, all signed by "The Committee," and a Movado clock, which vaguely indicated that it was closer to six than to nine. Annabelle finished towelling her legs, wincing as she brushed a fresh shaving nick on her shin, and tossed the towel toward the carpeted floor below four black-and-white magazine portraits—Jean Shrimpton, Jean Harlow, Jean Seberg, Jean Harris—that were Scotch-taped to the rough white paint of the wall. Nico sang "Sunday Morning" as Annabelle dressed, quickly, as if it was all prearranged, putting on her newest, smallest underwear and a pair of Dior stockings and a black herringbone skirt—one that her father complained was immodestly short—and tugging on an oversized white cotton sweater, ensuring that the shoulders fell to her elbows and the sleeves bunched on her knuckles and the crew neck dropped, exposing the vertical modeling of her neck.

While shutting the dresser Annabelle glanced at the cream-colored parchment envelope wedged behind the top drawer's edge, her name formally engraved across its already threadbare surface, and pulled out the card once again—

Mr. Theodore Patrick Winfield and Mrs. Peggy Romney Winfield
Mr. Percival John Winfield
Miss Betsey Ann Winfield
request the pleasure of
MISS ANNABELLE TAFT'S
company at their annual spring banquet
Dover, Connecticut
Saturday evening, June the thirteenth
at seven o'clock

kindly send reply to
2936 Union Drive, Dover, CT 06426 *Dancing*

Replacing the envelope, Annabelle crossed to the closet to postmortem the clothes she wasn't wearing, considering with some satisfaction the correctness of the card, the absence of the word "Anthesteria" and the appearance of her typeset name. She stood transfixed by the summer breeze, pulling her hair from the sweater and combing it with her fingertips so that it fell across her curved forehead and down her back, gazing toward the mirror, eyes half shut, lips parted, and as she bobbed her head to see around the residual masking tape from a fallen perfume ad the ghost of Lisa Sparrow sat down on the bed.

"I can't bear to see you," said Annabelle. "I can't take this."

"I am doomed for a certain term to walk the night," Lisa said over the music. "I'll be your mirror."

"I needed you with me once," said Annabelle.

"God, smell that morning air. You still do," said the ghost. "I have never left your heart because I was always beyond your desires. What can't you take?"

"The next four days," said Annabelle. "I mean, the last school day, big deal, another fucking Dover weekend, the party tomorrow night, and then graduation on Monday— I mean, right there, that's enough for—"

"What else?"

"Yeah—that goddamned note I got from Ralph fuckhead DiGrassi in eighth grade. Remember that?"

"You had just developed," said Lisa.

" 'If I looked like you I wouldn't do anything except stare at myself in the mirror.' I can't look in a goddamned mirror without being reminded of that."

"But what can't you take?"

"Do you ever— You know, if I could really do what I wanted, indulge some damn *whim* or something— I swear, what I really want to do sometimes is drop— I mean, school's *over,* but sometimes I just think I could drop out of school, you know, just tell Harvard to fuck off, save Dad ten grand and then, and then go back overseas, you know, or down to New Mexico or somewhere, and sort of— Maybe dye my *hair* blonde, blow some money on blue contact lenses, gain weight and maybe get a job as a diner waitress." Annabelle squinted at herself. "I'm *already* gaining weight, damn it. Might as well go through with—"

"Why?" said Lisa, an eight-year-old girl with an eighteen-year-old voice. "The last thing you need is another pose."

"Because everything moves so fast," said Annabelle. "All this shit, you know, and everything moves so fast." While speaking she moved toward her desk and strapped on the Tiffany black brass watch which had been holding open Schopenhauer's *Essay on the Freedom of the Will,* and then turned back to the mirror, like a moth, clinically scanning her eyes along the white cotton and the neck muscles and the angled jaw and cheekbones, the square teeth behind the pouted mouth, the wide dark eyes beneath the dark brows and the spill of curling black hair. Finished at the mirror, Annabelle dropped into the desk chair to pull on a pair of black high-heeled shoes, frowning at the inadvertent effect with the skirt and switching to flats while Lisa sat on the edge of the bed.

"You get dressed so reluctantly sometimes," the ghost said.

"I *do* keep hoping you'll tell me how to do things right," conceded Annabelle.

"It's very difficult to do," said Lisa. "Francis of Assisi would beat himself with branches."

"Oh, for— This again. It's not the same thing," said Annabelle. "It's not the same, 'cause— There's always some part of me that's not thinking about what I'm doing."

"There's always another part of you that *is,*" said Lisa, pointing to the book on the desk. "And there's always a part watching. Even at the worst times you're watching and you know what to do. If something happened—"

"But why," said Annabelle, "do you have to give me some *story?* Why can't it just be clear?"

"When they asked Christ why he spoke in parables he answered with a parable," said Lisa. "If you're asked what you believe you explain what you've done."

"But by acting in freedom you could discover what's right," Annabelle argued.

"No," Lisa said. "Examples aren't morality. Lessons of faith are understood when principles and events are cut apart."

"Cut with scissors?"

"Yes."

"I don't want to go," Annabelle said in dismay, nodding once, for punctuation. "The Thorn in my side, man—I'm not going to school."

"Then what will you do?" Lisa asked. "Since you can't bear to see me."

"Nothing," said Annabelle. "All the bullshit— I'll stay right here and— Fuck it, I'll just stay here. Tell you what—I'll keep translating the book, you know, to send to Carlo."

"When you make a mistake you know you're making a mistake," said the ghost.

"Talk about it," Annabelle agreed. "You remember when I was thirteen? Everyone has their crush on Jake Hackett, but when I was thirteen I saw that picture and I totally fell for Bonomi— I always thought it was so fucking *sad* that he was so damn unsuccessful writing in English that he was never even *translated* and people in his hometown couldn't read him." Annabelle stood still, elbows touching, fists to mouth. "I pictured this town—I wanted to show up with the books and he'd be there, Bonomi himself, sitting in the basement with the bottles of crushed tomatoes and I would say, Giuseppe, I brought your novels to the town and you don't have to stay down here any longer, you can drink with the townspeople, you can dance and maybe I can come along. Just like that. Hey, Giuseppe— I'm the American chick who brought your books home. And later he'd let me invent some nickname for him I could use in public, among the townspeople, later to the newspapers and magazines, later on, when it started to fall apart and I was talking to the magazines." Underneath Annabelle's stack of *Vogues*, the white bindings aligned vertically like architecture, was a hidden cache of airmail letters, addressed overseas and unstamped. "When the shit went down with Carlo I was older, I'd lost the dream and I thought he'd be good enough, I remembered the words and kept writing, each chapter a new letter, like he cared."

"It's time to see the world as it is," said Lisa.

"Annabelle!" called a male voice. Annabelle's brother, Douglas, was yelling through the bedroom door, abrasively, over the music.

"What do you mean?" asked Annabelle, looking at the magazines while hearing the ghost voice. "You're talking funny."

"Annabelle? You there?" Douglas yelled.

"I'm going away," said Lisa. "You won't see me again."

"You have to come back one more time," Annabelle told Lisa fondly.

"I can tell stories but I can't reveal secrets," said Lisa.

"Annabelle?" Douglas yelled. "Damn it— Would you turn the music down?"

"Goodbye," said Annabelle softly, turning to punch the tape-monitor switch on the stereo, watching the cassette hubs spin silently for a second, and when she turned back around Lisa was gone. "Douglas? You want something?" she called out.

"Are you coming?" yelled Douglas. "I'm taking off."

"Are you leaving right now?" Annabelle called back, peeling back a sleeve to look at her watch. "When did you get *up?* Did you get any sleep at all? Did you get the paper done?"

"Yeah, I crashed for a couple hours— I got eight pages together and typed it up."

"How'd it turn out?"

"How do you think it turned out? It's a piece of shit," Douglas called back. "I used so much Liquid Paper the fucking thing won't even *bend. Yes,* I'm leaving right now—I've got Chemistry. If I'm late, he'll kill me—" His voice walked closer. "Those bastards *love* to come up with stupid reasons we can't graduate—"

"You'll be fine," said Annabelle quietly.

"What? What? I can't hear you," Douglas complained, his voice now right outside the door, directly behind the Manet poster.

"Forget it," said Annabelle, collapsing on the vacated bed and sweeping her hair up above her ears.

"Can I come in?" Douglas asked.

"No. I'm indecent."

"What? What?"

"Go to school like a good boy. Go to school."

"What? —Look, Anna, any news on the weekend?"

"I told you— Maybe you're on the list, maybe not. Jack's very coy."

"What? Look," said Douglas, irritatingly close now, "are you coming or what? Can I open the fucking door? I can't *hear* you."

"No way. I'm not ready. Go." After a moment Douglas' footsteps retreated. "Sorry, Doug," she called after him.

"*What?*" said Douglas' distant voice, and then Annabelle heard the apartment's front door slam. She turned to look at herself in the mirror again, all dressed up and nowhere to go, and then reached for and gulped down the coffee and walked out into the wide bedroom hallway, listening to confirm that the apartment was otherwise empty before approaching Douglas' door. She entered and looked around the darkened bedroom and then lay on the unmade bed, concentrating, and after a moment she picked up his phone, took a deep breath, and dialed a number, waiting without exhaling through several rings.

"Thorndike School," said a female voice.

"Hi. Roberta? Annabelle Taft."

"*Well,* sweet child. Where you calling from?"

"I'm home. Listen, Roberta, I think I've come down with something—"

"Oh, here we go—"

"No, I'm serious," said Annabelle, faking a sneeze and then speaking with a constricted voice. "Excuse me. Roberta? You still there?"

"Why would I leave?"

"See, my parents are away—Dad had to go overseas as part of this, you know, this totally complicated business maneuver— See— There's this client using about twelve fronts to buy out British Petroleum and it's really serious and he'll have to miss graduation and all." Annabelle could hear several loud male students behind Roberta's voice. "And Mom went along too. So how about that anyway—neither parent home and missing graduation too— Well, maybe they won't have to miss graduation, maybe you'll see them there, and wouldn't you be surprised." Annabelle winced theatrically, as if being watched. "They'll be back Tuesday afternoon. Or Monday or whatever it is. I just—"

"Okay, okay, Annabelle. It's the last day— What's your mother's name again?"

"Giulia," Annabelle said, smiling without letting the smile affect her voice.

"Giulia Taft," Roberta confirmed. "But the big question is, when did she *call* me? Say quarter after eight?"

"Cool."

"And your brother's fine? This isn't family blood— Your doctor just said you needed to sleep it off?"

"Exactly," said Annabelle. "Family doctor—you want the number?"

"Nah, who cares. I've been here seven years, right—I think after seven years they trust me."

"Is that Steve Leonard I hear back there?"

"Yeah, and the rest of the team," said Roberta. "Feeling better, Annabelle? Coming in after all?"

"Jesus, my glands are *killing* me," gasped Annabelle, faking another sneeze. "I mean, can your *thyroid* gland flare up suddenly? Is that something I should worry about?"

"Have fun," said Roberta, breaking the connection.

Annabelle hung up the phone and looked around her brother's bedroom, safe and alone, waiting, standing, stretching, walking, collapsing into the battered desk chair and looking out the window at a cedar-clad water tower and a whitewashed wall and the featureless, brilliant blue sky. Carelessly opening the desk drawers, she discovered one of her issues of *Vogue* behind a box of Pilot pens and tucked it under her arm, alarmingly close to tears because she couldn't remember anything about Lisa Sparrow's face behind her battered plastic glasses above her crucifix necklace—it had happened long ago, before Milan, back when the summers smeared together, back in those strange years when Giulia held down the two jobs and Greg spent every weekday at Columbia and the summer weeks were hours and hours atop the dining room radiator, reading with everyone away.

Lisa was Annabelle's first friend from outside the school—they had met on the bus back when the buses were green and had Flash Gordon–style metal trim, and Annie and Giulia, riding across town every morning, would hunt for the odd, talkative girl amidst the bus-waiting crowds. Greg had been openly skeptical of Lisa during her first visit and Annie had surprised everyone by yelling at him, which cemented the bond between the eight-year-old girls and explained, later on, why Lisa happened to be around during what turned out to be the worst of those pre-move, pre-brokerage, pre-Milan weekends in Dover. It was early spring, shortly after the first Civil War House weekend, a time of window repairs, shutter openings, wall groutings, long before the beaches opened and the New England tourists flocked to the Lawrence Hotel, and "Sausalito" Jane, the Tafts' cat, had rubbed against the red leather Chevrolet car seats and against the children's legs all the way up to Connecticut, echoing their brittle mood. Giulia had had a particularly difficult week, and Douglas, who had been spending all his afternoons with Max Gantry, talked about nothing but the airplane that they were planning to build.

Saddened by the overcast and cold May weather, Lisa and Annie had sat around the Civil War House kitchen with coffee mugs extracted from winter storage boxes and filled with instant hot chocolate, talking about—Annabelle could barely remember—talking about their mothers, about the leaves and the sky, talking about God, until Jane crawled gingerly into the kitchen, slinking between the table legs and sneaking onto the basement stairs. Alarmed, Annie led Lisa down to the furnace room, where Jane lurked miserably on the cold cement beneath the gas meters, circumnavigating an abandoned basket of frayed and folded linen, and some terminal knowledge in the tiger cat's eyes spoke to Lisa, making her vault back up the stairs and burst out through the back-porch screen doors to interrupt an anguished math-homework argument between Giulia and Douglas. "What I'm asking, Mrs. Taft," Lisa said, her thin hair pulled back in flat sheets from her glasses, "is whether your cat needs extreme union."

"What?" said Giulia, stumped.

"Extreme— Wait—"

"Extreme *unction?*" Greg said suddenly, looking up from the regional paper. Lisa nodded, eyes wide, and Greg darted past them with an awkward speed that Annabelle still remembered, clattering downstairs, leaving them to wait while the wind picked up and scattered the abandoned newspaper across the porch's warped floor.

"Mom—" Annie began. "Jane's got—"

"Douglas!" Greg shouted wildly. "Annie! Lisa, everyone— Come look! Christ!"

They found him near the furnace, crouched by the oil drums waving for quiet with the basket between his knees, where the cat lay motionless, impaled on a diamond of contraband sunlight.

"Dad?" Annabelle whispered, her hands drifting to her mouth. "Is she—"

"She's giving birth," Greg said.

The children walked forward, staring through the starscape of dust—Jane lay panting on her side, hissing at Douglas when he reached for her trembling head like a blindfolded child approaching a wall, and when the blood came, burnishing the bedclothes and soaking the basket as the mass of kittens pulsed out like excrement, pink and bright within their placental tissue, born without eyes, Jane looked at them with proud grief, biting off the umbilical threads and eating the detritus—Annie turned away and hugged Giulia, who watched Lisa mimic a half-learned baptismal gesture as Jane moved the mass of uncounted kittens around, mashing one to death as she rolled, licking them as they staggered and cried, straightening their matted lines of fur, keeping them together and suckling them further into life.

"We'll leave them alone," Greg whispered, ushering everyone back upstairs. After that, as far as Annabelle could remember, she and Lisa spent several static hours cleaning her bedroom, trapped in the weekend, eventually facing off with books, but at some point, as Lisa laughed at the Christian comic book she'd brought with her,

Annie closed *The Wind in the Willows* and walked to the mirror, not knowing why—she stood stretching her small featureless body within her shapeless red turtleneck and blue corduroys and staring at her pale flat face, her braces, her thin brown hair pulled into pigtails.

Annabelle stood up and closed Douglas' desk drawers, returning to her bedroom to drop the magazine onto the stack that concealed the airmail letters and extracting a pack of cigarettes and a box of matches from beneath her mattress. "Sometimes I could really use some extreme union," Annabelle said as she walked through the quiet apartment, sliding open a plate-glass door and stepping out onto the living room terrace, where she stood for a long time, smoking as the late-morning sun slanted across the park, watching the cars and trucks and buses, the passersby far below, legs moving as they walked, their bright clothes shining in the summer sun and shifting into shadow.

chapter 8

Cars ran past the brownstone steps that fronted the Thorndike School, edging resolutely around the double-parked traffic, their fenders shining like floodlights in the bright early-afternoon sun as groups of students drifted across the streets and sidewalks with cigarettes and ice cream, enjoying the ripe summer wind that sifted through tailpipe smoke from the buses and trucks and blew the bakery's scents through the flapping plastic wrappers on the candy store's stacked newspapers. Friday had hit Thorndike as usual despite the latent emotions of the last day of school, and nobody seemed to mind—everyone had gone about their business, lugging notebooks and shoulder bags around the building as they shuttled themselves from classroom to classroom, retreading the linoleum floors and panting at the tops of the stairs like athletes, their eyes lingering on the industrial-issue wall clocks. Douglas Taft sat in his second-to-last class, feet up, legs itching, feeling transient and tired, his mind slipping out the window and across his Harvard acceptance letter and over the surface of the afternoon while the discussion rolled along underneath like a backbeat—he had handed in his last paper and signed a few yearbooks and was vaguely hoping that Mrs. Fischer wouldn't get around to discussing the Henry James novel that nobody had read.

"I think we can get to the Henry James in the remaining time," said Mrs. Fischer, looking at her hideous wristwatch, "before this *big weekend* starts, but I want to make sure there aren't any more questions from *Gatsby.* Wednesday we finished up with the last chapters—Gatsby's death, the discovery of the body—"

"That was a little contrived," said Tina Foster in her flattened voice.

"Contrived? How so?" said Mrs. Fischer, turning to her.

"Well—" said Tina, grimacing with the effort of complex speech, noticing Douglas watching her, continuing, "first of all, how can you fire a bullet into a man drifting on a rubber raft in a swimming pool and have it, you know, end up that he's drifting around with *blood* soaking into the water, dead, without the raft getting punctured?" Tina brushed strands of her copper-colored hair away from her oval face as she talked—she was wearing a T-shirt under brown overalls that hung along her tall body with a sort of elegant limpness, and her guitar case leaned against a nearby wall.

"It could happen," said Jack Winfield, crisp-haired and freckled, nodding critically.

"*How?*" demanded Tina, turning to him.

"You remember," said Mrs. Fischer, "on Monday, when we talked about Gatsby polluting nature, consuming nature. The oranges and lemons turning into rinds, the—"

"That's—" said Douglas quietly.

"Yes, Douglas?" said Mrs. Fischer, adjusting her hair along the edges of the bun it had been pulled into.

"That's— How can you have a big party without using up fruit? I mean, *any* big party." Douglas looked over at Jack Winfield, to Tina's delight, and then continued. "It's like that bullsh— That business with the shirts. Another, what, another 'consumption metaphor.' I don't see why Gatsby's shirts, you know, in order to make Daisy cry, have to represent something like 'societal abuse of wealth.' "

"What do *you* think they represent?" asked Mrs. Fischer.

"I think they're *shirts,*" said Douglas. "He's got a lot of nice shirts." Various people laughed.

"Douglas, I just don't see why you've been fighting this every step of the way," said Mrs. Fischer. "You're just refusing to accept this."

"I'm sorry," said Douglas.

"Can you see why the raft doesn't get punctured?"

"Well, I *like* the raft not getting punctured," said Douglas.

"It's *impossible,*" said Tina.

"I don't understand why he had that problem with the title you talked about last time," said Jack. "I mean, doesn't *anyone* know what they're doing?"

"Familiar things can get new names, Jack," said Mrs. Fischer. "I'm sure you know about that."

"Of course he does," said Stephen Leonard. "Visa used to be BankAmericard and MasterCard used to be MasterCharge, right, Jack? Or, should I call you Percival?"

"I— I wouldn't know, Steve, is that right?" said Jack, smiling at him.

"Look, let's move to the Henry James," said Mrs. Fischer resolutely. "I wish we had more time. I think we've come far enough this semester for it to be clear, the way Daisy looks, the hyper-American name, 'Daisy Miller,' the—"

"I thought it was Buchanan," said Stephen, looking up suddenly as if breaking out of a trance.

"Well, names change, Stephen— Did you know that?" said Jack drily.

"—Damn it," said Mrs. Fischer, looking at her hideous watch again, "it's five more minutes. Can't I have five more minutes of your time? It's just a *weekend.* This is my *job.*"

There was a brief electrified silence. "Sorry," said Jack.

"The trip to Italy, the scene in Rome, the death by polluted nature, the faltering faith of the narrator. Stylistic moral ambiguity, perversion of the reader's vicarious desires to the author's ends, reification of traditional tragedian story elements through inventive use of character and tone. There— All you need to know. Clear?"

"Whew," said Tina, shaking her head while furiously taking notes.

"I can treat this like a joke if you can treat this like a joke. Any questions? Douglas?"

"Um, well, I think this 'morality tale' argument is spurious," said Douglas. "How are you finding 'death by polluted nature' in the Rome sequence? You keep finding 'polluted nature' everywhere. How is that ever a *moral* question? I think all your symbols obscure—" Douglas broke off because Ralph DiGrassi was grinning insanely at him from outside the classroom.

"Obscure what?" asked Mrs. Fischer.

Spurious? mouthed Tina Foster out of Mrs. Fischer's line of sight.

"Sorry," said Douglas. "Obscure, ah, your straightforward appreciation of the story, just as, not as *characters* and *motivations* and *representations* but just—just as events, people and events," he finished awkwardly, looking over and seeing that Ralph had vanished as quickly as he had appeared.

"So that makes this a spurious argument?" asked Mrs. Fischer, sitting back down and brushing chalk dust from her fingers. "I can't buy that. The moral lesson is clear. I can't understand what— You're talking as if you're offering something *else*, something *instead*."

"I guess I'm really not," said Douglas. "I don't know. I'm sorry, I guess it *is* a, what do you call it, a morality story, because— Because even while reading we all have certain beliefs of right and wrong. I mean, certain courses of action— We all say, well, you know, it's circumstance, other cultures have their own beliefs and all that, but there are some things we won't condone."

"You mean like sins?" asked Tina, smiling.

"Well, maybe we don't," said Douglas, leaning back resignedly. "I don't know. Forget it."

"No, it's a legitimate argument," said Mrs. Fischer. "You can go on with that. It even gets back to the book, maybe." She grinned humorlessly.

"How?" asked Tina, looking perturbed. Jack Winfield laughed tactfully.

"No, I— I don't really know," said Douglas. "I mean, it sounded good but I'm not sure what— I'm not sure what my opinion about this really is." Embarrassed, he glanced down at his desk, where someone had written *Annabelle Taft is a Walking Orgasm,* the blue ballpoint writing smearing into the shopworn linoleum. While Douglas was noticing this, bearded and tweeded Mr. Nathan Chablis leaned in the door and cleared his throat in his best pseudo-Groton manner, waving a sheaf of computer printouts, and several students automatically sat up straighter and tried to adjust their facial expressions.

"Excuse me," said Chablis—Assistant Headmaster and history teacher—"I'm sorry, there's no avoiding this. Barbara, have you got a minute?"

"Hello, Mr. Chablis," said Tina.

"Hello, Tina," Mr. Chablis said threateningly.

"Dance, Mr. Chablis, Dance!" said Jack Winfield suddenly.

Chablis looked around the room as Mrs. Fischer smiled and several students laughed.

"Well, I'm—" began Chablis, smiling behind his grey beard and tortoiseshell glasses.

"Dance! Dance! Dance!" said everyone.

"Barbara?" said Chablis, escorting Mrs. Fischer to her feet with smooth curving motions of his arms and upper body, and the students cheered as Chablis and Fischer did a little soft shoe for a moment. Several people chanted a waltz rhythm, being the drums and piano of a dance band—first Jack Winfield and then Tina and Douglas and Charlie and the guy that nobody knew, reproducing the rhythms of the band. Eventually Mrs. Fischer stepped on Mr. Chablis' foot.

"Oh, I'm so sorry, Nathan," laughed Mrs. Fischer with great concern, peering down at Mr. Chablis' bruised loafers.

"Quite all right," said Chablis, also peering down at his shoes. "There's always that danger with a fox-trot."

"That was no fox-trot," pointed out Bill Coleman, adjusting his Kissinger glasses.

"The office is still processing the ceremony tickets," Chablis told Fischer, undaunted, wielding the printouts. "Could you spare a moment and help me double-check this thing?"

"*Oooh,*" everyone said, recognizing the list of graduating seniors.

"The list! The list! Money in the bank!" Stephen Leonard chanted incoherently.

"Shut up, Stephen," said Tina, wincing prettily, apparently overwhelmed with boredom.

"Hang on, I'll be right back," said Mrs. Fischer, standing and following Chablis out into the corridor—the class waited for the somewhat soundproof door to swing shut on its hydraulic arm, and then relaxed, and Stephen immediately threw a wad of paper at Douglas.

"*Spurious?*" Tina marveled. "You raconteur—"

"Douglas, did you read the book?" asked Jack.

"Of course not," said Douglas.

"So, anyone catch *Hill Street* last night?" said Stephen.

"Oh, fuck you, Taft," said Bill Coleman, pushing up his accountant's glasses. "You humanities people never have to do any work, you're always bullshitting your way through."

"*God,* I hate this," said Tina.

"You just made all that up?" Jack asked Douglas.

"Well—" said Douglas nervously, realizing that Tina was watching and betraying no interest. "Yeah, I guess. I mean it didn't *work,* or anything."

"Oh, man, this is such a lose," moaned Tina in her flattest cadences.

"Douglas, you busy this weekend?" asked Jack.

"Uh— Not especially, why?" Douglas answered in perhaps too bored a voice.

"Well," said Jack, leaning over and lowering his voice, hefting the textbook, "this is a *really good book,* you know. I mean I found it really *enriching*—I just thought, you're not doing anything this weekend you might as well make a pass through it. Just giving you some advice, you understand."

Douglas nodded. "Uh-huh. Thanks, Jack," he said. Jack nodded politely. Everyone watched the door, waiting for Mrs. Fischer to come back. "Hey, Jack," said Douglas suddenly. "Do you— Do *you* have any plans for the weekend? Because if not, you know, maybe you could come over tomorrow night and explain to me what Henry James' *deal* is—with this book here."

Jack smiled at him and said sadly, "Gee, that's really nice of you, Douglas, but I've got plans tomorrow night. Some other time maybe."

"Oh! Sure," said Douglas, smiling.

Jack resumed watching the door for a moment while the class sat still, bored and tense, watching time pass, and then Jack abruptly spun around in his chair, grinning as he flung a cream-colored envelope at Douglas, who caught it, knowing as everyone in the room did what it was, except, maybe, the guy that none of them knew. The front of the envelope was engraved MR. DOUGLAS TAFT. *"Répondez s'il vous plaît,"* Jack muttered pleasantly.

"Oui—merci beaucoup," Douglas muttered back, pocketing the envelope.

"We're out of time," Mrs. Fischer announced, briskly reëntering the room.

"Not really," said Jack politely, looking at his watch. "We've got five minutes still." Stephen Leonard grimaced, again out of Mrs. Fischer's line of sight, and slumped in his chair, absently scratching his arms under the frayed hems of his Lacoste tennis shirt. While Jack spoke, Douglas happened to glance beneath the windows and notice a red Thorndike spiral notebook lying beneath the radiator— He tugged it from the floor, read the name "Jill Brooks" on its cover, and looked around before casually slipping it into his bookbag.

"No, I mean, I've got to go," Mrs. Fischer was saying. "That damn computer— Now it looks like you'll get your tickets by the *end* of the day *if* they finish on time. Well"—she beamed at them—

"that's all, folks. Have a good summer— Seniors, thanks for dropping by and I'll see you at the ceremony on Monday."

"Unless the system crashes," Bill Coleman muttered.

Douglas left the classroom with the others and walked down the fourth-floor corridor and over to the water fountain, noticing that a few people he didn't know—freshmen and sophomores wearing lunar-landing sneakers—looked at him deferentially as he passed. Wally Patterson, dauntingly, almost dangerously good-looking, was sitting on the wooden bench by the fountain, wearing a white T-shirt under a drab V-necked sweater, his arms draped loosely across the bench's backrest, left leg outstretched, right leg pulled up so that his heel hung from the edge of the bench seat. Wally somehow conveyed confidence in other people's breathless knowledge about him—that he was on the wrestling team, that he had once almost gotten kicked out of Thorndike, and certain other more private details about him, the sort of private details that become public knowledge among strangers while remaining hidden from friends. Behind him on the wall was another one of those new posters of fifteen-year-old Brooke Shields with cigarettes in her ears and a caption announcing that "Smoking Spoils Your Looks."

"Hey, Douglas," said Wally.

"Hey, man," said Douglas, trying to sound world-weary, dropping his bookbag and self-consciously gulping water. "What's going on?"

Wally smirked and said nothing, and Douglas sat down, noticing Wally's shaved sideburns, white socks and black loafers. "Are you done?" Wally asked. "Ready to get off and get out?"

"Man, I'm so tired—" Douglas theatrically pinched the bridge of his nose. "No, I've got History."

"What—with Chablis?" said Wally, peeling open a stick of gum and sliding it into his mouth, gesturing with the pack at Douglas, eyebrows raised.

"No thanks— Yeah, Nate and don't be late."

"Right," said Wally. "That sounds like a lose. You *know* you're getting a real class. Asshole."

"We got *sort* of a real class in there," said Douglas, gesturing toward the classroom he had just come out of. "With Fischer. It didn't go anywhere, though."

"Yeah, Barbara the sidewinder babe," said Wally. "What happened in Chemistry?"

"Nothing. You could have showed up, you know—we just gave all the books back. I can't believe I don't have to lug that Chemistry book around any more. I mean, I dropped it on my *foot* once, it was like an athletic injury."

"Yeah," said Wally, nodding. "So, you know, where's your sister, anyway? Everyone's scoping for her."

"She didn't come in today," said Douglas. "I don't know what her deal was this morning."

Wally laughed. "Man, that's beautiful. I mean, everyone's going, oh, it's the last day, it's the last day, what a big deal, let's talk about the Winfield party—you know what I mean?—and what does Annabelle Taft do? Stay home. And you notice she's not around and you feel stupid for thinking it was a big deal."

"Well," said Douglas, a bit annoyed, "come on, it's *not* that big a deal. She just didn't want to come in. She was pissed off about something."

"Right," said Wally, leaning back and gazing contemptuously at a freshman boy who was wandering past them, manhandling a Mattel Electronics football game. "Yeah, but come on. She may—come on, now—She may have some grief but we both know it's a move, it's a fashion thing, right? Listen. Did you—"

"Take your feet down, Patterson," said Mr. Chablis, walking past with a stack of textbooks bound for summer storage. Wally took his feet down. Chablis spun around, favoring Douglas with an English-boarding-school grimace. "Taft, if you're late to class I'm taking you down to the office."

"Don't worry," said Douglas. Chablis walked out of earshot, sparing a baffled glance at the kid with the football game, who made a loud touchdown and sleepwalked out of view.

"Come on," said Wally. " 'Taking you down to the office'? What the hell is that, what is this, reform school? —Listen, Douglas. I got to ask you a question"—"ask" pronounced *acks*—"I got this question for you. That morning at your house? That I dropped the paperweight and you woke up? When she was sneaking me out?"

"Yeah?" said Douglas skeptically.

"Did your parents— Were your parents awake? Did they catch on? Your elevator man gave me this look."

"Don't worry about it," Douglas said. "I don't think—"

"Jill!" Wally called out, grinning past him at the stairwell door. Douglas tried to turn calmly, feeling suddenly trapped in voyeuristic property theft as Jill Brooks came through the stairwell door, small, blonde, and innocently erotic, with painted eyelashes and what passes for high cheekbones on high school students, her machine-tooled limbs exhibiting her health-club diligence. Behind her, for a second, Douglas saw Ralph DiGrassi gesturing, waving, pointing at Jill and grinning, somehow keeping himself—in that way that he seemed to have a particular genius for—precisely outside of her peripheral vision as he clowned behind her. "Oh, he's such a cock-sucking asshole," muttered Wally, continuing to wave at Jill.

"I have to get my library books in!" called Jill, pointing at her bookbag and performing a Marine Corps salute before dashing out of view.

"What the hell are *these?*" said Wally, picking from a stack of small blue pamphlets beside him on the bench. The cover said ASTROTURF, and, beneath that, THE THORNDIKE LITERARY MAGAZINE and SPRING 1981. "Shit! I don't believe it," said Wally. "It finally came out. On the last day— God damn, everything's Cadenhead poetry. Here, *you* take it." Douglas accepted the magazine and was glancing at a characteristic photograph of pigeons flying around a rooftop water tower when a hand slapped the pages and he flinched, looking up to see Charlie Dane looming over him.

"Charlie! What's going on?" he said.

"Yeah, how you doing," said Charlie tersely. "I'm late for class— But listen, Roberta said to snag you— You got some phone message downstairs." Charlie walked off, turning around to point theatrically down toward the first floor, parodying his role as messenger.

Douglas looked at his watch. "Shit, I've got ten minutes—" He stood up and jammed a copy of *Astroturf* into his bookbag.

"Run! Run!" said Wally, waving his fists rhythmically.

"See you 'round, Wally. Shit, I'll see you at the Winfield thing," called Douglas, enjoying yelling across a populated school hallway about a private party, walking to the stairwell and galloping downstairs, narrowly missing a pair of paint-covered art teachers in emerald smocks as he cascaded through the lobby stairwell door and swung around the corner toward the Dutch door of the switchboard office. The bulletin board was covered with flocks of folded-over slips of notepaper, each bearing a student's name, and he plucked the note bearing his name and read, *Call this number immediately*— there was a phone number—*important.* "Hey, Roberta," Douglas said, leaning into the switchboard alcove and holding up the note. "Excuse me— Do you have any idea who this was?"

"A mystery man," Roberta muttered, adjusting her phone headset as she turned.

"Can I make a call?"

"Sure, come in," said Roberta, unlatching the bottom half of the door. Douglas went to the back of the alcove and dialed the number and after several rings the phone on the other end picked up.

"Hello?" said a moderately deep male voice. It was a bad connection.

"Yes, this is Douglas Taft? I just got a message that—"

"Douglas! Man oh man. I didn't think I'd reach you."

"Hello?" said Douglas.

"Don't you recognize my voice?"

"What— What— I'm sorry, who—?" Douglas stammered, squinting and masking out the lobby noise with his hand.

"It's Max!" said the voice. "Max Gantry."

"Max!" shouted Douglas, laughing. "Jesus Christ. I don't believe it— Are you in town?"

"Yeah, I got in last night. I didn't mean to scare you with the 'important' crap—I just wanted to make sure I got through. I forgot you guys are still in school."

"Max Gantry. I can't believe it," said Douglas, smiling. "What the hell? I haven't— You haven't called me in decades, you—"

"*I've* been around, *you've* been in hiding," said Max over the static.

"—Flying Dutch— What?" Douglas squinted, straining to hear.

"I've seen everyone at parties but you're never around. Yeah, Choate's over and everybody else went to New Hampshire or wherever the hell they live—I tried DiGrassi but his phone's out. Listen, I thought we could meet for coffee or something."

"Yeah, great!" said Douglas, watching Roberta manipulate the buttons of the phone switchbox. "Whatever. You still down on Twentieth Street, or what?"

"Yeah. I can get uptown in half an hour."

"Well, you want to come here? I mean, I could meet you here, you know, at Thorndike." Jill walked past the doorway and Douglas leaned over to watch her go by.

"Actually, not really, you know?" said Max. "I'll tell you what, I'll meet you at the corner of Eightieth and Madison at—what is it now, two?—say, two-thirty."

Douglas looked at his watch. "Shit, I've got a *class* that started two minutes ago—"

"To hell with that," said Max. "School's *over.*"

"Yeah, you're right. Okay, I'll be there."

"Great. Two-thirty—see you then," said Max.

"Goodbye. Thanks a lot, Roberta," Douglas said, hanging up the phone.

"No problem," said Roberta. "Child, are you *graduating?*"

"That's what they say," said Douglas, taking off his sweater and picking up his bookbag.

"I can't believe it," Roberta marveled. "How's your sister feeling? Is she feeling better?"

"Oh, Wonder Woman? She's— Yeah, she's fine, I should think by now— You know, these eight-hour viruses—"

"I'm going to *miss* her," said Roberta, winking. "School won't be the same without you guys."

"Sure it will," said Douglas. "Come on, don't get all sad— Someone *else'll* come bother you all the time *next* year."

"Yeah, but Anna kept me up-to-date on the soaps," said Roberta. "Have a good summer, you hear?"

"You're coming to the thing, right? You'll be there Monday?"

"Yeah, I'll watch you all go. I always do."

"Right. Well, see you then. Thanks again," said Douglas, leaving the office. While crossing the north lobby he passed a squad of fifteen kids that must have been seven years old, returning from a museum trip. He waded around them, squinting and sneezing in the sun, and walked out and down the brownstone steps that fronted the school.

chapter 9

At two that brilliant afternoon Douglas headed down Madison Avenue past rows of psychiatrists' offices and drugstores, fiddling with the perfumed parchment of the Winfield invitation envelope and stowing it in his back pocket before moving it to his bookbag, where he shoved it somewhat violently between the leaves of Jill's notebook. Crossing Eighty-second Street, he walked under the awning of a store where he'd nervously bought a soda for a girl when he was in sixth grade and passed a bookstore that had the year-old, still-in-print *Official Preppy Handbook* stacked in its window and a wall of movie posters that repeated like postage stamps, advertising upcoming movies by means of barely clad women—*For Your Eyes Only,* where the woman held a crossbow, and *Tarzan the Ape Man,* where the woman was Bo Derek swinging on a vine so as to show off her impossibly concave stomach. He continued past a theater where a line of squinting kids was already forming for *Raiders of the Lost Ark,* several of them intently fiddling with Rubik's Cubes, and arrived on the corner of Eightieth Street, and while he was watching an old man with an eye patch board the Madison Avenue bus, Max arrived, almost sneaking up on him—Douglas immediately noticed that Max had gotten taller and that the modeling of his face was more pronounced, that his eyes looked darker and his shoulders wider. He wore black pants and a T-shirt and his hair was shorter than before—it had been cut in some artful way that exposed the bottom halves of his ears, and it swept back to reveal a square hairline.

"Douglas!" Max shouted, walking up and hugging him, and Douglas hugged back, feeling the muscles of Max's back shifting under the sun-broiled white cotton of his T-shirt.

"Max! How are you?" said Douglas, laughing. "I turn around and there's Mr. Emotion himself. You look great."

"Yeah, you look like your dad," said Max. "Wall Street mastermind—I'm not kidding. So what's the deal? Where do you want to go? You have to be home any time soon, or what?"

"Um, not for a few hours. I've got to get ready for the weekend," said Douglas, moving aside to let a couple past him into a flower shop. "You want to go to the Café?"

"Sure," said Max. They started walking and after a moment Max put his arm around Douglas, squeezing his shoulders. "God damn. I don't know where to start— I saw a photograph of you in the litmag last semester."

"Right," said Douglas. "My sister was— Nick Blanchard was over at our house taking pictures. She's mind-fucking Nick Blanchard."

"Nick the quick. Where you going to boot camp?"

"Harvard— You?"

"Yale. We can throw things at each other during football games."

"Right," said Douglas, laughing as they passed a row of pay phones. "Man oh man—I can't believe this. Hang on," he added, stopping and fishing in his pocket for a dime, his hand, Max noticed, trembling self-consciously.

"Who're you calling?" Max asked.

"I thought I'd see if Annabelle's still home," said Douglas, dialing his own phone number.

"Listen, don't bother," said Max.

"Why not? It's no big deal," said Douglas. Max raised his eyebrows and strolled away from the phone, looking up and down the street.

"Hello?" said Annabelle, answering after half a ring.

"Hi. It's me—I didn't know whether you were home or what."

"*Yes,* I'm here. What— Why aren't you in class?" Annabelle sounded like she'd been drinking coffee. "Don't you have Chablis?"

"Oh, figure you've got the moral high ground— Hey Annabelle, guess who's back in town. You won't believe it."

"Who, damn it? I'm busy."

"Max Gantry. Remember him?"

"Yeah, I think Mom said he tried to call last night."

"What?" said Douglas. "When did he call?"

"I don't know. Some damn time. It was on the board by the kitchen phone."

"Well— Why didn't you tell me?"

"I forgot. You get in touch with him?"

"He's standing right next to me. Choate ended earlier and he got into Yale and we're going to the Café."

"I'll be sure to stay the hell away from there then," said Annabelle. "Listen, Mom called from the office and we're bringing both cars—Dad's closing some deal and I've been running around getting my dress altered and *you've* got to figure out the driving, so don't—Don't go wandering around and get home late and fuck everything up, that's all. Did Jack get around to inviting you?"

"Yeah," Douglas said tersely. "Look, Anna, whenever you want to cut the bullshit, it's fine with me. I mean, it's so *patronizing*, you know? I went to *school* today and just for a change everyone's making *me* explain my gorgeous sister's midlife crisis or however the hell you'd prefer I phrased it—I can't even get a drink of *water* without—"

"Fuck off, Douglas," said Annabelle, breaking the connection.

Douglas hung up the pay phone, shrugging in response to Max's look. "She's got something up her ass today, I don't know," he said, squinting. "Come on, let's hit the Café."

"This is so strange," said Max as they resumed walking, "because one of my strongest memories of Thorndike is how all the high school people went to that damn café and I was always scared to go. God damn, it's good to see you, Douglas."

AN HOUR AND a half later Douglas and Max occupied the extreme front of the crowded Café De Gaulle, their small, black-cotton-draped table pushed against the brilliant plate glass that faced Lexington Avenue, stoneware cups of strong coffee and unfinished three-egg omelettes before each of them. Douglas had asked Max a loaded question while they were waiting to be seated, a question that he already half regretted, and they were both wondering when the question—which Max hadn't answered—would come up again. "So how was the end of Thorndike?" Max asked, cleaning an ear with his little finger.

"Strange," said Douglas, staring at the nineteenth-century engravings of Parisian cityscapes that covered the walls. "Quiet, you know, but stuff happened— Once it got warm everyone started hanging out on the staircases, you know, and someone would go around the corner and bring back some chocolate bars or something and the guys would play bridge, you know—"

"I can't imagine being in the city during the spring," said Max.

"Yeah, Choate must have been beautiful. I remember when you left I kept picturing it like those landscapes you'd paint for the F-111."

"Yeah," said Max, leaning back and lighting a cigarette, his chair legs scraping the floor tiles. "And I still can't believe I spilled that goddamned blue paint all over the living room floor that time."

"When we moved," said Douglas, trying to flag down the waiter, "I was so sad, you know, because I knew that— Annabelle wouldn't be able to sit on the radiator with a book like she used to. Mom and Dad kept talking about the damn terrace in the new place."

"You've got a terrace?"

"Oh, yeah," said Douglas, frowning and then grinning while holding up two fingers in an unconscious victory sign. "We've got *two* terraces, onto Fifth Avenue and then off the kitchen out the back. It's so cool— Dad got one of those big kettles and he goes and cooks out there sometimes. Which is not the right approach but who gives a shit 'cause he can grin in the elevator."

"What floor do you live on?" asked Max, leaning forward to allow an elderly man and woman to take possession of the next table.

"Fifteen. Anyway, we were moving and Annabelle was on the point of asking the new tenants if she could come over and read on the radiator after school."

"Annabelle is so funny," said Max.

"But. I was saying— Spare a cigarette?"

"Sure." Max fished out his last Marlboro and handed it over, tilting his brass lighter under it—the first time he had ever done this for Douglas.

"Are you sure? Your last one?"

"I've got some Drum," Max said, the blazing midafternoon light skating across his face as he leaned back.

"Thanks. When the— Whoa, shit, I forgot about Marlboros," said Douglas, blowing a stream of smoke across the tops of the coffee mugs. "When we were cleaning the last few things out of the apartment, you know, and there were ten million cardboard crates everywhere—"

"—Yeah?"

"The moving guys tore up the carpet in the living room and the goddamned blue paint was still in the floorboards underneath. I was looking right the fuck at it, you know? I couldn't believe it. Annabelle saw the paint and that was it—we were both sort of crying, but she lost it."

The waiter asked if they wanted more coffee and Douglas and Max both nodded. "Thank you. Everything was changing back then," Max said, squinting as he brushed his black hair away from his face. "I mean, before I left Thorndike, you know, there was that year when Annabelle wasn't around—"

"And when she came back—"

"Don't remind me. But she missed eighth grade, which was when I was—"

"She missed ninth," said Douglas.

"No," said Max. "It must have been eighth. I remember this— It must have been eighth because I remember being around, and after eighth I'd left."

"You're right," said Douglas, confused. "No—" He looked exasperated. "It was eighth grade for *us.* It would have been ninth for *her.*"

"Right," said Max.

"So yeah, the end of the year. Damn— It's *hitting* me, you know? I'm feeling how it's different. It's gonna be a summer, though."

"Yeah. It's gonna be hot," said Max. "It's gonna be good."

It was almost four o'clock and the light was changing—Douglas gazed out the window at the passersby along the bright street as an unfamiliar waiter went to crank open the transom windows, admitting the slight summer breeze into the café. "Oh, shit— Max, quick, look over there." Douglas pointed across the street, where a young girl was walking in the sun, tall and graceful in an emerald shirt and piped fusilier's pants, her long blonde hair blowing back, uselessly beautiful.

"Wow," said Max appreciatively.

"That's Louise Delany," Douglas said, grinning. "Remember her?"

"What?" said Max, smiling in surprise as the Café tape deck

began playing "Bette Davis Eyes." "*That's* Louise? She's *changed.* If that's how the *nondescript* Thorndike people are turning out—"

"Listen, you don't know the half of it," laughed Douglas, speaking over Kim Carnes' shredded voice. "You remember Mary Hofstadter? Remember how painful she was?"

"Oh, she was beautiful," said Max.

"You wouldn't *believe* how she looks now," said Douglas. "It's like a new art form, for Christ's sake. You know what she did at the beginning of this year? She'd just spent about fifteen months on the beach, she was all tan, you know, and she'd bleached her hair." Douglas shook his head. "She was so hot—she came in every day in, like, sherbet-colored T-shirts, white pants—the weather was beautiful, you know."

"Yeah, my dad was telling me. It was raining at Choate."

"Anyway, I woke up this one Monday morning and looked out the window and *autumn* had started. Anna told me it was supposed to be cold, you know, so we got all bundled up and went to the Thorn, it was windy and overcast, leaves from the park were blowing all over Fifth Avenue and when I got to class, there was Mary— Suddenly she was wearing a turtleneck and grey flannel pants and a herringbone jacket, penny loafers, all the fall colors—and she'd *dyed her hair black.*"

"Not really," said Max, grinning. "Hey, look, there goes Louise again."

They turned to the window in silence, sipping coffee and watching her pass the other direction, tossing her hair back and deeply drawing her breath as she squinted in the sun. "She's *really* got it," said Douglas, and whatever it was she had, it was there despite the caffeine and the closeness of the walls—in the early summer air it could all be found.

"It's funny, when you stop talking you look under the weather," said Max.

"I was up damn near all night writing my last paper. I mean, let me tell you how tired I am," Douglas said, wincing theatrically as he spoke.

"Yeah, you're looking baked," Max said, watching workmen in brilliant orange clothes adhered to the scaffolding of a distant building as they blew a tremendous amount of white steam through hoses into the air, and then looking back at Douglas, perhaps considering the loaded question that Douglas had asked as they entered the Café, perhaps giving Douglas an opportunity to forget it, perhaps not. "You're looking well, though, Douglas," Max finally said. "God, it's been so long."

"Yeah. Look, how was Choate, anyway? I can never get a straight answer."

"Over," said Max, smiling. "It's a hell of a place."

"How's the painting going?" asked Douglas.

"Really well," said Max thoughtfully. "I've been taking all these classes. How's— How's whatever it is you do going?"

"I don't 'do' anything," said Douglas. "Come on, tell me about the painting— Have you done *Max Gantry's Rapture* yet?"

"What?" Max looked confused.

Douglas gestured. "Come on— You used to always talk about how you had this, like, little scheme that you would do this major painting called *Max Gantry's Rapture*—don't tell me that's by the boards."

"Yeesh," said Max, looking away, embarrassed. "I'd *forgotten* all the— This is going to be going on for *days,* I can tell right now, with you bringing up all this quaint old shit that I barely even remember. Every time I turn around you're gonna have some story about when we were young—"

"Come on," said Douglas, smiling.

"No, I know," said Max. "Yeah, though, painting's going really well. I'm learning"—he seemed geared for a speech, but he tapered off—"I'm learning how to do it."

"And you're actually going to Yale," said Douglas. "I hope your dad's taking it well."

"Yeah. He thinks he's never going to see me again. And I know, you and— What happened, you and your sister bribed your way into Harvard? Is that how you did it? I mean, neither of you ever did any work, right?"

"Well," said Douglas testily, and Max cut him off.

"No— I mean, I'm just being, you know, reminded about Thorndike. That's all," said Max. "I mean going to school somewhere else I can forget."

"Come on, Max," said Douglas. "Don't tell me Choate's so *different,* with the, with how the college deal works. There's a brethren *there* too."

"No, it's just a question of perspective," said Max, pouring cream in his coffee, over the inverted spoon, continental style, and stirring it by blowing across its surface before taking a sip. "The city does things— It made Annabelle into a Club Chick."

"I'm not sure I'd agree."

"Well, you know, agree or disagree," said Max blandly.

"All right," said Douglas. "Look, what's up your ass, anyway?"

"Sorry. But look"—Douglas had shrugged his appeasement—"what you said when we came in— Were you *serious?*" Max asked abruptly, leaning forward and frowning. "I mean I can't *believe* you want me to come."

"But I do."

"Look, Douglas—" Max sighed theatrically. "Every time I see Annabelle we don't get along and it's just stupid to think you can sort of—conjure up this—*magical* weekend where we can overcome this—this grudge from before."

"I'm scared," said Douglas. "I mean, who knows, maybe it's all bullshit, all the Winfield Party stories, maybe nothing *happens,* maybe— Maybe it *is* all bullshit, in which case— Even if *that's* what it is, then I want to have someone sane there to assure I don't go nuts, you know, because my family turns into a bunch of maniacs every year during this weekend, and—"

"How come you never went before?" said Max.

"I was never invited before," said Douglas. "Jack changed his mind about me, or the tide changed, or something."

"It's not like you couldn't have just *gone,*" said Max, inhaling on his cigarette. "I mean, *reporters* go to that thing."

"I wasn't ever invited and I didn't go," said Douglas. "And with the grudge, whatever, with Annabelle, you know, I don't— Look, Max, damn it, there is no— I mean, if you *want* to, you know, you can keep contriving this *feud,* but, you know, it's ridiculous, really. I mean, you don't understand— Annabelle doesn't hate you, she just, you know, never thought you liked her." Douglas ate some of the rapidly cooling eggs and swallowed some coffee before continuing. "And the magic weekend thing, you know, we're graduating, and it's the Winfield party, you know? I mean, come on, you have to admit— You can get into the *idea,* can't you? I mean, *I* can— The idea that once a year you just hire all these cars and bring all the New York society people out to this huge house in Dover for this big decadent party, um, where they can— That you get the big *hotel* doing the food, and you bring in some Connecticut *register* types, right, and then add a huge *Thorndike* crowd, all Jack's friends, so that— See, my parents are like *double-bills* with our house up there and the *school*, right, but— I just like the idea that the *Winfields*, right, these people who have a wing at the *museum*, do this thing every year for the rest of us, so naturally it's like a, you know, a *base* people get used to touching, some kind of—"

Douglas had turned to look out the window and he stopped speaking, startled, because Annabelle was standing outside the Café, watching Douglas and Max through the window, still wearing the herringbone skirt, the white sweater, wearing her scuffed-leather bomber jacket, hands in slash pockets, looking at them. "Christ," murmured Max, turning away, putting his hands, Douglas saw, under the table with a sort of reflex action. "Is that *Annabelle?* She looks so different," Max said quietly. Annabelle was gone when Douglas looked back at the window, but then he felt her hands on his shoulders and he jumped.

"Invite a lady to join you, Douglas," she said, as Douglas observed her inverted face over his shoulder, all teeth and eyes as she smiled at him. "You're letting all your fashionable food get cold."

"I'm not hungry. How you doing. Sit down. Got any cigarettes?"

"Toss me a cigarette, I think there's one in my raincoat," Annabelle sang while pulling over a third chair, simultaneously producing her Zippo and a pack of Marlboros from the brass-zippered breast pocket of the bomber jacket, sitting down as she tossed both objects to Douglas, who caught them, lit a cigarette and blew out the first, butane-soaked breath of smoke as he watched Annabelle through his fatigue.

"Things okay? Things all right? Sorry about the phone," Douglas said.

"Take it easy," said Annabelle, smiling in surprise. "You'll have to hurry home. Mom called right after you— She's in a big rush."

"Some things never change," said Max, reaching for his coffee.

"Where the hell did you get that?" asked Annabelle, pointing at Max's baroque lighter on the tablecloth between them and stopping his hand halfway to the cup.

"It's an old World War II piece. Mr. Chablis got it for Tina Foster, ah, in Dresden, I think, and then she gave it to me, um, when I saw her at this club one time." Finished explaining, Max completed the grab for the coffee cup, glancing over its edge at Annabelle, who hadn't moved since speaking, as if still waiting for the facts about the lighter.

"Hello, Max Gantry," said Annabelle finally.

"Hello," said Max, swallowing coffee. "Hello, Annabelle Taft."

Douglas watched as they broke off the engagement of their eyes, assuming a Yalta Conference demeanor. "You weren't," Annabelle said finally, pointing at the elderly couple at the next table, "supposed to bring your *parents*, Max."

"They begged to come," Max said in a bleak, unimpressed voice.

"You look well," Annabelle told him. "You look *different.* Have you been athletic behind my back?"

Max hesitated and then nodded. "I did track. And a little lacrosse."

"Track and lacrosse— At Choate, right?" Annabelle tasted the words as if testifying, crossing her legs and adjusting the fall of her hair along the edge of her white sweater, and Max watched her perform the trick, still unimpressed. "Max, what happened? You were such the Encyclopedia Brown and then you got so cool. Man, it's so beautiful out," Annabelle said, looking out the window. "It's perfect, you know? Sweater weather with bright sunlight."

"So Annabelle," said Max, smiling privately.

"Yes, Max."

"I'm not sure you should have pulled that stunt with Ted Cox."

"Oh, no," said Annabelle, leaning forward on her elbows on the table, smiling away from him. "Here we go. Figure you *would* bring that up—"

"What?" asked Douglas. "What did she do?"

Max began rolling a cigarette, and Annabelle stared pointedly at his arms as they moved. "Has anyone told you about it, Annabelle? I mean, did anyone fill you in on how Ted reacted? There was—"

" 'Fill me in?' "

"—all this shit afterwards when we were leaving the city. Ted was upset, you know, and back at school we had to do all this stuff, talk to him, we had to stop him from— Ted had this, like, canvas canteen filled with vodka, you know, we came in with the food later on and we had to stop Ted from drinking seven gallons of vodka from this canvas canteen."

"Jesus," said Annabelle, shaking her head, reaching for the notchless ashtray.

"The other guys," said Max, loading Drum tobacco into a rolling paper, "we were over at McBee, you know, and all the other team guys were going 'Just a chick, man, she's just a chick,' slapping him on the back"—Max had used a passable football-player voice—"and taking this canteen away. I mean—"

"Why weren't you *there,* Max?" Annabelle asked petulantly.

"At the Gold and Silver? Come on."

"What happened? Ted Cox? Gold and Silver?" Douglas was saying.

"Why didn't you go?" said Annabelle.

"I wasn't interested in that shit," said Max. "I mean, Ted had this thing, he was going, you know Annabelle Taft? I was saying, Ted, come on, the whole Eastern Seaboard knows Annabelle Taft, she's not—"

"Fuck you," said Annabelle, tossing a wadded-up napkin at Max.

"Yeah, so—" Max licked the cigarette and twirled and tapped it shut. "So, you know, I can picture the train rides, you know, and Ted fiddling with this green fluorescent—"

"That green thing!" said Annabelle, suddenly leaning forward. "All the Choate guys had those green glowing things, those tubes. They were—"

"From the concert," Max explained. "At the Dead show—some woman was going around, you know, 'Mushrooms? Mushrooms?' and nobody wanted mushrooms but we all took these green things."

"*That's* what that deal was," said Annabelle, nodding. "Those guys with the yellow bow ties and the green things around their wrists. Football guys. What?"

"It happened." Max nodded at her warily. "It *did* happen, then."

Annabelle turned away and then back, waited and spoke. "Oh, get a clue, Max. It was so *funny.* Nobody could take that shit seriously."

"Ted wouldn't shut up for days. The things he *said*— Hand me the lighter?"

Annabelle lit Max's cigarette, quite intimately, using her other hand to steady his. "I don't know. Ted was— Ted had the V, you know? The shoulders and waist. He was— I mean, the whole thing he had. But, I mean"—Annabelle brushed her hair back with one hand—"but what an asshole that guy is, you know?"

"He's got all these family problems," said Max.

"Give me a break," said Annabelle.

"It's *true,*" said Max, watching her, trying, Douglas thought, to accentuate the joke. "Well, we don't all have the— Everyone's not blessed with, you know, doting parents letting you—"

"We don't have 'doting parents,'" Annabelle said contemptuously, oscillating a thumb between herself and Douglas. "*Nobody* has 'doting parents'— Hey, Doug, I ran into Charlie Dane. You've *got* to be more subtle about your crush on Jill. She's—"

"Subtle? What the hell, Annabelle—"

"You got him off vodka," said Max.

"What?" said Annabelle.

"Ted. After that night he says he'll never touch vodka. Hand him a bottle of vodka, he hands it back, he says, 'that bitch'—"

"Great," said Annabelle. "I'm not sure who's laughing here."

Suddenly Nick Blanchard arrived, swinging through the Café door and walking up to their table—nobody had seen him coming. "Nick!" Annabelle said brightly, leaning forward, chin in hand, elbow on crossed knee, smiling up at him.

"Hey, Annabelle. How you doing," said Nick in his unmistakable sandy voice, Leica slung from one hand, speaking very quietly as he pulled over a fourth wooden chair, flashing a hand signal at a waiter as he sat down. "Hello, Douglas. I haven't seen you around much recently." Douglas nodded back, frozen in the chilled air that had rolled through the opened door. "You know, I forgot what day this was?" Nick continued. "I went past the Thorn and everyone was hanging around the second staircase with the damn yearbooks and then I remembered. It's the kind of thing that—"

"Oh, come on, Nick, you've been away, what, three years, four years?" said Annabelle. "It hasn't been all that long." Immediately Nick's coffee arrived, its steam contrasting to the deadness of the other cups on the table.

"It seems like a lot longer," Nick said, sipping the coffee.

"So you'll be in Dover this weekend?" said Annabelle, luxuriously taking off her bomber jacket.

"Yeah, that's right," said Nick with exaggerated bleakness. "I'm driving up in the morning, you know, so I'll see you guys before the avalanche— I've got to go downtown and work out the Buzzman connection."

"Downtown? Don't get shot," said Annabelle.

"'Buzzman'?" said Douglas.

"You'll see," said Annabelle. "Nick— You're driving up in the morning?" said Annabelle. "What— You've got something on tonight?"

"I got an invitation to a party at Orpheum," said Nick, crossing his legs. "This chick who works for that gallery gave me a couple of tickets— I figure I can grease the magazine people."

"That's tonight? The hostages' benefit?" said Annabelle. "I got that too, it's sitting on my desk. Man, that's gonna be *packed*— You got *two* passes? Who're you taking?"

"I'm just going by myself," said Nick, swallowing the sentence somehow, using his much imitated technique. "They just give them out in twos. Yeah, I figure I'll have some coffee and drive up at around five and get some sleep before the Winfield thing. You need a ride up?" Douglas watched Nick's face masterfully handle the series of sentences.

"Well—" said Annabelle. "I don't know— I mean, I haven't got my evening worked out. I may at that. Orpheum, huh? We could have a major night." Annabelle squinted at Nick. "They do *not* give them out in twos—you've got something up your sleeve."

Nick shrugged, looking away, his voice growing more parched. "They give Nick Blanchard two, they give Annabelle Taft one. I guess they know about you."

"I guess they know about *you,*" said Annabelle, arching her chin and lazily kicking Nick's leg, for punctuation.

Douglas abruptly stood up, hitting the table with his thighs and rocking the coffee cups slightly. "Sorry," he said. "I'll be back in a minute." He threaded his way between the interlocked tables and practically dove into the De Gaulle men's room. A minute later Max came in behind him and soon they stood washing their hands, reaching for towel paper and speaking to each other's reflections.

" 'We could have a major night,' " said Max. "She's *changed.* What's this new deal of hers?"

"Beats me," said Douglas. "I bet we're going to find out."

"What do you mean?"

"I mean she's always— She always goes nuts about the Winfield thing, but not like this year. This year she's—I don't know. *God,* that guy pisses me off—" Douglas finished drying his hands.

"Nick? Pisses you off?" Max watched Douglas through the mirror's filed-down cleanser stains. "What's the problem? He's nice enough— I mean, you can't take a guy like that seriously."

"But Max, he's nice to me, right, but he doesn't— He doesn't *know* me, or anything— It's all for the hostages' benefit."

"Oh, nothing happened," said Max, rinsing his hands. "So what if he's nice? What's the difference? Come on, Doug— Blanchard's just this extremely polite guy."

"Yeah, you're right. Nick Blanchard—" Douglas shuddered theatrically. "Guys like him, they figure all this shit out, you know, watching everyone else, and then it's their turn—" He leaned on the wall, waiting for Max to finish washing his hands. "There should be some *rule* about people like him. I mean, some clear rule to reassure everyone else."

"Employees Must Wash Hands," said Max, tipping his head at the cardboard sign behind him.

"Right," said Douglas, slapping Max on the shoulder. "Fuck, twenty minutes and rolling already— It's good to *see* you, Max."

"What's this about a crush on Jill Brooks?" Max peered at him. "Is that for real?"

"Yeah." Douglas gave a resigned sigh. "Christ, Max, I can't get that chick out of my head."

"Jill *Brooks?* Come on."

"But have you *seen* her recently?" said Douglas as Max pulled towel paper from the brown roll on the windowsill. "She's stunning. Why does she—why does Annabelle have to *put* it that way, a 'crush.' I mean—"

"She's this little girl," said Max. "She eats Cocoa Puffs for breakfast. I mean, what are you, crazy?"

"No, it's like— 'Her grace creates a realm of glass/A watered world of heat,/And so I pray for night to last/Ere morning brings retreat,' " Douglas said, lowering his voice as they walked back out through the paneled oak door.

"What—" Max slapped his arm playfully. "You guys with the constant bullshit, applying fucking *Bonomi* to some moronic teenage girl on the beach—I mean, what is this, are you in love?"

"It's not a question of love—it's a question of drilling her," Douglas said, smiling.

"There's no hope for you," Max muttered as they returned to the table, where Nick was taking a few shots of Annabelle offhandedly, trying, Max noticed, to catch the sunlit cigarette smoke hanging in front of her face. They sat down, reaching for their cold coffee, and Nick immediately put the lens cap back onto his camera.

"I've got to go," Nick said, lunging to his feet and gliding away. "Buzzman's waiting. But thanks for the coffee, man—that was like absolutely what I needed. Oh, *Douglas,* man, I forgot"—He darted back toward them—"I've got something for you. Here." Nick shouldered his Leica and pulled a manila envelope from his canvas bag, handing it to Douglas before leaving, his overcoat flowing in the bright June sun as he slipped through the door and strode away.

"What's with the overcoat? It's not *that* windy," said Douglas.

"What'd he give you?"asked Annabelle, pointing. Douglas opened the envelope, grimaced as he extracted its contents.

"What is it?" asked Max.

"Take a fucking look," Douglas said, tossing over a stack of eight-by-ten glossy black and white prints of Jill Brooks in a bathing suit on a pier.

"*Nick,* you nut"—Annabelle had cracked up—"I haven't laughed so hard—"

Max leaned over and looked at the photographs. "Hmm," he said. "He's using some kind of filter— Nice printing— Washed-out sky— He could probably *publish—*" Douglas snatched the photographs back.

"I love when pornography is disguised as art," said Annabelle, covering her eyes and laughing. "It's just— Aaaaah! That guy is brilliant. I *told* you to be more subtle."

"All right, all right," said Douglas, stowing the envelope in his bookbag.

"He complains but he keeps the pictures. Take note, Max," said Annabelle.

"Damn right," said Douglas. "They're good pictures. *I* love when pornography is disguised as art."

"You just love pornography. I've got to blow," said Annabelle, pulling on her bomber jacket. "Hurry home."

"Wait," said Douglas. "Annabelle. What's the deal— You coming with us tonight?"

Annabelle looked annoyed. "Of *course* I'm coming. What do you think, I want to screw around at Orpheum and drive up at five in the morning in some fucked-up Volkswagen? With Nick *Blanchard—* What—talking about"—she waved her hand—"talking about *lens caps?* I'm with the family tonight."

"Good," said Douglas, sounding relieved.

"Take it slow, Doug. See you this evening, Max." Annabelle

followed Nick's path out of the Café, striding across the avenue, barely dodging the swerving cars before disappearing around the corner behind the florist.

" 'See you this evening'?" said Max.

"See?" Douglas pointed at Max with his coffee spoon. "It's a fucking foregone conclusion." Max gestured to the waiter for more coffee and lit yet another cigarette. "Max," said Douglas, "you are smoking those things like—"

"It's Annabelle," said Max, frowning as he exhaled. "Like Nick with the camera— She looks at me and it's like, you know, Do Something, so I light a cigarette."

"Nick's still doing all these pictures for *Astroturf.* So already, you know—"

"*Astroturf,*" said Max fondly, watching as the waiter poured more coffee into his cup. "That really— Jesus, time goes by and you forget. You remember in eighth grade when *Astroturf* was this, like, sublime document that was like, better than anything we could have done? I mean, and it's just another high school litmag. I should show you the crap they did at Choate— Who edited this year? I'm just curious."

"Mike Cadenhead. A-member him?" Douglas said. "He wrote that stuff back when you were around."

"That bullshit," Max said, grimacing, blowing smoke. "I mean, people should keep their bullshit in a *drawer.*"

"Look, Max," said Douglas, "are you coming up this weekend or not?"

"It's a big deal, right?" Max grimaced. " 'Amityville' or whatever—"

"Anthesteria," said Douglas, suddenly resolved.

Max gulped his coffee. "You're trying to, you know, become part of something that you're leaving at the last minute."

"Stop fucking around," said Douglas. "You're talking parties here and talking to Nick there and all this business that I don't— You're in the swing of things somehow."

"This— No, I mean, yeah, I run into a few people—but I don't have the old Thorndike hallways, right? And you've got the house up there and everything."

"That's right." Douglas' slow smile vaguely suggested Annabelle's grin, unintentionally evoking it. "The house and everything."

Max cast his eyes downward and then gazed across the table, his eyes fixed on Douglas, the first sustained look they'd had that day, containing all the causes and effects of the time gone by.

"I'll be over at around seven?" he said finally. "Is that okay?"

"Great," said Douglas, still grinning. "I'll show you the time of your life."

"You'll show me the time of my life," Max said woodenly. "The things I get myself into—"

"Well, you got me to cut Chablis," said Douglas.

"You got *me*— To cut Chab*lis*—" sang Max, snapping his fingers. "Hand me the check— Let's get out of here before someone *else* shows up."

chapter 10

By the late afternoon the direct sunlight had altered its attack and stopped hitting the East Side streets with the same razor-cut trapezoids of bright heat that had moved across the city all day, slowly shifting across unnoticed patches of asphalt, margins of tar and all the recently scrubbed plate glass of the storefronts, while the air had picked up its pace, blowing gusts of dry wind from Central Park that carried the aromas of the approaching summer. The beauty of the day had come out of nowhere, unexplained and noted by everyone with a sort of pleased bewilderment after the static, sweaty halfhearted heat that had interfered with the past week like an oil too thick to lubricate but too thin to stop things in their tracks. It had been the sort of day that demands attention, the summer being young enough for this sort of arrogant showmanship, calling other summers and other years to mind, filling the heart with the vaguest sort of memory and the strangest sort of longing.

Douglas had almost arrived home when he noticed Annabelle walking in front of him, carrying a large white box, white sweater tied round her waist, jacket off, and he hung back, watching his sister from behind as she stalked toward their building, before running to catch up. "Hey," he said, arriving winded, and Annabelle flashed him a glance. "Annabelle"— she ignored him, looking up and down Madison Avenue, figuring out where to jaywalk—"Anna, what the hell?"

"Douglas, leave me alone every once in a while, okay?"

They walked side by side for a moment, late-afternoon sun catching the brass fixtures on Annabelle's jacket, Douglas waiting before speaking. "What's wrong?"

"The thing is," Anna said eventually. "The— Damn it— I'm not a bitch. Douglas, I'm not a bitch, right?"

"You're not a bitch. You going to tell me the story?"

"Damn it—"

"Okay," said Douglas, kicking a bottle cap across the pavement. "Okay. Look"—she turned, glared at him—"look, just don't— I mean, don't overreact so much. This guy Ted Cox, this guy's an asshole, right? Everything isn't all dramatic."

"Douglas—"

"Just don't overreact so much."

"All *right*," said Annabelle, smiling eventually. "I just had this day, is the thing. Can you understand my not wanting to come in? I mean—"

"Yeah, I'm sorry about the phone thing," said Douglas. "What's in the box?"

"My dress for the party. They didn't alter it right and I had to wait while they fixed it. Waist in, chest out—I thought they knew me by heart."

When they had walked another half a block, Douglas said, "Annabelle, Max is coming up this weekend. The—"

"Yeah, great, Douglas, great." Annabelle turned away as she talked, grimacing, turning and turning back. "Good move. Jesus Christ—"

"What's the matter?" Douglas said, confused. "You were turning on the charm at the— You were friendly enough at the Café."

"Of *course* I was friendly at the Café." Annabelle stopped walking suddenly. "Douglas, don't you think enough is going on this weekend without some guy from Choate hanging around? Some guy who—"

"This is *Max*," Douglas said, stopping also, spinning to face her and gesturing with his arms as she stared and waited. "Max Gantry— He's not 'some guy from Choate.' What the hell is your problem? What's going on that's such a big—"

"Doug*las*—"

"All right"—spreading his hands—"so nine times out of ten you've got something up your sleeve, but I don't understand why you have to act like you've got something up your sleeve when there isn't a goddamned *thing* up your sleeve."

"Oh, no—" Annabelle said as they glared at each other, their faces inches apart, her eyes flickering past Douglas' shoulder.

"What—?" said Douglas, turning to see Michael Cadenhead

walking up the edge of the avenue, waving. As he approached, Douglas noticed his nondescript clothes and shoes and his somewhat overbearing grin.

"The Tafts in a catfight," Michael said, smiling as he arrived, looking small and pale behind his glasses. "How's it going?" he added.

"Catfight—" Annabelle conceded, laughing politely. "It's going."

"I was looking for you, actually," said Michael, trying as usual to hold Annabelle's gaze, giving up, dropping it, his eyes skating over the sidewalk and the awnings nearby. "I breezed by the Café and nobody was there except Duane, and he never *speaks,* you know— But they finally gave out the graduation tickets."

"Oh, *shit*—" Douglas said. "I knew I was forgetting someth—"

"I picked yours up," Michael continued, looking at both of them. "But I left them in the *Astroturf* office, so I'll have to— Listen, are you going to be *there* this weekend? At the Winfields'? Jack invited me— I was so surprised I almost had a heart attack."

"Oh, they wouldn't have it without me," said Annabelle, shocked. "Don't worry, I wasn't going to mention it first."

Douglas laughed. "I'll be there. Who you staying with?"

"I'm not sure," Michael said, looking pained. "I'll have your tickets, though."

"Thanks, darling. I cut school," Annabelle explained. "It would have been my last mistake. Oh, Michael," she added abruptly, touching his arm, "I read that thing you gave me."

"Oh yeah?" Michael said brightly, looking down at the sidewalk as cars and pedestrians passed.

"Well, it's— Listen, Michael, did you ever read any Bonomi?"

"Oh my God," said Douglas, laughing. "Now you've done it, Mike."

"No," Michael said.

"You're just getting, I don't know, you're getting too caught up— You're getting caught up in all this complicated shit that nobody understands. But in *Italian*— See— Even when Bonomi was writing in English he would lapse into Italian with the chapter epigraphs, right? And the—"

"Mr. Chablis makes fun of Bonomi any chance he gets," said Michael.

"Yeah, yeah," said Annabelle. "You going to listen to Chablis or are you going to listen to me? The—"

"Listen to Chab*lis*— Or listen to *me*—" Douglas sang, snapping his fingers.

"Both of you shut up," said Annabelle. "Look, Mike, Bonomi was— You never read *The Story of Jake Hackett?* Bonomi understood *simplicity.* At the end of *Jake Hackett* the main character's lost everything. Lost every fucking thing— But all along he keeps going, you know, I stand on the granite of memory. Every time he turns around there's the bedrock— So he's lost everything, 'cause this man named Morstan has produced a book of heresy, of lost scripture that's undermined his entire sense of faith and almost destroyed the Catholic church in the bargain, I mean really gone to Rome and almost, you know, dealt the death blow to Catholicism, and Morstan almost killed him in Venice, where he fell in love, and led him on a midnight chase by horseback across the city, and his Italian friend, this monk named Thomas, has died for him, you know, deathbed scene, and the woman he's in love with has renounced him, and at the very end he's boarding the railroad to return to America—"

"It sounds like a soap opera," said Michael.

"Oh, it's so great," said Annabelle impatiently. "Listen— Anyway, by the end of the book Hackett's leaving Venice and his entire reason for being there is stripped away— So on the last page, right, Hackett leaves the train station, you know, remembering the whole story, realizing it's important to remember it, and then he quotes Michelangelo— *Vivo su questo scoglio orrido e solo.* And he just, you know, he can just leave it at that. I mean it's—"

"What's that mean?" asked Michael.

" 'I live upon this fearful lonely rock,' " Douglas translated.

"But he leaves it at that," continued Annabelle. "*One* sentence. And maybe you go, so what, but then, but *then,* you realize that in this context it's the rock of the *papacy,* too— And suddenly it's clear that the papacy itself invites double reading 'cause we're going back to Christ's pun on St. Peter's name, which brings us back around to the fact that this story *ends* at fucking *St. Peter's,* on top of Michelangelo's dome. So he gives that *one quote,* and, like, ties together the whole bag of fish."

"That's really cool," said Michael. "You could teach English, you know that?"

"Yeah, right," said Annabelle. "But Jesus, Michael, I'm really not the person to give these things to, you know? It was sweet dedicating it like you did, though. It was really sweet."

"Well— Thanks," said Michael, looking down, and then, after a moment, at his wristwatch. "I've got to go meet someone," he told them. "I guess I'll see you tomorrow night."

" 'Bye," said the Tafts in vague unison—Douglas watched Michael dart away, moving like a child, before they continued walking. "He gave you a *story* to read?" he asked eventually.

"Yeah— It was really nice," said Annabelle. "I mean it was kind of naïve but it was nice. Jill Brooks and how she was— I mean, it doesn't *say* Jill's name but it's so obvious— How she's really a private eye, she wants to be one of those women on paperback covers, she wants to carry a gun— 'Swan in Love.' Proust reference and everything, and all because of *Jill*— You guys are crazy." Annabelle laughed. "*Astroturf.* I love it— Mike thinks he, like, walks among the stars."

"Yeah, Hollywood stars," said Douglas, "He told me about— You remember when he was hanging around with Nick Blanchard? When Mike was?"

"Please," said Annabelle.

"Yeah, he was telling me in the lunchroom— Nobody realized that Blanchard wanted little Mike to write poetry for that show he did."

"Yeah," said Annabelle, hunching to light a cigarette, cheeks hollowing as she blew a cloud of smoke that the breeze pulled away. "I guess I didn't realize that."

"Well, I think your buddy Nick wanted to keep it *quiet,* you know? He was— For when his *career* takes off, like he doesn't work for a fucking *carpet* company. But Nick was noticing Jill all the time and he *asked* Mike to write a poem to her— Actually, I heard this on the *staircase,* you know, that day after you left, that afternoon. Wally and Tina were talking about Mike— You remember, he was always staring at Jill and talking about Greek statues and embarrassing the shit out of himself real quietly. So I guess— So then Nick, you know, *stepped in.* He gave me this shitty grin when he came by school last month to pick— To pick her up."

"I remember that," said Annabelle.

" 'Cause he— 'Cause he'd invited her to Coney Island."

"Yeah," said Annabelle.

"And I guess that's when he got her to pose for the pictures," said Douglas, flicking the edge of the manila envelope that protruded from his bookbag.

"And then he drilled her into the mattress," said Annabelle.

Douglas looked at her and then back at the sidewalk. "She fucked him? Just like that?" he said wonderingly.

Annabelle looked exasperated. "Of *course* she fucked him. What do you think, that we're all just— That we're all just playing around here? Don't you understand what the deal *is* with these things?"

"But why?" said Douglas. "*Why* is that the deal? What's the *point*— Being so, I don't know, so casual?"

"That's just what the deal is."

"I think that's bullshit."

"Too bad," Annabelle said while tossing back her hair and hefting the slipping box. "Besides, it's not like you're *detached* or anything— You're just jealous because Nick actually nailed her and you didn't."

"All right, all right, who cares," said Douglas, putting his hands in his pockets as they crossed another street. "Wait— Mike *dedicated* the story to *you?* The thing about Jill?"

"Yeah, 'For the Little Scholar'— It was sweet, but then he had to, like, hand it to me on the second staircase with everyone around. Such a bad move— It was *charming,* though. I mean *he* wasn't embarrassed."

"You like him," said Douglas, looking at her as they walked.

"Shit, I don't know"—Annabelle squinted at the sky—"he's *nice* and he's certainly smart and all, but I just get tired of the *thing* about him, going beyond that he's such a pain in the ass all the time with his damn beady eyes." She impatiently scratched her ears as they approached their building's awning. "But his heart's like an ashtray and he won't empty it. Are you listening to me?"

"No. How you doing, Sport?" Douglas greeted the doorman, one of the series of marching-band conductors, who tipped his cap to Annabelle.

THEY GOT UPSTAIRS and Annabelle stormed into her room and slammed the door, causing the Manet poster to fall off the door's back side, and Douglas heard her say "Shit!" and found a roll of masking tape in his desk drawer, heading down the hall to whip it through the crack in her door. "Thank you," Annabelle shouted while Douglas retreated to his room, dropped his bookbag and lay down on the unmade bed in the dark, feeling his fatigue in an unexpected rush, listening to the faint sounds of Annabelle making brief phone calls from her room. He got up by force of will and sat at his desk, turning on the light and noticing that the desktop litter wasn't exactly where he'd left it, and as he was looking languidly through the piles of papers, Annabelle knocked at the door. "Come on in," he said sarcastically. Annabelle walked in and sat on the edge of the desk in front of him.

"Douglas, I'm sorry I was so—"

"Listen, were you fucking around in here today?"

"Yeah, I came in here this afternoon for a while— It's so *peaceful* without people and you get all the noon light. And you took the new *Vogue,* you asshole."

"Sorry, yeah, I just looked at it. Scoping out the models— Move over," Douglas said, flipping through stacks of spiral notebooks. "I'm trying to get these—"

"Douglas"—Annabelle squirmed out of his way—"is Amy *really* pretty?"

"What do you mean?" said Douglas absently.

"I mean with the older boyfriend, she thinks she's such hot shit. Is she *really* such a sidewinder? You've got a dick."

"Look, I keep telling you"—Douglas flipped the notebook closed and looked at Annabelle—"there's Amy and Tina and what's-her-name, Jill, the threesome—"

"But I figured it out," said Annabelle. "None of them are that pretty— They just realize that a group of three sort-of-pretty girls always looks like a group of three beautiful girls." Annabelle pushed her hand into her hair. "And you don't fool me for one second with that 'what's-her-name' crap."

"Yeah." Douglas drew another spiral notebook out of his bookbag and sat flipping through it, glancing at Latin quotes, physics equations, French dignitaries' dates of death. "I mean, I guess everybody thinks so, but come on. So, the threesome, then Louise Delany. Amy, I don't know, I think she looks like a pinup. I mean, *bad,* like a pinup."

"I thought only the chicks realized that," said Annabelle.

"Don't worry, we're not that stupid. The guys, I mean. Louise is a *serious* beauty— And Mary and what's-her-name, Jill, are *sophomores.* Jill, though— She's got—" Annabelle poked him gently between the eyebrows. "Besides, what the hell are you worried about? Aren't you satisfied? There's the threesome and then Louise and then there's you. Except"—Douglas laughed—"I heard Wally

Patterson talking today about how good Louise was looking. He went, Annabelle Taft should look out, you know, because it's starting to look like she and Louise are neck and neck."

"So how was school?" said Annabelle.

"Okay," said Douglas. "Weird. About what I expected. I ran off to meet Max so I guess I'll have to wait and see everyone at Anthesteria. How does this party *work,* anyway? What's the—"

"Nobody actually says 'Anthesteria,' " said Annabelle.

"—big game plan? I mean, um, most of the people there are from the city, right? So, I mean, Max'll stay with us, Jill's got her place, but there's hundreds of guests, right?"

"Didn't you know what— I thought you understood," said Annabelle irritably. "There's a group of cars that leave from the city late tomorrow afternoon, from, I think, in front of the museum, that the Winfields have there, that take everyone up. Except, no, they—"

"I thought you understood."

"—also have a charter bus. Most of *us*'ll be up there for the weekend, though. On the beach tomorrow and like that. I hope it's nice—"

"What families?" asked Douglas.

"Jill's parents go," said Annabelle. "Not that many Thorndike parents, actually— I think maybe the Delanys, um, and Tina's father, maybe. Mostly it's a set from Manhattan. Some Connecticut people, too, though, um, the conservative crowd from Sharon, some coastline art types, river people."

"So all your buddies," said Douglas, fingers drumming on the desk. "Where do they usually crash?"

"Duane and Amy and Tina crash at Jill's," said Annabelle.

"What about Jake and Elwood?"

"I think Steve'll just stay with Jack, in some Winfield guest room. Wally I don't know."

"Where's Nick staying?" asked Douglas.

"We'll see," said Annabelle.

"I'm sorry about that phone call," said Douglas, looking at her. "I just can't stay mad at you. 'Nobody can,' " he mimicked her in advance.

"Nobody can," Annabelle recited automatically. "Can I see the litmag?" Douglas fished it out of his bookbag, taking the opportunity to dump out all the accumulated paraphernalia from the last semester and start sorting through it, while Annabelle leaned back against the wall and started flipping through the magazine, the desk lamp shining on her skirt from a few inches away.

"Check it out," said Douglas, flipping the battered pages of one of his old Thorndike notebooks. "Actual Nate Chablis notes. They go on for— Gee, almost six pages here— Then suddenly we seem to lose track of European history— Notes back and forth with Bill Coleman—"

"What about?" said Annabelle, not looking up.

"You don't want to know," said Douglas. "The Van Allen radiation belts. But here's the thing from Tina's *party*—" He held up an envelope. "You remember this?"

"How could I forget?" Annabelle was still looking through *Astroturf*. "There's so much Cadenhead poetry in here. Oh, here's the 'Swan' thing—"

"Let me see," said Douglas, leaning toward the book in her lap—he saw an arrangement of three Blanchard photographs around two Cadenhead poems across the magazine's centerfold. "Those aren't up to Blanchard's usual standards."

"Well, the way Nick talks about it," said Annabelle, "he does stuff that's sort of deliberately in the dumb style of Thorndike photography, you know, as a sort of commentary."

"Or he gets lazy and runs out of time," said Douglas, rummaging in his bag again. "Here's my goddamned sneakers—"

"You know, Douglas," said Annabelle suddenly, "when you're hanging around with me you're so *funny*. I don't understand what happens with other people."

"I had no idea so much shit had accumulated in my bookbag— A pencil sharpener— Socks—"

"I mean, it's like you're being the little guy on the side because you *like* it or something."

"Check out the last poem," said Douglas. "Mike's big conclusion— It's pretty good."

"*This* thing?" said Annabelle, flipping through the pamphlet and frowning at the last page. "The words are all over the goddamned page."

"It's his best piece of work," Douglas argued.

"The *words* are all over the page. No, I'm sorry," said Annabelle archly, "but this is bullshit. There's no— There's no—"

"Yeah?" said Douglas skeptically.

"Oh, I don't know. I just want him to stop. I'm sick of reading all this crap."

"You want everyone to write romance novels," said Douglas, extracting Jill's notebook from his bookbag and flipping through it, finding reams of loopy math notes and then a page of poetic text. "Check this out, Anna—" he handed her the opened notebook—"Jill *Brooks* writes poetry."

"Douglas, these are fucking *song lyrics,*" Annabelle said, tossing the notebook back. "I mean, if you were *paying attention* you wouldn't fall for this crap all the time."

"Well— I guess I'll return this to her, then—"

"She doesn't *care,*" said Annabelle exasperatedly. "School's *over.*"

"I thought I could—" Douglas dropped Jill's notebook on the floor. "I thought she was keeping a journal or something. I thought I could understand—"

"You don't know *anything* about her scene," said Annabelle. "She closes all the *discos.* She meets *dealers.* She sleeps with *stockbrokers.* She never *reads.* I mean, don't kid yourself."

"Look, Anna," said Douglas, rubbing his temples, "are you going to have a problem dealing with Max this weekend?"

"Oh, Jesus, that's *right—*" Annabelle looked exasperated. "Look, you shouldn't have done that. I don't— I just don't think it's a good time for that sort of thing."

"Because of the party? That's—"

"You run into your friend from the *sandbox* and invite him to *Dover* for the *Winfield* weekend? Did he— Was this *his* idea? Or what? I mean, where's your head at? Sometimes I really wonder where your—"

"You're being so *stupid* about this," Douglas marveled. "So there was a bad *scene* one time, but— I mean clearly you couldn't care less about each other."

"I'm just looking out for you," Annabelle said more softly.

"Who's Margaret MacAffee?"

"What? What are you *talking* about?" Annabelle said, mystified. "Are you paying attention to me? I'm trying to make a point about—"

"I know, I'm *listening,* but I don't want to forget this 'cause it's driving me crazy. Yesterday there was this letter in the kitchen, a letter for Dad, um, from Margaret MacAffee, and, I mean, I've been meaning to ask you, you know, what that name is, 'cause it sounds familiar. Does it sound familiar to you?"

"Wait— MacAffee, you said? That's weird." Annabelle had picked up a pen off the desk and was haphazardly using its clip to clean her already immaculate fingernails. "That's not a name I know."

"Anna," Douglas said, "Why don't you just tell me who she is. I mean Dad never gets letters."

"I don't *know,*" insisted Annabelle. "I swear— Who can you trust if you can't trust me?"

"Nobody in the world. Got a cig?"

"They'll be home any minute," Annabelle said, fishing for her pack of White Camels and handing it over. "You know I saw DiGrassi try one last week?"

"Yeah?" Douglas smiled, pulling out a cigarette.

"He is *such* an idiot— So he stands there smirking, you know, on the third staircase and pulls out a pack of White Camels, and then he practically faked an *asthma attack* to make it look like it wasn't the *cigarette* making him sick."

"Watch what you say about Ralph," Douglas said, twirling the cigarette. "His dad'll have you up on charges— Can I get a *light* someday?"

"I'll have the fucking mob after me," laughed Annabelle, leaning horizontally toward him, face above his, bracing a hand heavily on his shoulder and flipping the Zippo lid open, spinning the wheel and slowly moving the bright flame toward the cigarette that protruded from Douglas' mouth.

"Annabelle!" their father called over the distant clatter of the front door.

"*Bull's-eye,*" Annabelle gasped, ducking her head to grin as she snapped the lighter shut and pushed off from Douglas' shoulder, swerving back upright. "Saved by the bell— No smoke for *you,* darling."

"What's *he* want?" Douglas said, leaning back and spitting the still-pristine cigarette onto the desk, where it rolled out of sight.

"I'll report back," Annabelle said briskly, heaving herself off of the desk, sliding to the floor and quickly leaving the room, shutting the door behind her.

Douglas shut off the desk lamp and collapsed into his frayed butterfly reading chair, knocking random paperbacks from the bookshelf, and after a few minutes he heard his mother entering the apartment and calling "I'm home!" Tensing, Douglas continued blindly thumbing through one of the toppled books—a science fiction novel—until he heard her inevitable footsteps in the corridor. "Douglas?" she called through his bedroom door.

"In here," Douglas yelled resignedly, automatically slapping the paperback shut, his index finger wedged between the pages.

"Hello, love," Giulia Taft said, swinging the door open—she looked unconsciously exotic in an immaculate Naget suit, the well-cut white fabric emphasizing her height and the varied darkness of her skin and flattering the richness of her wavy black hair, which was pulled back by means of a small bronze clasp.

"Hi, Mom. How was your day?" said Douglas, letting the book drop between the chair and the floor lamp—he sometimes became very sad at the thought of how easily he could confuse and frighten his parents by making some false, strange change in his behavior and then carefully maintaining it, suffering further as he forced himself to weather their resigned, carefully loyal reactions and knowing that the real fear was that they would not react at all.

"Not bad at all, considering— All I've been doing is talking about how my children have finished high school and sailed into the colleges of their choice." Giulia sat down in the desk chair, her eyes scanning the textbooks and magazines and missing the hidden cigarette. "Choices— I ran into Bob Foster at the bank and we talked about the elation of paying the last Thorndike bill. Did you just get home? I called a few times."

"I went to the Café with some people."

"Don't they feed you at that school?" Giulia smiled resignedly behind her large black-rimmed glasses. Her voice was contralto and precise, lapsing between the cadences of her father's Sicilian city language and the blunt diction of her mother's Brooklyn heritage. "Where are you getting all this money?"

"Same place you are. Listen, I *am* going to the thing, but I invited Max Gantry up for the weekend. Is that— Is that okay with you?"

"Well, it has to be, doesn't it?" Giulia said after a moment. "I won't ask you to rescind the— You've already asked him?"

"Yeah," said Douglas. "It was a spur-of-the-moment—"

"*Who* are we talking about?"

"Max. Max Gantry. Choate got out early."

Giulia beamed. "Max. It's been years. Will he get here in time for dinner? Your father's in there stewing crabs."

"Sure—before dark. Or whatever we said."

"Is he invited to the Winfield thing?" said Giulia, extracting the jacket of the Rolling Stones' *Sticky Fingers* from the desktop litter. "What is this, a joke?"

"What? It's an Andy Warhol photograph, Mom."

"A shame I've never met *this* man."

"Keep your hopes up," Douglas said, smiling at the attempted repartee. "I don't think Max is invited but I figured he could go as our guest. Right?"

"Of course," said Giulia vaultingly, waving her hand and squinting. "I could bring the entire Venezuelan navy and Peggy wouldn't mind."

"Or Granddad's extended family?" said Douglas, running his hands through his hair.

"That *might* cause a stir," said Giulia, nodding. "Fifteen or twenty Italian-ghetto urban blight victims in inappropriate clothing— I love explaining about how it only takes three generations to get from the Garibaldi family coming to America to me living on Fifth Avenue. It's so *heartening.* I told Peggy Winfield it was like a medieval dynasty. She loved that— Douglas, did you pick up those trousers at Dunhill?"

"Trousers?"

"The grey flannel trousers— They were altering the waist?"

"Right," said Douglas, wincing. "I forgot. Damn. Sorry— I've had things on my mind."

"Don't apologize to *me*— I just don't know what you'll be *wearing* tomorrow night. Annabelle darling!" Giulia sang out suddenly, her accent tightening.

"Oh, here's where everyone is," said Annabelle, leaning in the door and looking around. "Mom." She walked over behind the desk chair and hugged Giulia from behind. "I *thought* I heard you come in. What's up?"

"Not all that much. Mmmm—" Giulia reared back to examine Annabelle. "My, you look nice today." She kissed her daughter's cheek. "Smell nice, too— Is this that Naget from your father? He really *will* buy you anything you tell him to."

"Yeah, the old number-five. When are we leaving?"

"No great rush, if we take both cars— You can take the sedan at your leisure after we've left. Remind me to give you all the keys."

"Okay, Mom," said Annabelle, leaning her head on Giulia's shoulder. "Where's the big car? Is it still down in the garage?"

"That's right. Douglas, would you do me a favor?"

"Name it."

"Pick up Nathan Chablis?" Giulia squinted. "Some confusing car problem— Anyway, he needs a ride."

"No trouble at— Wait. Mr. *Chablis?* Oh, Jesus, he's coming for the weekend?"

"That's right," said Giulia archly, turning back toward Annabelle. "You *really* look spectacular, darling— When *I* was growing up I had one pair of nice shoes and I wore them once a year for the Christmas plainsong. What's the *occasion?*"

"Day of school. Nothing." Annabelle had walked over to Douglas' record collection, lamplight shining on her forehead.

"You go to school like that?" Giulia laughed. "How do the boys get their homework done?"

"They draw me on desks, right, Douglas darling?" said Annabelle, smiling malevolently, glancing at Douglas as she pulled out a record.

"Nobody ever does any homework, Mom," said Douglas, getting out of the reading chair with a lurch and walking over. "What the hell are you doing, I've got those organized, Anna—"

"Relax, man— This is mine," said Annabelle, tucking *Led Zeppelin III* under her arm, where it slid against her sweater. "So's this. And *this.* Jesus—"

"Well, I'll remember that when I'm looking at the Harvard bills and you're both calling asking for more money," said Giulia.

"Come on, Mom, money grows on trees on Wall Street," said Annabelle, scanning the records.

"Big trees. Like—ah—oak trees," said Douglas, grabbing a record back. "This isn't *yours.* I bought this in Dover last summer."

Gregory Taft walked in, wearing an apron and holding a spatula. "Hello, Doug— Hello, Anna," he said.

"Hi, Dad," said Douglas and Annabelle, still poring over the records.

"They're not hungry, they went to that café," said Giulia. "Give the food to the cat, I guess—"

"Give it to Jane? I'll go sell it in the street," said Greg. "You *are* eating, aren't you?"

"Yeah," said Annabelle. "And remember, the Gantry kid hasn't had a square meal in months, so, you know— Put a little extra on, because—"

"Oh, Jesus," said Douglas. "That's it—" He clumsily grabbed the entire stack of record albums out of Annabelle's arms. "You don't deserve *any* records. Not—"

"*None?*" Annabelle said petulantly.

"Maybe the *Grease* soundtrack," Douglas conceded, fumbling with the slipping stack of records. "Mom, what's the deal tonight? Which car, which luggage, and like that?"

"I thought I explained— Your father and I are taking the small car, and we've got to leave—"

"You can say 'the Porsche,' Mom," said Annabelle.

"—right after dinner because Greg's got to detour outside Dover and talk to someone about a closing. Or something like that. You've got the big car, and you've got to stop about forty minutes upstate and get Chablis—"

"Jesus Christ," said Douglas, grimacing again.

"I'm sorry, Douglas, but certain arrangements have to be respected. I told him you'd arrive around ten."

"All right, fine," said Douglas.

Giulia got up, adjusting the hem of her skirt, and walked toward the door. "Don't be late for dinner. I think we'll have time to read afterwards," she said, walking out.

Douglas refiled the records that Annabelle had dropped and brushed lint off of his shirt while Annabelle, at the desk, finished flipping through a pile of magazines and made to leave the room. "Listen," said Douglas, "could you go up with Mom and Dad? There might not be room for the two of us *and* Max *and* Chablis and all the suitc—"

"I won't be ready," Annabelle said, shaking her head, not looking at him as she moved toward the door.

"But the—"

"No way." Annabelle whirled and interrupted him loudly, pointing at him with a high-fashion angered look. "This is *your* thing. No one asked you to invite that guy up— Everything's already arranged and Mom's probably pissed if you didn't notice"— she took a breath, watching him—"and you *didn't* notice, but don't ask *me* to rearrange my—"

"All right!" Douglas shouted. Annabelle stopped talking. "All right," he said more quietly. "Forget it."

Annabelle looked at him and then walked out, stalking back to her room, slamming the door, and Douglas heard the Manet poster fall again. "And your masking tape sucks," Annabelle shouted through the doors.

Douglas sat down and retrieved the old science fiction book, trying to find his place. He slammed his fist on the wall and then continued reading, his eyes skimming over the words while his fingers broke bits of brittle paper off the pages, and five minutes later there was a knock at the door. "Is this going to be an Annabelle Taft kiss-and-make-up act?" he asked loudly.

"Certainly not," said Giulia, sticking her head into the room.

"Oh, Mom, sorry," said Douglas, automatically concealing the book's title with his fingers. "What's up?"

"Nothing— I'm sorry to bother you. When's the Gantry boy showing up?"

"We said seven," said Douglas.

"I was just having a drink out on the terrace. The evening looks promising— I was thinking of taking a quick walk in the park. Would you like to come with me?"

Douglas crossed his legs before answering. "Well, no thanks, Mom. I'm just— I've got things on my mind, you know? I'd rather not."

"All right," said Giulia, retreating from the room.

"Don't bother asking Annabelle," Douglas called through the door. "She's in one of her moods."

"Actually I wasn't going to," Giulia called as she walked away down the corridor.

This family shouts through doors too much, thought Douglas. After a moment he got up and walked out to the living room, where Giulia was absently polishing a jade statuette on the piano—he could hear the crabs stewing in the kitchen, where his father had the radio tuned to a classical station. "Mom?" he said. "I changed my mind."

YOU'RE ALWAYS COMING and going," the doorman said in mock surprise.

"Just can't keep track of me, Sport," Douglas told him, following Giulia out onto the sidewalk as the doorman laughed and resumed scrutinizing the three security video screens. A breeze brushed Fifth Avenue as they crossed, the evening light shining through the shrubbery at the park's edge, the brownstone border casting deep shadows across the hexagonal paving stones. They entered the park at Eighty-fifth Street and trudged up the hill toward the curving East Drive, where cars rushed by under the trees and the bike lane was filled with cyclists and joggers.

"My Lord, it's gorgeous out," said Giulia. "I wish Annabelle had come."

"Yeah, yeah," said Douglas.

"Douglas, don't be that way."

"Sorry."

Passing the museum's shining limestone corners, they crossed the highway and approached the Great Lawn's north edge, where a late softball game occupied the nearest diamond and a young girl's scarlet kite hung atop the pale and fading sky. "Everyone's out so *late*— I love June," Giulia said. "Have you got any coherent plans for this summer?"

"Is that what's on your mind, Mom?" said Douglas. "Is that what the walk's about?"

Giulia frowned. "Of course not. I'm not playing games with you, Douglas. I don't play games with you anymore."

"I guess not."

"You know, I think you learned that trick from your father— Where you make some accusation and then you just cover your tracks. You're very good at those non-comments."

"Yeah, I know," said Douglas.

"I don't know— I wonder whether I'd rather have Annabelle biting my head off or you just—shifting away like that. I think ultimately your method's far shrewder. You come off better in that regard." Slowing, they circled the cusp of the Great Lawn. "I happen to know that Senator Rollins is looking for an aide— You'll meet him this weekend."

"Oh, Jesus, here they come, the job offers," said Douglas. "Look, I'd kind of like to take things— I just— Next year's a big deal, you know? I mean, I wish things would *slow down* for a minute. All this business going on everywhere."

They stood side by side gazing south across the Great Lawn, where the afternoon's reddening light reflected from the edges of the mid-town towers that protruded above the distant trees. "You know," said Giulia, flicking back a cuff and glancing at her watch, "when we lived on West End I always— It always bothered me how long it took to get to Central Park. Remember all those weekends when your father had all those Saturday classes and I—"

"Which Saturday classes?" asked Douglas, watching a woman in headphones, kneepads and roller skates jerk around in circles.

"You remember, at Columbia," said Giulia.

"Right."

"And I would bring you and Annie over to the playground on Eighty-sixth Street?"

"Yeah," said Douglas, smiling. "That long walk."

"There was that one time that other boy from Thorndike—what were you, six years old?—when that boy pushed you off the swing? You came crying to me and demanded that I let you stay home from school?"

"Right, right," said Douglas, his loafers kicking dust from the asphalt path. During the summer of 1970, when Douglas was seven, he had awakened on the morning of his first interview at Thorndike and immediately been trammeled into one of those little suits that parents think the rest of the world wants to see their children wearing—Douglas vaguely remembered how sorrowfully sick he had felt that day, how every lurching of the crosstown bus was magnified, how Greg and Giulia flanked him like sentries as the huge posters for the movies *Let It Be* and *Fritz the Cat* drifted past the bright, milky windows behind the backlit head of the small, nervous boy in the crimson windbreaker who stared through the broiling air and belligerently avoided eye contact. When the Tafts left the bus the young boy tailed them, making the already queasy Douglas even more self-conscious as he stumbled up the cinnamon-colored staircase, following his oblivious parents through the buzzing bronze door and into the hot, harshly lit lobby while nervously noticing in an attack of panic that the boy from the bus had entered behind them, and when Douglas finally vomited he managed to splatter his force-fed breakfast all over this stranger, drenching his dirty sneakers and windbreaker, slick vomit speckling his ungainly nose and greasy black hair. The interview had gone well, despite all this, and Douglas was accepted by the school, as Annie had been the previous year, but several days later, having returned with his father for some "testing," Douglas found his way to a stainless steel bathroom and ran into the boy again.

"Hey, kid," said Ralph DiGrassi.

"How old are you? What's your name?" Douglas asked, his fingers dripping soapy water.

"Hey, everyone knows me." Ralph spoke with the rote bravado he'd already cultivated. "My dad's the Iron Fist, man, so watch your step. I've seen the *jails.* You going into first grade? What's your name?"

"Doug Taft," Douglas recited carefully. "Second grade."

"You got a sister named Annie?"

"Her real name's Annabelle. How do you—"

"Met her on the bus."

"She told you her name?" Douglas said. "Annie doesn't *take* the bus."

"You saying I'm lying, faggot?"

"No, but— How do you *really* know her?"

"I *fucked* her," Ralph said. "I told her you puked on me and then I fucked her and now she thinks you're a real rude kid." Ralph swung his eight-year-old fist and punched Douglas on the cheek, clanking his head against the bathroom tiles— Douglas fell to the floor and then regained his feet and Ralph watched him spend several minutes silently washing a small smear of blood from the wall.

Douglas and Giulia had begun walking west, veering onto the bridle path, and Douglas unbuttoned his cuffs and pushed up his sleeves. "Ralph DiGrassi. He was chasing the damn pigeons around and he noticed me acting like an idiot on top of the jungle gym, probably pretending I was in the F-111, right? Yeah, I remember that."

"That was DiGrassi?" said Giulia as they walked past the tow path. "The same boy from that first day? I remember meeting his father at the first Parents' Association meeting— He's a very odd man."

"Right. Always calling me a rude kid, and— Ralph would always call me a rude kid, and I would call him an ugly kid, and he'd call me a fag and then I would never know *what* to say. It was such a lose."

"My Lord— And here I thought I was raising my children away from the territorial squalor of *my* upbringing." Giulia gave her light, attractive laugh as they left the path and approached the playground.

"Don't worry, Mom," said Douglas, smiling and putting an arm around her waist. "You seem to have done all right."

"I have, at that. You've gotten *taller,* Douglas," Giulia said, looking at him warmly and observing the alignment of their heads. They passed the edge of the chain-link fence and entered the dim and deserted playground, where dark shadows gathered on the sand-strewn rubber sheets beneath the abandoned cast-iron seesaws and splintering swings.

"Everything's so *small,*" said Douglas quietly. "Right here"—he'd led Giulia forward, pointing at one of the low swings—"this one was my favorite. I'd always get this one and Annabelle'd sit there. You'd sit over *there.*" He indicated a bench by the fence.

"That's right." Giulia nodded. "I read most of Thackeray sitting right there. The—"

Douglas had started crying. He was crying very hard, face twisted, throat constricted, tears running over his cheeks and nose. He didn't seem to know what to do or how to move—he just stood with his arms slightly bent, looking straight ahead, crying.

"Douglas," said Giulia, stepping toward him. He hugged her, his cheek pressing the side of her head rather than her shoulder or waist as it had in the distant past, his face contorted in shame, his scuffed breath hitching erratically, his hands awkward and guilty on his mother's back for being so aware of its feminine contours.

"Mom—" He tried to clear his throat, noticing from up close the new lines along her aging neck. "Mom—" His crying shifted into a softer crying that was more subdued and he clutched her strongly and then let go and stepped away and wiped his face with his hands, and she handed him her handkerchief and he cleaned his reddened eyes and handed it back. "Thanks," he whispered, and when he looked at his mother he couldn't see her expression but then she tipped her head and looked at him and smiled and she looked sad. "Well, how about that," he said, looking away and then back, shaking his head, sniffing as he tried to breathe normally.

"I don't really know what to say," said Giulia softly. "You've been in such a state these days."

"Nothing to say," said Douglas, looking around again.

"We should get back," said Giulia, looking at her watch. "Your father's probably got dinner ready."

"Right," said Douglas, sniffing slightly, catching his constricted breath. "Let's get this weekend in gear." He turned and waited, letting her take the lead, letting her start them moving toward the playground gate, and then they left the playground and started walking back toward the east edge of the park.

chapter 11

"Jesus Christ," Max said, gazing around—he stood just within the apartment's broad white front door, which Douglas braced open, and he carried a suitcase with the predictable CHOATE sticker along its battered edge. "You've really come out of the closet about the money."

"Yeah," said Annabelle, walking forward while putting her watch on, "and how do you think it feels? Drop your stuff anywhere."

"This is such grotesque decadence," Max said, putting down the suitcase and wandering into the cavernous living room.

"Come on, no it's not," said Douglas, embarrassed, shutting the door and following.

"No, you're right. It's worse— It's *restrained* decadence"—Max examined a doorknob, a coaster—"everything carefully handcrafted to look off-the-rack."

"Right!" Annabelle said, beaming.

"You've got all these Bonomi books," Max continued, looking at the bookcase's rows of threadbare first editions. "I hate that shit."

"Oh, come on," said Douglas. "Don't start this *already*— "

"Too bad," said Annabelle. "You won't enjoy Dad's reading. You know what Bonomi said."

"What," said Max, "you mean besides 'Where am I going/And why do I know the way?' "

"Right," said Annabelle.

"Well—start right there. What the hell does that mean?"

"It means a lot. He also said"—Annabelle was running a fingertip along the spines of the books—"he also said 'Disdain this room, Disdain the world/Disdain these miles and miles of night,/

Sail on beneath the sails unfurled/Past sight of dark and distant light.' "

"Beautiful," said Max, looking at Annabelle. "Like a Hallmark card— And Douglas is giving me the 'realm of glass' quote— I mean he's clueless but you're turning into one of those *moonies.*"

"Right!" said Annabelle.

"Are you serious?" said Max.

"Of course not," said Annabelle, wandering away toward the kitchen. Max followed Douglas around a series of double doorways, gazing at the views of Central Park out the windows, the terrace off the kitchen, the high ceilings, the Steinway, the Barcelona chairs, his sneakers creaking against the whitewashed shining floors. In the dining room a Prokofiev piano concerto was softly playing and Greg and Annabelle were laying out place settings—near-burlap napkins, thick-handled silver knives—while Giulia selected a bottle of wine from the rack by the kitchen door.

"Max! How are you?" Greg said, putting down the last fork and striding over, hand extended, grinning his tight smile behind his antique glasses, still wearing an apron over his shirt and tie. "Christ, it's been years."

"Hello, Mr. Taft," said Max, shaking hands, noticing Greg's slightly older face and short-cropped greying hair. "It's good to see you."

Greg smiled, taking off his apron. "Just Greg, please."

"Max, dear," said Giulia, walking over with a sanctimonious look—or so it seemed to Max—and kissing him on the cheek.

"Hello, Giulia." Max fumbled around with the physical protocol, kissing her back, conscious of his breath.

"This is getting cold," said Greg, prodding at a steaming ceramic pot on the table with a wooden spoon. Everyone sat down in the baroque chairs, Greg and Giulia facing each other from opposite ends of the table, Douglas with the windows behind him, Annabelle and Max side by side across from him. Greg doled out crabs and rice and passed the plates around while Giulia filled and distributed seamless wineglasses.

"This place is beautiful," said Max.

"That's right, you haven't been here before, have you?" said Giulia.

"No," said Max just as the phone delivered its odd electronic hum. "What the hell is *that?*" Max said, looking around.

Annabelle dropped her napkin beside her plate. "I'll get it," she said, dashing off through the white swinging door into the kitchen.

"So in the interim while you haven't been here you've been going to high school?" asked Greg, attacking his plate.

Max nodded fervently, struggling to swallow a mouthful of rice, watching his reflection bobbing outside the indigo windows. "I went to Choate— I'm starting at Yale in September."

"Douglas is going to Harvard," said Greg.

Douglas looked pained. "Obviously he knows that, Dad."

"Well, I'm just making conversation," said Greg.

Annabelle came back in and pointed her thumb back over her shoulder at the kitchen. "Mom, that's Nathan Chablis— He wants to make sure everything's arranged properly."

Giulia got up as Annabelle sat down. "You might have said I was eating, Annabelle," she said, swirling off into the kitchen.

"I thought everything had *been* arranged," said Douglas, unfolding his napkin with an absent flourish.

Annabelle flared her eyes and nodded at Douglas, swallowing a bite. "Mm. He's such an asshole. I'm so sick—"

"Annabelle—" said Greg.

"—of deferring to him. I mean, Christ, we're shuttling him to Dover, where he has no idea what's going on—"

"Annabelle, he was with the Lineage Institute. He could be anywhere—he's at Thorndike because he likes high school students."

"I'll bet," said Max, glancing at Annabelle.

"He's at Thorndike because he likes *money,*" said Annabelle. "And, yeah, he was with that stupid outfit, and so what?"

"Well," said Greg, leaning forward, "he wrote an important *letter,* too— A couple of important letters for this family, so— You know, you can just put up with him."

"Yeah," Annabelle said finally, looking intently at Greg, her voice grown quiet, "but do you *like* that, Dad? I mean, is that your idea of how things should be?"

"Well, *I* worked for the Institute, remember? The—"

"That's not what I meant," said Annabelle. "And besides, you're not coming off that well if we look at that whole series of events, so—"

"Annabelle!" said Greg sharply.

"What? What the hell?" said Douglas, looking back and forth between them.

"Sorry, Dad," said Annabelle.

"Are we picking up Nathan Chablis?" said Max smoothly. "I'm sorry, have I interfered with some tight scheduling?"

Greg smiled. "No, not at all, Max."

Giulia returned carrying a stack of odd-sized envelopes. "Douglas, your father and I will leave at eight-thirty," she said, looking at her watch as she moved back to her chair. "Can you make it to New Wye by nine?"

"No problem," said Douglas, sipping the red wine, fatigued. "Right, Annabelle? We can make that, right?"

"Of course, Douglas darling. Anything good, Mom?"

"I'm sorry to do this now," said Giulia, shaking her head as she flipped through the envelopes. "I just didn't want to forget— Thorndike, Thorndike—"

"*More?*" said Greg. "I paid everything."

"It's labeled 'Alumni.' I guess it's official— Harvard, Harvard—"

"Is it checkbook time?" said Greg. Douglas and Annabelle reached for the identical envelopes, ripping them open simultaneously as Max finished his food, laying the heavy-handled silverware along the edge of his plate.

"Room assignments," said Annabelle, looking over the mailing. " 'We look forward to meeting you in September—' "

"I look forward to receiving the first bill," said Greg.

"I'm sorry, Max, we've got all this hectic business and we haven't had a chance to talk to you," Giulia said, tabling her napkin and leaning back. "It's such a pre-college madhouse here."

"It's the same at my house," Max lied.

"Shall we retire to the other room?" Greg asked expansively, looking around at all of them as the Prokofiev ended.

"Darling," said Giulia.

"We've got some time— I can get a chapter in," Greg said. Douglas had started collecting the dishes, and Max got up to help him.

"ALL RIGHT," said Greg, reclining in the reading chair before the piano and opening his Scribner's first edition of Bonomi's *The Story of Jake Hackett.* Giulia sat at one end of a white couch, Annabelle at the other, and Max in a black chair with Douglas cross-legged at his feet, leaning back against the black marble proscenium around the fireplace. " 'Chapter Twelve,' " Greg read. " 'In Which I Discover a Way to Elude Mr. Morstan and Reëstablish my Innocence.' "

"What's the chapter epigraph?" asked Annabelle, examining her fingernails.

"It's Dante," said Greg, reading it—

Aciascun'alma presa e gentil core
nel cui cospetto ven lo dir presente,
in ciò che mi rescrivan suo parvente,
salute in lor segnor, cioè Amore.
Già eran quasi che atterzate l'ore
del tempo che onne stella n'è lucente,
quando m'apparve Amor subitamente,
cui essenza membrar mi dà orrore.

"Cool," said Annabelle, smiling, having been nodding along. "Wait—*cui essenza*—"

" '*Cui essenza membrar mi dà orrore.*' 'In a form, or guise, which is—repellent, I guess, or horrifying to recall," translated Giulia without looking up.

"That's what I thought," said Annabelle. "Go on, please, Dad."

Max looked puzzled. "That's what Mike Cadenhead used to do all the time," he said. "Put some foreign quote without explaining it."

"Who the hell are you to complain? You're not telling the story," said Annabelle. "Dad, let's go."

" 'When I regained my composure,' " Greg read, " 'I ascertained that an hour of reckoning had arrived unasked. Regardless of my failures and despite my dreams and desires, the wheels of fate had spun me towards this mysterious rendezvous, wherein my quest for the profane and unfortunate text in Morstan's foul hand would be waylaid. No sooner had I regained my feet and gazed about the courtyard that I discerned a dark figure approaching towards me—a woman clothed in the simple habit of the local chapter—and while awaiting her arrival I examined my whereabouts. The baptistry appeared softer now in its countenance, the harsh stonework hushed by the advancing nocturnal hours—' "

"Wait, hang on," said Douglas, looking up from the floor. "Sorry, Dad— He's in the *church courtyard* already?" He looked around. "How'd he get *there?*"

Greg, legs crossed to reveal argyle socks, looked over at him. "Don't you remember?"

"The chapter last weekend," said Annabelle. "Come on— You've *got* to remember."

"Vaguely," said Douglas, squinting.

Annabelle sighed. "Jake was in the town square, where he saw Morstan the first time, remember?" Douglas nodded. "So Morstan has those three Giovannian monks with him, who beat Jake over the head, and the last thing he sees— The last thing he sees is the stars whirling over his head, right, with, like, the Venetian haze, as they carry him off down away from the Grand Canal and into the depths of the city— Right?"

"That's it," said Greg, shaking his head while flipping the old book's pages.

"And wait," said Annabelle. "I remember it, Dad— 'The stars shone brightly over the vast and ancient city as they had in the bygone times of the Medicis, and then the swirling of the starlight abated as rough hands bore me over bridges and down darkened alleys and then for a time I knew no more.' "

"What a memory," said Greg. "That's exactly out of the book."

"Yeah— Get *to* it," said Douglas impatiently.

"I love that paragraph," said Annabelle, embarrassed. "But, anyway, Doug— So he wakes up in the baptistery courtyard, he smells the canals and knows they haven't taken him far, and he doesn't realize they've taken his crucifix and rosary, and then here comes the woman—"

"All right, all right," said Douglas. "Jesus Christ. I know where we are. Dad—punch it."

"Somehow I don't think we're going to get very far with this tonight," Greg said, looking around, his eyes lingering on Max politely, raising the book and continuing. " 'I discerned a dark figure approaching'—yes, yes, yes—'the harsh stonework hushed by the advancing nocturnal hours as the cold wind of dawn approached. I remembered the drama of the previous evening, the spires of the city bathed by the winds of evening fire before the still waters of the night, and as I awaited the good woman's arrival I believed that the solution to the horrid puzzle had presented itself—I fancied that I had been blessed with a divine intuition, vouchsafed the briefest of clear visions of the clockwork of the universe, and my meager story seemed then a mere reflection of grander stories, a pale shadow of the vast forces of good and evil casting their influence across the lives of every denizen of this troubled world.

" 'As the lady arrived by my side I perceived, with some surprise, that it was none other than Anna. I must surely have blanched in my apprehension and she must just as surely have perceived my disquietude in the morning light. The—' "

"Wait," said Douglas. "Anna from the gondola? *That* Anna? The one that Morstan gave the flowers to?"

"*Yes,*" said Annabelle. "Would you pay attention?"

"Sorry," said Douglas. "I lose track of all this mumbo jumbo."

Greg continued. " 'The good woman gazed at me with an expression of indefinable melancholy—' "

"*Oh,* yeah," said Annabelle, smiling. "How could you forget *this,* Douglas?"

"I'm an idiot," said Douglas.

" ' "*Signorina,*" I began, but she placed a pale hand on my arm.

" ' "For that there is no need, Signor Hackett," Anna said in a halting voice. "As I have come to understand your origins I have gained a command of your language."

"Yeah— She learned English in two seconds," Douglas muttered.

" ' "Let there be, then, no secrets between us," I said,' " Greg continued, sparing Douglas a sharp glance. " ' "I am plagued by nervous vapors," said Anna. "Were we within the walls of the church I could speak frankly with you, sir, but as things stand I can say only that you are in great danger, far greater than you may suspect."

" 'I recoiled at her words but endeavored to speak calmly, not wishing to upset the good woman. "Anna," I began, "if I may be so bold— Were events cast in a different shape I would hasten you to a church with utmost speed and there enact vows with you that would insure an eternal frankness between us. When we first met by the Grand Canal I felt sure of this, as sure as I have felt of anything that has transpired, good or ill, since I entered this country. I endeavored to guide you within the Cathedral *San Marco* but my actions were swiftly curtailed by Morstan's untimely arrival."

" ' "It would seem, sir," said Anna, her eyes cast demurely downwards towards the cloister's paving stones between us, "that we two have been detained between churches far too often."

"Greg," said Max, "Did you name your daughter after this crazy nun?"

"You bet your life I did," said Greg, smiling at him and then continuing to read. " 'There was a moment of silence between us in that calm and holy place—a moment during which I considered how best to extract from Anna the information concerning Morstan's foul book that I desperately needed.' "

"He's such an asshole!" Douglas exploded, laughing.

"Douglas!" said Greg sharply.

"Hackett?" said Max, smiling.

"*Yeah,* Hackett," said Douglas. "Anna, why do you *like* this guy so much? Here he's got the babe in *front* of him and all he's thinking about is that damn book."

"Darling, we've got to go," said Giulia, examining her wristwatch.

"Oh yes?" said Greg, looking at her and then closing the book around one of the Harvard envelopes as he stood.

"I think if we push things you can make it," said Giulia, standing also. "Would you mind calling the elevator while I get the bags?"

For the next several moments Greg and Giulia moved around collecting objects from the living room—wallets, eyeglasses—and then sped off together toward the group of suitcases by the bedroom hallway, and, with amazing rapidity, had everything stacked by the elevator door before Douglas or Max could intercede. Everyone stood around in the vestibule while the elevator needle moved toward fifteen. Greg grinned blankly. Suddenly the elevator man wrenched the door open and everyone clambered around loading the elevator. "Yes sir, Douglas," said the elevator man.

"Hey, Sport," said Douglas.

"All right," said Giulia, standing in the elevator door. "I left the BMW keys and Chablis' directions to his house on the kitchen table. The car needs gas. Questions? Annabelle?"

"What—" Annabelle laughed confusedly. "All clear with me, Mom."

"Fine. Don't lock yourselves out," said Giulia, apparently overwhelmed by strategy. "Have a nice drive— See you in Dover."

"Drive carefully," said Greg. "Enjoy the drive, Max."

"That I will," said Max, nodding gravely.

The elevator man looked back and forth between Greg and Giulia. "Okay?" he said.

"Let's go," Greg said, turning back to his children as the ornate elevator door closed across his clamped smile.

"Jesus *Christ*, they move fast," said Max.

"Come on, darling— Let's get drunk," said Annabelle, poking Max in the stomach and slipping in through the front door.

"Man, I was having trouble keeping a straight face while your dad was reading," Max told Douglas as they reëntered the apartment. "I'm liking the pad, though."

"Money has its moments," said Douglas. "But yeah— I mean, that Bonomi stuff is such crap. Even *Mom's* had enough of Dad's nostalgia trip. We've been doing it for *years.*"

"But he only wrote four books!" said Max. "You must know them by heart."

"I never remember what happens at the end," Douglas said as they got to the dining room, where Annabelle was already crouched on the floor, her posture hiking and tightening her skirt, her hands pinwheeling open the beige bar cabinet. "Max, are you ragging on Bonomi again?" she asked without looking up.

"Well—" said Max.

"We *both* are," said Douglas.

"Oh, Bonomi's beautiful—if you can't see it, you're fucked in the head," said Annabelle disgustedly, poring over the liquor cabinet.

"I'll be back in a minute," Max said, heading off toward the bedroom hallway.

"*Now* we've got a ball game," Annabelle said, pulling a bottle of Cointreau from the cabinet and standing up. "I've had my eye on this for weeks. Douglas"—she turned to him while reaching toward the racked glassware—"you caught everything that morning with Wally Patterson, didn't you?"

"Uh— Yeah, more or less," said Douglas, watching her get three glasses down.

"Less, believe me," said Annabelle. "What a nightmare—"

"Two," said Douglas, holding up two fingers.

"What?"

"Two glasses. I'm driving."

"Right," said Annabelle, shaking her head distractedly and filling the glasses. "You heard me outside the elevator, right? When I yelled at him?"

"Oh yeah," said Douglas, taking up the hushed voice she was using. " 'So *what* if the myth's true?' Pretty cold."

"I didn't say *that.*" Annabelle screwed the cap back onto the square bottle. "But actually, I did, didn't I? He's no sidewinder. Shut up," she said sharply as Max returned. "Come on, Gantry, we're drinking a toast, you and me."

"We are?" said Max, walking over. They picked up their glasses.

"*Yes.* To the Ivy League, right?" Annabelle and Max clinked their glasses, and Max moved to sip his drink, but Annabelle stopped him. "Hold on," she said. "Do it right." With her leading, they intertwined their arms and drank the liqueur that way, standing in enforced proximity, while Douglas sat down in one of the dining room chairs and watched.

"To the weekend," Douglas said.

"You don't have a glass, driver— We'll do the toasting, thank you. Again," she told Max, moving to refill the glasses.

"Can I get some ice?" said Max.

"Plebeian," said Annabelle.

"Well, okay," said Max.

He and Annabelle each had another drink.

"Great— Are we ready to go now?" asked Douglas. "I want to get this Chablis business over with."

"I'm making it painless," Annabelle said, replacing the bottle. "Let's rock."

chapter 12

Much later Max learned that each horror is made of the unfinished pieces of the next perfect union of events, as every perfect hour is a picture of decay—not because pain leads directly to pleasure but because a disaster contains nothing but elements of the next epiphany. Now he sat shotgun in the Tafts' BMW gazing into the dusk, admiring the speed with which they'd emerged from the hidden garage and crawled through scattered traffic past housing projects toward FDR drive, slipping between toll gates and onto the expressway, leaving the city behind as the evening faded. They were ambling along a deserted two-lane farm road forty miles north of Manhattan, and Douglas, hands at the worn wheel, glanced at Max's unshaven and bleary-eyed face in the passenger-side rearview mirror and thought back across the years of their strange and awkward friendship. Before they were even ten years old Max had shown up at Thorndike as the kid with the strange hands who had a habit of banging the open lockers shut as he ran down the school corridors, and nobody had known how to speak to him until a winter afternoon in the early seventies—wide ties, Watergate—when Douglas had discovered him crying in a locked bathroom stall and had climbed over the metal barricade and hugged him, still not knowing what to say. The alliance had grown against its impediments, like the crystal growth of winter ice on a windowpane accepting the edges of the glass, past the first time Douglas had brought Max home, the uncomfortable night that Annabelle had reacted in disgust to Max's hands and gone to her room, refusing to eat, and soon they'd decided to build an F-111. Everything got very serious and Max filled homework margins and huge newsprint drawing tablets with aeronautical design schematics while Douglas accumulated, in a closet, the necessary materials—light bulbs and coaxial cable and wood and a white steel steering wheel from an abandoned truck—but the collection was always far from complete, lacking sheet metal and safety glass and headlights, printed circuits, transistors and tubing, crash cushions, nylon webbing, washers and white paint. They spent Dover weekends rearranging the furniture of Douglas' room into the F-111 interior, Max bringing his paintings for the views from the windows, and Douglas watched Max's mangled hands move across paper to create an airfoil or a mountain range and envied his grace, but when Douglas started asking when they'd begin construction and who wanted to telephone the airspace commissioner, Max officially terminated the project on the grounds of "reality."

"You're not driving fast enough," Annabelle said from the backseat. She was leaning against the starboard door's Bavarian upholstery, arms around her knees, scuffed sneakers on the seat, old Army duffel bag beside her, her blank white T-shirt shining blue against the deep country dusk—it was dark enough for the windows to reflect their faces and the trees had lost their detail and faded to heavy shadow. Max looked around at her irately and saw her smooth knees protruding through the fray of her worn jeans, caught her eyes, and dropped his staged frown as he turned back to face the road.

"Lock your door," said Douglas.

"I love your concern, Douglas," Annabelle said. "The way you—"

Douglas reached over and used the driver's-door control to lock all the car doors, the sudden quadraphonic thump startling Max.

"This is great," said Annabelle. "I feel like the girl with two bad dates at once."

"I'm watching for signs, Annabelle," said Douglas, flicking his gaze between the road and the odometer.

"Sorry," Annabelle said, lunging suddenly forward between the front seats and straining to slip a cassette into the dashboard tape deck. Douglas swerved the car, and when the Police's *Zenyatta Mondatta* started playing he twirled the volume down a bit.

"Damn it, that's *three* miles since the turnoff," said Douglas, looking at the odometer. "Max, what does that thing say?" While he spoke they drove past a small grocery store the size of a roadside house, with two cars parked beside it and a pair of faces briefly visible within the bright window. "What do you think, should we stop and go ask those people?" Douglas asked.

"Well, I can't—" Max had unfolded the sheet of Giulia's stationery and was squinting in the fading light, scanning the directions. "Your mother's handwriting—"

"Let me see," said Annabelle, leaning forward and looking over Max's shoulder, bracing her forearms along the edges of the front seats, her hair brushing the muscles at the back of Max's neck.

"See," said Max, "the parkway— Yeah— Exit eight— Fine— Turn off on Randall Drive— Uh huh—"

"You can't read this?" said Annabelle, almost in Max's ear— He turned his head to look at her and recoiled at the proximity.

"I was *saying* that— Look." He pointed at the directions, one by one, ticking them off. "We did that. Did that—"

"Are you sure?" said Annabelle.

"Did it," said Max, nodding and moving down the list. "Did *that*— I think we're *here,* you know, but there aren't any signposts this far out."

"Not a one—" said Douglas, watching the road slip past, progressing into a more heavily wooded area, and he turned on the headlights, bringing the dashboard to life.

"This says drive all the way down Randall and then left at the yellow barn," read Annabelle, leaning farther forward and pointing at the handwriting. "That's Emory Street. Then it's the fifth house."

"Yeah, the fourth mailbox and then the shortcut under the porch— And between the blades of grass and then over behind the tool shed," said Douglas. "And Chablis does this every *day?* I mean, what is he, insane?"

"It's not that far," said Annabelle, leaning even farther forward to tap the gas gauge, and Max fixated on Douglas and Annabelle's side-by-side arms, both wristwatches silver and gold. "I mean, it's been, what, forty minutes— You've got to get gas soon." Douglas swatted irritatedly at Annabelle's arm and she withdrew it.

"Here," said Max, pointing as they approached an intersection. The roads since the turnpike turnoff had gotten narrower, less well paved and populated, and all around them almost by design was precisely the sort of abandoned-object's flirtation with decay that had inspired Victorian homeowners to rust their own bridges—the red steel of the farm equipment and the rusted cables held their color against the dusk like a drunken man swaying late at night, withstanding the wind of the homeward road.

"It's really pretty here, actually," said Annabelle.

"Yeah— There was a field near Choate a bunch of us went to sometimes on weekends," said Max, looking out his window. Douglas signaled despite the lack of traffic, making a left as Annabelle sat back down. "You guys really missed out, going to school in the city."

"I didn't miss out," said Annabelle.

"Yes you did. Here's the fifth house, Doug." It was a small one-story affair—Douglas flashed another futile turn signal and took them in, killing the engine and stopping the tape in midsong, leaving the driver's door open as he trotted around a battered picket fence toward Nathan Chablis' front door. Max could barely see Douglas frowning comically back at the car before disappearing into the house, and he moved his head to watch a squirrel make its inverted way down a birch tree.

"So Chablis lives here. God, I'm so thirsty," Annabelle said, climbing over the seat and landing next to him. "I used to do that all the time," she said, twisting her T-shirt back into place. "But I used to be a lot smaller."

"Right."

There had been noise from the highway and music and now, by contrast, the car was quiet—a damp breeze tossed the grass and trees and sifted fragrance from the surrounding flowers in through the opened door, and Max caught Annabelle's scent, the Naget perfume that she somehow augmented, and noticed again how she had changed. He remembered again being frozen on a bed, Douglas' quilt adhering to his trembling legs as Annabelle screamed in anguish, slamming doors, not just once but rhythmically, like a die press, and he remembered that she'd been sent into this fury by a small blue airmail envelope carrying soaped stamps and stuffed with crumpled and illegibly scrawled tissue paper. As Max gazed deliberately away toward the phone poles standing against the twilight beyond the trees, his memory of the letter lying on the old Taft hallway floorboards lingered and combined with the bitterness of the black coffee that Greg had wordlessly handed to all of them, the coffee that they had obediently drunk, the squint to Greg's mouth and eyes and the perverse horror of the afternoon. Greg had always had a specific blindness about him, a practiced distractedness—Max knew that Greg had wept for Kennedy and abstractly hated him for it—but Giulia's face had betrayed the enormity of the upset balance, the momentum with which things had gone wrong, the lost peace, and Douglas had angrily done nothing while Max had finally spoken, said something, he didn't remember, but talked through the broken bedroom door in some soothing way that had panicked Annabelle completely. Looking at her now against the slow quartz ticking of the dashboard clock, he realized that her features spoke with greater authority than he remembered—she had once been half-pretty in a half-understood way but something had happened to the shape of her face, over the years, a natural enhancement that an adult might have forseen, awakening dormant shadows, and the effect startled Max with every change in her expression, every glance past the horizon, in her drowsiness or impatience, her narrowed eyes of anger or contentment, and with every new angle that he saw her from.

Annabelle was gazing out the car window and absently rubbing her jeweled ear, and Max took advantage of her looking away and indulged in a long stare, sliding his eyes down her T-shirt to confirm his suspicions about the dimensions of her chest, which were actually exceeded now that he had a clearer view. While he stared Annabelle winced and he slid his eyes toward the house just as she twisted around and stretched back across the car, rummaging in her Army bag with her waist inches from his eyes, and then collapsed back down holding a monogrammed platinum cigarette case.

"Jesus Christ," said Max. "What's wrong with the damn boxes they come in?"

"This was a gift from a man I knew in Italy," said Annabelle. "A painter named Carlo Giolitti— And besides, you know, invite me over when someone gives *you* a silver cigarette case so I can watch you throw it away. 'No thanks, dude, the box is just—' "

"It's platinum," said Max.

"What?"

"It's not silver. It's platinum. Platinum's about fifty times as rare as silver. You don't even know what—"

"It doesn't *matter* what the—" Annabelle grimaced as she interrupted him. "Don't be such an *appraiser,* all right?"

"Sorry," Max said quietly.

Annabelle looked at him and then smiled. "No, I'm—" she said, trailing off and waving her hand vaguely.

"You going to smoke in front of Chablis?"

"Max"— Annabelle snapped open the cigarette case and he saw that it was full of cotton swabs— "could you do this for me? I'm not trying to revolt you but my ear is driving me insane. My hands are shaking," she added, holding out the platinum case. "Could you—?"

Max sat up straight, selecting a cotton swab and tamping down the end while Annabelle snapped the case shut and inclined her head, as if listening, her face immobile while Max eased the swab into her ear, slowly, sliding it along the sides and guiding it back into the deepest recesses of her ear canal, thoroughly pressing against the smooth tympanic membranes, twirling and withdrawing the stick, which emerged brown with wax. "That's almost it," Annabelle murmured in a businesslike fashion, brushing her hair more completely out of the way. "Go deeper."

Max repositioned, using his free hand to steady her neck before sliding the swab's other end into her ear, pushing it back, and Annabelle winced. "Does it hurt?" Max asked, drawing the swab away. "I think I got it all— There's only two ends on this thing."

They both heard the screen door slam and drew apart, Max taking his hand from Annabelle's neck as Douglas emerged from the house carrying a nondescript suitcase, followed by Mr. Chablis, who turned to lock the faded door, the bending leather patches on his corduroy elbows darting in the dark like diamonds while Douglas hefted the suitcase into the trunk, blocking the back window. Max and Annabelle got out of the car, Annabelle returning to the backseat, Max pausing to shake Chablis' hand and then ducking to push Annabelle's Army bag out of the way before following her. Douglas slammed the trunk, courteously opened the shotgun-seat door for Chablis, and then circled round to the seat that Annabelle had just vacated, cautiously fastening his seat belt before starting the engine. The tape deck blared back on, making everyone jump. *Her friends are so jealous— You know how bad girls get,* Sting was in the middle of screaming. *Sometimes it's not so easy to be the teacher's pet.* Douglas jerked his hand over to snap off the stereo.

"Well, this is quite a nice automobile," Chablis said in his familiar mid-Atlantic accent, looking around at them, the dashboard light catching his smooth glasses and the flecks of silver in his beard. "Is this yours, Gantry?" Max smiled but the cotton swab snapped in two in his hands.

"How are you, Mr. Chablis?" asked Annabelle.

"Please, call me Nathan. I'm doing just fine, Annabelle." They had pulled out into the town again, such as it was, and Max saw that the grocery store had closed. "Well, Douglas, how do you like my little town?" Chablis asked, spiking the sentence with half-hidden sarcasm.

"Nice town," said Douglas. His unlined hands twirled the BMW's wheel, and soon they were back on the highway and the salmon fire along the western notches of the barely visible horizon had faded to a cool dusk shining through the telephone poles.

"Have I interrupted a pleasant evening?" Chablis asked after a moment.

"Not at all," Douglas assured him.

"We've been— I got to hear *Jake Hackett* read aloud, for one thing," Max said.

"By Bonomi?" said Chablis. "Oh my God. That old trash novel?"

"Yeah," said Douglas. "You've read it, Mr. Chablis? Nathan?"

"I made a pass through it at Groton," said Chablis. "Bonomi was still rather fashionable in the late forties—he would be introduced as exemplifying a retrograde eddy in American letters."

"American— Wait, how long was he *here?*" Max asked. "I thought—"

"I *knew* you'd get interested," Annabelle said, flipping on a blinding ceiling light while extracting her purse from the Army bag and fishing through it, shuffling club invitations and credit cards and an international student ID and extracting a folded clipping, which she handed over. Max opened the thin paper sheet, which he recognized as having been cut from some sort of reference book.

BONOMI, GIUSEPPE (1901–1945), Italian-American novelist, poet, and short story writer, born in Inganno, a village near Naples. The illegitimate son of an impoverished priest, Bonomi learned English as a schoolboy and worked as a correspondent for the New York *Post/Dispatch* and the Toronto *Star.* Having published several traditional romantic sonnets in *Collier's* magazine, Bonomi migrated permanently to the United States in 1922. A collection of epic poems, *The River of Angels* (1925) received a lukewarm reception and the disheartened author turned to fiction, penning stories that introduced Americans of great intelligence and faltering faith into European locales and situations. *August Light* (1931), a novel about a young woman's troubled visit to Paris, was moderately successful, and having thus secured a modest reputation Bonomi began moving within celebrated literary circles. "Too dreadfully young and at the same time too old," GERTRUDE STEIN commented upon meeting him in Paris, allegedly adding, "Beautiful warm Italian eyes but he will not be invited back." *The Story of Jake Hackett* (1935), a tragic romance about a fledgling priest pulled into a web of clerical intrigue, remains Bonomi's best-loved and most successful book. In 1938 Bonomi married the well-known New York débutante DIANA FOXWORTH, with whom he had a daughter, Miracola, but the marriage ended in abrupt separation and Bonomi soon departed for the American West, settling finally in Montana. During a sojourn in California Bonomi spent several weeks with JOHN STEINBECK, whom he revered, and this experience was later recounted as a fictionalized episode in *The Windmill* (1941). This dark and somewhat lengthy magnum opus, concerning an ensemble of characters facing growing premonitions of European war, is generally considered a failure, and Bonomi attempted to revise and re-publish the novel several times to no avail. Bonomi never attained the sort of lasting popularity that he desired and was found to be destitute when he died in a railway accident in Shelley, Idaho while beginning a fifth book, *The Country of the Saints.* According to EDMUND WILSON, "[Bonomi] was better than he knew, for his fascination with American landscapes allowed a freshness of vision and informed a fearless simplicity of intention that remains unmatched." SEE Mizener Kazin's biographical study "Bonomi and America" in *Examinations of American Literature* (ed. Alfred Turnbull, 1959).

"What's going on back there?" Douglas asked, peering toward the rearview mirror.

"Insurgence," Annabelle said, turning out the light. Max blinked and handed the clipping back.

"I really do get very tired of these immigrant philosophers," Chablis went on. "Dvorák, Rand, all these uninvited guests burdening us with their condescending yet daunted perspective on our cultural precipitates—I mean it takes a supremely adolescent personality to be so colonial as to abandon the riches of one's own civilization. All this childish fascination with puerile archetypes—these expatriates following teenage children down our highways looking for John Wayne or Aaron Copland or Norman Rockwell as if—"

"All those people are great," Annabelle said.

"—hunting for sentiment. Well, I suppose every age has its required reading," Chablis finished resignedly.

"You mean like the Romantic Age?" Douglas asked.

"I mean every age group," said Chablis.

"So what *happens* in this beautiful story, anyway?" Max asked brightly.

"Why are *you* in such a good mood?" asked Douglas.

"Ignore them, darling. What happens," said Annabelle, "is that Hackett gets, um— There's a sect of monks living in this concealed abbey near Venice, the Giovannian Order, and they've been there actually for hundreds of years, you know, generation by generation, this ritualized life, hidden atrocities committed, ritual murder as punishment for heresy, and what they've been doing is getting ready for these events, um, that they believe are ordained as commencing near the beginning of the twentieth century, which is going to be this sort of rebirth of the Counter-Reformation. So all these—"

"Well," said Chablis.

"—monks are— All right, but that's close enough. All these monks are led by Brother Morstan, a transplanted Englishman, who is the only one, at least as the novel begins, who moves around in the secular world, and when we meet him he's spent all this time mingling through Western society and he has all these great lines about how contemptuous and afraid he is. You getting this?"

"Sure," said Max.

"So when Hackett gets to Italy he doesn't know that he's arrived at this, like, crucial moment that the Giovannians have been planning for centuries. They're called Giovannian monks for the same reason they're located in Venice."

"I'm not getting you," said Max.

"Pope Leo the Tenth," Chablis explained, "was Giovanni de' Medici, whose father was Lorenzo the Magnificent. Naturally Leo was a great patron of the arts, given his lineage, which is almost all one can say about him, save that the Reformation began in Germany during his rule—he never quite grasped what was happening and his only countermove was to ban Martin Luther in 1521."

"So in Bonomi's book," Annabelle continued, "the secret order is founded on the principles of Leo's papacy, which was taken to be a great alignment of Roman Catholicism and the Venetian Renaissance, as well as the beginnings of the Counter-Reformation."

"It's a yin-and-yang thing, Max," Chablis said. "Bonomi believed that the Reformation and the Counter-Reformation started at the same time."

"That's silly," said Max.

"What do you mean, silly? It's brilliant," said Annabelle impatiently. "So Morstan has investigated the process by which the Giovannian Rule is copied down, generation to generation, and buried among their ancient manuscripts he's discovered and authenticated a lost deuterocanonical scripture translated from the Hebrew Septuagint Canon and realized that it's the key to their order, since it reveals that all Latin translations have subtly misinterpreted the visual iconography used throughout the New Testament. See, the Giovannians believe that the Venetian Renaissance laid the groundwork for the Enlightenment through manipulation of sacred imagery, and once the West is dominated by egalitarian societies founded on Enlightenment philosophy—meaning America and this century—then by scholastically challenging the papist interpretation of scripture they can reinstate the Church as the dominant force in Western Civilization."

"You're amazing," said Douglas. "You've got this, like, one thing you know and you never let us forget it."

"And now here comes this young American priest," said Max. "I think Bonomi was really confused."

"He was a poor novelist," said Chablis. "It's all a lot of simple tricks and nonsense."

"But all that's just background to the plot," Annabelle said. "Once Hackett hits Italy it's a love story pure and complicated."

"Oh, Douglas," intoned Chablis. "I've got a bone to pick with you."

"You do?" Douglas said, switching lanes.

"Yes— I brought Western Civilization to an end this afternoon, without you, sad to say."

"Douglas, you *didn't* cut Mr. Chablis' last class?" asked Annabelle nastily, yawning and curling up against the car door.

"Everybody else made an appearance. I'm not personally offended, needless to say," Chablis continued in vaulting tones. "I'm just saddened that you deprived yourself of the lecture. I mean, naturally, I can understand how—*humdrum* history can seem in the face of other temptations for the—"

"Gee, Mr. Chablis, this arrangement sure is lucky," said Douglas, watching the road. "I mean, I guess you were planning on taking a Greyhound bus to Dover, ah, or were you planning something else?"

Chablis took a moment to answer. "Yes— Have I told you about that interminable bus ride to Boston? The only relief I had from the monotony was my good fortune in chancing upon a friend of mine from the Harvard admissions office."

Douglas looked over briefly and he and Chablis smirked at each other.

"Good to have you with us, Mr. Chablis," Douglas said.

"Well, I enjoy talking with my best college-bound students," said Chablis. "They provide a unique perspective."

"So, Annabelle," said Douglas brightly, trying fruitlessly to find her in the rearview mirror, "what do you think, we've got Max Gantry with us, it's like a *reunion*—next thing you know Lisa Sparrow will show up." There was no answer. "Annabelle?"

"She's asleep," said Max, looking at her.

"No, I'm awake," murmured Annabelle, opening her eyes. "What'd you say?"

"Sorry. I couldn't see you— I thought you were awake."

"What did you *say?*"

"I said maybe Lisa Sparrow will show up."

"No way," said Annabelle.

"What happened to her, anyway?" said Douglas.

"Wait, I remember Lisa Sparrow," said Max. "I talked to her once in fifth grade."

"Last I heard she was at boarding school in Virginia," Annabelle said.

"She wouldn't talk about anything except devils and exorcisms," Max said.

"She *was* a bit odd," Annabelle said quietly. It had grown fully dark and Annabelle turned her head, pressing her forehead to the cold window and looking up at the starry sky. "Star light, star bright," she murmured, pivoting her face on the safety glass, watching the shadow of Chablis' head bob to look at Douglas and then straight ahead at the road. The car was dark and quiet save for the hum of the engine and the whisper of passing cars and the green etched glow of the dashboard, and Max turned in his seat and stared out the window, twirling the ends of the cotton swab absently in his hands and staring at the pale darkness of the passing trees.

THE TAFT COUNTRY house—the Civil War House—is on the outskirts of Dover on a hill that screens the view to the rear but allows passing cars a glimpse of the architecture, and every so often some motorist stops at the foot of the drive, presumably admiring the façade, before moving on. During Gregory Taft's Columbia Business School days, before the move, before her trip to Milan, before the Dover house was repaired and renovated, Annie would constantly sit out on the manicured lawn reading Kenneth Grahame or A. A. Milne or dozens of frayed British editions of *Asterix the Gaul* or *The Adventures of Tintin,* hunting for the next book through the jovial wreckage that filled the study—the overturned boxes of paperbacks, the Warren Report, Eldridge Cleaver, stacks of *Life* magazine, the bottles of Liquid Paper by the typewriter and the old basket for the cat that had to be moved out of the way of the black-and-white TV so that they could watch one of the moon landings or, later, Nixon's resignation. The Tafts had an old Chevy Malibu in those days—Douglas remembered the young Jane riding in the car, perched with her front paws atop the front seat, head and whiskers twitching in the hot breeze—and they would take the Malibu to the stores in town, before all the town stores changed. During those seventies summers they would spend weekend days at Dover Beach or on the porch of the Lawrence Hotel, returning to the house after ice cream or coffee late at night, when candles were put on the hotel tables and the stars shone through the huge summer trees down Union Street. The car radio played the Byrds, the Rolling Stones, the Doors, and while Giulia hummed along randomly Doug would, from time to time, ask her again whether the school would allow him and Max to descend onto its roof each morning in the F-111.

In the evenings after returning to the house Annie would take a bath towel out to the back lawn, choosing a place where there were no trees nearby and the horizon was a perfect band-saw circle, and after a while, bored with whatever he'd been doing, Douglas would join her, sometimes sneaking up and diving onto her back, wrestling her from behind while quoting their father's homemade bedtime stories—"Watch out! The Red Ghost!"—and pinning her face-up in the grass, wrists framing her head as she bucked around, her turtleneck streaking with grass stains, and finally pushed him off. Then they would lie flat on the cold ground, the damp grass sharp against their shoulder blades as darkness flowed like ribbons from the Old Woods and the last evening light faded across the hill and behind the vast and misted expanse of the lake—Annie would be silent and the stars would be high and distant and Doug would imagine the F-111 taking off from the field, from *exactly right here,* he would think, and sailing them over the lake and beyond the hills toward a bright place where the sun had not begun to set. They lay on the grass and the stars shone and then they stood and stretched and climbed the hill, past the lawn chairs, already damp and cold in the outdoor air, past the screen door where the local newspaper blew around and drifted against the screens, and into the bright house, and everything all around the house was dark, was close to darkness.

Before going to sleep Douglas would sit in his small wooden chair listening to the crickets and the wind and the family's voices downstairs, and at the end of each summer, as the wind got colder and the days got shorter, autumn approaching, September beginning and ending, when those days came, Douglas would think of the approaching school year, and, turning off the lights, would shuffle across the black room and kneel on the bed to face his window, leaning forward, breath frosting handprints against the glass, and sometimes he would be frightened, and whenever he was frightened he would remember being very young, when his father would ease his night fear with gentle stories of how the Red Ghost could be kept away. Outside beyond the glass and stone Douglas could see the ghostly grass stretching off toward the forest, and he would wonder if a company moving through Connecticut, a band of horsemen passing for some strange and noble purpose, might enjoy the momentary comfort of the Taft lawn chairs before moving on into the night.

chapter 13

They were progressing along a curved and wooded two-lane road, passing mailboxes and occasional small roadside buildings, and Douglas reached down for the main window controls, like a jet pilot grabbing for the throttles, and cracked all four windows at once, admitting a bracing draft of clean, clear country air. They had just stopped at a Connecticut Shell station, an hour and a half after picking up Chablis, who had insisted on paying for their gas with, as Annabelle described it later, "these ridiculous crumpled-up singles"—as they approached the town, cars were passing in the other direction, mostly station wagons owned by people who lived in Dover year-round and who characteristically forgot to turn off their high-beams, so that Douglas was routinely squinting and blinking as he drove.

"Is it much further, Douglas?" Chablis asked.

"No, we're almost in Dover," said Douglas. "A couple miles—we always stop at that gas station. It's routine."

"Come to Shell for Answers," Annabelle said, fishing through her Army bag for a moth-eaten brown cotton sweater that crackled with static.

"I can't believe how *short* the drive is," said Max, sighing with mild evening fatigue. "It used to seem to take forever, you know, during the seventies."

"I'm curious to see the town," said Chablis.

"You've never been here?" asked Annabelle, yawning, curled up on the car seat. "Do you know the town history at all?"

"Oh, Jesus," said Douglas. "Not this again—"

"No, I'm curious," said Chablis. "Enlighten me."

"No, I mean, I don't know all that much about it. There's an exhibit in the Lawrence lobby about— You know the Lawrence Hotel?"

"Peggy Winfield showed me an old engraving," said Chablis.

"Well, the Lawrence is where the town council puts all their memorabilia. Three families owned the town land, Winfield, Hatch, and Sher—"

"No," Douglas interrupted. "That's wrong—the Sheridans are from the olden days but the *Winfields* bought their estate from the Van Hausmanns back in the fifties."

"Right," said Annabelle, shaking her head.

"I mean, if you're going to subject us to this get it straight," said Douglas.

"Sorry. The Sheridan house is north of Union Street and the Van Hausmann house became the Winfield house, off to the west, and that's in all the guidebooks— You've been there, right? It's a beautiful house but Jack told me it's a huge tax drain somehow and they'll have to sell it someday."

"So what about the Hatches?" asked Chablis.

"Right," said Annabelle. "Frederick Hatch, the last one, turned out to be this religious eccentric, right, who gave this *unbelievable* amount of his grandparents' money to this nondenominational church in New Mexico— He sold the house to my grandfather and moved out West. It was, you know, it was in bad shape for a while, weeds and shutters, but we picked it up pretty cheaply. Since Dad hit, uh—"

" 'Financial maturity,' " said Douglas, changing lanes.

"Since Dad hit financial maturity he's sunk a lot of money into the place."

"Why do you call it the 'Civil War House'?" asked Chablis, grinning back at her.

"Yeah, what the hell is that?" said Max. "I never understood that."

"We always have," said Annabelle, shrugging. "Take it, Douglas."

"What? Oh, it has to do with these shenanigans between the Hatch family and the state senate during the 1860s—the house was supposedly built with money embezzled from the war fund. I don't know."

They passed an ornate sign, adorned with the Connecticut state symbol, that said ENTERING TOWNSHIP OF DOVER—Douglas sped the car around down the hill and onto Main Street and as they waited at the intersection of Main and Union, Chablis and Max looked around at the town. It was nearly ten-thirty and more than a few people were walking the sidewalks, where several of the closed shops were brightly lit and yellow lamplight shone through the windows of the old balloon-frame houses that flanked the curved and cobbled side streets—Max noticed the brick sidewalks and the wooden architecture and smiled at the pseudo-Colonial shingles identifying the oddity shops and the "package" store and the groceries. The façade of the Lawrence, across the intersection, was brightly lit and several people sat at the summer tables that had been put out on the big porch, having after-dinner drinks around small ruby-glass candles sheathed in plastic fishnets.

"What a charming town," said Chablis, hotel light reflecting from his glasses. "This is the Lawrence Hotel?"

"Yeah," said Douglas.

"Peggy Winfield's directions were that I was to call her from the hotel and she would send a car to get me," Chablis explained.

Douglas looked at him. "Right," he said, "but that was when she thought you were coming up by bus. The buses stop right in front of the hotel, is the deal, so she was expecting you to wait there. I mean, I can drive you right to the house."

"Well, I think perhaps it might be best if you just dropped me off here," said Chablis.

"That's silly. I can drive you right to the Winfield house—it'll take ten minutes."

"I appreciate that, but I've already imposed on your evening a great deal. It's already very late."

"Are you sure?" said Douglas, idling. Another car drifted up behind theirs. "Damn it," said Douglas. He signaled and then crossed Union Street and pulled over into a parking place across from the hotel. "Look— Really, Mr. Chablis, it's no trouble at all."

"But I've never had a chance to see the town. I won't mind waiting."

"It's ten-thirty, for Christ's sake," said Annabelle, yawning, curling up into another position. "Everything's closed." Douglas killed the engine and they could hear the wind in the trees and the murmur of voices from the Lawrence's porch.

"Look," said Chablis, "really, I appreciate your offering but it wouldn't sit right with me. I'll go to the hotel and wait for a car from the Winfields."

"All right," said Douglas, getting out of the car, sprinting around to let Chablis out, retrieving the teacher's suitcase and then accepting his handshake.

"Good night," Chablis said, leaning in the window and giving Max and Annabelle a charming smile. "I appreciate your patience."

"Oh, don't worry about it, Mr. Chablis, it was a pleasure," said Annabelle, and for Max, who was watching, her smile was somehow refined and coarsened by the fragrance of the country air.

"Good night," Max said.

As Douglas reëntered the car and started the engine they watched Chablis in his jacket and tie walk across Main Street and dart up the steps of the Lawrence, hefting his suitcase. Douglas looked around and then performed an imperfect U-turn and started back down Union Street, toward the intersection with Hopewell Street, which would take them past the town's final buildings, and Annabelle rolled down her window and leaned out, looking up. "Oh, yeah," she said. "You can see all the stars. Man oh man—"

"Chablis is such an idiot," said Max.

"I know," exploded Douglas, turning the tape deck back on. "What the hell was that?"

"He doesn't want to embarrass *us,*" Annabelle said, sitting up again, nodding with the music and lighting a cigarette against the wind—the particular aroma of the woods entered the car as Douglas turned off Hopewell Street and started down Blackfoot Road. "You know, he's *terrified* of Peggy Winfield— He didn't want to show up with the three of us, you know, dressed how we are or whatever."

"And he just ordered five vodka martinis," said Max, cracking them up.

"Man, you're *really* in a good mood," said Douglas, grinning around at him.

"I don't know why," Max said.

"You don't *have* to know why," said Annabelle, reaching to shake Max's shoulder. "It's the Dover air— It doesn't matter."

"That's the back of our property," said Douglas, pointing at a saw-toothed forest edge. "The Old Woods."

"I remember this," said Max.

Douglas dodged the car around the tiny carcass of a small, struck animal and continued winding along the dark deserted curving road, past mailboxes and reflectors that swept aside like sentinels, headlights flashburning the blacktop and the overhanging leaves, knowing every turn by heart. They passed a field of flowers with running water and Annabelle saw starlight shining in the stream and felt far away from the city.

MAX STOOD LEANING in the doorway of Douglas' small bedroom in the upper recesses of the Civil War House, feeling the softness of the threadbare floral carpet against his dirty bare feet, watching Douglas move around—he had pushed his bed on its casters over underneath the dormer window and was busy unrolling a thin mattress across the floor and draping sheets and a quilt over it, which, because it involved a lot of kneeling and lunging, was amusing to watch. The room was underlit by an old, nautical-looking cracked-porcelain table lamp, wearing an almost-shredded yellow shade, that stood on the floor next to a small blue-painted wooden bookcase.

They'd arrived and Max and Annabelle had hunted round the dark kitchen and made mugs of instant hot chocolate from the "boiling water" spigot on the sink, while Douglas had moved back and forth unloading luggage from the car and stacking it at the foot of the stairs. Max and Douglas had begun relaying the luggage up to the bedrooms—quietly—while Annabelle moved the BMW into the garage, where the Porsche was parked on the cold cement. The burglar alarm was flashing its red lights and they'd all felt the contraband adrenaline of the chocolate and the clean, clear air and the quiet country darkness that amplified their movements. Before going upstairs Max had wandered around the dark expanses of the ground floor, noticing the considerable amount of work that had been done on the house since he had last been there—the newly stripped and varnished woodwork, the distribution of a lot of furniture that he recognized from the old West End Avenue apartment, the redone kitchen and laundry alcove—while Annabelle had gone to have a cigarette on the back lawn, looking up at the stars, and had just leaned in to say good night.

"Watch out," said Max, pointing at the mug of hot chocolate on the floor near Douglas' knee. "Don't knock that over."

"Thanks," said Douglas absently, folding the bedcovers under the mattress and reaching to move the cup onto a chair. "You want to open the window and get a breeze through here?"

Max went over and raised the stiff wooden sash, admitting cool air and cricket sounds and peering through the screen at the near-total darkness outside the house. Stepping around the room, he scanned his eyes across the bookshelf's collection of aging children's books and tapped open the bathroom door to put his toiletry bag above the sink. "Look out!" Douglas said sharply as Max approached another door. Startled, he withdrew his hand from the new-looking doorknob and looked at Douglas. "Sorry. Just don't open that door— It doesn't go anywhere."

"What are you talking about? Is this new? I don't remember."

"Well," said Douglas standing up and retrieving his chocolate, "you remember back in the old days, that door wasn't there?"

"Wait, wait—" said Max, squinting at the door.

"It was just an outline on the wall. Maybe at the end in sixth grade there were some grooves in the plaster—"

"Sure," said Max, nodding. "It was for the sun deck, right?"

"Right," said Douglas, kicking off his loafers and collapsing on the quilt-covered bed, leaning against the wall by the open window. "It was Mom's whole idea— She wanted to put these doors here and over in Annabelle's room and have a deck in the gap in the house between them, and have a sort of outdoor terrace off the kitchen downstairs."

"So how long can that take?" said Max. "I mean, come on, that was years ago."

"I know," said Douglas, "but they had all these problems with the house—the stone superstructure turned out to be much more complicated than the original appraiser thought. Some restoration guy came out here and got the plans from the archives at the library and realized that it was, ah, that puncturing the back facade was a bad idea, so Mom got some New York architect to figure out a way to do it with some sort of freestanding structure."

"Yeah?" said Max, yawning, sitting cross-legged on the floor and reaching over to pull a book from the bookcase.

"But the doors were already put in," said Douglas, noticing the crisp night air from the window, the wind and insect sounds contrasting with the charged night atmosphere outside windows in New York. "Mom was berserk with this thing and Dad couldn't stop her from doing the doors. They had this big fight. So Anna and I have these two stupid doors that don't go anywhere— I mean, we're old enough that they can trust us not to wander through them or anything."

"Man, I am tired," said Max, yawning again and looking at his digital watch. "Let's hit the sack."

It was around eleven-thirty when Douglas and Max finally settled into bed, Max under the window, Douglas hospitably on the floor mattress, all the lights out, the windows casting dim mullion shadows on the ceiling.

"How you doing?" asked Douglas, leaning on his side and staring at the hazed night sky between the windowpanes.

"Not bad," murmured Max, obviously very tired. "Your parents are always so nice to me."

"Yeah, damn right—" said Douglas, yawning. "They really like you, Max. I can tell— My Dad gets this look on his face." Douglas absently rubbed his neck. "They've always liked you— I mean, it doesn't *bother* you, does it?"

"I don't know. No, of course not," Max corrected, speaking softly. "There's just— Jesus, have the last six months been as weird for you as they've been for me?"

"Maybe not," said Douglas. "What don't I know?"

"Well, Choate was so complicated—I went out with this girl for most of the year and it ended really badly, and I had some bad trouble with my mom."

"Oh yeah?"

"Yeah, usual routine shit— She's pleased about Yale and all that, you know, but there's a limit to— Every time I see her, I feel more and more like we just can't—we can't really talk like we could back before Dad left. She met my *girlfriend* once and it was total cold war, 'cause she's got— My mom's got these strange-as-hell views about what I should be doing with myself. She was really pissed about this weekend."

"Really?" said Douglas. "Why?"

"Well," said Max, "you know, she got involved with this leftist journal last year, you know, and she'd been with those people when she met me yesterday at the train station. So I was out last night, you know, and I overslept and she saw me for about five minutes before I left to meet you. I was gone a couple hours, right, and I got home and she was all set to have this big weekend with me— She wanted to take me out to meet this *man* again, she wanted to have this big sit-down talk with me about Dad and the financial aid forms and the summer, you know, and suddenly I'm packing to go to Connecticut and go to this big party. She was pissed— I needed some money, you know, and—"

"Look, Max," said Douglas, "you know you don't have to worry about paying for anything this weekend."

"Yeah, well, I appreciate that, thanks, Douglas," said Max, "but it's this pride issue for Mom. You know, she's got these revolutionary articles she writes and she *hates* the damn *Absolution Journal* set and William Huxley, you know, and Thorndike and the Winfields and all of that— I mean, she keeps going, I mention the Winfields, and she goes, don't— She gets all mad— She goes, don't you know who Ted Winfield *is?* I mean, what are we talking about with the Winfields, we're talking about oil money, right? Or what the hell is it? I mean—"

"Max—"

"No, I'm just saying, about my mother— She's like, that son of a bitch Winfield, you know, and I say, Mom, come on, and then— It's like in the old days, I'd go over to Ralph DiGrassi's house and Mom would get all worked up about *that.* I remember, she'd always be, like, Frank DiGrassi, that gangster. I'd go, Mom, Frank DiGrassi's just a lawyer, and Mom would be, oh, mob connections, evil money, this and that— She would always say, you know, there's this fucking *Brethren* everywhere, you know, so watch your step 'cause they're so crafty. I mean she sees me as a spy." Max sighed lightly, winding down. "And spies pay their own way," he finished.

"A Brethren. That's pretty good," said Douglas. "So your mom messed the thing up with this Choate girl?"

"Well," said Max, "I mean I should have seen it coming, when it— When she started, the chick would call, and she'd get on the other phone and talk to her. She kept saying she just wanted to talk to her—I'd be going, hang up, Leigh, just hang up now. So Leigh was in the city one weekend, spring break, you know, and Mom got back from some thing one night with the big man and she wanted to talk to Leigh and she wouldn't let her out of the house. It was a bad scene."

"Jesus."

"Hey Douglas!" said Max suddenly. "You know what? I'm really glad I came up. I'm actually looking forward to this Winfield thing."

"Cool," said Douglas. "Listen— Why are you so pissed at me about Jill Brooks?"

"Oh, fuck," murmured Max, rolling over. "Good night, Douglas."

"No, come on," persisted Douglas, hoisting himself on an elbow and smiling.

"Well, shit," said Max. "I mean what's the big deal? Just some— blonde little girl— That's all— Little baby cheekbones— With the *sportswear*— It makes no sense, Douglas."

"Damn it, why not have—"

"Forget it, Douglas. You're wasting your time. I mean she's beneath you. I'm serious, I know it sounds so arch and all, but she's beneath you."

"I wish she *was* beneath me," said Douglas, smiling.

"Come on," said Max, sounding disgusted. "I mean, what are you, some operator like Blanchard? You're this— I mean, you don't want to get caught up in that bullshit— You're this quiet thoughtful guy."

"Max, I don't want to debate philosophical issues with her. I want to drill her into the mattress."

"Wait," Max murmured after a moment. "Is this— Douglas— Are you looking for someone to deflower you?"

"Well— Yeah, actually," said Douglas, his voice very quiet.

For a moment they could both hear a distant car behind the night wind. "All right," Max said. "All right, I'm sorry— But you've got to watch what you're doing, Doug. Don't be so damn pitiful about it. Look, I *know* about Jill. She's a pro, she's a sidewinder. I mean from what I hear she's a fucking acrobat."

"So?"

"So you don't know any better. And you've got to watch out for the sidewinders— They can really fuck you over."

"Look," Douglas said, "Max, if I'm going to be— If I'm going to be *told*— I mean, damn it, hearing all the stories and with this 'watch out, watch out' all the time? I mean, I'm supposed to say, Okay, I understand, I'll leave it alone, I've learned some, you know, some lesson just by being *told* about it?"

"Yes."

"Fuck that," said Douglas. "I've got to actually find out."

"It's your show, man," Max yawned.

Douglas' night vision had arrived and the room looked clear, clear enough for thousands of things to be suggested by the outlines of the walls and by the bright stars out the window. "Max?" he said.

"Max?" Max was asleep. Douglas resettled and closed his eyes and soon slid smoothly into sleep himself, guided downward into darkness by the muted murmurs of the Dover crickets and the soft sounds of the quiet, random wind.

chapter 14

Douglas and Annabelle had known the Civil War House all their lives and they slept the sweet sleep of childhood whenever they were there, awakening without knowing the year. The comparative quiet, Connecticut after Manhattan, disoriented their dreams, and today was no exception—Douglas was curled in the quiet of his familiar room upstairs, and he could have been any age in that moment of waking. The bright morning sunlight filtered through his eyelids until he remembered Max's presence, which reminded him of all the Saturday mornings when he had been eight years old and Max had been visiting—Greg and Douglas would take the Malibu to town, meeting the bus at the Lawrence and taking Max home to greet Giulia and shyly wave to Annie, who would run away behind a white pillar as he and Douglas dashed upstairs.

"So what's this?" Max asked during one of those mid-seventies weekends as Douglas showed him F-111 drawings—inept schematics that Max would follow when he made his tempera paintings.

"That's the view out the window. Out the front window. There's us flying around. I called yesterday— Where were you?"

"Oh! I was at Ralph DiGrassi's house," said Max in a mad rush of energy. "We went up on the roof and looked at pigeons. Will the F-111 fly over ocean?"

"Yeah— Let's set up the fake plane in here so we can play the game." It would generally take twenty minutes—they would push furniture around to resemble the airplane interior and unplug all the room lamps and push the cherry dresser so it formed a corner with the bed, and while this was going on, Annie would walk into the bedroom, her red turtleneck and blue corduroys emphasizing her smallness, a clam chowder stain on her upper lip, poking Douglas in the ribs, and they would wrestle until he finally pinned her arms. "She still hate me?" Max would ask after Annie had left, and Douglas would ask Max what he'd brought—a gauge from a bike pump, a few square cutouts of worn radial tires from the abandoned car lot near Max's apartment downtown, all fodder for the closeted collection of bits and pieces of the airplane. When they had arranged the F-111 it would always be identically immaculate—two stools, exactly aligned, sat before Max's carefully painted window view, four lamps illuminated the corners of the room, the rug was aligned down a skewed axis and Doug's steering wheel sat importantly on his desk, while tinfoil and cardboard created the impression of contoured walls and string and paper formed a ceiling low enough to give the boys adult stature. "How long will it be?" Douglas would always ask, his mouth full of a slice of browned apple from the plate they had brought up from the kitchen. "How long can it take?" One Dover weekend Max finally announced that building the airplane was impossible, but by then who cared? They kept acting it out, alighting on the West End Avenue rooftop and adjusting their sweaters against the crisp morning air, the amber streetlights buzzing as they were extinguished up and down the avenues, their trousers flapping in the Hudson River wind as they stared uneasily down the sides of the building to the streets, empty save for a butcher's truck or a man on a brown delivery bike approaching the florist's, and the F-111 was perched on the rooftop, glowing and evil—they would dramatically swing back the steel clamps that kept the airplane anchored to the roof and pull the canopy back, and, once aboard the cramped cockpit, check various hand-built meters before firing the Air Force engines that would throw them from the roof with tremendous momentum, as if from an aircraft-carrier deck—they would watch Manhattan swing by silently as they aimed the plane straight up into the morning sunlight over New York Harbor and at eight years old fly unencumbered across the earth before returning to the dim upstairs bedrooms of the Connecticut house.

SO WHEN DOUGLAS woke up that Saturday morning in June of 1981 it took him a moment to remember the last day of school and realize that this was the day of the Winfield party. When he checked his watch it was almost noon—"Sausalito" Jane was asleep on Max's rumpled and empty bed, curled beside a folded paper shopping bag, and Douglas stroked her awake before wandering to the window in his underwear. The sky was bright and clear and a breeze stirred the hot wind through the trees behind the house—from this height he could see telephone poles in the distance behind the Old Woods, toward town, and the midday air was clear enough to allow a faint view of the tidal water of the sound far beyond. As he watched several redwing blackbirds flutter round the bird feeder, he heard the sound of dishes downstairs, and so did Jane, who left the room, and Douglas took a shower and put on jeans and a T-shirt and a pair of moccasins and went down to the kitchen, where Jane was restlessly pacing the floor around her milk bowl and Giulia was sitting at the table reading the local paper.

"Morning, Mom," Douglas said, putting a pot of water on the stove. Giulia flinched and then turned around.

"Douglas! Give me a kiss," said Giulia—she was dressed in black trousers and an orange turtleneck. Douglas walked over and kissed her and then went to get out a box of cereal and a bowl. "How was your drive?"

"Fine," said Douglas, pouring cereal. Jane, assuming that Douglas was feeding her, paced between his feet, craning her neck and yelling at him. "We ferried Chablis and everything. Annabelle talks so damn much— She gave her spiel on the Dover families and started in on Bonomi. Shut up, Jane, damn it."

"I assume you found enough blankets for your friend."

"Oh, sure, Mom," said Douglas, sitting down opposite her and reaching for the back section of the newspaper. "No problem— I gave Max the bed and used the thin mattress from the upstairs closet."

"Good of you," Giulia said absently.

"Mom, did you put some shopping bag on my bed?"

"Your trousers," said Giulia. "Your father and I stopped by Dunhill before leaving town last night—the man was very gracious. You should try them on."

"Great—thanks, Mom, I owe you one. Man, this has got to be the worst regional newspaper in the country— Where is everybody?" Douglas asked, getting up to put a pair of bread slices into the toaster. He looked around for Jane, expecting her to bother him again, but she had gone over to chase an imaginary speck through the air and into the laundry alcove.

"Well," said Giulia, putting the paper down, "your father went into town for groceries and to check in with the Lawrence porch crowd, you know, Paul Brooks and that bunch, and catch up on town news—"

"Right, right, as usual—" said Douglas, running water over his bowl and spoon and turning off the heat under the steaming kettle.

"—and Annabelle and Max got up before we did, I think. Annabelle left a note— Some person named Blanchard showed up early and they drove off with him."

"Nick Blanchard took them somewhere?" said Douglas, pouring coffee beans into the mill. "Oh, Jesus—"

"Something's wrong with that?" asked Giulia. "Should I not trust this fellow?"

"No, no—" said Douglas, loudly grinding the coffee before resuming the conversation. "I mean, not that you *should* trust Nick Blanchard, I didn't mean that— I just wish some people would stay in New York where they belong, you know, and not follow everyone *around* all over the place. And if I hadn't slept so late so I could've gone with them. Damn it— "

"Their note said they'd be back by noon. You should go outside," said Giulia, standing up and stretching. "It's a beautiful day— I thought maybe when everyone got back we could go to the beach."

"Good idea," said Douglas, waiting for his coffee to pour through.

"You don't sound too enthused."

"No, I mean, yeah, great idea," said Douglas, pouring a mug full of coffee, lacing it with milk and going to get his toast. "Is the note around here somewhere?"

"It's on the bulletin board," said Giulia. "I think you should pay attention to how much coffee you drink, Douglas. I don't want you to turn into a nervous wreck."

"Oh, of course not," said Douglas, getting out the butter and tangerine jam and sitting down. "I realize you're concerned about that happening."

"I'm going out back," Giulia said tersely, gathering up the paper and leaving the kitchen. Douglas sat for a few moments watching the leaves outside the kitchen window shift silently in the soft summer breeze, sipping his coffee, listening to the ticking of the old clock above the refrigerator. He made an omelette and another slice of toast, clumsily folding some cheese into the omelette, and he had just sat down to them when he heard a badly mufflered car pull up outside the house, followed by loud voices and the noises of car doors, and then the car drove away as the screen door slammed and Annabelle and Max rushed loudly into the kitchen.

"Hey hey hey! Good *morning,*" Annabelle yelled, dropping a plastic shopping bag by the refrigerator and lunging over to swipe a piece of Douglas' toast—she was wearing a grey THORNDIKE T-shirt rolled up around her waist and some navy blue janitor's pants. "You finally woke up, you jerk— Isn't it *amazing* out today?" she said, her mouth full, brushing a crumb off her tanned navel.

"It's a beautiful morning," Max sang, slapping Douglas on the head with another copy of the local paper—he was wearing Nick's sunglasses and carrying his camera.

"Douglas, you should go outside, you're so *pale,*" Annabelle overlapped, chewing toast, collapsing into a chair and picking up the magazine section.

"What the hell is with you?" asked Douglas, smiling and pulling his feet onto the chair's rim. "You guys shouldn't have done those *lines* when you woke up— Max, how'd you con Nick out of the camera?"

"Jesus," said Max, taking off the sunglasses. "I have so many memories of when I was ten years old connected with this kitchen. What?"

"I said how did you con Nick into lending you his thousand-dollar camera?"

"He has two of them," said Max. "It was just a whim— I thought if we did anything today I'd try to take some pictures. I always wondered what the big deal was, you know, what the hell the difficulty was in just *taking* pictures, you know, like these people do."

"Good— I thought it was just me who was sick of this photo business," said Douglas, glancing at Annabelle.

"What's happening today?" Max asked, flipping on the kitchen stereo—a nineteenth-century waltz was playing and he suddenly started dancing. The clouds had shifted and the noon sun brightened to further dazzle the room, catching Max now in profile, now backlit as he danced over and grabbed Annabelle, pulling her to her feet, newspapers dropping, taking her hand and waist and waltzing her around.

"Max, Jesus! Getting ready for *tonight,*" laughed Annabelle as Max moved her around. "One two three— One two three— Why, Mr. Gantry, you fox of a dancer!"

"Why, Miss Taft— You pretty much suck at this!" said Max. It wasn't true. While they danced they knocked against the edge of the table, causing Douglas' coffee to spill.

"Damn it!" said Douglas, leaning over and grabbing some towel paper. "Listen, we're going to the beach today."

"Cool," said Max, releasing Annabelle, sitting down and picking up the newspaper. "So, Doug, you were so baked last night I decided not to disturb you."

"Yeah," said Douglas. "I just woke up. Where did you guys go? Whose car was that?"

"Didn't Mom tell you?" Annabelle said, getting some coffee from the decanter. "You want some coffee, Max?"

"Sure," said Max, looking over. "Thanks."

"No problem— Nick Blanchard called so I told him to come on over. He's staying with the Sheridans. We hit the town and drove around real fast. His car is ridiculous. It's got a peace symbol on the hood."

"I've seen it," said Douglas. "Did you scope Dad?"

"Yeah," said Annabelle, "with the morning crowd on the porch— we didn't stop or anything," said Annabelle. "Have you noticed the way he blends right in up here? I think it's amazing the way he blends right in."

"Well, come on, Annabelle," said Max, looking up from the paper. "Aren't you going to tell him the news?"

"*Max,*" said Annabelle, laughing and tossing some of Douglas' wadded-up towel paper at him—Max caught it deftly and lobbed it into the sink and then turned back to the paper. "Lacrosse star, I keep forgetting," said Annabelle. "Yeah, Nick keeps trying to get a commercial assignment, and—"

"Right, he's Mr. Integrity," said Douglas.

"—he's trying— Well, you don't work at a *carpet company,*" said Annabelle. "He's got to pay his goddamned bills, Douglas."

"Yeah, forgive me," said Douglas. "Look— Could we talk about something else?"

"You don't even know why she's so pleased," said Max, grinning.

"Why are you so pleased?"

"Nick wants me to model," said Annabelle.

"Oh, Jesus, this again?"

"No, it's totally different this time— This is the real thing. He had some pictures of me—you know, those pictures from that day—and he showed them to this guy he met from Flash. He talked to this guy at Orpheum last night."

"Is that right?" said Douglas.

"That's right," said Annabelle. "So this guy, apparently he was *really* encouraging. Nick got off a couple of good ones at the Café yesterday and he brought them, too— All these pictures— So I'll see these people, you know, the formality, face-to-face thing, but if it works out they might sign me."

"Yeah—except, how do you know this isn't some bullshit?"

"Come on, Douglas," said Annabelle angrily. "Don't be such an asshole. This is *Flash Models.* The big-deal agency— I mean, it doesn't *get* any better than that. Flash is the fucking pinnacle."

"Yeah," said Douglas, sipping coffee, "but if I were you I'd make sure you can trust this guy. I mean, he could be, like, just some jerk."

"He's a *vice president.* Would you face the music?"

"Wow," said Douglas.

"Give him the quote," said Max, smiling.

"Right— The guy was *really* impressed, and—"

"Yeah, you said that already," said Douglas.

"No, wait," said Annabelle. "He looked through the portfolio and he said, 'She could go to the top.' I mean offhand, you know, but he *said* it."

"Jesus Christ. That's great—my sister the Flash model." Douglas took another sip of coffee and then shook his head. "Anna, I'm sorry, it's just startling."

"Talk about it," agreed Annabelle. "I should get a grip on myself."

"Some woman is going to try to make it to the party tonight," said Max. "Right? You left that out. Some Flash agent— But, you know, who can say, Douglas— We're going to have to, like, go to college and everything— There's no way we can skip that shit. Maybe I should play the guitar."

"It's not—" said Annabelle. "It's not that sort of thing, Max, damn it— Why do you have to—" She trailed off as Max made a truce gesture.

"That's really cool, Annabelle," said Douglas. "You know, it's weird— You look different. I mean"— he laughed —"you still look the same but you look different. I can't explain."

"She doesn't look different," said Max.

"I *feel* different," said Annabelle. "It's weird. I should go tell Mom—"

"Did you go anywhere else?" asked Douglas, going to get a third cup of coffee.

"We hit that little area at the end of Hopewell," said Annabelle. "I haven't been out there since last fall. Did you know it's totally changed? There's like four new stores or something— There's even an Aztec Clothes outlet."

"Really? From Madison Avenue? Aztec's up *here?*"

"I finally bought one of those Kamali swimsuits," said Annabelle, picking up the newspaper and flipping through the back pages.

"Jesus," said Douglas. "I can't believe what's happening to the town."

"Yeah, all of you people of course have nothing to do with it," said Max.

"We're fine," said Douglas. "We're Knickerbockers, damn it."

"Is anything good showing at the Triplex?" asked Douglas.

"The 'Triplex'?" said Max, grinning.

"It used to be the Palace," said Douglas. "You remember—at the end of Union, with the bijou lights."

"*The Four Seasons, Outland,* and *Xanadu,*" said Annabelle with sarcastic enthusiasm, having found the listing.

"That crap's still around? Jesus," said Douglas. "They're such a fly-by-night operation. Hey, Flash model, what's at the Showplace? —Oh, right, that's where *Raiders* is."

Max shrugged. "I'd see it again."

"I can't believe you'd even *think* of going to a movie on a day like this," said Annabelle.

"Yeah, we *are* going to the beach, aren't we?" said Max.

"When Dad gets back," said Douglas. "You want to go toss the basketball around?"

"Sure," Max said absently, downing his coffee. "Like the old days."

chapter 15

At one-thirty in the afternoon Annabelle sat on the stone steps of the Civil War House, leaning back against the front flank of the house, facing the sun, which hit her directly, shining off her gold wristwatch and her silver anklet—she still wore her THORNDIKE T-shirt and navy blue pants and she could feel the warm gravel between her toes and the hot sun along her legs through the dark cotton of her pants, making her knees particularly hot. With her sunglasses on she could stop squinting and thus get a clear view of her parents, who were loading a plastic picnic cooler into the BMW's trunk—Greg Taft was wearing a weightless white oxford, worn-out moccasins and olive- and grey-striped bathing trunks which cuffed above his knees, his shirttails flapping with the trees in the mild wind, and Giulia—who was folding a towel—wore her maroon-colored one-piece bathing suit under a white summer dress. Douglas leaned against the steel-colored Porsche farther down the driveway and Max was shooting the basketball at the hoop attached over the garage door.

Annabelle closed her eyes and listened to the breeze and her family's voices, the words like languid insects drifting over and back away with no force or urgency. "We ready to go yet?" came Douglas' voice. "I mean, we've been *standing* here for—"

"Relax, man," Max said softly. With your eyes closed during the summer, thought Annabelle, it's so easy to read everyone's mind.

"Just hold your horses," Giulia said, and Annabelle smiled. "Douglas, did you try those trousers on?"

"Oh, Jesus. Yeah, I did, as a matter of fact, Mom," said Douglas, dribbling the basketball, which, of course, bounced erratically on the hot gravel.

"They fit properly?"

"What? Yeah— The guy replaced the zipper, though— I'm going to need a welding arc to get it open."

"Do you want me to get some thread and—"

"*No,* Mom. It's just for tonight. Who cares."

"Annabelle, are you coming with us?" said Greg. Annabelle opened her eyes and looked down to see him squinting at her and shielding his eyes with his hand.

"I can't move," said Annabelle.

"What?"

"I can't move," Annabelle said more loudly.

"What— You?" said Giulia, laughing. She was using her chin to hold the edge of the towel that she was folding against her chest. "My daughter? I don't believe it."

"Hey, Dad, heads up," said Douglas, tossing the basketball to Greg, who weaved and caught the ball and tossed it to Max.

"Come on, Annabelle, come to the beach," said Max. "They've got this living room you can sit around in."

"Rotate, Gantry," said Annabelle automatically, her head still leaning against the front door frame.

"Hey, Anna, if you blow this off," said Douglas, "will you call Roberta? Or, you know, how *will* you do it?"

" 'Rotate?' " said Giulia, shaking her head.

"I feel so suburban," grumbled Annabelle while Greg slammed and locked the trunk lid, characteristically jingling the car keys around, dropping them, and grunting while leaning to pick them up. "Forget it, I'm not going," said Annabelle.

"Of course you say that," said Max, walking over, dribbling the basketball. "Come on—it's the first real day of summer. It's brilliant out."

"I know," said Annabelle. Max hopped from foot to foot on the hot gravel—the air was still and the sun burned undisturbed.

"Yeah, all you day-school chicks are the same," said Max. "What are you going to do—sit around the house and read *magazines?*"

"You sure you want me to come?" asked Annabelle. "I'm not sure I can keep up, you know, keep up with you boarding-school guys."

Max caught the basketball, tried for an ostentatious lay-up and missed, and Douglas got the rebound and made the shot. Annabelle jumped to her feet and wandered down to the car, hands in back pockets, Max following. "How 'bout it, Mom? Should I come with you? Can you wait while I change?" she said.

"Why not change at the beach?" said Giulia. "We'll swim a lot and have some lousy hot dogs."

"Come on, Anna, Jesus," Douglas blurted, lobbing the basketball into the garage and walking over. "What's the big deal? Just get your stuff and let's go."

Max looked around calmly, hands in pockets, bouncing on his toes. "Yeah, let's go," he said indifferently.

"You absolutely want me there?" said Annabelle. "You've never seen me in a swimsuit." Douglas abruptly swung around and began to wrestle her into the car.

"Cut this shit out and let's go," said Douglas, laughing. Inside the car, holding Annabelle's arms to the car seat, he muttered, "Don't make a fool of yourself."

"Get your hands off me," said Annabelle, writhing. "All *right*— I'll go with you. Let me get my stuff together." She glanced quickly at the view of Max, Greg and Giulia out the opened car door before continuing more quietly. "Should I wear the new swimsuit or my old one?"

"I don't even know," Douglas said, grimacing. "It's just the same Diver Beach as—"

"Dover Beach."

"—the same Dover Beach as from when we were six years old. Anna, I'm not the guy to ask about what to wear all the time."

"I guess not."

"Why are you acting like this?" asked Douglas, catching her arm as she opened the other car door. "Are you trying to act some new way?"

"I'll wear that new one," Annabelle said, walking off, leaving the car door open.

Douglas shrugged and leaned back in the car seat, putting his bare feet on the worn blue carpeting between the front seats near the parking brake and looking up through the rear-window defogger stripes at the bright sky. Max got in the other side, holding a small canvas bag with his blue-and-orange Walkman and Nick's Leica and a couple of books in it. "I feel like a press secretary," said Max.

"Oh, Jesus—" said Douglas.

"What?" said Max.

"Nothing. I just— It just occurred to me—"

"*What?*"

"Sorry. It's just I'm so used to the beach rhythm up here, you know? I've been thinking for the last ten minutes how nice it'll be to have some peace for a few hours. You know? Peace and seagulls. But I forgot."

"Forgot what?" asked Max.

"I forgot what weekend this is," said Douglas, rolling down the window and leaning out to watch his parents lock the house while Annabelle's arms closed her upstairs window. "I forgot that everyone from the damn school's going to be on the damn beach."

THAT AFTERNOON WAS the first time that Max rode with the Tafts since his own driver's exam in Manhattan, and he caught the way that Greg moved the BMW around the Connecticut roads like a professional and noticed the look of the land between the house and the beach. While watching the road Max fielded Giulia's questions about Choate as best he could while admiring the gold-ripening trees and brittle wooden houses spinning by. "It's so good to have you back," said Giulia warmly.

"You know, Max, during those summers when you were up here, we almost regarded you as a member of the family," said Greg, speaking as if to a board meeting.

"Well, you know, I almost *felt* like one," said Max, ignoring Douglas' glance.

"Yeah. Listen, what's the deal?" said Annabelle, fiddling with the plastic box that contained her new swimsuit. "Are we going right to the beach or into Dover for a drink or what? I want to try this thing out."

"What—like it's a piece of artillery?" said Max, grimacing. Greg and Giulia laughed.

"Well, no, but—" Annabelle stammered, turning red.

"Oh, look at that," said Douglas, leaning over and grabbing his sister's chin, grinning. "Somebody take a picture! Annabelle embarrassed!"

"Max," grumbled Greg gravely, "I think you're eligible for some sort of family prize." Giulia was still laughing.

"Oh, you can all go to hell," said Annabelle, trying resignedly to wrench out of Douglas' grip.

"Shall we go to town?" said Greg, looking around in his birdlike fashion.

"Watch the road, Dad," said Douglas.

"Well, it's up to the kids," said Giulia. "Into Dover? Right to the beach?"

"Um," said Max, "I'd kind of like to do some swimming before I eat anything."

"Make up your minds, here comes the turnoff," said Greg.

"The beach," said Annabelle. "Rock and roll. Let's do it."

Greg turned down the turnoff and drove around the sandbar and into the Dover Beach parking lot. It was murderously bright and many cars had been parked at haphazard angles and newspapers and crushed wax-paper cups had blown against the running fence that zippered the beach's hilltop edge. Greg found a parking space and everyone got out of the car and helped unload the trunk and then stood around squinting and exploring the burning film of sand on the parking lot surface with their toes while Greg locked the car. They walked up over the crest of the hill and through the gap in the fence in rough formation.

"All right, Mom and I are going to go change," said Annabelle, gazing around at the wide, crowded beach. "You going to the soda stand?" she asked Douglas.

"Give me a chance to sit down for a minute," muttered Douglas, hearing distant seagulls. Max stood looking out over the soft sand, past the blankets and people and toward the calm waters of the sound.

"Right, right—" said Annabelle. "Come on, Mom." She and Giulia started off toward one of the wooden buildings over by the trees, and then Annabelle spun back around. "Hey, Max."

"Yeah?" said Max, taking off his shirt.

"That 'artillery' line? That really wasn't all that funny."

"Didn't mean to offend."

Greg led Max and Douglas down toward the clearer areas of clean sand about halfway down the beach. "Man, this is so nice," said Douglas, kicking sand as he walked.

"What the hell is her problem?" said Max.

"Well— What did she say? I didn't hear her," said Douglas.

"Never mind," said Max. They found their territory and spread a large blue towel and sat down and took off their shoes.

"You know," said Greg, "Frederick Hatch lived in Dover for thirty years, at our house, twenty minutes away, and he *wasn't even aware* of the beach?"

"Oh yeah?" said Max, assuming that Greg was talking to him.

"Unreal," said Greg, shaking his head. Max got out Nick's camera and peered through it experimentally. Greg looked over. "Is that a Leica M5?" he said.

"Yeah," said Max.

"That's a very expensive piece of equipment," said Greg.

After a moment, Max said, "Well, obviously it's not *mine*— I borrowed it from Nick Blanchard."

"Well, I'm no Polonius," Greg said. "Does he know you've got it on the beach?"

"They brought them to *Vietnam,*" Max said, looking at Greg. "They're expensive because they're good at surviving *trench warfare.*"

"Right, of course," said Greg, smiling.

Douglas took off his shirt and leaned back awkwardly on his elbows, which made his shoulders stick up like parentheses. His usual beach apprehension waned when he noticed that he had more of a tan than Max did—Max's body was more precisely defined and muscular, but Douglas had the same dark and unblemished skin as Annabelle. Greg smiled at them automatically and then pulled a sheaf of computer printouts out of his bag and began poring over them, brushing away an occasional sand grain.

"Oh, Dad, you can't be serious," said Douglas, squinting over.

"What do you mean?" asked Greg.

Douglas waved at the printouts. "Come on, Dad— We're on the beach, for Christ's sake."

"Douglas," began Greg sanctimoniously.

"Oh, shit," said Douglas suddenly, waving his hands in appeasement. "I take it back, I'm sorry, Dad, I'm sorry—"

"No, I just think you might have a bit more perspective," said Greg calmly. "This is a blow-off summer for you, the last of a long series, and you can sit on the beach and not do anything and that's fine. I, on the other hand—"

"Dad, all right—"

"—am facing some pretty unbelievable bills and I've got to get these accounts nailed down this week."

"All right. I'm sorry, for Christ's sake," said Douglas. "And since when is this a fucking 'blow-off summer'?"

"And that's another thing, Douglas," said Greg, looking up again. "I've noticed more and more profanity peppering your—conversation."

"What, more than Annabelle? Come on, Dad—"

"It just makes a—I'm not sure it's the sort of impression you want to make." Greg laughed suddenly. "I'm sorry. I'm sounding like one of those fathers. Gosh, who would have thought?"

"Who indeed?" said Douglas.

"Doug," said Max lazily without opening his eyes, "you're gesticulating too much too."

There was a pause and then Greg and Douglas laughed. "You're on a roll, Gantry," said Douglas.

"Well," said Max, sitting up, "I'm just getting used to this. I mean, you guys— All four of you, it's incredible."

"Time to flatter the hosts?" said Annabelle, walking up behind them. Max and Douglas turned to squint up at her. She wore a white T-shirt tied round her waist with the sleeves rolled above her shoulders, over her new black swimsuit, a sleekly designed one-piece strapless affair which had been deliberately fashioned so as to look several sizes too small—on the sides, it barely came down below her elbows. "What do you think?" she asked. "Have I wasted some more money?"

"No—that looks *good,*" said Douglas. "I love those high-cut hips."

"Isn't that gonna, like, drive you nuts when it gets wet?" asked Max.

"Good question," Annabelle said, frowning while running her fingers over the swimsuit's bottom hems, which exposed her tanned pelvic bones. "I don't know *how* well this works in the water."

"If that thing just *stays on,* it'll be a miracle," said Giulia, walking up. "You want some glue for when you swim?"

"Jesus fuck, *everyone's* on a roll," said Douglas while rummaging through Max's bag of tapes.

"Watch your language," said Max.

• • •

IN THE BEGINNING Max just wanted to swim and Douglas just wanted to avoid the inevitable Thorndike crowd at the beach and Annabelle was not very interested in swimming or in avoiding the crowd. After a while Max went out into the water by himself—he swam a few powerful laps across the gaze of the crowds on the beach and then staggered back to the encampment of towels and collapsed, the sand gluing to his wet legs and the small black cord that he wore around his neck.

"Whoa," said Max, panting. "Man oh man."

"You swim very well. I was watching you," said Greg.

"Thank you," muttered Max breathlessly, still face down in the sand.

"Nobody seems to be around," said Annabelle. "You can relax, Douglas."

Douglas took off Max's blaring headphones and turned to Annabelle. "What?" he said.

"I said, nobody seems to be around, so you can relax."

Douglas nodded and put the headphones back on.

"You're determined not to pay attention to me, aren't you, Douglas?" said Annabelle. Again, he seemed not to hear. Annabelle abruptly picked up the Walkman and hit the "talk" button and yelled "Douglas!" into the mike. Douglas flinched and grabbed the headphones off and glared at her.

"What?" said Douglas, sounding beleaguered.

"You're determined not to pay attention to me, aren't you?"

"Annabelle, leave your brother alone," said Giulia, lying back on her wicker bag and reading the *New York Times.* Annabelle and Douglas looked at their mother and then back at each other, and then Annabelle shrugged, and Douglas mirrored the shrug and then put the headphones back on. Max sat up and began brushing the sand off his chest and then drying his body off.

"Hey, Max," said Douglas, stopping the tape, "do you still have all those Civil War lead figures?"

"What? Yeah, in a box at home," said Max. "About ten billion of them— Dad always asked what they were *for.* He would say, aren't you a little old for toy soldiers, Max? And I would say, you know, they're not toy soldiers, Dad, they're *Civil War figurines.* Remember— We went down to that store in Madison Square to buy them? Back when that whole D&D thing was going on?"

"Right," said Douglas. "Hey— Do we still have that bet about whether Luke or Darth Vader's gonna win?"

"You said it was Vader, right?" said Max. "Yeah, bet's still on."

"You guys want to go up to the concession stand?" said Annabelle.

"Sure," said Max, pulling on a CHOATE TRACK TEAM T-shirt from his bag. "I'd love something to drink. You coming, Doug? Hey, man—" Douglas had started the tape again and Max reached over and clicked it off. "Come on, let's go get something to drink," he repeated to Douglas.

"Fine," said Douglas, widening his eyes blankly.

"We'll be back in a little while, Mom," said Annabelle, standing and picking up her bag, and the three of them walked across the sand and over the dune ridge, passing the running fence and approaching the concrete bungalow that contained the concession stand and the strange bathrooms. "Where the hell *is* everyone?" Annabelle asked, pushing her sunglasses back as they entered the shade, where quite a few people stood at the chest-high Formica tables in bathing suits, drinking sodas out of big wax-paper cups, and a big stereo radio was belting out Styx's "The Best of Times." Max ran his eyes over the prices of hot dogs on the corrugated plastic "Sprite" board and bought a small Pepsi, handing a soaking-wet dollar to the blasé person behind the counter and then wandering back over to the Tafts, gulping soda, the cold crushed ice hurting his teeth.

"Annabelle!" someone called—they turned to see Jack Winfield standing by one of the wooden posts, wearing surfing jams and a T-shirt, his short hair sticking up Army-brat style, his legs pale.

"Hey, Jack," said Douglas, "you hitting that Henry James real hard?"

"Douglas, you psychopath," said Jack, wandering over.

"Hey, Jack, what's up, man?" said Max, swallowing the "man" as if it were a punctuation mark.

"Max Gantry! Wow," said Jack, walking over and shaking hands with Max, gold Rolex flashing. "How's it going? Are you here for the weekend?"

"Yeah," said Max. "These guys brought me up."

"Well, you *are* coming tonight, right?"

"If it isn't a problem, yeah," Max said, grinning. "Wouldn't miss it."

"Great," said Jack, frowning. "Except, Mom's got the driveway guard slaves— You may need an invitation."

"Oh— Come on, *Jack,*" said Annabelle. "You giving my people a hard time?"

"No, no, no," said Jack. "No way."

"Well, good."

"Are you psyched?" Jack grinned, squinting in the sun.

"Talk about it," said Annabelle, nodding. "Mom knows Senator Rollins— That's one thing."

"Cool," said Jack, nodding.

"Why are you— Jack, are you here with your family?" asked Annabelle. "You know where everyone *is?*"

"No," said Jack. "I mean, yeah, I do—I just came looking for Duane. The rest of us are over at the Lawrence bar having some drinks."

"That's what I thought," said Annabelle. "Man, Duane and Amy are so cute."

"They're not here, though," said Douglas, suddenly doing a Bronx accent. "They ain't here, they ain't here—"

"Gee," said Jack, rubbing his neck, "I wonder what they're doing right now."

"Maybe *she's* on top this time," Annabelle said, prompting Max and Jack to laugh. "Wait, they're *serving* you at the Lawrence? How the hell did that happen?"

Jack gestured with both hands, resignedly indicating himself—"Hey, I'm Jack Winfield"—his last-minute sarcasm saving the answer.

"Of course," said Max, looking away.

"Well, let's *go,*" Annabelle said, looking back at the running fence and then at the others.

"Annabelle," said Douglas. "Shouldn't we tell—"

"Oh, come on, *Douglas,*" said Annabelle. "Would you lighten up?"

Annabelle led the others over the fenced ridge to the parking area, approaching their car and opening the doors for the others. "Man, I never even saw you swipe the keys," said Max.

"Oh, you guys taking the Beamer? Um," said Jack, "look, I've got my car here and I don't think I'm coming back to the beach— I think I'll just follow behind you."

"Okay," said Annabelle. Jack walked over to his dark-green MG, got in, started the engine and pulled out of the parking lot, and Annabelle drove out behind him, Max in the backseat, Douglas beside her. "Put your clothes on, you guys," she said. "They have that rule in town."

"Right," said Douglas, struggling to pull his jeans on while Annabelle screeched the car around the signpost onto the road into Dover, slamming into each gear with minimal attention to the clutch. "Jesus Christ, watch it!" Douglas shouted. "Annabelle drives like a maniac," he said over his shoulder to Max.

"Great, get us all killed," said Max, contorting himself in order to pull his pants on. They followed Jack's car around the corner into Dover and parked behind him on Union Street next to the side of the Lawrence. Annabelle killed the engine and they got out just as Jack walked over, squinting in the sun, hands in pockets, kicking the sidewalk curb while he waited.

"Annabelle, come on," said Douglas. "You can't go into the Lawrence like that."

"What?" Annabelle said, locking the car and hopping around barefoot on the hot asphalt of Union Street, still wearing her swimsuit and T-shirt. "That's right, that's right," she said suddenly, leaning to reopen the car door and pull out the "Aztec Clothes" shopping bag, squinting and brushing her hair back as she pulled out a folded pair of white cotton trousers, cut off the price tags with the Swiss Army knife that Max handed her, and leaned against the trunk lid to put them on, pulling the drawstring tight around her waist and then ducking back into the car to fish out her shoes.

"We shouldn't stay too long," said Douglas as Annabelle relocked the car.

"I know," said Annabelle, tossing the keys to Douglas, who had pockets. "Jack, can I have your car?"

"If it were mine to give—" said Jack.

"Jack, darling, everything's yours to give," Annabelle said. "Can I call you Jake?"

"No," said Jack.

They mounted the white wooden steps onto the Lawrence porch, threading their way between various local people and bus tourists who sat around in the wicker rocking chairs. "Where is everyone?" Annabelle asked, holding the screen door for the others.

"Follow me," Jack said, leading them through the dim, ornate lobby, past revolving racks of postcards and well-dressed people in armchairs by the fireplace. They crossed a Colonial dining room, where several senior citizens and a few newlyweds attacked a very late lunch, and ducked through an archway into the Lawrence bar, which had a low wooden ceiling and was decorated with pewter tankards along the walls. Jack nodded at the waiters as he guided them through a pair of plain French doors and back outside, toward the faint sounds of silverware and voices, onto a shaded brick terrace that faced the hotel's courtyard, which was arranged in a way that drew attention to the centuries-old architecture, half sunlit by a square of flawless blue sky—there were a great number of round, glass-topped metal tables beneath lemon-and-white-striped umbrellas, cluttered with frost-beaded exotic drinks and smooth pie-slices that caught the sun and flanked by nondescript people in cast-iron chairs who all seemed to be wearing tennis or golfing outfits. Jack led them across the flagstones and white gravel toward a loudly occupied table beneath a white trellis.

"Hey!" said Wally Patterson, turning around—he looked almost exactly as he had the previous afternoon, wearing a T-shirt with a sweater vest, cutoff jeans, loafers and sunglasses. With him were Stephen Leonard, Nick Blanchard, Tina Foster, and Michael Cadenhead, surrounding two of the round tables that had been dragged together—the tracks in the gravel were still visible. A sixth chair had been pulled out and draped with a white sweater.

"Amy and Duane are AWOL," said Jack, tossing a fresh pack of chewing gum to Wally and moving to drag up three more chairs. "But I found the Tafts."

"Obviously," said Wally. "How's it going, Annabelle—you fucking *truant*. Hey, Douglas." Douglas and Annabelle said hello.

"Hey, girl in white," said Tina, cocking her head, holding an arm out toward Annabelle—she wore a yellow sundress and her guitar case leaned against Wally's chair. "What's up, girl?"

"Hey, Foster Girl," said Annabelle, moving over next to Tina, taking her hand as she leaned against the side of her chair, arm around Tina's shoulder, Tina's head against her waist. "Who's sitting there?" asked Annabelle, indicating the empty chair.

"Local fool," said Wally, sliding a stick of gum into his mouth.

"Oh, now— Come on," said Tina, releasing Annabelle, who joined Douglas and Max in sitting down.

"Sorry, sorry," said Wally. "The local sidewinder. Jill Brooks— Hey, Tina, you going to carry that damn banjo around the rest of your life?"

"Until the end of the world," Tina said dully.

"Hello, Mike," said Douglas, glancing at Michael, who looked uncomfortable, his hair sticking up in back, glasses sticking out, turtleneck incongruous in the heat.

"Hey, Douglas, how are you," Michael said, brightening.

"Not bad," said Douglas. "I saw *Astroturf*—it's looking good."

"Thanks," Michael said eagerly. "It was all right—we had some altercations with the printer so we couldn't get it till yesterday."

"Altercations, huh?" said Wally, finishing his drink, chewing gum.

"Excuse me. Excuse me," said Jack as the white-jacketed waiter walked by. The man paused and looked at Jack politely—he was probably in his mid-twenties. "I'm sorry. Could we have another round, please, when you get the chance?"

"Of course," said the waiter. "Let me just make sure I've got it straight— That was a Tom Collins, two gin and tonics, a vodka tonic, a screwdriver—"

"And another vodka tonic for me," said Jack. "Annabelle? Max? Douglas?"

"Gin and tonic," said Annabelle, smiling at the waiter, who smiled back.

"Same," said Douglas.

"Scotch on the rocks for me," said Max.

"All right," said the waiter.

"Could you just make out a new check?" Jack said, holding a platinum American Express card out between two fingers to the waiter, who took the card, nodding.

"Can I see your fake ID again?" asked the waiter. "I'm sorry, it's this check-by-check state law."

"Sure," said Jack, handing over another card, which the waiter accepted before leaving.

"I like *him,*" said Annabelle, watching the waiter walk away. "He's cute."

"I know," agreed Tina, nodding, flaring her eyes, her enthusiasm not reaching her voice. "Local boy— *I* should get a house up here."

"Hey, Bill Coleman's coming to the party, right, Jack?" said Stephen.

"You bet he is."

"So Duane and Amy weren't at the beach?" said Nick, speaking for the first time, his voice cutting through the others somehow—he was leaning back in his chair with his legs crossed, unshaven behind yet another pair of vintage sunglasses, looking urban in pinstripe trousers and a thin silk tie.

"I can't *imagine* where they'd be," said Annabelle, and everyone laughed as Jill returned to the table.

"Oh! Hello," Jill said, having suddenly noticed that the others had arrived. She wore a teal-and-white-striped dress, her hair flatteringly pulled back.

"What's up, kid," said Annabelle, pointing. "You know Max Gantry?"

"Of course," said Jill, sitting down. "Hey, Max."

"Hey, Jill," said Max, smiling benignly.

"Hey, *Douglas,*" said Jill.

"How you doing," said Douglas weakly, and Tina and Nick laughed covertly as the waiter arrived with the drinks, distributing them atop green-rimmed paper coasters.

"I reached my Dad, Mike," Jill said brightly. "You can stay with me tonight."

"Oooh," everyone said, drawing glances from other tables—Jill looked startled and then flustered as Michael reddened shyly and Douglas came close to spilling his drink.

"So, Mike, how are you?" said Max.

"You remember the time we put shaving cream on everyone while they were asleep?" said Wally. "We put all that shaving cream on Steve and it evaporated, and he woke up and was like, hey, somebody put a *little bit* of shaving cream on me."

"How are *you?*" Michael said, reaching over to shake Max's hand. "I haven't seen you since—"

"Eighth grade," said Max. "So you did *Astroturf?*" Douglas had nervously folded a paper placemat into quarters, and he stowed it in the back pocket of his swimming trunks.

"That's right," said Nick, who was obviously keeping his sandy-voiced comments to a minimum, confident of everyone's attention. "Every time there's some thumb action Mike's got the words."

"Right," said Michael. "And Nick's got the pictures— Soon it'll be pictures of Annabelle everywhere, right?"

" 'Thumb action?' " Max said skeptically.

"Oh, Christ, Mike, keep quiet," said Nick, fiddling with his camera, which shone blindingly in the sun as it moved.

"What?" said Tina, looking between Mike and Nick. "What are

you guys, Starsky and Hutch?" Everyone laughed. "Anna, what do you think, now we've got *these* two, you know, riffing off each other all the time. I mean would you ever have predicted?"

"Never," said Annabelle. "But, you know, it's not that weird— I mean they're, you know, practically the same *guy.*"

"Ex*cuse* me," said Nick, exhaling roughly.

"*Come* on, Nick. I read the litmag," said Annabelle, smiling impishly, looking at Jill, who was looking at Wally. "My own *brother* did the footwork here— Nick the quick going around with the 'I like Mike' routine— They're both after the same thing."

"What? I don't get it," said Jill, looking around—her gaze slid over Douglas' and he smiled slightly, and she smiled back, a bus-waiting smile, and he looked away and reached for his drink.

"Wait," said Tina, "what's this, Nick? Pictures of Annabelle everywhere?"

"No comment," said Nick. "Ask Cadence-head."

"Mike?" Tina said doggedly.

"Nothing," said Michael. "Nick mentioned something about a modeling contract."

"Well, it's about time," said Wally, looking at Annabelle.

"Really?" said Jill. "Wow. Annabelle, I'm so jealous."

"Don't be," said Annabelle. "Nothing's happened yet."

"I think Ralph DiGrassi may be in town," said Stephen, leaning back and fiddling with a box of Lawrence Hotel matches.

"Oh, shit," said Nick, while a few other people groaned. "That asshole—"

"Is he going to crash the party?" said Wally. "I'll throw him in the fucking duck pond."

"Wally," said Annabelle.

"Don't we have to go, Annabelle?" said Max, somewhat abruptly.

"In a minute, in a minute," said Annabelle. "Wait, is this a big deal? Jack?"

"I think *Ralph* shot J. R.," said Tina, provoking some mild laughter.

"No way— It was Cliff," said Jill.

"Oh, I don't know," Jack was saying. "It's not like *Brezhnev's* gonna be there. I just wish— Well, maybe he's not coming. We'll see what happens. DiGrassi. Damn it—"

Everyone sat sipping their drinks silently for a moment. "Ralph came up to me yesterday," Michael began, "and said the magazine was for shit but he liked the pigeons."

"Hey, you know who *else* had a pigeon fixation?" Wally said. "Bert on *Sesame Street.*"

"You really know how to hit a guy where he lives, you know that, Wally?" said Max.

"Sorry, Max," said Wally. "I don't want to demean your childhood or anything."

"That's not what I meant," said Max.

"Wait, relax," said Jack. "Calm down, Wally. What's the matter with you?"

"Sorry," said Wally.

"I don't know," said Tina. "I always *liked* Bert. I thought he was cute."

"Did he have a high F.Q.?" said Annabelle, smiling fiendishly.

"Well, I don't know about all *that,*" said Tina.

"What's F.Q.?" said Wally.

Tina and Annabelle looked at each other. "Should we tell them?" said Annabelle.

"It's really embarrassing," said Tina. " 'Fuckability Quotient.' "

"What?" said Jack, cracking up. "Wait, that's hilarious—"

"That's from ninth grade," said Annabelle, stretching and rolling up her T-shirt sleeves.

"What— You'd sit around *rating* everyone?" said Stephen. "Is that what you were doing all those times?"

"Well, yeah, we did," said Tina, smiling at Annabelle.

"I heard about that," said Jill.

"Yeah, we'd look through magazines," said Annabelle, "and then we'd talk about people at school, right, Foster Girl?"

"So who scored high?" said Wally, leaning forward and grinning at Annabelle.

"Anna, we should get back to the beach," said Douglas.

"Yeah, yeah, in a minute," said Annabelle.

"We had a list," said Tina. "Well, I mean, for *me* it was a list— You know, a top ten list or whatever. For Annabelle it was more of a *checklist.*"

"Oh, fuck you," said Annabelle, flinging a wadded-up Lawrence coaster at Tina.

"What—" said Tina, laughing. "It's not true?"

"Well, thank you both," said Wally. "I'm flattered."

"Naturally I made a few mistakes," said Annabelle, looking at him.

"I hope you do as well with this chick from Flash," said Nick quietly.

"Amen," said Jill, nodding.

"It's not this fucking solemn thing," said Annabelle.

"No," said Nick. "Their list pays better, that's all— I mean, find the cultural mainline, you've found the money. As we know, right, Jack?"

"Oh, shit, don't remind me," said Annabelle. "I'm so nervous about this business."

"Nick," said Jack, "my people didn't find any cultural mainline, whatever you said. They just found the wells."

"Brilliant, Nick," said Michael, shaking his head. "It's just fashion photography."

"*Just* fashion photography?" said Nick incredulously.

"Blanchard philosophy," said Wally. "*How* many Thorndike classes did you fail, Nick?"

"Annabelle, we've got to go," said Douglas. "Mom and Dad are going to be real happy not having the car."

"All right," said Annabelle, standing up. "I'm sorry, we've got to get back to the beach. Thanks for the drinks, Jack."

"My pleasure. See you tonight," said Jack.

"Take it slow, Foster Girl," said Annabelle.

"See you later," said Tina.

Douglas and Max said goodbye and followed Annabelle back out through the hotel. "Nice bunch of people, the Thorndike crowd," said Max as they crossed the porch.

"They really are, is the thing," said Annabelle as they trotted down the hotel's front steps. "I'll meet you guys at the car," she added suddenly. "I'm hitting the store."

"What?" said Douglas.

"The package store. You know," said Annabelle, spinning back as she walked off. "This round the brunette chick's paying."

chapter 16

Max stood at the edge of the water and looked out at the surface of the sound and at the row of sailboats moored near the shore, and he was standing there squinting in the still-bright late-afternoon glare off the whitecaps in the water when Greg walked up, greying hair whipping in the wind, his hands in the pockets of his striped shorts beneath the hem of his white oxford, sleeves rolled, Rolex band catching his arm hairs. Greg stood next to Max and silently joined him in looking out at the sound.

"It's quite a beach, isn't it?" Greg said.

"It's beautiful."

"You're enjoying your stay, Max? You know if there's anything you want or need, anything that— Anything that Giulia and I can do for you, just ask."

"Thank you," said Max, returning Greg's look. "Thank you. I really couldn't think of anything. This is—" He waved his hand across the view of the beach. "I mean you know I love it up here. I've always loved it."

Greg smiled blandly and turned toward the water, and then turned back, as if something had just occurred to him. "Max— I don't know how seriously you take this thing tonight. God knows I can't imagine anyone taking it less seriously than me— But it's— There's a certain polemic of appearances around here, and at the Winfields'— You know what polemics are?"

"Yeah," said Max. At the edge of his vision, near the shore beyond the beach, toward the sailboats and the hills farther away, a woman stood in a scarlet catamaran, dropping and folding a white mainsail.

"My wife is constantly stressing these things to me," Greg went on. "If you need a cufflink or a necktie or you want your shoes polished or you want to borrow a shoehorn, please don't feel the slightest hesitation in asking me. God knows I've got enough of that sort of stuff to last me decades. I just wanted to make sure you were comfortable in asking."

"Thank you," Max said, turning back toward Greg.

"I mean it. Don't— Don't think anything of it. Douglas tells me you plan to study art history at Yale?"

"Yeah, that's right."

"Giulia and I just thought we'd drive into Dover and have a drink at the hotel," Greg said. "You mind if we leave you here for a few hours?"

Max shook his head and then realized that Greg was also watching the woman in the catamaran and couldn't see him. "Sure, fine," he said. "Take as long as you want."

Greg smiled and patted him on the shoulder and walked away, and Max continued watching the sailboats twirling gently round their moorings in the shifting wind. He stood for a few minutes alone and then suddenly something pinched his waist from behind, making him flinch violently and turn around.

"Come on, Max darling," Annabelle said, releasing him and grinning whitely through the strands of black hair curling across her face. "Mom and Dad leave, we hit the south dunes with six-packs— You coming or what?"

Max reached for her waist, his fingers slipping against her smooth rib cage before she pulled away, the T-shirt catching his fingers. "Yeah, of course I'm coming," he said. "Lead the way."

Annabelle sprinted toward the parking lot, jogging up the hill and passing her parents, who moved more slowly, and by the time Max had rejoined Douglas at the towels she had returned, panting, lugging the paper bag she'd gotten in town and dropping it in the sand.

"All *right,*" said Douglas, grinning. "Annabelle, babe, you pulled it off— I tried to stall Dad with the basketball—"

"*That* was real effective," said Annabelle, sitting down.

"What—?" said Max, smiling.

"Well, damn it, everyone was *outside,*" said Douglas, trying to peek in the bag, getting slapped away by Annabelle.

"And I barely got the shit out of the car before Mom and Dad took it away," said Annabelle, still a bit winded.

"Amazing," said Max. "You two could pull anything off."

"Anything at all," said Annabelle, rubbing Douglas' shoulders. "We going to the dunes?"

"Fine with me," said Max.

"Max, you *do* have a nice body," said Annabelle, squinting at him.

"Thank you," said Max, shifting his legs and waving his hand in a beckoning gesture. "Come on— What's the catch?"

Annabelle smiled with one side of her face. "I guess that 'nice' is just 'nice.' How's that?"

"Nice," said Max, looking away.

"I mean," said Annabelle, still rubbing Douglas' shoulders, "anything less than 'nice' you don't even *say.* Jesus, are you always this *tense?*"

"Yeah, but—" Douglas twisted to look at her. "It's also— I mean, it's like something's going to *happen* tonight. Not just the damn party but something happening."

"You guys are in for something. To hell with this." Annabelle relinquished Douglas' back and he shrugged and rolled his shoulders. "Let's hit the dunes."

"You go ahead," said Douglas, standing up and stretching. "I'm going to get a pack of cigs."

"Get White Camels," said Annabelle, hefting the sodden paper bag.

"Get Marlboros," said Max, slinging Nick's camera over his shoulder.

"I'll get both," said Douglas, sprinting off.

MAX AND ANNABELLE sat on the edge of a high dune surrounded by sand and tufts of grass, several empty beer cans and the wet paper bag between them, a bristle of extinguished cigarettes sprouting from the sand near Max's foot. The beach had gotten darker and the shadows longer and Douglas had gone down to wander near the shoreline, and they watched him from a distance as the waves erased the black dots of his footprints and the gulls cleared a path for him.

"The last of the sun," said Annabelle. The threadbare clouds had cleared and they watched as the new sunlight, clear and bronze, brushed the water that followed the waves. Max took off his shirt and felt the sun on his pale shoulders and stretched, his arms raised, his hands on the back of his neck, and Annabelle reached over and stroked her fingers along one of his arms. "Wait, do that again," she said.

"What?"

"Flex your arm again." Max clenched his arm and Annabelle ran her hand over the muscles of his shoulder and his upper arm. "Man, you were lying before, weren't you? You *did* do some weightlifting."

"Yeah, I did some for track, you know, but it was stupid."

Annabelle pulled off her T-shirt as Max took another beer from the sodden bag, his head swimming in a way that was enhanced by the renewed beach heat, and he lit another cigarette as Annabelle began spreading sunscreen onto her legs and hips and then onto her arms. The beach was nearly deserted and they could faintly hear the seagulls that drifted overhead—a rusted and tilting orange oil drum stood square against the clear sky, flecked with topographical rust and shining along one edge like a crescent moon. "Max," Annabelle said, "would you do my back?"

"Sure," said Max, putting down the beer can and screwing it into the sand so that it stayed upright. He put out the just-lit cigarette with the others and took the tube of sunscreen, walking on his knees to position himself behind Annabelle, and as she arched her back he began thumbing the sunscreen into her shoulders, his eyes fixed on the brown water's edge down past the orange surface of the dunes—Douglas had sat down in the sand a ways back from the edge of the water, elbows on knees, the wind whipping his hair, facing the sound, far enough away for his face to be unclear.

"That's it?" Annabelle said as Max released her back and stood up. "You barely—"

"Hang on," said Max, sitting back down. "My legs were killing me." He crouched directly behind Annabelle, his knees in the blazing sand on either side of her waist, adjusting his balance on his ankles and the pressure of his thumbs on her back.

"You were telling me about Choate," said Annabelle.

"Yeah." As they watched, Douglas got to his feet and and ran toward a group of gulls that were circling above the water.

"Your friend Jeff, right?"

"Jeff Cohen," said Max. "He played the drums and he had this girlfriend. *Phoebe,* that was her name—Phoebe Maxwell." His arms moved as he oiled Annabelle's back. "And then they broke up."

"Was she pretty?" asked Annabelle.

"Phoebe? I don't know," said Max. "Yeah, she was. Kind of but not really."

"Was she pretty or wasn't she?" Annabelle asked again. "It changes the story."

Max felt Annabelle's fragrant hair blowing toward his face as he kneaded her shoulders, looking down at her exposed hipbones and her thighs arching across the sand. "No," he said. "Just, I don't know—cute. But there's one story I remember—"

"One story," Annabelle said after a moment.

"Right. Sorry, I was just— She was from some small town in Massachusetts, you know, the whole Mayflower-stock reactionary attitude, which faded pretty damn fast at school— But the time I was with her and Jeff we'd all gone to the city after the game to hear Elvin Jones." Annabelle tipped her head to tell him to keep talking and Max shifted closer and continued rubbing her back, his legs reacting to the proximity of her waist—from close up he saw the tortoiseshell plastic of her sunglasses curving over her ear, trapping a few black strands of her hair. "She was wearing an Army jacket with MAXWELL on the lapel. Her father's Army jacket. And she went to get some matches and when she turned around I noticed that the jacket had this jagged hole in the back. So I said to Jeff, you know, what's the deal with the jacket? Jeff explained how one afternoon she'd gotten bored and taken her dad's jacket and hung it on a tree and went and got his rifle and blew a hole in the jacket from across the lawn. And I looked over to Phoebe, at the bar getting matches, and I noticed that the hole was—well, it was perfect marksmanship, you know? Under the shoulder blade, left of the spine. You've got a beautiful back."

"And then he just gave her the jacket," Annabelle said quietly, nodding.

"Right," said Max. "But we danced a few times and then she danced with this other guy, not someone with us, some guy who really knew how to twirl her around. She went to get a beer for him but he'd left, so she gave the beer to Elvin Jones and when she got back she had his number— He'd told her to keep asking for him even after his mother answered the phone. She didn't get the joke."

Clearly Annabelle's back had been completely oiled, but Max had continued rubbing her shoulders, moving up to the vertical muscles of her neck and down to the groove of the hollow of her back as he slipped into familiar back-rub motions. "So I didn't see her for a while after that, but I ran into her at Orpheum—"

"When were you there?" Annabelle interrupted, moving her shoulders under his hands.

"That time was last summer— I was supposed to meet this chick Leigh but she never showed up. They had shrubbery everywhere and I was trying to get through the room and I saw Phoebe with about five guys giving them all her phone number."

"On Orpheum matchbooks."

"Right. That business— But we were talking and I said, you know, Phoebe, why're you giving out your *number* to these guys? And she said she only knew Jeff's friends and she was lonely and wanted to make new friends." Max's face had been drifting forward until his chin was almost touching the smooth protruding bone at the base of Annabelle's neck, between the slopes of her shoulders. "I *think* that's what she said," he murmured. "We were *screaming* at each other, the beat was so loud. I never saw her again."

Max gently brushed his lips across Annabelle's neck.

"Stop it, Max," said Annabelle quietly.

Max moved diagonally back, settling on the sand a few feet away and fruitlessly adjusting his swimming trunks as he pulled out another cigarette and lit it. "That makes me think of Jill," Annabelle said, stretching, running her fingers through her hair. "When she became such a big deal. Going from party to party to party"—Annabelle rhythmically bobbed her head—"making out with some guy at somebody's coming-out ball and throwing up on the sidewalk outside some club at five in the morning, time goes by, time goes by and now she's— I mean what is she now? She's arrived, she's returned, she's redesigned, she's at the clubs with the lawyers and the pictures of the Hampton parties— Actually the funniest thing is the shit she got into."

"Shit she got into?" said Max, looking out over the beach.

"Yeah. Actually I don't think you'd have heard this. I mean this is a secret."

"Okay."

"See," said Annabelle, "Tina Foster brought Jill down to hang around at this recording place she's always going down to— She, like, knows all these people down there, you know, industry people, music people, right? But Jill's got this, I don't know, her family is fucked up or something, but she's got this problem. I mean I don't know if you heard about the Marine, but she's— It's always— She gets into these situations, is all. She gets into these situations. So Tina took her down one time, and I guess maybe it was a mistake."

"Uh-huh," said Max.

"So at this point the details get hazy, but as far as I know from the Foster Girl, there was— Let's see, how did it start— Well, there was a guy, is what I'm getting at. There was this music business guy, and things started to roll, 'cause this isn't exactly unfamiliar territory for Jill. I mean stories go around. So this guy supposedly is selling himself as this big deal producer, he's friends with— There's a *real* guy involved, Tina's friend, who as far as I can tell really *is* a producer, a nice man, and of course he's supposed to be really good-looking, too, according to Jill, but this guy who Tina met, he's someone else, he's some kind of record-business sleaze. I mean I think he's just a dealer, really. So Jill got into this situation, where—"

"*What?*" said Max. "What happened?"

"Jill got into the market," said Annabelle. "I mean I think this guy took her around to some of the dance places, you know, where the Studio 54 people ended up. I mean, Jill was one of the people when we were freshmen who were at Studio all the time, but— But she started spending time with this music dealer guy, but he was really after the Thorndike drug money— I mean he wanted to deal a blow to all the rich kids and I guess Jill had this stupid moment when she did this really stupid thing."

"Which you're not going to tell me," said Max. "Come on, everyone knows drug stories. At *my* school—"

"Yeah, but with Thorndike, you know, things are *mild.* It's always been grass, right? I mean, now things are changing, now there's this coke connection, last few months, you know, with Nick and Jack Winfield, I mean, Blanchard knows who he knows and Jack has the money, right, but back when I'm talking about there was *nothing.* So Jill got some money together, you know, borrowed from people and her parents and all, right, and bought coke from this guy, you know, thinking she'd deal at Thorndike, thinking it would be the thing to do— She moved the shit into school, brought some of it to school."

"Jesus Christ," said Max. "Jill *Brooks?*"

"But she fucked everything up," said Annabelle. "The guy had her number, he took the money and was gone, and the shit she bought was worthless. I mean, I don't even mean it was cut, it was *worthless.*

The guy must have taken one look at her and burned her—Jill brought the shit to school in a monogrammed *handbag* and Tina laughed at her, gummed it and laughed, so Jill dumped it."

"She flushed it?" asked Max.

"No, she *dumped* it. I mean she didn't do a single thing right. It's somewhere in the basement. Down one of the gratings or something."

"She must have panicked when she realized what she was doing," said Max.

"Yeah, she's a little slow," said Annabelle. "No secret about that— But Tina told me the whole thing and now Jill's being extra nice to me. She could get so fucked even now, make no mistake."

"But all she has to do is take the shit out of the school building," said Max, confused.

"She *can't*," said Annabelle. "She can't get it. She *tried.* It's way the hell down there— Only one of the *janitors* could get it out, you know, with the building keys, go down there into the plumbing conduit and get it. We're talking about a *grating.*"

"Wait, I thought it wasn't real," said Max.

"It's real enough. She'd get expelled. I mean she's got two years left."

"Wow," Max said.

"So Jill's so fucking scared of me— I mean *Tina* doesn't give a shit but Jill thinks I'm going to get *mad* at her or something, and she's *desperate* for me not to talk— You know, she'll do *anything* to keep me quiet, she's so damn shameless."

Annabelle lit a cigarette and Max used his hands to shield the lighter from the wind that was moving across the dunes.

"It's a *great* story," Max said. "I thought we were talking about something, though."

"We were," said Annabelle. "Your friend. This chick. I was listening."

"If you're not in the mood to talk, I unders—"

"What's the *deal* with you, anyway?" She glared quizzically at him. "Don't you *ever* have— I can't just *bring things up.*"

"I'm sorry," said Max.

"It can't be this *hard,*" Annabelle said distantly, shaking her head and staring off, pressing her crossed arms to her chest. "It *can't* be. I'm beginning to think it's just *me,* my problem, or— I don't know, maybe Mom's right, maybe it's Taft trouble."

They both looked past the beach sand at Douglas, running around startling the seagulls, his feet slapping the shoreline froth. "For him too?" Max said.

"He's got things simpler," Annabelle said, watching her brother dance among the birds, which scattered. "He just needs to get laid. Or I don't know what he needs— There's not— There's something he expects someone to just *give* to him."

"I'm sorry, Annabelle," said Max. "I don't mean to cut into you. It's just that it's been a long time, you know? You've changed."

"Not really," said Annabelle, looking at him, shrugging, looking off again. "Same old girl trying to make the same old moves." She turned back to him. "I mean everything *else* has changed, you know? Things are getting electric— You guys were building a goddamned *airplane* back before, running up and down the motherfucking *stairs*, you'd turn around, I was there. I was there and it was the same, right? I never had much to say. I'm the same old girl."

"Different look," said Max, lighting a cigarette.

"You know better than that," said Annabelle.

"Maybe I do," Max said, gazing across the sand toward the water.

They sat side by side in silence, drinking, their legs across the sand. "Max," Annabelle said, "you know how sometimes you're walking around and you see someone and you think it's a friend of yours, and you smile and wave? And then you get closer, and it wasn't who you thought it was?"

"And you get all embarrassed," said Max.

"Well, yeah, but"— Annabelle squinted—"but sometimes that person looks back at you? And you think, that wasn't my friend but it was someone *like* my friend? And that person sees you and thinks— Maybe that person has a friend like you? Maybe you see something in each other and you keep walking?"

"Yeah," said Max. "I know what you mean. And you think, look at all these people I'm passing by."

"No, but— What I'm saying— It's just how people *look,* right? And— If somebody's beautiful they *always* look familiar? If they're beautiful enough?"

"And you don't want anything you need to pass you by."

"Well, *you* think it, right?" said Annabelle. "You walk around and you watch, sometimes you see someone and it's like, every lock has a key, right?"

"So Douglas needs some specific thing," said Max.

"Some kind of relief of tension, yeah," said Annabelle. "Boy, does he ever." She waited and then suddenly continued. "*Nobody* deserves the world's longest, most violent fuck more than Douglas. You know? *Nobody.* All his problems would be solved—he'd stop dwelling on the shit he dwells on, *Jill,* scared of Nick *Blanchard,* the hair-trigger, all of it. I mean, you know how you can just *tell* about people. Douglas has this thing in his brain that he doesn't understand, that he doesn't even know is *there.* I mean, I keep thinking, he's so close, one of these days, I don't know, that—*switch* is going to get flipped and he's going to *wake up.* I mean, you know, he *talks* about chasing after all these chicks, people *see* him— He just never *moves,* you know, he's so frightened all the time. I mean, he doesn't realize, you know, that so many girls would *immediately* jump into bed with him."

"Really?" said Max skeptically.

"What? Oh, yeah," said Annabelle, squinting and nodding emphatically. "What—you don't think so?"

"Well, it's just— He's not—"

Annabelle was shaking her head critically. "That's— And you don't even know. *You* see him and you don't know. It's strange— You guys are so *mystified,* I mean, you can't, what I'm saying, you can't tell about each other, you think you can see it but you can't."

"Come on," said Max, smiling. "I mean, I *know* what you're talking about— At school, you know, there would always be these certain guys who would scare the hell out of me and the chicks would say, you know, Him? No way—and then they'd all, like, fall down dead when some bland guy showed up. But *Douglas*—"

"Oh, absolutely," said Annabelle, smiling gently, looking down. "I mean, he's my brother, you know, but I'm not *blind.*"

"Well, you know what I'm thinking," said Max, looking over at her.

"What?"

"I'm thinking it wouldn't be so difficult. I mean, I'm thinking there's this idea of what we could do— Not that it's possible but there *is* this idea." Max looked over at her, seeing that she was squinting, concentrating. "You getting my drift?"

"Yeah, I'm getting your drift." said Annabelle, beginning to laugh. "Oh, you bastard. Beautiful."

"It's just this idea, but if we could do it—"

"If we could do it that would be something. That would be good. Later on, maybe, without the— Aaaaah!"

Douglas, who had been sneaking up the back of the dune, grabbed Annabelle's shoulders from behind and wrestled her down onto the sand, shouting, "Look out! Look out! It's the Red Ghost, it's the Red fucking Ghost!" Annabelle screamed laughter as they wrestled and Max fumbled with Nick's camera and took a picture—the only one he took that day—as Douglas finally pinned her, gyrating under him, her knees flanking his waist.

"Uncle," Annabelle panted, finally relaxing. Douglas got off of her and sat down and they both adjusted their clothing.

"Where the hell did you get that 'Red Ghost' shit?" Max asked, replacing the lens cap. "I'd forgotten about that."

"Oh, God, it's so old," Annabelle said as she and Douglas sat up. "*When* did we start doing that?"

"Christ, so long ago." Douglas put on a navy sweatshirt from his bag and pushed the sleeves up and then lit one of the new cigarettes, ducking behind Annabelle's shadow to do it. "When we were born. It's from—"

"It's from when we were really little," said Annabelle. "I mean, long ago, back when we had nightlights. It was— See, Doug and I would get scared at night, you know, after Mom read to us, and we'd cry and Dad would come in and quiet us down and he would say that nothing could hurt us, that we were safe."

"He would say," said Douglas, "I mean, I barely remember, but he would say that he could protect us, that he would protect us because nothing could hurt us, right, nothing, and we would say, not anything? And he would say, well, there's one thing that can hurt you, just one thing, and that's the Red Ghost, but, don't worry, I can keep it away. So there's—"

"Keep *her* away," said Annabelle. "*Her.* The Red Ghost was female. I remember."

"No," said Douglas, confused. "Really? I just remember it being 'it.' "

"No, it was a female ghost," said Annabelle. "Mom thought it was so funny that she wouldn't let him forget it— But Dad would say, don't listen to her, because I know— The only thing to be scared of is the Red Ghost, and I can keep her away. So then I guess it became this joke, when we were growing up— 'Look out!

Look out!' all the time. So that's what that is, Max. Glad you asked?"

"Glad I asked," said Max, prying another can of beer off the current six-pack and cracking it open. The three of them sat quietly, feeling the brush of the wind that stirred the sand, letting their eyes wander over to the tall grass and the shadowed square of the concession stand and the bait shack and the sadness of the empty, sand-covered parking lot.

"Look at that guy's bathing trunks," said Annabelle, pointing out a young man who was standing toward the concession stand rolling up a volleyball net, the muscles in his arms moving obtrusively as he worked. "Right out of the catalog."

"For fifty dollars they're yours," said Douglas, glancing over.

"Check them out," said Annabelle, staring. Eventually the man—a beach employee—noticed Annabelle looking at him and quickly looked away, smiling, and chose that moment to break off the fray from the end of the net ropes, grimacing and flexing his arms across his chest. "Max, I'm gonna put you in one of those catalogs."

"Right, I'll be one of those, like, fucking idiots standing around on a sailboat, you know, *smiling.* Forget it."

"No, come on, Max— Just wear the shorts and you can afford all those palette knives and turpentine and everything. Cut your hair and we'll give you a stage name."

"Yeah, like what?" said Max.

Annabelle stretched backward across the sand on her elbows, pushing her T-shirt upward, her fingers skating over her black Lycra swimsuit as she felt for her Ray-Bans and put them on. "How about 'Carlo'?" she said, squinting at the shore. "That's a good name." The man packing the volleyball net was glancing over again, clearly trying to look bored and powerful. "Look, I'm turning him around without moving."

"You are, at that," said Douglas, smiling.

"We're going to have to go back and get ready soon," said Annabelle. "The sun's going down soon."

"Let's clean this shit up," Max said to Annabelle, catching her eye.

Annabelle got up and joined Max in moving around and collecting the empty beer cans, picking the cigarette butts out of the sand and dropping them into the cans.

"Are we going to do this?" whispered Max.

"Shh," whispered Annabelle, juggling empty cans. "Not now— We'll get a chance to talk."

"But are we going to do this?" whispered Max.

"I think so," whispered Annabelle, smiling beautifully at him.

"Look, Mom and Dad are back," said Douglas, pointing. They hadn't noticed the car's return, but it was there, alone in the lot, and across the near-empty beach they saw Greg and Giulia walking over the sand toward the towels, looking out across the water. Douglas took the empty beer cans from Max and he and Annabelle brought them to the orange oil drum, dropping them to clatter in the rusting dark, while Max watched, from a distance, as Greg put his arm around Giulia's waist and Giulia put her head on Greg's shoulder.

chapter 17

The tape reels spin and the clock paces me as I fight to master the truth of what happened and imprison it in this account, fight the quiet battle, but while the battle commences I can hear the other clocks—once again I can hear all the clocks running out, marking time, standing ground, looking on as all time and memory wrestle, events their weapons, the worth of our lives in the balance. So the battle rages, and time has no visible weapons besides these tape reels, where events are common ground, framed fragments of rapture and remorse, objects of love, ragged pictures of sweetness and evil, yet memory persists, changing the rules, fighting the tide, capturing its dark and barren ground until the tapes and typewriter force structure onto the story, this straight line of words, this charade, until the bloodied frontline blurs and shimmers with memory and illusion of memory, until the weapons of time falter and fade, until the battleground is gone.

The sun was setting as Giulia and Greg and Douglas and Annabelle Taft and Max Gantry drove toward the Winfields', sitting in silence and staring out the BMW windows at the golden landscape of early twilight—the sun had finally vanished behind the furred, emerald edges of the serene hills that faced the night as they had since before they were named by the Blackfoot. From the darkness of the backseat Douglas could see the glowing green stripes of the dashboard shining off his father's white cuffs and glinting cuff links—Greg's smooth, freshly shaven face pinched into agreeable dimples as he smiled, his face and hands flattered by a flawless white button-down shirt, a yellow bow tie, and a dun-colored wool suit, early-evening headlights reflecting in his gold-framed glasses as he twitched the steering wheel and guided them along Union Road. Giulia sat beside him wearing a white Naget gown that complemented her dark, smooth skin, her thick black hair pulled back, her face serene, her fingers clicking together the pearls of a necklace that Annabelle had given her upon her return from Milan as she gazed past her husband's profile at the passing fields and fragrant farmland and the shadows of the hills. She had once said that her daughter looked old, not personally ancient or mature but archaic, somehow, her face having more and more to do with history as time passed, and it was true tonight—Annabelle sat calmly, slim legs pressed together beneath the hem of her black evening dress, her pale gold shoes protruding forward between the plastic push-button seat-belt sockets, hands together holding her small purse in her lap, her wide-set green eyes untroubled beneath her dark brows, her black hair framing her face like velvet ropes round a sculpture. Douglas sat to her left, compressed against the driver's side door, his profile turned toward its barely visible reflection in the window glass, light hair brushed back, hands in his lap, wearing a charcoal grey wool suit, a white shirt and an olive-and-burgundy striped tie with a silver tie pin, face still rounded with youth, deep-set eyes absently pinched and squinted. Max sat on her other side, black hair falling over his forehead, blue eyes in shadow, sharp jawline dusted in stubble, dressed in a secondhand black suit jacket and pleated grey trousers and a thin black tie, his mangled fingers holding Nick Blanchard's camera against his lap.

They had sped through town, passing the oddly deserted Lawrence Hotel and the stone-flanked swell in the edges of Union Road where the "Private Property" signs had begun appearing along their route, and Greg finally slowed the car and flipped the turn signal as they arrived at the mouth of the Winfields' long, wide, tree-lined gravel drive—seeing it for the first time, Max privately admired the abandoned gatehouse, the first glimpse of the lake down the descending and artfully overgrown slope of the hill, the second glimpse of the lake, the first glimpse of the house, the final glimpse of the lake as they made their final approach, joining the procession of nearly identical silver, blue, and black European automobiles that wound onto the circular drive together. They had skirted the edges of the western hills that had blocked the road from the setting sun, and the tremendous white stone surface of the house was flooded with final sunlight, columns catching long shadows from the distant trees, windows shining like melting ice—later, Annabelle remembered, as it got darker, the majestic stone promenade behind the house would resemble a long and narrow operatic stage, lit from behind, lit from beneath, lit from above with indoor and outdoor light, and dozens of men and women would stand together talking and laughing and dancing by candlelight, the lake still glowing beyond the dampening lawn beneath the dark shifting trees.

Greg pulled up behind another car, and after a moment a drably uniformed driveway attendant stepped up and opened Giulia's door, and then Max's door, while Greg and Douglas and Annabelle clambered out by themselves on the driver's side—the attendant nodded to Giulia and Annabelle as he accepted the keys and got behind the wheel, carefully inserting their car into the herringbone weave of automobiles that already flooded one area of the rolled lawn. The five of them stretched their legs, noticing party sounds that blurred in the wind as they adjusted their clothing—Greg fiddled with the knot on Douglas' tie and Annabelle held her hair above her head, wincing while Giulia disentangled its strands from her gold-chain necklace—and strode across the gravel toward the house, the sunset casting their shadows on the front door, which stood just slightly ajar. They bounded up the smooth, rust-discolored granite steps and Greg knocked on the enameled door, which was opened almost immediately by an extremely thin middle-aged woman in a peach-colored gown who was facing backward toward a dimly lit congestion of guests—the woman turned to beam at the Tafts, cheek-kissing them one by one as they entered the front foyer, ladies first, and then reaching for Max's hand. "Mr. Garment, isn't it?"

"Gantry. Max Gantry," said Max.

"Oh, I'm *terribly* sorry, dear," the woman said, crestfallen. "Peggy Winfield."

"Please don't worry about it," Max reassured her, finally relinquishing her warm hand.

"She thought you were Leonard Garment," Greg muttered, patting Max's shoulder affectionately as they stepped forward. "Now she thinks you're James Bond."

The Tafts walked into the house, Max following, wading forward against a tide of sound, music and dozens of voices, clattering china, footsteps, laughter. In the foyer several people were standing around with champagne glasses at the foot of the curving staircase—one of them was a partner at Greg's brokerage and Greg walked over and started talking to him, while Max wandered in a tight circle with his hands in his pockets, his eyes picking out details, and Douglas stood at the room's edge, listening to the muffled roar of the party going on through the double doors in the living room.

"Get that stupid-assed grin off your face," Annabelle said, arriving behind him as Max walked tentatively toward the loud living room doors.

"I can't," said Douglas. "I can't believe it— This *really is* the Winfield party. Where's everybody from Thorndike?"

"*Relax,*" said Annabelle. "Just relax— It's still early. I'm sure everyone's around. The important thing for you is to take it—*Jesus!*" she blurted, flinching.

"Don't say a word," murmured Nick Blanchard, having stepped up behind Annabelle and tapped her shoulder, pointedly speaking only to her. He wore a dark brown plaid jacket and a green shirt with a black tie, his face unshaven behind clear-framed, green-lensed vintage sunglasses, his hair slicked back from the precise right angles of his hairline, his second camera hanging from his shoulder, and to Douglas' eyes he looked spliced-in, like a piece of New York street crudely grafted onto the party.

"Hi, Nick. Great jacket," Douglas said.

"Hello, Douglas," said Nick, glancing at him and then back at Annabelle. "Listen, Anna. Don't go into the living room yet. It's the same as last year, pretty much the same deal— Same shit going on— But there's someone here I want you to meet."

"Oh yeah?" said Annabelle.

"Yes. Excuse us a moment, would you please, Douglas," said Nick, his sandy voice shifting oddly around his unusually formal tone. "We're all set up in the Piano Study. There's—"

"Nick," said Max, suddenly walking up.

"Max! How are you?" said Nick, shaking his hand.

"Fine. Here's your camera," Max said, handing over the Leica.

"Did you get anything?" Nick asked, making an exaggerated show of inspecting the camera for damage.

"Just one shot," said Max. "I'm no good at it. I'm not— I have absolutely no idea what I'm doing."

"One shot is one shot," said Nick cryptically. "Maybe you'll— Aha," Nick broke off as a door off to one side of the foyer swung open to reveal a small young woman with thin blond hair and glasses, wearing an Italian business suit and carrying a suitably feminine

Mark Cross briefcase, who came through the door and stopped abruptly, leaving the door ajar.

"Annabelle?" said Nick, offering his arm again, which Annabelle took, and they began walking together toward the woman at the door.

"I shall return," Annabelle said over her shoulder. "Relax, Douglas—it's going to rain tonight."

"If you say so," said Douglas, staying where he was, some distance away from the threshold of the living room, nervous now that Annabelle had gone, watching Max wander toward the living room door and the clatter and noise behind it.

"Claire Plittman, Annabelle Taft," Nick was saying.

"Good to see you," the woman said, shaking Annabelle's hand and looking at her pointedly. "I'm sorry, I've just got to ask if that's your real name."

"How do you do," said Annabelle. "Yes it is. I have crazy parents."

"You know," the woman was saying—Douglas could barely hear her—"I'll let you in on a little secret right now— I could get in trouble for saying it but John sent me out here with strict instructions to sign you as fast as I could. Have you spoken to anyone else?"

"No," said Annabelle. "John *Bogart*? The, like, the man who invented Flash?"

"The one and only. As we talk I'll describe our operation to you, how we're the most prestigious agency in the business, what we do for our clients, how our standard contract operates, and make sure that all your questions are answered, but, meanwhile—"

"Fine," said Annabelle. "Can we get some drinks?"

"Right— Shall we go to the Piano Study?" said Nick, gesturing toward the door that Plittman had just emerged through— Douglas could make out dim, table-lamp-lit view of red lacquered walls and a hearse-length full-grand piano and doors leading off into other rooms.

"How did Nick get a hold of— of John Bogart?" asked Annabelle.

"Any friend of this 'young photographic genius,' " Plittman said. "They call him a 'young photographic genius.' You'll *like* John— He's done everything you can do, he takes a *personal* interest in his clients, which is, you know, which is rare in this business— I mean he's slapped girls for eating but he's also bought them boats."

"Jesus," said Annabelle. "That's quite a life."

"Well, when you've spent your career with a visionary like Bogart you're always learning," said Plittman reflectively, touching Annabelle's shoulder and guiding her toward the doorway. "I can tell you stories but I can't reveal secrets."

"Come on, Annabelle," said Nick, a bit too eager, breaking or at least bending the trance. "Could be the most important event of your life. Douglas"—he spun around to point at him—"we'll catch you upstairs." The three of them vanished through the door and Douglas watched it close.

MAX HAD HIS first real brush with fame that evening—not with individually famous people or objects but with the texture of fame itself, the low-voltage, high-octane substance behind the arrested movement of everything he saw, and he also saw the irreproducible effect, not of mere money or mere love, but of that greater substance upon scores of people lingering casually in the blind spot of the public eye, feeding off the current, waiting for that certain forthcoming moment when their lives, they were sure, would abruptly assume the contours that they expected and deserved all along. Later, as he probably assumed, he would develop that particular reaction, that particular deadening, but that night he had trouble enough just watching it all happen, watching the smaller-than-life actors chuckle with complacency, the life-sized politicians smile with discomfort and hunger, watching the walls and windows of the Winfield house waver in his gaze like an after-hours trading floor or the ruin of an ancient stadium, and as dinnertime approached Max found his equilibrium, like a pendulum coming to rest, somehow, at the top of its arc, found his axiomatic reaction to all forms of formalized vice, pinning it down finally like the lost cause that it was.

Now Max stood framed in the opened French doors of the tremendous Winfield living room, squinting in the pale horizontal glare of the evening's final weak light shining quietly through the doors and windows of the opposite wall. Across the room, silhouetted by the bay windows, a middle-aged, balding man with a mustache and a pipe stood talking with a group of teenage girls who all had a buffed-and-polished look, their small bodies sheathed in tight, pleated gowns made of shining, pastel-colored cloth, as if each of them had gotten ready for the party by having themselves shrink-wrapped—the teenage girls flanked the middle-aged man, turning their earnest faces up to him, flaunting the war paint on their cheekbones and the shadows that their earrings cast on their necks. Max weakly stepped forward and approached a white-linen-draped table that stood against a far wall bearing various hors d'oeuvres and drinks and attended by waiters in white coats, in the middle of which, on a small white marble pedestal, stood a peach frozen into a foot-wide cube of melting ice—shining drops of cold water were collecting along the top of the marble pedestal, which, Max saw, had small canals etched into its surface, like the canals in the butcher block that rare steak is carved upon.

Max stood staring at the frozen peach long enough for the ice to visibly melt a few millimeters—like watching a clock's hour hand move—as the ice absorbed the room's latent body heat, and when some random man hurried to the table and mixed himself a gin and tonic, dropping a wedge of lime into the crystal tumbler, Max caught himself watching the thousands of air bubbles rising from the lime, mesmerized. The room was bright and hushed, its flutter of subdued sound punctuated suddenly by the clatter and babble of more guests arriving out in the hall and by the sudden, incongruous noise, dimly audible, of a Led Zeppelin album being played somewhere upstairs, playing for a few seconds and then being abruptly silenced.

"Did you hear that?" said a man at Max's left—tall, grey-haired, balding, mustachioed, draped in a crisp Savile Row suit—it was the man who had been talking to the shrink-wrapped teenage girls. Max hadn't seen him move across the room. The shrink-wrapped teenage girls were nowhere in sight. "You know what that is?" the man said, gesturing toward the ceiling with his pipe. "That's the beautiful sound of the seventies."

"I beg your pardon?" Max had suddenly realized that he was speaking with Theodore Winfield.

"The beautiful sound of the seventies. You remember the seventies. I don't care how young you are."

"Sure," said Max.

"I mean," said Theodore Winfield, "you think these things make a difference. They don't make any difference. Twenties, thirties, forties, fifties, sixties, seventies, eighties—honor shifts around, styles change, but only for everyone else. Not for us—up here things stay pretty much the same."

"I think I understand what you mean," said Max tactfully. "But look, go back far enough and you begin to see a difference. Victorian times. Edwardian times. Napoleonic times. You begin to see a difference."

"*Yes,*" Winfield exclaimed, poking Max in the shoulder, "eventually I'm sure you would. But it becomes *hypothetical,* what *could* be seen. Nothing that's encompassed by a human lifetime."

"Right," said Max.

"You know, the very poor are different than you and me," said Winfield.

"Yes," said Max. "They don't have as much money."

"You're an extremely observant young man," Winfield said. "What's your name?"

"Max Gantry."

"Is it really," Winfield mused keenly. "How very interesting— Have you decided to stay? Have you made your decision yet?"

"I beg your pardon?" said Max, startled.

"You're the young fellow who was going to move in here, aren't you? Moving in with Betsey Ann, moving in and engaging in carnal activities which are illegal in most states. Isn't that you? The clever young man?"

"I think," said Max, swallowing, "that you must be mixing me up with someone else."

"No, I'm *sure* it's you," intoned Winfield, leaning closer to Max, his yellowing mustache concealing the movements of his upper lip. "I *recognize* you. I've *seen* you before. You finally arrived—the young man who hunts geese and parts his hair and drinks rubbing alcohol and never goes to church. Did I ask your name?"

"Yes."

"Did I give you a gift?"

"No."

"Don't know what's coming over me these days," Winfield mumbled, reaching in his breast pocket. "Forgetting everything— Here you are, a small token." He handed Max a miniature calfskin address book, which Max took and looked at quizzically.

"Thank you," Max said.

"Don't mention it. Look," Winfield went on, smiling in a tight way that puffed his cheeks and narrowed his eyes, pulling his chin toward his neck, "I understand what you're doing but I'm willing to say that we'll keep it between ourselves. Certain matters should remain secret, should they not?"

"Oh yes," said Max.

"The fact that it cost me"—Winfield's voice sank into a scratchy clandestine whisper for the three words—"*six million dollars* to restore the outside of this damn house, to extend the Corinthian columns to a more manly length and undo all the restoration-related damage that that bitch Emily Van Hausmann caused— That should be a secret, shouldn't it?"

"I suppose so," said Max.

"Well, *good,*" said Winfield, heartily, mustering a Tammany Hall grin and slapping Max on the back. "I don't mean to startle you. Understand that I've had a good deal to drink. Come on, young fellow, I'll set you up." He moved toward the bar table, and Max followed, gazing at grandiose vistas down through rows of opened, aligned French doors. "Now, be straight with me, young fellow," Winfield continued. "Did my daughter ever take you hunting?"

"No."

"Damn good thing too— What's yours?"

"Scotch on the rocks."

"Good man," said Winfield gruffly, beaming as he selected one of the round crystal tumblers of subdued design with the engraved W's and the indented teardrop shapes in the centers of their thick crystal bases and loudly dropped several ice cubes into it, and, as Max watched, poured what must have been less than half an ounce of Johnnie Walker Black Label into the glass from a huge bottle that had been pinioned into a silver pouring stand, the infinitesimal amount of scotch barely staining the ice cubes brown. As Max continued to watch, Winfield topped off the glass from a frost-beaded silver pitcher of ice water. Max received the "drink" and stared at it for a moment, seeing the tiny amount of scotch making dim wavering lines through the cold tap water.

"How do you like this thing over here?" Winfield asked as Max performed an exaggerated pantomime of relishing the drink. Max looked up and saw that Winfield was pointing at the ripe peach in the block of ice.

"It's very nice," Max said.

"You're damn right," said Winfield. "It's *perfect.*" He waved at Max's glass. "Don't want to be hauled in for contributing to the liquancy of a minor," Winfield confided, waiting a moment and slapping Max on the back. "Enjoy the party, young man, and remember what we talked about."

"I'm sure I will," said Max, widening his eyes. He waited until Winfield was out of sight and then put down the stained tap water, picked another glass off the tray, and made himself a proper drink, and while he was standing there sipping it Douglas and Greg Taft walked up together, both holding their hands in their pockets in the same unconsciously casual way, both grinning.

"Well well," said Douglas.

"This is quite a scene," said Max.

"You ain't seen nothing yet," Greg said, smiling his tight smile at them. "One year there were paramedics."

"That's not *true,*" Douglas said, squinting. It was necessary to speak somewhat loudly in order to be heard over the mounting sounds of the music and conversation coming from the rest of the house. "You shouldn't be trying to scare us, Dad."

"Fair enough. I'm going to reclaim my wife," Greg told them, wandering away to join Giulia in greeting a group of people from Dover that were just arriving. Max realized that he was absently fidgeting with the address book that Ted Winfield had given him and he stopped and stowed it in his breast pocket, where it would poke him in the chest the rest of the evening.

"Your parents' marriage is just so cool," Max said fondly.

"Yeah," said Douglas, leaning to make himself a gin and tonic. "It is pretty miraculous. I'm glad you're here, Max."

"Me too," said Max. "Nice house, huh?"

"Talk about it— I thought I knew what to expect, you know, with Annabelle explaining all the time, but this is something else. Maybe some tourists will come watch the party."

"It's going to rain tonight," Max said, catching his arm.

"What?" said Douglas, confused. "What the fuck are you talking about?"

"The rain's on its way," said Max, still holding Douglas' arm. "When the rain comes you can go home."

"If you say so," said Douglas, leaving him to find his way to the ballroom—the source of the music—a large red room where a small "combo" played swing triplets and people were dancing in one corner and others were sitting with drinks in another. He took an hors d'oeuvre off a tray—something involving toast and fish—and munched it down, standing near the edge of the room and looking around, and while he was wiping his mouth with a napkin from another tray Annabelle leaned into the room, saw him, nodded exasperatedly, and walked over, carrying herself with a slightly fluid gait, somehow looking intoxicated yet alert.

"*There* you are," said Annabelle. "This is like fucking musical chairs."

"Well?" said Douglas, almost shouting over the brackish horn solos. "What was that all about?"

"What?" said Annabelle, smiling.

"Come on— When you went off with Nick and that—"

"I'm a Flash model," Annabelle said, smiling as she held up the folded sheet of paper that she had been carrying.

"No shit?" said Douglas, grinning. "Wow, Annabelle, that's great." He leaned to kiss her on the cheek and noticed something slightly mannered about the way that she kissed back. "That's it? A contract and everything? You just signed the thing they gave you?"

"Jesus *Christ,* Douglas"—Annabelle squinted in disgust—"*Yes,* I signed what they had. It's their standard three-year agreement, it's what *everybody* gets— Look, there are girls all over the *world* who would *kill* for a chance at that thing, so, you know, don't give me a hard time. I need a drink," Annabelle said, looking around the red ballroom and then taking Douglas by the hand and leading him back toward the living room. "Come on, more musical chairs, I can't hear, I need a drink," she said breathlessly, leading Douglas through the French doors and over to the linen-draped table with the peach in the block of ice. Douglas watched as Annabelle picked up a glass of champagne and gulped it down, reeling for a moment and flaring her eyes, putting the empty glass on the floor behind an ornate chair in the same movement.

"So soon I'll be seeing you in all the magazines," said Douglas. By now the almond-colored light from outside had almost entirely faded and reflections of the lamps were visible on the inside surfaces of the windows.

"Yeah," said Annabelle, laughing. "Soon you will. Jesus—"

"Calm down, Anna. Come on," said Douglas.

"Sorry."

"So is anyone else here?"

"What?"

"Is anybody else from school here?"

"Yeah. Remember it's still early— Nick says everyone's upstairs. This is a Dürer sketch," Annabelle said, peering suddenly at a framed drawing on the wall behind Douglas.

"Makes *me* feel at home," said Douglas.

"Oh, don't be such an asshole," said Annabelle disgustedly. "There's no reason to be so—"

"Hi, Mom," said Douglas brightly—Giulia was walking up to them with a middle-aged, thick-haired, sunburned man in an ostentatiously off-the-rack suit.

"Senator Rollins, Douglas and Annabelle Taft," Giulia said, smiling politely.

"I *knew* Giulia *had* to have beautiful children," said the man as he shook their hands ingratiatingly.

"Thank you," said Annabelle, nodding. "I've heard your name. I mean"—she was smiling shyly—"besides the usual way."

"Oh, your mother and I go *way* back, don't we?" Rollins said, grinning at Giulia, who nodded confidently. "At the Porcelain Club there were all *kinds* of—"

"Giulia, darling!" said a woman emerging from the crowd that danced at the other end of the cavernous room.

"I'm *sorry,*" said Giulia regretfully, ducking away.

"I do that all the time," Rollins told them, with renewed attention. "What do *you* both do?"

"I'm a model," Annabelle said, smiling politely.

"Of course you are," said the senator, flaring his eyes oddly.

"I'm starting at Harvard in the fall," said Douglas.

"Went there myself," Rollins said, waving and squinting dismissively, as if to reassure him. "That's *right*"—pointing at Douglas as if picking him from a lineup— "*you're* the man who can save me."

"Save—"

"My most recent aide—who *believe* me I don't relish discussing—has gone far away and won't be back. How do you feel about the Beltway?"

"I don't like it," Douglas blurted impulsively.

"Perfect," Rollins said, peering keenly at them both. "As they say, you can trust a Taft— Or— Or—"

"Or not trust them," said Annabelle, smiling.

"That's right," Rollins said blankly—he had been fumbling with his breast pocket. "We have a relationship of trust, Dennis— You'll learn what that means. I'm afraid I have something—" Douglas and Annabelle caught each other's eyes and tried not to laugh as Rollins reached into his jacket pocket and produced a long, flat package wrapped in tissue paper, which he handed to Annabelle. "This is my new idiosyncrasy— I've been giving these to everyone. Meant for your mother but I'd really rather give it to such a lovely young girl as yourself."

"Thank you very much," Annabelle said curiously, accepting the package.

"Oh, please," said Rollins, gesturing self-effacingly. "Well, it was a pleasure finally meeting Giulia's children, but there's a young fellow named Hopkins who's looking for me. Call the *Delaware* number, son—the WATS line's down. Ask for Peter Feldman."

"Thank you, sir," said Douglas as they shook hands.

"Annabelle, I'll see you looking at me from magazine covers," Rollins said, shaking her hand.

"I enjoyed meeting you," Annabelle told him, waiting politely while the senator nodded and weaved away and then tearing the tissue paper from the package to reveal a turquoise TIFFANY AND CO. box, which she opened, dropping the shredded tissue—within the box, nestled in new cotton and a felt bag, was a gold-plated pair of barber's scissors. "Uh-huh," Annabelle said, flexing the sharp scissors and then closing the package and stowing it within her handbag. "I'm not looking at *him* from any magazine."

"I can't *believe* it," Douglas was saying. "I guess they really talk that way and everything really goes on that way. Well, there's my summer—"

"Oh, Douglas, that was beautiful," said Annabelle, putting a hand on his shoulder. "You bastard— Delivering letters for fifteen dollars an hour—"

"Well, it's not like you've got anything to worry about," Douglas said.

"That's right," said Annabelle, hugging him and breaking away. "Oh, Douglas, we're going to rule the fucking world."

"Maybe just a small portion," Douglas said distractedly. "Jesus—"

"You are just such a jerk, it's incredible," said Annabelle, checking her watch. "What's wrong *now?*"

"Nothing. I've never been to this before," said Douglas, breaking into a grin.

"This is my fifth one. More champagne," Annabelle observed, reaching for a passing waiter's tray—nearly knocking him over—and taking two new fluted glasses.

"I wasn't the hot eighth-grader," Douglas said, clinking glasses with her.

"Mmm— *Somebody* thought so," Annabelle said, swallowing.

"What— Really? Who?"

"Not telling."

"Who *was* it, damn it?"

"A man's got to know his limitations. Come on"—Annabelle laughed, wiping champagne from her chin—"everybody's upstairs. Buzzman'll be here soon."

"Who?" said Douglas, smiling.

"Buzzman—" intoned Max fiendishly, crouching and waving his fingers like a conjurer, having crept up behind them and caught the last sentence. Douglas and Annabelle turned and laughed, startled, Annabelle's hand lingering on Max's shoulder.

"Who the hell is Buzzman?" said Douglas.

"All those years of Thorndike?" Max said, gulping from his second scotch, obviously relaxed, putting an arm around Douglas' shoulders. "And you've never heard of *Buzzman?* Take care of this boy, Annabelle."

"I'm way behind you guys," said Douglas, taking Max's drink for a bracing sip and returning it as the three of them began moving toward the foyer and the staircase.

"Time to catch up," said Annabelle, having linked arms with both of them. "Come on— Let's get *up* there."

chapter 18

Sitting on couches and in chairs and on the carpet or on the floor in the large Winfield upstairs study were Douglas and Annabelle Taft, Max Gantry, Nick Blanchard, Jill Brooks, Tina Foster, Amy MacIntyre, Wally Patterson, Michael Cadenhead, and Duane Sudler. Wally and Nick and Duane were drinking bottles of beer and Duane was characteristically peeling the labels off with his fingernails, and Stephen Leonard and Wendy LaSalle had been in the room briefly but had wandered out, leaving behind the people who had referred to themselves as "the gang" in eighth grade. Jack Winfield had just left, hunting for another pack of cigarettes, and while he was out of the room Ralph DiGrassi had walked in and balanced precariously on the edge of one of the couches, wearing a retina-burning red jacket, and everybody was studiously ignoring him, enmeshed in various conversations, handing each other fresh beers. Jack returned, dressed in a handmade dinner jacket and yellow socks, smiling shyly and whipping the cigarette pack across the room to Nick, who caught it despite his sunglasses and the dimness of the room.

"Ah— Don't you have anything besides these fag cigarettes?" Nick said.

"Cigarette fags," laughed Annabelle as several others groaned at Nick's comment.

"Oh, Jesus," said Duane.

"Oh, that's— Fuck you," Tina called toward Nick—she was leaning against the wall picking arpeggios on her white Telecaster, which wasn't hooked to an amplifier, so it could only be heard during those random moments when nobody was speaking. "When you were at Thorndike you smoked White Camels like everyone else."

"Oh, leave Nick alone, Foster Girl," said Annabelle absently.

Jack produced his twisted grin. "I'm sorry. That's all we've got— If you want I can find out if any of the kitchen staff are running into Dover and have one of them get other cigarettes, you know, when they go."

"Jack's such a nice guy," said Amy, who had been standing by the window looking at the candlelit tables on the lawn behind the house. She walked over and kissed Jack on the cheek, and Jack grinned shyly, and then Amy crossed back and sat next to Duane on another couch and leaned her blonde head on Duane's shoulder.

"Yeah— Are we gonna get some real drinks up here, Winfield?" said Nick, twirling the cellophane top off the pack of cigarettes. Tina wadded up a cocktail napkin and flung it at him—the napkin missed his head and sailed into a dim corner of the room, landing next to an Atari video game and several cartridges—*Missile Command, Breakout, Superman*—that probably belonged to Jack's younger sister.

"Whoa," said Nick, cringing and squinting as if watching a home run. Annabelle leaned over and extracted a cigarette from the pack, and after a moment she got another one out and handed it to Douglas next to her without looking. Michael watched their hands during this maneuver, shifting his unobtrusive position on the floor, wiping his hands on his cross-legged knees and reaching inside his lapels to pull his shirt cuffs back inside his jacket sleeves.

"You think—" Duane loudly told Nick, sitting upright suddenly and letting Amy's head slide from his shoulder and bang against the back of the couch. "You think—" Everyone quieted down and turned to Duane respectfully, listening as he stammered.

"Yeah?" said Nick quietly.

"Ouch," murmured Amy, rubbing her head.

"You think that just because you're some kind of Marxist or *artist* or something you're supposed to— Supposed to be rude to *Jack,* or you're supposed to have some— Cut that out, damn it." Nick had raised his camera and was unnervingly snapping portraits of Duane. "Have some stupid— Act like this is all just about class *struggle* or whatever. I mean, you say—"

"Nothing to do with *class,*" murmured Nick, taking more pictures.

"—you say everything like you're showing us you're—*free* or something, but you're sitting here in a tie drinking beer. Forget it— forget it—" Duane collapsed back onto the couch, waving his hand in a gesture of dismissal or deference as Amy replaced her head on his shoulder.

"Nick, you're wasting film," said Jack, looking concerned, as Nick took still more pictures. "It's really dark in here. You want a flash?"

Amy shook her head against Duane's shoulder. "Such a nice guy," she said absently.

Nick grimaced, smiled, took another picture, the motor drive grinding while the camera brushed his wrist. "No way. See, Duane—" He turned to Duane, getting both Duane's and Amy's attention, which meant waiting for them to complete a kiss and turn back to him. "That's my point, Duane. You don't have to have some attitude—I mean not that I don't *have* this attitude, but you don't *need* it. You just have to have, you know, *detachment.* A slow hand. There's always enough light."

Annabelle started moving slowly toward Nick, hands and knees across the carpet like a wildcat, approaching where he sat. "Tell me about your slow hand, Nick," she said, leaning forward and gazing at him.

"Oh, Jesus," said Amy, burying her face in Duane's shoulder. "Here she goes, the fucking master operator—"

Annabelle shot a grin at Amy, breaking character, and then turned back to Nick, doing the moves, drifting her face toward his, lifting her chin, lowering her eyelids, parting her lips. "Tell me about your slow hand," she murmured again, settling beside him and moving even closer—Nick was as frozen as an animal in the headlights, his hands tapping the camera.

"Oh my God," laughed Jill, watching in disbelief.

"Tell me about— Tell me about—" Tina said quietly from the floor, reaching for the amplifier cord and hooking it to the Telecaster jack. "Wait—" She suddenly started picking the guitar and singing, *"I like a man with a slow hand—"* She sang the chorus and a few people joined in, Michael very quietly, and they stopped when Tina couldn't remember the next verse and settled on a G-minor-seventh chord. There was scattered applause—Annabelle had cracked up and Nick was photographing her embarrassed, hand-on-eyes laugh.

"So anyway," said Jack Winfield after a minute, "the guy should be here in a minute with the drinks."

"One of the slaves?" said Wally, looking at Nick. Annabelle had sat down next to Nick on the floor, her back against a bookcase, legs out straight, gold shoes in the middle of the carpet by Nick's abandoned beer bottle, having placed herself precisely so that their thighs lightly touched.

"Did you explain it to him so's he'll get it right?" asked Max, doing a passable imitation of Nick's voice, prompting scattered laughter like wind through power lines stirring a resting flock of birds.

"Yes, Nick, I did. He'll have it—" One of the French doors began to open, and Jack stood up, smiling. "Right now," he added redundantly as a waiter in an elegant white jacket wheeled a linen-draped steel cart into the room, bearing a bottle of Absolut vodka, a basket of oranges, a brass orange-squeezing press, a knife, a cutting board, several tumblers, each with a W etched in the side, a frost-beaded silver ice-bucket supporting a pair of silver ice tongs, and a plate of toast.

"Here you are, sir," said the waiter to Jack, bowing incrementally.

"Thanks," said Jack briskly, taking off his jacket and rolling up his sleeves. He put his cuff links on the cart and began to make screwdrivers, his arms pumping up and down as he cut and pressed each orange.

"Do you— Would you like some help, Jack?" Michael asked.

"First fag cigarettes, now fag drinks," said Max, again imitating Nick's voice, again provoking laughter.

"Oh, please— Don't trouble yourself, Mike," said Jack, his arms in the ice bucket, smiling kindly. "I can manage." As conversation resumed Jack started distributing drinks, first to Tina, Amy, Jill, and Annabelle—when Jill shifted her position on the floor to accept her drink, Michael noticed that she wore a silver anklet with a small key hanging from it.

"You should all stop giving me a hard time," said Nick, his voice apparently weakened by Annabelle's proximity—he was trying to sound bored, which made his tone all the more marginally awkward.

The door opened and Stephen Leonard reëntered the room. "Hey, guys," he said.

"Stephen!" said Amy lazily. The others greeted him as he ambled forward, performing a wrestling-team hand clasp with Wally and nodding at everyone else.

"Where'd you go, Steve?" asked Annabelle.

"I was dancing with these society babes downstairs. They have these ridiculous women at this thing. Nick, you try and take my picture I'll kill you."

"Oooh," said Nick, smiling privately, taking Stephen's picture.

"You watch your back, man," said Stephen, returning the grin. Jack was still distributing drinks, handing them now to Wally, Stephen, Michael, and Douglas.

"Hey, Steve, where's everyone else?" asked Tina in her flat voice. "Where's Bill Coleman?"

"Bill had something to do, I think a summer-job interview or something," said Stephen. "He's driving up later— Like after dinner or something."

"Cool," said Tina. "I can't wait."

"He had a *job interview?*" said Wally, his face twisting in near-comic disbelief. "We *need* him."

"But he'll be here soon and he's bringing so much weed," Nick whispered dryly.

"He is?" asked Jill shyly in her high voice, grinning. Nick did one of his charismatic facial maneuvers, pivoting his head to peer at Jill, smiling with his mouth closed and his chin protruding. "Oh," said Jill, widening that angelic grin of hers as Michael and Douglas watched, each unaware of the other's watching, both noticing that her smile didn't seem to have anything to do with her, as such—it seemed to come through her from somewhere else, like a movie projected on a good screen. Jack, having finished bartending, had begun walking round the room, subtly inspecting it as if looking for scratches or damage.

"Um," said Stephen, "Bill says he might call Louise Delany."

"Hoop hoop hoop," chanted Wally and Stephen, pointing rhythmically, hand-jiving like backup singers, while Jack and Max, and then Nick, and then Michael and Douglas all reacted similarly, repeating Louise's name painfully, whistling, blowing air, collapsing, making flailing motions and otherwise feigning angina pectoris.

"Not really," said Max, smiling.

"You bunch of creeps," said Tina distractedly, strumming the guitar quietly.

"Hoop hoop hoop," Wally and Stephen continued chanting. "Hoop hoop jinga jinga hoop hoop."

"You said it, Gantry," said Wally. "There's like *no way.* Forget it, man, she's not coming— She'll *never* go to a party—"

"I swear," agreed Amy, looking at Tina.

"That's *right*, she hasn't even been to *any* of them, has she?" said Stephen, still standing.

"That bitch," said Annabelle, leaning back and smiling so the light shone off her teeth. "She's showing *up?* Why?" Everyone was laughing again. "She's so— She doesn't even *like* parties. She never even *says* anything, man, she's so *strange.*"

"Uh-huh. Uh-huh," said Nick, nodding.

"Fuck off, Nick," said Annabelle. "I may not like *her,* but she—*definitely*—doesn't like *you.*" Tina, Jill, and Amy applauded as Stephen, Douglas, Max, Wally, and Jack—from the drink cart at the other end of the room—winced in sympathy for Nick. While walking round the room Jack suddenly noticed Ralph DiGrassi, still perched on the edge of the couch, grinning silently, beyond the edge of Jack's previous vantage point by the door—everyone's laughter died slowly and they all silently watched and waited as Jack stood facing Ralph, who hadn't moved.

"Ralph!" said Jack brightly. "I guess you— Did you get your invitation? I guess it was lost in the mail. My apologies." Douglas could see Jack's face betraying his sarcasm.

"I'm just waiting for Buzzman to arrive," said Ralph, grinning around his obtrusive teeth, his eyes fixed on Annabelle, who was manipulating the orange-squeezing press, her arm muscles moving.

"You called—" said Jack.

"But—" said Duane, launching forward in his seat, accidentally knocking Amy's head back with the momentum, "you're not supposed to *call* Buzzman, asshole."

"Look, Ralph, could you not sit on the edge of that couch?" said Jack. "It's an antique."

"Ouch, damn it," said Amy, rubbing her head again. "Duane, stop making points, it hurts my head."

"Oh, right," Ralph said to Jack. "Sure it's an antique."

"Watch your step, man—" said Nick, very quietly, so that Douglas could barely hear.

"Downstairs some *Smithsonian curator* was trying to do a fucking handstand on the couch in the library, which I insist is an exact duplicate of this one," said Ralph, his tone betrayed by his grin. "I didn't see any Winfields stopping *him.*"

"They were bought at the same time by my grandfather," said Jack.

"You're missing the point, dickhead," Duane suddenly exploded. Amy was glaring at Ralph.

"Hey, Ralph— You know Dustin Hoffman's about to do a movie where he plays a woman?" said Stephen calmly. Tina continued playing very quiet blues licks on her unamplified Telecaster, watching.

"Stop leaning on me, man," said Ralph, still wary and motionless, still on the couch.

"Oooh," said Stephen.

" '*Nobody* leans on Sharkey's Machine,' " said Wally, who hadn't moved from the floor, drawing more laughter, while Nick stood up, slowly, almost regretfully, and started wandering over to where Jack and Ralph were standing—after a moment Annabelle also stood and followed, walking behind Nick, and Ralph watched her.

"I mean it's just a couch, I'm not doing anything wrong," said Ralph.

"You're still missing the point," said Duane, still stroking Amy's hair, "dickhead."

"Ralph," Max said quietly, pressing the palm of his hand against his eyes and then waving the hand at Ralph, looking down, "just get off the couch."

Ralph got off of the couch, sliding to a standing position. Annabelle looked at Max, and Douglas looked at Annabelle and then back at Ralph—Nick had turned away, almost casually, Amy had her head back on Duane's shoulder, and Michael watched everything. Suddenly, horribly, Ralph started shouting.

"When I don't have my Dad's muscle you can *talk,*" Ralph shouted. "It's easy to get the drop on *me,* Sudler, it's easy to give *me* a hard time, when you've fucking got it made, when you're living the fucking *life,* doing all the bullshit moves, doing the *bullshit,* free drinks and all, slipping it to *her* not just once but whenever you *want,* living like a fucking—"

In one move Nick swung around and punched Ralph across the mouth—his camera, still on his shoulder, swung to bang Annabelle in the arm and then slipped off and fell, and Jack caught it miraculously before it hit the floor and put it on the cart atop a dark patch of spilled vodka.

"Get my camera out of the vodka," Nick said, his voice quiet, not looking, watching Ralph, who had fallen to his knees, his shoulders shaking, hand on jaw, two drops of blood on his chin, trouser cuff riding up to reveal a pale, shaved calf above a white sock. Jack took Nick's camera out of the vodka, putting it next to a Fabergé egg on a piece of velvet atop the piano while Nick stepped forward, and Annabelle, who was already moving, arrived in front of him and put her hands on his arm. "Asshole," she whispered, glaring at him. Michael heard a clicking sound, very briefly, from behind him.

"Shit. I—" Nick seemed speechless. "Damn it, Duane's a buddy. He's a buddy."

"Yeah, what are you, Gary Cooper? Jesus, Nick."

"She's not impressed," said Amy, languidly looking over while beside her Duane stared fixedly at the floor.

"Well, I didn't say *that,*" said Annabelle, prompting general laughter. Max grimaced as he walked over to crouch next to Ralph, who was probing his jaw experimentally. Michael, still sitting cross-legged on the floor, took a sip from Annabelle's abandoned screwdriver, pausing before the second sip to brush a bit of lipstick from his mouth, and while his head was turned he happened to catch the sound of the clicking behind him and peripherally saw a quarter hit the window.

"Shit— There are quarters— Somebody's throwing quarters at the window," Michael said.

"Oh yeah?" said Tina, furiously strumming another blues progression.

"Buzzman's here," said Ralph from the floor, accepting a linen napkin from Max, who had filled it with ice from the bucket on the cart.

"That's— Buzzman? *Now?*" said Jack.

"Right," said Nick, facing the wall. Jack dashed out of the room as another quarter hit the window.

"I'm sorry," said Nick, very quietly, to Ralph.

"Fuck you," said Ralph, sounding close to tears, holding the bloodied napkin to his mouth. Jack reëntered the room carrying a canvas duffel bag, which he put on the floor and unzipped, the buzz of the zipper making everyone realize how quiet the room had gotten—quiet enough for the sounds of the party downstairs to be noticeable, waxing and waning like waves. Jack got the bag open and pulled out a ladder made of aluminum rungs connected by links of steel chain with big hooks at one end.

"What the hell, is that actually one of those house-on-fire escape ladders?" said Max, standing up.

"That Gantry mind," Annabelle said, walking up behind him and stroking his shoulder.

"Yeah, my parents are amazing," said Jack, intently fitting the pieces of the ladder together while Max casually put his arm around Annabelle.

"Hands off," Annabelle said absently, sliding away.

"Well, the Chase Manhattan Bank must think so," said Nick quietly. Jack smiled politely as another quarter hit the window.

"What's going on?" said Jill, looking around, and Douglas watched her head pivot.

"Where's the damn screwdriver?" Jack muttered—he was holding some wing nuts and frantically hunting through the canvas bag.

"Yeah, like there aren't enough screwdrivers in the room," said Tina—one of the few still sitting down—still picking her guitar. Max wordlessly handed over his Swiss Army knife with the screwdriver open.

"Thanks," said Jack, looking at him as another quarter hit the window. "Just a minute, damn it," he muttered, tightening the wing nuts and then crossing to a small window behind the piano. He slid it open and gently reeled out the ladder, and Nick helped him attach it to the windowsill. "Watch the paint," said Jack.

"How's it going?" Nick stage-whispered, the breeze stirring his hair as he leaned out the window. Douglas watched while the ladder shook and then Jack and Nick helped Buzzman in the window. He was a tall thin man, about twenty-six, with a curved, pocked red face and long reddish hair tied in a ponytail—he wore old-fashioned black horn-rimmed glasses, white pants adorned with grass stains, sneakers, a red Boston Red Sox baseball cap, and a green plaid flannel shirt over a red turtleneck. He had a sort of slow-moving, dazed facial expression and was carrying a small satchel on his shoulder.

"Hey," said Buzzman, gazing wide-eyed around the room, his voice rough and quiet. "Bunch of gangsters," he said, grinning.

"Buzz, what's up," said Nick as they clasped hands. "Nice dreads. Nice threads. Nice treads." Buzzman reached to swat Nick on the top of the head.

"Blanchard," said Buzzman finally. "Winfield— Sorry I took so long, dude."

"Hey, listen," said Jack dismissively, shaking Buzzman's hand. "Let me introduce you around," Jack continued, beginning to point at everyone. "Amy MacIntyre, Duane Sudler, Max Gantry, Tina Foster, Steve Leonard, Wally Patterson—"

"Yeah, I know all you guys," said Buzzman.

"—Mike Cadenhead—"

"Hi," Michael said from the floor.

"Hi," said Buzzman finally, wide-eyed, nodding at Michael. Jill laughed.

"Douglas Taft," Jack said.

"Anna Taft's brother, right?" said Buzzman. He clasped hands with Douglas, looking at his eyes. "Whoa, shit, this guy's been at it already. Black *basketballs*— Where's Anna Taft?"

"Yo," Annabelle said.

"Annabelle, man, give me a kiss," said Buzzman.

"No way. All right," said Annabelle. Buzzman stepped over and touched Annabelle's face with surprising gentleness, his dull expression not wavering but his eyes narrowing as he arched out and kissed her gently and drew back, his baseball cap's visor brushing against her hair. Various people applauded, laughing.

"Think it'll rain tonight, Annabelle?" Buzzman said.

"Oh, *Jesus,*" laughed Max, twirling away.

"What've you got?" asked Nick, poking at Buzzman's bag.

Buzzman turned to him. "Anything you want," Buzzman told him. Nick raised his eyebrows and went over to the bar cart to refill his glass. "Yeah, this is a pretty good scene," Buzzman said, looking around and noticing Ralph DiGrassi, who finally got up off the floor and walked over.

"Hey, man," said Ralph, grinning.

"Di*Grassi,*" said Buzzman, sounding more dazed, angrier. "*There* you are. Hey, Gratso, man, listen, I don't care who your father is— I mean, *never* call me when I'm not in town. That's a bad scene, man. You just— You've just got to wait for me to show up." Ralph had fished out his wallet and was holding out two crumpled fifty dollar bills. "What the fuck?" said Buzzman. Ralph mumbled something, apparently unable, in his embarrassment, to keep a grin off his face. "What?" said Buzzman. "Speak up, man."

"For Joe Fly," Ralph said.

"I'm confused," said Buzzman, looking it. "I barely know the man."

"But we said," said Ralph, holding the money out toward Buzzman, who was already shaking his head.

"I know we said, man, but I barely know the man, and it was *two* hundred, and it was last month."

" 'Joe Fly'?" said Annabelle, looking from Buzzman to Ralph.

"Oh, Jesus, what an asshole," said Nick, still facing the wall, grimacing, turning around. "Are you going to put up with this shit, Winfield?"

Jack pulled out a calfskin wallet and produced a crisp hundred-dollar bill. "No," he said quietly. "No, I'm not." He took the two fifties from Ralph, who held on to them and then released them and then handed the three bills to Buzzman before turning back to Ralph. "Okay? Now goodbye. Please."

"I want to know who 'Joe Fly' is," said Annabelle.

"What's the difference? Get the hell out, DiGrassi," Nick said harshly. "Get in your crappy car and go."

Ralph looked back and forth between everybody and then turned to Jack. "Where's the men's room?" he asked politely.

Nick grabbed Ralph's jacket by the lapels, jerking him forward, making the others jump, and spoke loudly, directly in Ralph's face. "Look. Huh? Jack off on your own time, hey, Ralph. Get the hell out."

"Jesus," said Annabelle.

"Nick, you idiot," said Tina quietly, shaking her head sadly, still sitting on the floor, still playing the guitar. Buzzman was folding the money and tucking it into the edge of his sneaker. Ralph looked around, walked out the door, and slammed it. Amy, Duane, and Jill started applauding and Max and Michael joined in.

"You people clap too much," said Buzzman.

"You're applauding?" Douglas said quietly, so that only Max could hear.

"Shut up," said Max.

"But you're applauding?"

"I was invited," Max said, looking intently at Douglas.

"Okay," said Buzzman. He walked over and sat on the floor, opened his satchel and pulled out some cellophane bags and a pipe, and then stopped moving suddenly and stared at Michael, tilting his head and waiting before speaking. "How'd *you* get in here? You look like the boy accountant."

"I'm— I—I don't know," said Michael. "I'm not an accountant. I'm a writer."

"A *writer?* A *writer?* Kid—" Buzzman gave Michael his wide-eyed stare. "You never even made out."

"Oh, don't pick on Mike, Buzzman," said Tina tiredly. "He's all right."

"I guess I—" Michael began powerlessly.

"You're a high school dude like all the rest, man," said Buzzman, continuing to look at Michael. "No shame in that. Been there. Been there. The funny thing though, kid, the funny thing is that you *look* like a high school student. I mean, these other gangsters, I don't know—"

"Don't worry about it," Tina whispered flatly to Mike, leaning toward him while Buzzman filled the pipe and handed it to Jack. "He's harmless. I mean he's like a teddy bear."

"Thanks," said Michael, noticing that Tina's face looked different from up close.

"You got it, man?" Buzzman was asking Jack.

"Yeah," said Jack, moving the pipe to his mouth, squinting, moving his other thumb on Max's lighter. "Give me a second to get the—" Suddenly one of the gilt doorknobs clattered and there was a light knock at the door.

"Oh, *shit,*" said Jack, panicking, vaulting up and lunging to grab Buzzman and yank him to his feet, clutching the pipe and lighter in his fist. "*Come on,*" Jack whisper-shouted, shaking Buzzman, who had barely snatched the duffel bag before Jack grabbed him again and yanked him across the room, shoving him into a closet and slamming the door in his face before racing across the room, scrambling around a couch and diving to sit in a chair by the far window. "Come in," Jack called out casually. The door opened and Nathan Chablis entered.

"Mr. Chablis!" said Jack calmly, turning to the door as if surprised. "How are you? Make yourself comfortable, please— Would you like a drink?"

Chablis slowly wandered into the room, hands clasped behind his back, taking his time, giving stern, bemused glances to everyone, weaving with intoxication. Wally and Stephen were vibrating and turning crimson, approximating cardiac arrest in their efforts to keep from laughing.

"Well hello," Chablis said finally. "Here you all are. You're missing the hors d'oeuvres."

"Oh, Mr. *Chablis,* there is so much food, you wouldn't believe," said Jack.

"I guess there is at that," Chablis said. "You're all talking over old times, I presume? Years and years of Thorndike memories? Didn't you all play in the sandbox together or something along those lines?"

"Something along those lines, Mr. Chablis," Annabelle said, her teeth shining.

"Dance, Mr. Chablis, dance!" said Jack suddenly. Max had started rolling a cigarette. Stephen, Tina, and Douglas started laughing.

"Not this time." Chablis was sadly shaking his head. "Barbara is nowhere to be found— Still around, Blanchard? You survived our dishonorable discharge?"

"I'm still around," said Nick, finishing his drink and putting the glass on the floor.

"Glad to see it can be done," said Chablis strangely, wandering to the open window, hands still clasped behind his back, standing and squinting at the ladder hooks, beard jutting. He stood motionless for a few more moments, the breeze from the window rippling his trousers as he stared at the ladder hooks. Finally Chablis turned to Jack, pointing at the hooks. "Jack— You clever boy, have you arranged for an emergency exit?"

"That's the idea," Jack said.

"Brilliant," said Chablis, looking at the ladder. "Ingenious. If you decide to make the getaway, you won't leave me behind, will you?"

"Of course not," said Jack. "You'll be the first to know."

Chablis stood examining the ladder for another moment and then sighed briskly and turned back to the door. "Well, I'll leave you to your devices," he said, hand on the knob. "Whatever gives you a buzz. Farewell."

They waited while Chablis left the room and closed the door and then everybody exploded into laughter. "Jesus *Christ,*" said Duane, gasping for breath.

"What the *fuck?*" said Buzzman, coming out of the closet. "Man, I thought that guy would never leave."

"Sorry about that, Buzzman," said Jack, taking the duffel bag as everyone resumed their seated positions.

"Who *was* that?" said Buzzman, still dazed.

"Man, we didn't fool him for *one second,*" said Amy.

"I'm ready to begin," said Buzzman. "Let's go." He adjusted his cap, retrieved the cellophane bags and the pipe from his pocket, and began refilling the pipe.

chapter 19

Douglas watched calmly as a curl of smoke drifted across the ceiling, curling around the cornices and spreading, lit from below, making him notice the ceiling, fully notice it, for the first time—the darkness near its center, the moons of light above the yellow-shaded lamps, the moldings and the dark white paint. The study was filled with people, all of them motionless and limp—it was pleasantly warm, the Oriental carpet was soft and smooth, and the furniture was also soft, but hard, Douglas supposed, looking at the mahogany feet on the furniture, where it needed to be. The room's air was warm and still save for the fragrant breeze that brought the countryside's aromas and the sounds of wind and trees through the opened window. Douglas looked back at the curl of motionless smoke, which seemed to have the scale and complexity of a celestial object. "Jesus," he said.

"You watching that band of smoke?" said Tina.

"Yeah. Jesus, Tina, I barely know you."

"Don't worry about it." Tina was playing some delicate classical guitar and she stopped to brush her hair out of her face.

"Oh, man—" said Nick, lying on the carpet, sunglasses on. "Tina, babe, don't stop. That sounds so good." Tina continued playing. "Hey, Tina, when's your album coming out?"

"Somebody hook her up," said Wally, lying on the floor with his eyes closed.

"What?" said Jill.

"Hook Tina up. Hook her up with an *amplifier,*" said Wally.

"Man oh man—" said Annabelle.

"Hey Annabelle," said Wally, "can I borrow some of these famous photographs of you sometime?"

"Go screw," said Annabelle absently.

"Leave her alone," said Nick. "Whoa, *shit!*" Nobody had ever heard Nick speak so loudly. Tina and Michael turned to look at him.

"What the fuck?" said Amy, sitting down on the floor next to Wally.

"Sorry," said Nick. "I was just noticing that curl of smoke."

Douglas and Tina laughed. "Right!" said Douglas exuberantly.

"He's one of us," said Tina.

"That's right," said Douglas. "Hey, Nick, you see patterns in the smoke?"

"He probably sees f-stops," said Annabelle. "Motor drives. Lenses."

"I see mountains," said Nick quietly, looking up at the smoke.

Annabelle and Max looked at each other and started applauding. "Man, cut that out," said Duane, wincing. Annabelle and Max stopped clapping.

"Nick's sensitive side," said Annabelle. "I can't believe it. I think it merits applause."

"Don't kid yourself, babe," said Nick.

"My eyes are closed," said Wally. "I can't see the smoke."

"Someday they'll glue them shut," Nick said.

"Talk about it," said Tina dully. "I was going to go down to the Power Station but the guy I knew went to the Marley funeral."

"What else should we know about?" Jack asked Tina.

"Um," said Tina, "well, you know about the new Stones album, right? They finished down there—it'll come out in a couple of months. They're touring in the fall."

"Oh my God," said Amy. "Did you *meet* them?"

"What's it called?" asked Wally.

"I think *Tattoo.* I met Bill Wyman," said Tina casually. "We got along. They had a basketball hoop put into the big room down there. It's still up."

"Oh my God," Amy said again.

"Bob Marley *died,* man," said Buzzman, wide-eyed, over at the piano. "That was, like, such a *drag,* man."

"What the hell, Tina— Was that drugs or what?" Stephen asked.

"It was cancer," said Nick. "All the Wailers were there. They glued his eyes shut."

"Oh, shit, what a buzzcruncher," said Wally. "Change the subject—"

"Hey, Duane!" said Tina.

"What?" Duane said weakly from across the room.

"How come you never say anything?"

"The beasts of the field, the birds of the air, the fish in all the seas— They toil not, neither do they spin," Duane said, "and they don't fucking *talk.*"

"Shut up, Duane," said Wally languidly. Jack had slowly wandered around the room and found an amplifier cord—halfway back, he stopped in the act of stepping over Wally and started laughing wildly.

"What's so funny?" said Douglas.

"I was just— I was just—" Jack said, sitting down weakly on the floor, laughing. Douglas tapped Tina on the shoulder and pointed at the white amplifier cord wrapped around Jack's fingers, and Tina smiled.

"It's like a snake," Tina said.

"You talking about me?" said Wally, not opening his eyes.

"Will you quit advertising your claim-to-fame?" said Duane, who had walked to the window.

"Jealous?" Wally said.

"Why were you laughing, Jack?" said Douglas.

"I'm imagining—" said Jack, laughing, his eyes watering—"I'm imagining— Okay, so Wally and Nick are in a bar and they go up to some woman and at the end of the bar there's—a little museum, you know, a few paintings, right there in the bar, and Nick and Wally sort of wander up and Wally starts off by saying— He starts out by saying, 'Yeah— I like art too. Can I fuck you up the ass?' "

"Uh-oh, Winfield's lost it," said Nick. "Because— Because— Jack! Guess what— *We would never do that.*"

"Oh, Jesus," said Annabelle, laughing uncontrollably and then coughing.

"You want a drink of water, Annabelle?" said Michael.

"Probably the only thing she doesn't want," said Wally.

"Hey, Nick!" said Amy. She was sitting next to Wally, looking down at his face and his closed eyes, her voice echoing around the room, and Douglas, just for the hell of it, imagined that he could see the visible traces of the echoes—when Max and Annabelle applauded again, the sound shone like nailheads shimmering along the room's edges.

"You want a drink of water, Annabelle?" said Michael.

"Hey, *Nick!*" said Amy.

"How many times is she going to say that?" Douglas asked Tina.

"Say what?" Tina gently played the guitar.

"What?" Nick said to Amy.

"Come over and take a picture of Wally," said Amy.

"Why?" said Nick.

"Someone asks Nick *Blanchard* to take a photograph and he says *why?*" said Wally. "Besides, it should be obvious."

"Right," said Amy, stroking Wally's hair. "Because he's so pretty."

"Temperature's rising," said Tina, announcing the news, her voice pounded flat. "You're pretty too, Douglas. Don't let these bastards get you down."

"Thanks, Tina," said Douglas.

"How's my F.Q.?" Wally said, opening his eyes, still lying flat.

"Off the scale," said Amy.

"*Him?*" said Annabelle, who had ended up over at the bar, fixing another drink. "Don't be fooled, Amy. Size isn't everything—"

"It's the *only* thing," said Tina, eyes glittering.

"But wait, I have to know, Wally," panted Amy hysterically, "I have to know if it's really as long as they say."

"It really is," said Wally, grinning.

"Are you kidding?" asked Stephen. "Are you not kidding about the *man?* The man who needs a goddamned garden-hose reel?"

"Tone it down, tone it down, tone it down," said Jack. "Remember what the—"

"I remember I remember I remember," said Max. "Wait, I remember something— You remember back in seventh grade or whatever when Nick asked Amy out?"

"I *like* you, Max," said Nick.

"Everybody likes Max," said Annabelle. "Even the little kids."

"Shut up, Annabelle— So it's a dance at the gym at Thorndike and there's Nick surrounded— This was sixth grade, right"—Max looked around as he talked—"and there's Nick surrounded by, like, this whole semicircular ring of all his friends facing Amy, right, surrounded by a semicircular ring of all *her* friends, right, and Nick says, 'Will you go out with me?' "

"I remember this," said Tina.

"So Amy goes, *'Yes,'* " narrated Max. "And then, like, a moment goes by, and then she, like, *spins around real fast*"—Max was almost acting it out—"consults with the ring of girls, buzz buzz buzz, and then she turns back around and says— And says— And says *'No.'* "

"Yup," said Annabelle, nodding. "That happened."

"Evil woman," murmured Wally on the floor, gently scolding Amy, who was stroking his shoulders.

"E-vil wo-man," Tina sang, playing the guitar. Douglas laughed.

"Oh, *shit,*" said Jack, still on his knees, falling to the floor in slow motion, suddenly sounding like he needed air or had some similar problem, so that everyone else suddenly stopped talking. "Oh, *shit, shit, shit—*"

"What?" asked Michael, mildly enough to get a mild laugh.

"Shit. I just realized the *schedule,*" said Jack, rolling on the floor between all of them, his face in his hands. "I just realized that we're going to have to do the goddamned dinner *stoned.* We have to be there or Mom'll kill me, and it's in fifteen minutes and we have to do it stoned and shit, shit, we don't even have any *coke—*"

"Where's Buzzman?" said Douglas.

"Right behind you," said Buzzman.

"There's a *wall* behind me," said Douglas without turning around. "I'm *leaning* against it."

"Yeah, but like, *nevertheless,* man," said Buzzman from behind him.

"Douglas doesn't catch on," said Nick, smiling and lighting a cigarette. "Man, I love the way the taste of cigarettes is affected."

"Even fag cigarettes," said Annabelle.

"Cigarette fags," said Nick.

"Buzzman? Buzzman?" said Douglas.

"I haven't gone anywhere," said Buzzman from behind him. Douglas suddenly pivoted to look at the wall behind him. Everybody laughed. Amy kissed Wally and Duane stormed out of the room.

"Uh-oh," said Annabelle, giggling.

"Jesus, go somewhere else, have some tact," said Jack, flat on the floor in defeat. "Could you play more quietly, Tina?"

"Of course," said Tina. "Sorry." Douglas looked over at what felt like the next moment and Wally and Amy weren't there anymore, and as he watched Annabelle got up and walked over to Max and the two of them walked over to Jill, who was lying on the couch with her eyes closed, and shook her awake, and Jill stood up and the three of them walked toward the door. Douglas hurried over, head spinning as he stood, and caught Max's arm.

"Where are you going?" Douglas asked.

"What?"

"You heard me— What are you doing with Annabelle? Why'd you wake up Jill?"

"Don't worry about it," said Max.

"We'll be right back, Doug," Annabelle said, poking her head back into the room. "Take it easy."

"I can't believe you bought that piano for so much money," Stephen was saying to Jack.

"That's how much it costs," said Jack, shrugging. "You pay it."

"I could never figure out Robert Redford's hair," said Tina, playing "Casey Jones." "Even when I met him."

"I'm not sure you've got that right," said Nick.

"Oh, of course not," said Tina, cutting the song off.

"I was *around* back then," Nick said quietly.

"What's Mick Jagger really like?" asked Amy, out of the blue.

"Stupid question," announced Wally, covering everyone's embarrassment, moving for the vodka and orange juice, which had been transferred to the floor. "Have another drink, Amy."

"Where did Duane go?" Douglas whispered to Tina, having sat back down.

"I'm not getting involved in that shit," said Tina.

"Hey, *Michael!*" said Douglas.

Michael jumped—he had been writing furiously on a cocktail napkin. "Yes, Douglas?"

"What've you got there?"

"I'm embarrassed," said Michael.

"No, come on," said Nick. "Let's go."

"Read it, Michael," said Tina.

Michael started reading, sitting cross-legged on the carpet, his glasses askew, and Tina accompanied him with a barely audible modal progression that flattered the words. " 'I always knew this day would come,' " Michael read, " 'and wondered what it would bring, but when it came I learned that I have a secret knowledge, and I was afraid, and lost in a deep sadness, knowing that something that I had always needed and always owned was gone. A familiar voice taught me of the paradox of love and contempt and asked if I was fit to judge because time had passed and made me wise, or because I had been made blind, and hearing the voice I discovered an uncharted sorrow. I have seen the wounds of time and the mystery of a silent hour, and I have loved these things without regret, because I will travel far, but a part of me will remain as long as I save this sad and secret knowledge.' "

"That's really good," said Tina quietly, a few silent moments after Michael had stopped reading. She stood up and walked over to hug him, from behind, her thin hair drifting down above his shy and sudden smile.

"Damn," said Douglas. Amy and Wally walked back in, their faces red, closing the door loudly and causing Douglas to flinch.

"Hey, it was a duet," said Tina blandly, squeezing Michael's shoulder. "You're brave to make secrets public."

"Just my own secrets," Michael quietly told Tina. "Just words. But thank you."

"What's going on?" said Wally, looking around.

"We're thinking about leaving Thorndike," said Tina more loudly, reclining away from Michael and staring at Wally and Amy in a bored fashion.

"Oh, shit," said Wally. "Bunch of saps. Come on, Amy, let's go." While he spoke, pivoting on the carpet, the door opened again and Annabelle, Max, Jill, and Duane walked back in, almost smashing the door into Wally's face—Wally and Duane exchanged glares and then ignored each other.

"I leave for five minutes and everybody gets so somber," said Annabelle.

"We found Duane," said Jill, pointing at Duane.

"I think we're coming down," said Nick.

"Where's Buzzman?" said Douglas.

"Well, *some* of us are coming down," said Wally. "Hey, Douglas, get a clue, why don't you."

"What?" said Douglas, reeling to his feet.

"You all right, Douglas?" said Tina.

"Where the fuck is Buzzman?" said Douglas, stepping forward, his nose running a bit.

"I keep saying I'm right here, man," said Buzzman from behind Douglas. Douglas whirled around and Buzzman was right there. "I'm here but I have to go."

"Don't go," said Tina.

"I have to," said Buzzman, courteously leaning to wipe Douglas' nose. "You all right, man?" he said gently.

"I think so," said Douglas.

"Hey, Buzzman, what's the deal— Are you going home?" said Annabelle. "Where do you *live,* anyway? Can I visit you?"

"You wouldn't like it," said Buzzman, keeping his hand paternally on Douglas' shoulder. "And I can't go home till the rain comes."

"Oh, Jesus Christ," said Douglas, reeling—he almost fell and Max caught him. "I'm okay," said Douglas, standing up.

"Goodbye, Buzzman," Jack was saying. Douglas watched as Buzzman put on his satchel and climbed back out the window.

"What did that professor dude say? I'll leave you to your own devices," said Buzzman. "Well—" He stopped halfway out the window, his leg hanging in the starlight outside, and fished another nickel bag out of his jacket pocket, tossing it to Jack. "Check it out."

"How much?" said Jack.

"Another half," said Buzzman.

"But how *much?*" said Jack.

Buzzman waved his hand, slipped out the window for a moment, caught himself, looked outside, seeming to notice for the first time how high up he was, and then said, "Forget it. On the house. Like me right now— Maybe next year I can use the pool."

"Deal," said Jack. "Thanks, Buzz." Jack stepped forward. "Dinner's kind of important to me, you understand, family thing, certain people—" As Jack spoke he produced a bill of some unspecified denomination that no one could make out and slipped it smoothly under the visor of Buzzman's hat. "So, a few bills—"

"I can't believe I'm hearing this," said Tina.

Buzzman smiled, reached in his pocket, and produced another cellophane bag, this one smaller and white-translucent. "A few bills, my ass. I don't do this the way anyone else does. Here's some flour— Bake yourselves for dinner."

"Thank you, sir," exalted Jack, tossing the new bag to Nick. "Find a smooth mirror in the bathroom, Blanchard," he ordered, pointing at him.

"Jesus, Jack, calm down," said Tina, laughing and putting an arm around his shoulder, her other hand still holding the guitar. "Stop showing off— Don't worry about dinner."

"Douglas," said Buzzman, still half out the window, pointing at Douglas, "I can dig your not seeing things when they're right behind you but you've got to learn to see things when they're right in *front* of you." Buzzman touched his finger to the visor of his Red Sox cap and hoisted himself the rest of the way out the window and they heard him climbing down the ladder.

"Got it," said Douglas. "Oh, shit—"

"Goodbye," called Buzzman from some distance outside as Nick pulled up the ladder and Jack closed the window—he flung a last quarter against the glass and was gone.

"Wait a minute, wait a minute," Douglas said, reeling around. "The Red Sox have a *black* cap, not a red cap. Make him come back, make him come back—"

"You poor little jerk," said Wally, walking up to Douglas, veering while Douglas wiped saliva from his chin. "You look so *lost*— What are you *doing* here, Douglas? I mean, why are you really here? Is *everyone* going to take advantage of Jack being a friendly guy?"

"Hey," said Max, stepping forward around the ottoman. "Hey, Wally, come on—"

"Watch it, Gantry," said Wally, shoving Max's shoulder—Max reeled and the backs of his knees hit the ottoman and he lost his balance and toppled backward, sitting down hard on the ottoman and knocking it back against Michael's knees.

"Come on, Taft," said Wally into Douglas' face—Douglas rubbed his red eyes, sniffing as he cowered. "Why don't you make it *clear* you don't know what you're doing when Buzzman shows up?"

"Son of a bitch," muttered Max, trying to stand. Only Michael heard him.

"Ride your sister's coattails— I mean, shit— Does this seem right to you? I mean does this seem right to you?"

"Hey," said Annabelle, finally arriving between Wally and Douglas, stepping between them very quickly. "Hey, Wally, you asshole, leave him alone."

"What are you calling me now?" Wally said incredulously.

"You heard me, asshole," said Annabelle, moving forward and causing Wally to back up a step. "Leave him— Hey! Leave him alone." She shoved him in the chest with her fingertips and he stepped back again and everyone watched, electrified. "Huh? Leave him alone."

"Annabelle," said Wally, smiling incrementally down at her as she faced him, trying not to pose but posing anyway, shoving him in the chest again. "Jesus, Anna, are there any *limits* to your arrogance? I mean"—he looked around at everyone else and back at Annabelle—"I'm sure *everybody's* been wondering."

"Don't worry about it," said Annabelle quietly, staring at him. "Leave my brother alone."

"Why?" said Wally. "What difference does it— Why should I? I mean, one hopes he can fend for himself." His voice hardened as he backed up, his calves brushing against a small table.

"Oh, Jesus, watch the furniture," said Jack, spinning away. "Not *another* fight—"

"Leave him *alone,*" said Annabelle again, glaring at Wally, several strands of hair falling in her eyes as she closed on him.

"Why? Tell me why," said Wally.

" 'Cause he's *better* than you," Annabelle said tightly.

"Annabelle, watch your step," said Wally. "You want me to say how good you thought I was after a— During a certain night last month?"

"Look, can't we all just, I don't know, *agree to disagree* or something?" Jack was saying plaintively.

"I don't care," said Annabelle, lifting her chin. "I know what I said and I don't care." Douglas couldn't see her face but he could tell how angry she was from the way that her head moved. "Is that how you—how you *decide* what people are *good for?* Douglas could fuck you in *half*— He's more of a sidewinder than any of you *assholes.* See"—she poked him again—"see, if Douglas cared he could beat you at your own stupid games, if he *cared,* if he didn't have better things to do." Max looked down, smiling, and then over at Douglas, who didn't catch his gaze, and Max realized that nobody else was smiling—Nick was still sitting behind the piano, leaning his head sideways on his arms on the sheet-music rack, watching.

"Annabelle, have some tact," Wally said.

"*Tact?*" said Annabelle. "Leave him alone or I'll throw you out."

"You're going to throw me out?" said Wally, laughing. "Come on, Anna, that's— You're out of your mind, you know that?"

"Don't mess with her," warned Nick from the piano, his voice quiet and sandy.

Wally stopped walking back, suddenly, and his smile faded—he tilted his head and looked down at Annabelle. "Okay, cut it out, Annabelle. Game's over."

"The *wrestler,*" said Annabelle. "The fucking *wrestler.*" She pushed Wally again, a series of shoves, lightly and then more strongly. "Apologize to Douglas."

"Annabelle, this is ridiculous. Will you just—"

"Say you're sorry, you— Say it. I'll kill you."

"Will someone *get this bitch off me?*" said Wally, voice sharpening. "Why don't you people move, for Christ's—" He cut himself off as Annabelle suddenly reeled, swayed on her feet, and began to fall down—Nick started moving immediately, probably because he'd been watching Annabelle more closely than anyone, but she almost hit the carpeted floor before Wally caught her, sagging under her sudden weight and almost losing his balance. Everyone was on their feet—Nick and Wally began moving Annabelle toward the couch, stumbling a few steps, and as they did so nobody could miss the fact that she was completely limp, eyes closed, mouth open.

"Annabelle?" said Nick gently, looking down at her. "Annabelle?" One could forget all about Nick, watching him do this, Tina Foster told Michael an hour later. "Anna, are you all right? Anna—"

Annabelle stirred and woke up, got her bearings, stood up roughly, and pushed Wally and Nick away—Wally let go of her waist reluctantly. "Leave me alone," she whispered, swaying, reaching to lean on Nick's shoulder as she held her bowed head.

"Take it slow," murmured Nick, supporting her. "Shh— Take it slow. Breathe easy— Are you all right?" Annabelle nodded weakly, standing straight, rubbing her eyes.

"Anna, I'm sorry— Jesus, are you all right?" said Wally, moving toward her.

"Back off," said Annabelle, cringing from Wally. "It's— I just— It must be the dope. I just got light-headed. I'm all right." Jack walked in and handed her a glass of water, the white cloud of vapor in the top half of the glass still fading upward. "Thanks, Jack," whispered Annabelle, smiling at him, still avoiding everyone's eyes. She went to sit down on one of the floor cushions by the piano, and Nick sat beside her and took the glass when she held it out, and glared at Wally, who had been walking cautiously toward her, and Wally turned away. "*Whew*— Sorry about that," said Annabelle, alert again. "Everyone stop looking at me. I'm fine, damn it— Nothing happened."

"I guess," said Jack, leaning against the piano and gingerly opening the first of the two bags that Buzzman had given him on his way out the window, "I guess if we're still rolling we might as well just do ourselves in for dinner. How is everyone?"

"*Man,* what a host," said Annabelle happily. "We're coming down."

"Then get over here," said Jack.

chapter 20

The menu was Jellied Consommé of Lobster, Salmon Roulade with Oysters and Riesling Sauce, Breast of Baby Chicken and Squab in Greek Pastry, Cleaned Champagne Grapes with Wild Blackberry Sorbet, and (upholding the traditional Anthesteria theme) Athenian Tea Cakes, all prepared by two chefs borrowed from the Lawrence Hotel and served by a team of waiters from somewhere in the area, although nobody really knew where the waiters came from. Douglas, Max, Annabelle, Michael, and Nick were all seated at various positions around one of the twenty-nine white-linen-draped tables on the stone court behind the house, drinking in the darkness as the cool evening breeze stirred their hair and clothes and swung the lanterns in miniature arcs, their orange and yellow light reflecting in the brilliant surfaces of the bay windows behind them. They had no real way of knowing what was going on at the other tables, but the five of them were in the final stages of being heavily stoned, and the food tasted better than anything they had ever tasted in their lives—they were all in a sort of unmentionable private ecstasy as they devoured the main courses, spearing oysters with their thick-handled forks and wiping their mouths with the Winfield napkins, glad that the outdoor darkness kept their ferocious eating out of any conspicuous notice. At a certain point Max caught Nick's eye and Nick did a little clandestine pantomime, squinting and turning the corners of his mouth down with satisfaction while indicating his food and then giving Max a solemn "OK" sign with his hand, signaling profound approval—Max, despite himself, had to grin and nod, and he never forgot that moment between them.

Besides the three others, there were no familiar faces at the table—Douglas had been seated to Max's left, with a large middle-aged woman in a red dress and pearl earrings between them engaged in a conversation with the thin elderly woman to *Douglas'* left, but the red-dressed woman somehow impeded all conversation, so Max turned to his right, where, to his surprise, he found little Betsey Winfield, ten years old. At the beginning of the dinner, during the business of shuffling around looking at the chart and at the little name cards, Max had been terrified, experiencing that particular drug-related paranoia, afraid of knocking over a chair or spilling wine or somehow making an ass of himself, but now, safely parked at the dinner table, he felt fine, eating the salmon and chicken and squab and losing his balance in several minor, hidden ways as he looked around the huge promenade at the other tables and the bright lights from the kitchen door, where all the white-shirted waiters raced primly back and forth with trays of food, and through the kitchen door at the rows of fluorescent soft-drink cans and the beer kegs and the champagne bottles chilling in entire steel garbage cans filled with ice water.

The vast lawn between the house and the distant trees was almost like the fields and forests around Wallingford, near Choate, close enough to fill Max with sudden, unexpected emotion at the thought of what he'd left behind—the cool air felt like the air that had rolled over the campus in the spring, reminding him of the last days of the school year, already more than a week in the past, and of all the final evenings when he had sat with his Choate friends in sweatshirts and shorts on the edges of the athletic fields, and although he had never spoken a word to anyone about it, during those evenings he'd come closer to seeing the colors and contours of *Max Gantry's Rapture,* the painting, than he ever had before. Max smiled as he remembered the shouting of the Choate athletic coaches ("The ball comes in—Where were *you?* Where were *you?* Up your *ass,* that's where you were") and the sodium lamps during the games, and when he finally let his gaze settle on Annabelle, who was sitting across from him deep in conversation with Nick, he suddenly felt something alarming that he'd never felt before, the first brush of a particular insight that seemed to cast shadows in all directions—sitting unnoticed and staring at her, watching her talk to Nick and brush her hair away from her face, Max felt a surge of emotion that had nothing to do with Dover or Thorndike or the Tafts or the Winfield party or

Choate or anything else that he could compare it to, and after a moment he tore his eyes away. Looking out across the black surface of the lawn, he saw the dark saw-edges of the windswept trees by the shore, and as his eyes adjusted to the darkness he could see the shimmering reflection of the moon on the hidden surface of the lake, and when he gazed straight up, beyond the heavy black eaves of the house, Max could just make out the distant, silver stars.

"Are you gargling?" Betsey Winfield asked.

"What?" asked Max, startled, looking at her.

"I thought you were gargling," said Betsey, laughing, covering her closed mouth with her hand. "I'm sorry. My brother's friends are so strange."

"You're Betsey?" said Max, pretending he didn't already know.

"That's right. I don't believe we've met," recited Betsey.

"Not just Betsey," said Max. "Betsey *Ann,* right?"

"Yes," said Betsey. "But that's a secret."

"I'm sorry," said Max, smiling in what he hoped was a congenial way. "I met your father, and he was— He seemed confused, he thought I was a friend of yours."

"My father plays games," said Betsey. "I think he likes to pretend things. You can call me Betsey Ann if you want."

"Thank you," said Max, smiling again.

"Go for it, Max!" said Annabelle from across the table, watching. "Younger women!"

"I'm Max Gantry," said Max, ignoring Annabelle.

"How do you do," said Betsey primly, smiling at him. She was quite small, her hair center-parted and pulled back with barrettes, which were made of brown Woolworth's plastic and were incongruous with her small green evening gown. She was clearly too young to be wearing an evening gown, Max saw, but she sort of pulled it off—when she smiled Max saw that she had braces.

"You're right," said Max. "Your brother's friends are very strange."

"You have weird fingers," said Betsey, pointing at Max's hands and then quickly repeating her hand-in-front-of-mouth gesture, this time with alarm. "Oh, gosh, I'm sorry."

"I know. Aren't they strange?" said Max, trying to put Betsey at ease, conscious peripherally that Annabelle was still watching. "I was born this way."

"I was born with normal boring fingers," said Betsey, squinting and examining her outstretched hands clinically—she was so small and her voice was in such a high register that this little performance was somehow majestic. "So," she said, more quietly, leaning toward Max, almost whispering, "tell me about all of your friends."

"Well," said Max, quietly, leaning forward, taking a sip of water and spilling a few ounces onto the linen tablecloth, "which ones do you want to know about? Oh, damn, sorry," he finished, noticing the spilled water.

"Don't worry about it. Hey," said Betsey suddenly. "Are you stoned?"

"Shhh! No," Max said.

"You *are* stoned, aren't you?" said Betsey. "Just tell me. I have to go to bed soon. I'm turning eleven soon. You might as well tell me."

"Yes," said Max.

"Oh," said Betsey, looking a bit sad, and Max suddenly regretted the answer he'd given. "So tell me about your friends," said Betsey, brightening as she leaned closer to him. "Who's the girl over there?" Betsey tipped her water glass, pointing at Annabelle.

"Which one?" whispered Max, as if he hadn't noticed.

"With the black hair. You *know,*" whispered Betsey. "Right over there."

"That's— Her name's Annabelle," said Max.

"Is she a friend of yours?" said Betsey.

"Yes," said Max. "Why?"

"She's so beautiful," said Betsey. "How old is she?"

"She's nineteen," said Max. Betsey frowned.

"Is she a senior at Thorndike? My brother's only eighteen."

"She skipped a year," explained Max. "She skipped a year and went to Italy."

"She's just so pretty. Who's the guy next to her?"

"Shhh," whispered Max, giggling. "Watch out. That's Nick— don't mess with him, he's *dangerous.*"

"What?"

"I mean, of course I *say* he's dangerous, but what I'm really doing is just—giving him some free *publicity,*" Max explained, laughing a bit more, so that the woman in the red dress to his left looked over sharply.

"You *are* stoned, aren't you," said Betsey.

"*Whew.* Yes," said Max, exhaling and regaining his composure.

"Sorry— That's Nick Blanchard. He's twenty-two," he added, anticipating the next question, "and he's a photographer."

"He's not a teenager any more," said Betsey reflectively. "Is he Annabelle's boyfriend?"

"No," said Max. "Look— Over there to our left, behind that woman— That's Douglas, Annabelle's brother."

"Uh-huh," said Betsey. "He looks like a nice boy."

"He is a nice boy," said Max.

"I can tell. He's cute, too. You're *all* cute— Who's the fellow with the glasses?" Betsey pointed with her fork.

"Shh," said Max, pushing her hand down. "That's Michael. I just met him today, really—I used to go to Thorndike but I didn't really know him."

"Are your parents here?"

"No," said Max.

"You're all *alone?* You came by *yourself?*" said Betsey, her eyebrows climbing.

"No, I—" said Max, trying by some visual means to get Betsey to lower her voice. "A lot of people did. I think people got rides all different ways. Some people haven't even gotten here yet. There's this guy Bill Coleman who's coming later, and he might bring some other—"

"They'll miss *dinner,*" complained Betsey, seemingly overwhelmed by the incorrectness and injustice of the arrangement. "And I won't get to *meet* them. I'll be in *bed.*"

"You can meet them on Monday," said Max. "You're going to the Thorndike graduation, right?"

"Are you finished, sir?" asked a waiter, looming over Max suddenly and making him jump.

"Of *course* I'm going. My brother's graduating. Hi, Angus," Betsey said, waving at the waiter.

"Yes, I'm done. Thank you," said Max. Angus, the waiter, took his plate. "You can meet Bill on Monday, then," he said to Betsey. "Angus scared the hell out of me."

Betsey laughed. "He's nice," she said. "So you came by *yourself?*"

"I'm not—" Max drank his water. "I'm staying with the Tafts." He gestured at Douglas and Annabelle, realizing that he hadn't given their last names.

"Oh," said Betsey, staring at Annabelle again. "Is Annabelle your girlfriend?"

"If she were," said Max, "wouldn't— No, she's not." Out of the corner of his eye Max saw Jack wandering over to the table, weaving a bit, smiling and waving, and Max waved back. Eventually Jack arrived behind Max and Betsey, leaning on the backs of their chairs.

"Hey," said Jack, smiling. "Betsey, Mom wants to talk to you."

Betsey looked crestfallen, pouting and then making an exaggerated show of folding her napkin and getting up. "Bedtime," she said, rolling her eyes. "You will excuse me, Max— It was delightful to meet you."

"The same, I'm sure," muttered Max, smiling—before he could react Betsey leaned forward and pecked him on the cheek, and then bolted off, skidding around the table, recovering and dashing across the damp grass over toward the table where Peggy Winfield was sitting. In the moment she was close to Max she had smelled of toothpaste and Ivory soap and no perfume at all.

"Hey, man," Jack said, collapsing into Betsey's just-vacated seat, his dinner jacket still immaculate. "Hey, Blanchard— Annabelle— Douglas—" Jack tipped his head as each of the others waved at him. Max leaned back and fished a package of Drum tobacco from his pocket and started rolling a cigarette, provoking a startled glance from the thin elderly woman to Douglas' left.

"How you doing, Max?" said Jack, leaning suddenly toward him.

"Not bad," said Max, nodding.

"You all the way down yet?"

"Shh! Not just yet. You?"

"Wally and Stephen and I just had a few more hits," Jack said, pointing toward the house. "Listen, Max— I'm sorry you had to put up with my sister. She's such a pain in the ass."

"She's all right," said Max.

"I'm glad somebody thinks so," said Jack. "God damn, I don't think there's *ever* been this many people at this thing."

"What time is Bill Coleman arriving?" asked Max.

"An hour or so," said Jack, looking at his Rolex. "Do you know Louise?"

"Not really."

"But you've seen her." Jack smiled.

"Oh yes," said Max. Angus, the waiter, was distributing plates of Athenian Tea Cakes and taking orders for coffee and brandy, making his way down the other side of the table and apparently memorizing everything. "I saw her yesterday— We were at the Café and she walked by."

"She's something," agreed Jack, as if Max had actually made a comment. "She's such a strange girl. I mean, you know, strange in the Thorndike sense. Parents are millionaires. She never says anything. She never goes to parties and she's never gone out with a guy, and she gets perfect grades, and she goes right home after school and never hangs around with us, and it's fucking impossible to make her laugh. I don't know. You figure it out. What a waste of a body— Every time a visiting team comes to Thorndike, you know, for a home game, I find myself wishing that she'd walk by, and she does, and then the visiting team sees her, and they don't know any better, so they get all nervous and maybe it affects the games. Who knows? Not me. I just play defense."

"She can't be that bad," said Max. "Hey, Angus. Just coffee for me."

"Yes sir," said the waiter, still unflappable, having made his way around to them. "Mr. Winfield?"

"Coffee, brandy." Angus, the waiter, moved on, and Jack turned back to Max. "Max— You know the *help?*" he whispered incredulously.

"Not really," said Max. "Dancing's starting again soon, isn't it?"

"Yeah, the orchestra's here," said Jack. "I *hate* those bastards—I keep telling Dad to get a band from Hartford or something, but he couldn't care less. Dad always makes these weak-as-hell drinks for the conductor." Max looked to his left and saw Peggy Winfield leading Betsey by the hand into the house, through the bright kitchen door. The woman in red to Max's immediate left got up, dropping her napkin, and walked toward the house. Jack brightened. "Douglas!" he called, beckoning to him. "Scooch over. Scooch over."

Douglas got out of his conversation with the thin elderly woman to his left and moved over into the vacated seat next to Max. "Hey, guys," he said.

"Hello," said Max.

"Listen, Max"—Douglas abruptly leaned forward to whisper in Max's ear, embarrassing him—"what happened between you and Anna and Jill?"

"Nothing," Max whispered back.

"Please tell me," whispered Douglas. "I have to know."

"It was nothing," Max said. "Don't worry about it."

"Douglas, you aren't still angry at Wally, are you?" said Jack, having misheard.

"I guess not," said Douglas quietly. "He kind of had a point—I'm still not down." He tipped his head, pointing at the woman he'd just been talking to. "This woman thinks I'm crazy."

"Check it out, here comes all the coffee and everything," Jack said, leaning forward and pointing toward the kitchen. "I'm sorry, Douglas, what was that?"

"Nothing."

"Nothing at all," muttered Nick, having walked around the table to crouch between them, taking photographs. "How you guys doing." Max looked over and saw that Annabelle had left the table.

"No, no," said Douglas, flinching, raising his hands as Nick pointed his camera at him. "Come on—"

"Nick, you spilled wine on your jacket," said Jack, concerned, pointing at the stain.

"Hey Nick— Is Annabelle feeling better?" asked Max, looking down at the top of Nick's head, which was bobbing with his camera as he tried to frame Douglas in the viewfinder.

"Come on, Taft, give me the look— What now, Max?"

"I said 'Is Annabelle feeling better?' "

"Annabelle is feeling so good, you have no idea," said Nick, weaving, pointing the camera up at Douglas, crouching buoyantly. "Come on— Come on, Taft— That's it— Move left—"

"Nick, *please* don't photograph me," said Douglas, projecting real anger, dropping the thin coffee spoon he'd been fiddling with.

"Oh, Douglas, please," said Nick, in a completely charming and deferential comic voice. "Please, please, man— Just let me do it"— He was shifting into some sort of dialect, bowing at Douglas' elbow, and Max and Douglas felt the power of his terrifying charisma— "Just let me take one meager little picture of your beautiful face— Douglas— Just let me have this one thing— And I'm sure your life will turn out beautifully— A perfect life— We'll pray for it together— And you'll walk off into the horizon with a beautiful girl on each arm."

Douglas looked down at Nick. "They'd get into an argument," he said finally.

"Oh, I hear you, man," said Nick, laughing, shifting his crouching position, camera hanging from his hand, patting Douglas on the arm. "I'm sorry, Douglas. I won't take your picture if it bothers you."

"Nick, you're going to have a stain," said Jack, staring at the dark patch of wine on Nick's jacket. "Why don't you borrow a jacket of mine? Just go upstairs and help yourself and I'll have that one cleaned."

"Does it ever make a difference?" Douglas asked Nick. "Does it make a difference what bothers people and what doesn't? I mean, you know, sometimes I wonder, Nick." Douglas and Nick were both smiling—it reminded Max of the baited exchanges between Douglas and Mr. Chablis the previous evening.

"Of *course* it does," said Nick, trying to brush the wine off of his lapel. "What do you take me for? Just some asshole? I am *so sensitive.* I thought everyone knew how good at thumb action I was."

" 'Thumb action?' " said Max exasperatedly. "For Christ's sake—you people are driving me crazy. What the hell is 'thumb action'?"

"You guys don't know about thumb action," Nick rasped sadly in his buttery, sandy voice, still crouching on the flagstones, shaking his head as he raised his thumbs. "See— When you talk about a man's *sensitivity*— You are talking about a man's *thumbs.* Pure and simple. The rest is bullshit."

"I'm sorry, I just don't understand," said Jack. "It must be me."

"It's not you," Max said.

"A man's thumbs serve the sole purpose," explained Nick, "of wiping a woman's tears off her cheekbones." He grinned at them, emphasizing the shape of his face, the arched eyebrows, the stubble. "If you can do that right—I mean do it *perfectly*—then everything else falls into place."

"It's good to be able to snap your fingers, too," Jack said.

"So that's it?" said Douglas, examining his thumbs. "It all boils down to that? Wiping the tears—"

"I guarantee you," said Nick, finally standing up, clapping Douglas on the back paternally.

"Oh, for—" said Max, utterly disgusted.

"I don't know. That's kind of cool, actually," said Douglas, smiling. "I guess it's a foregone conclusion that you've made her cry."

"Well, Douglas," said Nick, walking away, "for you it would be."

• • •

"YOU KNOW," SAID Jack, pushing his chair back, sipping coffee, smoking a Marlboro that Max had lit with his brass lighter, "I had the strangest dream about Louise Delany." A short while had passed and the formal arrangement of the table had fallen into disarray, and Jack, Max, and Douglas were still sitting in a loose semicircle where they'd started, but the rest of the people who'd eaten at that table had drifted away—the dishes had been cleared, save for their coffee cups and Jack's brandy snifter, which was too large for his hand and looked somewhat comical. It was cooler than it had been during dinner and all the hired hands were busy down by the orchestra tent, where a sequence of small spotlights had been turned on and several small tables had been adorned with red-glass-globed candles in fishnets, and where about a hundred people had already wandered, after-dinner drinks in their hands, to watch the band set up. Max could make out Nick's figure down there, wearing a white linen jacket of Jack's, leading Annabelle to the dance floor, talking to her while the band warmed up. Max strained to watch but they were some distance away.

"The dream wasn't much," continued Jack. "I don't want to, like, set up some huge deal here. In the dream I was marrying Louise. Well— I wasn't *really* marrying her. It was really just me and her standing around on a street corner near Thorndike talking, but there was a moment— You know how you just sort of *know* things in dreams— There was this moment where I just sort of *knew* that we were going to get married. It was, I don't know, old-fashioned or something, like something our parents had arranged. And, you know, it was also—"

"Yeah?" said Max politely after Jack trailed off—he had begun rolling a pair of cigarettes, his blunted fingers twirling the Drum paper. The band were into their first number now, and Max glanced over again and saw couples dancing and saw a group of waiters uncorking champagne, a couple of discreet photojournalists taking flash photos, and Peggy Winfield wandering around presiding over everything. As he caught sight of Annabelle and Nick dancing, Max flicked his glance away.

"Mmm," said Jack, frowning, sipping more brandy and beginning, as if by some afterthought, to swirl the brandy around in the snifter with a calm, rhythmic movement. "I'm sorry. So in my dream I'm talking to Louise, and we're having this big conversation— Which is strange because I've never had any kind of real conversation with her, right? *Nobody* has. But we're doing it, we're talking, and it's turning out, you know, despite her shyness, that we have a lot in common. And all the time in the back of my mind I'm realizing that later on we're going to get married. And you know how everyone says that Louise— See, Max"—Jack turned to Max—"if you'd stayed at Thorndike you'd know what I mean. Everyone says about Louise that after Thorndike she's going to just drop totally out of sight, because she doesn't give a flying fuck about any of us. And, you know— That makes sense. But in this dream we're talking and I'm realizing that we're getting married, and that really, it's just the Thorndike thing, that we're leaving behind, which makes her just be this, like, frustration for everyone. And finally— I swear to God this is true, from my dream. Finally I'm making some gesture, you know"—Jack moved his arms, miming his dreamed gestures, which were uncharacteristically flamboyant—"and I'm moving my arms— She's got that *unbelievable* body, you know, almost like Annabelle's body, you know, but different. Excuse me Douglas. But I'm moving my hand and it brushes across the front of her chest, by accident, and I'm so embarrassed, you know, I can't believe how rude that is, I don't know what to do."

As the music stopped, Douglas and Max both looked over toward the distant dance floor. Max saw Nick and Annabelle walk over to a small candlelit table by the edge of the orchestra's tent—Nick diverting over to get two fluted glasses of champagne—where eventually, as Douglas and Max would see, Jill would join them, and one of the discreet photojournalists would snap a picture of the three of them together, and soon Mrs. Winfield would clap her hands for attention and make some remarks, standing by the saxophonist and speaking to the crowd. Her announcement would be shrouded in amusing pleasantries that the crowd laughed at, but nobody up by the house would make out what she was saying, and then after her announcement, Annabelle and Nick would leave the table and wander with a large group of people across the field and down a pathway into the woods—Max and Douglas would both watch as this group of about twelve couples wandered farther and farther away, toward the back of the moonlit field and then into the foliage and the trees leading down to the lake, their path lit by the crazy light from the flashlights that several of the staff were waving around, until eventually the entire group would disappear from view.

"And then Louise apologizes," said Jack, smiling gently. "Damned if she doesn't apologize, with this little sad smile on her face." Jack widened his eyes, sipping his brandy, looking at them. "Then I woke up."

"Damn," said Douglas, accepting a freshly rolled cigarette and a light from Max.

"But that's what the dream's about," said Jack, putting down his snifter and stubbing out the cigarette. "Leaving."

chapter 21

Michael Cadenhead stood in the damp grass beside the house, beyond the perimeter of the red lanterns, looking across the lawn toward the tables and the dancing platform while smoking his first cigarette of life, all alone, watching as two hundred people shifted around the Winfield property, drifting over the lawn and in and out of the house, eating and drinking, dancing and talking, arriving and leaving. Amy and Duane shared a small table at the edge of the wooden dance floor, tossing bits of shrimp into each other's mouths, and as Michael watched they both spoke emotionally and stared at the ground and then Duane moved over to Amy's chair and they hugged for a few minutes, rocking back and forth, eyes closed. Ted Winfield sat stroking his mustache while talking to a young actress, sipping a weak scotch, and his commentary seemed to enthrall the actress but Michael was too far away to hear.

Annabelle was dancing with Nick, her teeth flashing with the white spotlights and the candles on the edges of the platform that they danced on. She was an amazing dancer. Nick was having some trouble—he was better at club dancing, where you don't touch your partner, the dancing he'd noticed Annabelle couldn't really do as well as someone like Tina, who danced downtown with authority when she danced—but Nick was managing, holding his own, grasping Annabelle by the waist and hand and finding the swing groove of the orchestra's music. They ignored the occasional peripheral flashbulbs as the trumpet started moving into delayed triplets, loud syncopated eighths, and Nick started taking some chances, lunging and withdrawing, smiling down at Annabelle, who smiled at him as she noticed that other, older couples on the dance platform were watching—she saw them silhouetted by the spotlights, their thin hair backlit, as the breeze moved the huge trees and brushed her legs, waving the warm white linen of Nick's jacket beneath her fingers, and she could smell his aftershave—he wore aftershave—against the minted air of the summer night.

The song ended with a double-bass glissando octave, as it was meant to, and as the couples stopped dancing and stood clapping, winded, Annabelle leaned on Nick's shoulder and bent to take off her shoes, thumping down to her natural, considerable height and standing again in stockings, still leaning on him. "You want to sit the next one out?" Nick asked, slipping his arm off her waist and glancing at a trumpet player fiddling with his mute.

"Yeah— Let's get something to drink," Annabelle answered. "Come on, we should book before they start again and we get caught." She took Nick's arm, leading him between the pausing dancers and over to the tables—they passed Senator Rollins, on his way in with his diminutive wife, and he and Annabelle nodded to each other.

"Are you sure you're feeling all right?" asked Nick.

"I'm fine," said Annabelle, smiling at him from close up. "Really— Stop being so sweet, it's making me shake." She tugged his arm suddenly, pulling his face down, but then she faced back ahead and they began to walk over to a table, her arm in his, her gold shoes hanging by their heels from her other hand. "Were you saying something?"

"Just now?" asked Nick. "You weren't listening?"

"I was *dancing,*" said Annabelle. "What were you telling me?"

"Nothing"—Nick deftly plucked two gold-stemmed glasses of champagne from a nearby tray and joined her at the table, where he'd left his camera under a napkin—"I'm sorry. Hey, did you have a good time this morning?"

"Not as good a time as I'm having now," Annabelle said, sipping champagne, giving him another look and gently hooking his calf with her shoeless foot.

"Yeah, but it was nice driving around with you guys. Max is all right."

"You must think so— You gave him your *camera,*" said Annabelle, leaning back and squinting. "That was— I couldn't believe that."

"I'm changing," Nick said.

Annabelle glanced toward the distant house and saw that all the tables were deserted except the one nearest the bright French doors in the back façade, where she could just make out Douglas, Max, and Jack in silhouette—she thought she had caught Max's eye, but then he turned his head to look somewhere else, and she decided that he hadn't seen her and turned back to Nick, who was still talking. "Anyway, it's going well, and I don't have to drag the carpets all day anymore— I've got a clipboard to carry around now. Your brother—"

"Douglas," said Annabelle, sipping champagne and smiling at him. "Say Douglas."

"—Douglas seems to think I'm not a good artist."

"He thinks you could be," Annabelle said.

"Yeah— So I talked to these people I was telling you about, right, and they want to see what I've done," Nick went on, "so I'm getting my stuff together to show them. I mean, who knows, I could be lugging *carpets* all my life, but I think I've got some talent and you've got to— You've got to take what you've got and *push* for it. I mean *you* did it."

"I did it," Annabelle said.

"Your brother's doing good tonight," said Nick. "He's all right— He's quiet but I like him."

"*You're* quiet," said Annabelle.

"You know what I mean," said Nick. "He's cool."

"Douglas is very cool."

"I'm sorry, I took yours," said Nick, mixing up the champagne glasses, doing a double take on the lipstick smudge that he had been lifting toward his mouth. "Hey, Anna, I got a question for you."

"Uh-huh," said Annabelle, leaning toward him.

"A big question," said Nick, grinning, his chin flicking toward her.

"Yeah?"

"What the hell is Nathan Chablis doing here?" Annabelle touched his arm and laughed, dipping her head. "That's my question— I mean what's this thing coming to, anyway? I thought this was supposed to be a nice party."

"He's here because Jack's going to Princeton."

"Uh-huh," Nick said, leaning back and adjusting the white jacket.

"And you *knew* it," said Annabelle, swigging the champagne and tapping the empty glass back down onto the table. "You already *knew* it, you wanted to hear *me* say it"— she touched his nose with her forefinger—"I know you just wanted to hear *me* say it, Nick Blanchard, you can't hide these things from me."

"I can't hide anything from you, Annabelle," he said—her face was very close to his and he smiled his sideways smile and looked back at her through his sunglasses.

"There's Jill Brooks," said Annabelle, looking past him. "Check—her—out. *Jill!*" Nick turned and watched as Jill moved somewhat clumsily between the dancers, her white dress fluttering as she arrived.

"Hey, Anna," Jill said, leaning deferentially against Nick. "Hey, Nick—"

"What's up, Jill," said Nick, wincing. "Son of a bitch—"

"What?" said Jill, startled, moving to sit down.

"Nothing," said Nick. "How can you be old enough to look like that and not old enough to vote?"

"Now, Nick, don't make me feel insecure. I always feel so insecure," Jill said.

"Well— Get over it," said Annabelle, looking at her watch and then, for no good reason, up at the starry sky.

"So we've all been watching you dance," Jill told Nick and Annabelle. "You look so cute together."

"Shit, watch these guys," said Nick, pointing to the two society photographers, who had occupied territory near the bar table and were flashing shots of groups standing with drinks. "With the strobes getting these sweaty-looking pictures. It's not *that* dark— What are they using?"—he squinted—"Nikons. Figures."

"So what do you think, Annabelle?" Jill said. "I mean, this is your last one."

"My 'last one?' " said Annabelle, still looking up.

"Your last *Winfield party*— Me and Amy are going to have to do it alone next year. I mean what's it *like,* now that it's over?"

"Hey, we come and go, but Anthesteria endures," said Annabelle, dropping her chin and smiling at Jill. "That's a beautiful dress, Jill," she acknowledged.

"Thanks. Yours is better. But right? It's over for you—I mean, in '83 it'll be *our* turn, but you guys will be *gone* and it won't be the same— I'll probably be off crying somewhere."

"Oh no," said Nick slyly, leaning forward, having noticed a photographer bearing down on their table.

"You'll be off *laughing* somewhere, believe me," said Annabelle. "Look, I remember— When you're a sophomore life's forever, you can't imagine leaving, but a second-semester-senior, Jill, you're walking wounded, make no mistake." The photographer—a round, bearded Greek-looking man in shirtsleeves, with thick forearms and a handkerchief tied on his head—was approaching the table, making a big show of changing lenses.

"Really?" said Jill, taking off her own shoes and putting them under her chair. Nick had manifested his camera from under the napkin and was photographing the photographer. "Annabelle, we didn't cause a scene sneaking out before, did we?"

"Okay, quick draw," the photographer said to Nick. "What the hell is that, an R3?" The orchestra started the next song, which was faster, and the couples started dancing again—Nathan Chablis was dancing with Peggy Winfield, presumably taking care not to get stepped on.

"*No,* Jill," said Annabelle, stopping a waiter and taking more champagne glasses from his tray—two for each of them. "We didn't cause a scene— Come on, chill out."

"R4," said Nick, brandishing the camera, cocking his head and squinting at the photographer. "Why the strobe?"

"Was Douglas angry?" asked Jill.

"Because it's dark," the photographer said. "I'm wide-open and it's still dark. I said it's still *dark,*" he repeated over the sound of the orchestra.

"Douglas doesn't *get* angry," said Annabelle, hungrily gulping champagne. "You won't have that problem. It's the chick's dream—no fights."

"What, 'wide-open,' what's that, 2.8?" Nick said. "The Nikkor excuse for speed?"

"I thought the chick's dream was *winning* the fights," said Jill, delicately sipping champagne. "I don't want both of these." The orchestra suddenly stopped and Annabelle looked around, bewildered.

"It's 1.4," the photographer said, "but I need the speed for these people, they won't stand still for candids. You mind if I get a three-shot?"

"Sure, blind us," said Nick, beginning to shoot more pictures of the photographer. "Right, girls? Try to look embarrassed and unkempt and drunk for the candid man."

"A photograph?" asked Jill. "For a magazine?"

"Why'd the music stop?" asked Annabelle, watching Peggy Winfield clap her hands for attention and gazing back up at the house, where Jack, Max, and Douglas were still sitting at the dinner table, drinking brandy and talking, far enough away for their faces to be featureless. While she was looking at the house, the photographer snapped a shot of the three of them, Annabelle gazing off, Jill grinning, Nick with the camera, blinding them with his flash.

"Good job," said Nick, still taking pictures of the photographer. "Nice timing."

"I'm gone," said the photographer, leaving.

"How will he get our names?" asked Jill.

"Shut up," said Annabelle, trying to hear Peggy Winfield, and failing—the quiet and the attentive dancers gave the lawn and the platform a night-rally aspect for a moment, and Annabelle turned to glance down at the woods and the obscured dim view of the lake.

"Nick, you look *different,*" said Jill, looking at him. "I've never seen you dressed like that." Nick *did* look different, somehow—the jacket made a difference, flattering his roughness into experience.

"Doesn't he look good?" said Annabelle.

"I hate this," said Nick. "I feel like I'm in disguise."

"What did she *say,* damn it?" asked Annabelle, peering toward Peggy Winfield and lighting a White Camel. "Stop *talking,* damn it."

"What? The pathway's open," Jill said. "The path to the lake."

"Oh man, I am so *happy,*" Annabelle said, beaming as she suddenly stood. "Come on, Nick, get up—"

"What?" said Nick, standing also, looking disoriented.

"*Boats,*" said Annabelle. "The *lake,* Nick. Come on— Take me out in a boat."

"Yes ma'am," said Nick, shouldering his camera. "Should I grab a bottle?"

"I've got a flask. Come on, Blanchard, we got a date. Catch you later, Jill."

Annabelle leaned on Nick to put her shoes back on and then led him down to join the lake-bound crowd, leaving Jill behind. Michael was still watching from a distance and he could make out the way that Jill looked at the table's contents—the six champagne glasses, the White Camel putting forth its vertical cloud—and he couldn't see her face, but he knew that the table already meant nothing, just abandoned glass and smoke, and he wished he could tell her that he had seen her moment alone with Annabelle and Nick, that he could always help her remember, if she wanted, but then Jill happened to glance at the flashbulbs still flashing nearby and he knew she felt documented and safe. Michael watched Jill as she watched Annabelle and Nick and the others make their way toward the lake, moving together like monks, vanishing around the bend in the trees, into the woods and out of sight.

''DOUGLAS TAFT,'' said a woman's voice. Douglas adjusted his coffee cup and turned away from the serving table toward the person who'd addressed him—he was finally sobering up as the last vestiges of the dinner were cleared and most of the party converged indoors, where more coffee and dessert were being served as an overture for the third round of champagne that would be cracked later on ("Yeah, like New Year's Eve," Jack had apologized one year. "Doesn't make any goddamned sense, I guess"). Douglas and Max had been dancing together to old Cole Porter and Billie Holiday songs on the stereo, surrounded by adult strangers, and Douglas had wandered over to the edge of the living room so as to find and refill his coffee cup when the large, ungainly woman in the red dress who had sat next to him during dinner had suddenly approached him. "You look so much like your father," she was saying.

"It's not *that* startling, is it?" Douglas said, giving his altar-boy smile. "I mean I hope I haven't *alarmed* you."

"Oh, it's just interesting. I've seen so many photographs— Of course, there's a limit to what a wallet photograph reveals. A limit— You're— What, in your late teens, obviously. What do you"—the woman suddenly leaned close—"what do you think of all this?"

"I'm not the best judge," Douglas said diplomatically. "I live too close—I'm not used to it."

"Oh, you're not?" said the woman. "That's interesting. I mean, I have to admit to being surprised, or, should I say, somewhat pleasantly startled— I mean I don't know about *you* but I tend to find these things disarming, but then, I'm afraid I'm doomed to never being the conventional, the typical party conversationalist—but then I guess you aren't *either,* are you? As you just said. Forgive me—My point simply being that I find these things disarming, but, after all, I think I must stand apart from the others, not in any way that couldn't be politely overlooked, but I do stand apart if only because I work for a living— I'm not trying to put you *off,* Douglas, I'm just *talking.* I mean, I'm just beginning with the pleasantries, some pithy facts about myself, just to get the conversation moving, and one pithy fact about myself happens to be that I work for a living, in an office, every day. And I realize— Isn't it funny? —But I realize, I stand chatting so pleasantly with you and I find myself realizing that I couldn't afford the drink in your hand, Douglas, the glass and the drink, with a week's pay, odd as that may seem, *ironic* as that may seem, and you're wearing such a beautiful shirt— You'll permit me to admire your shirt, won't you, Douglas? —Such a beautiful shirt, which I mention only in passing because it reminds me of another shirt— Not like that, of course, much coarser, much rougher— Well, of course I mean a *machine-made* shirt, really—that I bought for my son, recently, my son who's younger than you by five months *exactly,* can you believe it? On his birthday, the thirteenth, after he graduated—graduated from public high school—he had, since you ask, he had a bit of trouble in school, oh, just some minor difficulties, nothing so dramatic as a learning disability, nothing so sophisticated, just what might be called some mild motivational difficulties, which had the unfortunate effect of impeding his collegiate plans just a bit, Douglas, and all I could do for him was buy him that *shirt,* that machine-made shirt that this *understated* shirt of yours happens to remind me of. Your uncle gave you that one, am I right? Hard to keep these things straight, I suppose, but it *was* your uncle, wasn't it? Or perhaps you have as much trouble as *I* do keeping these things straight, keeping straight which gift comes from which person, Douglas Algernon Taft, the shirt, the drink, the glass, the poise— I mean allow me to at least admire your *poise* now that we're away from the dinner table and the dinner conversation and you don't feel quite as *safe* any more, now that I've gotten you all unfashionably shaken up because it's your birthday soon and maybe you'll get a *car,* a brand-new—"

Before he realized what he was doing Douglas had grabbed the woman's arm, making her falter for a moment, noticing her age and the odd look to her eyes and asking "Who are you?" before she kept talking.

"—car, an expensive one of course, money, of course, being, as they say, no object, isn't that how they put it, no *object,* nothing at all between you and the miraculous Germanic engineering, and believe me, I know all about that, all there is to know, you could say, all he could tell me in between these absolutely *charming* anecdotes about you and your sister, and how he talked about *her,* talked about what an absolute gem she is, such an absolute *gem*— I mean, the details, forgive me, but the *details,* the facts at hand, the fact that aside from her beauty and her tremendous, tremendous *intelligence* there's that particular *sad* aspect that makes any story about her that much more interesting and educational— I mean one has to assume the point of all these stories and anecdotes is to be educational, to *teach,* it's certainly all I can assume, being lacking in the apparatus for finding whatever *other* point there is—making any story about her that much more a sort of gift to the listener, a gift of, I don't know, a gift of *wisdom*—or maybe, looking back, maybe *not* a gift of wisdom, maybe just a gift of wit. But looking back changes everything, doesn't it, changes things so that even when it ended, even when he couldn't be reached, no answer in New York, phone off the hook in Dover, I still had these, I can't complain, the experience was so *enriching,* so *vital* because I still had these poignant memories of the conversations, of the way he could talk, talk so beautifully about both of you, which *is* regrettable since we can't have scars, traces, marring of surfaces, so it had to happen and it had to end and when it ended it had to be so irretrievably over, no calls, no letters, a rethinking of *priorities,* perhaps that's the bond-market way to put it, which is, after all, the best way to put it, I'm sure you'd agree, a rethinking of *priorities* that leaves me with the spare antique glasses and the wallet photographs and leaves me with you, Douglas, blithely politely facing me and I'm sorry but I have to say, I have to conclude that it's all such a shame, all such a fucking *shame.*"

Douglas looked at her as she leaned close and her whisper was barely audible. "So pray you never learn what it means to be swept under."

Douglas looked at her. "Under what?"

"The carpet, Douglas. The Taft carpet." As quickly as she'd arrived, the woman in the red dress walked away, turning to smile at Douglas lovingly before being enfolded back into the living room crowd.

Douglas realized that he'd saucered his coffee, so he peeled a paper napkin emblazoned with another W—"We're going to be seeing W's in our fucking sleep," Annabelle had said—from a stack and cleaned the coffee out of the bone saucer, hoping nobody was looking, and then refilled the cup. He was just adding the cream when a pair of arms grabbed him from behind, around the shoulders, making him spill the coffee all over again—he turned around and Jack Winfield was grinning at him, Max and Stephen Leonard standing behind him.

"Douglas!" wheezed Jack happily, leering at him. "Douglas! Douglas! We came *looking for you*"—he indicated Max and Stephen—"I mean, dinner ends and you and Max are dancing like the two faggotty homosexuals that you actually are"—Max hit Jack on the arm, Jack flinched—"and I came to fucking find you because I have *very good news.*"

"Yeah?" said Douglas, looking down at his coffee cup.

"I'll tell you in a second," said Jack, waving magnanimously toward Douglas and toward the table. "Go ahead— Have some coffee. Don't be such a slob."

"No, I— I don't think I'd like any coffee, actually," said Douglas, putting down the cup and turning to them. "What's the good word?"

"Shhh," said Stephen, leaning forward conspiratorially. "The news is, Bill Coleman just arrived— He brought his stupid car with the cellophane on the back windows and he brought a shitload of dope, and he brought *Louise Delany.*"

"Really?" said Douglas, raising his eyebrows. "Oh my God— Louise is at *a party?* She's at *this* party right now?"

"Really," said Jack. "I'm just like, thank you God. I mean—Bill *Coleman,* man, I don't know how the fuck he did it but he took a blowtorch to the ice goddess and she's *here.*"

"Well," said Douglas, looking around through the haze of the living room, "where are they?"

"We're out by the pool toking it up," Stephen said, putting an arm on Douglas' shoulder. "Douglas— What's *wrong?* Would you relax?"

"Some woman was just cutting into me," said Douglas.

"Well it wasn't Louise," said Stephen, "so who cares? Come on— Everyone's out by the pool house."

"You go," said Jack, heading off in the other direction. "I'm going to swipe some scotch from the kitchen." Max, Stephen, and Douglas threaded their way through the house and down the flagstone path through the shrubbery, where the pool was bathed in light and a knot of people stood by the pool house. "Don't wait for me," Jack called back at them.

THE SKY WAS clear and starry, the damp air blurring the stars, but off beyond the edge of the lake, beyond the dim and distant trees, the horizon glowed a deep blue, shining with the light from the distant town, and below that haze of dim light the starlight shone in cold patterns on the water and obscured the reflected shore. Out here behind the island the lake was calm and mirror flat and silent save for the sounds of Nick's oars gently dripping lake water, with no other sound, no crickets or voices, and the nearby rocks and trees of the primeval and deserted island and the dim, distant lakeshore and all the land they could see was dark and grey. The other boats were almost out of view, closer to shore and nearly hidden by the island, their paired points of flickering yellow candlelight shining on the motionless ebony lake, and the candles on Nick and Annabelle's boat danced the details of the soft wind that they couldn't feel, dripping hissing wax into the water and cresting the bright ripples that traced the boat's path.

As they'd arrived onto the the cold ground of the dock before the fleet of antiquated rowboats, outfitted with candles that shone through the mist, like the boats that take you to Avalon, Annabelle had whispered in Nick's ear for him to hurry, a thrill in her whisper, biting his ear, and Nick could still feel the marks of her teeth. They were farthest out, and Nick had stopped rowing and sat straight between the oarlocks, resting and rowing again, gently guiding them toward the island shore, sunglasses off, sleeves rolled up, Jack's jacket lying in a soft bundle in the darkness of the bow and pillowing the abandoned camera. He pulled the oars and watched Annabelle, who lay almost prone across the stern of the slim wooden rowboat, drinking gin from her platinum flask in the starlight, her legs over the gunwale, one gold shoe dangling precariously by its toe from one silk-swathed foot, the other foot bare, its gold shoe glowing on the keel, stretching her muscled neck and staring through her lowered lashes at the clear and starry sky. "Mmm," Annabelle murmured, her soft voice carrying through the silent air. "My ears are ringing."

"Mine too," Nick whispered. He had moved them close to the shore, the trees looming over them, and he held the oars up, letting them drift along the steep bank and under a willow tree, the hanging branches whispering over the boat, and Annabelle reached up to break off a strand of foliage and wrap it around her head.

"Star light, star bright," she murmured, watching the stars through the hanging willow branches as they brushed past, drinking from her curved flask—in the pale darkness Nick could barely make out the engraved "AT" on the flank of the bottle as he moved their boat farther from the others and into the recesses of the shabby island shore, sculling them to a stop and shipping the oars, laying the grips on the keel, stretching his back muscles and gazing at Annabelle, the candles shining in the silent air.

"Oh, Christ, Nick," Annabelle said softly, looking at him.

"Annabelle?" said Nick, seeing her face change. "Are you sad?"

"No," Annabelle whispered, voice cracking, eyes gently watering as she looked back at him. "I'm so young," she whispered. "I'm only nineteen."

"It's all right," Nick said.

"I know," said Annabelle, giving him a sweet stricken look, her body bent across the boat, back arched, willow branch hanging from her head, and Nick swung slowly forward across the boat, rocking it silently, his elbows hitting the oars and sending them sliding to splash in the water, his knee knocking the clattering flask, reaching for her waist and back and pulling her into his arms, stroking her back as she held him.

"Don't cry, Annabelle," Nick whispered, her hair in his eyes. "Don't cry."

"I'm sorry," Annabelle said, moving against him. Nick moved his head, stubble scratching her, and when Annabelle raised her face he slowly kissed her.

They kissed for a moment, Nick pressing forward, the boat rocking, the kiss hardening as he stroked his fingertips across her collarbones, his thumbs pressed into the edges of her neck, and as his mouth ground gently into hers his hand moved up to the back of her head, the other hand finding the angle of her jaw, his thumb jamming against her cheek as their teeth clicked together. His hands knew what her face looked like—he stopped to catch his breath and Annabelle smiled as she kissed him back, her arms around his shoulders from beneath, slipping her legs against his, the boat splashing, gin dribbling on the beams and soaking his knee. They drifted from the shore as they kissed and when the second kiss ended Annabelle sank back against the gunwales and Nick lay atop her, gently brushing his fingers across her neck and smooth jaw and the hollows beneath her cheekbones.

"Is— Is the boat— Is this breaking your back?" he asked softly.

"I won't break," Annabelle whispered.

"I'm sorry," said Nick, stroking her hair. "Touching you— You're like a Michelangelo."

"Mmm— Don't worry about it," said Annabelle, closing her eyes as she kissed him again.

"I'm just worried about your *back,*" said Nick, hands down to her waist. "I'm sorry I don't have the routine down. I don't want to hurt you."

"Have the what?" asked Annabelle, squinting as Nick's hands drifted up her sides, audibly brushing the black dress.

"Nothing," whispered Nick, pressing against her again, hands on her thighs now, guiding her legs apart, ducking down to kiss her neck—Annabelle was moving under him, moving the wrong way, and when he brought his mouth to her face she twisted her head to one side. "Come on, Annabelle," Nick murmured. "Get it straight."

He finally pinned her mouth, trying to guide her into another kiss, and she murmured a moment and then made sharp sounds with her throat, pulling away from his mouth, getting her breath, startled. "Mmm— Wait," she murmured, but Nick was pressing down on her, pressing her back into the boat. "Wait— Wait— *Wait!*" she said finally, the word carrying sharply in the silent dark air as she got her hands under him and pushed him back, pushed him away from her.

"*You* get it straight," Annabelle said, glaring at him, sitting up as he backed off.

"What are you doing?" asked Nick. "Damn it, that's not fair, Annabelle."

"What am I— Blanchard, *you* dove across the fucking boat." Annabelle retrieved the flask, leaning in a way that gave him a view of her chest, and he looked away and then helplessly looked back.

"Come on, Annabelle, don't— So I made a wrong move." She glared to one side. "I mean you can't expect—"

"Nick— For Christ's sake don't *talk* about it," Annabelle said, taking a breath and adjusting her dress, squinting in the candlelight. Nick took the opportunity to reach out and grab one of the sodden oars and begin, ineffectually, to use it so as to fish out the other oar.

"I never understand how you just—change gears like that," Nick muttered. "Like with Wally Patterson— Go down on a guy and then practically beat him up— I mean, what the fuck—"

"You don't have the routine down," Annabelle said tightly, hunting for her other shoe in the darkness and putting it on, her voice carrying across the lake.

"I'm sorry," said Nick. "I thought you were into it."

"I *was* into it," Annabelle said weakly. "I was into it— Damn it— Jesus, what's wrong with me?"

"Annabelle—"

"Do you think I'm crazy, Nick?"

"Annabelle—"

"I mean, I must be some— And *you're* sitting there"—she took a belt from the flask, hand shaking, and looked at him—"You're sitting there, when— I mean we have everything in the fucking world and we can't even— I guess you might as well row back now." Annabelle took another gulp of gin and capped the flask and then she drew her long legs back aboard the boat, and when she looked at Nick he was shaking his head and then nodding tightly and she reached for his arm but he pulled away.

"Nick," she said in a different voice. "Nick, I'm sorry. It would have just been a fuck. Like a— I don't know. Like driving a car."

"Never stopped you before," he said, his voice doing its trick.

"Don't be too sure," said Annabelle, drawing back, resettling on the seat.

"Why not me?" Nick said quietly.

"I'm sorry. I can't explain."

"Please try."

Annabelle squinted and gestured, taking another sip of gin while he waited. "You know what you're doing too well."

"Like you *don't?*" said Nick.

"You fake it better than me."

"That's not—"

"I mean, I don't *try* to fake it."

"You're not making sense," said Nick, leaning on an arm on the gunwale and looking off at the ripples the boat was making as it drifted. "I mean, you're *good* at not making sense. You're better at it, you're as good at not making sense as I am at waiting. I can wait while you figure it out but I can't understand."

"I know," said Annabelle. "I realize that."

"Please, Annabelle."

"Oh, Nick, don't make this more difficult."

"It doesn't have to be difficult at all."

"But, Nick— I could tell you what to say but you'd just be saying what I'd told you to say."

"Annabelle— It *wouldn't* have been just a fuck. I mean I just want— I want to be proud, you know?"

"You'd better stop talking, Nick," Annabelle said tightly. "The more you talk the longer you're going to wait."

"And now you twist the knife," said Nick, stroking his forehead and staring at the deck of the rowboat. "You should be sorry."

"I am sorry," said Annabelle. "Now row back."

chapter 22

The north edge of the Winfield house overlooked a steep and moss-covered slope, cut by a jagged flagstone path leading down to the wide slabs of tiled concrete that encased the pool. The small, grotto-like area was brightly lit by insect-clouded spotlights concealed at irregular intervals among the trees, the leaves around the lights glowing emerald above the pool, which shone like smooth glass, aided by small underwater lamps, and at its southern, shallow end, among the tall birches that crowded the house, beside a padlocked wooden outbuilding, Douglas, Wally, Max, and Michael stood in a vague circle lit by the flame of Jack's Zippo while Stephen approached them from the pool's edge. "Drugs II—The Sequel," Stephen said, looking around fiendishly. "Where's Coleman?"

"He had to go out to his car," said Wally, brushing cigarette ash from his trousers, looking Jazz-Age for a moment as he pulled his blond hair back from his forehead.

"Hey, dudes," said Bill Coleman, walking up, adjusting his IBM-executive glasses and producing a wax-paper bag from his jacket pocket. "Anthesteria—rock and roll." Bill was unquestionably loved by the other Thorndike students despite his computer-programmer's demeanor, his penholders and shiny cuffs, in a way that confirmed the correctness of their criteria and their blindness to the invisible cues and forces that guided his actions. "Wally, give me the fucking lighter."

"Man, this is pretty good," said Wally, handing over the Zippo and getting the first hit off of the joint that Bill had rolled as easily as uncapping a pen. The music from upstairs changed, Led Zeppelin to the Rolling Stones—"Moonlight Mile"—and Wally sucked back half the joint before Stephen tackled him from behind, laughing, grabbing the joint and straightening his tie.

"So I hear I missed all the action," said Bill. "Buzzman came and left, right? And things got heavy with DiGrassi, am I right?"

"Bill, you brought *Louise,*" gasped Wally, finally blowing out a cloud of fragrant smoke. "You missed a couple of technical knock-outs, you didn't miss *anything.* Oh, man, Bill, this is some good shit."

"Taft's next," said Stephen, grinning, offering the remains of the joint to Douglas, standing to cup the flame with his hands, standing casually closer to Douglas than he ever had before and clapping him on the back when he coughed.

"Okay," Douglas whispered hoarsely, after he had finished coughing. "Hey, where's Jill?" he asked casually.

"Douglas actually wants to know where Jill is again," said Stephen loudly, looking around at the others and pointing at Douglas as if at a classroom exhibit. "Jill's getting into some coke with Tina, last I heard."

"Yeah, that's where they are," said Wally.

"Well, where's Louise?" asked Douglas.

"She's inside, I think," said Bill, adjusting his glasses. "She's nervous—we had to get all these gas station directions and when we hit the driveway she saw the house and froze."

"Hey, Wally," Stephen said, turning suddenly toward him. "I bet you can't talk to Louise without acting like an asshole."

"Max," whispered Douglas, leaning toward Max unobtrusively, "*what the fuck happened* between you and Annabelle and Jill before dinner? Would you please tell me?"

"What makes you think that, Steve-o?" said Wally brackishly.

"What the hell is your problem?" Max asked quietly, glaring at Douglas. "Would you leave me alone?"

"You went off with my sister and Jill for five minutes and I haven't seen either of them since," Douglas hissed into Max's ear.

"What? Oh, nothing, Wally," said Stephen with merry sarcasm, "except that your line with the chicks doesn't really work with Louise, you know, because she is not one of those chicks. She's just a normal person."

"Don't be so—" Max whispered back at Douglas. "Look. Douglas— Believe me, you'll figure it out someday."

"Steve-o," said Wally, "Louise is one of those chicks. Wait and see, keep your eyes on me."

"Hey, guys," said Louise, walking up, looking pretty in ways beyond the ways that could be mentioned out loud.

"Louise!" said everyone, looking at her in disbelief—Douglas, Wally, and Michael stared blatantly before catching themselves. "When did *you* get here?" Michael asked.

"One drink ago," Louise explained. "I came with Bill."

"Hoop hoop hoop hoop," chanted Wally and Stephen, pointing at Louise from behind her.

"You got a place to stay?" said Bill suddenly, doing a turn as Groucho Marx, grinning and wiggling his eyebrows up and down over the rims of his glasses and waving an imaginary cigar—it was somehow so inexpressibly funny that everyone laughed hard enough to make themselves light-headed.

"Don't listen to him, he's nuts," said Wally, smoothing his voice, smiling gently. "How are you, Louise?"

"Here he goes," Stephen told Douglas under his breath while lighting Douglas' cigarette, which tasted thin and hard, like water, after the dope.

"I got it all figured out," said Louise. "You only need a place to stay when you need a place to *sleep,* right? I figure I've lost my mind, I'd better lose it all the way."

"What the hell, are you going to wander around town, for Christ's sake?" said Max.

"Hoop hoop hoop hoop hoop," Wally and Stephen chanted.

"Is that Max *Gantry?* I don't believe it," said Louise. "Far out."

"Watch Bill— This is going to be great," Stephen was telling Douglas. "Bill gets stoned enough, he starts speaking FORTRAN."

"Hi, Louise," said Max. "Didn't mean to snap at you."

"I spoke FORTRAN when you were learning to talk, Stephen," Bill said, fingers still moving, not looking up. "But then you *never* learned, did you? I'm sorry."

"What?" said Louise, leaning toward Max, showing her ear.

"Nothing, nothing," said Max. "Good to see you, Louise."

"Bill, do the Groucho Marx again," said Louise. "That was so funny."

"Well—" said Bill, flustered, fiddling around with the bag of marijuana.

"Or do the Karl Marx," said Wally, managing by bad luck to insert this weak joke into a moment of silence while everyone rearranged themselves in the glow from the spotlights.

"You stupid idiot," Stephen said, increasing Wally's embarrassment.

"Your ass is grass, Steve-o," said Wally hopelessly. "I told you, man, *never* call me that."

"You got off a funny line," Stephen persisted, taunting Wally happily, "and you *could* have left it alone—"

"You're begging for it, Leonard," said Wally, standing up, grinning.

"—but *no!*" Stephen finished, imitating John Belushi.

"You want to fight, Leonard?" said Wally, trying to loom over him.

"Anytime at all, Patterson," said Stephen, smiling.

"Can we get the dope moving around again?" said Max.

"No, no— Don't fight—" said Louise, looking perturbed.

"Don't worry, relax, don't worry," said Bill, his Adam's apple moving above his bow tie.

"I can't *believe* Louise is here," Michael whispered shyly to Douglas.

"Shh! She'll *hear* you," Douglas whispered back.

"Sorry," whispered Michael. "But my God."

"Can I get a cigarette? What a body," mumbled Wally, having walked over to Michael and Douglas to obtain a cigarette.

"It's a new age," said Douglas randomly. The trees sighed with the wind as Jack circled the edge of the shrubbery holding a bottle of Johnnie Walker Black by the neck, looking around, and everyone nodded at him.

"Hello," said Jack pleasantly. "Hello everyone— Hey, it's Coleman."

"My respects to your family and your house," said Bill, still sitting on the rock, concentrating on the joints that he was rolling, the muscles of his thin arms brushing the synthetic cuffs of his short-sleeved dress shirt.

"Louise!" Jack said, beaming. "I don't believe it— My fiancée. I'm so glad you showed up."

"Hello, Jack," said Louise, smiling dazzlingly. The contrast with the way she usually acted was remarkable to everyone—she seemed possessed by a benign demon as she walked over and kissed Jack on the cheek, and Jack looked so happy that he was almost unrecognizable.

"You know," Max whispered in Jack's ear, having characteristically snuck around behind him, "she's a *serious* babe."

Jack looked at him incredulously. "Of *course* she is," he hissed back, smiling pleasantly again. "I mean, Max— What'd you think I was doing? *Kidding?*"

"Oh, shit!" said Douglas, pointing toward the swimming pool in alarm.

"Uh-oh," said Michael, looking where Douglas had pointed.

"Jesus, don't do anything dangerous, please," said Jack, looking also.

Stephen and Wally were walking over to the swimming pool, silhouetted against the spotlight, their shadows crossing the tiles—as everyone watched, Wally and then Stephen removed their suit jackets, carefully draping them across a woven deck chair before climbing onto the diving board, its cold, rough surface quivering as they helped each other up.

"Who's up for the dope?" asked Bill, not paying any attention, holding up two fresh joints without looking, concentrating on the Drum paper and other paraphernalia in his lap. Max took the joints and Bill lowered his arm distractedly.

"Are they both wearing waterproof watches?" Jack asked anxiously.

Wally and Stephen were now facing each other like Sumo wrestlers, balancing with their feet spread on the diving board, their gleaming leather shoes gripping its sandpaper surface, symmetrically poised to attack each other—the wind blew the other way but everyone vaguely heard them speaking in unison. "Ready— steady— *go!*" they chanted, suddenly grabbing each other by the upper arms and struggling, their fingers clamped around soft white Brooks Brothers cotton, their leather shoes scuffling for purchase on the diving board.

"Jesus Christ!" exclaimed Bill from where he was sitting, laughing in disbelief, having finally looked up and noticed what was going on. *"Come on!"* He surged to his feet, stowing all the dope equipment in his pants pocket and leading everyone over to the poolside deck, Jack trailing behind, carrying the bottle of scotch by the neck. As they approached, Wally and Stephen's struggles became more pronounced, each of them careening wildly back and forth, overbalancing and correcting, their reddened faces straining with concentration as they wrestled—finally Stephen, grunting with the effort, managed to shove Wally off the diving board, but as he fell, Wally held on to Stephen's arm so that both of them splashed into the pool at almost the same time, hitting the water like cannonballs, spattering water onto the tiles around the pool and soaking all the spectators. The diving board quivered and clattered like a struck tuning fork and Louise screamed with laughter as Wally and Stephen both resurfaced, their hair plastered to their foreheads, the motion of their limbs as they treaded water illuminated by the Kirlian underwater lamps.

"You two assholes," said Jack weakly, moving their jackets out of the way and collapsing onto the deck chair, putting the scotch bottle down beside him where it clanked against the tiles, and sucking on the joint, which had gotten around to him. Louise sat next to him, folding her hands in her lap, arranging her feet.

"That was *great!*" said Michael, stepping forward. "Why don't you—" He suddenly slipped on the wet tiles and twisted in the air as he fell, legs above his head for a moment, landing on his lower back on the concrete lip surrounding the pool—his glasses twirled through the air, splashing into the water beneath the diving board with a quiet, quick sound like a pizzicato cello note, sinking slowly, reflecting the underwater lights as they drifted downward. Everyone lurched forward and Jack stood back up again, and after a moment so did Louise.

"Come on in, Cadenhead!" said Wally, treading water.

"The water's fine! It's a fucking heated pool!" added Stephen happily, his tie floating out from his neck.

"We're sorry— Are you all right, Michael?" said Jack, crouching next to him.

"Hoop hoop hoop hoop hoop," Wally and Stephen were chanting.

"I'm fine," mumbled Michael, soaking wet. "Um— Could one of you guys dive for my glasses? I can't see a thing."

"Smoke some more shit," suggested Wally from the pool. "Everyone."

They sat on the tiles as the joint went around again, and got back to Bill, who sucked back its remaining length, flicked the roach into the pool, and said, "I just might go in."

"If you do," Louise told Bill, "I'd like to watch."

"Bill," said Michael politely, "if you go into the pool, could you get my glasses?"

Abruptly everyone heard footsteps tapping on tiles and turned to look—some distance away, back by the flagstone path and the shrubbery and the looming black wedge of the house, a young man was walking slowly toward them in the lunar glare, hands in pockets, a cigarette in the corner of his mouth, his damp hair carelessly swept back, sunglasses obscuring his expression. Michael squinted in vain at the approaching figure, his face naked without eyeglasses. "Who *is* that?" he asked.

"Hello, Nick," said Jack. "Watch your feet— It's slippery."

"I'm not going to fall," Nick said, walking up to them, hands still in pockets—he had changed back to his original jacket, wine stain and all, and had Jill been there she probably would have pointed this out, but most of the others hadn't even seen him change the first time, and Jack didn't say anything.

"Nick, do you know Louise?" asked Jack.

"You're making a *mistake*—" Stephen and Wally gleefully chanted, their heads bobbing in the pool.

"Hello, Nick," said Louise. "You used to go to Thorndike."

"Pleased to meet you," said Nick, shaking her hand. "Jack, let me get a slug of that, would you?" Jack handed over the scotch bottle and Nick sat cross-legged beside the pool and lit a cigarette. "Bill," he said suddenly, "you ought to give that stuff a rest. You'll never get a job with the State Department at this rate."

"Yeah, but I wonder," said Bill, sucking on a joint that nobody had seen him roll or light. " 'Cause that's the political manifestation of morals, right?"

"What the hell is he *saying?*" shouted Wally from the pool.

"Yeah! We can't *hear* him— Speak up, Coleman!" shouted Stephen.

"When it's obviously just perceptual epistemology creating the *illusion* of an ethical dilemma," Bill said distractedly. "I mean who needs *Nietzsche*—"

"Right," said Nick, crouching clinically beside Bill, listening with exaggerated keenness.

"—when you've got *Babbage?* Sacrifice sobriety for direct current and society gets *analog,* that's all—"

"Right," said Nick, nodding.

"What the hell did he *say?*" shouted Wally from where he was bobbing in the pool.

"Yeah," shouted Stephen. "What was he *saying?* Clue us *in.*"

"Will you two homos *get out of the pool already?*" yelled Jack suddenly.

"Hey, Bill, is it true you solved Rubik's Cube in ten minutes?" asked Max.

"He just *looked* at the fucker and it gave up," said Nick.

"You're brilliant," said Louise, smiling at Bill dazzlingly.

"He's a charlatan," said Nick, smiling sadly.

"What's with you, Blanchard?" Bill said. "You seem under the weather."

"I'm fine," Nick said quietly, patiently returning Bill's gaze. "Don't worry about it— It's nothing."

"Is Annabelle here?" asked Louise, shivering, looking around at all of them.

"She flew to Cuba," said Max.

"That's right!" said Nick, beaming at Max with sudden surprise.

"All right, you guys," said Douglas abruptly, sucking on a cigarette.

"Wait, where *is* she, though?" Max asked Nick. "I thought she was with you."

"I don't know where she is," Nick said hoarsely. "Inside somewhere— I think she went to find Tina and Jill. What's the difference?"

Wally and Stephen had finally climbed out of the pool, and they joined the circle of people sitting beside the cold metal posts that supported the diving board. "Mike! Your scopes," Stephen said after a moment, holding out Michael's glasses and failing to get his attention. Nobody remembered seeing him dive for the glasses. Jack and Louise, who had been talking quietly between themselves, got up and walked back toward the pool house.

"Jesus—" whispered Wally, shivering, as soon as Jack and Louise were out of earshot. "I can't *believe* she's here. I keep thinking I'll blink and she'll go away."

"Jack seems on top of the situation," whispered Stephen.

"Maybe he's proposing right now," said Max.

"She's hot," said Wally, as if just noticing. "She's almost as hot as Annabelle." He paused, considering. "Actually, no. No, she's not nearly as hot as Annabelle."

"Hey, Wally!" said Bill. "Is Annabelle really a sidewinder?"

"You're asking the right man," said Nick halfheartedly, turning his head away and looking the other direction.

"Annabelle?" Wally laughed incredulously, rocking back and forth, soaking wet, hair plastered to his forehead, talking as he shivered. "Annabelle the fucking human lathe?" Douglas stared at Wally and then slowly the others noticed the way Douglas was looking at him and they quieted down, except for Bill, who was beside himself with laughter. "Oh, shit," said Wally. "Douglas, man, I'm sorry— I wasn't thinking. Sorry, man, really."

"It's all right," said Douglas, staring at him, hands on his thighs. "Hey, Bill, can I get another hit of that?"

"What? —Sure, Douglas, here," Bill said, still laughing, wiping his eyes. "Lathe— God, if I'd thought of that I'd be so happy—"

"If you'd had *occasion* to think of that you'd be so happy," wheezed Stephen, still shivering, his teeth chattering, his sodden clothes adhering to his body. "Oh, shit, sorry Douglas," he added quickly.

"Oh, can we stop *apologizing,* already?" exploded Wally sneeringly, having just taken a meager hit off the joint and held it out to Stephen without looking. "I'm so *sick* of this shit— I mean, come *on.* So she's his fucking *sister,* he's got *eyes,* we're not *offending* him— I mean, if she had *one* reputation this would be bullshit, with the *apologizing,* but come on, we're talking about Annabelle *Taft* here. Douglas, are we *bothering* you, or can you, like, face the facts?"

"I can face the facts," Douglas said.

"Hey," said Bill, getting up and staggering around, "anyone ever been to an *air show?*" He collapsed into helpless laughter at his own wit.

"The funk is born in Bill Coleman," Nick said, smiling with his lips pressed together and patting Bill on the back.

"Never forget it, son," said Bill, adjusting his plastic penholder with one hand and thumb-thwacking an imaginary fretless bass with the other. Suddenly all the lights illuminating the pool area went out, all at once, and they were plunged into near-total darkness. "Shit! An air strike!" Bill shouted.

"What the fuck—" said Stephen.

"Whoops," said Max, grinning. "Power failure."

"We blew out the *generators,*" said Bill. "Winfield's gonna get *sued—*"

"Everybody relax," Nick said quietly, hissing the word's stretched sibilance, the voice clearly his, even disconnected in the darkness as it was. "You can still see."

After a moment their eyes adjusted, grey retinal fog yielding to light and dark, and Douglas could see faint yellow light from the house and the shadows of the trees against the sky, Stephen's shadow flawed by the joint's floating coal, Bill's thin arms moving nervously back and forth and Wally's profiled nose silhouetted against the dark shimmer of the pool. Michael heard all the sounds surrounding them, the ghostly clatter and laughter from the house and the moan of the wind moving through the trees and across the distant water. "Nobody fall in the pool," said Max, chuckling.

"This is really nice," Douglas said quietly.

"Yeah," said Wally lazily, shivering, "except, where are the fucking *women?*"

Two shadows approached, clearly male and female, their footsteps clicking on the tiles, each holding a long, flat object in front of them, almost like pallbearers—everyone watched, trying to identify them in the darkness and figure out what they were carrying.

"Hello?" Stephen said nervously. Bill had put out and concealed the joint.

"Hi," said Jack—Michael squinted through his wet, chlorine-smelling glasses and saw that it was Jack and Louise. "You all got so quiet."

"We thought it was the cops," said Bill.

"The *cops?*" said Jack, laughing as he and Louise shifted their parcels around so that they were identifiable—they had brought a stack of thick, folded white cotton towels the size of bedsheets and they handed them to Wally and Stephen and then sat down.

"Thank you, thank you, thank you," wheezed Stephen, wrapping a towel around his shoulders and shivering convulsively.

"Did *you* turn the lights out?" said Bill. "Where *were* you?"

"Just getting towels for these guys," said Jack, smiling. "I just thought it was too bright out here, you know, like a prison exercise camp or something."

"We got some other stuff," said Louise, lighting a sputtering match and then igniting two of the familiar candles in red glass bulbs and fishnet webbing, which she put on the tiles between them all, the yellow candlelight reflecting on the swimming pool in oily, shifting patterns.

"You are the best host," said Douglas.

"Thank you, Douglas," said Jack.

"What *took* you so long?" asked Stephen, shivering. "We were *freezing.*"

"What took us so long?" Jack asked, sitting down next to Louise and accepting the bottle of scotch that Nick handed over. "The pool cabin's locked— We had to go into the house. Oh, we found Tina and Jill and Annabelle— They're upstairs in one of the bedrooms moving through the coke. And Amy and Duane left."

"What?" said Wally incredulously. "They *left? When?* What the *fuck?*"

"Shhh," said Nick in his quiet, buttery voice. "Take it easy, man."

"Jill and Tina and Anna are 'moving through the coke'?" Douglas repeated in a startled voice. "*What* coke? The coke from Buzzman?"

"Everyone has to relax," said Bill, producing a second plastic bag from somewhere in the pockets of his high-water pants and beginning to roll another joint. Nick had retrieved the scotch bottle. "This is the real stuff, not that ice water. Louise"—Bill suddenly looked up at her darkly—"Louise, you just have to relax."

"I guess you're right," Louise said, looking over at Jack and then back at Bill.

"No, Tina and Jill brought some," Jack was telling Douglas, putting down another object he'd brought from the house—a battery-powered, suitcase-sized stereo. He popped in a tape, and a Creedence Clearwater Revival song—"Have You Ever Seen the Rain?"—started playing.

"Is this your mix?" Stephen asked Jack, gesturing toward the radio.

"Yeah," Jack said, adjusting the volume so that the music was unobtrusive.

"She sees me coming," muttered Nick, "she better cross the street."

"ALL RIGHT," BILL quietly announced, finishing a new joint that was thicker than the others. "This is the real stuff— That other shit was Newtonian. Here we have some relativistic dope."

"About time," said Nick, grinning.

"This is some serious shit," said Bill, holding the joint up ominously. "Inconstant simultaneity. Where's the lighter?"

"Give it to Douglas first," said Nick, his smile barely discernible in the candlelight. "He needs inauguration. Then Max."

"That's *right,*" said Jack. "Douglas, are you happy?"

"Yes," said Douglas.

"What about the rest of you first-timers? Max? Michael? You happy?"

"Yes," said Michael.

"I'm happy," said Max.

"It's my first one too," said Louise impishly.

"Oh, don't you *worry,* this is coming *right to you,* Louise," said Bill fiendishly, fiddling with the joint.

"It's just a joint," said Wally quietly. Stephen immediately hit him on the arm, and they both laughed, their movements bathed in candlelight and deep shadow—the Creedence song had ended and "Fly Like an Eagle" had come on, which had been almost too much of a joke, and then "Cowgirl in the Sand," but then "Wish You Were Here" had followed, and by the chorus everyone was singing along. The joint moved around in a sort of ritual silence and Douglas felt close to panic and then far away from any fear, and it seemed that they were all sitting much closer together and the surrounding landscape seemed darker and larger, and much wilder, also, as the wind blew loudly across the swimming pool, and Douglas was coughing and reeling and then he was all right.

"This song is so good I can't believe it," he said quietly.

"It's like mainlining it's so good," said Stephen in a fake voice.

"You stupid idiot—" said Wally, who was lying back on the tiles, still wrapped in the towel.

"You want to fight? Forget it, we'll both drown," said Stephen.

"Man, this is rapture," said Max quietly.

"Shit," said Douglas weakly. "Oh shit, I think I'm beginning to understand something."

"Can you feel it? Can you feel it?" said Bill happily. "Can you feel the *tachyons?*"

"Bill," said Wally, "I love you, but you are one insane motherfucker."

"He's not crazy," said Louise, stretching, so that everyone noticed her body all over again. "And I'm glad you're understanding it, Douglas."

"He's waking up," said Nick gently.

"His blood's too clean, that's all," said Wally. "Happened to all of us."

"I'm frightened," said Douglas.

"But Douglas, it's so beautiful," said Bill, his white socks shining. "It's so simple— It's just waking up."

"—Just waking up—" repeated Douglas dutifully.

"Can you see it?" Nick asked, his voice cracking like flesh in the desert.

"I see everything," Douglas said, almost bursting into tears. "It's like everything before this was a grey blur. I know it's stupid, but it's all color— Everything's gold. I mean it's *all* gold, you know? Even the other colors are gold behind the edges."

"Gold only comes from supernovas," Bill said, smiling. "It's totally true."

"Oh my God," Douglas whispered, awestruck. "It's so sad where we're going. Goodbye Douglas."

"Come on, man," said Stephen, looking like a stranger, patting Douglas on the arm. "We're all here. We're all here." Douglas smiled and tipped his head back momentarily and involuntarily up at the sky.

"We're here, man," said Nick.

"How can you guys stand so straight, you know, sit up without moving and stand so straight when everything's moving so fast?"

"It's a technique," said Nick, not kindly, not unkindly.

"Someone's coming," said Michael, pointing toward the house.

Douglas and Max and the others looked over as "Band on the Run" began playing, and Douglas realized that this wasn't anything like what had happened hours ago, upstairs. "Is it just me, or are these songs going by way too *fast?*" Michael asked, and nobody answered, because everyone was looking toward the flagstone pathway, where a woman was walking toward them, her silhouette not yet identifiable against the lights from the house.

"Who *is* that?" Louise whispered, while Bill once again extinguished the joint and threw the remains out of sight. Everyone looked over their shoulders at the approaching woman, trying to identify her—they could see that she was tall and graceful but little else, except for some sort of grandeur to the way she approached them, making everyone wonder who she was and what would happen when she arrived.

"Well well," the woman said. "*Here's* where you all are."

"Annabelle!" said Max, smiling as he recognized her. Michael looked over and saw Nick seemingly frozen in place, impaled by the candlelight.

"Annabelle," said Douglas, his voice projecting real happiness.

"Douglas," said Annabelle, as Douglas stood up and walked over to her.

"How are you?" Douglas laughed giddily as Annabelle hugged him. "I *missed* you."

"Never mind me— How are *you?*" said Annabelle, examining his eyes merrily. "You all right, brother?"

" 'Brother, where you bound?' " sang Stephen.

"I'm just fine," said Douglas. "Annabelle, you look so pretty." Douglas squinted. "You should be proud. Annabelle"—he lowered his voice and leaned closer—"do you have any idea what they've been *saying* about you?" Everybody laughed, like a Greek chorus, like a studio audience, like a multitude of concertgoers. "Bill's been explaining the fundamental human question," Douglas went on.

"Just beer and city wind," said Bill, shrugging. "That's all it is, but country wind will do just as well or maybe better." He looked at Douglas slyly. " 'Fundamental human question'— You must have some further brain than me."

"I'm so glad to *see* you," Annabelle said, hugging Douglas again. "I've been looking for you, Doug," she whispered into his ear. "This is all turning into such shit."

"Are you all right?" Douglas whispered back. "Where the hell have you been?"

"Out in a boat. Upstairs with Tina and Jill. Never mind, we'll discuss this later— Shit, am I glad I found you." She examined his pupils again before stepping away, ostensibly still gauging his condition for the others.

"How's he doing?" asked Nick, his voice catching.

"He's all right," said Annabelle, cocking her head as she spoke, and Douglas could tell that she was deliberately not looking at Nick but he didn't understand why.

"Louise, you know this chick who's about to be making a lot of money?" Jack said pleasantly.

"Making *money?*" said Bill incredulously, squinting at Annabelle, brushing leaves from his Brillo hair.

"Didn't you hear?" said Stephen.

"Bill didn't hear," mumbled Nick hoarsely, audibly scratching his unshaven face.

"Shut up, Blanchard. Making *money?*" Bill repeated.

"Annabelle's a model," said Douglas.

"*Wow,*" said Bill, reaching for the scotch bottle. "Wow— You know what *happened* with Annabelle? You know what happened on the *assembly line?*"

"Oh, Jesus," said Nick.

"What assembly line?" asked Douglas.

"The *assembly line,*" said Bill, adjusting his Kissinger glasses. "You know— How it happens, there we all go, down the conveyor belt, and some jerk wasn't paying attention, you know—" Bill laughed convulsively and then continued. "Talking to the guy next to him, they're all there dripping the stuff in as we go by, little vials and spice jars and such, and so when Annabelle came by the guy was screwing around and not paying attention, and he just"—Bill mimed it with his hand, delicately, like a man pouring cream into coffee or vermouth into gin—"he just, you know, totally fucked up and dumped too much of this certain thing into the mix, fucked the thing over, and to *hell* with the Hubble constant—" Douglas was still listening but other conversations had started and Nick was looking at the candles and up at the extinguished outdoor spotlights, probably wondering if he had enough light to take pictures. "—And then he realized he'd fucked up, but it was too late"—now Bill mimed watching something as it traveled away—"It was too late because— there she went—with the recipe destroyed, with way too much of this damn stuff in her. I mean, face the facts, she's designed by the Big Guy— Why *shouldn't* it pay her grocery bills?"

"Fuck you, Coleman," said Annabelle absently, picking up the scotch bottle and having a belt—and then handing it to Douglas, who still had his arm around her shoulder.

"That's all bullshit," whispered Nick, so quietly that only Michael heard him. "We're *all* designed by the Big Guy— Annabelle invented herself."

"Did you say something, Nick?" Douglas asked brightly.

"Shut up," said Nick.

"Douglas," Annabelle whispered, suddenly leaning close, "they're all assholes. Come inside— I want you to meet someone."

"They're all assholes inside," said Douglas.

"Yeah"—she moved even closer to his ear—"but there's nobody to *talk* to in there and it smells like fucking Woodstock out here. Come on, Douglas, let's leave. Oh, fuck—"

"Is she all right?" asked Jack considerately, looking up from the level of their knees.

"What's wrong, Anna?" said Douglas quietly, taking her shoulders and looking at her.

Annabelle shook her head, sniffing, and finally raised her head and looked back at him. "I'm okay," she said, nodding. "I'm okay. Douglas, let's just leave. I mean, the party, the town, all of it— You and me, let's just get in the car and go, right now, just keep going and never look back. Whatever we don't have we'll buy on the way."

"Anna?"

"Doug, I'm so worried— Will you come with me?"

"All right," said Douglas quietly, stepping away from her and putting his hands in his pockets, looking down behind him—as far as he could tell, nobody was catching their conversation.

"We're going to go inside and get some food," Annabelle said more loudly, her voice back in shape. "Maybe we'll come back out later."

"Great," said Stephen, waving absently.

"So, um," said Bill, suddenly turning toward Annabelle, pushing his glasses up his nose, "so I guess you're a Republican now, Annabelle."

"*What?*" Annabelle said, looking down at him. "Why is that?"

"All models are Republicans," said Bill.

"What do you mean?"

"What I mean," said Bill, "is that nobody could want to have their millions taxed when they're nineteen. Hey, that rhymes." Bill coughed explosively. "But we are talking about millions of dollars. Make no mistake— Enough to buy everything."

"I'm a little sick of your art-and-money line," Annabelle said, as she and Douglas turned to go. "I mean, get a new joke."

"No joke. Facts are facts," said Bill, his voice slurring. "You know about Roosevelt's letters to Princeton? There was a war going on." He adjusted his glasses and reached for the scotch bottle. "They *bought* relativity."

chapter 23

Ten minutes later Bill suddenly remembered a case of Weideman's that he'd left in the trunk of his car. "And it's probably still cold, too," he told Michael. "You're the only one still coherent— You want to come with me?" Michael agreed, and soon they were rounding the dark southern edge of the Winfield house, wading gingerly through the ferns and shrubbery in the darkness, the crickets very loud in their ears. "I hope we don't set off any goddamned alarms," Bill said, looking back at him as they came around to the front of the house. "This place is probably a fucking minefield. Protecting the assets for future generations and all that—" They got to Bill's housepaint-covered two-door Chrysler, the silver gaffer's tape that held cellophane stretched over the triangular frames of the rear passenger windows shining in the glare of a single spotlight atop the house, and the same spotlight cast dim shadows of their feet against the gravel. Bill kicked the trunk, which popped open, and dove headfirst into it, emerging with two beers and handing one to Michael, and they leaned against the side of the car, enjoying the quiet.

"What's this drift I'm catching with Wally and Annabelle?" Michael asked after a moment.

"Oh, didn't you hear that whole story?" Bill intoned, raising his eyebrows, projecting his usual Kissinger dryness.

"What whole story?" Michael asked, cracking the beer open, realizing that they were already far into the night, past the arch of the evening and into its downward slope.

"Well," said Bill, "I'm not sure how to explain it— Actually, it's funny, you're asking the right man. I mean, everyone was there, but

I was the one who *saw* it. This was, what, six months ago, whatever, a while back, when everyone was sending off their college applications. There was a party at Tina's house— You know the one I mean, right? That party at Tina's house."

"I'm not sure." Gusts of wind from the lake were cold knives against their thin shirts, making the freezing beer taste better, like a part of the landscape or of the evening.

"Anyway, Wally was on the wrestling team back then. Right? They had— What?" he said suddenly, looking at Michael.

"Nothing," said Michael. "I just remembered that championship season."

"Right," said Bill, who told ugly stories as correctly and confidently as he wore ugly bowling shirts. "Tina's parents were out of town, buying guitar strings or something. Or *she* was buying guitar strings. Or *I* was buying guitar strings for the purpose of strangling all of *you.* Anyway. What happened was— *No,* I'm sorry, this *wasn't* at Tina's party. Stupid of me. This was earlier. It was snowing. Why can't I remember it right?"

"You're not exactly clean and sober," said Michael.

"That's true. All right. That day was a Wednesday in October— I mean, a Friday in January, shit, I'm really fucked up— It was that big snowstorm, and we all had that big test in English— Remember that? Barbara Fischer— Anyway, Tina was home sick. She had some virus or something and she'd been home for two days, and the big snowstorm was going to hit— It was *already* dark when Wally and I went over to visit her after school. We went in there and Tina was lying around in her room— You ever been to Tina's house?"

"No," said Michael, remembering the week that Tina had missed several English classes due to illness.

"Her room is crammed with all this junk and Tina was in bed surrounded by a million Kleenexes and her guitar. She was so happy to see us— We made her tea and we sat around in her kitchen and watched the snow coming down. We had to tell her everything that had happened in school. All the details— She comes on so bored, but don't think she doesn't pay attention. She asked Wally about Annabelle, because, you know, Tina had brought Annabelle to the wrestling match, when Wally had won the set. Wally hadn't noticed. He hadn't been paying attention. Tina goes 'Annabelle' and Wally's going 'Who? Who?' all the time. Snake-oil salesman. She has pots hanging against the window. The snow fell for hours. It was peaceful.

"So we stuck around for hours and the three of us sat around in the kitchen, with steam everywhere, because Tina's mom had turned the radiators up, 'cause Tina was sick, you know? —That's right, Tina's folks *weren't* out of town, they were at the opera or something twelve-toned like that. So the radio keeps going 'big snowstorm, big snowstorm, twenty inches,' all that crap, 'big snowstorm,' every five minutes, and we had our bookbags and everything— There were already these amazing snowdrifts over the cars outside and there was all this thermal convection going on all over the kitchen and Wally and Tina and I sat around drinking tea and watching the snow fall.

"Around nine at night Tina had perked up and she was re-tuning her guitar and using some kitchen implement—a garlic press or something—to do slide guitar, and Wally and I started calling people and inviting them over. Tina started putting brandy into the tea, and eventually Stephen came over, and then Amy and Duane— They're so *boring* when they're together, you know, Mike? And he never says anything anyway. Yeah, did they get into some spat tonight?"

"It looked like it."

"Son of a bitch," said Bill. "That's too bad."

"I guess."

"So by now it was eleven and we'd been at Tina's since *four-thirty*, for Christ's sake, and we didn't know what it was *like* out until people started showing up—Stephen walked in and his hair was *filled* with snow, he was *caked* with snow, and his face was *crimson*, like, the color of his *liver* or something. So eventually, around midnight, a lot of us were there, Blanchard arrived, Jack Winfield, even some sophomores, you know, Jill Brooks and some friend of hers that never spoke but had tea and said 'thank you' a lot and admired the *apartment* a lot. Very uncool, don't you know. So where was Annabelle? That was the question. It wasn't *my* question, but it was the question, you know what I mean? It was Wally's question."

"Uh-huh," said Michael.

"Well," said Bill, sipping his beer, shrugging, shivering, "he'd just won the big match, he was the star of the team and Annabelle had seen— The next few days, everyone was looking at him and needling him in the ribs and going 'Hoop hoop hoop' all the time. You know— 'you've got *Annabelle* after you!' Wally was going, you know, 'Cut the shit,' getting shy. But he knew. By the day of the snowstorm he knew."

"What did Blanchard say?"

"That's *right,* you hang with Blanchard, don't you?" said Bill, startled, poking Michael in the shoulder. "I always forget. Damn, Mike, we never talk— What did Blanchard say? He said 'Let her do it.' I think he was tired of waiting, he was tired of waiting for chicks to find out about Wally, and like that. Finally we all gathered around in Tina's room, with the tissues and crap, and we got Tina to stop with the guitar for a minute and everyone was handing Wally the phone. He wasn't used to this, I think he realized he was exactly as scared as he was letting on, he was used to it being different— I think he felt like a girl or something, but then again, you know, he felt like a man. Wally's dialing the Tafts' *house,* saying I can't believe I'm *doing* this, I must be out of my *mind,* she doesn't even know who I am— Stephen started in on him—"

" 'You stupid idiot,' " said Michael, badly imitating Stephen's voice.

"What?" said Bill, startled. *"Me?* —Oh. Yeah, like that— Finally *Tina* called her. 'Wally's here,' she says, all casual. Hangs up. 'Anna's coming right over,' says Tina— She's on her way to some club but she'll divert, bring some antihistamine or something from the corner. Everybody screams. When the doorbell rang Wally was getting into the brandy heavily, but when Annabelle came in he was so casual. She was wearing this black outfit with white polka dots with her stomach exposed, you know. I mean, she meant business. All that shit Blanchard always talks about. He thinks she's a genius.

"Anyway Jack suggested we all go out in the snow, into Central Park, and we all got our coats on— This was one in the morning, and I'd been indoors since four, in my *socks,* you know, so I was desperate to get out. It was incredible out there— Huge and dark and the sky was *bright,* you know, like it gets at night sometimes, it was *still* snowing hard and everyone had gone home and no one had walked the streets for hours. The only sound is our voices echoing across the snow. I mean, that's *it*— No cars, no airplanes, no sirens, no pedestrians, nothing. I don't think we saw one other person the whole time we were outside. It was *so* quiet, all the snow sculpted into fractals—fractal math, man, that's what it all gets down to—and I *saw* it that night, but who gives a shit? Blanchard's taking pictures all over the place, trying to get Annabelle into the picture, and Annabelle and Tina are throwing snowballs at him. They're both in these *overcoats,* you know, the new thing— Everyone else in normal down coats, having a good time. Annabelle never gets cold. You notice that? She's got *reptile blood* or something. Her coat's unbuttoned and she's throwing snowballs and she throws them overhand and the coat flaps and you see her stomach. I think the trick to her is that she *really does* that shit, stuff that other chicks understand but don't bother with. Drives guys nuts— Wally's jumping off walls into the fresh snow and climbing trees and shit, impressing her. I still can't— I wish someone else had done the dirty work."

"I can picture it," said Michael.

"You weren't *there,*" said Bill intensely. "Heisenberg would have eaten you for breakfast, you know that, Cadenhead? Anyway, we got back to Tina's at two in the morning and stacked up our coats and boots and everything by the elevator and Blanchard made Irish coffee in the kitchen. He does stuff like that. Tina's parents got home and we joked around with them for a couple of minutes and then they went off into the bedroom to procreate and we stayed in the kitchen."

"Maybe they went to sleep," said Michael.

Bill looked at him. "They were just at the *opera,*" he said. "You know these people, they get these ideas about themselves." He laughed, shaking his head. "I'm such an asshole— Anyway, there we were, and at some point Annabelle must have taken Wally off somewhere, but the thing is"—Bill looked at Michael—"the thing is that *none of us saw her do it.* It was just, Hey, where'd they go. They'd been gone five minutes and the next thing I knew, they both reappear with their coats on, real harried, about to leave. Don't leave, says Blanchard. He's got some self-control, that man. We've got to go, Annabelle and Wally say. Our parents. It had been *five minutes.*"

"Jesus," said Michael, finishing his beer and putting the can down on the gravel.

"So we saw Annabelle and Wally to the door and said good night, and went back to the living room, and there was Annabelle's scarf by the chair— So I went, you know, Oh, shit, and raced back to the door, you know, hoping the elevator hadn't arrived."

Bill finished his beer. "So I scrambled back there and opened the door, and went, you know, 'Hey, Annabelle, your scarf'— And it had taken her *that long* to get his pants open. Man, I can still see it, with the two overcoats, and Wally with his head back against the wall— And Annabelle with the *New York Times* under her knee— And the sound of the elevator on its way."

"Jesus Christ," said Michael, shivering, looking at Bill. "What did you do?"

"I shut the door," said Bill. "Tina's still got the scarf. You know, I *saw* it." Bill pointed and they moved toward the beer in the trunk, getting ready to tow it back to the pool. "I *saw* it. And you know, listen, let me tell you, that guy Wally— They are *not kidding,* what they say about him."

ANNABELLE AND DOUGLAS climbed the crooked flagstone path toward the spotlit, furtive-looking side door that led back into the house, entering a tiny vestibule lit only by means of an opened bathroom door to one side. They stopped there by unspoken agreement and Annabelle fumbled in the darkness, withdrawing a slightly bent White Camel from her purse, and Douglas produced some damp poolside matches and by their sputtering yellow light noticed that her fingers were trembling—a limp strand of willow-tree foliage was caught in her hair and Douglas drew it away, holding it before her eyes and dropping it to the tiled floor.

"Thanks," said Annabelle, puffing the Camel alight. "You want one?"

"Mom and Dad are around," said Douglas, waving vaguely toward the rest of the house. "They could come over here any m—"

"I don't give a shit," said Annabelle, shaking her head.

"I feel like I haven't seen you in hours," said Douglas. "I mean, not since dinner— Are you all right? I mean, you know, physically, are you feeling all right?"

"Yeah," said Annabelle, head down, eyes closed, hand on her forehead.

"Are you sure?" said Douglas. "You're looking a little pale—"

"I'm okay," said Annabelle, leaning to close that door against the mild draft it had been passing, settling back against the wall and putting one gold-shoed foot up on the wall behind her, so that the hem of her black dress slid back to expose her thigh. "Where's Max?" she asked in the same dogged tone. "Is he around?"

"He's right down there," said Douglas, concerned, gesturing toward the pool. "What— Didn't you see him?"

"I didn't really notice who was there," said Annabelle. "It was just that it was that crowd."

"Louise is down there. She's causing a sensation," said Douglas.

"Yeah, talk about it," Annabelle said wearily. "Man, people are so *dumb*— I mean it's not even that she's not doing it correctly, not that she *is,* you understand, but it is *such a simple trick* she's pulling. I mean, there's the act, but she thinks she's such hot shit."

"She seems all right," said Douglas. "She seems fine."

"Is Max still getting these funny looks?" asked Annabelle, squinting at Douglas through the vestibule's dim, grey air. "People looking because of his hands?"

"No," said Douglas. "He was keeping his hands in his pockets for a while there, like he used to, you know, but he relaxed. I thought you were taking me somewhere."

"Did you actually tell him to keep doing that? I mean, did you *used* to tell him to keep doing that?"

"I used to tell him to stop," said Douglas, leaning closer to Annabelle so as to allow a smiling bald man past him into the bathroom. "Did I make a mistake? Inviting him?"

"He scares me," Annabelle said as the bathroom door shut and locked, leaving them in relative darkness. "He just *stands* there with his pretty stubble— I mean nothing *gets* to him, you know? How can you deal with someone who nothing *gets* to?"

"You never could figure him out," Douglas said. "Things get to him."

"Come on," said Annabelle, standing up straight, suddenly, and reopening the outside door to flick the still-full-length cigarette outside before taking Douglas by the hand and leading him farther indoors. "Thanks for the light."

"You sure you're okay?" Douglas said, pulling her back toward him.

"I'm fine," said Annabelle. "I'm just confused. I'm fine. Come on."

She led him past a sequence of corridor doorways, and through one opened door they glimpsed their father standing alone in the Winfields' mahogany library poring over a book—*I Heard the Owl Call My Name*—that he'd pulled down from one of the towering shelves. "Hi, Dad," they said together—Greg looked up, distracted, and then grinned and waved. "Having a good time?" Annabelle asked, leaning into the room.

"Hmm? Oh, sure," said Greg, waving at the bookshelves. "Always remember— No *great house* is complete without literature. Look"—

he pointed—"there's a first edition of *Gatsby.* Perfect condition—Pages cut and everything. I don't think it's real, though— I think it's one of those"—his hand fumbled rhythmically for the word—"facsimiles."

"We'll see you later, Dad," said Douglas, waving, pulling Annabelle after him. "That's right, you told me every year it's the library," he said softly as they continued down the corridor toward the living room. "Didn't he *give* them *Gatsby?*"

"Yeah—Dad's slipping sometimes," said Annabelle, frowning. "I get worried."

They continued down the corridor, passing another doorway, and Douglas glanced into another sitting room—one that connected to the Piano Study—wallpapered with wide canary-yellow-and-white vertical stripes, and within this room Tina Foster and Jill Brooks reclined on the edge of a pale Oriental carpet flipping through piles of battered record albums, three champagne glasses between them. Douglas saw what little he did of the room, saw enough, saw Jill, and hurried past, pulling on Annabelle's arm.

"That's right," Annabelle said without humor. "You have no courage—I have all the proof I need. Jesus, you *told* enough people— I mean, if you would calm *down,*" she added contemptuously as they approached the living room, "if you would just calm down it's not so crazy. Why'd you *tell* everyone, though, Doug?"

"I don't know," said Douglas helplessly. "You *do* think there's a chance, though? Is that what this's all about? —I mean, I'm hoping. Or is this something else?"

"There's a chance," said Annabelle. "I'm not telling you what this is all about. We can get some food, waste time—but we're going into that room, Douglas."

"Whatever you say," Douglas said brazenly. "Man, she *is* like a swan in the white dress—I don't care what anyone says."

"Jesus, you've got it bad," said Annabelle. She abruptly diverted before they reached the loud living room and pulled Douglas around a corner toward a Brobdignagian set of French doors, twisting the fluted brass handles and propelling them out onto the deserted back balcony.

"You're taking me in circles," Douglas said, hugging himself against the mild breeze as they wandered toward the parapet. They were ten feet above the dark, damp lawn, hearing dim speech and laughter echoing through the foliage from the direction of the pool, and the yellow light from the house touched Annabelle's shoulder blades and the back of her neck, glittering in her eyes as she glanced back toward the house before joining him at the stone balustrade to gaze across the dark meadow—the dance platform was deserted, looking long-abandoned, several of its red lanterns still lit, and beyond the dance platform the lawn curved away toward the dark drypointed trees beneath the clear night sky.

"It's going to rain," said Annabelle.

"No way," said Douglas, hands in pockets, sniffing at the ozone charge in the air. "They'd have to go cover the boats and everything. I'm glad I don't have *that* job— I'll bet that path"—he was pointing—"becomes a fucking mudslide."

"Maybe they'll forget," said Annabelle. "Maybe the boats will fill. Maybe they'll sink."

"I thought you were cheering up," said Douglas, leaning backward against the balustrade.

"The rain's coming," Annabelle said softly, still looking out.

"It's an absolutely clear sky." Douglas stared upward at the house's heavy shadows and the dark edge of the looming trees where the wind sifted them. "I'm not expecting rain."

"Like I say," Annabelle said. "You never *expect* anything."

"Uh-huh," said Douglas—he was peering through another French door into the living room, which was filled with adults drinking champagne and dancing to dimly audible piano music. He glimpsed their mother for a moment, standing with several middle-aged women, and as Douglas watched Giulia moved a few feet to one side so that a mullion in the door blocked her face from view—when she moved Douglas was suddenly alarmed to see Ralph DiGrassi standing alone in his scarlet jacket, devouring handfuls of salted nuts.

"Ralph's still here," Douglas said, amazed.

"Oh, I don't *believe* it," Annabelle murmured, moving behind Douglas and looking over his shoulder. "Everywhere you turn—Jesus, can't he just *give up* and *go home?*" Right then Ralph happened to look up, glancing through the glass and locking eyes with Douglas, before a young couple wandered over to the French doors, blocking the sightlines.

"He's not really doing any damage," said Douglas, stuffing his hands into his pockets and furling his shoulders against the wind. "I mean, it could be worse."

"He makes my *skin crawl,*" said Annabelle. "He's always staring at me. *Always.* Day and *night.* Passing me *notes*— I mean, with the— You know, if he expects *Max* to come deal with him he's dreaming. Max is *long* gone."

"You see that woman there?" said Douglas, pointing, so that the motion caught the eyes of the couple indoors. "I want you to take a look at her and see if you—"

"Jerk," said Annabelle, laughing as she pushed his arm down. "We're undercover— You want *Ralph* coming out here? And now you've got *those* two watching us—"

"Cut it out," said Douglas, laughing. "Stop changing the subject— I'm trying to *point out* someone."

"They're *really* staring," Annabelle said, mildly surprised, standing straight and sidling up to Douglas, putting a hand on his arm as she looked over his shoulder back at the house. "This is so annoying—I thought we were hiding."

"Anna—"

"*Who,* damn it?" said Annabelle. "Come on— If they think they're eavesdropping they'll stop." As the couple inside the house watched, she pulled him closer and stood up, her chin touching his shoulder. "Okay, I'm looking— Who am I supposed to see?"

"You see the woman near Mom?" said Douglas looking over Annabelle's shoulder, across the field and toward the woods as he stroked her back. "You see the woman— Is she still there? The woman by the mantelpiece? The, like, large woman? With the red dress?" There was no response. "Annabelle?"

"Wait," said Annabelle, the point of her chin brushing Douglas' shoulder as she craned her neck toward the house. "*Yes.* Oh, shit, I know who *that* is— That's Margaret MacAffee." She moved her head to look at him. "You didn't recog— Didn't you meet her before? She was next to you during—"

"I know," said Douglas. "But the weirdest thing happened before— She, like, *grabbed* me, right after dinner, and said all this— She was really rude to me."

"Uh-huh," said Annabelle, sadly, her voice shifting as she put her head on his shoulder. "Poor Douglas."

"You know her?" asked Douglas. "I mean I think we should talk."

"By reputation," said Annabelle. "I hope she wasn't too cruel. Jesus, listen to m—"

"Anna, I think we've got to talk about her."

"*No,*" said Annabelle, her grip tightening on him. "No, we are *not* going to talk about her. There's some shit you never discuss, Douglas, things you can't *say,* there's things you— Oh, God, *please* don't make me talk—"

"But she said—"

"Douglas, she's history, she's dirt, she's not the point, she's far away, she's *gone*— You have to *understand* some things."

"*What* things?" Douglas slid his hand along the bare muscles of her back, feeling her stroke his neck in response.

"You're so fucking *close,*" said Annabelle, speaking softly as Douglas moved his hand to her hair. "Jesus, everyone's giving you such a hard time— Look, Wally's an asshole. I wish I could explain things to these guys."

"I wish you could too. I would if they would listen to me."

"I know you would," said Annabelle, hugging him suddenly.

"You knew I was awake when Wally was leaving that morning, didn't you?" Douglas shifted his posture, stroking Annabelle's smooth back. "I mean, you said the thing about—"

"Let's not get into it."

"But you *knew,*" Douglas said.

"You're always awake," said Annabelle into his lapel. "Let's drop it, all right, let's not get into it— What did he say, Wally, what did he call me, 'arrogant'? And I'm supposed to be so tough. Oh, fuck, I am not enjoying this—"

"I'm sorry."

"Oh, let's get drunk, Douglas"—she shook him by the jacket sleeves, lightly back and forth—"let's get really, really drunk and go into the other room and maybe we can do some lines."

"Drinks, yeah, but I'm not touching the blow," Douglas said. "You know I've never— Hey, look who's here," he said suddenly, gazing through the doors into the living room, where Jill and Tina were dancing together, spinning with the other couples to the rhythm of a barely audible waltz.

"She can't dance," Annabelle murmured, grinning.

"What's funny?"

"Nothing— Walking home yesterday. Me having things up my sleeve."

"You *not* having things up your sleeve."

"Either way," said Annabelle, abruptly straightening and pulling him back toward the house. "Come on, darling."

"I'm scared," Douglas said, his grip slipping from her waist.

"That's why I'm taking over," said Annabelle, guiding him back into the loud bright warmth of the house. "At the Lawrence you were *dead*— And upstairs, I kept waiting, she fell *asleep.* That's no way to—"

"Yeah," he said tremulously, "but maybe this isn't—"

"Douglas," Annabelle whispered, turning toward him as they approached the living room doors, "who can you trust if you can't trust me?"

"I don't know. Annabelle—" He awkwardly pulled her back.

"Jesus— *Now* what?"

"I'm afraid I won't know how to kiss her. It's stupid, but—"

"Is that *all?*" Annabelle looked away, distracted, freezing their movement halfway back to the French doors. "Look, Douglas, would you do me a favor?"

"Yeah?"

"When you're *there*— I mean, don't get me wrong, I've never *seen* the Brooks house— But when you get—"

"Maybe it won't come to that."

"—to the house I've got this *package* I want to hide." Annabelle was laughing. "You understand, just a *small*— Down a storm drain or something—"

"Come on," said Douglas. "Stop screwing around— Is there a real favor?"

"Yeah," said Annabelle suddenly. "Yeah, there is. Doug, what is it about her that gets to you?"

"She's—" Douglas stared at the flat white surface of the French doors, mesmerized. "She seems sweet. She's pretty and she seems sweet, you know, like underneath all this shit going on at school, you know, maybe she's sensitive, you know, or shy or something— I mean maybe she's an interesting person."

"But what *gets* to you?" asked Annabelle.

"I love the way she looks," said Douglas. "The way the cheap clothes hang on her. I mean they're not really cheap but she never looks wrapped in money. I love her smile. I love the way she moves. I love her *back.* How smooth it is. I know it's dumb— I can't help it. I just love looking at her and I can imagine, I can imagine talking to her, spending time with her, without all of the other—"

Annabelle kissed him abruptly, her tongue puncturing his mouth while he talked, and then just as abruptly pulled back.

"That's how she'll do it," she said. "She'll get you talking and then do it. Remember."

"Oh yeah?" said Douglas, leaning forward and reaching for Annabelle's face. "This is how *I'll*—"

"No, no," Annabelle said, swerving away. "Wrong— You *warned* me. I didn't warn you."

"Oh," Douglas said. "I get it."

"No— You don't. But you will," Annabelle murmured, clinically narrowing her eyes as she straightened his tie and brushed his shoulders. "Have a shot," she told him, pulling the near-empty flask from her purse and handing it over. "Come *on*— Belt it down. Let's go." Shuddering, Douglas complied, draining the final drops of gin. "How's that?"

"Pretty fucking good," Douglas said, holding the empty flask toward her and reeling as heat washed over him. "That's— So I look okay?"

"Oh, you look good," Annabelle said, nodding intently. "Let's do it." She took his arm as he staggered and recovered and then led him toward the living room doors, through which they could hear the recorded waltz getting louder as they approached.

MICHAEL AND NICK sat side by side on the tiles beside the pool drinking the last two Weideman's, Nick smoking a cigarette, watching Wally and Stephen swim laps in their underwear, and Jack stood with Bill and Louise at the other end of the pool, fiddling with the padlock that held the small outbuilding's door shut.

"What time is it?" Michael asked.

"It's almost three," said Nick. "It's the afternoon of the night."

"What?"

"Midnight is high noon of the night," said Nick, staring at the pool water. "Sunrise is the sunset of the night."

"If you don't have a job."

"Right."

Michael sipped from his can, the cold aluminum brushing his lips, and stared at the house. "Looks like we're finishing Coleman's beer," Nick said.

"I don't think they'll mind. Everyone's gone," said Michael. "God, I'm really going to feel this in the morning—"

"Yeah, where *is* everyone?" Nick said. "Tina and Jill are inside—

Amy and Duane left— Buzzman left— Gantry's dancing— DiGrassi's gone, Wendy was here ten minutes, Charlie Dane never made it—" As Nick trailed off, Jack got the outbuilding door open, and he, Louise, and Bill disappeared inside. "I guess we're the thing."

"I don't have a place to sleep," said Michael.

"Is Jill dead?" Nick said absently.

"During dinner," Michael explained patiently, "she told me something had come up and I couldn't crash there."

"*That's* a low blow," Nick said, looking at the outbuilding.

"Well— Where are *you* sleeping?"

"I'm driving back," said Nick. "You can come."

They sat quietly, sipping beer and looking across the pool, and suddenly they heard a door slam and voices descending the crooked flagstone path—they stared at the shrubbery, waiting, and eventually a thick-haired, sunburned middle-aged man in a bland suit stepped out onto the tiles, followed by a woman in her late twenties, tightly wrapped in an ankle-length strapless gown made of shimmering green fabric, her hair twisted up and fastened above her head. Nick and Michael watched as the newcomers approached them, the woman stumbling in her high heels, the man supporting her.

"Hello," said Nick.

"Good evening," the man said agreeably.

"Intro*duce* yourself," chided the young woman, leaning on his arm. Behind them, Wally and Stephen had stopped swimming and were treading water, watching. "He never intro*duces* himself. He's so *modest.* This is Senator Rollins."

"Nick Blanchard."

"Pleased to meet you, Nick," said Rollins, who clearly was more sober than the young woman. "And you?"

"Michael Cadenhead."

"We thought we'd do some *swimming,*" said the young woman, putting her head on the senator's shoulder.

"I've been trying to talk her out of it," said the senator, his hand on the woman's bare shoulder, while behind him the outbuilding's door opened and Jack came out and slammed the door, the padlock falling audibly onto the tiles, and then walked up the path and away—Michael and Nick heard the house door slam, distantly, and then the outbuilding door drifted open a few inches, revealing a wedge of blackness, before it, too, was slammed shut from inside.

"*Nonsense,*" the woman protested. "Look— *These* boys are swimming"—she waved at Wally and Stephen—"and they don't have bathing suits. I've been *telling* him"—she was standing, now, without the senator's support—"I've been *telling* him that at Anthesteria people have been known to swim in their underwear, and here's the proof. I don't know what else you need to see."

"Please," Rollins said, smiling as the woman undid fastenings on her shimmering green dress and then pulled it off and dropped it on the tiles and stood there in her small lace underwear and high heels. "Please, not in front of these fellows—"

"Hoop hoop hoop hoop hoop," Wally and Stephen chanted loudly, staring at the woman while treading water. "Hoop hoop jinga jinga hoop."

"They're big boys," the young woman said fervently, ignoring the catcalls from the pool. "You'd better *join* me." With that, the woman kicked off her heels and dove into the pool, and after a moment Rollins shrugged, smiling benignly at Nick and Michael as he took off his wristwatch, jacket, tie, and shoes, and then dove into the pool after the woman.

Michael and Nick looked at each other.

"It's getting cold," said Nick, squinting with his eyebrows raised.

"Yeah, you're right," said Michael. "Maybe we should see what's going on in there."

"I don't really want to—*phew*—go join the others, really," said Nick, standing up and putting out his cigarette in Senator Rollins' shoe. "You want to get some good beer and sit in the Piano Study?"

"Sure," said Michael, standing also. They walked the length of the pool and approached the crooked flagstone path, Michael glancing back at the senator and the young woman and Wally and Stephen, who were all splashing each other, and as they passed the outbuilding the door opened and Bill came out, almost furtively, shirttails flapping, holding his bow tie and looking flushed.

"*I FUCKED LOUISE DELANY!*" Bill triumphantly whisper-screamed at them.

DOUGLAS SAW JILL'S back first, because she and Tina were dancing, their paired arms brushing the other couples in the after-midnight crowd—the party had settled into the distinct pieces it had looked for all night, and this room seemed to be enjoying the incorrectness of the late dancing, to recorded music, after the band's departure. Annabelle led Douglas straight up to Jill and Tina and interrupted their spin, grabbing Tina, while Douglas stood back, feeling the wildness of the second round of dope and the dead heat of Annabelle's gin.

"Slow it down, Foster Girl," said Annabelle into Tina's ear.

"Girl in *black,*" Tina said, almost falling over. "Where *were* you?"

"Hey," said Jill, smiling at Douglas, the curves of her mouth emphasizing the smoothness of her face and the damp darkness of her eyes. "There you are."

"Hi," said Douglas. "Hi, Jill."

"Hi, *Douglas*— What's going on?" Tina and Annabelle were talking while the music continued and the other dancers kept moving, and soon they started dancing.

"Not much," said Douglas, hands in pockets, avoiding Jill's eyes and then catching them again. "I mean, all this— I just got stoned with the guys out by the pool."

"You were at the pool? Let's dance," said Jill, moving up to him and pressing against him.

"Yeah," said Douglas, dancing, beginning that particular languid shuffle, speaking too loudly down toward Jill's ear, incredulously feeling her arm on his back, catching the scent of her hair. "Wally and Stephen were swimming."

"Those guys," said Jill into Douglas' shoulder, moving him as they danced.

"Standard—" Douglas coughed, wheezing a bit at the afterbite of the gin. "Standard move for those guys."

"That's right," said Jill against the music. They kept dancing, moving around, and as they turned Douglas realized he'd lost sight of Annabelle and Tina.

"It's nice to dance with you," said Douglas.

"Thank you," said Jill, moving her arm on his back. "It's nice to dance with you."

"Sorry I'm not the world's best at this."

"You're doing fine," said Jill. "You don't look a lot like Annabelle."

"What? Annabelle got all the family charisma," Douglas said, pressing closer to her as they turned, feeling her waist against his.

"What?" said Jill, straining to hear over the music. "I couldn't hear you."

"Annabelle got all the beauty."

"You've got nice eyes," Jill said, looking up at him.

"You've got beautiful eyes," said Douglas.

"Thank you," said Jill, smiling. "You know, I saw your dad— You look like him and Annabelle looks like your mother."

"Right." Douglas shook his head, smiling.

"Your family's got a lot of style."

"Uh-huh," said Douglas, looking down at her as they danced, amazed at the effect of her face this close up—the dark eyebrows, the wisps of blonde hair that drifted forward toward his chin.

"Your family's got a lot of class."

"You've got a beautiful back," Douglas said, stroking her smooth shoulder blades.

"Oh yeah?" said Jill, looking at him and then back along the lines of dancing couples.

"It's like glass," said Douglas, sliding his hand down the hard muscles of her lower back.

"Like a glass of gin?"

"Like Steuben glass," Douglas said, pressing against her, feeling her legs shifting against his with her dress and his trousers between them—they kept turning and Max was there, up close out of nowhere, watching him across the low shoulder of his dance partner, Giulia Taft. *Acrobat,* Max mouthed, watching Jill dance before vanishing back into the crowd. "You're an acrobat," Douglas told Jill, pulling her waist toward his—their lower bodies were blatantly pressed together, which was having a serious effect on Douglas, one she could feel through the fabric and didn't seem to mind.

"Some nights," Jill said, pressing back, turning her face up to him. Douglas slid his hand down the silk along her spine and kissed her, right there in the middle of the crowded room.

"*You're* aroused. Wow," said Jill, stroking his shoulder.

"Every time I look at you."

"Wow," Jill said, shaking her head, laughing, and he kissed her again, recovering and pulling back—over her head, Douglas could see Annabelle dancing with Jack Winfield, and then the view was blocked again.

"Every time you see me?"

"Every time," said Douglas, smiling by rote, flaring his eyes. "I swear to God." The taped waltz ended and they slowed, stopped and separated with the other dancers, standing for a second together before Jill tugged Douglas' arm, leading him past all the dancing spectators and toward the double doors, where Max was standing, waiting to pull Douglas aside.

"When you move you move fast," Max whispered in his ear like a lawyer. "There's hope for you yet."

"Goodbye, Max," Douglas whispered happily, grinning as he gently pushed Max away into the crowd while Annabelle stepped up to them out of nowhere, stepping between them, putting one arm around Douglas' shoulders and another around Jill's.

"Come on, you two," Annabelle said. "Let's get a bottle of champagne—we're the new club."

chapter 24

"The first time I photographed Annabelle" —Nick rubbed his chin as he spoke—"the first time she was *ever* photographed—I mean there'd been snapshots, yearbook shit, family pictures, whatever, but the first time she was ever *photographed*—I remember this so clearly, Mike— This was, what, October, I guess?" Nick took a breath, pulling half an inch from his cigarette, took a sip from a bottle of Rolling Rock—one from a six-pack that he'd swiped from the kitchen—and fiddled with his camera as he looked around at the otherwise deserted Piano Study. "It was perfect, raining all the time, white sky, sad, sad weather. I was— This is funny. Everything I did, you know, Mr. Ballard would tell me I was taking these great pictures and then ruining them." Nick smiled. "He thought it was so *perverse,* but he had a heart— After he was in that car crash old Ballard sold me one of the enlargers. That fucking darkroom, they have so much money, the school— But he sold me the enlarger and the first thing I did was file down the edges of the negative stage. He thought I was out of my mind, what was I doing to his Leitz enlarger, but I wanted the sprocket holes around the prints— I did it by mistake one time, got the old KODAK on the edge, and that became part of the style. I did that before all the fucking magazines."

As Nick talked, Michael was remembering when he had been very young, remembering the babysitter who liked to take him to the park and feed him a plastic tub of something called Neptune Salad, the first Cadenhead apartment, the story Michael's mother had told years ago about how she and his father had first arrived in New York and gotten married and how during their first evening together in their first apartment they had innocently carried a barbecue grill into the park for a picnic and been told by a policeman to put out the fire and move along. Just telling or remembering one story from those times brought all of it back, and as Michael sat in the Winfield Piano Study listening to Nick, who was smoking and talking more than usual, he remembered fifth grade, and the things that had happened to Douglas Taft and Max Gantry, like the thing with the soft-hearted turtle—the story he couldn't remember at all—and the other thing with the cheating and the teachers and the way that Max ended up with a pencil point in his thigh.

"But Ballard, he thought I was nuts, the way I would print— I was solarizing prints, you know, fluorescent light while the thing was in the stop bath, I was shooting at a fifteenth handheld, pushing the film to 1600, something like that, grain and depth-of-field— And Ballard would always say, you know, Nick, you're cheating." Nick smoked, fiddled with the f-stop ring on the camera. "I'm so glad I left Thorndike, man. What an asshole— He thought I was spending too much money on *equipment,* you know, nine hundred for a lens, here and there, all this money. But, Mike"—he looked at Michael—"Mike, I have to do this. I mean, a Leitz lens, you know, center-to-edge is just *perfect.*"

" 'Stop in the Name of Love,' " Jill screamed from behind Nick. She and Douglas and Annabelle had taken possession of a gilt-legged white couch in a large adjoining parlor with brightly striped wallpaper and Michael gazed past Nick's head and saw the three of them framed in the opened French connecting doors, loudly laughing and talking and poking each other, while Tina reclined at their feet flipping through a stack of records and a guy that none of them knew stood by the window drinking an Irish coffee.

Back years and years ago, Michael was remembering, he used to own a pair of blue serge shorts with a clip hanging from a strap on the belt buckle, Boy Scout shorts, and Michael could remember all those days riding the bus to school with his mother, who would be on her way to work, holding his notebooks, walking into classrooms in his shorts and sitting at the tables that only came up to adults' knees when adults stood next to them, leaning over with their hands on their knees and looking at the students' handwriting, bits of cursive writing carefully carved into paper with a dotted line across the middle of each line of prose, indicating the small-letter height, or looking at the drawings that students would do on pieces of manila paper when they had some free time. Michael remembered the day he had sat on a miniature chair in that one classroom at the back of the fourth floor of Thorndike, writing on the paper with the horizontal lines and watching Max Gantry and Douglas Taft get into an argument.

"So Annabelle, you know, she was always hanging around, and I had been thinking about faces, you know, looking at people, thinking about their faces," Nick was saying. "Watching people talk— Once I started paying attention I couldn't stop. There's always such a difference between someone's— The image in your head when you hear their name, and their actual *face,* you know, the flesh and bones of their face. These chicks have it all figured out, you know, from the magazines, they're saying, oh, great cheekbones, big eyes, dividing and conquering, but a guy just says Oh— A pretty girl. Right? Doesn't understand what he's *seeing.*"

" 'Stop in the Name of Love,' " screamed Jill, who had a beautiful smile, drawing Michael's gaze past Nick's talking head and through the distant French doors—the sky had deepened from burgundy through shadeless grey to blackness behind the clean reflections of the wallpaper and Jill and Douglas and Annabelle were tossing wadded-up pieces of towel paper at each other as they occupied the couch. A record had recently ended and Tina had begun fiddling with the stereo, trying to figure out which song to put on next, and Jill, drunk and happy, was screaming out the names of songs. " 'Stop in the Name of Love,' " Jill screamed. " 'Hotel California.' 'Casino Boogie.' 'Tuesday Afternoon.' "

"So Annabelle was hanging around," Nick continued, "playing the thing out, high school chick, in the background, in the foreground, in the background again, with the knee pants, with the sweaters, the whole deal. Mike, you saw— It was so *charming,* what she was doing, but I don't think anyone was watching as closely as *she* was, you know? Except me." Nick lit another cigarette. "Douglas— He's a smart kid, you know, giving me the look, you know, like, I thought you left. So I asked Annabelle if I could photograph her and it was all right. I did not fuck up— I asked her *specifically* before that party Wally Patterson had, you know, in the park or something, I was saying, you know, this is not a date." Nick smiled. "It was not a date. I did not fuck up. So I met her after school and I had this new motor drive. I remember Jack thought I was going to take pictures of guys making touchdowns or something, he didn't understand how the motor's for *portraits.* Portraits of Annabelle." Nick stopped and looked around, his sandy voice catching. "The *last* thing they are is portraits. That's the one thing— Annabelle, she's a model now, but she *became* a model that overcast day. What I did to her, I did something, she woke up and they stopped being portraits. Poor girl."

" 'Stop in the Name of Love,' " screamed Jill. Douglas and Annabelle sat on either side of her, trying to get her attention, both their heads bobbing as they smiled at each other and at her, and Michael could see Jill's blonde hair sliding around and she swung her upper body forward and back, happily laughing, her hands on her forehead and her elbows on her knees, feet pointed inward, hair spread out in a corona around her upturned and laughing face. The three of them had obviously found a fresh bottle of champagne somewhere, because three fluted champagne glasses stood on the floor by their feet, each half full of champagne—Douglas kept picking his up and sipping from it until some of Annabelle's towel paper landed in it, and then he lit a cigarette and dropped ashes, calmly, into Annabelle's glass. " 'Take Me to the River,' " Jill screamed. " '(Just Like) Starting Over.' "

Michael remembered how the whole fifth-grade class had been compelled to write little five-page book reports, and how, as tended to happen with these room-by-room fifth-grade projects, there were those who could do it without any problem and those who couldn't—and at this point in remembering the story Michael began to doubt his facts, because it didn't make sense for fifth-graders to be writing book reports. But in any event, even if it *had* happened later on—and it *must* have happened later on, Michael reasoned, because he remembered that it was during an oil embargo or something that specifically dated it—he could clearly remember that Max had had no trouble doing his book report but Doug had gotten into some kind of big mess and had had trouble getting it finished on time—which had, as Michael remembered, created a dilemma between the two of them, since they were in the midst of designing some sort of aircraft.

"I met Annabelle near Thorndike," Nick said, his voice characteristically catching, hoarse on some words, fluid on others. "On the corner— We faced each other across the street, a truck moved and there she was. I was leaning against a wall, carrying all my camera crap, drinking a beer, she probably thought I'd been standing there a while before she showed up, you know, like a little kid thinks the refrigerator light is always on. We went to the park, by the track, burned some rolls, but it wasn't working out— She was awkward, she felt like a fool— So we went back to her place. You should see the Taft place. Fucking huge— I mean it's *obscene* how much that pad must have cost. She and Douglas are going to get so much money— But I realized we'd get some good pictures. I asked her to change and she puts on these old jeans and a sweater and when the light was right I got her by the window. It's always like, I don't know, like a ballet. Annabelle— She gets against the glass of the window, there's no sound, she's moving slowly and meanwhile, there I am, blam-blam-blam-blam, six frames a second, getting off multiple shots, roll after roll. She's nervous, breaking the trance, but then it starts to happen, you know, she starts to move away, become *unfamiliar,* become a stranger, become a model."

But if Doug and Max had still been in the midst of designing their airplane, thought Michael confusedly, then it *couldn't* have been during the oil embargo, it *must* have been earlier on, because nobody continues with childish things like believing themselves capable of designing and building aircraft all the way forward into the same period of time that they're doing five-page book reports—nobody continues with those childish things for that long—but then maybe that was what had started Douglas' and Max's fight.

"On the third roll," said Nick, "on the third roll, it's starting to get dark outside, I'm running out of light, we've got to get going, you know, because ostensibly we're going over to Patterson's house— So I say, are you going to try on clothes before leaving, figuring out what to wear to the party? Annabelle's shy, people don't like to admit shit like that, but she says yes. And where the hell are her parents, by the way? They have some dinner they're going to after work. Okay. So she's going to change, and I ask if she'll do it with the camera. Wait, Mike, don't—" Nick grinned without showing his teeth. "This isn't about to become one of those stories, all right? She finally put on this dress, I was in the other room looking at the coffee table books, shouting in through the bedroom door, real knowledgeable. You know— Oh, hey, *Cartier-Bresson!* What a great book! And Annabelle's in her room going 'What? What?' Then Douglas came home."

" 'Imagine,' " Jill was screaming. " 'Bridge over Troubled Water.'

'Aqualung.' 'Hopelessly Devoted to You.' 'Black Dog,'" she screamed.

The book reports had been turned in and soon Max had been going around making fun of Doug to the other people in the class, and Michael, who was still wearing the blue serge shorts with the Boy Scout clips on them, watched as they argued about the F-111 and was lectured in eleven-year-old tones of derision by Max, since Max had reached that impasse where he no longer believed their construction of an airplane to be feasible, and then Douglas had called him several names, bravely conjuring his father's worst mild insults, and Max had gone to the teacher and revealed that Douglas had falsified the last three pages of his five-page book report. The teacher had been angry at both of them, and the whole class, including Michael in his blue Boy Scout shorts, had laughed, and then Douglas had jammed a pencil into Max's thigh.

"So Douglas walks in," continued Nick, "and he'd been hanging around record stores for three hours or something— He calls the elevator man 'Sport.' Real cute. He gives me this look and says, Nick! What am I doing there? I'm photographing Annabelle. Great, Douglas says. Annabelle comes out all embarrassed. The way they deal with each other, it's so interesting— So Annabelle and Douglas are talking and I took some more pictures, blam, blam, blam with the motor drive, the two of them talking— It's like, four different locations and four sets of clothes, one of those scenarios, one of those damn photo series where the woman fucks around by herself with the clothes and shit, all narcissistically and everything, and then the man arrives, so here Douglas has arrived and they're talking and just when there's *not enough light anymore*"—Nick leaned toward Michael—"just when the lamps are being turned on and I'm down to a sixtieth at 1.2 with the Tri-X pushed to 800, there they are, the two of them, and the light's all gone." Nick smiled. "We asked Douglas to come to the party, but he wasn't in the mood. Annabelle got angry, she's saying you're *never* in the mood, it's so stupid, you'd fit right in, Jill's going to be there, but Douglas didn't come."

"'Tenth Avenue Freezeout,'" screamed Jill in the other room. "'Sister Morphine.' 'Oxford Town.' 'Comfortably Numb.' 'Brown-Eyed Girl.' 'Tempted.' 'Sweet Hitchhiker.' 'New York State of Mind.' 'Alison.' 'Last Chance Texaco.' 'Canary in a Coal Mine.'

'Roundabout.' 'Maybe I'm Amazed.' 'Country Girl.' 'Venus in Furs.' "

"God damn it, someone put on a record," said the guy that none of them knew. "Anything, damn it."

Jill stopped laughing and screaming out the names of songs and stared at Annabelle's feet. "I can't believe you wore gold shoes, you bitch," she said finally.

chapter 25

Max wandered down a dark corridor alone, the living room music diminishing behind him as he passed a series of French doors—behind one was loud female laughter, and the next afforded a glimpse of the Piano Study, where Nick and Michael sat talking between stacks of old Schirmer piano music. He crossed the deserted marble foyer, skirting the staircase, and continued toward the library, which was lit by amber-shaded brass lamps on low side tables that projected blurred, bright parabolas on the oak walls and the dim white ceiling. Theodore Winfield and Nathan Chablis shared an antique couch—the twin of the one upstairs—Winfield sitting back silently, legs crossed to reveal silk-shod ankles, smoking his pipe and frowning severely as he listened to Chablis, who broke off his intent lecture as Max opened the door.

"Excuse me," Max said, turning to leave.

"It's the young man!" said Winfield, frowning pleasantly at Max. "The clever young man. Chablis, have you met this remarkable young man?"

"Hello, Gantry," Chablis said threateningly, lamplight flickering in his glasses. "Feel free to join us."

"Thank you," said Max, stepping into the room and then noticing that Gregory Taft was standing by the bookshelves behind the door, immersed in a book.

"Pray continue," Winfield said to Chablis.

"When we did *Principles of Supremacy* at the Institute it was the same argument and Huxley and I always make the same point," Chablis said. "We are not discussing the legitimacy of a pursuit—

we are attempting to approach the notion of methodological underpinnings."

"Hello, Greg," said Max, putting his hands in his pockets.

"Max," Greg said, flashing a weary smile. "This is my favorite room. Are you looking for Annabelle and Douglas? I saw them not long ago—"

"I know where they are," said Max.

" 'Methodological underpinnings'— We just don't read the same way," Winfield told Chablis. "Right, Taft?" He turned toward Greg, pointing. "Taft, you're Porcelain, you understand. I mean these Elis don't know how to read— You're a Yale man, aren't you, Chablis?"

"It's not a Yale thing," said Greg. "Nobody knows how. I forgot years ago."

"Do you know what time it is?" Max quietly asked Greg, scanning his eyes along the bookshelves, noticing the Schlesinger and Sorensen books about Kennedy, the Durant *Story of Civilization* series, Italian art books the size of attaché cases, leather-bound Jefferson collections, John Updike novels.

"Don't they teach you Yale men to shoot muskets?" Winfield said, leaning back on the couch and stroking his yellowing mustache. "I thought in New Haven they went and shot muskets all the time."

"Three-ten," Greg said, glancing at his Rolex. "And that's not all. Look carefully"—he waved his arm at the books, moving closer to Max—"these are *not books-by-the-yard.* Do you understand the *brilliance* of that? You have *no room* to object."

"Come on, it's been done," Max said, shaking and then nodding his head.

"Not a bad shot. Quite a library, isn't it?" Greg abruptly slammed the book he'd been reading, frowning with the effort as he replaced it on its high shelf. "I've been loitering here for years."

"I don't blame you," said Max. "The Bonomi books are here, aren't they?"

"Well," said Greg, gruffly stretching, arching his back, hands laced behind his downturned, grimacing head, "I gave Ted a copy of *Jake Hackett* back, what, fifteen years ago. I remember I'd spent months trying to find *The Windmill.* They're all out of print, but *Windmill*'s hardest to track down— I cling to college memories like a fool, Max, but I remember when that book meant a great deal to me, when Giulia couldn't let a day go by without my standing at her window and reading from it."

"Things can get lost in the shuffle," Max said, running his hand through his hair so that it flopped against his forehead. They looked at each other for a moment and neither of their expressions changed in the slightest.

"You know these people," Greg said.

"I'm sorry," said Max.

Greg smiled with his lips shut, as usual looking like Douglas as he moved to pat Max's shoulder while gesturing toward Winfield and Chablis. "This is dueling banjos— Maybe you can keep score," he finished, moving toward the doorway.

"I'm sorry to disturb you," Max said. "You don't have to leave."

"No, no," Greg said briskly, halfway out the door, lamplight shining on his glasses and his short graying hair as he reached for the knob. "I should go find my wife. Nathan, Ted—"

"Taft," said Winfield, waving distractedly at him. "Don't leave without saying good night."

"Of course not," Greg said. The three middle-aged men nodded at each other before Greg left the room, closing the door behind him, and Max wandered toward the window.

"From a historiographic standpoint," Chablis went on, "we shall perform contrasting examinations of the text, but the contrasts themselves, as determined by philosophical and cultural influences, ultimately comprise the true objects of our epistemological inquiry."

Max leaned on the cold window glass, staring out at the dark lawn where all the cars had been parked—way off to one side, before a housepaint-covered Chrysler with gaffer's tape on its back windows, a pair of abandoned beer cans cast razor-cut shadows on the spotlit gravel, and as he gazed across the manicured grass, Max suddenly heard faint voices to his far right. He watched as two barely visible figures came into view and after a moment he recognized them as Douglas and Jill.

"Nice turn of phrase, that," said Winfield. "Where did you prep?"

"Groton. Therefore the postulates underlying our methods of examination must conform to strictly rational principles so as to overcome subjective disjunctions between reader and text."

"Elementary point, but it fools everyone," Winfield agreed heartily.

Max pressed his face to the window glass, watching as Douglas and Jill waded into the sea of automobiles and stopped as they arrived at a battered blue Volvo—Jill fished in her purse for the car keys as Douglas massaged her back, leaning to whisper in her ear, and Jill moved her head and kissed Douglas, quickly, without turning around, the spotlight shining harshly through her hair, casting shadows on the smooth curves of her cheek.

"The philosopher provides nothing but a rudimentary rhetorical structure," Chablis argued, "but the reader may manipulate the selection and examination of the tacitly agreed-upon postulates so as to be in accord with what will correspond to the subjective requirements of the text. Our discourse concerning Eros is constrained by this rigorous ontological framework regardless of subjective nuances—the object of examination has particular aspects or qualities which may be revealed by means of exemplification. Each example creates a subjective resonance that may be challenged by the resonance of a subsequent example, and through this process of exclusion the philosopher defines the commonality of discourse. This methodology transcends historical and cultural difference and in so doing approaches a poetic understanding without sacrificing its rigorous examination of the object. You must acknowledge the sustained deliberate fiction of universals."

The kiss complete, Jill opened the passenger door and went around and they both entered the car—Max could clearly hear the doors slamming—and after a moment the headlights came on, flashing bright and dimming down before the Volvo edged out of its parking place and drove off. Max watched the car weave as it vanished among the trees, reappearing near the distant gatehouse, and he barely heard the engine surge as the car vanished from sight.

"Come on, Chablis, I'll mix you a drink," said Winfield, grandly rising to his feet. "My blood's in safe hands—you could have taught Michelangelo."

"Michelangelo would have gone to Groton," said Chablis, standing also. Max stared into the dark window, blankly watching the lamplit reflections of the two men as they walked out of the room and closed the door, leaving him alone in the library. Glancing around at the bookshelves, he suddenly spotted an ancient copy of *The Story of Jake Hackett.* He gingerly took it down, examining the slippery-looking 1930s cover, with its near-abstract painting of the Piazza San Marco, and flipping the novel open to its first page.

Chapter I

In Which Under Compromising Circumstances I Leave My Father's American Rectory and Depart for Italy

Omnipotente Dio, benchè del fato
invittissima legge e lunga pruova
d'esser non sol mie' prieghi invano sparsi,
ma al contrario esauditi, mi rimuova
dal tuo cospetto, io pur torno ostinato,
tutti gli altri rimedi avendo scarsi.
Che s'altro Dio potesse pur trovarsi,
io certo per aiuto a quel n'andrei.
Nè mi si potria dir mai ch'io fosse empio,
se da te, che mi sacci in tanto scempio,
a chi m'invita mi rivolgerei.
Deh, Signor, io vaneggio; aita, aita!
pria che del Senno il tempio
divenga di stoltizia una meschita.

Tommaso Campanella

IN THE LAST decade of the Nineteenth Century I began my service as a newly ordained Priest in the Catholic church, making my home (as I always had) in my late father's small farmhouse on the outskirts of a certain small Middle-Western city, studying the scriptures under the tutelage of Father Sigourney. Having little or no desire to remain in the several square miles of tranquil American countryside that comprised all that I had known since my birth, I decided to make my way to Italy, intending to travel by foot and by rail through that lush and bright countryside and to arrive eventually, after (I secretly hoped) no small measure of adventure and fortune, at the great Vatican City, where I would ascend the steps before Bernini's great basilica as had thousands upon thousands of pilgrims before me. I should mention at the outset that I did eventually arrive upon the Vatican steps, but in a manner altogether different than I had expected—when I did cross that great court beneath the moonlit stone shadows of the Saints and arrived at Bernini's steps it was moments before midnight, under some heavy pursuit, at great risk to my own life and to the lives of two others, and several months in advance of my planned arrival. The circumstances of my final, death-defying flight across Rome, on horseback and by torch-light, a unique volume of scripture clutched beneath my cloak in a deathgrip, are rather complex, I fear, and their understanding depends upon my telling this story with more patience and reserve than I am accustomed to. Even as I set pen to paper, secure as I am now amongst the Jesuits of the hallowed St. Mary's Mission within Montana's Bitterroot Valley, I find it difficult to properly recall the bright torches and clattering cobblestones of my Italian adventure. As I write these words, beginning my infernal confession and praying for absolution, I may hear the soothing voices of passing priests beyond my chamber door, reminding me again of the strange journey that has brought me to the Valley of the Saints in the noble footsteps of Ravalli—the voyage that began many months ago in New York City.

It was early in a summer's day in 1915 when I arrived in the vast expanse of Manhattan, an absurdly young and callow Priest of genteel appearance, my few possessions bundled into the small bag I carried, my senses offended by a cosmopolitan wind tainted by the fires of coal-burning stoves and the stench of the slaughterhouses standing upon the shores of the rivers. I had been directed by Father Sigourney to find one Father Morstan, a Priest of some renown and of considerable wealth and influence within the rather shabby and ill-kept structure of the Eastern American church. Had I remained in that great city as long as I had planned, I would indeed have run across Morstan, he of the crooked teeth and kind eye, and my story would have transpired in an altogether different fashion, but for better or worse, I cannot say. No, I did not encounter Morstan until our paths crossed in Venice months later, for it was my good fortune to make the acquaintance of one Lady Ashley after the passage of two days and nights in New York. Lady Ashley was at that time (as you may or may not recall) a widely known and rather splendid figure within the ballrooms, clubs, museums and great hotels that comprised the gilt and velvet-lined world of New York society. She was descended from one of the great New York families (which it is superfluous to name) and had been glimpsed during the 1880s with such Worldly figures as Prince M——, who declared her a great sportswoman, as well as a certain Mr. O——, a young novelist whose flights of narrative whimsy, I recall, had strained the patience and offended the critical faculties of many a modern reader. I would indeed meet many of these characters during my brief sojourn in New York, but my Manhattan adventures began the night that I witnessed a calamitous street accident while I walked across one of the stinking and overrun boulevards for which, I fear, that city has become rather well-known. I had been visiting with a cousin in the old "Ladies' Mile" district—a wizened and gentle English beekeeper possessed of a vast and quiet intelligence—and was returning to the Rectory adjoining the Church, when an old-fashioned Hansom Cab, festooned with decorative gilt carvings and propelled at some tremendous velocity,

Max abruptly shut the book, returning it to its slot on the bookshelf before turning to leave the library, wandering out past the Piano Study toward the living room, where a few couples were still dancing, the noise and brightness growing as he walked. He made his way to the bar table to pour himself a scotch, noticing, with some surprise, that the block of ice which had encased the peach had completely melted—the white linen of the table was soaked with a dark, spreading ice-water stain, and the peach itself lay nude on its side atop the white marble pedestal, looking very small without the magnifying effects of the ice. Max looked around, picked up the peach, and experimentally took a small bite—it was still cold and soaking wet and tasted terrible, and he put it back on the marble pedestal and turned away. The next time Max looked, someone else was taking a bite of the peach, and the next time he looked it was gone.

MAX WAS HELPING himself to a second slice of Key Lime pie when he noticed Annabelle standing at the other end of the room, drinking more champagne and talking to the young, athletic-looking Lawrence Hotel waiter who had served them that afternoon, and he walked over and joined them. "Max!" Annabelle said, somewhat drunkenly, breaking off whatever she had been telling the waiter. "Have you met— Um— I'm sorry, what was your name again?" The waiter told Max his name, which Max immediately forgot as he shook the man's hand, feeling its anatomy-textbook perfection and noticing the waiter's slight revulsion at the touch of his truncated fingers. "Max was with us this afternoon at the hotel," Annabelle explained.

"Right!" said the waiter, tearing his eyes away from Annabelle and registering Max's appearance. "I'm sorry— I've got to go help them pack everything. I enjoyed meeting you, Max."

"Oh, me too," said Max, returning his hands to his pockets, watching the waiter leave and turning to Annabelle.

"How you doing?" Annabelle asked, touching Max's shoulder, closing her eyes for a moment.

"I'm okay," said Max. "I'm sorry, I didn't mean to make him leave."

"Yeah, big tragedy. Jesus, I've got to stop this—" Annabelle looked around for a place to put her champagne and Max saw the way that she was weaving and gently took the glass, putting it down, finally, on the edge of the floor.

"You doing all right?" Max said, touching her warm, bare shoulder.

"I'm just tired," said Annabelle.

"Is Nick around?" said Max a bit too casually. "You could use a ride."

"Nick's not around." Annabelle raised her voice against sudden, surrounding laughter. "I can't believe it's so *loud* in here."

"You want to go sit down?" said Max. "You're looking a bit pale—"

"I am not pale," Annabelle insisted, glaring at him. "Everyone's saying I'm pale— I'm *fine.* It's just *loud* in here."

"We don't have to stay," Max said.

"Let's go out to the car," said Annabelle suddenly, not looking at him as she took his lapels and pulled him toward the doorway. "It'll be all nice and cool and quiet."

They left the living room and headed down the corridor to the foyer past groups of people and then out the massive front door and into the fragrant night air, down the granite steps, ears ringing, their feet kicking the driveway gravel, and they walked onto the wet grass and across the meadow, wading into the herringbone weave of professionally parked cars that stood at random angles shining in the starlit mist. They finally located the familiar Taft BMW, its wet flanks and dew-covered windows reflecting the house's lights—Max stood shivering in the cool air watching Annabelle open one of the unlocked back doors and clamber into the car and then followed, shutting the door.

"It's late," Annabelle said, leaning back against the car seat and resting her feet between the backs of the front seats. "It's very late. This is ending soon."

"It's winding down," said Max. "Jesus, what a party."

"Here we are talking in this fucking car again," said Annabelle, smiling, eyes closed, fingers on her forehead, leaning back to rest her head beside one of the flush-set car-stereo speakers.

"Is your ear bothering you again?"

"Oh, Christ, Max"—Annabelle gave a strange, dead laugh, looking out the window, up at the black sky—"my ear always bothers me. That's why I need you around."

"I guess we're leaving soon," Max said.

"I guess so," said Annabelle, still not looking at him. "I've got the spins. Do you have the spins?"

"Yeah," said Max. "Look— What's with you, anyway?"

Annabelle sat looking out the window, bringing a leg up to rest a foot on the edge of the car seat, adjusting her shoe without looking. "Jill and Douglas just left," she said. "Did you know that?"

"Yeah, I saw," said Max. "I watched them go—I could see them from the window. Everything worked fine."

"I guess so."

"You sure you're all right?" Max asked, slowly edging toward her across the car seat, in a way that she didn't seem to notice.

"I'm just tired," Annabelle said. "And I've got the spins."

"You don't look tired," Max said softly. "You don't look tired at all—you look better than you did when we arrived."

Annabelle finally moved her head, moved her gaze away from the window, smiling at him. "That's so sweet," she said.

"I saw you with Douglas and Jill," Max said, reaching up to stroke her cheek. "You should be proud."

Annabelle raised her eyes to his as Max caressed her face, slowly moving his hand to her neck as he arched his mouth toward hers, his other hand gently finding her waist. Startled, Annabelle lost her balance, slipping back against the car door as he pressed forward, and then quickly raised her arms, pushing him roughly away—Max fell back, staring at her, hands quivering as their eyes locked over the ticking of the dashboard clock.

"You son of a bitch," Annabelle said in a tone of quiet disbelief.

"I'm sorry," said Max finally, moving his head tightly, glaring back at her, exhaling as he spoke. "I got the wrong idea. I'm sorry."

"Max, will you take the fucking hint?" Annabelle said, rubbing her eyes. "Don't you think I have *enough* to deal—"

"You led me on," Max said, suddenly, not having moved. "God damn it, this is not all my fault. You've been leading me on."

"No," said Annabelle softly, rubbing her eyes, squinting as she pinched the bridge of her nose. "I'm sorry, Max— I'm flattered, but you've got it wrong."

"Well, *I'm* sorry," said Max, collapsing back into the seat, facing away from her. "I mean, it's not like I wasn't being *careful*— I tried to—"

"All right, *careful*, so you know the careful guy thing, but—" Annabelle looked out the window again. "You think it's all so fucking *easy* for me. After what we decided to— After what we did, you think—"

"It was your idea," Max said, brushing his hair away from his face.

"It was *not*— It was *your* idea."

"It was a good idea," Max said slowly, glaring at her.

"But it was yours. After— With the suntan lotion—" She waved her hand at him in a beckoning motion. "Remember? The suntan lotion."

"All right," Max said. "Look—you *wanted* it then."

"What?"

"On the beach. You wanted it."

As they stared at each other his face tilted, drifting toward hers again, and she sat up straight, raising her hands. "I'm serious, Max— try it again and I'll scream and they'll throw you out of here so completely you'll never come back. I mean it."

"I'm sorry," Max said, collapsing back against the car seat. "I'm so sorry."

He opened the car door, gently stepping out and clicking it shut, and the house shone before him like a yellow furnace against the shadows of the trees.

chapter 26

When Jill shifted gears she punched the clutch like it was a bass-drum pedal and then resumed stomping on the gas, and while making mild turns she pumped the brakes in a way that Douglas imagined he could feel in the fillings in his teeth—Jill almost seemed to be able to move the Volvo's center of gravity forward, to distort physics itself, the way she drove. The tires crunched along the lunar-landscape Winfield gravel and then thumped onto the blacktop of Union Drive, headlights flashing wildly on the rusticated Florentine stone of the gatehouse, making flickering emerald fire of the foliage of the twisting texture of the trees beside the gatehouse, and Douglas cowered in the bucket seat, knees hitting the dashboard, terrified that Jill would hit the gatehouse and that the hood would accordion-fold into them and the car would explode in a gasoline-fireball, but it didn't happen and the car whispered onto the dark road and Jill laughed at his fear.

"Don't be so jumpy," Jill said.

"You drive so *fast*—"

"I like to drive fast," said Jill, leaning forward to adjust the white fabric of her dress against the car seat, moving quickly enough to lock her shoulder belt, swerving the car so that the headlights shone against the rough blur of passing tree trunks. "Fasten your seat belt." Douglas, who had been losing little two-minute parcels of time, so that he barely remembered how they'd gotten out here from the wallpapered room where they'd been sitting with Annabelle, fastened his seat belt, his forehead bumping the Volvo safety glass as he turned in his seat to do it. "You want to get some music going?" Jill said, reaching to punch the button that opened the sunroof, immediately creating a horizontal blade of wind that tugged Douglas' hair back from his forehead.

"Um— What should I—" Douglas was leaning forward against his own seat belt, his mouth tingling, squinting down in the dimness at the carrying case of cassettes on the rubberized floor, picking through the racked TDK cassettes whose white labels had been marked in the rounded, loopy handwriting that he recognized from her stolen notebook. He pulled out a tape at random and fumbled it out of the box, thumbing it into the Blaupunkt stereo and trying to find the right buttons.

"Just shove it in," said Jill, reaching over, while driving, her fingers brushing Douglas' face to jam the tape into its slot, igniting the amber lights of the stereo and accelerating even more as Douglas flopped backward into the bucket seat and Paul McCartney's "Maybe I'm Amazed" started blaring into the car. Jill swerved around a corner, almost sideswiping the ENTERING TOWNSHIP OF DOVER sign as she turned right, and Douglas was propelled centrifugally into her.

"Sorry," he said, straightening, recovering from the perfume that had coursed across his face as he'd swung against her body, trying to relax against the car seat as she sped down the hill into town, where there seemed to be no other traffic. They were surrounded by the dark, hulking shapes of dew-covered parked cars, and Jill drove down the edge of the meridian toward the Main and Union intersection—the McCartney song ended and "Naked Eye" began, making Douglas realize that the drive had been going on longer than he had realized.

"Whoa, whoa, whoa," said Jill in her high voice, squinting and spinning the Volvo's wheel as a station wagon sped toward them from out of view behind the curve in Main Street, slamming on its brakes at the same moment that Jill hit her own brakes, headlights shining directly into Douglas' face like gigantic frosted moons—Douglas screamed as Jill got them into a tailspin and the back wheels of the car jogged on the sidewalk's edge and the other car's brakes squealed as Jill recovered and shifted gears, launching them forward again, and the other car's horn rang out angrily. The station wagon sped away behind them and Douglas turned to watch it go as Jill began accelerating again, rushing past the dark, looming façade of the Lawrence Hotel.

"We could have been killed," Douglas said weakly. "That was almost a major—"

"Are you kidding?" said Jill, shifting the 5-speed gearbox, the bracelet on her wrist snagging the hem of her dress and pulling the white fabric up to expose her muscular leg as it pressed forward to propel them even more rapidly up the hill. "None of us are going to die, man. Hey"—she suddenly performed a loud, skidding U-turn across the mercifully deserted top of the hill—"I got it, Douglas— Let's go get some bottles."

"What?" said Douglas over the rough sound of Roger Daltrey's voice. "What?"

"Let's go hit the store and get some bottles," said Jill, glancing to smile prettily at him as they cruised back through town. Douglas stared incredulously at the two sets of curving tire tracks from their near-collision shining in the intersection street lamps.

"Yeah— Good idea," said Douglas, reaching to loosen his tie. "But, except, what's open?"

"Good point," said Jill, squinting as the last lights of the town whirled by and The Who began playing the smooth hi-hat triplets that would end the song. "We can hit that place out by the, you know, where those new stores are— Aztec Clothes and all that."

"Right— You ever been there?" Douglas asked, looking over at her as she drove.

"What?"

"Ever been there?"

"All the time, man," said Jill, smiling at him. "I go to—"

"Watch the road," said Douglas, terrified.

"—Aztec Clothes to get the, you know, to get— That's where the hot swimsuits are and everything." They were approaching the small "mall" of stores, and there was, sure enough, one convenience store open, its lit window shining across the deserted asphalt lot where one other car was parked beneath the flapping plastic banners from the store's opening, the reflectorized letters that spelled ICE on the big steel machine near the front door glowing as the Volvo's headlights brushed them. Jill parked at a weird angle and shut off the engine, extinguishing the headlights—she was already getting out, sending warm country air and the sound of crickets into the car, and Douglas, after taking a moment to find the oddly placed door latch, fumbled with his seat belt and then clambered out. Jill waited impatiently as he stood, his head spinning, and weaved toward her, turning in a sort of panic and slamming the car door behind him, nearly losing his balance. She smiled sweetly and took his hand, the points of her high heels clicking on the cold asphalt as she led him toward the store's glass door, and Douglas put his arm around her waist but then let go in order to yank the door open.

The store was air-conditioned and brilliantly lit, filled with quiet music that almost sounded classical until some fake vibes came in, and deserted except for a sparsely mustached boy their own age sitting on a stool behind the counter in an REO Speedwagon concert shirt with three-quarter sleeves, reading an issue of *Road and Track*, and an elderly man in a red flannel shirt standing on the other side of a shoulder-high shelf of white bakery boxes, staring at a wall-mounted rack of motor-oil cans. Jill and Douglas wandered in, Douglas still queasy and disoriented, the fluorescent light reflecting off Jill's dress as she led them past an acre of magazines and comic books and around the back of the store.

"Where's the—" began Jill, looking around in confusion, finger in her mouth as she frowned.

"Behind— Behind the counter, I think," said Douglas, his voice sounding very loud to his own ears. "You want to just get some beer?"

"No. Behind the counter?" Jill was already stalking down an aisle between stacks of DieHard batteries, and Douglas followed.

"Jill—" said Douglas, laughing nervously as Jill arrived at the counter, her blonde hair brushing the bottom of the cigarette rack as she leaned forward over the counter—the boy had noticed her approach and was looking at her rather incredulously.

"Hi," said Jill, smiling at the boy, who closed his magazine just as Douglas arrived behind her. "How are you?"

"I'm okay," the kid said in a mannered, sullen voice. "What can I do for you?"

"Could we have—" Jill said, stretching luxuriously forward and peering down at the various bottles on the rack behind the kid, "could we have a fifth of Absolut? Cool?" She looked back at Douglas across her bare, tanned shoulder, diamond earrings flashing in the fluorescent light.

"Fine with me," said Douglas, shaking his head in agreement, stepping forward to begin massaging Jill's shoulders.

"You got an ID you can show me?" the kid said, giving them a movie-cowboy squint.

"No," said Jill, teeth glittering. "Left my purse at home."

"It's true, she did," said Douglas. Jill elbowed him.

"Sorry," said the kid, looking at Jill, reaching behind his neck to adjust the collar of his shirt. "No can do."

"Please," said Jill, leaning farther forward across the Formica counter and staring into the kid's eyes. The kid, flustered, looked away and then back at her, glancing around the store.

"Wait till the old guy leaves," the kid whispered finally—Douglas turned around and saw the elderly man lumbering toward the counter with a gold can of motor oil, and he looked down to make sure that his shirt cuff covered his wristwatch as he and Jill cleared out of the way. The kid rang up the man's purchase, bagged the gold can and waited for the bell on the store's door to signal the man's departure before reaching down for a bottle of Absolut and another paper bag. "Anything else?"

"Pack of White Camels?" said Douglas, rubbing Jill's shoulders.

"What?" said the kid. He mustered another skeptical squint, pausing halfway through the vodka-bagging operation as he glanced over to see that Jill had her hands behind her, on the trouser fabric between Douglas' thighs, and looking away.

"Camel Filters," Douglas explained somewhat tersely. "Sorry."

"*O*-kay," the kid said, drawing the cigarettes from the overhead rack and taking Jill's money with his other hand, not looking. Douglas took the bag and they walked back outside, the air fragrant and warm after the air-conditioned chill of the store. They reëntered the car and Jill ignited the headlamps and revved the engine loudly as Douglas refastened his seat-belt and soon they were back on the road, driving fast, music blasting, emerald foliage shining in the high-beams, and Jill was reaching for the vodka bottle, which Douglas had spun the cap off of and was gulping from, the cold glass clicking against his teeth—Jill had scanned forward a track on the tape and now they were hearing "Tempted" as the Volvo roared down the dark road, weaving in the slight slipstream of occasional passing cars, Douglas noticing the bobbing orange needle of the speedometer touching seventy as he reached to poke the cigarette lighter, wind from the open sunroof blowing his hair. Jill didn't bother to turn off her high-beams as cars approached, and they flashed theirs reproachfully but Jill didn't seem to notice—her face was set in eager prettiness as she gulped vodka and handed the bottle back and Douglas cracked his window and pulled the cellophane and foil off the pack of White Camels and drew out a cigarette. *"Tempted by the fruit of another,"* Douglas sang along with Glenn Tilbrook. *"Tempted but the truth is discovered—* This is a great tape, Jill."

"Yeah," said Jill, glancing in sudden disgust at the rearview mirror. "Oh, *shit—*"

"What?" said Douglas, his voice obliterated by the sudden blare of a police siren—he swung his head around, squinting in the sudden glare from the police car that was bearing down on them at great speed, flashers lit. The siren stopped as Jill slowed down, hugging the road's edge as the cigarette lighter popped back out, and Douglas frantically recapped the vodka and rolled the bottle under the seat, his head slamming into the glove-compartment door as Jill hit the brakes. In the sudden quiet Douglas sat up and rubbed his head as Jill wound her window down, admitting a gust of warm Dover air into the car. Through the back window, which was clouded by the police car's headlights, Douglas saw the policeman walking toward them—the Squeeze song had faded out and "Have You Ever Seen the Rain?" was starting, and Douglas reached to turn off the stereo as Jill frantically adjusted her appearance.

"You kids from that goddamned party?" said the cop in a grim, beleaguered voice, speaking in advance of leaning in the window, the police car's headlights shining in his pale blue eyes—he was a young man with crew-cut sandy hair and a small horizontal scar across the hollow of his chin. "I want to know right now. Is this that damn Winfield thing?"

"Yes," said Jill, cocking her head, looking at the cop from inches away. The cop nodded knowingly, frowning in frustration, looking away. The radio on his belt hissed and then spoke unintelligibly and he ignored it.

"Son of a bitch. You kids—" The cop looked back at Jill, still frowning, beckoning at her resignedly, "Come on," he sang. "License. Let's do it." Jill reached on the floor for her purse and the cop looked at Douglas merrily. "You having a good time? I sure am," he said sarcastically while Jill hunted for her license. "What's *your* name? I'm Officer McNulty. What's your name, anyway— Mister Scotch?"

"Douglas Taft," said Douglas, slurring a bit. Jill had found her license and was handing it over.

"Thank you! Thank you *very much,*" Officer McNulty said happily, producing a flashlight. "Let's see about Mrs. Scotch here. Jill Brooks!" He beamed at her. "How about that—I even know your *dad.* Paul Brooks, right? Always at the Lawrence— What a coincidence!" Officer McNulty's voice was climbing into an even higher sarcastic register as he opened his ticket book. *"He's* a square G— *All* you summer people from the city are so *nice.* I clocked you going so *fast,* sister—"

"Don't call me sister," said Jill, her quiet voice sounding even younger than usual. McNulty looked at her, delighted.

"I'm sorry, Jill," McNulty said equitably, grinning at her from very close and then clicking a ballpoint pen and beginning to fill out the ticket form. "I really am," he continued distractedly, concentrating on the ticket book, standing straight, stowing his flashlight and tilting the book to catch the headlights, the radio on his belt hissing again as he walked toward the back of the car for the license number. Jill looked at Douglas, a startled, frightened, amused glance, and their eyes locked together, their faces softening and hardening as they leaned toward each other and kissed in the police headlights, the policeman's shadow coursing across them, a sudden warm fragrant breeze whispering in the trees and entering the car as they took each other's shoulders and continued the kiss, shifting their legs on the car seat, the gearshift between them. "All right, break it up," McNulty muttered impatiently, having arrived back at the driver's door, and Jill and Douglas pulled apart, a bit breathlessly, Jill turning back toward the window and accepting the ticket. "Here you go— Merry Christmas," McNulty said, grinning and touching his cap, saluting them from his hands-on-knees bent-over position. "Wasn't that a fun process? Let's do it again sometime."

"We're sorry we were going so fast," Jill said meekly, raising her eyebrows. "I didn't realize how much I was—" But McNulty was already walking back toward his car.

Douglas' head was reeling—he squinted at the dashboard's digital clock as the police car made a U-turn and drove off the way they'd come and saw that it was almost four. Jill waited until the police car had driven out of sight and then started the engine, tossing the ticket out the window before rolling it up, shifting into gear and then swinging out into the road, reaching to turn the stereo back on, making Douglas jump as the Creedence song started again, and he looked out at the dark passing landscape and said, "I know what you're thinking."

"Like hell you do," Jill said, laughing, and they drove another couple of minutes, Douglas beginning to panic in his drunkenness—for a moment he thought that they were back in the convenience store, and then he realized where they were—and then Jill was pulling off the road, the hum of the engine decreasing in pitch, and approaching her small, dark, one-story house, headlights shining on the wooden wall panels and reflecting off the shaded windows and the gas meter, shining into the ghostly darkness inside the opened, empty garage, flashing onto a rolled garden hose and a few bags of what looked like grass seed and a bracket-mounted shelf of nail-filled Mason jars and cans of Spackle that cast shadows on the painted brick wall.

"Home sweet home," said Jill, clicking off the car stereo and killing the engine, opening the car door and admitting the humid garage air, and Douglas leaned his spinning head back on the seat and looked up through the sunroof at the dim wooden beams of the garage ceiling, listening to the crickets. Jill turned off the headlights and got out of the car, which was in complete darkness save for the digital clock and the ghostly moonlit glow from outside, and Douglas unfastened his seat belt and opened his own door, pausing to pull the cassette out of the stereo and return it to its plastic box, and then, after looking to see that Jill was facing away, walking toward a door in the garage wall, sticking the boxed cassette into his lapel pocket. He retrieved the bottle from under the seat and got out of the car and slammed the door, looking out at the trees beyond the driveway as he joined Jill at the door, which had a pair of concrete steps beneath it, leading up, and a cheap-looking brass doorknob, like a hotel door, and he put his hands on her shoulders again, feeling her flinch and then relax—he felt it, too, the haunted silence of the moonlit country outdoors, the deserted, lonely calm in which anything could happen miles from anyone else.

"Let's see," said Jill, examining the door. "Fuck. —Oh, right." She leaned over to detach the key from her anklet and then opened the door, the clicking sound of the lock very loud against the dim quiet.

"Come inside," she said, taking Douglas by the hand. "I'll show you around."

Douglas followed Jill inside, his ears ringing in the silence, feeling slippery linoleum tiles against his feet. "Hmm. I'm *really* drunk," he said, feeling Jill's hand leave his and then blinking in the sudden brightness as she turned on a flickering overhead light—they were standing in a small, sparse kitchen, a table at one end with plastic salt-and-pepper shakers flanking a small stand-up cardboard calendar from the Lawrence Hotel, a black window reflecting the motion as Douglas put the bottle down next to a toaster-oven.

"Mom? Dad?" Jill called out, putting her purse down on the kitchen counter and then turning to Douglas, tilting her head and looking up at him, her white-silk-sheathed body incongruous against the bleakly lit kitchen appliances, her high heels tapping as she stepped closer, her perfume brushing him—Douglas reached for her and they stood there kissing each other beside the open garage door, Douglas still conscious of the quiet country darkness behind him as he slid his hands over Jill's muscular back and felt her forearms on his shoulders, moving a hand to the back of her neck under her soft hair and pressing his mouth into hers. They pulled apart and Jill looked up at him and he was amazed by the harshly lit view of her face from this close as she reached to swing the door shut.

"They're not home," she said, smiling sweetly up at him.

"No," Douglas said, stroking her hair. Jill pulled away and got him by the hand again and led him toward another door, waiting while he hooked back to get the bottle, dropping his hand and turning on a shaded chrome standing lamp, which shed a dim light, leading them into a thickly carpeted, low-ceilinged living room, long and wide. Douglas lurched as he followed her to a white couch and they sat together on the couch, lit by the dim hotel-like standing lamp and by the bright kitchen door, entwined together on the couch, alone in the deserted house, wind blowing the trees in the darkness outside.

"What have you heard about me?" murmured Jill, pulling away from Douglas' face and sliding her hands in his lapels. "Everybody's heard something about me."

"I heard about the Marine," said Douglas, reaching for the vodka bottle that was sitting on the glass coffee table, lensing the kitchen light onto Jill's smooth leg.

"Oh yeah?" said Jill, startled. "I didn't think that— Look, that was a certain situation, okay? I mean, look, you can't expect—" She was still speaking quietly, from up close, taking the bottle as he held it out, eyes glittering at him. "You can't expect— That was just this thing that happened, I mean, that you wouldn't understand, so let's not, you know, we shouldn't talk about it."

"Well, you asked," said Douglas.

"I mean," said Jill, "You can't just *talk* about something as if it's public knowledge."

"But it *is* public knowledge," said Douglas, taking the vodka bottle.

"What else do you know?"

"Nothing," Douglas admitted, staring at the bottle. "Absolute nothing."

"Do you know about the grating?"

"The *what?*"

"Never mind," said Jill. "Fuck, what a party."

"What a party," said Douglas, looking past Jill's dimly lit hair at the blank white walls, looking around at the chairs that matched the couch and the electrical outlets and the edges of the carpeting against the baseboards and the lack of any other furniture besides a small chrome-and-mirrored-glass bookcase with a rounded top which he hadn't noticed before because it was next to the kitchen door.

"Hey, could you believe that Nick actually *hit* that asshole?" Jill said as he reached to stroke his hand along the outer edge of her thigh where it was catching the light. "I mean, someone finally *hit* him."

"No," said Douglas, barely remembering what she was talking about, feeling the hard muscles of Jill's leg, arching to kiss her again, then drawing away, closing his eyes against the sudden imbalance he felt.

"You coming down?" said Jill, squinting at him. "I was worried about you there."

"I'm not sure," said Douglas. "I'm all right."

"Just don't panic," said Jill. "You're all right. I mean, don't freak out on me."

"I think I need to sit here a minute."

They sat there together on the couch and the wind rose and shook the trees outside.

"You never come to any parties," said Jill.

"I'm generally not invited," said Douglas, taking the bottle as she held it out.

"It's not that kind of thing," said Jill. "You can— You can just go."

"I never did," said Douglas weakly, feeling the room as it spun.

"It's too bad," said Jill. "I mean it's too late. It's over."

"Nick Blanchard's still around," said Douglas. "I mean— What I mean is— What I mean is that it's never too late. I can still come back. Because Blanchard does it— Blanchard does whatever he wants."

"That's different," said Jill. "Sometimes he does what you say. Believe me."

"You're right— Jesus, you're *smart,* Jill," Douglas said, squinting, leaning forward and rubbing his face with his hands.

"So what do you do all the time? Since you never go to anything?" Jill was asking, as if from a great distance.

"Play pinball," said Douglas, slurring. "No, I mean, just—try to just— You know, even when I go *home,* right, I've got my *sister* to deal with and my *parents* all the time, and— And it can get to be a mess sometimes. Oh, man, I am totally drunk—"

"Your sister's so cool," said Jill quietly. "I can't believe how cool your sister is. I mean, she's scary."

"She's very cool," said Douglas, leaning back against the couch again, taking the bottle as Jill held it out.

"She's *scary,*" said Jill, shaking her head. "Nobody should be that cool. It isn't *natural.* I mean, you know, you see her at *home,* right? Do you see her, like, in the morning, you know, figuring out how to look so *perfect?* I mean, is there, like— How *long* does it take her?"

"She's not as cool as Officer McNulty," said Douglas, laughing suddenly, wheezing with the vodka. "I mean, if Annabelle was— If she'd been— She would have met her *match.*"

"What?" Jill smiled at the joke, her pretty eyes flashing.

"Nothing. You're so pretty," said Douglas, looking at her.

"You mind waiting here a second?" Jill asked, raising her eyebrows again. Douglas shook his head and Jill got up and walked to the kitchen, and he watched her walk, seeing the kitchen light that shone through her dress and silhouetted her body as the wind moaned wildly around the house, reaching again for the bottle, losing his grip on its neck for a moment so that it clattered against the smooth glass of the coffee table. Jill walked into the kitchen and around the corner, out of view, and then reappeared with a thick glass ashtray, which she brought back over and put down on the coffee table next to the bottle. Douglas obediently fished the pack of White Camels out of his breast pocket and offered her one, and then took one himself, finding the matches from the convenience store in the same pocket and noticing that they had a driving-school advertisement on them, and lighting the cigarettes as Jill sat back down.

"Are you all right?" asked Jill, inexpertly inhaling cigarette smoke.

"I'm fine. I don't want this," said Douglas, stubbing the cigarette out in the ashtray.

"You're not going to freak out on me?"

"I'm fine."

"I don't want this either," Jill said, leaning to put her own cigarette out as well.

"Hey, we could go through the whole pack like that," said Douglas, and they both laughed.

"My mom smokes," said Jill.

"Yeah, that's— You *don't*, right?" said Douglas. "You're an athlete, right, you're an acrobat."

"I'm not an acrobat," said Jill, squinting at him. "You said my *back* was glass, too."

"You don't like that?" said Douglas. Jill shook her head contemplatively.

"No," she said. "No."

"Why not? It was a compliment," said Douglas, taking the vodka bottle again.

"It's breakable," said Jill. "It's fragile. Glass."

"I meant it was smooth," said Douglas, handing her the bottle. "That's all."

Jill smiled. "That's nice," she said.

They looked at each other and it seemed to Douglas that wheels that were very large were sliding together as he glided his mouth to hers, her hair casting a harsh shadow across her mouth in the dim light, both of them shaking as she leaned to put the bottle on the floor, Jill kissing him back, pressing against him on the couch, moving her hand to his leg and then up to his waist and then down and over to his groin, stroking him as he pressed his fingers into her shoulders—they slid backward, Jill falling on her back, Douglas on top of her, their clothes sliding against the cool leather of the couch, Douglas' foot nudging one of the coffee table's legs, Jill's hand reaching to unbuckle Douglas' belt, Douglas shifting his waist out of her grip, somehow, his grip on her shoulders lessening as they separated.

"You're nervous," said Jill, looking up at him. "You're into it but you're nervous."

"I've never done this."

"That's not exactly good news."

"I'm sorry," Douglas said, feeling the room spin, reaching for the back of the couch and finding the leverage he needed to pull himself up to a sitting position.

"What's wrong?" said Jill, sitting up, squinting with concern, touching his shoulder.

"I'm sorry," he said. "Give me a minute— Lost my balance there for a second."

"You all right?"

"I don't know," said Douglas, coughing, leaning forward.

"Do you want some aspirin?"

"I'm fine," said Douglas, the coughing spell passing, feeling light-headed, turning back to her and feeling a cold wave as he stared. In the kitchen the refrigerator suddenly clicked and hummed and they both jumped and then Jill reached over and lightly pulled his shirt-tails out of his trousers, roving her fingernails along the crease of his lower back, and Douglas didn't move except to adjust his arms as she moved her hands across his back.

"What's slowing you down?" Jill asked.

Douglas stood up suddenly, Jill's hands dropping off of him. He stepped back a few steps, stumbling as his calves hit the coffee table, and Jill stood also, facing him, looking flatly at him—he reached for her face and she moved away and then reached down and pulled her dress over her head and dropped it with a hiss on the carpet beside the couch.

"Jesus," said Douglas.

"Be good to me," Jill said.

He stood there and looked at her and then reached to pick up the vodka bottle and stow it in his jacket pocket, and Jill stood there watching him and she watched as he turned, stumbling, and began walking toward the kitchen, and there was nothing to hear besides his footsteps on the carpet and then on the linoleum and he walked toward the garage door, and stopped, and turned, looked through the two rooms back at Jill, who stood in her heels and underwear, not having moved, looking at him, looking very small.

"I'm sorry," Douglas said, the chilled breeze brushing his knuckles as he opened the kitchen door.

"I'm sorry too," said Jill, from the distance.

Douglas stepped down the concrete step into the garage, closing the door and standing in the darkness before walking into the fragrant outdoor air, away from the house and toward the pale darkness of the road.

AT THE FOOT of the driveway Douglas began walking north, or what he was sure was north, following the asphalt, having some trouble maintaining a constant line along the highway, watching his shoes glide into view on the pavement ahead of him, seeing flashes of glass gittering in the asphalt, and when a car approached, sound and light, tremendous engine and headlights, he shambled into the wet roadside underbrush and over a low fence of cables and silver-painted cement posts. He caught his trouser cuff on the fray of coaxial wire and fell to the muddy ground, blades of grass against his face, the cold grass soaking him as the vodka bottle smashed, not hurting him but bursting like brittle fruit, dousing him with cold vodka, and he cowered in the damp sand and grass as the car roared past and then lay there, hearing the wind, his cheek on the cold ground, and eventually he rose, head spinning as he sat in the tall grass, which wasn't so bad, and stood to brush himself off as best he could, picking the bottle shards from his pocket and dropping them to the ground, the broken glass scratching him as he straddled the cable and stepped back onto the road. He kept walking and as he walked the wind picked up, twisting his jacket and sifting his hair, and his dress shoes, obviously not made for hiking any real distance, almost immediately began hurting his feet, but he continued along the downward curve of the road, sparing a glance back in the direction of Jill's house, where a light was still burning in the square cutout of the living room window, and as he watched the light went out and the house was dark, and that made Douglas afraid—he imagined Jill coming after him, changing somehow and chasing him, but as he looked at the house through the dim and gentle trees he became calm and he turned and kept walking, and soon, as he crested a hill and started down the other side, the house was hidden from view and he felt safer and kept walking, his breath fogging, stumbling in the starlight and hunting for the road's edge, stranded in the darkness. After a while he found that his eyes had begun to adjust and he could follow the road by tracing the line of orange reflectors nailed to the concrete posts that the coaxial cable had been strung along, and using this new system he continued north, cresting the next hill, looking back at Jill's house, farther away but still within view, showing that he still had far to go, so he kept going, saying under his breath, "I can't see the fucking road," whispering the words as he walked. He passed a sign that warned of an approaching curve and another sign that said DEER XING, which was absurd because he had never seen any deer anywhere near Dover, and after about fifteen minutes he was far enough away from the Brooks house to be in complete country darkness, hearing only crickets, the air still and cold, the road bending through the woods, and he tried to remember how far it was into town, remembering the drive, standing still, hearing the crickets and the wind and the sound of an owl and the other forest sounds all around him, his head spinning as the wind picked up again, a backwards wind that sang, flipping forward his lapels, and Douglas cringed and started running, running for a few minutes, panting, stopping, starting again, hearing a car's roar building from the quiet behind him and moving to the edge of the road, still running, panting as a pair of headlights dawned over the hill behind him, casting his twin running shadows on the silver-painted concrete posts as he stopped running and walked along, winded, expecting the car to slow, but the car sped up, the sound building, and finally Douglas spun around and saw a dark red Honda Civic moving toward him, Wally Patterson leaning precariously out the driver's window as the Civic sped past, and maybe there were others in the car, maybe not, impossible to see, but Wally gave Douglas a demented look as the car passed, leering at him through the window, shouting "Douglas Taft, you're a sidewinder," revving the engine and accelerating but still leaning out the window screaming "Sidewinder! Sidewinder! Fucking *side—winder!*" and laughing insanely as he ducked his head back into the car and then sped off around the next bend in the road, vanishing from view, faint headlight afterimages fading as Douglas stood looking after the car, his ears ringing as he kept walking, the road doubling, tripling, stretching so that the same tree and the same moss-covered rock and all the same details passed several times, until eventually he got to a sign that said DOVER 1 MI. and he stopped walking and hit the sign with his hand, striking the reflectorized 1 with his wrist and making the sign clatter back and forth so that the STATE OF CONNECTICUT logo on its base blurred. The sky was bright enough to silhouette the tops of the roadside trees, which seemed gigantic, towering over him as a cold wind blew out of the woods and streamed across the road, and

Douglas reeled again, his breath catching painfully as he stumbled to the silver-painted wire and leaned over it vomiting for a few moments and then walked a few steps farther along the road, wiping his mouth with his wet hand, gathering water from the silver coaxial roadside cable onto his hand and wiping his mouth, wailing, "I can't see the fucking road!" and then reeling conclusively and falling down, mercifully falling into the soft sand and closing his eyes, lying in the sand at the edge of the road without feeling the passing time, eyes closed, fingers clutching the roadside dust, the ground spinning in tight circles as he cried and lay still beside the dark and barren road, until there was light, a bright glare from very close that shone in his face, making him open his eyes and stare into sudden sunlight.

"Can you stand up?" said a man's quiet voice. "At least stand up."

The flashlight moved away from Douglas' eyes and he twisted his head to look at the black figure bent over him, bent down from very close, and then got his palms on the cold sand under him and hoisted himself, looking past the black silhouettes of the man's legs and over at the road and seeing a dark car with a long low hood and luxurious tailfins and smooth patches of chrome that gleamed in the weak starlight as the car's twinned headlights cut bright triangular columns through the mist. Douglas rolled over in the dirt and sat up, looking up at the dark, featureless figure standing over him, groping for his balance as the man took hold of his arms in a strong grip and hoisted him to his feet and then shone his flashlight up and down Douglas' body as he leaned on the man's arm and they stood facing each other in the road.

"I'm a mess," Douglas said.

"Yeah," said the man slowly, "but it's just dirt. It'll wash off."

"I guess so," said Douglas, blinking at the afterimages from the flashlight, and the light moved but he still couldn't see the man's face.

"My sympathies," the man said. "I know your line, Douglas."

"You do?" said Douglas.

"What are you doing here?" the man said, playing the light up and down Douglas' clothes. "What's happened to you?"

"I was— I was over— I'm going home," said Douglas. "It's a dark night."

"Yeah, I guess so," said the man. "You want a lift?"

"Maybe I should walk," said Douglas, taking a breath. "Jesus— I don't know how long I was out on the road—"

"You sure you can make it?" the man said as he adjusted the satchel on his shoulder. "I've got places to go but I could take you to town."

"It'd just be farther to walk," said Douglas, squinting at the man's face. "I'm glad you came."

"We're on the same road, man. No walk is short," the man said in a quiet, almost dazed voice, and Douglas looked behind the car and around the flanks of the road into the woods and then turned back to look at his face.

"I'm scared," said Douglas, flinching in surprise as the man clapped his hand on his shoulder.

"Relax, man. It's just a country walk, right? During the day it'd be a snap, make no mistake."

"Right," said Douglas, smiling. "Thanks a lot, Buzzman."

"Hey, we aim to please," Buzzman said, starting back toward the car. "It's a pretty night, man. Hurry home."

Buzzman slammed the Chevrolet door and gunned the engine and Douglas heard the car approach behind him as he began to walk, watching his shadow flicker in the glow of the headlights, walking until he saw the lights of the town behind the trees, stopping as the Chevrolet swerved around him and sped up, its tailfins and taillights glowing, Buzzman waving out the window and speeding down the road, cresting the next hill and leaving a momentary glow, the misted headlights bobbing with the car as it moved out of sight, and as Douglas reached the hilltop the town was spread before him, lights shining from the back of the supermarket and the Lawrence façade, the church's steeple facing the sky like a knife, and he stopped and waited, his breath fogging as he looked down at the streets and the water beyond, waiting and then walking the ten-minute stretch to the Blackfoot Road turnoff and across the deserted turnoff and down the dark tunnel of the trees of Blackfoot Road toward the Taft property, blind to passing time but finally arriving at the field at the point where the stream cut through the iron pipe under the road, and he left the road, drifting toward the black sawtooth edge of the forest, insects chattering across the wind that rose from nowhere as he drifted through moonlit goldenrod, wading the waist-high weeds, water from the weeds soaking his feet and legs as he started across the field and stopped in the field's center, the road out of view, stopping and gazing around at the reflected starlight and the moonlight that blotted the starlight out, waiting before starting through the underbrush toward the forest, stopping at the forest's edge to hunt for the path while a car drove past on the road behind him, its headlights drifting slowly along as he found the narrow leaf-littered path and entered the woods, pulling off his tie and stowing it in his pocket among the few remaining vodka-bottle shards, the dim grey clouds moving across the dark country sky between the heavy shadows of the shabby ancient trees as he advanced through the forest, his feet knocking against the wet tree roots and the ferns and the moss, falling down and coating his trousers in mud and getting up and finally arriving at the twin pines that broke the chicken-wire fence that ran away in both directions beneath the black shadow of the yellow PRIVATE PROPERTY—NO TRESPASSING sign that marked the Taft property line, stumbling as the moonlight guided him into the vast shadows of the Old Woods, the foliage that sealed him into darkness, making him lose his footing and twist his ankle and stumble before he could see the yellow-misted glow of the Civil War House shining between the trees and casting long shadows across the lawn as Douglas found the path and penetrated the final copse of trees to walk onto the newly cut lawn that surrounded the black wedge of the house, downstairs windows shining, fishing in his pocket for the key, finding his way to the porch door, quietly clicking it open and slipping into the house, closing the door against the grey brightening light, leaning his damp forehead on the warm rough paint of the door, shivering in the familiar scented darkness of the laundry alcove, where it was warm, where Annabelle's black dress hung from a horizontal broomstick pole, where he dropped his jacket atop the clothes dryer and weaved through the dark kitchen, rubbing his cold arms through his sodden shirt as he entered the living room, colliding with the coffee table, where a pair of empty brandy snifters flanked his father's cuff links and tie beside his mother's purse, his muddy ruined shoes tracking softly across the floorboards as he turned to climb the carpeted stairs, ears ringing, head spinning as he pulled himself across the topmost step and stood soaking wet and freezing cold facing the dark wall and the half-open door.

OUTSIDE MY WINDOW the streetlight wanes and the room darkens—my shadow falls before me as I pull a page from the typewriter and stop the reel-to-reel tape, thrust back years and years into a childhood that I have barely remembered, almost forgotten, and when I lean to rest my tired eyes the games I've played for so many years seem unfamiliar and unknown, fall from view leaving nothing but the sadness of passing time. I have been alone in this room for so long, remembering other people's pasts, and I may still believe, if only for a moment, that I can see the truth, explain and so be saved, but the solitude of the night prevails and I am hopeless and lost. As I read over this near-complete text, looking through my notes and thinking about the way that Max arguably saved Douglas' life, I remember so many things that have gone unmentioned, so many days that can only be hinted at, so many years barely recalled, and I remember the one time that I saw the Tafts at Harvard—or, I should say, the time that I glimpsed and briefly spoke first to Douglas and then to Annabelle, on a wet, overcast day during October of our sophomore year. I had spent the weekend in Concord, taking advantage of a break in classes at Swarthmore to travel around New England, and I arrived in Boston by train, bringing my suitcases over to the house that belonged to my mother's first cousin and her husband, a retired lawyer—I heard the patient ticking of their grandfather clock as I told them about my life and then eventually excused myself, changing my shirt and calling Stephen Leonard, who was also at Harvard. I told this story to Annabelle during our first interview, and as we sat at her kitchen table talking to the microphone I narrated how I'd been getting along up to then, how I'd decided on journalism, and Annabelle interrupted and said that she was *sure* I was getting it wrong, because she would have remembered if we'd seen each other that autumn, but I continued talking, explaining that I hadn't *spoken* to her, I'd just *seen* her, and decided not to disturb her, and as I told the story Annabelle began to remember—"It was the thing with the ghost," Annabelle said, leaning on the table, the reels of the tape deck turning slowly beside her. I explained about how I'd caught the Metro train over to Cambridge, where I had to wade through the construction in Harvard Square, stepping over pieces of concrete-reinforcing steel before wandering onto the campus, and where I loitered for a long time, talking awkwardly with Stephen, who had to go off to a "Hellenistic Archeology" class—Stephen was drunk with big words—and sat in a threadbare coffee shop that I can't remember the name of, listening to the erudite clamor of the breathless undergraduates and trying to look like I was waiting for someone. ("You *were* waiting for someone— You were waiting for *me*," Annabelle interrupted.) I had, in fact, entertained some vague hope of running into the Tafts, since I'd heard a few stories about how they were doing, none of which really agreed—according to some, they were taking all the same classes, according to others, they hadn't spoken in months. I followed Stephen's directions to Douglas' dorm and spent an awkward half-hour with his roommate, who was listening to the new Stray Cats album and folding his clothes the entire time, and who said just enough to me to make it clear that he didn't like Douglas at all—he thought Douglas was arrogant and moody and perhaps, he hinted, "off his head," which seemed, at the time, an odd colloquialism coming from the sort of person that the roommate seemed to be. ("I *do* remember this," Douglas said at this point when I was telling him the story. "You showed up that shitty day.") Douglas came in briefly to grab some textbooks and was happy to see me, but somewhat bewildered and disoriented, not nearly as much as he was four and a half years later during the night at St. Mark's Hospital that was the next time I saw him, but distracted nonetheless—he kept talking about the stint with Senator Rollins, which he'd had mixed feelings about, and about how difficult he was finding the situation of living in Cambridge. Douglas was late to a class and had to go, and he promised to call me later that day, but he never did—he was clearly preoccupied with an imminent midterm and I'd told him not to trouble himself. ("I guess I *did* blow you off," Douglas interjected apologetically. "I'm sorry.") I suppose it was a pleasant day, but it had been growing colder, and Harvard Square was jammed with construction equipment and European cars and students who walked around in the particular, distracted way that college students have, edging around passersby with their casually entitled demeanor. I was watching everyone's faces looking for my friends, fruitlessly, and I'd finally given up and decided to head back to my cousin's house when I saw Annabelle walking across the other edge of Harvard Yard in a green sweater, deep in conversation with two other women—I watched her wave goodbye to her companions as they walked off with their bookbags, and I was still trying to decide whether or not to try to catch up with her, when I saw her stop, and stare at the face of the building she had been approaching, moving her hand in an odd gesture, staring at the face of the building as she brought her hand to her eyes, standing motionless for a moment as I stood and watched her across the quad. "It wasn't long before I left school," Annabelle said years later in her kitchen. "It wasn't long before I dropped out and came back to New York. I mean, that's *incredible,* Mike, that you were there right then— When I was going to leave, when I was going to set things straight— There was that afternoon at school, that October afternoon, and it was the ghost." I mentioned that there seemed to be many things that I had been around for, noticed or not. "Sure," said Annabelle, remembering. "It was Lisa— She *said* she would return, and I swear to God I saw her that day. Just for a moment, but she was there, and she didn't speak, but she waved goodbye— She was in front of me waving goodbye, and then she was gone, and I knew that I had to leave." I finished my half of the story, explaining how I'd stood watching Annabelle regain her composure in the courtyard and begin walking purposefully toward a campus building, soon disappearing within, and I headed back to the Square, hurrying in the hopes of making the next train.

chapter 27

Douglas pushed the door open and peered into the darkness, reeling forward as he tripped on the antique carpet's hemmed edge—he weakly waved his arms but failed to slow his toppling crash against the bed and Annabelle opened her eyes and her face was below his and her body stirred beneath his. "Oh, Christ, Anna," Douglas whispered, ears ringing, close to tears, watching Annabelle's face as she slowly awoke and gazed up at him.

"What—" Annabelle whispered, half asleep. "What time is it?" She stretched a bare arm toward the night table, where her watch was draped beside the opened box that held the gold scissors, and as she brought the watch to her face she noticed his wet hair and reached to brush it out of his eyes. "Is it raining?"

"I told you it wouldn't rain. I fell down," he whispered, his eyes adjusting to the darkness as Annabelle returned the watch to the table, squinting with the effort. "In the— In the woods, the woods behind the house— I've been through town. I've"—closing and reopening his eyes—"I'm so glad I made it home."

"What *happened* to you?" Annabelle whispered, gazing up at his face. "My God—"

"Oh, Jesus, Annabelle"—he caught his breath—"it was so bad, so— It was just so *awful*— I got so *scared*, and— What can I— I can't find a way to— I can't—"

"You're still pretty drunk," Annabelle whispered, not moving, soft strands of her hair falling over her cheekbones and across the pillow.

"Yeah," said Douglas. "I'm sorry I'm not—" He stayed where he had fallen, his weight along her body, his cold hands wedged against the dry weave of the wide bedspread where it tugged upward, flanking her waist. "I left. Jill's house. I left."

"I covered for you," Annabelle murmured, absently stroking Douglas' hair from his forehead. "Said you were staying, and someone would— What'd did she *do,* throw you out?"

"I just left," Douglas said helplessly, his strained neck muscles giving out as he let his head sink downward, his eyes burning. "It was so terrible, Anna, so fucking— I feel so—"

"Shhh," Annabelle whispered, closing her eyes, gently stroking her fingers against his temples. "Shhh— You don't have to tell me."

"I *want* to tell you," Douglas murmured, raising his head, voice catching again. "I want to tell *someone*—goddamnit, things can be so goddamn—"

"I know," Annabelle said, raising her chin as she stroked his hair, soothing him. "I know how it can be."

"I just— I mean I just walked *out,* with—"

"I know," whispered Annabelle, shaking her head with measured contempt. "That stupid girl. That stupid girl. I know."

"I felt so alone—"

"Poor Douglas," Annabelle said, shifting her position slightly, her hand having moved across his sodden shirt-collar. "Look, at least she didn't *throw* you out."

"That's true," Douglas murmured, smiling slightly, his head sinking, closing his eyes as his face settled against the pillow beside her head. "But God *damn,* that walk was rough— I thought I'd never—"

"Douglas, I just made the bed," Annabelle whispered, her hand still collapsed across his shoulder, turning her face toward the damp back of his head beside her. "Your clothes are all wet from the woods."

"God, I'm tired," Douglas murmured, voice muffled by the pillow. "I walked so far—"

"Douglas—"

"Just my shirt," Douglas whispered, wincing with the effort of hoisting himself upward, off of her, cringing as his cold shirt brushed against his skin, closing his eyes and reeling with fatigue while Annabelle undid the buttons of his shirt, and then he pulled the shirt off and dropped it beside the bed, sighing as he slowly lay back down, shifting back on top of her and closing his eyes. "I'm so tired," he whispered, kicking off his muddy shoes and hearing them thump to the carpet as he rested his head beside hers again, his bare arm across her. "It's so quiet in here," he whispered. "So warm and quiet—"

"You must have been cold," Annabelle murmured, brushing her arm across his back.

"Annabelle." Douglas raised his face and gazed down at her, their faces very close. "You never told me. You never"—Annabelle pivoted her head to look at him, her hair brushing the pillow—"You never told me what he— What Carlo said in that letter."

"Long ago," Annabelle whispered, gazing upward as Douglas moved toward her, gently reaching to brush her hair from her face. "A long time— He— He said it hadn't meant anything, that he"—she took a sharp breath, her green eyes narrowing—"I mean he blew me off, just like that, wrote the whole— He said it was *circumstance,* that— I mean he didn't know the word but just things *happening,* tending to happen but not meaning what you think." Douglas stroked Annabelle's hair as she remembered. "But those days back then— I was fourteen and he was twenty-eight and we could barely *speak* when we saw each other— We could barely *speak,* Doug."

"Wow," Douglas whispered, gazing at her eyes and brushing his fingers along her jaw, and she slowly arched her head backward as he skated his fingers down the smooth lines of her jaw and neck. "That bad, huh?"

"No, I mean we couldn't *speak*—he didn't know English and my Italian was all phrasebook bullshit but he had those *eyes* and he wanted to see me again"—Annabelle's eyes fluttered shut, her lashes touching her cheeks—"and he wanted to make me a model and I kept telling him I wanted to teach kindergarten and I think I bought that line back then too. God, that feels nice."

"You look like one of those soap opera—" Douglas brushed a finger along her cheekbone and then around her jaw and down her neck to the hem of the bedsheet, where Annabelle was moving her arms, taking her arms upward, her hands absently roving upward toward the headboard. "You know, the woman in bed with the demure bedsheet—"

"It's—generally a bit more immodest," said Annabelle as Douglas slid the sheet downward until it lay draped across her chest, his fingers catching on its thick and wrinkled white cotton hem.

"The sheet is so sexy," Douglas whispered.

"Oh— The *sheet*"—Annabelle squinted, moving her body slightly—"thank you very much— But the thing is, he was— The thing is that Carlo was an asshole, you know? Just another— I mean, it's never, there I was for the first time and he looked so sweet, looked so good but he was another asshole, and it's never— It's never—" Annabelle's breath was catching in her throat as she began to close her eyes and her voice was hitching as she tried not to gasp while Douglas stroked his hands over her breasts. "It's *just*—never *possible*—to know beforehand. Jesus Christ that feels good," Annabelle whispered.

"Was he still in— When he wrote did he still feel it? Like he would remember?" Douglas moved his face down as he whispered, brushing his mouth over Annabelle's forehead and then across her hair as she let her arm drift over to settle on his neck where he felt the heat and weight of her smooth arm against his still-damp skin. "Does he— You think he still— Still thinks of you?"

"I think he does," Annabelle breathed as Douglas slid the smooth sheet down farther and pressed his hands more firmly around her breasts. "I think he does, 'cause there's— 'Cause there's— You take a certain guy, and there's something— Something *about* me"—her head was pressed back, her fingers spread against his shoulders—"Can't you tell?"

"I can tell," Douglas whispered, watching Annabelle's eyes as her fingers caressed his neck, continuing the movement she'd begun as she spoke, her eyes sharply clearing as she gazed at him. "I can tell— I can *feel* it," he whispered. "I can feel it."

Douglas felt her body arch under the sheet, felt the warmth of her navel and thighs against his damp body under the sheet and it took the abrasion of her movement to make them both realize what was happening to him. "Oooh. I can feel *that*," Annabelle whispered.

"Yeah"—Douglas moved again without intending to move as he whispered—"Yeah, you can, can't you"—and Annabelle arched her back, slowly, her breathing shaking as Douglas inclined his head and bit her ear and Annabelle slid her hand down Douglas' back and toward his waist and then around between them, on his side of the bedsheet, slid her hand while her legs drifted, hissing against the smooth soft cotton.

"That feels painful," Annabelle breathed, both of them barely audible now.

"You're so fucking beautiful," whispered Douglas, his face immersed in the heat near Annabelle's neck, whispering almost into Annabelle's ear.

"Douglas," Annabelle whispered as his hands lightly touched her smooth face, feeling the warm perfect shape of her face. "Douglas, you remember our conversation about Jill's house—"

"Yeah," whispered Douglas, face drifting downward as if weighted. "Oh my God, yeah—"

"There was a *package,*" breathed Annabelle. "I had a package, something you would—"

Douglas brought his mouth to hers and their lips grazed gently while her mouth opened and he kissed her gently, softly, slowly, withdrawing and hefting himself upward with his arms while he looked down at her and saw the way that her face was transformed, saw her barely open mouth and eyes and the strands of hair that curled over her flushed face, looking a way that he had never seen, a way that nobody had seen, breathing audibly, breathing and gazing up at him. "Douglas, take— Take your pants off," she whispered. "There's mud on your pants— Take them off."

Douglas was already pulling his unfastened belt away, dropping it as he struggled with the stuck zipper on the newly tailored trousers, trying more and more frantically to wrench the trousers open, Annabelle lying softly under him, relaxed like wire, stroking her fingers up and down the wool stretched across his thighs, her hair over her flushed face, breathing quickly. "Shit—" he muttered breathlessly. "I can't—"

"Hang on," Annabelle breathed, lunging to draw the scissors from the box and sliding the narrower of the two blades behind his waistband, the thin gold-plated blade touching his abdomen and shooting liquid fire through his nerves as she cut his trousers open, making a jagged vertical cut down the front of his trousers and pulling the scissors away as he wrenched the trousers off and dropped them to the floor. "*Socks,* Douglas, *fast,*" Annabelle panted while Douglas twisted in place, frantically peeling off his sodden socks and flinging them away as he looked back at Annabelle where she was lying, reaching down with his index fingers and drawing the sheet down to her waist while she drifted a hand to the outside of his arm, drifted her hand while Douglas drew his fingers slowly backward up her arching rib cage, his fingernails lightly brushing the soft muscles of her stomach as she slowly closed her eyes and opened her mouth and then bringing his fingers very lightly around the outside curves of her breasts, his hands turning to curve over her shoulders, tightly taking her shoulders so that nothing moved in the warm and quiet room except for his arms and the small changes in Annabelle's face as her breathing got quicker, louder, less regular, her head stirring slowly back and forth, his grip on her shoulders tightening as he pulled her toward him, her hand holding his arm, holding it, feeling his thin biceps bulge as he lifted her from the pillow with her head limply hanging and then slipping forward onto his shoulder as they looked into each other's eyes, eyes locking as she stroked her hand over the front of Douglas' tented underwear and he put his warm hand on her warm rib cage and slid his other hand around her body and across her wide shoulders beneath her hair, wrapping his arms around her and pulling her toward him while her arms came up around his shoulders from underneath as their heads tilted and their eyes closed and they darted their faces forward and kissed again, very thoroughly, for a long time, for minutes, their mouths grinding together as Douglas' hands moved along the smooth muscles of Annabelle's back and her hands locked onto his shoulders and her cheeks sucked inward with the kiss, her hands tugging his bare waist toward her as her stomach pulled inward with their shared breath, and Annabelle knew how to give a kiss, knew how to push her jaw forward so that Douglas could feel it in his fingers and toes, push forward once and then again until they both gasped for breath and the kiss gently ended with their faces still together, eyes drifting open, and Annabelle was moving, rising to her knees, breathing quickly, the sheet falling away as Douglas rose to face her and she held his neck and kissed him again while slipping her other hand under the waistband of his underwear, stretching the cheap elastic to slide against his skin as she pulled his underwear down before both her arms pulled him down on top of her and Annabelle knew his nerves, knew how to move so that right then everything *slowed down,* slowed, kept moving but slowed, became precise, became like fire, turned into glass as they moved together, panting, out of breath. "Hold off," Annabelle gasped, eyes closed, the tip of her tongue against her front teeth.

"I can't," said Douglas.

"Hold off"—Annabelle pounded a fist on the bedsheet as she whispered— "Hold off, hold off—"

"I c—" Douglas jammed his teeth together.

"Yes you can, goddamned Douglas Sidewinder Taft—"

"Oh, you bitch," gasped Douglas, squinting, his thigh muscles tightening.

"Ahhhh," breathed Annabelle. "Oh, God—"

Douglas' arms gave way and he slowly toppled forward with his face buried against Annabelle's neck, long black hairs catching in his teeth, his sweat-drenched muscles relaxing as he collapsed over her, strained arms hugging her, her arms hugging him back.

"I'm glad you made it home," whispered Annabelle, crying, hugging him tightly.

"I'm home," whispered Douglas.

"Oh Christ, Douglas," Annabelle whispered fearfully, looking into his eyes.

He felt her jaw move against his face as she bit her lip, crying as he moved his face against hers, cheek to cheek, wincing with grief as the bedsheet wound its way down and their hips touched. "Annabelle," he whispered softly, choking, lips to her ear, "oh, Annabelle, Jesus, I wish I could— I wish I could keep them away, I could *save* you from everyone, from all the pain, from— If I could just *do* that, do it for you, I'd do anything to save you, but— But nobody can."

"Nobody can," Annabelle whispered, tears on her face, breath catching like a blade.

"If I could," Douglas breathed.

"Oh, Douglas"—her fingernails scratched his sides as his hands glided toward her chest, their forearms colliding as they swerved together—"Douglas, you could have— Could have showed them, fucking showed them *all*"—her mouth darted breathlessly forward, finding his between her words as she stroked his shoulders—"Made them see what it's like— God, your *skin,* your beautiful skin, your shoulders— Your body's like a *sculpture*—"

"I don't have any muscles," Douglas whispered.

"You're weak but you're so *smooth*"—her face turned as he leaned with awkward grace to kiss her again, his mouth grinding downward—"so beautiful and smooth— You're just the prettiest mess— Oh, Douglas, I was— I was—I *knew* I was right about you, knew I just *had* to be— Had to be *right*"—she smiled as she roved her hands over his back as if desperate to feel every part of him—"All those people— all those people—"she was kissing him as she whispered—"my darling Douglas"—Annabelle tenderly pulled their foreheads together, her hands laced behind his neck as she stretched her long legs around him and their bodies slid against each other, slid like a dream as he grazed her gently, pulling away, arching backward and returning as they kissed again and his eyes closed, and when he pulled away to look at her face through her hair, see her smiling with her eyelids half closed, he slid down against her, grinding firmly against the contours of her body, their hardened muscles gleaming in the dim darkness as they panted.

"My God, Annabelle," he whispered, tenderly stroking her face.

"Stop," Annabelle murmured, moving her hands between his legs, rolling him over, the flattened bedsheets cool against his sweat-soaked back as he stared at the ceiling, stretching his shoulders, his legs stirring as her hair brushed his thighs, letting his hands drift down to her head as he arched his back, watching the room shift and spin at the edges as he gazed down at her, amazed, clutching the bedsheets in his fists and watching her head move up and down with absolute assurance—the dim haze of the darkened room flared in his eyes as he heard her swallow and then crawl to collapse against him, panting as she lay in his arms, exhausted and warm, her thighs interwoven with his, and they lay together without moving for a long silent moment, their eyes closed, muscles aching, until Annabelle moved, her leg brushing forward with the first twitch of sleep, waking him up, making him stir, making him move to push her upward, turning her over and finding the rhythm again and this time he was *concentrating* on prolonging it, holding off as carefully as he could, holding off, but again it was like an electric current was inside him and by the end they were at each other like wild animals, like tigers, grazing each other's necks like horses as they gasped for breath, arching and collapsing, falling together, closing their eyes, content.

"I meant it," he whispered, voice catching.

"Don't start," she whispered, hugging him fiercely, beginning to cry again.

"I just—"

"No, don't"—her voice thinned out—"don't do it, *please*—"

"Anna—" Their eyes were open in the darkness, finding each other's stricken gaze.

"Douglas, what did we—"

"I meant it," he whispered, brushing her tears from her cheekbones with his thumbs, watching as she pulled her head backward to the pillow, away from him, drawing in her breath as she looked into his eyes, her face vivid.

"You got me," she finally whispered, gazing at him. "You really got me. You just should know. That's all."

"Annabelle, every *day,* I"— his voice caught, slurring finally with fatigue—"every *day,* I can't help it, I'm with you."

"Douglas," she said, gliding her lips against his neck, her hair softly brushing across his face. "Douglas."

DOUGLAS HEARD A voice in the darkness calling his name, and as the voice spoke again he felt a hand on his shoulder, shaking him, and he opened his eyes—the room was lighter, its haze fading, the window visible, indigo and distant, weakly glowing. "Damn it, Douglas— Wake up," Annabelle whispered, and he let his eyes close again, curling his arm back around her waist before she pulled out of his grip, shaking him again. Blinking, Douglas peered at the lightening window as Annabelle reached for her watch and brought it close to her face as if blind. "Jesus, it's almost five-thirty— Douglas"—she was shaking him again, her frightened voice scratching—"Goddamnit, you're *not* falling asleep here—"

"I'm awake," Douglas murmured, struggling to sit up. Annabelle's dim silhouette crouched beside him, crying again, hands to her face, and he reached for her shoulder.

"Stay the fuck away," Annabelle sobbed roughly, terrified, slapping his hand down.

"Annabelle," Douglas whispered, his hot eyes blurring as he caught her arm and held it as she tried to push him away, quivering in his grip—their breathing hitched as she stroked his arm and then they were kissing again, burning eyes closed as they held each other, losing their threadbare breath as they quickly separated.

"No, no, no," Annabelle sobbed, jamming her fist into Douglas' shoulder, pushing him roughly away—the room was brighter and he saw her shoulders trembling.

"Annabelle—" He heard the tears in his voice as he shivered, his hands drifting to his face and toward her and away and back toward her in blind fear, touching her arm. "We can—"

"Don't touch me, don't touch me," Annabelle whimpered, turning away and pitching forward, curling around the pillow and crying as Douglas wiped his eyes and slowly got to his feet beside the bed. He retrieved his clothes, his head spinning with the sudden effort, and stumbled in the darkness, wandering naked and blind toward the dark, drafty corridor and closing the door behind him.

He found his bedroom by touch and stood outside the door shivering as he pulled his underpants on, gently turning the knob, holding his breath and entering—Max lay asleep in Douglas' bed, face down, paisley bedspread stretching across his wide back, arms flanking the pillow and framing his dark head, and Douglas dropped his crumpled clothes in a muffled heap on the threadbare floral carpet, still shivering, his exhausted arms and aching legs trembling as he groped in the darkness for the bathroom door, found the doorknob, pushed the door forward, and stepped through. It was the sundeck door and he lost his balance and toppled forward into the cold wind, feet slipping, plummeting downward against the cold stone façade of the house but managing to twist as he fell so that his arms slammed downward into the aluminum door sill as his face cracked against the limestone cladding beneath the door and exploded with pain—he hung three stories above the concrete embankment, hands slipping on the carpet, bare legs slapping the freezing stones, feet groping for purchase and finding none as his arms continued to slip outward, the doorsill grinding into his biceps, and he heard himself screaming as his slipping wrist slammed into the door frame, the impact blunted by the bracelet of his tank watch, which snapped, the watch tumbling onto his face and sliding coldly down his chest, striking his foot and dropping, and he screamed again and pulled himself upward, hearing the watch smash against the concrete, tearing a muscle as he clawed at the carpet and felt his fingers touch something solid. He grabbed desperately at what he'd touched, still screaming as he pulled himself upward, but he'd grabbed Jane—the cat dug her claws into the carpet and snarled in panic as Douglas pulled her out the door, squealing as she thumped against Douglas' face, her claws scratching him as she slipped away and fell with a diminishing feline scream and then Max was grabbing his sweat-soaked wrists, powerful lacrosse-team muscles hardening as he heaved Douglas into the bedroom to stumble on the carpet, gasping for breath as he tumbled forward, trembling, arms burning, falling onto the warm soft floor and hearing distant crashing footsteps and yelling voices, dull diminishing echoes that faded into black.

chapter 28

The rain finally came in the early morning while Douglas and Max and Annabelle slept, and the air was quiet and still beneath a distant wind that moved all through the night. The waiter that Annabelle had talked with at the party showed up early to work at the Lawrence Hotel, moving the sodden courtyard tables and lowering the awnings, but it rained hardest long before dawn when no one was awake or around—the rowboats in the lake behind the Winfield house filled with water as the Anthesteria napkins and coasters melted into the grass and the stream behind the Old Woods swelled, flooding the pipe beneath Blackfoot Road, but there were clear slashes through the clouds at dawn and the shattered glass shards of the vodka bottle near Jill's house shone in the overcast sunrise.

As the sky grew brighter Max awoke from his light sleep, blearily blinking as he stepped over Douglas' body to pull jeans and a white T-shirt from his duffel bag and duck into the bathroom to shower and dress. After quietly gazing from the steamed bathroom window at the white misted landscape and listening to the whispering rain, Max hunted through the cluttered medicine cabinet and found a bottle of Tylenol and then headed down the narrow back stairs, damp bare feet hissing against the carpet as he entered the deserted kitchen, where he poured a glass of brackish tap water and swallowed the bitter, chalky tablets, and he was refilling the glass when he heard dim television sounds. Carrying the water glass, Max wandered through the still-dark dining room and out into the low-ceilinged living room, where Annabelle was collapsed sideways against an ottoman, head on hand, gazing with boredom at the big Sony Trinitron in the varnished cabinet and using her free hand to repeatedly change the channel—she was also barefoot, her white T-shirt tucked into a pair of faded jeans that ended at midcalf, and her hair was disheveled and wet enough to reveal rivulets of scalp where it pulled from her temples but not wet enough to drown its waves. She was yawning without covering her mouth as he walked in, not noticing him, and Max, who hadn't expected to find her, stood for a moment before crossing to sit beside her on the floor, looking at the television, where the bright primary colors of a familiar Warner Brothers cartoon were washed to pastels by bright reflections of the overcast morning windows against the glass screen.

"Hi," Max said.

"Hi," said Annabelle, looking over, startled, using the same scuffed, woolen voice that he'd used. "I didn't see you," she yawned, narrowing and then widening her reddened eyes, wincing in fatigue as she gestured vaguely toward the television. "The reception up here is so bad."

"Uh-huh," Max said, leaning back against the couch.

"You feeling it?" said Annabelle, leaning forward on the ottoman to look at him.

"Yeah," said Max, widening his eyes. "I guess I survived the Winfield party."

"It is," said Annabelle, "a *very good thing* that it only happens once a year."

"Once a decade would do it," sighed Max, stretching his legs across the soft rug and watching drops of rain hit the ivy foliage against the bottoms of the windows. "I love summer rain—where's everyone else?"

"Mom's in town, I think." Annabelle changed the channel again, over to a Technicolor Western. "Is what's-his-name asleep?"

"Yeah," said Max. "He's going to sleep all day, I think— He was so fucked up when he got home last night."

"You were awake?" Annabelle glanced over.

"Hey, that's Gary Cooper," said Max, smiling, pointing at the TV.

"That's not Gary Cooper," said Annabelle. "That's Lee Van Cleef."

"That's Gary Cooper."

"Were you awake when he got home?"

"I think I heard him come in," Max said. "I had some trouble getting to sleep."

"It must have been really late," said Annabelle, glancing over again. "I don't know how he got back— He must have *walked* or something." On the TV, the man they'd indicated had entered a saloon and ordered some controversial drink, stopping all conversation.

" 'Morning," Greg whispered, leaning in the living room door, wearing mint-condition jeans and a red wool sweater.

"Good morning," said Max, looking over. "We didn't realize you were here."

"You don't have to whisper, Dad," Annabelle said as Greg came through the door. "It's just some old Western." Max happened to glance around the room and notice a small ceramic bowl of milk resting on the carpet's margin—the window's light shone on the milk's surface, which had been stained a light pink, as if by children's breakfast cereal.

"Hmm," Greg said gravely, hands on his hips, thumbs in front, squinting at the television. "I was in the other room— I thought I heard the paper boy. Max, is Douglas still asleep?"

"Douglas is still asleep," said Max.

"Good."

On the TV the man in the saloon had received his drink—it had been slid down the bar to him—and he tossed it back and then slammed the glass on the bar and looked around ominously. "You're right," Max said to Annabelle. "That *is* Lee Van Cleef."

"I told you," Annabelle said. "Gary Cooper, my ass—you don't *forget* what Gary Cooper looks like."

Greg looked at the TV again. "That's not Lee Van Cleef," he said finally. "That's James Arness."

"Oh," said Annabelle. Greg beamed at them and then walked out and they heard him open the front door for the paper and head for the kitchen.

"Was he drunk?" asked Annabelle. "When he got home?"

"He fell out the door."

"*What?*" Annabelle looked over intently. "He's all right, isn't he?"

"He's fine," said Max. "No, he didn't *fall* out the door. He just—

I think he was confused, you know, or really fucked up, because as far as I can tell he just opened the door, and, like, stepped out."

"Jesus Christ," said Annabelle quietly. "He's one lucky son of a bitch."

"Yeah, he *must* have gotten lucky last night," said Max. "The wind from the door hit me and I got over there in time and pulled him in."

"He *did* get lucky," said Annabelle. "Those goddamned doors—"

"Yeah, what kind of place has doors like that?"

"Check this out," said Annabelle, pointing at the TV. "I think this is the big confrontation." Lee Van Cleef, or Gary Cooper, or James Arness, or whoever he was, was standing in the saloon facing a "villainous" man with a mustache and a black shirt, talking obliquely about the dangers of the particular part of Montana that they were in. For a moment the illusion took hold and both Annabelle and Max actually managed to believe that they were witnessing nineteenth-century events before the Western snapped back into focus as the charade that it was.

"Wow," said Max. "They should have the paintings at the end of the bar."

"Paintings?" said Annabelle. "What?"

"Paintings— An art gallery in the bar. You know— 'I like art too. Can I—?' "

"What the fuck are you talking about?" said Annabelle, mystified.

"Come on— The art gallery in the bar." Annabelle stared at him. "Don't you remember? Jack Winfield's joke from upstairs. The joke about Wally and Nick."

"*What* joke about Wally and Nick?"

"You really don't remember?"

"No," said Annabelle. Max settled himself on the living room's carpeted floor, watching the Technicolor gunfighters and trying to imagine the mountains of Montana surrounding them.

DOUGLAS WAS IN a state of profound pain and had been for several hours, his deep slumber progressing into a tight, dry, painful dozing during which he had the same dream—himself drinking a glass of water—over and over at regular intervals, enduring dozens of despaired moments as he confused the dream with reality. Finally he opened his dry, burning eyes and gingerly sat up, taking care to move his throbbing head very slowly, wincing at the sharp aches in his back and shoulders and the tender bruises along the edges of his arms. Fruitlessly swallowing to clear the copper taste from his mouth, he noticed his wristwatch on the chair next to Max's unmade bed—it was hopelessly scratched, bits of concrete and grit adhering to the marred case, and the crystal now had a long vertical crack, but the watch was still running, indicating that it was almost three in the afternoon, and he strapped it on.

He stumbled to his feet and wandered dazedly to the bathroom mirror, where he was badly startled by the dried blood on his face and the rain and roadside mud that had dried into his caked and tangled hair. His head began spinning as he noticed his dark, hang-over-tinged urine and he reeled dizzily against the wall, his knees buckling as he sank to the floor and vomited, painfully and at great length—he tried to keep his eyes open, desperate to avoid the images from the previous night that were battering his vision as he crouched against the tiles, trembling, arms pressed over his head, eyes clamped shut. He shivered on the floor for a near-unendurable span of minutes until his head began to clear, and then he stood, flushing the toilet and reaching to turn on the shower, the hissing hot water and the soap's aromas helping him forward—as he watched blood from his cut lip wash between his feet and swirl down the drain, a tiny brass screw clattered onto the porcelain, and he bent to rescue it, baffled until he realized that it had dropped from his watch.

By the time he stood drying his hair and watching the rain stir the blurred trees out the window, Douglas' strength was returning, and he pulled on some cotton trousers and the navy sweatshirt and moccasins that he'd worn to the beach and clattered down the back stairs to the kitchen. Greg sat alone at the table reading the *New York Times Magazine,* the rest of the paper strewn out behind him next to the radio—the sink was piled with egg-stained stoneware plates, the globe of coffee in the machine was half full, and something looked wrong, but Douglas couldn't place what it was.

"Good morning, Doug," Greg said without looking up.

"Morning, Dad," mumbled Douglas, wandering to the cabinet for a drinking glass and then heading to open the refrigerator, bleakly staring at its contents and trying not to be sick again as his eyes caught sight of all the lurid-looking containers of food. He finally found a white half-gallon carton of orange juice and poured himself a glass and brought it to the table.

"The air's cool today," Greg said, closing the magazine. "Cool for June. How do you feel?"

"Like shit," said Douglas, rubbing his face, gulping the orange juice. "Mmm. Sorry— Too much profanity."

"Your mother and I are leaving early," said Greg. "The office called and I've got to go in this evening."

"Uh-huh," said Douglas, looking around the kitchen, feeling sick again, closing his eyes. "Something's wrong here. Something's—"

"Your mother's in town running an errand," said Greg. "I want to leave as soon as she gets back, actually. Look"—Greg paused, looking uncomfortable, and then continued—"Max didn't want me to wake you up, so I've been waiting."

"Mmm," said Douglas, leaning his forehead on the heel of his hand. "Waiting's good. Worse things than waiting— You get sick of waiting, but—"

"Douglas, I can't tell you how horrified I was last night," Greg said.

"Talk about it. No," he added quickly, seeing Greg's face. "I'm sorry, Dad. I'm sorry." He blearily looked around the kitchen again. "Damn it, something's not right here— I'll think of it in a second—"

"Douglas, is that—" Greg was pointing at Douglas' wrist. "Your watch fell, didn't it?"

"Yeah."

"I'll buy you a new one."

"No, I—" Douglas tilted his wrist, looking at the watch. "This one has the inscription, you know?"

"I can have the same inscription put on a new watch," said Greg.

"Come on, no you can't," said Douglas, sipping orange juice and watching the light rain spatter the kitchen window.

"Douglas, do you want to go for a walk?" Greg suddenly asked, crossing his legs and running a hand through his short, greying hair. "Your mother'll probably be a while."

"Where's everyone else?"

"Max and Annabelle are watching TV," Greg said, gesturing vaguely in the direction of the living room. "I thought we could walk through the woods. What did Annie used to call them—'the ancient woods'?"

"The Old Woods," said Douglas. "Sure, Dad— Let me just get

some coffee." He got up, still feeling weak, and poured himself a cup of coffee, using one of the old HARVARD CLASS OF 1958 mugs with the VERITAS seal and the network of tiny, fine cracks in the porcelain surface, laced it with milk, and brought it back to the table, looking at it and realizing that he didn't want it, but nevertheless frightened of the imminent conversation. While Douglas sipped his coffee, Greg had picked up the Sunday edition of the local paper off the table and was going through it methodically, glancing once at Douglas and then back at the paper, and suddenly Douglas realized what was wrong.

"Where's Jane?" Douglas asked, looking around.

"How's the coffee?" said Greg, not looking up from the paper.

Douglas put down the coffee mug, sighing with dread. "All right, Dad," he said. "We're going for one of those walks— I understand."

"All I meant was that that coffee's been sitting there for hours. I made it—"

"Let's go," said Douglas, standing up. "I'll bring this with me."

"If you want to talk to Annie and your friend—"

"Let's just go."

Douglas went and got an old raincoat out of the laundry alcove, putting the coffee down on the clothes drier while he swung the raincoat on, and Greg joined him and they walked toward the back of the house, past the sound of the living room television, and Douglas found himself looking at every corner of the floor for Jane and not seeing her.

"We've got some things to talk about," said Greg, holding the garage side door open for Douglas and then gingerly closing it behind them. "I guess you realize that." They walked outside and started toward the Old Woods.

THE RAIN HAD abated by the time Douglas and Greg stepped away from their view of the Civil War House, their feet brushing the moss of the path as they walked farther into the cathedral of trees, the slight rain tainting Douglas' half-full, rapidly chilling coffee cup, misting on Greg's antique glasses and soaking the rumpled ground.

"Mmm," said Douglas, wincing after a sip. "Great coffee, Dad."

"It's been sitting there," said Greg, hands jammed in denim back pockets, pushing the raincoat back. "I told you it was terrible. You kids never learn," he added, smiling.

"I should have had some tomato juice," Douglas said, wincing again.

"That's right"—Greg squinted—"you were very sick with drink last night, weren't you?"

"Yeah."

"Douglas, would you like a cigarette?"

Douglas had been sipping his rapidly cooling coffee and he swallowed, staring as his father pulled a fresh hard-pack of White Camels out of his shirt pocket. "This is your brand, isn't it?" Greg said, pulling the gold cellophane band from the pack. "I picked these up in town."

"You went to the Lawrence?" Douglas asked hoarsely, watching his father's hands crack open the top of the box and pull out the flashing foil shield.

"This morning," Greg confirmed. "You know I had to make the rounds. Everyone was on the porch, all the usual people, drinking tea and whatnot. I talked to Paul Brooks for a while. You know, I saw that daughter of his last night— Have you seen her? She's really quite attractive."

"I've seen her."

"Here, have a cigarette," said Greg, proffering the pack again. "Come on, it has to complement the coffee, right?"

"Right," said Douglas, prying a cigarette from the pack, as if pulling teeth, and a match from the big folder of Lawrence Hotel matches to light it, Greg expertly shielding the match. Douglas drew a breath and nodded at his father, feeling the smoke smother the tightness in his throat, and they stepped apart and Douglas dutifully sipped the cold coffee as they resumed walking.

"We've got to head back to the city," Greg said apologetically, looking away, handing the cigarettes and matches to Douglas, who pocketed them. "I wish I didn't have this commitment— I just finished packing and as soon as Giulia gets back we'll leave."

"Where's Jane?" Douglas asked again, waiting for a while, as he was used to, before getting an answer.

"Well," Greg said finally, "I guess it was quite a fall she took. Last night— She was lying on that, you know, on that concrete embankment, the concrete from the sun deck. You remember, it was 1978 when that crew came to sink the concrete, back when—"

"How is she, Dad?"

"It looks bad," Greg conceded. "I brought her inside and she was doing that constricted breathing of hers— I put her on the carpet in the living room, your mother gave her a bowl of milk, but she didn't seem interested. There was some blood, not much, but a little bit. Cat blood is so *dark.* She was still lying on the carpet when your mother and I went back to bed. This morning I went to feed her and I couldn't find her but your mother located her— She'd gone down— This was a couple of hours ago— She'd gone down to the basement. You know that—"

"The basket."

"—basket down there by the furnace, you remember that. That's where she went, that's where she is now. She's an old cat, Douglas."

"I know," said Douglas. "I know. God, I feel—" He caught his catching voice and continued. "I feel so guilty. I mean I can't help it. I feel so sad."

"Put it out of your head, Doug. You should be very thankful to your friend that he was there. Listen," Greg said suddenly as Douglas dragged on the cigarette. "Douglas, I've got something to say to you."

"Uh-huh," Douglas said, dragging on the cigarette.

"I have to try and confess something. It's going to be difficult for me to get this out, but I think that—"

"Dad."

"—once I've come clean with you, you'll—"

"Dad."

"—understand what— Douglas, please just let me speak for a moment. Once I've come clean you'll—"

"Dad— Margaret MacAffee. I know."

For a thick moment Douglas couldn't see any reaction in his father's eyes, but then Greg's face moved, betraying its age at last. "Yes," he said. "I heard she— Chablis noticed her speaking to you and I figured it was time. Douglas, I— I told Annabelle about it. I explained it to her once and it helped me come to grips with the thing."

"I know you did. I understand, I guess. But why?"

"Because it's"—Greg gestured helplessly while the wind picked up, tossing the trees and shaking down secondhand rainwater—"it's the sort of thing you tell Annabelle. It's not the sort of thing you tell Douglas. You've both got—"

"No, Dad, I'm not talking about that— What I meant was, why? I mean, why do something like that? What was the—" Douglas trailed off, dragging on the cigarette, dropping ashes among the wet leaves.

"It's difficult to explain," Greg said helplessly. "I never told you about when the Winfields started doing their spring banquet— After Giulia bought the house, shortly after Annie was born, the Winfields had their historic first party. It was already a big conspicuous affair— I remember the Kennedys were up in Massachusetts and they came down and made an appearance. That poor bastard had five months to live."

"I remember you telling me," said Douglas. "Mom has that story about talking to Jackie."

"Things were different— I hadn't gone back for my MBA yet, so I was— I'd known Margaret at school, and I remember being surprised that she was at Ted's party. I can't remember how she got invited. I saw her talking with that Rollins fellow—"

"Senator Rollins."

"He wasn't anything yet, just your mother's old flame. Rollins gave you a summer job, is that right?"

"Yeah."

"Take it," said Greg, shrugging. "What the hell—I would. At any rate, I remember talking to Margaret that night. It was '63 and she was wearing one of those Audrey Hepburn dresses, but it was red. Margaret was always— She was against the war, back then, and I even remember how she hated Kennedy but she loved shaking his hand. She worked as a fund-raiser for the Lineage Institute, she got me involved with that for a while, so I did a bit of financial work for them, back in the early seventies, before that beer company got involved, and she got married and divorced in the late sixties, and that's about all I know. She never did very well, I guess. We met several times over several years, I guess until '76 or thereabouts, and then that was it. I've heard she's had some trouble recently—she wrote and told me she would be at the thing last night, but I didn't see her."

"She's got a kid," said Douglas.

"Yes, a little boy. I can't even remember his name now. I don't remember that much. Of course I remember the whole thing but I don't remember the right details. She always wore red, Margaret did. Even back at school— Several times, I remember, there was this Brattle Street place where—"

"The Red Ghost," said Douglas suddenly. "She was the Red Ghost."

Greg didn't answer at first, and Douglas watched the shine of the late-afternoon light on his smooth glasses and on his rain-soaked shirt collar. "That's right," Greg said.

"Jesus," Douglas murmured, looking away through the sodden leaves. "Jesus."

"I always protected you both," Greg said, putting his arm around Douglas' shoulder. "That's what it was about back then. I always remember those days—I would see both of you on the grass, and you were such young children and I knew I had to protect you. You were always so frightened and I wanted to tell you the truth." Greg took a breath, and Douglas transferred the coffee mug to his other hand, fingers feeling the rain, and walked more closely to his father. "All the times we had back then," Greg said, waving a hand at the surrounding landscape. "It's so damned nice, what you've all given me. It's all so damned good." They had both stopped walking and they stood on the wet ground, looking at the pale overcast light shining through the weave of the trees, and they heard the sound of a car approaching the house.

"Mom's back," said Douglas.

"Just in time," said Greg, tossing his head toward the sound, looking at his watch, wiping rain from the waterproof gold. "The three of you can close the house, right? I can trust you to remember about the burglar alarm and the garage door?"

"It's no problem, Dad."

"Douglas," said Greg, "when was your first kiss?"

"It's hard to remember," Douglas lied. "I remember. It was in sixth grade. During a party game. I was so scared."

"Who was it?" asked Greg, hitching up his mint-condition jeans.

"It was Amy MacIntyre."

"Don't believe I know her," said Greg, concerned.

"It was Amy," said Douglas, assured.

"How did it feel?"

"It wasn't really a kiss. Well— It was a kiss. It was soft. You remember your first kiss, Dad?"

"Of course," said Greg, smiling quietly.

"It wasn't Mom, was it?"

"It was Giulia, yes."

"At college?" asked Douglas, walking slowly.

"At college, during the winter. I think it was during the winter because there was snow outside."

"That would do it," said Douglas.

"It was a good winter. There were bottles of gin. There were pennants. Football season—I was picturing the wedding. It wasn't long before I could imagine raising a family."

"You already knew?"

"I already knew," Greg said, the shadow of a pine tree branch passing across his face. "I've made mistakes but I've done the best I could."

"You did all right, Dad," said Douglas. "You kept the Red Ghost away."

"The rain's letting up," Greg said. The clouds had moved as they left the woods and a soft glow touched the house's eaves, the whitewashed bricks shining against the heavy gray shadows of the sky. "Yes indeed."

THE CLOUDS HAD darkened the passing day and a weak overcast light shone the damp breeze into the kitchen through the weave of the screen door, the damp breeze gently tapping its frame against the soft sound of the rain. Max and Annabelle sat around the newspaper-strewn table drinking mugs of strong coffee that Max had just brewed, and Douglas stayed where he was, leaning in the dining room doorway with his hand in his pocket, his raincoat still on, holding the cold, empty HARVARD coffee mug and hearing the thumping footsteps of his parents packing their suitcases upstairs.

"Are you all right?" Max asked, rolling a cigarette, not looking up from the blue plastic tobacco pouch on the table before him. "Really, man— What the hell happened?"

"I—" Douglas stared out the screen door at the rain-beaded edges of the porch. "I opened the wrong door. I guess it's—" He finally looked over at the table. "I guess it's funny, 'cause— 'Cause Dad was always so worried— You remember, Anna? When the sun deck thing started? Anna— I'm talking to you."

"Yeah," Annabelle said, cross-legged on the kitchen chair, staring at the Sunday comics and reaching for her coffee without looking. "I never th— Yeah, I remember."

"What happened with Jill?" Max asked, frowning around the act of flicking his old brass lighter at the fresh cigarette.

"You sure you want to—" Annabelle was pointing at Max's cigarette.

"I'm a guest," Max told her, trying for a sarcastic nonchalance. "Really, Douglas— What happened? I've been hearing about this chick all weekend and you finally—"

"Yeah, what *did* happen with Jill?" Annabelle said, turning a page. "I *wondered* where you'd gone last night."

Douglas finally entered the room, skirting the table and moving through a cloud of sweet-smelling Drum smoke to pour himself some of the fresh-brewed coffee, scalding his fingers in the process. "I went home with her. What—" he said, facing away from the table, staring at the rattling drainpipe and sipping the nauseating coffee. "What's the big deal?"

"And you struck out?" Max said from behind him. "Come on."

"No," Douglas said, examining the cracked porcelain edge of the steaming coffee mug. "I didn't strike out. Can we not—"

"That smells good— Can you roll another?" Annabelle said. Douglas turned around and fished the pack of White Camels from his raincoat pocket, tossing it onto the table in front of Annabelle, who flinched.

"From Dad," Douglas said.

"Well, all *right.*" Max smiled, holding out his lighter, but Annabelle had pried the Lawrence matchbook from the cigarette's cellophane and was using that. "Not bad at *all.* I mean she took so *long* getting you out of there—I saw you guys leave, out the window, and it was like, 'about fucking time.'"

"What's her house like?" Annabelle asked suddenly, looking up at Douglas.

"Like the last twenty-five centuries never happened," Douglas told her. "You made that joke about—" He stepped forward and put the coffee cup on the table, looking back and forth between them. "Wait."

"Weren't you afraid her parents—" Max was grinning.

"I *remember,* Annabelle"—Douglas was standing at the table's edge looking past her head as he spoke—"You made that joke about her house. On the balcony— You were so sure she was going to take me home."

"I just wanted you to make your *move,*" said Annabelle dismissively, loudly turning pages and smoking the cigarette. "Come on, I had to practically shove you guys together. Max, you missed that shit, you know, when they were playing some—"

"No," said Douglas, his raincoat rustling as he glanced back and forth. "No— You were *sure.* Max, you said 'about time'? And when we were upstairs, and you left—"

"What are you talking about?" said Annabelle, tapping ashes into her coffee. "That was an alcohol thing— Just one of the—"

"Okay," said Douglas warily. "But you *knew* she would take me home. Max"—he pointed at him—"you wouldn't tell me what you were doing with Jill. I couldn't get you— I kept asking and you just got pissed."

"Don't drink that," Max warned Annabelle as she raised her cup. "There's ashes. Here—" He slid his jar-lid ashtray toward her and surged to his feet, taking her coffee cup to the sink, as if following stage directions.

"You said I'd find out," Douglas suddenly remembered. "You guys set the thing up, didn't you?"

"Come on, Douglas, chill," said Max, opening the coffee can and removing the filter basket from the machine. "Don't get *mad*— I mean you've been talking—"

"Don't get *mad?*" Douglas turned to face him. "Don't get *mad?*"

"Would you take that *raincoat* off?" Annabelle said painfully, dropping the comics page onto the table and pinching the bridge of her nose.

"What did you do?" asked Douglas tightly, leaning farther forward, almost knocking over his coffee cup. "Tell me— Tell me what you did."

"We didn't do anything, Douglas," Annabelle said contemptuously, stubbing out the half-smoked cigarette. "It came up in conversation that Jill thought you were—"

"He was *watching*"—Douglas waved a hand at Max—"out the *window, watching* us leave—he stood there *watching us go* and he said *'about time.'* "

"We talked on the beach about how you and Jill were both—"

"On the *beach?*" Douglas said incredulously, dropping into Max's vacated chair.

"—looking for—"

"Where do I put the coffee grounds?" Max asked, confused, holding the filter basket.

"In the sink," Douglas said woodenly, looking out the screen door at the darkening lawn and hearing Greg gallop down the stairs with several suitcases.

"There's a big garbage thing over by the laundry," Annabelle said, pointing. "You have to—"

"No, he can— He can just put them in the sink," Douglas told her. "Dad says—"

"Dad *clogs* the sink," Annabelle said quietly, leaning her face on her hands. "Max, you have to go through—" Max had crossed to the screen door and he pulled it open, admitting the chilled rain for the moment that it took him to fling the coffee grounds into the flower bed, and the screen door slammed behind him as he circled the table.

"I'm sorry," Annabelle said, reaching for another cigarette, her hands shaking. "Douglas, please don't give me a hard time."

"I'm not giving you a hard time," said Douglas, catching Annabelle's gaze, finally pulling off the raincoat as she looked away. "I didn't even want to talk."

All that afternoon "Sausalito" Jane lay curled in the laundry basket, unobserved—some sure knowledge had led her to that basement corner, content with the discarded pillow, and there she had curled in the dark and waited, after a youth of floorboards and hot country grass, knowing that at a certain silent moment, in that quiet place, her broken body could find grateful peace in the evening light, and there would come the brief shudder, the last humble movement, the simple wordless stopping of a heart.

chapter 29

By that evening the rain had ended and the sky stood close to sunset, filled with quiet color, and the darkening clouds cleared to admit a pale evening light that shone in the pools of clear rainwater, reflecting the soft grey lines of the sodden trees. After Max and Annabelle had silently finished their coffee and left the kitchen in separate directions, Douglas had eventually descended the basement stairs and found Jane moments from death, and had dropped the HARVARD mug to shatter on the cement floor as he ran to summon Annabelle. They galloped back down the stairs and Annabelle dropped to her knees beside the ancient wicker basket, Douglas crouching beside her in the feeble basement light, watching as Jane slowly raised her battered head and peered blindly at them, her body resting in a crumpled, twisted position on the bloodstained cushion, feeble eyes filming, bruised paws twitching, mouth crusted with dried and darkened blood—Douglas reached to touch the fur along the cat's neck and began to cry as Jane flinched, trembling with quiet fear.

"She's dreaming," Annabelle murmured, wiping her eyes. "Already her hands— She's starting to dream—"

"She looks cold," Douglas whispered, his voice scratched and hoarse.

"Wrap some blankets around her," said Annabelle, shivering in the basement's concrete chill. "I'll get some blankets—"

"We could get"—Douglas sniffed and continued. "Maybe we could get her— We could get her to drink some warm milk—"

"She's gone," said Annabelle, her hands rising to her face, crying as she moved to avoid Douglas' accidental touch. "Oh, sweet Jane, baby Jane—"

Jane's eyes flickered closed as the damp fur along her abdomen rose, shuddered and fell a final time, and Douglas and Annabelle did not touch each other during the silent moment that followed. "Jane," Douglas whispered. "We can— We can take—"

"Leave me here," Annabelle said in a weak and broken voice, turning her shining face toward his. "Just go— Give me a minute alone. Then I can— Then I don't care."

Douglas mounted the stairs, not looking back, and when he returned to the basement door twenty minutes later Annabelle was gone—he heard her and Max moving around in separate upstairs rooms, packing their luggage, as he carefully picked up Jane's stiffening, still-warm body and carried it out of the house and across the soaked lawn toward the Old Woods. He lay her across a soft bed of ferns and forest litter as he used a silver serving spoon to dig a hole in the hardened, mulch-covered soil between the clotted roots of an oak tree, wiping his aching wrists across his blinded eyes and smearing earth over his face for the hour that it took, and when he had finished, and had placed Jane's body within the ground and filled the grave, pushing the damp soil across her fur and covering her at last, the details of the trees had faded and the air was blue with approaching night.

MAX AND ANNABELLE sat side by side in the backseat of the BMW before the house's front door, the windows down, drinking cans of Coke that Annabelle had half emptied and refilled with Grand Marnier, looking back through the rain-beaded safety glass at the darkening sky. "Is he *coming,* or what?" Annabelle said, squinting in annoyance—she'd pulled on her motheaten brown cotton sweater over her T-shirt and she folded her arms against the mild, rain-scented breeze that entered the car.

"He's got to be packing," Max said, sipping the spiked soda and leaning to peer up at the lighted upstairs windows. "He'll be down soon."

"You in a hurry to go?" Annabelle said, leaning her chin on her knees.

"It's not that," Max said, shaking his head and looking at her. "I'm just— Annabelle, did we make a mistake?"

"You know what we did," Annabelle said, frowning mildly, her disheveled hair silhouetted against the foliage outside. "So now you're angry too? Now we can all be angry."

"Oh, please," said Max. "I'm sorry, all right? I mean give me a break— I'm just wondering if we should have told him."

"He got so mad," Annabelle said, slowly drinking and staring forward. "I didn't expect— I mean, it was just Jill."

"What?" Max said, as if he hadn't heard.

"It was just Jill."

"I thought I heard you right," Max said, looking away.

"All right," Annabelle said, crushing the emptied scarlet can. "So you're a fucking detective— So congratulations."

"Well"—Max resettled against the seat as he turned to her—"Well, now, wait a minute. I *realize* things are complicated."

"Things are simple," Annabelle said, looking directly at him in the fading light. "The weekend's over."

"Not yet."

"It's over. You want to get it straight in your head, you want to try, go ahead, but it's—"

"I've *got* it straight. It's no mystery," said Max, scratching his eyelid as he moved his face to return her gaze. "It's no secret."

"Wait—" Annabelle gave him a sharp stare, motionless for a moment. "Are you saying— You're giving me that look."

"All right," said Max, evading her gaze. "Okay, Annabelle— But the thing is that— I mean, of all the obvious ways to *go,* you know— Everyone warned me about you and I was so smug, damn it. But in the end"—he looked back at her hopelessly—"in the end of *course* I just couldn't help it."

"Couldn't—"

"I fell for you." He widened his hands, making a subtle shrugging gesture as he looked back at her. "I'm sorry."

"That's too bad," Annabelle said, looking out her window.

"Yeah," Max said. "It's too bad."

"Well, look"—Annabelle swung her head and gave him a dull stare—"don't *overdo* it, all right? I mean I *am* flattered."

"Of course you are," Max said. "You're always *flattered.*"

"Well, all right," Annabelle sighed, turning away.

The car was flanked by bright pools of rainwater that shone amid the dark wet gravel, and Max finished his drink as he stared out at the water. "Look," he said, "do you think— You think you can just say you're confused, say you can't do things, and it's that easy?"

"Max," Annabelle said wearily, closing her eyes.

"I mean, you can do any damn thing and then afterwards you think, Oh— I did that, and that's—"

"Leave me alone."

"—all it takes? I mean look what—"

"Leave me *alone,*" Annabelle said again, painfully widening her eyes. "If I don't think about it and— And he doesn't think about it then you can't talk about it."

"Well, I'm not *enjoying* it," Max said sharply. "Talking about— Look, it wasn't on *purpose,* how I feel. I don't fuck these— I *can't* fuck this kind of thing up. I don't have the *slack.*"

"And I do." Annabelle nodded, voice breaking. "Well, thanks for—"

"No—"

"—pointing it *out.*"

They looked directly into each other's eyes and then Max looked away. "I shouldn't just talk," he said. "I just— I'm sorry, I just shouldn't have come."

"I keep telling myself," Annabelle said, head lowered, wiping her eyes. "I say these things— It's a question of time and I have to be brave. Years go by"—her voice constricted as she hid her anguished face for a moment before continuing—"but what a fucking night, what a night, and in the morning the pine tree filled the window like long ago and I was sick but I took a shower and felt fine so what am I worth? I can sit in the sunlight, but then I realized, thought and realized, remembered the windows in the winter at home, reading stolen library books and stopping to watch the snow, long ago, and that was it, that's all. It's not my fault, Max," Annabelle said earnestly, locking eyes with him again. "It was never my fault, and I— But I— But I came so close. I came— I mean I *felt* it, Max, a nightmare but this shining light. I can't explain." She shook her head. "Just that I'm not that bad."

"Anna, I"—he was breathing in, breathing out—"I'm sorry. I'm sorry it's all been so hard."

"Not your fault," said Annabelle, raising her face to look at him. "I'm glad you came. It was never going to be a normal weekend."

"I know."

"And someday I'll—" She swallowed. "Someday I'll fall for someone too."

"I know you will," Max almost whispered.

"You're all right, Max," she said, smiling at him, her voice soft and smooth, the way he would remember. "You're all right."

"Are we friends?" Max asked hoarsely.

"Oh, we're friends," Annabelle said, nodding firmly. "We always were."

They reached for each other and hugged, Annabelle resting painlessly in Max's arms as he gazed through the lines of the window defogger at the shadows of the sky.

DOUGLAS SAT ON his dim and deserted bedroom floor beside his packed suitcase, twirling the gold scissors in his hands and looking out the rain-beaded window past the single visible treetop at the hushed grey sky. After washing his face and hands and gathering his clothes he had made a circuit of the upstairs, and when he spared Annabelle's room a brief glance he had noticed the scissors resting on the bedside table in their Tiffany box beside a worn-out hardcover copy of *The Story of Jake Hackett,* which now lay before him on the floral rug, opened to its last page.

began my great voyage to America, and to the humble life that awaited me amongst the Cheyenne Tribes and the Copper Kings of the great Treasure State. I recalled my Italian adventures as the Venetian spires retreated down the Grand Canal, fervently vowing that I would commit to undying memory the tragic secret that Morstan had yielded before his death, and as my train left the vast Italian city behind, affording a final glimpse of the *campanile,* I was stricken by the vivid memory of Anna's sweet smile upon the baptistery steps, and her bold courage as she stood lashed to the column of the San Marco Cathedral and the hoofbeats of Morstan's arrival clattered from the Bridge of Sighs—but I remembered, too, greeting the joyless dawn atop Michelangelo's dome where Thomas had met his tragic and untimely end. If I had learned too late of the depths of Thomas' unshakable faith, and had dallied too long in my unspeakable sin, I had also come to understand, as Anna had told me, and as Morstan had forbidden me to believe, that over the dark centuries the good church may rise from its knees to stand without remorse upon the fields of ignorance in the bright light of faith. *Vivo su questo scoglio orrido e solo.*

THE END

Douglas shut the book and stood, flicking off the nautical cracked-porcelain lamp and hefting his suitcase, stashing the boxed scissors and the Bonomi novel in its front pocket. He heard the car horn blasting outside and he knelt on the bed, raising the window sash and yelling, "Just a minute, damn it," down toward the car—the horn stopped and Douglas closed his eyes against the window screen, forehead bending the metal, and then shut the window and left the room, heading back downstairs. Leaving his suitcase in the foyer, he threaded his way through all the darkened downstairs rooms, closing windows and double-latching the garage and the porch door, and he was setting the controls for the burglar alarm when the car horn sounded again. He grabbed the house keys from the newspaper-strewn kitchen table and returned to the foyer, retrieving his suitcase, going out the wide front door, and closing and locking the Civil War House.

"About *time,*" Annabelle said lazily as Douglas got behind the wheel and Max moved to the shotgun seat.

"Sorry," said Douglas, pulling the *Zenyatta Mondatta* cassette from the stereo and flipping it back toward Annabelle without looking. "I couldn't find something."

"Did you close all the windows and lock the doors?" asked Annabelle. "Did you check all the rooms?"

"Just give me the goddamned keys," Douglas said, flinching as Annabelle tossed them forward—Max caught them before they could crack the windshield and handed them over. "Are we set?" Douglas asked.

"We've been set for a *long* time," said Annabelle. "Hit it."

Douglas gunned the engine and started down the gravel driveway and Annabelle settled in the backseat, gazing back at the shadows of the deserted house. Soon they were driving along Union Street, through Dover—the sidewalks and parking spaces were empty, the wet pavements shining, the buildings unlit save for the lanterns on the porch of the Lawrence Hotel, and by the time they had passed the Shell station and were merging onto the parkway it was full dark.

• • •

IT WAS NEARLY eleven as they crossed the Harlem River and Annabelle and Max were both asleep—Douglas maneuvered through the heavy traffic of FDR Drive and took the Twenty-third Street exit, immediately stopping for a red light, and Max stirred beside him, stretching as he looked around at the harshly streetlit corner. "It's warm out," Max said in a groggy voice, cracking his window and admitting the sounds of traffic and air conditioners and the brackish summer air.

"Where the hell are we?" murmured Annabelle, brushing her hair out of her eyes, checking her watch and bending to peer up at a street sign. "Oh— We're in Gantry Town," she said, leaning back against the seat again.

"You have to direct me, Max," said Douglas starting across the intersection.

"Make the next left," said Max, rubbing his eyes. "Now right."

"I remember this," said Douglas, starting down Twentieth Street.

"This is fine," said Max, pointing. Douglas pulled over and shifted into neutral. Max opened his door and Douglas got out of the car and circled around to the trunk, getting Max's suitcase out and handing it to him.

"Thank you," Max said awkwardly, accepting Douglas' handshake—Douglas again noticed Max's odd, truncated grip. "Be sure to thank your parents for me."

"Thanks for coming," said Douglas. "And keep in touch—you've got my number."

"Yeah," said Max. "If you're around this summer, what the hell— You can meet some people from *my* school."

"Sure," Douglas said. "Listen, Max, graduation is— The thing's at noon tomorrow, at the Thorn— Maybe you can stop by."

"Mom's taking me to meet her new boyfriend," said Max, shaking his head. "I'll be downtown all day."

"Well, if you change your mind," said Douglas.

"She's awake," Max said, peering past Douglas at the building. "Shit, maybe I'll go have coffee for an hour until she packs it in."

Max looked back at Douglas and then put down his suitcase and hugged him, and after a moment they separated and Max picked up his suitcase again. He started onto the sidewalk, stopping at the car's back window and leaning down. "Goodbye, Annabelle Taft," he said.

"Goodbye, Max Gantry," said Annabelle from inside the car, her voice obscured by the door, her face in shadow.

Max walked away toward his building as Annabelle got out and moved around to the front seat, and then Douglas got back into the car and started the engine, and he was about to drive off when Annabelle put her dashboard-lit arm against the steering wheel next to his hand. "Stop," she said.

"What?" said Douglas, following Annabelle's gaze as she corkscrewed in the car seat, watching Max climb his front steps, and as they watched, Max stopped, moving his hand toward his face before passing through the glass outer door and bending his head toward a switchboard—they dimly heard a buzzer as he hefted his suitcase and vanished from view.

"Carry on, driver," Annabelle said, staring straight ahead.

"Why'd I have to wait?" said Douglas, putting the car in gear and pulling away.

"I just wanted to make sure he got in all right," Annabelle said, settling back in her seat. "What did you think?"

"I was just asking," said Douglas, his voice hoarse as he turned the steering wheel.

"We won't talk any more," Annabelle said.

AT ELEVEN-THIRTY on a Sunday night in early June of 1981, Douglas Taft—by his own account—had unpacked his suitcase and was opening the Tiffany box and extracting the gold scissors when he heard the intercom buzzing in the kitchen, and he headed out past the ghostly illumination of the Central Park sky in the living and dining room windows, flipping on the kitchen lights and leaning across the butcherblock for the earpiece receiver. "Hello?" he called into the silent static.

"Hey, Sport," said the doorman, his voice garbled by the old wiring. "Friend here to see you."

"What?" said Douglas, confused. "Who is it?"

"Michael."

"Oh," Douglas said. "All right, send him up."

Douglas waited at the apartment entrance and after a moment the elevator's ornate door clattered open and Michael alighted in the foyer, his hands in the pockets of a navy blue windbreaker, smiling behind his glasses. "Hello, Douglas," he said.

"Mike?" said Douglas, rubbing his eyes. "What's—"

"I've got your tickets," Michael said, fishing in his pockets and producing a red checkbook-sized envelope. "I'm sorry to come so late—"

"—But we need them to leave," Douglas finished, accepting the envelope. "Thanks, Michael."

"Is she all right?" Michael asked quietly, tipping his head toward the muted, faraway sounds of Annabelle crying in her bedroom. "It's none of my business but—"

"Take him down," Douglas told the doorman, glancing past Michael with his reddened eyes.

"Douglas—" Michael said as the doorman reached for the buffed chrome lever.

"Good night," said Douglas as the steel door slid closed between them. Michael closed his coat as he fell and soon stepped out into the cool night air, and Douglas stared at the indicator's counterclockwise spin, hearing the dull sounds of the elevator's descent and waiting while the world was dark.

book III

chapter 30

It was a cold November morning and it had been getting colder as the morning progressed and the wind blew the river's random chill across Manhattan, and I stood against the cold wind on the narrow cast-iron fire escape outside the tremendous Mussolini windows of the Metropolitan newsroom with my reddened hands curled round the overpainted cast-iron rail, a battered cordovan suitcase between my feet, my breath fogging under the paper-white overcast sky, the lapels of my overcoat and of my recently purchased black suit flapping in the bitter breeze as I smoked a White Camel and stared at the birds that fluttered around the surrounding commercial buildings. I remember that sleep seemed a fond and distant memory as I stood perilously on that fire escape and tried to stay awake, concerned that I would begin to doze only to fall to the canyon of the street below, in which case many people would rush down to view my destroyed body and nobody would be concerned with the contents of my ancient suitcase, yet unreasonably confident, in a way that I'd recently learned, that my face and manner betrayed none of this simple fear. It was nine o'clock on that Monday morning when Rachel Geisler found me on that cast-iron balcony, startling me with the sliding scream of the heavy, rusted aluminum window frame as she wrenched it upward and stuck her head out into the wind.

"Don't jump," Rachel called above the drone of the traffic far below. "How long have you been out here?"

"A little while," I said, reaching to help Rachel step over the soot-caked granite sill and out onto the fire escape. "Why—am I missing something in there?"

"Not really," Rachel said, waving dismissively at the brightly fluorescent-lit newsroom, at the ceiling fans and the glowing ATEX screens and the self-important interns and copy editors who circulated in shirtsleeves and ties as they distributed the morning edition through the sparsely populated maze of desks. "Somebody called for you—I thought I saw you go out the window but I didn't know how to find you," Rachel told me as she gazed around at the vast vertical landscape of midtown Manhattan and shivered in the winter wind.

"Now you know," I said, coughing with the effort and turning my head toward her. "Wilson come in yet?"

"He called—he'll be in soon," Rachel said, her halting movements betraying her acrophobia. "I told him you were back. How *was* your week, anyway? Odd time for a vacation. You *look* rested."

"Are you kidding?" I said bitterly. "Maybe I look *groomed,* but not— What's the matter?" I asked, my inevitable shortness of breath interfering with the words as I sucked on the stale, five-year-old cigarette. "You seem depressed."

Rachel grimaced. "Just a bad morning," she said.

"Which means you had a bad night, right?" I smiled at her, shrugging the overcoat more tightly around me.

"You're learning," said Rachel. "No, it just— I guess I went out when I should have stayed home. We had that drunken thing where the man says 'I'll call you again—will you make it home all right?' and you want to go 'Listen—don't bother, okay? Don't say that on my account.' I'm never going to be good at this routine." Rachel reached to pry the cigarette from my cold fingers, having difficulty until I saw what she was doing and handed it over. "And I do miss my husband—it's a shame."

"It'll work out," I told her, and as I spoke I heard a motorcycle's distant drone and caught sight of a flurry of white, a small cascade of paper that floated in the distance and transfixed me.

"Oh, you're just saying that automatically," Rachel said, smiling somewhat wisely at me and returning the cigarette, having taken a token puff. "How do *you* know? It's not as if things *tend* to work out."

"All right," I said amicably, reaching to adjust the heavy suitcase, which had been tipped by the gusting wind and now leaned against my leg, and noticing that a young woman in her early twenties was standing within the window, a small woman with curling brown hair wearing a white turtleneck and gold eyeglasses who looked hesitantly out at us.

"This is my daughter," Rachel told me, following my gaze and then beckoning to the young woman. "Come on out," she called, speaking so as to be heard through the thick, dirty glass.

"The Collegiate Woman," I said, remembering.

"Be careful," cautioned Rachel as the young woman climbed awkwardly though the window. "Hildy, this is Michael Cadenhead—one of our new reporters."

"Hello," said Hildy, reaching to shake hands. "Have you been here long?"

"No," I said hoarsely, removing the cigarette from my mouth.

"Hildy spent the summer at a regional weekly, but she wants to—"

"Mom," Hildy muttered, reaching to light her own cigarette, turning to shield the match against the building's cold granite façade. "I want to be working here," she told me.

"Yeah, that's what I did," I told her. "The Suburban Supplement. You'll make it."

"What *is* it with you this morning?" Rachel said in mock alarm. "You're Mister Happiness today."

"No, I'm Mister Tired, if you want to know," I said, gazing down the avenue toward the grey morning haze.

"Hellzapoppin' on the fire escape," Wilson said, sticking his head out the window, ambient morning light shining in his thinning red hair as he gestured at the street. "I tried to arrange ticker tape for your return, Cadenhead, but no soap— Meanwhile I have this little theory that the two of you could come back in here and get some work done."

"Hello, Wilson," I said, picking up the heavy suitcase. "How've you been?"

"Is Natalie Wood out here *singing?*" said Wilson, leaning his hands in the unheeded windowsill soot and squinting at Rachel's daughter in feigned confusion. "Are you Natalie Wood? Is this a doomed love thing?"

"Wilson, this is—" I began as Wilson darted back inside, perhaps a bit too quickly.

"I'll introduce you to him later," Rachel told Hildy as I crushed the cigarette against the railing, leaving a charred grey spot and sending flakes of ash sinking down through the cold air toward the early morning darkness of the street, and turned to follow Rachel and her daughter back inside the newsroom. My desk was as I'd left it, ten days before, its battered surface still hidden by debris—a mess of papers and floppy disks, the dormant ATEX terminal, marked-up Xerox copies of Tommy Hopkins' press releases from the previous month, the phone tap, the microcassettes, the tacked-up photograph of Annabelle, the notes from my three days' worth of frantic phone conversations, the newswire printouts announcing Ralph's death, several drafts and the page proof of my obituary notice, and a dog-eared index card diagonally inscribed with all my hard-won phone numbers.

"You said someone called me?" I asked Rachel as I draped my overcoat over the back of my chair and heaved the suitcase onto the desk.

"A couple people while you were outside. I wrote it down," Rachel said, handing me a pink phone slip. "What's with the suitcase, anyway?"

"That's what they're calling about," I said, looking down at the slip and frowning. "These are the wrong people. Damn it—" Consulting the battered index card on my desk, I picked up the phone receiver and dialed a number, blinking the burn from my eyes and watching Rachel and her daughter mill around between our desks while I waited for the call to go through.

"Good morning—Flash Models," said a young man's voice.

"Claire Plittman, please? It's Michael Cadenhead again," I said.

The young man wordlessly connected me to a recording of Madonna singing "Live to Tell," and I took the opportunity to sit down at my desk and sip experimentally from an hour-old Styrofoam cup of lukewarm coffee that tasted like motor oil. "You're Annabelle's friend," Plittman told me once she was on the line. "She said to expect your call— You're trying to get a hold of her today, right?"

"That's right," I said. "I left a message—"

"It's going to be difficult," said Plittman, audibly shuffling papers. "She's got a fitting this morning and an editorial spread this afternoon, and— She's pretty much booked solid through the week, actually, with an advertising series starting after the—"

"Octane Jeans?" I asked, staring up at the bright fluorescent lights that depended from the pressed-tin ceiling and watching the fans spin silently between them.

"That's not till next month," Plittman said briskly. "Are you in the business?"

"No."

"Then do you know"—Plittman was suddenly almost whispering—"*why* she's *doing* that Octane nonsense?"

"It's complicated," I said.

"Well, you're her *friend*—there's still time to talk her *out* of it," Plittman said. "I'm teasing you. Actually she's leaving the agency so it doesn't matter what she does—I'm going to miss mothering her."

"She's an interesting person," I said cordially, noticing that Wilson was threading his way toward me between the desks, devouring a glazed donut and carrying a torn-off sheet of newswire paper in his other hand.

"She was turning into a real cash machine for us," Plittman said. "Her look is money all the way—I think she would have made us a killing."

"You'll survive," I said, looking at my watch. "Thanks for your help."

"I think we might want to *call* the mayor's office," said Wilson without overture, arriving next to me and speaking with his mouth full as he held out the newswire paper, the harsh fluorescent light revealing several unnoticed smears of window soot on his yellow broadcloth shirt, "and get the word on this purported zoning deal, just to make sure that—"

"I did it," I said, hanging up the phone and pointing at the wire. "Before you came in—they wouldn't give me a statement but I think that they're worried that auctioning the subway renovation contract is going to have all those community boards up in arms."

"Hilarious city we live in," said Wilson thoughtfully—one of the overhead lights had begun flickering and buzzing. "Did you talk to Daniels?"

"Furillo—he gave me the usual phony squirrel tail." I saw both Rachel and her daughter watching me with interest and looked back at Wilson. "It'll be a complex story in the next few months but I think it'll be possible to simplify it on paper."

"A complex story simply told is a simple story badly told. Nice suit," Wilson mumbled, wolfing down most of the glazed donut as he looked at my cuffs. "What are you—Valentino?"

"I've got a funeral today," I said apprehensively. "Didn't Margot tell you? I left a—"

"Will the corpse be there?" Wilson asked, narrowing his eyes.

"What? No," I said. "What do you—"

"Then it's a memorial service, not a funeral. Read the AP Style Book," Wilson lectured expansively. "Precision in life—that's the ultimate smart thing. Listen, Michael, some joker named Holly Martins has been leaving messages for me—Do *you* know what that could be all about?"

"Today is Monday, November Third, 1986," I told him, reaching for my overcoat again. "In twenty-four hours the voters of this city will—"

"All right, all right," said Wilson, chewing on a mouthful of glazed donut. "But who the hell is Martins?"

"He's the flack at Reed Gardner Grant," I explained. "Tommy Hopkins is announcing his withdrawal this afternoon, um, and he's interested in setting up an exclusive interview—I said I couldn't do anything until I cleared it with you. Wilson, I'm sorry—I've got to go out," I said, stowing the pink phone slip in my pocket and looking at my watch with mild alarm.

"What— You just got here," Wilson said, spreading his hands in profound resignation. "What gives with you?"

"No, *you* just *got* here. Look, I just have a couple things to take care of—it shouldn't take long," I lied. "And if you put me on the transition I'll be your galley slave for the next two months, so—"

"I get tired of these jack-in-the box maneuvers," said Wilson. "But they certainly won't keep me from putting you on the transition if you think you can swing it."

"Good," I said, looking at him.

"So I take it you've learned something?" Wilson asked.

"What? I've learned to get my facts straight," I said, pulling on my coat and rubbing my eyes again.

"That's it?"

"Jesus, Wilson," I mumbled, yawning as I hefted the battered suitcase, "I don't know. I haven't slept—"

"Be like me," said Wilson, nodding. "You'll sleep."

"Wilson, this is my daughter," Rachel began, stepping forward suddenly. "Hildy's studying journalism at—"

"Pleased to meet you, pleased to meet you," Wilson chanted distractedly, waving regally at Rachel's daughter as he began to walk away, pointing at me without making eye contact. "Follow him around—he's the new generation. He'll tell you what you want to know."

• • •

AT ELEVEN-THIRTY that November morning I sat on a bench in Union Square Park beneath the paper-white overcast sky with my wool overcoat wrapped around me fruitlessly and the battered cordovan suitcase wedged between my feet, hands stuffed into my coat pockets, collar turned up, tapping my feet on the cold cement beneath the bench as I watched the sparrows that grazed across the heavy sky above the surrounding storefronts and buildings. "Jesus, it's *freezing,*" said Tina Foster in her flat voice, sitting next to me on the weather-beaten bench, huddled into her own odd-looking overcoat—green with large buttons, 1986 Retro-Cool, as she put it. "It isn't supposed to be this *cold,* is it, Mike? I mean this is ridiculous."

"Yeah, the weather's been funny," I said, looking around at the cars that were slowly lurching past, watching the crowds move along the sidewalk in front of the cars. "It's supposed to warm up later today."

"You sound pleased with yourself," said Tina, looking at me, the cool breeze catching some coppery strands of her flat hair and blowing them around her dark oval face.

"What? No"—I smiled shyly, pointing at my eyes—"it's just that it's dry weather, you know, and, um, my old contacts used to give me a hard time on days like this. Now, you know, nothing— I feel like I've got perfect vision."

"You've got time for this, don't you?" Tina looked at me with concern as I compulsively checked my watch, seeming mildly amused by my haste. "I'm sorry I couldn't meet you anywhere else."

"No—this is fine," I said apologetically. "I've got at least an hour—I'll just walk east"—I gestured around at Union Square and immediately regretted removing my hand from my warm pocket—"and then catch a cab uptown."

"So you've got the goods," Tina said, tipping her chin at the suitcase.

"That's right," I said, tapping my feet against the chill.

"Can I see?" Tina asked. "Can I take a look?"

"No," I said apologetically. "It's not really my place. Look, Tina." I pointed at the birds circling round the buildings, moving like a parade baton, and Tina leaned forward suddenly, like a whiplash victim, to check my wristwatch.

"You shouldn't be so nervous, Mike," said Tina, sitting back up and sighing theatrically. "I mean just show up—it doesn't matter, you know, how well you knew Ralph, how much you liked him."

"It's not that," I said, shaking my head gratefully. "It's seeing everyone together again, in formal clothes, you know, and having it be this."

"Do you remember graduation?" Tina asked after a moment.

"Yeah," I said, smiling. "That beautiful day."

"It was hot enough," said Tina flatly. "I had this itchy dress that was just wrong for a summer afternoon. I remember watching my parents walk around the Thorn, you know, and how bizarre it was. I remember Roberta hugging me. And all the flash cubes."

"Electric flash. It was all electric flash"—I smiled and felt the cold wind on my cheeks and teeth—"God, what a long time ago."

"Remember how Wally and Stephen and Charlie and Bill threw their caps in the air?" Tina smiled blandly. "Remember that?"

"Louise got hit in the face," I said, glancing at Tina. "Those ridiculous caps—the corner of a cap landed on her face. Right? Or I guess it was Amy."

"It was Amy," said Tina, squinting. "She had an ice pack all day. I left mine on the second staircase—I just sort of stupidly put it down—and I when went back to get the tassel—my Mom made me go back—there was this little kid standing there, this little girl in fourth grade or something, so I took the tassel and gave the cap to her. It might've been Jack's kid sister." Tina stared intently across the cold landscape of Union Square, breath fogging as she ran a hand through her flat hair. "I remember hoping Max would show up—I think the Tafts asked him to come. Or maybe it was just Douglas who asked him. You remember the state I was in at the ceremony? Annabelle and I?"

"It was just Douglas," I said. "Who asked him. Yeah, come to think of it, you were barely there—I remember noticing how *pale* you both looked, both of you with the pale skin and the Ray-Bans and how you stayed side by side through the speeches, um, and during the applause, and how— And how fast you left."

"We spent the morning at my house getting drunk," said Tina. "The phone kept ringing and Anna made me not answer 'cause she knew it was her family. I begged my dad to tell them Annabelle wasn't there. But I'll always remember that morning—the way I woke up and played the guitar before changing, delaying putting on the clothes I'd wear under that stupid gown, and when she arrived the doorman just let her come upstairs, Annabelle, just ushered her in, my dad in his suit, Mom changing, Mom coming in and talking to Anna, insisting on bringing her cough medicine but confused by scandal she couldn't see." Tina tightened her overcoat as she spoke. "And that was when Annabelle told me everything about the weekend, sitting at my house in our caps and gowns, and we made Irish coffee while we talked and it reminded me of the snow day, the day I was sick when everyone came over— You weren't there. I'm sorry."

"Poor Tina," I said, reaching to stroke her shoulder.

"And I haven't thought about all that stuff in so *long,*" said Tina, shaking her head. "It's funny. But it was like that night, warm air-conditioned summer instead of snow but the same feeling as we talked, without the crowd. I don't blame the babe for skipping this part when she talked to you—it's something about June nights, maybe, what gets said and what gets hidden. Of course she came to me," Tina said, leaning her head toward my hand for a moment's perfunctory gesture. "The ghost was gone and I had to whet her almost blunted purpose."

"Well, this is a gruesome twosome," said Max Gantry, shoes clicking on the pavement stones as he arrived, wearing a black coat, black hair tied back, somehow having managed to stay out of our line of sight until the last minute.

"Max!" said Tina as Max leaned to kiss her cheek, breath fogging out from both of them. "We didn't see you."

"I'm *always* sneaking around Union Square. Hey, Foster Girl," said Max, sitting down beside me on the park bench and gazing strangely at me. "Michael? You all right?"

"What do you mean, Max?" I asked, squinting at him as he stuck his mittened hands into his coat pocket and produced a pack of Marlboros and the brass lighter, tucking a cigarette into his unshaven face, and I leaned to shield the flame against the dry wind.

"Nothing—you look pretty refried is all. Wow—is this it?" Max asked, puffing the cigarette and glancing down at the suitcase. "Listen, is it true you're not coming?"

"Who told you that?" I asked—I had noticed that Max was wearing a dark suit under his overcoat. "I'm just all over the place today, that's all."

"I can't believe you've got it right there," Max said, his foot clapping against the suitcase.

"Here it is," I said, looking at him, stamping my feet against the cold.

"When did you realize you were going to make it?" Max asked. "I'm just curious."

"Around, um, around five this morning, actually," I told him, remembering how I had glanced wearily up from the typewriter toward the storm window to catch the first increment of grey dawn light, the oval desk-lamp reflection floating before me like a celestial object and superimposing my haggard face on the glass. "I just looked at the notes and there wasn't really anything left but the end—it reminded me of college."

"Do you guys know if Douglas is going to make the service?" asked Tina, looking over, squinting in the bright late-morning sun.

"Beats me," said Max, looking away.

"I've been trying to find him," I said, after shrugging. "Carol can't find him either."

"The woman who thinks she looks like Annabelle?" Tina was absently scratching her face as she spoke.

"She's got the hair," I argued.

"Without the face," Tina rejoined.

"So, Mike"—Max was indicating the suitcase again—"what happens now?"

I reached to accept one of Max's cigarettes, which he lit for me. "Do you want to just take it?" I asked.

"Your only copy? That's hardly fair," said Max, looking at me, his blunt but kind face focusing on mine.

"Well, I was thinking we could make some Xeroxes, but that'll be expensive," I muttered, stamping my feet again. "In the meantime you can take it and then I'll just pass it along to Douglas or to Annabelle, or— It's really up to the three of you," I added weakly, not bothering to make another point, because Tina and Max were looking at each other, both leaning forward on the battered park bench to look past me at each other, their expressions unreadable.

"So you surprised the hell out of me, Tina," Max said. "Five years of nothing and then today you call me up out of the blue—I never even thought you liked me."

"I liked you. I just kept my mouth shut," said Tina. "No, we all did. Right, Mike? Everyone likes Max—even the little kids."

"I'm not going to *touch* that one," said Max, gazing at Tina so as to gauge her mischievous smile.

"She's on to you," Tina told him.

"Uh-huh," Max said distantly, hunching forward with his hands in his overcoat pockets and looking away.

"Yeah, she found out a couple days ago," Tina said. "Annabelle Taft big as life on the phone. Woke me *up*—"

"Uh-huh, uh-huh," Max repeated as he rocked forward on the park bench, cigarette sticking out from his mouth FDR-style. "Woke you up, huh? Strange thing to do."

"Annabelle's a strange girl," said Tina. "Max— You really like her, don't you?"

"She's cool," said Max.

I was flicking my head back and forth, listening to this.

"Oh, come on," said Tina goadingly. "She's got a great body, doesn't she?"

"Well, yeah."

"Look, are you going to take this thing, or what?" I asked, kicking the suitcase toward Max. "Everything you said is here."

"I don't want it," Max said finally. "I'm sorry, Mike, but I don't think— Look, I think the four of us went a little nuts, you know, just a little off the beam last week, and you had to—"

"Max—" I began.

"I *know* what happened," Max said—he had looked suddenly at me, cigarette smoke drifting from his mouth as he spoke. "I knew five years ago, all right? Maybe it's not for me."

"Max, listen," said Tina. "There's going to be something at this club downtown this weekend, so if you want—" Max had grimaced comically, making us laugh. "No, it's a good place, and there's going to be dinner, 'cause there's this new Cajun place Raymond discovered, so if you want—"

"No thank you," Max said.

"But she's going," said Tina finally. "She'll be *there,* Max."

Max turned and gave an unexpected look to Tina—he had held the look in check, the way I'd seen him do, several times, during that weekend five years before, but this was an older Max, and the effect had matured—Max gave Tina a look that for a second was naked and pure, a simple picture of longing and hope.

"Why don't you just call her?" I said. "Stop this business."

"I've been calling her for weeks," said Max, embarrassed. "Look how that turned out."

"I mean *really* call her. Listen," said Tina—Max was already shaking his head—"listen, you don't know how she walks down streets with me. She looks at me when she's on the couch— You've never even been *down* there, Max, you're so missing out— And the—"

"It's true," I said. "It's a great couch. It's green."

"—way that— Shut up, Mike. The way her face changes, the way that her face can change—"

"And she oversleeps and she waters plants," Max said, still nodding. "*Everyone's* got detail."

"She must remember what you said," I told him while stepping out the cigarette against the yellow autumn leaves that littered the paving stones beneath the park bench.

"It's *true,*" said Max. "I dreamed her face. I always forget the— I can't picture her face right. No, really— I was always afraid I'd run into her on the street, you know, and wouldn't recognize her."

"She's a *model,*" said Tina. "*Everyone* knows her face."

"Yeah, that's my point," said Max. "Why I couldn't recognize her. But when Ralph died I had a dream about her, and I dreamed her face— In my dream I ran into her, in the dark, outside on the street somewhere, I just ran into her, and said her name, and she turned and I saw her face and there was no question about it."

"Call her," said Tina. "Call her right now."

"Tina," said Max, standing up, looking at his plastic digital watch, which he had to pry out from between his mittens and his suit jacket and overcoat cuffs, "you know, if I had my boots on I'd kick you across the earth."

"Just do it," said Tina.

"I don't think so," Max said, smiling kindly. "Thanks."

"You are so frustrating," Tina marveled.

"One was a beauty queen, the other was her friend," Max quoted as he stood before us. "I've got to go—I'll see you down there."

"You'll see *him,*" Tina said, tilting her head to indicate me. "I may not make it."

"All right," said Max, walking away into the Union Square crowd, black hair bobbing as he disappeared from view.

"It's just so nice to see that," said Tina after a moment.

"What do you mean?" I asked.

"Someone falling for someone," Tina said, pointing with her chin along the pathway that Max had taken out of the park. "But sometimes it can just be sad."

"You were so encouraging," I said, frowning.

"You have to encourage people," Tina said, tipping her head, smiling at me with the side of her mouth, the way she had always used to do. "You agree?"

"Yes."

"I've got something for you," said Tina, fishing in the pocket of her retro-cool overcoat and producing a thin envelope, which she handed to me—it was smooth and featureless except for the FLASH MODELS logotype in the return-address corner—and I looked at her as she brushed a strand of coppery hair away from her smooth forehead and shrugged her coat more firmly around her shoulders against the cold autumn wind.

AT ONE-THIRTY that November afternoon I emerged from a taxicab and walked along the white stone surfaces of an underpopulated and leaf-strewn residential block off Madison Avenue in the mid-seventies, my suitcase continuing to thump against my legs as I approached the sandstone flanks of a postwar apartment building, stepping down toward a small subsidiary door that was cut deep into the building at just below ground level, like a mine entrance. A smooth brass plaque confirmed my location, and I pressed a doorbell and was electrically admitted to a plain, unoccupied waiting room, where I hung my overcoat on a hotel-style theft-proof hanger and then gratefully collapsed into a soothing green couch and picked through a stack of dog-eared magazines from the previous year, wondering how long I could sit on the couch and keep from falling asleep. After a moment the rightmost door opened and a tall, rotund, and greying man stood framed in its aperture, fluorescent light accenting his precisely cut short cream-colored sideburns and steel-framed lozenge-lensed bifocals, several moles and fine wrinkles visible on his kind, putty-colored face, wearing a dark suit and humble button-down shirt, his yellow paisley necktie affording meager distraction from his sharp gray eyes—as the man stepped toward me I clumsily rose to my feet, transfixed by his eyes, and nearly knocked over the cordovan suitcase.

"Young Mr. Cadenhead," Dr. Karl Pershing sighed conclusively in his guttural, accented voice. "Please come in." Having shaken his hand, I followed Pershing past the other office door, which according to the brass plaque outside belonged to somebody named William

Hays, and into a dim, cluttered office, where I stepped softly behind the doctor toward a pair of leather armchairs that stood before a gigantic cluttered oak desk supporting an elaborate microcassette recording system and a brass desk lamp with a green frosted-glass shade. The lamp was turned off. I squinted around at the room, dust motes dancing in the weak light that filtered through the thick-slatted Venetian blinds, seeing stacks of heavy books, vacant flower-pots, framed pictures skewed round the carpeted floor at random, and several unidentifiable shrouded shapes surrounding us—blocks of heavy furniture, evidently—draped in furling white cloth like scenery for a modern dance.

"I see you received my message," Pershing began awkwardly, plucking his trousers as he crouched precariously above his leather chair, waiting for me to sit, and as I watched him sink ponderously into the chair I heard the sounds of traffic and the laughter and muted speech of passersby beyond the windows, identical to the sounds on Douglas' recording.

"Yes," I said a bit too loudly, loosening my necktie. "I'm sorry I wasn't able to answer you when you called the newspaper. I've been—"

"I have a patient arriving in twenty minutes or thereabouts," Pershing murmured, plucking a facial tissue from a box on the floor and beginning to clean his glasses, which flashed dimly in the grey horizontal light. "If you feel this time together is insufficient we may arrange another meeting."

"I hope that won't be necessary," I assured him, blinking in the darkness and looking around at all the cloth-shrouded furniture.

"The office is about to be painted," Pershing explained, following my gaze.

"It's a busy day for me too," I said.

"Your classmate is dead," Pershing said colorlessly.

"Well, yes."

"I was not expecting Douglas to contact me," Pershing mumbled, carefully replacing his glasses, "but last week—Friday or Saturday—I received a rather terse phone call from him concerning you, the substance of which placed me in a somewhat peculiar position."

"It must have been strange," I said noncommittally.

"I was already in quite a predicament, as I attempted to explain when we spoke on the phone last month." As Pershing talked my eye was drawn to a Victorian mahogany claw foot which protruded from beneath a white drop-cloth hem onto the carpet at the edge of my vision—as the meeting continued I found that for some reason I was incapable of keeping my eyes from the claw foot and I spent several minutes trying to identify the shrouded item of furniture that it belonged to. "You see, Mr. Cadenhead, following our final session I was legally constrained from communicating with Douglas in any way."

"And why is that?"

"Because I am merely a therapist," Pershing grated, "and as such I cannot interact with a patient once that patient has attempted to end his or her own life."

"You couldn't have explained that to me on the phone?" I asked, my voice betraying mild frustration. "When I called you and you said it was a matter of law?"

"Merely broaching the subject with another person is forbidden," Pershing explained.

"That makes us all parishioners," I realized.

"It would if I were a priest," Pershing said mildly, "but there is a difference between faith and law—as a journalist you must understand. Douglas' case was a cause of great frustration for me, since I am not— I should explain provisionally that I am not accustomed to having therapy abruptly terminated without notice in the middle of a"—here Pershing gestured for the first time, moving his hand in an arc as if sidearming a softball in reverse—"period of treatment."

"But you've done it once before," I said, suppressing a yawn. I had decided that the protruding claw foot belonged either to a corner cupboard or to a *tête-à-tête* couch but the shrouded silhouette beneath the drop cloth supported neither theory. "With Annabelle."

"Did she tell you that?" Pershing asked. "Discontinuing Annabelle's therapy was a mutually agreed-upon decision."

"All right," I said. "Look— Do you know what I've done?"

"I know that you have done something very dangerous," Pershing said. "Something potentially quite harmful that I would have quite urgently warned you not to do, had I known of it in advance."

"Well"—I grinned at him—"I tried to contact you."

"Have you completed the manuscript?"

"This morning," I said, indicating the suitcase. "It's right here."

"I see," said Pershing, arching his neck so as to squint through the bottoms of his bifocals at the suitcase. "It is partially based on the notebook diary that I directed Douglas to complete?"

"Which you never saw. Yes," I said, reaching to open the suitcase, feeling its ancient brass latches giving way as I pulled out the thick stack of purloined newspaper printout paper on which I'd typed the story of graduation weekend, my fingers catching on the "jumbo"-sized rubber bands that I'd wrapped round it as I held it toward Pershing. "But only initially. The bulk of the text is directly based on the interviews I did last week."

"Interviews," Pershing echoed, reaching to accept the block of paper and almost dropping its unexpected weight, "with Douglas and with Annabelle?"

"And with someone else—a friend named Max Gantry, whom I spoke to the first two nights."

"Ah," said Pershing, flipping loudly through the typewritten pages without removing the rubber bands. "Max Gantry."

"We agreed I should start with him," I explained, covertly checking my wristwatch as Pershing peered at my typing. "I mean, I shouldn't say we *agreed*, since there were never more than two people, me and someone else, um, in the same room together, but— I got everyone's consent individually and spent two nights with each of them, and then, um, then it took me four days and nights pretty much straight through in order to collate the—"

"Douglas has explained," Pershing said, looking at the manuscript.

"Did he explain how he stayed at— How he didn't leave his house or speak to anyone for more than a week?" I asked. "Did he explain the sutures or the broken door?"

"He did not," Pershing sighed, reaching for a battered business envelope that had been resting atop his cluttered desk and holding it toward me, "nor did he explain the meaning of this particular document."

I took the envelope and looked it over—Pershing's office address was scrawled in a familiar script, the stamp's cancellation date was 22 OCT, and there was no return address. "The day Ralph died," I said, opening the envelope and extracting a single sheet of thin lined paper with a jagged vertical tear along its left edge and a single ballpoint inscription:

She lay caressed by the twilight wind, unfurled in slumber, and when she stirred, shining in the moonlight, he yearned for her and made to speak, but with a kiss she silenced him, teaching of love amid the sweet grace of a darkling hour. So he found her, and as her face strained toward heaven the night was outside the world, for with her silken touch he entered a dream of beauty, and with her breath upon his lips he was blind with redemption. Thus he learned of peace in her clasping hands and beheld a realm of light, an enduring truth to surpass the ravages of time.

—GIUSEPPE BONOMI
The Story of Jake Hackett (1935)

"Can you explain what it means?" Pershing asked after a moment.

"It's the last page of Douglas' notebook," I told him, refolding the thin sheet and returning it to the envelope. "He tore it out."

"I confess that I have never understood the significance of the *Jake Hackett* novel," Pershing mumbled, his eyes reflecting the room's weak light as he spoke.

"Annabelle loved it all her life," I said. "I'm sure she told you about that."

"But that was simply a paternal sexual fixation transferred onto the author," Pershing said absently, "whereas Douglas has always acknowledged the book's dubious value. Why did his thinking change?"

"Well, that's not really a very difficult question. I'm sorry," I said, after mustering my courage, "but may I use your phone?"

"Certainly," mumbled Pershing, limply waving his arm toward his ornate, leather-inlaid desk. I was tired enough that my head spun as I stood and my vision greyed out for the moment that it took me to cross the obviously genuine Persian carpet and reach Pershing's complex-looking digital phone—I dialed by dim lamplight, waited through the rings at the Lineage Institute switchboard and then quietly asked the siren-voiced operator to connect me to Carol Casey.

"Michael?" Carol said without overture. "Have you found him?"

"No," I said, sighing with my barely concealed disappointment. "Not at home, not anywhere—I was hoping he'd, you know, shown up there."

"He has not," said Carol over the sound of distant typewriters clicking quietly, like a battle heard from a great distance. "The important thing is that I've been arguing his case with the board of directors and they're not entirely unsympathetic."

"Really?" I said. "They're still willing to take him back?"

"It's possible," Carol said, "provided it's reasonably soon—like he should talk to them today or tomorrow. Look, I thought you told me he was— That he had confronted his— That you'd seen him. That he would finish this thing with you by today, and then he'd be—"

"I've seen him," I said, spinning Pershing's expensive-looking desk scissors on their screw point. "Maybe I was wrong. Maybe he's changed his mind. I'm so tired—"

"What am I supposed to do?" Carol asked. "How am I supposed to reach him?"

"Christ, I don't know," I said. "I've put all this— I've been thinking about this damn day for so many hours, I don't— I'm sorry, Carol, but I don't really know what to say. Wait—you know about the funeral, right? The memorial service?"

"Several of us are going," Carol said. "From the Institute—several of the people, you know, the ones who deal with Frank. This is a busy day, Michael, so I might not be here—did I give you my beeper number?"

"If I find him I'll track you down," I said. "Look, even if Douglas doesn't show up for the service this guy named Max Gantry will be there, um, and he might know something about Douglas' whereabouts. Although by the time—"

"What's he look like?" Carol asked.

"Good-looking guy, roughly our age, long black hair, probably unshaven, disfigured hands."

"Stop it, you private eye. Max Gantry," Carol reflected as she audibly took notes. "Sounds like a bum steer—will you introduce us?"

"If I make it there in time." I had nervously glanced over at Pershing as I was speaking and seen that he was poring over the manuscript, flipping covertly through the white pages and tapping his foot in the air before him with a pianist's precise rhythm. "Listen, Carol, this isn't my phone, so—"

"All right," Carol said. "The day goes on. We'll talk again."

"Good luck," I said involuntarily.

"Good luck," Carol echoed before hanging up.

"You have certainly done a tremendous amount of work," Pershing said immediately. As I turned back toward my chair I saw that he was straining to hold the heavy manuscript toward me, and I accepted it in passing as it began to sink through the air in his weak grasp. "Did Douglas' notebook ever explain about the intervening years?"

"Without much detail," I answered, sitting back down and finding myself once again mesmerized by the concealed item of furniture. "He wrote about that summer, um, about the time he spent working for Senator Rollins, and about going— About how he and Annabelle left for Harvard in the fall."

"I met Annabelle Taft in December of 1983," Pershing said, the muscles of his smooth, sagging face relaxing by degrees, "following her aborted sophomore year. It was only in our final session nearly a year later that I discovered almost by accident that she had managed to avoid all contact with her younger brother for three years—she refused all my invitations that she speak about him or about her past, destroyed her notebook diary, and the following week failed to appear. Several weeks later I received a telegram from Milan informing me that she no longer wished to continue treatment, and shortly thereafter I was fully compensated for my services by means of payment transferred from an overseas bank."

"Did her telegram say anything else?" I asked.

"There was a brief apologetic message," Pershing said almost inaudibly, adjusting his glasses, "but I have forgotten it."

"And then?"

"In 1985—the following year—Annabelle wrote to inform me that she had returned to New York for business reasons and explained that she had contacted her brother."

"Really?"

"I will have to take my leave of you in a few minutes," Pershing said as he glanced at a Roman-numeral clock on the desk. "By that time Douglas had taken his degree and begun his employment at the Lineage Institute, procuring a rental apartment and subsequently withdrawing from any interaction with his family save for the financial support that he still received from his father, and it was by means of these transactions that Annabelle relayed her messages. Her letter explained that— Annabelle felt that she had failed in her obligation to reveal the facts of her life to me, and for that she was very remorseful, but she allowed as how I had presumably come to know her well enough that I might understand her reasons. She went on to say"—a buzzer sounded from somewhere in the room, and Pershing grunted and leaned to press a black button mounted on a small wooden base that I'd failed to notice—"she went on to say that she hoped to persuade Douglas to make amends by speaking in her place—she had enclosed a check for a very large sum with which she intended to finance Douglas' therapy."

"Did you ever see her again?"

"No," Pershing continued, clearing his throat, "but shortly thereafter Douglas availed himself of my services—his therapy began slightly less than a year ago today. Annabelle telephoned me on one occasion several months ago but it was simply a logistical matter—she had considered attending Harvard's 350th Anniversary Celebration and she wished to know if Douglas had similar plans, in which case she intended to cancel her own."

I had returned the manuscript to the suitcase as Pershing spoke, and I leaned to close its clasps and then looked up at him. "You told him not to go to the fund-raiser that night," I said. "That's what you were talking about on the tape. He'd told you about Carol?"

"He had," Pershing said. "R. D. Laing instructs us that while refusing to acknowledge one's difficulties itself becomes a difficulty, it need not become the principal difficulty—in *Knots* he proceeds to show that the idea of being good and the idea of being loved are as connected as the necessity of forfeiting another's respect allows. You have heard the final session, during which I cautioned Douglas concerning his amorous intentions—the young woman clearly had designs on him."

"That's right—I heard the tape, but I couldn't figure out what you meant about 'reactive denial.' Now I can." I was looking again at the draped furniture with the claw foot—its curving organic shape was completely baffling, and I concluded that it was definitely not an antique gun rack or a rolltop desk or a hobbyhorse or a musical instrument.

"I do not understand your role," Pershing said suddenly. "I confess that your behavior completely baffles me."

I had heard the street door opening when Pershing, prompted by the buzzer, had pressed his electric switch, and as he stopped speaking I clearly noticed the sounds of someone outside in the waiting room turning the pages of a magazine. "I can't explain," I said helplessly. "Not now. I actually thought *you* might understand, but—"

"Why have you done all of these things?"

"Because we're not all parishioners," I said, blinking with dazed fatigue.

"I beg your pardon?"

"Because the battleground is gone," I continued, but as I trailed off Pershing glanced past me at the desk clock and then stood up, and I stood as well, picking up the suitcase and rubbing my eyes, which had fully adjusted to the darkness of the room, and checking my watch again, transferring the heavy suitcase to my other hand to do so.

"Would you like to come and see me?" Pershing asked, looking at me, and I avoided his gaze by peering past him toward the blinded windows, where I'd heard the growing metallic roar of a passing motorcycle.

"I can't afford it," I answered finally.

"My fees are actually quite reasonable," Pershing said while leading me toward the office door. "I tend not to like the doctors who—"

"I mean I can't afford it," I said.

Pershing opened the office door and waved apologetically at a mildly obese young woman in a dark overcoat who sat in the waiting room, and as I stepped to retrieve my overcoat I heard the motorcycle's roar as it approached the sidewalk directly in front of the building, where its engine was cut. "I am sorry that my time is limited," Pershing told me as the woman closed the magazine she'd been reading and stood to meet him.

"Dr. Pershing," I said suddenly, turning to face him and pointing at the claw-footed object under the white cloth, "What's that piece of furniture?"

"A spinning wheel," Pershing told me, smiling.

AT TWO O'CLOCK that November afternoon Max Gantry arrived at Tom Allen's, the Lower East Side bar, noticing the midafternoon underpopulation as he located Nick Blanchard at a small table near the back, behind the pool tables, dressed in oversized black flannel pants and a white T-shirt and black scarf. Nick picked up his camera and overcoat and came forward, clapping Max on the shoulder with an odd, brusque awkwardness and then joining him at the bar.

"Hey, buddy," said Nick, smiling in the way that Max remembered, stubbled cheeks and arching eyebrows emphasized by the sunglasses as he beckoned to Barry, the bartender. "How you doing? It's been years and years."

"Hey," said Max, removing his overcoat and draping it over the next barstool as Barry moved to stand before them, red hair freshly combed, a sour expectant look on his pockmarked face.

"Stendhal," Nick told Barry, who nodded and looked over at Max.

"Um—Johnnie Walker," Max said.

"Red or Black?" asked Barry.

"Take both," Nick advised quietly.

"Okay," said Max.

"Two Stendhals," Barry announced, moving away.

"How you bearing up, man?" Nick asked more quietly, turning back toward Max and clapping his shoulder again. "Seeing you reminds me of the old days."

"I'm all right," Max said over the loud clinking of the shot glasses.

"So you're working, right?" Nick asked. "What's that job of yours?"

"Advertising graphics," said Max. "I get so tired of everyone's moronic fantasies."

"Uh huh," Nick said, tilting his head. "Who are your *friends,* Max?"

"Oh, come on, man," Max said, chuckling slightly. "What is this?"

"I'm sorry, I'm just— I guess I'm confused," Nick said, gazing forward. Barry returned with their four shot glasses, deliberately placing them on the bar as if demonstrating a chess deal, and Max and Nick raised glasses in tandem and knocked them back. "Man, why'd it have to be DiGrassi?" Nick asked the ceiling after swallowing.

"That's the question," Max wheezed, returning the shot glass to the bar. "That's the hammer."

"I couldn't believe it when I found out he was gone," Nick reflected, shaking his head and staring at the empty glass in his fingers. "I mean I'd just gotten off the train, right, I'm standing in the station and there's Cadenhead with the news."

"Yeah, thanks to Mike," said Max, pulling his second glass forward.

"It makes it"—Nick mimicked his motion—"so much *harder.* That it was Ralph, I mean," said Nick, looking to Max for the cue, and after a moment Nick and Max both took their second shot. "Feel the difference?" Nick said, smiling slightly.

"*Oh,* yeah," Max gasped, shuddering as he returned the empty glass to the bar.

"Red—and—*Black,*" Nick emphasized. "Listen, I shouldn't be there, man."

"I thought you'd say that. Look," said Max, "it's your choice but I would go."

"It's just hard," said Nick.

"Talk about it."

"Talk about it," Nick echoed weakly. "I'll drink to that. I mean I realize"— Nick had placed his camera on the oaken surface of the bar and he tapped his fingers against it—"that I'm the guy that threw him out of that party and all that. I realize all that."

"Nick, no one's going to *blame* you for anything," said Max, looking at the glasses on the bar and hearing the mild clicking sounds of the pool balls colliding in the nearby darkness. "You might as well come."

"Yeah— Listen, have you gotten in touch with what's-his-name? With Douglas? I mean you guys used to be so tight, and I haven't—"

"We talked last week," said Max, ponytail bobbing as he reached to pull cigarettes and his lighter from the breast pocket of his black suit. "Actually, it's funny, 'cause we've got Mike to thank for that. After I'd finished he called Douglas, and— What's wrong?"

"It's driving me batshit," Nick said as Max ignited the lighter. "Suddenly Mike's doing this goddamned thing and nobody's calling me. Listen"—Nick had leaned forward as Max lit his cigarette and was now almost whispering—"listen, is it true? Did Mike really fucking *tape you talking?* The three of you? And write a little, you know, write down a little story about the past?"

"Yeah," Max said, staring through the blue cloud of near-motionless smoke that hung before the brilliant front window. "He finished it this morning. He's"—Max made a sound like a sob as he laughed, choking a bit on the scotch—"he's carrying it around."

"Really? You're kidding," said Nick, grinning carnivorously. "What's it look like, anyway?"

"A suitcase full of paper," Max told him.

"Damn that little guy anyway. So listen, man, my question is, could I *see* this famous thing? Could I, you know, if I asked him, would he show it to me?"

"What—you want *my* permission? Sure," Max said, staring inexpressively at Nick. "Except maybe you'd better not."

"Squeamish, huh?" Nick said wisely. "I got a model in Montana like that—she'll open the clothes but I can't watch. So Cadenhead did it. That screwball—"

"What are you— Mad at him?" asked Max.

Nick tipped his chin forward, grinning in his way that made his cheekbones protrude below his sunglasses. "Mike is Mike," he said, shrugging. "I just think you should stay tight with Douglas, you know, 'cause he's a good kid."

Max frowned down at his necktie, brushing away a stray droplet of scotch that shone like a glass lens. "Why'd you want to meet me, Nick?" he asked, and right then a song began playing over the bar speakers, presumably from some patron's jukebox selection— "The First Time Ever I Saw Your Face."

"You know," Nick said eventually, "I *met* that guy Raymond once."

"Really?" Max said, drawing on the cigarette.

"Yeah, last summer," Nick said, momentarily ducking his head as if clearing an overpass. "Down at Annabelle's house—I'd stuck around, you know, in the afternoon, and he showed up early." Nick winced and then cocked his head to look askance at Max.

"All right," Max said, nodding and looking away. "So what's he like?"

"What? Oh, very nice, very nice," Nick said, grinning. "Hey, Barry, hit us again, would you? Max?"

"Sure."

"Two more." Nick held fingers up. "Yeah, Raymond— He's got the usual tricks to hide how slow his mind works. Very expensive suit. Very *fast*-moving son of a bitch, that guy—thinning hair, meek but just darted in the door. Beautiful old-world *composure* this guy has, don't you know."

"He's seventy-eight, right?" said Max, watching Barry prepare the drinks.

"He's forty-five spinning at thirty three." Nick grinned privately. "So he's there, Annabelle brightens—*you* know—and he glides in, kiss on the cheek, 'Hello, Peach,' and very soon I'm leaving."

"Look, she's never been stupid," said Max, laughing humorlessly and gulping down one of his new drinks, ignoring the bartender's glance at his disfigured hands. "I'm sure this guy was all right."

"I get the feeling he may be back in the picture," Nick added in his sandy voice, pushing his camera along the bar with a finger.

"Really?" Max said, reaching for his remaining drink. "But I thought you hadn't seen her since months ago—since way before your trip."

"Yeah," Nick said, looking at Max. "But I get the feeling."

Max squinted at Nick, weak afternoon light shining on his pulled-back hair. "Look— So *what,* man," he said, gulping scotch and gasping. "You're wasting your time telling me."

"That sounded good—nice and sincere," said Nick, tossing a shot back.

"Nick"—Max ducked his head as if in exasperation—"what are you *basing* this on, anyway?"

"Oh, you're *real* mysterious," Nick said. "Mike said he *knew* who was calling her—I just narrowed it down, that's all. You want to keep telling me how nice Raymond is?"

The pool game continued in the dark shadows beyond the front room and the quiet clicking and thumping of the billiard balls somehow emphasized the song's rhythm.

"All right," Max said after a moment. "I should have known when you called. I haven't— Look, last month I *saw* her, all right? I was just minding my own business, you know, getting lunch, and there she was at the, you know, at the farmers' market. So, like, I was *terrified*— I stood on the sidewalk and looked at her, made sure it was her, you know, and then I just left before she noticed, but it *killed* me, Nick—I was so ashamed. I mean, who am I kidding? I've just got to face the fact that it's been five years. I don't even know— I don't even know what she's, what she's like any more."

"You'll run into her again," Nick murmured, tapping his fingers on the camera. "Give me all this business of liking pain and shit but I'm telling you it could happen any day and with her you got to watch *out*—you may have your whole world in order but she's there five minutes and you'd do anything."

"Speak for yourself," said Max.

"Just be careful," Nick said earnestly. "That's all I wanted to say."

"But you don't understand," said Max, lighting another cigarette and looking away. "I wish I could just, just *show* you the look on Annabelle's face this one time at the museum— It was during an eighth-grade trip to see the Caravaggios and it was the last time I saw her before I left for Choate."

"Max," said Nick, his voice changing as he signaled Barry for the tab, "all right. You're talking to me, I already know. Just make up your mind"—he leaned forward—"make up your mind, Max, 'cause you've got a *choice,* right? I mean, you've *got* the choice. You can have her in your head all your *life,* if that's what you *want.*"

" 'You should do what I would do if I were you'—that's an old song," Max said, firmly shaking his head as if dazed by the scotch. "Really—I'm fine, Nick."

"So prove me wrong," Nick said. "You know how."

"You're not worth it," said Max, smiling as he returned Nick's close stare.

"All right," Nick said intently from behind the reflections of the bar lights in his sunglasses. "But this is it, man—Last Exit Before Toll."

"God *damn* you," said Max, standing to fish his wallet from his back pocket.

"You better get up there," said Nick, looking at his new watch and then gazing up at Max. "Drinks are on me, buddy."

"Thanks, Nick," Max said sincerely, picking up his overcoat and turning to go.

AT JUST AFTER two that November afternoon I stood in the bleak and bright overcast cold outside Dr. Pershing's deep-cut door facing the motorcyclist that I'd heard approach the office—Hector Costanza sat astride a tremendous axle-driven 1200-cc Harley-Davidson that he'd parked at an ostentatious angle across the orange and yellow fallen leaves covering the mica-flecked sidewalk directly before me, his arms crossed and his unshaven face puckered as he bit his cheeks and stared at me through gold-and-black-framed mirrored Cazals while audibly tapping his chamois-gloved fingers against the dark leather lapels of a familiar-looking bomber jacket, his orange helmet before him on the gleaming gas tank, his black jeans pulled tightly over worn steel-toed boots, his white T-shirt protruding like a bird's breast between the brass zippers and shining in the cold and humid air. "Hey, man," Hector said in his pleasant Bronx accent. "You coming with me or what?"

"I guess I am," I answered, squinting in the glare and hefting the cordovan suitcase. "Don't I know that jacket from somewhere?"

"This?" Hector raised his eyebrows, extending his arms as if about to take flight so as to admire the jacket's cracked sleeves. "Could be—a babe I met recently, this jacket belonged to her a long time ago."

"That's what I thought," I said, stepping forward and accepting Hector's hand, fumbling for the proper handshake. "Listen, are we in a rush? I've got this suitcase."

"No sweat," Hector said, twisting to indicate the chromium-steel luggage rack over the 'cycle's back fender. "But we don't got all day—secure that shit and we can roll."

"What's this?" I said, indicating Hector's new eyeglasses while adjusting my overcoat more tightly around my shoulders against the November chill. "You decided you're ready to die for your eyeglasses?"

"Not in this wealthy area, man," Hector said, grinning. "How you going? I haven't seen you since that night we played pool downtown."

"I'm fine," I said, wrenching the heavy suitcase onto the luggage rack, where Hector and I secured it by means of a series of green bungee cords. "How about you?"

"Chick trouble," Hector said, feigning a sinus problem. "I got this girl, I say to her listen, I don't have looks but I've got integrity so call me when you're tired of crying."

"Maybe she's not tired," I said, attempting to be witty.

"That's dope. Treat her like a prostitute, man," said Hector, nodding wisely and adjusting his Cazals as I awkwardly climbed onto the saddle behind him. "I'm just playing with you."

"New love in your life?" I said almost into Hector's ear, my view of the quiet residential street half obscured by Hector's dark hair as I gingerly wrapped my arms around his waist from behind. "What's she like?"

"Like the rest—she'll drink the water but you got to lead her to the well. You look like shit, man." Hector had turned to smirk back at me, igniting the motorcycle engine as I adjusted my overcoat, tucking it above the fender so as to keep it from harm.

"I'm very tired," I told him.

"You *must* be wiped, man, you look like Syd Barrett on a good day. Here"— Hector handed me the helmet—"you got to wear protection when we do this."

"Nothing personal," I agreed, wedging the bulky padded helmet over my head and adjusting the straps beneath my chin. "I can't even keep *straight* how long I've been awake anymore. It's been night after night—" Hector had pulled out into the meager traffic and I raised my voice over the motorcycle's roar as we sped east, the loud wind and rattling motion deafening and shaking me.

"I met DiGrassi once," Hector shouted as we swerved loudly around the corner onto Park Avenue, merging with the roaring southbound traffic that rolled between the high canyon walls of apartment buildings, racing past dark residential awnings and yellow-leaved trees. "With Nick— He seemed like a nice guy."

"That's not what you said last time," I shouted back, the helmet sliding around on my head—it was my first time on a motorcycle and I was terrified by the freezing wind and the top-heavy swerving motion and the cars, mostly taxicabs and luxury sedans, that boxed us in, rushing past inches from my splayed knees.

"*What?*" Hector twisted his head toward me, swerving the motorcycle, which bobbed back upright as he sped through a yellow light—I caught a sideways glimpse of angry flinching pedestrians and advancing delivery trucks—and then coasted to a stop at the next intersection between a child-filled station wagon and a silver cylindrical oil truck.

"Would you pay attention?" I said fearfully in the sudden quiet, tightening my slipping grip around Hector's waist, sleeves slipping on the smooth leather of Annabelle's jacket.

"Just hang on," Hector responded, gunning the engine as the signal changed and surging forward while more sluggish vehicles fell behind. We had a run of green lights, seven in a row that shone in a diminishing chain before us, glowing against the hoods of distant cars—over Hector's alternate shoulders I could see the distant gilded battlements of the Helmsley and Pan Am buildings standing against the sky, windows winking like scattered sugar as we approached, and as we suddenly pounded across a series of thick steel plates that had been placed to cover street repairs, rattling my teeth together with their impact on the tires, I glanced backward at my suitcase and made sure that it was still securely lashed against the luggage rack.

"You're going to get a *ticket,*" I shouted toward Hector's ear, but the wind pulled my words away before he heard them. Now the buildings were larger and taller—as we continued south between the corporate battlements I watched the Ritz Tower and the Seagram Building and Saint Bartholomew's Church and the Waldorf Astoria course past behind the flowing foliage and flower beds in the traffic islands, crowds of people striding across the sculpture-strewn marble courts and fountained mesas that fronted the skyscrapers, the motorcycle's fleeting reflection flowing like water across acres of plate glass. We nosed forward into the irregular sea of occupied yellow taxicabs that resolutely drifted toward the growing obelisk of the Pan Am Building like lemmings, approaching the stone-sided traffic inlets that gave into the dark stone portals puncturing the Helmsley Building and rattling over the steel plates in the street, my grip on Hector instinctively tightening as the motorcycle cleared the stone archway and sped into the the tunnel's loud yellow-lit darkness, rushing forward along the congested asphalt ramps and soon swerving both directions through horizontal daylight past vertical views of Vanderbilt Avenue's traffic far below—Hector yelled something incomprehensible as we passed the Yale Club, where from our flying second-story vantage point I looked through oversized French windows into a clean well-lighted place where men in mandatory ties and women in twill suits stood in mahogany lamplight as we sped across the top of Grand Central Station, rounding the corner where Nick had abandoned me and turning once more before crossing the cast-iron bridge spanning Forty-second Street and then descending another ramp onto Park Avenue South, and as Hector ran a red light while turning east I checked the suitcase again and continued holding on, watching the passing buildings as we joined Forty-second Street near the base of the Chrysler Building and continued east past the Automat and the Daily News Building and the Ford Foundation and finally skirted the south edge of the United Nations, speeding up the roadway past Hammarskjöld Library and south onto the FDR Drive's approach ramp, merging into the heavy traffic that skirted Manhattan's edge, and I gazed out across the sparkling river at the tugboats and barges and the surface of the sky.

Later I would dream of how it had happened, my dreams as precise as their inaccuracy allows—I remember the tremendous view that I enjoyed on the last of those late-autumn days as we sped along the river's edge, the view of the water beyond the slipstream of passing cars, the passing grass-green signs for off-ramps and inroads florid with extravagant graffiti tags with their edges as sharp against the cold grey sky as razor-cut flower stems and the wind that whistled beneath the edges of the helmet that I wore and sang between my ears and the helmet's padding like flute music. Soon we'd passed Williamsburg Bridge and rounded Manhattan's southeast curve and as the tremendous mass of solemn towers around Wall Street and Battery Park were finally visible far in the distance occluding the horizon like a mountain range I might have heard the sound of singing and realized that Hector was lost, overcome by the sensations of the motorcycle's journey as he signaled to change to the inside lane, and I might, in those few seconds, have had the cleverness necessary to realize that my presence had created a blind spot in the rearview mirror, had the wisdom to look for the source of the sound before the gypsy cab sped out from behind my shoulder and roared past us at tremendous speed with its braked wheels screaming on the asphalt and its horn blaring as it plummeted past inches away, causing Hector to squeeze one brake and heel-toe the other and nearly send us spinning through the air to crash against the highway's low concrete embankment but expertly managing to control the swerve, slowing further and tipping us far to the left so as to actually scrape against the embankment in his successful effort to keep the motorcycle upright. I suppose that my breath stopped in that moment or that my heart became arrhythmic or that I suffered whatever individual symptoms account for that particular loss of sequential perception, and before I recovered I grabbed Hector like a drowning man and lost contact with the motorcycle, swinging forward into the air and falling back as Hector righted our course, gunning the engine and guiding us forward out of the slow-motion traffic pocket we'd created and back up to speed. My breath returned and I heard my own voice calling out, saw Hector's head bob like an apple before my view of the grey afternoon sky, saw the yellow-stickered gypsy cab pulling ahead in the distant traffic, already on the far side of five consecutive cars, and some instinct made me twist backward, my heart laboring in my throat, and look down over my shoulder to see that my ancient, beloved cordovan suitcase had been destroyed—the oil-stained bungee cords had been plucked downward off of the luggage rack and scraped clear, nearly breaking, and the suitcase's clasps and hinges had snapped like matchsticks so that the suitcase now hung upside-down across the rear fender like a tent flap, handle resting serenely against the chrome exhaust pipe, completely empty—and I stared fruitlessly back along the traffic, the shaking helmet and automotive fumes obscuring my vision as I managed to catch a final glimpse of the unfurled ribbon of computer paper streaming across the sky and of one or two torn leaves of white paper floating in the air near the low steel embankment and settling by the highway's edge in the receding distance. My grip on Hector tightened as he thumbed the turn signal and began approaching an exit into Manhattan, and as I turned to face forward again I found that I was shaking with a cold emotion that felt like rage but was only fury's flush of tainted blood, containing no anger, presenting little reason to move or cause to destroy.

"What an *asshole!*" Hector was shouting incredulously, becoming audible as we turned onto an escape ramp that curved down and away and split in half so as to flank the ancient stone foundation of the Brooklyn Bridge, bringing us back to ground level. "You okay, man? Hope that didn't scare—"

"I lost my *package!*" I yelled furiously. "You son of a bitch—"

"What happened? What?" Hector called back maddeningly. "Are you okay, or what?"

"Look, stop the bike, will you?" I yelled more quietly, embarrassed by my rage. "Can we—"

"Almost there, man," Hector shouted, slowing down as we approached an intersection. "Did you *see* that fuckhead? How he cut me *off?* Fucking Arabs, man, can't do a goddamned thing right—" We had begun threading our way through a confusing snarl of subsidiary streets leading us along Chinatown's edge, past outdoor produce markets, warehouses, and pedestrians who glanced at our passage, and taking us by means of this roundabout path into the north end of Foley Square. It was close to two-thirty in the afternoon when we arrived there, sprinting loudly between the automobiles and the narrow sidewalks toward the island of asphalt and orange- and green-leaved trees before the New York County Court House, and after I'd gazed bleakly around at the surrounding municipal buildings and up at the Court House's Roman-temple façade, reading the pediment's inscription—something about *The True Administration of Justice*—I saw over Hector's leather-clad shoulder that there was a small crowd gathered on the courthouse steps, some sort of bright amber light shining down on the people, orange barricades visible in vertical strips between the shifting bodies of the crowd, but deep fury and despair had blindsided me and I found it impossible to make out what the people were doing there or what they were watching. Hector noisily shifted gears and brought us to an abrupt stop next to a family of newpaper-vending machines that were chained to a traffic-light post, cutting the engine, and we both got off the 'cycle, Hector immediately reaching to pull a dirty chain from beneath his luggage rack and drape it around the light post while I stepped dazedly onto the sidewalk, wrenching off the helmet and reaching to retrieve the empty, crushed and inverted suitcase from under the luggage rack's useless green bungee cords and carry it onto the sidewalk in my extended arms like the body of a stillborn child.

"What happened, man?" Hector said, securing the motorcycle, standing up and stepping over, his mirrored sunglasses reflecting my stricken face. "What was all the yelling about? Did you—"

"I was carrying a *manuscript,*" I told him furiously, shoving the cordovan wreckage toward his face and making him flinch, a cold wave passing over me as I felt the suitcase's ridiculous weightlessness, "in *this suitcase,* and it"—I pointed my thumb past my shoulder—"and when that— And it fell off— Fell off the *bike* when we—when you avoided that collision. Off the bike and into the air."

"Oh, *fuck,*" Hector said, sagging visibly, looking around at the surroundings. "That's terrible. That's— Mike, listen, I"—he had spread his arms helplessly—"I'm so sorry. That fucking gypsy cab, that was *totally* that bastard's fault. Driving like that— Do you want to go back?"

"What?" I asked, stepping toward him.

"Do you want to go back there? We could—"

"It's *gone,*" I said, tossing the destroyed suitcase into a steel-mesh trash can, where it crashed against the dented metal, rattling the can against a light post as it collapsed atop a pile of pizza boxes and waxed paper—Hector stepped back, clearly startled by tremendous crashing of the suitcase, which had caused several people in the crowd on the courthouse steps to turn curiously toward me.

"That was— Look, though, buddy, don't you want the suitcase?" Hector said in a soothing voice, looking nervously around. "Maybe you're—"

"Forget the *suitcase,*" I yelled at him, furiously embarrassed at the momentary attention the crowd had given me before turning back toward whatever they were watching. "I'm sorry. I don't want the suitcase," I added. "It wasn't your fault, Hector."

"Well, we picked a great time to stop littering," Hector said, slapping the metal "Don't litter" ideogram that was bolted onto the trash can and then leading us toward the back of the crowd. "Come on." He turned toward the courthouse steps and I followed dazedly, squinting in the sudden brightness as we advanced—there were, I saw now, three unspeakably bright lamps on tall metal poles on the other side of the small group of businesspeople who were crowded on the steps, each lamp trailing a thick orange power cable and creating eye-smearing heat shimmer above its aluminum casing and adorned by a weightless-looking white umbrella that billowed in the slight breeze, creating an almost nautical atmosphere above our heads. As Hector elbowed politely but firmly through the crowd, giving apologetic looks to the closing ranks behind him, I noticed a peculiar sound, a mechanical clattering rhythm that began, as I stepped forward, to overshadow the street noises, and through the gap created by Hector's passage I caught a glimpse of what the crowd was watching—behind the single barricade and the protective vigil of two large, self-important men in jeans, T-shirts, and gaudily colored mountaineering coats wearing earphones and wielding walkie-talkies, an excessively thin and tanned bearded photographer with close-cropped white hair and a light meter hanging from his corded neck was crouching over a gigantic chrome-plated large-format camera tipped backward on a weighted tripod that looked as if it had been designed for the space program, peering into a ground-glass focusing screen and talking ceaselessly as his finger held down a shutter button and created the railroad rhythm I'd heard. An assistant in a baseball cap stood beside him, holding a featureless white board in front of her so as to flash overcast sunlight upward past the camera's lens to where Annabelle Taft stood atop the pagan temple's granite steps between the bases of two fluted Corinthian columns, arching her back with her arms outstretched and pressing her hands against the columns in a Samson pose as she was photographed. All the random-looking light made sense when I saw her—it had all been cleverly aligned so as to shine on her in a way that presumably would appear natural in the resulting pictures but from our vantage point was absurdly overdramatic, theatrically highlighting the undersized liquid-silver cocktail dress and short gold-embroidered burgundy sequined toreador jacket that she wore and shining off the silver fabric like chain mail as she swiveled her position, tossing her black hair back and slowly lowering her chin to fix her familiar under-the-lashes erotic stare on the camera. Hector stood with his arms patiently crossed, watching, reaching to scratch his stubble, turning to murmur a gracious apology to the man he'd accidentally hit in the ribs with his motorcycle helmet, and I also watched from where I stood on the sidewalk, gazing at her over the heads of the spectators, my deep fatigue flooded out by the angry adrenaline of the lost manuscript—as Annabelle turned and put her gloved hands on her hips, stretching her waist and glancing back at the camera, I found myself thinking pathetically about all the plastic IBM typewriter ribbons I'd gone through and thrown away, and whether they were retrievable, since the words I'd typed were possibly visible on the ribbons. Thinking ruefully about the various opportunities I'd had to make Xerox copies of what I'd written, I suddenly noticed Douglas Taft sitting on the nearby steps watching me—he had been leaning back against the stone embankment in a relaxed posture, away from the crowd, his hands in the pockets of a flawless soft-looking black suit and pushing back the flanks of his oversized tweed overcoat as he calmly gazed in my direction, and once I had noticed him Douglas slowly smiled in greeting, very knowingly, like a patient king.

"Douglas!" I called out, walking over and collapsing gratefully on the steps at his feet. "Jesus, I thought I'd never find you."

"Hello, Michael," Douglas said fondly, punctuating his quiet words by reaching over and jovially brushing his fingers through my disheveled hair. "My God, you look awful— Have you gotten any sleep? Did you"—he had retrieved his fingers from my head and was grimacing comically at them—"did you even take a *shower* any time recently?"

"Oh, God," I said weakly, letting my exhausted head sink forward as I slumped against the stone. "Douglas—"

"Take it easy," Douglas murmured in pleasant alarm, tapping his fingers on my shoulder—from up close I had seen that his face still showed the signs of recent strain, but there was a trace of something else in his clear expression, something almost unrecognizable. "What's wrong? What's got you so worked up?"

"I finished," I said hoarsely, looking up at him. "I'm done."

"Really?" Douglas said, smiling distantly. "That's good. That's good, Mike."

"It's gone," I said.

"What?" Douglas had raised his eyebrows. "I'm sorry, I don't— Hey, is this the guy?" He suddenly looked upward and I turned to see Hector standing over us, his face shielded into MacArthur-style dispassion by the mirrored sunglasses.

"This is Hector," I said, confused. "He just brought, um, brought me down here. I thought—"

"Oh, you must be the brother," Hector said, putting a hand out. "What's up, man?"

"Douglas Taft," Douglas said, reaching up and surprising me by accurately returning Hector's street handshake. "How do you do. She should be done with this pretty soon."

"Yeah, looks like it," Hector said absently, resting a foot on a higher step next to me and leaning an elbow on his knee as he gazed back toward the photographer. "Valjean's supposed to be very fast. I think he's—"

"Is that Annabelle *Taft?*" said an incredulous young man, roughly eighteen, lurching toward us suddenly from around the edge of the steps, where he presumably had been watching.

"Yeah," Hector told him.

"Wow," the young man said, heading over to join the crowd.

"He's supposed to be fast," Hector continued, sparing the young man a dull glance, "because what do you expect when you've got all these swabbos creating your famous trademark lighting for you. I'm saying it, man—"

"Yeah, the gaffers were here when we arrived," Douglas said, leaning back against the cold stone and squinting as he smiled up at Hector, "but Valjean hadn't shown up yet."

"Everything's free for these assholes and what do they do? Rush through things. I'll just be over here," Hector said disdainfully, adjusting the jacket as he turned and headed away, walking back toward the crowd.

"Is he wearing Annabelle's old jacket?" Douglas asked me bemusedly, watching Hector walk away.

"What? Yeah," I said weakly, resting my head on my hands again and feeling the chill of the stone steps seeping through my clothes and into my flesh.

"Poor Michael." Douglas looked at me with concern, reaching again to pat my shoulder. "You said you lost the story? How did you lose it?"

"On the way down here, off the—off the back of the motorcycle," I told him. "Now I've *found* you and I can't *give* it to you. I mean"—I shook my head in confusion—"after all the time we all spent—"

"It's all right," said Douglas, removing his hand from my shoulder as I looked helplessly around—although my eyes were beginning to fill I could see the deepening November afternoon light sift down across the surfaces of the square.

"But I blew the whole thing," I said, hearing my threadbare voice as my throat thickened and realizing how upset I'd become. "I made the whole— I made the whole thing into a waste, Douglas, and now you won't be— If only Max had *taken* it."

"Max didn't want it? That's interesting," Douglas said distantly, gazing up at Annabelle's vigil at the top of the steps—she had removed the toreador jacket and was standing still spotlit in the cold wearing only the strapless silver cocktail dress, rubbing her hands outside her clenched arms and hopping up and down while waiting for the photographer's assistants to load a new film magazine. *"Me,* I might have taken it."

"What the hell are you so *calm* about?" I said, trying to control my voice. "Don't you understand that the story's *gone?* I mean what— What do you mean you *might* have taken it?"

"I'm sorry, that wasn't very polite given the circumstances," Douglas said, continuing to watch Annabelle. "I think I might have, actually. Then again, the way things are now—"

"I've still got all the tapes. I could do it again," I said, staring at the soothing geometry of the Federal Building's radiator-grille façade and finally noticing the featureless black photographer's van that had been parked across the street.

"See, I never *planned* this," Douglas said, looking at me. "Nobody made *plans,* Mike, and now"—he gestured gently with hands and head, almost as if weaving in preparation to catch a football—"now, Max didn't take it, I probably wouldn't have taken it—"

"But are you sure you don't want it?" I asked, feeling a bit more composed.

"Oh, I want it," Douglas said, leaning his head back and returning his gaze to Annabelle. "Sure I want it. I just wouldn't have taken it."

"I'm sorry I got upset," I said, watching the session continue—Annabelle was posing in the dress alone, and I could hear the staccato rhythm of the camera varying as the photographer endeavored not to catch Annabelle's breath, which the lights tended to emphasize as it fogged around her face in the brisk autumn air.

"I hope she's not too cold," Douglas said. "I hope she's all right like that."

"She's a pro," I told him, smiling inadvertently at my words' confident sound.

"Lights," the photographer shouted, and all the floodlights flared with a unanimous concussive sound and then extinguished themselves, and I peered into the comparative gloom of the now-unlit

location, blinking in the sudden darkness and watching the assistants immediately begin unhooking generators and other equipment as the somewhat embarrassed-looking crowd of businesspeople begin to disperse.

"I'm sorry, I haven't even asked about you," I said, suppressing an involuntary yawn. "How are you, Douglas?"

The crowd continued to break apart as two of the large mountaineer-jacketed assistants flanked Annabelle and ushered her down the steps and toward the waiting van, moving like a Peloponnesian phalanx with their arms raised to ward off spectators. "I don't know," Douglas said, intently, as if I had made a good point. "You would say you were having a strange day, right? That's how you would put it?"

"I'd say that."

"So would I," Douglas said, nodding slowly. "I'm feeling all right, though. That's the interesting thing." As we spoke the five assistants moved around, folding the tripods, winding the cords, removing all traces of the session, and Hector stood by himself watching with what looked like mild interest. "Come on, Mike, let's go bother these good people," Douglas said, sighing and stretching as he stood, and I weakly stood as well, closing my eyes and reeling with fatigue before following him toward the curb and then across the street to the now-crowded area around the windowless black photographer's van—a few spectators had remained, perhaps in hopes of catching another glimpse of Annabelle, and Douglas led me past everyone, Hector following lazily, moving around the flaked trunk of a shedding tree toward the closed doors at the back of the van.

"Excuse me," a large young man called out threateningly, darting forward, speaking in loud, vaulting tones. "Excuse me, this is— Oh, you're with *her.* I'm sorry." The man's voice altered, softening to a confidential murmur as he recognized Douglas. "She's just changing—she'll be out in a minute."

"Thank you," Douglas said considerately.

"Anyone got a match?" Hector called out.

"Listen, where the hell have you *been* all day, Douglas?" I asked, brushing dust and leaves off my overcoat and looking at him as we stood on the cobbled pavement. "Carol and I have been trying to—"

"Are you and Carol really *tight,* now, or what?" Douglas asked blandly, looking the other direction toward the courthouse steps.

"Could you guys move your feet?" a large red-faced man in a plaid flannel jacket and a Mets cap asked us—Douglas and I looked down and saw that we'd been standing on one of the orange power cables.

"I'm terribly sorry," Douglas instinctively told the man as we stepped backward out of the way, and as the man retrieved the cable my foot knocked against a raised pavement stone and I stumbled and almost fell down. "Are you okay?" Douglas asked with concern, reaching to block my fall and then squinting clinically at me. "Really— You're all right?"

A breeze tossed Douglas' dark blond hair and stirred the nearby trees, releasing leaves that floated slowly downward like snow, and I looked for Hector and found him leaning against the side of the van, accepting a light from one of the assistants. "I don't know," I said, dazedly shaking my head. "I'm just so tired, I can't even— All I wanted to do was finish by today, and—" I trailed off as the van's rear doors loudly unlatched and opened and Annabelle climbed out of the van's artificially lit interior, now wearing jeans and a white NAGET T-shirt and black cowboy boots, gold watch and backswept wet hair glinting in the overcast light. The assistants who had crowded around the back of the van immediately moved to her aid, taking the coat and bag she carried and needlessly helping her down, and as Douglas and I stepped unobtrusively forward Annabelle closed the van doors, allowing the red-faced man to help her into the heavy, hooded navy blue cashmere duffel coat that she'd handed him, and gazed calmly at the ground, shivering as a small young woman in a green coat with a clipboard spoke inaudibly in her ear, nodding several times, and then, as the other assistants cleared out of the way, looking up and seeing me.

"Michael," Annabelle said, smiling beautifully—there was a moment when we were both clearly confused by the physical protocol, and as we stepped toward each other I remember almost reaching for her hand before we hugged, very simply, and there was a moment where I was looking across the back of Annabelle's head at the shining black surface of the photographer's van—I remember this clearly—before we released each other. "Thanks for coming," Annabelle said from up close, her voice muffled by my overcoat lapel. "It's good to see you— This has been such a ridiculous day. Where's my bag?" she called out, looking around in sudden confusion.

"Here," said the red-faced man from behind her, handing over a large tapestry-patterned handbag as Hector pushed himself away from the side of the van, dropping his cigarette and lofting his chin in greeting.

"Thanks for getting him," Annabelle told Hector. "That's another favor I owe you."

"Not really," Hector said, leaning comically so as to look at Annabelle's watch and pointing at me. "I probably wasn't the man for the job."

"Yeah, Mike had some misfortune," Douglas said, hands in pockets, rocking on his heels and watching the assistants as they performed the silent-picture routine of loading the steel light stands into the van.

"Misfortune?" said Annabelle through the cigarette that she held in her teeth while fumbling in her bag for a pack of matches—I noticed again that she had switched to Camel Lights. "What'd you do to him, Hector?"

"Let *him* tell you," Hector said, gazing somewhat overearnestly at Annabelle's face while waving an arm, awkwardly signaling his departure. "I've got to take off."

"*Why* is this a work day?" Annabelle muttered intently, squinting with indignation while lighting the cigarette and then favoring Hector with a disproportionate stare as she shook out the paper match. "You're really leaving? When do I get the big ride?"

"You should just *buy* one, man, I'm telling you," Hector said, the mirrors over his eyes reflecting her face. "It's the way to go."

"Yours is axle-driven, right?" Annabelle asked.

"That's right," Hector confirmed.

"Thanks for the ride," I said, waiting for Hector to stow the helmet beneath his left arm and then fumbling through another of his handshakes. "I really appreciate it, Hector."

"Hey, no problem, man," Hector told me with the strange earnestness that I suddenly realized had to do with Annabelle's proximity. "Any time."

"Pleased to have met you," Douglas told him courteously, and Hector nodded strangely and then suddenly sprinted away, heading across the street and back to where he'd locked his motorcycle.

"He didn't say goodbye," Annabelle said, frowning through a cloud of fragrant smoke. "That's strange."

"*Let's roll,*" someone shouted as the diminutive woman in the green coat arrived briskly beside me.

"Everyone's going," the woman said, looking up at Annabelle—she looked to be in her forties. "Your car's on its way—if there's nothing else you need I'll just get a ride with these guys."

"That's fine. I'll be right back," Annabelle told Douglas and myself, touching our arms, and heading off to confer with the black-coated, white-bearded photographer, and as we watched, the van's engine abruptly ignited, propelling a cloud of exhaust fumes across Douglas' shins and prompting him to back away in near-comic alarm.

"Listen, Douglas, really, where've you been?" I asked again.

"I've been spending the day with Anna, actually," Douglas said quietly, putting his hands in his pockets as he gazed past me and around at the civic buildings that flanked the square. "We've just been hanging out—she was supposed to have a fitting or something this morning but it got canceled, so we, um, we had breakfast at her house and kind of sat around for a while, and then she had to come do this, so I figured I'd tag along."

"Oh," I said, startled. "How'd that happen?"

"You know, I think it's beginning to warm up a bit," Douglas said, sniffing the air as he adjusted his beautiful overcoat. "What? Oh, you know— She called me up a couple days ago, actually. Once you guys were done I gather she just ended up in a particular mood, and I guess"—Douglas pushed his hair back from his smooth forehead—"I guess I must have been in the same kind of mood, 'cause this morning I was walking around and I called her and asked if I could drop by. We actually don't live all that far apart."

As we watched, Annabelle hugged the photographer goodbye and waved into the van's passenger window at the assistants, who had crowded into the car like clowns and now called out appreciative comments about the work she'd just done, promising that they'd see her soon and then loudly slamming the doors. "But she called you *days* ago?" I said. "You might have told me."

"You were busy. What do you mean?" Douglas asked, turning toward me as the van lurched toward the pavement's edge, its engine heaving as the driver peered backward before merging into the south-bound traffic.

"I just thought you might have—" I trailed off as Annabelle slowly rejoined us, and we stood together on the cobblestones, surrounded by quiet traffic, the municipal buildings framing the overcast sky.

"I'm so glad that *worked,*" Annabelle said eventually. "Sending Hector to get you, I mean. He *is* an odd one, though."

"You sound intrigued," Douglas said pleasantly, still rocking on his heels.

"Not me," said Annabelle.

"Well, um— You must have gotten my messages," I said, noticing her state of mind as she dragged on the cigarette and checked her watch, prompting me to gesture toward the courthouse and the vanished evidence of the fashion shoot. "I've never seen you do this before. It's amazing."

"Listen, I've got something for you," Annabelle said, fishing in the handbag again and finally pulling out a large steel microphone with a round omnidirectional head and holding it toward me, cord dangling back toward the handbag. "This is yours, right?"

"Right," I said, nodding in recognition as I reached to accept the microphone. "That's mine. I was *wondering* where this—"

"You left it at my house the second night," Annabelle said, as my hand brushed her fingers where they curled around the microphone's shaft. "I didn't see it until you'd left, and then I kept forgetting. Look at Michael, he's wearing *tailored* suits now."

"What do you mean?" Douglas asked, grinning. "What was he wearing before—sackcloth?"

"No—he just had this suit that didn't fit him, that's all. I'm sorry, Michael."

"It was my father's suit," I said, embarrassed.

"We've got him here, we can make fun of him," Douglas said, smiling covertly, as he'd often done long ago, and I realized how much I'd failed to convey in my manuscript.

"All right, you two," I said, feeling my face flush.

"Listen— Did Frank ever call you?" Annabelle asked, turning toward me suddenly.

"It's getting late," Douglas said pointlessly.

"Yeah, last night," I told her. "Thanks for saying whatever you said—Holly Martins called my editor and I think I've got that interview, but I'm not sure I—"

"You missed all that work," Annabelle said. "I thought you could use his—"

"Regardless of what you thought," I began, "I'm not sure it's ethically—"

"I enjoy doing favors for friends," Annabelle said doggedly, swiveling her head heavily in my direction. "If it didn't bother me it shouldn't bother you."

"All right," I said. "Then that's that."

"I'm going to be late again," Annabelle said, checking her watch, miming frustration as she looked across the windy square. "Did something happen to you, Michael?" she asked neutrally, as if passing the time.

"I don't want to think about it," I said wearily, speaking over the sounds of surrounding traffic. "It's over and done with."

"Never mind that routine," Douglas said, smiling as he continued rocking on his heels. "*Tell* her."

"I've finished the manuscript," I said, "as promised, and I— And I've lost it."

Annabelle nodded, not seeming at all startled as she stared contemplatively past my shoulder at the looming towers of the Municipal Building. "You don't seem surprised," I said after a moment.

"No," said Annabelle, turning her green eyes toward me.

"I might," I said weakly, "be able to do it again. I've still got the tapes, and the typewriter ribbon, if you can believe it, tends to keep a legible imprint of—"

"I don't want it," Annabelle said, staring calmly forward and speaking slowly as the minted November air moved her hair around her lovely face. "I had a whole speech to give you. I'm actually glad it's gone, because—because I really don't want it."

"You didn't have to prepare a speech," I said gently, noticing how carefully Douglas was listening.

"Yes I did," Annabelle said intently, "because having told you I don't want it I would then have to find an elegant way to *ask* you for it, to ask if I could read it, 'cause I think—I thought and still think—that I really should read it."

"Well, I—" I began, trailing off hopelessly, transferring the microphone from hand to hand.

"Oh, where the hell is my *car?*" Annabelle moaned, staring fruitlessly across the approaching traffic.

"You've made up your mind, Anna?" asked Douglas, watching her curiously.

"Yes."

"Well, listen," Douglas said, stepping forward and smiling fondly at her from close up, his gaze again accented by that hint of something unrecognizable, and as Annabelle returned his glance I saw a mild trace of the same odd cadence in her eyes. "No big deal, but if you're so sure you know what—what you're doing why're you so nervous?"

"You've never seen me scared?" said Annabelle, adjusting her bag with a shrug. "We've *established* I'm strange—I mean I thought *every* girl had a soft spot for Mr. Spock."

"Mister Scotch?" I hadn't heard her properly—A mild panic had prompted me to check my wristwatch as I felt us sinking further into the fatigued haze of the overcast day.

"Spock," Annabelle said as Douglas laughed. "No emotion. What—you thought I'd said *Scotch?* Is this some joke between you guys?"

"No, it's— It was leaving the party," Douglas explained, still laughing. "After the Winfield party— A cop on the road called me Mister Scotch."

"Did you get pulled *over* that night?" Annabelle laughed, touching Douglas' arm. "Wait, you never told me you got pulled *over.* Was it ridiculous?"

"Listen, the funeral's starting soon," I began, "and I really should be getting—"

"Yeah—I'd totally forgotten that until last week," Douglas said. "Mike was on a *roll* our first night—he asked a good question and I remembered the cop. See, Jill was speeding," he explained, "and we happened to get this guy who—"

"Um," I interrupted, drawing their glances as I tapped my watch, "it's three-twenty. I hate to—" I broke off as a black limousine hummed toward us, boomerang TV antenna on its trunk lid shining in the afternoon light, its arrival seeming to have been slowed by our own melancholy until I realized that the car's driver was looking for a way to approach the cobblestoned island without blocking traffic. Anticipating his solution, Annabelle led us across the island to the courthouse side, waiting while the limousine—a stretched late-model Mercedes sedan—circled round to meet us and the unseen driver cut the engine, the sudden scarlet burn of his brake lights emphasizing the early afternoon darkness—the wind brushed yellow leaves across the irregular cobblestones and I could clearly hear the gentle chiming of the car's ignition-key reminder.

"Let me use the phone," Annabelle said, beckoning toward the electrically lowered window, where a black-sleeved arm emerged holding a cellular telephone, yellow buttons glowing against the platinum shadows in the cold afternoon light. Annabelle rapidly dialed a number and raised the handset to her head, staring across the car's roof as she waited. *"C'est moi—oui, je suis ici,"* she said after a moment, covering her other ear. *"Écoute, j'allais aller directment au—comment on dit?—au défilé de mode, mais il y a quelque chose et je serai peut-être un peu en retard."* Annabelle nodded, listening. *"Dis-leur ce que tu veux mais gagnes du temps. As-tu des nouvelles de Victor?"* There was a brief pause during which Annabelle absently began twisting her manicured fingers in the phone cord, inadvertently pulling it across the driver's jacket like a shoulder seat belt. *"Laisses-moi voir— Ah, oui! Tu as donné le RSVP aux femmes de la leucémie au musée? Ah, et aussi il faut voir si je peux aller à ce truc des Baltiques. Qu'est-ce que j'oublie encore?"*—another pause—*"Oui, prends donc les billets d'avion. Je paierai—Victor s'en occupera plus tard."* Annabelle listened intently, closing her eyes as she nodded and then suddenly glancing at Douglas and myself before continuing more quietly. *"Je viendrai peut-être même pas,"* she said. *"Et je n'aurai pas le job—et alors? Ca, c'est important."* I continued waiting as Annabelle lowered her head and turned marginally away, her voice thinning as she shyly smiled. *"Un homme que je n'ai pas vu depuis des années. Jamais je croyais"*—another pause—*"Oui, c'est très romantique. Il n'est pas là, je dois aller le chercher."* Nodding again, Annabelle unconsciously straightened her back and head, phone buttons glowing behind her fingers, full voice returning, sighing as she spoke. *"Bon c'est tout. Merci, hein! Et dis-moi merde, j'ai drôlement peur,"* she concluded tersely, flipping a switch on the phone before handing it back to the driver.

"When are you leaving?" I asked, tapping the microphone absently against my leg—I had tried and failed to fit it into my overcoat pocket.

"Next month," Annabelle said, twitching her head toward the car and then smoothing her hair with a related gesture, and I courteously ignored the crack in her voice. "We'll be in Paris locking down the Naget details—I've hired an assistant to help me get through this while I complete the move from Flash over to Anodyne."

"Aren't you in a rush?" Douglas said pleasantly, pointing at the car, where the driver lurked patiently in the shadows.

"Yeah," Annabelle said distantly as she reached to opened the car's waxed black door, heaving her heavy handbag onto the backseat. "I'm very very late."

"Well, Anna—" Douglas said, stepping toward her as she turned around, his voice roughening as he spoke.

"Douglas," Annabelle murmured haltingly as they fumbled for each other's calm embrace.

"Thanks for breakfast," Douglas said, sniffing as he spoke. "Thanks for calling me."

"Thanks for coming," Annabelle whispered, closing her eyes.

I gripped the microphone in my hands as they pulled together, arms around each other's backs, Annabelle's green-eyed gaze brimming as she stared over Douglas' shoulder.

"I'm so sorry," Douglas whispered as her voice gently broke.

"I—" Annabelle's breath hitched as she nodded her head, crying as she pulled him closer, face against his cheek. "I— Oh, Douglas, I'm sorry."

"Shh. We've got time," said Douglas, holding Annabelle against him as he stroked her back, speaking almost inaudibly as the November light reflected on his calm wet face. Afraid to move, I watched them gently draw apart and stare soberly at each other, the corners of Annabelle's mouth twisting upwards as she reached to wipe Douglas' reddened cheeks with her thumbs.

"Would I hate her?" Annabelle asked quietly, leaning her forehead on Douglas' brow.

"No," said Douglas. "No."

"She's good, then."

"She's very good," Douglas said firmly, his face breaking into a sad, helpless grin.

"We can do this," Annabelle said, raising her head.

"I know," Douglas said. "I know we can. Come on, get it together," he added, his voice firm, rocking gently back and forth and reaching past Annabelle's head to wipe his fingers across his face before releasing her. "You've got places to go."

"Michael, I—" Annabelle turned her heartbreaking face awkwardly toward me, haltingly trying to speak before lurching compulsively forward and pulling me into a stumbling, out-of-balance hug, clutching me with a fervent grip that I could barely return before she released me and swerved around, climbing into the limousine—I caught a final glimpse of her eyes as the car door slammed and in the moment before she glided away I was looking in the smoked-glass passenger window at the flattened shadow of my own face framed by the white reflected sky.

• • •

AT THREE-FORTY that November afternoon Max Gantry stood on the smooth granite steps before the ornamented wooden portals of a large Romanesque cathedral in midtown Manhattan, wearing a black pinstriped flannel suit with a single white rose boutonniere, holding a thick stack of handsomely reproduced programs imprinted with the cathedral's symbol and looking out across Lexington Avenue—as two blue-coated policemen hauled a wooden POLICE LINE transom barrier across the bottom stair, Max gazed at the landlocked Sargasso Sea of near-identical black limousines that blocked the cross-street traffic and glanced down at the men and women who moved almost furtively across the sidewalk toward the steps, their black formal clothes visible beneath their expensive overcoats, several of them stepping around the edges of a windowless white local television news van and giving a wide berth to the pair of headphoned cameramen who were turning in place, pinwheeling their shoulder-mounted Betacams and their wire-shielded, headlamp-sized spotlights and focusing them on a pair of garishly lit, teal-coated yellow-haired women holding silver microphones who were systematically accosting the formally dressed arrivals. Max stood rooted in the tide of mourners that threaded their way through the police barricade and up the steps, each accepting a program without meeting his eyes and several clearly noticing Max's hands as they did so, while the reporters and cameramen raced toward each arriving limousine so as to ascertain who it contained—William Huxley had arrived, as had a photogenic man with brushed-back silken black hair wearing a double-breasted silk suit whom Max recognized to be city councilman Tommy Hopkins. From atop the granite steps Max couldn't hear the journalists' questions at all, and the clouded, irritated facial expressions that washed with the spotlights across the faces of the mourners—mostly Reed Gardner Grant partners and associates and their husbands and wives—as they snapped their practiced refusals, clamping their hands on their spouses' arms and waving the cameras and microphones away, seemed all the more eloquent when robbed of their ambient sound. Wondering vaguely what he was supposed to do when he ran out of programs, Max looked upward past what he knew to be supremely expensive formal arrangements of white roses that Amelia DiGrassi had personally directed be placed within the blank niches between the cathedral's indentured columns, feeling the cold wind toss his ponytailed hair against his starched shirt collar as he gazed at the band of white sky that shone between the midtown office towers.

"Did you know Ralph well?" one of the reporters asked someone—the wind had shifted direction and the clamor from the sidewalk was now distantly audible to Max as he continued watching the sky.

"I have no comment," a man's rough voice responded to the reporter.

"What sort of person was he?"

"No comment," the man said again. Thinking that he knew the voice, Max returned his gaze to the street, squinting at the man who had just dodged the reporter's microphone and not recognizing him.

"Thank you," another voice said almost in Max's ear as another program was taken from him—looking over, Max saw that he was face to face with Tommy Hopkins, who was, he realized, shorter than he appeared in his television advertisements. "What a tragedy. Are you Michael Cadenhead?"

"No," Max said, startled, clearing his throat. "No, I'm sorry but I'm not."

"Mr. Hopkins! Mr. Hopkins!" One of the yellow-haired reporters was urgently yelling as she strode forward toward the barricade. Max glanced over and was completely blinded by the spotlight that a following cameraman was waving around behind her.

"If he arrives," Hopkins said covertly, ducking his head toward Max's ear after glancing apologetically toward his wife, who despite her severe black clothes looked like a host of a cable-television morning exercise program, "would you tell him that Hopkins is inside?"

"Sure," Max said, glancing past Hopkins' shoulder and suddenly noticing that Stephen Leonard and Wally Patterson were ascending the cathedral steps together—at first they looked to Max almost exactly as they had five years before, but as they approached, doffing their dark overcoats with mirrored movements to reveal grey business suits, as if performing a striptease, Max realized that their faces had changed marginally through time, easily acquiring mild age lines as if they were liquid assets. "Stephen!" Max called out as Hopkins and his leotard-worthy wife slipped past him into the cathedral.

"Max," Stephen said, stepping up, his voice laden with quiet ballast. "I'm so sorry."

"I'm glad you came," Max told him as they shook hands. "Hello, Wally."

"Max," said Wally, waiting for Max to transfer the slipping programs under his arm and then powerfully shaking his hand.

"He goes by Walter now," Stephen said, hooking a thumb at Wally.

"I'm sorry," said Max, reaching to hand out another pair of programs. "Walter."

"I work in a bank," Walter explained.

"I heard you're going to say something?" Stephen asked, pointing at Max's hair. "You're looking pretty radical."

"Unfortunately, yeah," Max said, nervously squinting back toward the big cathedral doors. "I wrote some stuff down but I may end up just, um, extemporizing for a couple minutes and then panicking."

"Well, we're going to be watching you like a hawk," Stephen said, grinning very nicely as he squeezed Max's shoulder. Within the cathedral the organ had begun playing, and at that moment Max happened to glance toward the sidewalk and was suddenly transfixed by his view of a tall woman with long black hair emerging from a limousine—she was facing the other direction, obscuring his view of her face, and as a middle-aged man followed her out of the limousine Max stared intently at her hands and at the back of the coat she wore but was unable to identify her. "I guess we're starting," Stephen was saying. "What do I need to know about the service?"

"What? It's a Catholic Mass," Max explained, catching his breath and staring at the woman's long black hair as he waited for her to turn around. "Just do what everyone else does. Do you know who else is coming?"

"That's right—I hear Jack keeps up with you," said Walter, not having noticed Max's fervent, heart-stopping stare past his wide shoulder.

"I see him sometimes," Max said distantly.

"That isn't *Annabelle,* is it?" Stephen asked pleasantly, having followed Max's gaze.

"Where?" Walter asked in perhaps too bored a voice, peering intently along the direction Stephen had indicated as a second middle-aged man emerged behind the first from the obscured limousine door. "I haven't seen that woman in years."

"I hear she dates some forty-year-old," Stephen said.

"I'd heard that too," Max said, straining to see as the second man audibly shut the limousine door and gestured at the driver.

"That's not Annabelle," Walter said derisively as the black-haired woman finally stepped into full view, skirting the television van and approaching the sidewalk with her two companions in tow. "You guys are seeing things."

"I guess we should find our seats," Walter said, scanning his eyes critically down the front cover of the program that Max had handed him. "I never knew his middle name was Emerson."

"Listen, find us afterwards," Stephen said, heading toward the opened wooden doors and the shadowed stone pillars within. "No kidding."

Max waved them into the cathedral and then turned back around as the black-haired woman and her greying male companions rounded the blue barricade and mounted the granite steps, sighing heavily as he prepared to offer his diminishing stack of programs, and as the woman looked at him she stopped walking, stepping toward him only after the men behind her had touched her shoulders and ushered her forward. "Max Gantry?" the woman said in a soft, rich voice, drawing his attention to her clear blue eyes and the edges of the brown dress that protruded from her coat's lapels.

"Yes?" Max said, blinking at the woman in confusion.

"Oh, good," the woman said with apparent relief. "I'm glad I found you so quickly. Have you— Save me a seat, I'll meet you inside," she instructed the backup men, who nodded and followed the crowds through the wooden doors. "I realize we haven't met, but I'm trying to find— Oh, you're the one with the *hands,* " the woman noticed suddenly, flaring her eyes at Max's fingers as he stowed the remaining program in his breast pocket and then registering her sudden embarrassment. "I'm sorry—that wasn't very diplomatic, was it?"

"Are you a plastic surgeon?" Max asked, smiling somewhat kindly.

"I'm Carol Casey," the woman said while extending a hand, which Max took. "He used to tell me about you—describing the hands and saying he missed you. I'd forgotten," Carol continued almost elegiacally. "He called you Mister Emotion."

"*Who* called me Mister Emotion?" Max asked.

"Douglas," Carol said decisively, closing her eyes luxuriously, as if clearing her head. "And I thought *he* was scatterbrained— Listen, did he show up? I mean"—Carol gestured at the church—"is he *here?*"

"You mean Douglas *Taft?* I haven't seen him," Max said, shivering again in the autumn air as the organ music continued and realizing that the barricaded area surrounding the cathedral steps had emptied and that all the mourners were inside. "Not in years."

"Damn it," Carol said, looking into the cathedral and speaking over the tremendous racket of a passing produce truck, her eyebrows lifting with nervousness. "I was *really* hoping he'd show up, but— I need some advice, Mister Emotion. Are you a kind man?"

"Yes."

"Do you think," Carol asked intently, "that to be attractive a woman should look hard and be soft or look soft and be hard?"

"No," Max said after a moment. "Not with that boy."

"I see," said Carol.

"With Douglas you have to wait," Max said while glancing into the cathedral, where his sun-bleached retinas registered nothing but darkness and dim patterns of stained glass and candlelight. "I don't know how well you know him but he's— He's not very good at spur-of-the-moment things."

"Well, I can't wait forever," Carol said.

"Yes you can," Max assured her. "You'd be surprised—it's not as hard as it looks."

"I like you," Carol told him, smiling with sudden clarity. "Look, we should go inside—this thing's beginning."

"Well, it's about time," Max said, graciously extending his arm and following Carol into the cathedral, reaching for the iron handles on the heavy wooden doors and swinging them shut.

AT CLOSE TO four that November afternoon Douglas Taft and I wandered south from Foley Square, crossing Reade Street into the overbearing shadows cast by the Municipal Building, and as we skirted the stone arcade that cradles Chambers Street I gazed upward past the severe colonnade at Adolph Weinman's statue of *Civic Virtue.* "The days are getting shorter," Douglas said absently, hands in pockets, slowing our walking pace as he spoke.

"Today went very fast," I agreed—the autumn air had inexplicably warmed through the afternoon and the sky had begun to clear, soft hazing highlights appearing in the streets, shadows deepening as we came in sight of the stone wall surrounding City Hall.

"Did you ever meet this guy Raymond?" Douglas asked suddenly, looking at me.

"No," I said, startled. "She's told me about him."

"Was she— When she talked about him did she seem serious?"

"Yes," I said, compulsively switching the silver microphone from hand to hand.

"She's been mentioning him to me," Douglas said, stepping off the sidewalk.. "I guess it's the life we lead, right? I mean I guess he sounded all right."

"But you wouldn't want him to marry your sister," I said, filling the pause.

"Never said that," Douglas said, shaking his head in advance of speaking. "Never said that." By mutual decision we'd turned west onto Chambers Street and were approaching the Hall of Records and skirting the edge of City Hall Park—it was a miniature street, an antiquated remnant of an absent age, and there were so few pedestrians that I felt utterly freed from passing time, as I might have felt walking through a daguerreotype.

"Are you going back to work?" I asked, looking at Douglas' profile. "Because—"

"Not yet," Douglas said. "Not *today,* anyway—it's too late. Soon," he added, squinting as he gazed upward past the soot-streaked pediments of the Court Square Building at a flock of pigeons that had drifted into view.

"One thing at a time, maybe," I said, craning my neck as I also watched the pigeons.

"Yeah— It's still strange to be walking around out here, you know, seeing people after the time locked up in my house."

I continued flipping the microphone from hand to hand as we walked. "What was it like?" I asked.

Douglas led us forward, walking slowly and taking a deep breath. "All that time," he said after a moment. "Days and days—I didn't really know how to eat. I got sick once."

"Really?"

"Yeah, it was very strange. I almost didn't know what was happening to me, just that I couldn't sleep without pain and I didn't have any, um, any *energy,* you know, and I'm so dumb sometimes that it took me a couple days to realize I was cold and sweating 'cause I had a fever. I didn't—"

"Jesus, Douglas," I said, moved. "You should have called someone."

"It was all right," Douglas said quietly. "I had my little room and I had quiet—I had the bricks across the air shaft, the morning light on the bricks always the same way. I took a lot of aspirin and I was fine. See?" He turned to me and held his arms out, humbly exhibiting himself. "That was the worst of it. Hey, Mike, you remember on that tape I said I have no past? The tape Pershing made?"

"Sure," I said, remembering.

"Well—" Douglas pushed his hair back contemplatively from his forehead—"during one of the weeks I was confused, I knew I was missing something, and— When I got sick I remembered my mother taking care of me when I was a little boy. Remember baths at night?"

"Yeah," I said, politely swallowing a mild irrepressible yawn.

"The night my fever broke I took a bath and it was *familiar*, the night wind on my body, the smell of soap, and I remembered how my mother used to give me a bath before bed and the way the room would smell before bed. All my life I would dream the door," Douglas said, tugging at his overcoat lapels as the wind gusted from behind us. "It's different on the—on the other side, and with Pershing I knew to get close— You get close enough to the door that every difference is behind you."

"That's through the door," I said.

"I know," Douglas hoarsely agreed. "You understand— I was *trying*. Every time I tried to buck the thing, something would happen and I'd be back in the mess. I mean, going to Annabelle's party, a stunt like that and I ended up completely back in the—"

"That was my fault," I said, "and I'm—"

"No it wasn't," said Douglas. "How could either of us know that when Annabelle told you graduation weekend she meant her *contract*, of all things? So you told *me*, but that was a misunderstanding, that's all."

Turning south onto Broadway brought the sounds of traffic into greater proximity—the provincial scale of the streets we'd walked on gave way to the vast spaces of the avenue, revealing deep diminishing views north and south, the machine-age financial district towers standing against the fading sky, their thousands of illuminated office windows shimmering through the haze of distance. "It's four o'clock," I said.

"Yeah," said Douglas, sighing heavily. "I guess the funeral's starting."

"When you talked to Max," I asked gently, "did he say anything about Ralph?"

"What—" said Douglas. "You mean the Toldran overdose? Or no— You mean the other part, don't you?"

"That's what I meant."

After a moment, Douglas said, "Look, Mike, some things should be secret, right? I mean Annabelle was trying to keep that damn Naget offer secret for *months,* so that Frank could get her that sweet deal, but Ralph— Are you asking me to tell you?"

"Yes," I said, my voice sounding less cavalier than I had feared.

"See— Max *knew* the psychosis and even *he* didn't understand how Ralph could be *frightened* of Annabelle, you know, wanting the power but scared— Someone had to lash him to the mast and I guess only Frank was safe. I wish Max *hadn't* told me what Amelia said"—Douglas stared down at the sidewalk—"about how she found Ralph in, you know, in that black dress and the black wig with the Toldran pills everywhere, and the lipstick on the wall with his father's name and Annabelle's name—"

"He had to see them together," I said, shaking my head. "It's so—"

"It was bad luck." Douglas brushed his hair back and then returned his hands to his suit pockets. "Nothing's expected—you can eat fish and you can eat in New Orleans and it doesn't mean you ate fish in New Orleans. This is a dark decade, Mike," Douglas said distantly, reaching to squeeze my shoulder with his hand. "It'll turn us all into thieves and liars before it's over."

We turned east at the small statue of Nathan Hale, the schoolmaster with but one life to give, passing the plaque to Joseph Pulitzer and entering onto the wide promenade that cut through City Hall Park. "This used to be where all the newspapers were," I told Douglas, looking at a discolored statue of Horace Greeley and across at the warm colors of the turning autumnal trees' remaining foliage. "When the city was young. You know, I never finished *Jake Hackett,*" I recalled. "How does it turn out, anyway?"

"What? Oh, it's melodramatic," said Douglas shyly. "See, Anna almost dies, right, and Thomas gives up his life for the new scripture, the book that Morstan and the Giovannian Monks have brought to Rome, you know, to challenge the papacy, and only at the last moment does Hackett discover"—Douglas had closed his eyes as he remembered—"that the book isn't real. The scripture—it's just this clever forgery that Morstan created, right, something he wrote after his time in cosmopolitan society that he based, you know, on the fears and desires of the age. So the Giovannian book's a fake—its only value is what Hackett and Thomas and Morstan and Anna *imparted* to it. They were trapped by their own faith—I mean is that stupid or what?"

We had slowed to a near standstill as we approached a pair of wood-slatted park benches, damp with days-old November mist, and as we sat side by side, Douglas adjusting his overcoat beneath his trousers, I felt my legs aching with relief and realized how long I'd been standing. "Hey, Douglas," I asked after a moment's consideration, "if you're not going to work, why are you all dressed up?"

"Because of the funeral," Douglas said, looking at me in confusion. "Why do you think?"

"Well, we're missing it," I said, automatically consulting my wristwatch.

"Why are *you* so intent on going?" Douglas said. "You and Ralph weren't—"

"I was hoping we could get everyone together," I said without thinking, and as Douglas looked at me I regretted having spoken.

"You've got some funny ideas," Douglas said with a trace of Annabelle's surety.

"I've been told," I said. "I'm sorry. Jesus, I can't believe the *time* I've spent," I added wearily, rubbing my face with my hands. "All that typing—"

"There's one thing we didn't do," Douglas said suddenly. "Something we didn't talk about."

"The night everything started," I said. "I mean—"

"I know what you mean," Douglas said, nodding as his eyes narrowed. "See— The thing is that I really thought I was all right when I got home. I mean, after the, after the fund-raiser we kept drinking, right, and in the morning I was feeling—"

"You were hung over."

"In the morning I was hung over and there were black"—Douglas coughed —"these black hairs in my mouth and an empty bed, a note from Carol beside the bed and she'd gone into work. I tried to wake you up, the note said. Love." Douglas had made quotation marks with his fingers. "So I went home and had some more to drink, right, like anyone would do, and by that afternoon I was seeing—"

"Yeah?" I said gently, tapping my fingers against the soft wooden slats of the bench.

"Right, seeing double." Douglas laughed fondly as he nodded.

"That was the trick, the Carol trick, seeing double— I found the scissors. Found them actually very *easily,* you know, what with the small apartment, no luggage, and naturally I busted the door—I mean what would *you* do if your hand kept slipping on the doorknob and you were seeing double and had to get out? I warmed up by spinning. I was spinning anyway but this was circles, around the stairwell landing—I remember it was so nice and cool. I'd always noticed the crack in the banister, and deciding that the thin part of the scissors would hurt less—hurt my heart less, right, and the skin— And then the gaffer's tape—"

"But the banister broke."

"It broke," Douglas said. "The neighbor—"

"She must have found you on the floor," I told him. "Sturgis and Martinez said you were screaming on the floor when they—"

"Who?"

"The two paramedics," I explained as Douglas nodded. "They explained that part. But I think when she saw— When your neighbor saw the damage to the hallway she assumed a crime had been committed," I continued, "which frightened her, so she *would* have gone with you in the ambulance, but—"

"But by then it was dark," Douglas said. "It was night."

"It was the night"—I had nodded—"that Nick Blanchard called me for the first time in five years and we went to the hospital."

Douglas stood and stretched, and I stood as well, the sudden rush of blood and disorientation nearly causing me to pass out. "All right," said Douglas, looking past me. "All right. Look, I've got to go do something, and I'm afraid I might actually lose my nerve, so—"

"Yeah," I said looking at my watch. "I guess I've got to go too."

"Friends?" Douglas awkwardly asked, looking into my eyes as he extended his hand.

"Friends," I told him, my small sudden smile surprising us both as we shook, and after he had nodded and turned purposefully away I stood watching his receding back as he crossed the park the way we'd come and soon vanished from view.

AT FOUR-TWENTY that November afternoon Max Gantry sat stiffly on the meager velvet cushion draped across the cathedral's front pew with his perspiring hands clasped nervously between his knees, as the heavily amplified organ pipes funneled their harmonics directly into the reverberating stone foundations of the building, staring obdurately forward at the ornamental gilt cross atop the overscaled altar, not looking at Frank or at Amelia DiGrassi as they settled into their strained positions on either side of him while the crowd of black-clothed businesspeople quietly finished finding their seats and gazed expectantly forward toward the flashing of Father Matteotti's spotless white vestment as he stepped humbly across the scarlet-carpeted stone floor toward the pulpit, his movements gracefully synchronized with the heavy reverberation of the hymnal's concluding major chords, gold-framed eyeglasses and crooked teeth glinting he waited for their silent attention. "The grace of our Lord Jesus Christ and the love of God and the fellowship of the Holy Spirit be with you," Father Matteotti began, his subtly amplified voice projecting across the soft wood and cloth surfaces of the cathedral.

"And also with you," the congregation replied, their murmured voices blending smoothly together, the dark and cool high stone vaults of the cathedral echoing the sound as the priest stepped to the altar, stained-glass shadows shining on his white vestment as he knelt beneath the gilt cross to kiss the altar and then stood, swinging the glittering silver censer through its static and fragrant fumes. Having incensed the altar the priest turned to face the congregation, spreading his pale hands as he invited a moment of silent prayer, and Max tipped his face downward and closed his eyes, hearing car horns and traffic outside the cathedral and Frank and Amelia's hushed breathing amplified by the humid and unmoving air.

"God of faithfulness," Father Matteotti continued, "in your wisdom you have called your servant Ralph out of this world. Release him from the bonds of sin, and welcome him into your presence, so that he may enjoy eternal light and peace and be raised up in glory with all your saints. We ask this through Christ our Lord."

"Amen," the congregation responded, Max's voice following the voices of the others and echoing oddly in his ears as the white-haired priest opened an inconspicuously threadbare leather-bound book.

"I was a derision to all my people, and their song all the day," Father Matteotti read. "He hath filled me with bitterness, he hath made me drunken with wormwood. He hath also broken my teeth with gravel stones, he has covered me with ashes. And thou has removed my soul far off from peace: I forgot prosperity. And I said,

My strength and my hope is perished from the Lord: Remembering mine affliction and my misery, the wormwood and the gall. My soul hath them still in remembrance and is humbled in me. This I recall to my mind, therefore have I hope: It is of the Lord's mercies that we are not consumed, because his compassions fail not. They are new every morning: Great is thy faithfulness. The lord is my portion, faith my soul; therefore will I hope in him." Matteotti turned to another part of the book, the pulpit's microphone exaggerating the heavy flopping of the pages, and then continued. "For if by one man's offense death reigned by one; much more they which receive abundance of grace, and of the gift of righteousness, shall reign in life by one, Jesus Christ. Therefore, as by the offense of one judgement came upon all men to condemnation; even so by the righteousness of one the free gift came upon all men unto justification of life. For as by one man's disobedience many were made sinners, so by the obedience of one—"

At that moment the cathedral's calm quiet was sharply broken by a shrill sound, startling the congregation, and Father Matteotti stopped reading and looked up, waiting as the appalled mourners twisted in their places, peering around and attempting to locate the sound's source. The shrill electronic chirp was eventually recognizable as the sound of a personal paging device, and Max's ears rang with the priest's heart-stopping silence as he glanced at the tear-streaked angles of Frank DiGrassi's face glaring backward across the expanse of the cathedral and then twisted his own head around, watching as Carol Casey stood up in the middle of the cathedral, fumbling at her waist to shut the beeper off and shuffling slowly past the mourners that blocked her way out of the pew, pointedly not watching, the clatter of her heels against the granite floor soon thankfully blunted by the carpet, her face set in dispassionate shame as she hurried down the cathedral's center aisle and out of view.

"So by the obedience of one shall many be made righteous," Father Matteotti continued. "Moreover, the law entered, that the offence might abound. But where sin abounded, grace did much more abound: That as sin hath reigned unto death, even so might grace reign, through righteousness, unto eternal life, by Jesus Christ our Lord."

"Are you sure you want me to speak?" Max whispered in Frank DiGrassi's ear a few moments later as Father Matteotti continued the Mass of the Resurrection, reading from the New Testament so as to conclude the Liturgy of the Word and beginning the Intercessions that preceded the Eucharist.

"Yes," Frank whispered tightly, his waxen face as pale as an ivory carving.

"Our brother in Christ Ralph has gone to his rest in the peace of Christ," Matteotti murmured, bowing his head. "May the Lord now welcome him to the table of God's children in heaven. With faith and hope in eternal life, let us assist him with our prayers."

"Lord, hear our prayer," the congregation self-consciously responded.

"In baptism Ralph received the sign of the cross," Matteotti prayed. "May he now share in Christ's victory over sin and death."

"Lord, hear our prayer," the congregation repeated as Max nervously scratched his face and leaned toward Frank again, putting a hand on the attorney's shoulder.

"This isn't what you're thinking," Max whispered. "I really loved him."

"I know you did," Frank responded, wiping his eyes as his shoulder moved beneath Max's hand. "I know you did."

"God of those who hope, look upon our brother tragically taken from our midst. Do not consider his sins nor judge him with the haste of a human heart," the priest pleaded, his eyes fervently shut. "For Ralph's family, especially his mother and father, that they feel the healing power of Christ in the midst of their pain and grief, we pray to the Lord. Let us pray to the Lord also for ourselves— May we who mourn be reunited one day with our brother; together may we meet Christ Jesus when he who is our life appears in glory."

"Lord, hear our prayer," said the congregation over the intruding sound of a car horn.

"I'm afraid, Frank," Max said. "You're being so—"

"It doesn't matter," Frank whispered heavily, his words sagging through the torpid, dust-spattered air. "Max, I— Just say what you should say. It's all right."

For the next ten minutes Max sat in a sort of trance as the Liturgy of the Eucharist proceeded around him, standing as the other mourners stood, following their example as they bowed their heads and sitting back down at the proper time without listening, absently accepting the wafer and the wine when the time came, until finally all the surrounding motion concluded and Max realized that Father

Matteotti and the others were looking at him, and he nodded in response, ignoring the singing in his head as he breathed deeply before standing up. Amelia reached to squeeze Max's hand as he stepped away, walking nervously across the altar's carpeted edge toward the pulpit, feeling the heat of the cathedral's concealed spotlights on his face as he deliberately wrapped his truncated fingers around the oaken top edge of the pulpit before him and looked out at the gridwork of white motionless faces that stared expectantly back at him through the cathedral's dry and silent air.

"I wish I didn't have to talk about love," Max said. "Ralph loved his parents very much, he loved his father, and that love was very humbling— His father had been a great success and all Ralph wanted was to suffice at something. It's not my place to say what Ralph meant to any of you—if you knew him you understand that he was good." Max took a halting breath as if forcibly smoothing and slowing his voice before continuing. "One night during college before I betrayed our friendship Ralph took me to a double feature of *The Maltese Falcon* and *My Fair Lady* and after Sam Spade had explained that he wouldn't play the sap for anyone because he didn't care who loved who and Henry Higgins had asked why a woman can't be more like a man, since a man talks of Keats or Milton and a woman only talks of love, Ralph told me that they both had everything backwards in their heads and that I had the same problem. Ralph was the only person I've known who—"

Max stopped speaking and stared past the silver microphone at the dim view of the congregation, noticing the empty space that Carol had vacated and eventually locating Stephen and Walter where they sat. "I never told anyone about a certain thing Ralph did when we were very young," Max continued, deliberately unfocusing his eyes. "He used to go bring me up to his roof and catch pigeons. He was adept, as he was with most things— He filled an atomizer with chloroform and misted it over the pigeons' heads until they stopped walking and began moving their heads like they were seeing visions. Then Ralph would grab one pigeon from the roof ledge, never the one I expected, and gently pull its wings back and tie them together with sewing thread. Ralph borrowed my copy of *Gray's Anatomy* and spent some time figuring out how to tie the wings together so the bird couldn't free them"— Max's voice had roughened— "and while the bird was struggling he would stroke its feathers as he cradled its body in his hands, and he said"—Max wiped his eyes—"he said that he loved the bird, truly loved it. Then he dropped it off the roof and watched it fall."

Max tightly shut his eyes and gripped the pulpit, breathing deeply before continuing, looking around and finding that his eyes had adjusted to the spotlights and that he could clearly see the details of Frank and Amelia's faces as they watched him. "At first I believed that Ralph was destroyed by the delusion that only beauty provided surcease from pain," he said, his voice regaining its cadences. "Now I understand that Ralph simply believed that beauty was love's face—that beauty was freedom."

Max stared through the shadows at the stained glass shining against the blackness of the granite walls, leaded lines lacing the glass panes like the veins of a leaf or the cracked and latticed surface of aging porcelain. "I fell in love once," he said. "Just once, as far as I know, so I don't— I don't think I understand how falling in love is supposed to happen, but when— When it happened Ralph was there. We were almost children—I'm sure you can remember. He was there and I treated him badly, I was blinded by my—by my desires and what I now understand"—he looked out at the congregation—"Today, I understand that Ralph never despaired because he knew that love could prevail."

AT FIVE O'CLOCK that November evening I stood halfway across the Brooklyn Bridge looking out over the darkening waters at the clear haze that shone across the overcast sky, inhaling the wet and salted air as I gazed at all the city's downtown buildings, their flanks shining proudly in the brightness of a winter's early sunset, their distant windows flaring with cold fluorescent light as the endeavors of the business day approached their conclusion. The wild winter wind pulled my hair from my face, freezing my fingers where they curled round the cold steel coaxial cables of the pedestrian walk, and beyond the downtown towers I could see boats moving across the vast smooth surface of the harbor and the distant figure of the Statue of Liberty, her newly-gilt torchlight glinting above the horizon as she continued her serene vigil—the statue reminded me of the past summer and I gripped the microphone and turned away from the elevated highway where I'd lost my manuscript, hearing the roar of automobiles clattering in both directions across the antique bridge's traffic level as I gazed toward the Brooklyn Heights Promenade where I'd spent my summer nights. When I had gone to pick up my new contact lenses several days before, my father had suddenly surprised me by awkwardly knocking his hand against my arm, attempting to express his affection, and I was moved by the realization that it was the closest that he could come to a spontaneous gesture—I remembered my father's satisfaction at the new lenses as I continued my journey across the bridge, descending into Brooklyn to walk well back from the curb as I navigated the quiet, oddly angled streets, adjusting the fabric of my ridiculously new suit within my overcoat sleeves and hoping that I didn't look excessively out of place or lost to those passersby who happened to glance my way. I suspected that I was dangerously tired, capable of wandering into traffic or into a lethal neighborhood without noticing, but the clear way that the world looked to me through my new lenses and the sensation of reaching protectively down for the suitcase and realizing that I was free of its leg-bruising, hand-wringing weight combined to keep me from finding the shortest route home.

And so I believe that day's single coincidence to have been deliberate—I have mentioned my recent discovery that the world contains a margin of fire, and as I walked into Carrol Gardens early that November evening and saw a lone street vendor in denim overalls and sneakers and a denim cap standing in the shadowed sidewalk near a street corner selling small orange-and-green puppets contrived to squeal when their mouths were operated, I finally recognized the calm place to which my own endurance of fulfilled longing had led me. As I wearily crossed that narrow residential street, the weather-beaten young man lowered the puppet-draped hand that he'd offered toward me, tightening his grip on the white cotton bag of puppets that he carried as his shopworn eyes met mine. "I've seen you before," I told him over the whispering of leaves against the pavement and the gentle tossing of the trees.

"Are you sure?" the puppet vendor asked in a gentle, teasing voice, raising the abstract-looking orange-and-green puppet and loudly opening its squeaking mouth—from up close I could see the puppet's matted synthetic fur and machine stitching and the noise-making apparatus that had been glued into the puppet's mouth. "I don't remember you."

"Where do you get the puppets?" I asked, squinting at his silhouette as the evening sunlight shone on the bricks behind him. "Do you make them?"

"They're commercially available," the vendor said, extending the puppet toward a pair of passersby and shrugging at me as they headed away. "I wanted to play a violin or something, compose violin music, but instead I just do this."

"It's like the violin?" I asked him.

"The puppet is a friend," the puppet vendor explained. "I wanted to keep them but nobody could listen. It's not my voice," he explained, surreptitiously, as if I was having trouble grasping the principle. "The voice is for other people."

"I have seen you before," I told him, smiling as I continued my homeward journey. My apartment was as I'd left it, early that morning, and as I shut the door and moved to turn on a lamp against the approaching darkness, winded by the walk and by the narrow flights of stairs, I was reminded of my frantic departure by the living room's disorder—the typewriter still stood on the table against the window as it had for the past ten days, surrounded by legal pads and handwritten notes and square, stacked boxes containing reel-to-reel tapes and empty blue boxes that had contained fresh typewriter-ribbon cartridges and dozens of crumpled paper sheets that littered the desk and the surrounding floor—and as I stepped over the boxes of fresh computer paper that leaned against the desk's base I saw Douglas' Pershing Notebook still propped against the tape deck with the gold-plated barber's scissors bracing it open, and I extracted Dr. Pershing's battered envelope from my coat pocket, unfolding the final page and returning it to its place so that the matching halves of the jagged tear intermeshed. Removing my overcoat and dropping it onto the couch, I pulled the aluminum kitchen chair away from the desk and over to the window, where I sat, resting my feet against the windowsill's cracked paint, removing my tie as I surveyed the cluttered floor—the overturned Bonomi book and the white Federal Express carton and Jill's TDK audiocassette in its scratched plastic box and the glossy black ANTHESTERIA 1981 matchbook were all still strewn across the floorboards, and I turned away in utter exhaustion, gazing past the storm window's reflections at the darkening sky.

I have no idea how long I sat there looking out the window before falling asleep but I remember that I had reached to switch off the desk lamp and before long I was dreaming—the room grew darker and in my dream I was wandering in a strange place that became familiar by degrees, being led by the hand toward a place that I'd seen before, and soon, as my friend began ushering me down overbright corridors and hurrying me beneath eerie fluorescent lights, I realized that I had arrived at the hospital—*No, Nick, not again,* I weakly tried to call out—*Please don't bring me here again*—but Nick was gone, and as I tried to increase my pace, stumbling along the white antiseptic walls and passing doorways through which I could see glimpses of bloody figures hidden in the darkness, I remembered that I was carrying some sort of precious burden beneath my arm and that I had to warn somebody of something, and I became more and more alarmed as the maze of white corridors led me further and further astray. As my sluggish flight continued I heard clattering footsteps that echoed oddly throughout the hospital and realized that someone was running in front of me, remaining just out of view, and I tried to call out, knowing that the secret I carried—the knowledge that the Red Ghost and the Ghost of Lisa Sparrow were the same ghost—was desperately important to the dark-haired woman in the black dress that I was chasing, but as I caught up to the woman and she turned around, and I saw her face and learned that I had been chasing the wrong woman and that my secret knowledge was useless, the woman stepped closer and wasn't a woman at all but was a man my own age. I realized right then that I had lost the object that I had been carrying and that I was in greater danger than I had imagined and I ran through a doorway into cool night air, knowing that I was pursued as I stumbled blindly down a damp, barren road through a dark and terrifying countryside, and looking behind me I suddenly understood who it was that followed me wearing white hospital clothes, but as I left the road and crawled through the underbrush that led toward a nearby forest I heard a horrible sound, a deep and booming thumping sound that came from all directions, and as I began to moan in deep terror I was jolted awake. Outside the storm window it was full dark and softly raining, the night sky shining dimly through the glass, and as I rubbed my burning eyes and reached to turn on the blinding desk lamp, having no idea how long I had slept, the booming sound repeated, almost stopping my heart as I realized that it was coming from my front door.

"Who's there?" I called out fearfully, standing up and staring across the dark apartment at the door, trying to clear my head and wondering if I was still dreaming as the pounding on the door was repeated. "Who is it?" I called out again, hearing the tremor in my voice as I approached the door.

"It's *Nick,*" came the sudden, irritated reply, the familiar sandy voice blunted by the thickness of the door. "What are you, *deaf?* Open up, Mike."

Still shaken, I unlocked the door and pulled it open, squinting as I peered fruitlessly into the drafty corridor, which was feebly illuminated by a small low-wattage fixture on the cracked plaster of the opposite wall. "Nick?" I said blearily, seeing a silhouetted figure standing silently in the darkness. "Is that you? What time is it?"

"It's almost five in the morning," Nick muttered, stepping forward as I reached to flip on the overhead light near the front door, his face and hair misted with rainwater. "You going to let me in, buddy?"

"Five—?" I repeated, shocked at the length of time I'd slept in the chair, clearing my throat as I noticed his dark overcoat and boots and the disorienting effect of his raw, direct eyes not being shielded by sunglasses. "I was— What are you *doing* here, Nick?"

By way of responding Nick held up the object that I hadn't realized he'd been holding—a thick, heavily damaged stack of accordion-folded computer paper, stained and slightly crumpled, an automotive tire track clearly visible across one of the orphaned single sheets that protruded from the unkempt edges. "We've got to talk," Nick told me. "I just spent the last nine hours reading this thing of yours, Mike, so I figure you can spare me some time."

"You've been reading—"

"You bet your ass," Nick said, carrying the manuscript past me into the apartment, his camera nearly bashing against the door's metal edge and his soaked, mint-condition cowboy boots tapping the worn floorboards. "You going to turn some lights on in here?"

"Is it really five in the morning?" I asked, locking the door, tucking my heavily wrinkled shirt into my tailored trousers and blinking to clear my head before following Nick's stalking form down the dim corridor, arriving behind his swaying overcoat as he crossed the ransacked room and flipped on the desk lamp. "Christ, I slept almost eleven hours— You can move all that stuff and sit down, Nick," I apologized. "You want me to make some coffee? I've got—"

"You son of a bitch," Nick marveled sweetly as he turned to face me, camera swinging, holding out the manuscript, his pale, red-eyed face revealing his barely repressible fury. "You fucking son of—"

"Keep your voice down," I urged, wincing as I raised my appeasing hands. "What's wrong— Are you angry about how I described you?"

"What? No, of *course* not— Who do you think I am, *Sinatra?*" Nick rasped as he stepped closer, looming heavily over me as I stepped backward. "You think *I* care? I mean you did a fucking great job with the fucking *boat*"—Nick's hands gripped the sheets of paper like mountain climber's hands on ropes as he backed me up against the wall, the light switch painfully poking beneath my shoulder blades—"I mean that was a nice hazy memory before tonight, but no, Mike, I'm really not all that interested in how you talk about *me.*"

"You going to hit me, Nick?" I asked quietly.

Nick stepped heavily away, his momentum nearly causing him to trip over the Bonomi book, his other foot crashing down on Jill's plastic tape box and crushing it into splinters. "Look, you're supposed to feel *ashamed,*" Nick sighed finally, dropping the manuscript on my desk and turning tightly to face me. "With a secret you can feel ashamed— When you tell people it stops bothering you."

"Are you saying I've hurt them?" I stepped away from the wall and glared sarcastically at Nick, realizing that I wasn't tired at all. "That I've hurt Annabelle and now you'll protect—"

"*Hurt* her? No— You *can't* hurt her," Nick said, facing me across the room's cascade of wreckage and speaking over the soft whisper of the rain. "Don't you understand that even now? It's not *possible* to make a—"

"She could have trouble ahead," I argued. "Like any—"

"She'll do very well. Heat *rises,*" Nick insisted, poking me in the chest. "This is what famous people *do*—fuck their way into celibacy. Look, something happened to her when she was abroad, that's all, and no amount of—"

"You're really calling her a broad?"

"Overseas," Nick corrected, squinting contemptuously, turning away. "But I should have *known* it's nothing rare, it's *all* just chick suspense, right, like with any professional dick magnet. That's it, man, without—"

"*Stop it,*" I nearly shouted, my sharp voice sounding less shocked than bereaved. "Nick— Just stop. Why are you *talking* like this? What's the—"

"It's something you wouldn't know about," Nick said. "And let me *tell* you, man, you may have spent your whole *life* over your head but this is— You finally beat me, right? You finally found a secret for yourself, something nobody had and made it your own— You think this is *your* thing, Mike? You think the right to surprise me with a hidden secret is any—"

"But you knew," I said, confused.

"What?" Nick said, his voice sounding more incredulous than offended as he stepped marginally away, shoulders sagging. "What the fuck are you—"

"When did you tell Annabelle that Max was the man calling her?" I asked.

Nick slowly lowered the overcoated arm he'd waved in my direction and stepped across the paper-strewn floor toward my second-hand couch, clearing a space and sinking wearily, his tired eyes finding mine. "What makes you think I did that?" he asked finally.

"Because there were *results,*" I told him. "Today—or yesterday, I mean—Tina contacted Max and started urging him to see her. I was there."

"Okay— But why was it *me?*" Nick asked intently.

"Because you're the only one who *could* have," I said. "The only people who knew that Max was calling Annabelle were"—I ticked them off on my fingers—"Max himself, Gregory Taft, from whom Max got her phone number last summer, and then me—I don't think there's much chance Greg and Giulia would be talking to *anyone* about her, let alone *you,* but that doesn't even matter, because they've been out of the country for the past few months while all of this was going on. But ten days ago I mentioned to you," I explained, "that *I* knew who was calling her—I made the mistake of assuming that you'd never guess who I meant, because I forgot that you knew the story of the weekend."

"I'm not getting you, buddy," Nick said, elbows on sodden knees, voice echoing in the building's early-morning silence. "What makes you so sure I had the goods?"

"You called the Lineage Institute in *June,* asking for Douglas," I said. "That's *two months* before you found out about the Naget deal, Nick—right around the time you started hanging out with Annabelle. And we *know* your phone number was at Douglas' apartment—it must have been, or that neighbor could never have called you the night he got hurt."

"I called Douglas, it's true," Nick said. "But how does that—"

"What kept bothering me," I continued quietly, undercutting Nick's voice, "was that I never understood why Annabelle suddenly decided to tell me everything. It actually took me a while to figure it out, since I'd made a mistake—I kept thinking you called Lineage from *Kathy's* house because I spoke too fast and Carol Casey thought she recognized the name. But it was the night you were with Tina, wasn't it? The night you mentioned to me at the hospital, when you said that Tina had asked after me—she told me that you'd been having a rough night and you took her out to dinner. Carol *heard* Tina's guitar— You might as well say. You must have *really* wanted to reach him."

"Yeah, I called Lineage from Tina's house. It's true," Nick said, leaning his head back against the wall, glaring past me as he extended his boots into the dimly lit room. "Nobody had the kid's number, but Tina knew where he worked. What's your point?"

"It must have been a *big deal,* when you and Tina talked," I said, moving a box of computer paper out of the way and sitting cross-legged on the floor. "You both played it cool, but it must have been a hell of a conversation, Nick. So what made you go to Tina?" I asked gently. "What happened that night?"

"She didn't say?" Nick asked quietly, his sandy voice wavering. "Annabelle never told you?"

"No," I assured him. "I promise."

"The night I made a move on her," Nick said hoarsely, looking at the floor between his feet. "During the summer, when we were hanging out after we'd gotten back to being friends again—I mean, we'd just been out walking around the Village, this beautiful summer evening, and we'd sat on that damn couch for hours and finally I couldn't help myself any more and I reached for her face"—Nick was barely audible—"and suddenly she was crying, flinching away like a fucking child. And I *apologized,* I kept saying I was *sorry,* but she just got up and ran upstairs to her bedroom, slammed the door, and I just— I couldn't figure out why it had been so *bad* for her, being touched. So finally I left, and I don't really know what kind of dangerous state I was in, but I ended up calling Tina." I watched Nick's eyes, waiting for him to continue. "Tina said come on over, we had dinner like she told you, and finally I asked her about Annabelle. I was *desperate,* Mike—I'd just gotten her back, you know, and I didn't want to lose her again—and finally Tina asked me if I could keep a secret, and she told me this weird story about graduation weekend."

"So what made you decide to call Douglas?"

"Tina begged me not to," Nick said, smiling gently as he audibly scratched the damp back of his neck. "I guess she might have had a point—I mean, there really was no way I could get the Tafts back together, get them to see each other, and even if I *could,* you know, that was no guarantee it would break Annabelle's fucking mental block—but after seeing Annabelle pull that shit, you know, I was willing to try anything."

"Tina must have been angry," I said, fiddling with the plastic shards of the ruined cassette box.

"Yeah," said Nick, smiling distractedly as he remembered. "I think she blamed herself—I mean, breaking Anna's *confidence,* you know, finally betraying the secret after all these years. So finally Tina realized she couldn't talk me out of trying to reach Douglas—I remember she was so angry, she just went into the other room and played the guitar while I called and talked to that babe at Lineage." Nick yawned with deep fatigue as he resettled against the dark rainwater stain he'd printed onto the couch, rubbing his eyes and then eventually looking at me. "Listen, Mike," he said quietly, "I'm sorry I fucked you over. The hospital, the Naget deal, what I—what I did to you both."

"If you hadn't done it Tina never would have urged Annabelle to talk to me," I told him. "A couple days after Ralph died I went down to Annabelle's house for my, you know, for my so-called DiGrassi investigation, and after I'd made a mess of things and left, Annabelle was in such a state of distress that I'm *sure* she called Tina and told her about all of my questions." I stood up off the cluttered floor, stretching as I looked at Nick and rubbing my eyes with my other hand. "You say Tina felt guilty during the *summer,* talking to you, but once she knew *I* was poking around she must have been *amazed* at the damage she'd thought she'd done by telling you the secret. And the next day they both contacted me."

"I was so *furious* at that bitch when she wouldn't get me the Octane deal," Nick said distantly. "But the important thing was to *deserve* the job."

"I thought all you wanted to do is beat the system," I said, frowning in confusion.

"Beat the system and you gain nothing," Nick said firmly. "It's better to lose. But I did have to hurt her, and now—" He shook his head as he trailed off and then leaning forward, retrieving his camera as he slowly lunged upward to stand next to me.

"So you did tell her it was Max," I said, glancing over at the manuscript on my desk.

"Well, of course I did it," said Nick angrily. "What did you think? Remember, I'd *seen* Raymond. Tina told me all his— Look, Mike, do you think I enjoyed seeing her with that middle-aged *fuck?* I'd missed her for *years* and she looked so *young* this summer, so full of life, Mike, and— And it's all such a fucking waste." Nick had slung the camera under his arm and had begun leading me toward my front door. "After I left your house the night you started writing," he continued wearily, "I was sitting on the express train and I realized Max was the one, and when I got home I called Annabelle and told her. But look, buddy, let's just not pretend it's anything but pure *futility,* all right?"

"How'd you get over her?" I asked quietly.

Nick had led us down the dark corridor to the doorway, retracing his wet footprints, and I stood behind him, watching the wet back of his motionless bowed head and waiting as he faced his own shadow before turning back.

"I didn't," Nick said. "Until today."

"You didn't *go,* did you?" I asked. "The memorial?"

"Neither did you," said Nick, his sandy voice echoing against the featureless corridor walls with the distant pattering of the rain. "I'll bet everything I've got in my bedroom. Listen, buddy"— Nick was suddenly grinning at me as he touched my shoulder with his finger— "didn't *Bill* put a cigarette out in Senator Rollins' shoe? I mean, it sure as hell wasn't *me.*"

"I changed a few things," I admitted.

"I should go," Nick sighed as he checked my watch and then looked around as he pulled his overcoat shut. "I've got to leave for Billings in a few hours, damn it— I've got just enough time to make it home and pack as it is, and now you've got me doing—"

"Billings?"

"Billings, Montana," Nick explained. "I've got to get out there to finish the Octane session—I've been hanging around New York too long anyway. I'll get back around Thanksgiving—maybe I'll give you a call and you can meet me at the station."

"All right," I said, nodding as I reached to unlatch and open the apartment door. "Well— Have a good trip."

"Wait a minute," Nick said, looking at me suddenly. "Stand still."

"What—" I stood transfixed as Nick slowly raised his camera to his face and pointed its lens at me, seeing myself reflected in the lens before the strobe blinded me—blinking away the flash's retinal aftermath, I peered through the dark apartment air and saw Nick grinning as he lowered the camera.

"You and me, man," Nick said, nodding as he caught my eye, his overcoat swaying heavily as he stepped into the dark hallway and reached to pull the door shut. I locked the door behind him and returned to the living room window, leaning against the storm window's metal age looking out into the soft rain, stretching my cramped and aching back and gazing above the black outlines of the slumbering nearby buildings as the first hint of grey dawn light touched the sky. I stood there for a while, feeling oddly rested and awake, noticing the beginnings of my morning hunger as I checked my watch and realized I'd be going in to work soon, and then I suddenly remembered the crumpled, ancient pack of White Camels that I'd carried in my overcoat all through the previous day, and while hunting through my coat pockets in search of the pack of Anthesteria matches that were on the desk I came across the envelope that Tina had given me in Union Square and ripped it open to extract a single sheet of notepaper containing a handwritten message—

MICHAEL—THANK YOU—XOXO—AT

—and suddenly the telephone rang and I dropped the note, the last White Camel dropping unlit from my mouth as I inadvertently jumped and then reached to pick up the receiver, clearing my throat before answering. "Hello?" said a very young female voice, her voice strangely garbled and distorted, as if she spoke from within a subway tunnel. "Is this Michael Cadenhead?"

"I can barely hear you," I said, suddenly hearing a clipped electronic tone.

"Okay—that was the speakerphone," the young woman explained, her voice having jumped into clarity. "Listen, I'm sorry to bother you but Hector said— I just got your number from Hector Costanza and he said you kept funny hours and I could call. Hey, you're the guy that wrote that *thing,* aren't you? That big story— Are you a writer or something?"

"I'm a journalist," I said.

"Well, I saw a few pages—it looks *really* juicy," the young woman told me. "Listen, I'm trying to reach Nick Blanchard, actually—he said he went to see you but he's been *gone* so long—"

"Is this Kathy?" I asked suddenly as I remembered. "Kathy *Schall*, right?"

"That's *right*," Kathy answered brightly. "Listen, no big deal—I was just hoping to reach Nick and get him to come home 'cause I'm going to have to get to *school* in a few hours and I don't have money for a cab—I've been cramming for a test all night and I've got to get there on *time* for once."

I stood there with the phone pressed to my face and my other hand jammed into my hair above my forehead, absolutely unable to free my face from the smile that paralyzed me while I tried to talk.

"Hello?" said Kathy.

"He's on his way to you," I finally answered. "You won't have to wait long."

"Cool," said Kathy. "He's a good guy but I was afraid I'd have to take the fucking subway out of this bad area— You're in Brooklyn, right? Near Coney Island— Shit, maybe I should be seeing *you*. Anyway, thanks a lot, Mr. Cadenhead."

"Goodbye, Kathy," I said, hanging up the phone.

THOSE WERE BROOKLYN days for me and I was far away but I know what finally happened at five-thirty that November afternoon—how Max Gantry emerged from the Lexington Avenue cathedral into the bright daylight, standing still against the outward tide of black-clothed mourners and gazing at the surface of a flawless white building that stood before the sky as if sculpted there like ice against glass. Max felt a clean wind across the cathedral steps as he breathed the cold air with a surety borne of the great weight that had lifted from his heart, hearing the slamming limousine doors and smiling openly at the welcome clutching of his throat as a wild flock of indistinguishable high-altitude birds shimmered across the distant fading sky.

"You've done a man's job," Walter Patterson said, stepping easily forward and reaching to grasp Max's hand. "You should be proud."

"Thanks, Walter," Max said, grinning at him and feeling a hot shimmer in his own eyes.

"It's true," Stephen Leonard affirmed from Max's other side. "I think you really got to everyone."

"I'm so glad you guys were here," Max told them, his voice catching heavily in his throat as he turned his head back and forth, looking fondly at them both.

"Well, it's the whole wrestling team at once," said a distantly familiar overblown male voice behind them—Max, Stephen and Walter turned and were surprised to see the lean, mildly aging figure of Nathan Chablis standing behind them, his overly tight-fitting bottle-green suit and stern double-breasted worsted coat emphasizing his stooped flower-stem posture like a bandaged arm. "I was hoping to come across some of the old crowd," Chablis told them warmly, adjusting his familiar tortoiseshell glasses above the trimmed edges of his greying beard. "Hello, boys."

"Mr. Chablis," Stephen said as they all turned fully around, ignoring the jostling passage of the men and women leaving the cathedral, bouncing on his toes as he took Chablis' warm, narrow hand. "How are you?"

"Oh, I'm getting along quite passably," Chablis told them, skating his eyes between their faces, the effect of his well-remembered classroom scrutiny dampened by their increased height. "The usual assortment of ignorant young scholars are creating the usual havoc. And you? I assume you've all turned into figures of Herculean importance?"

"Well, we're managing," Walter said, awkwardly extending the handshake.

"Stephen, Wally, and—*Garland,* is it?" Chablis recited, squinting severely at Max as they shook hands. "I'm sorry."

"Gantry," Max said, laughing. "Max Gantry."

"So tell me," Chablis said sternly, peering at them with exaggerated collusion while continuing to shake Max's hand. "How does it feel to be five years out?"

Max held Chablis' gaze, looking into the teacher's grey eyes as his beard bristled against his well-starched collar. "It feels good," Max said.

"You spoke beautifully," Chablis gravely told him, as he held on to Max's hand. "I was privileged to have known Ralph quite well. He was in all respects a remarkable young man—had he been able to witness the size of this gathering I'm sure he'd have been humbled and proud at such a demonstration of friendship and love."

"Thank you," Max managed to say, sniffling as his voice finally broke and reaching to wipe his eyes. "Thank you."

"I'm sure you're right," Walter said as Stephen nodded, his eyes flashing.

"Listen, Mr. Chablis," Stephen said, hunching his shoulders as the city wind picked up, "we were just thinking of hitting the Oak Bar—would you want to join us for a drink?"

"Well, I've only an hour free, unfortunately"—Chablis had extracted a platinum pocket watch from within his lapel and he fumbled it open, frowning over his glasses at its ornamented face before raising his head and then his eyebrows—"But I'd like that very much."

"Great," Walter said, stepping with a trace of his former athlete's grace out of the way of the lumbering pair of Reed Gardner Grant partners that were the last of the departing crowd as Max casually gazed into the cathedral's open doors, vaguely discerning the darkened altar and the outlines of the gilt cross. "You've got to be somewhere?"

"Thorndike," Chablis told them self-effacingly, following Walter's lead toward the sidewalk while Stephen began scanning the traffic for taxicabs. "I share the dubious honor of preparing this year's seniors for their College Board examinations—we spend a dreary ninety minutes every Monday night."

"Max?" Stephen called from between two parked cars, arm in the air, gazing inquisitively back toward the others. "You coming with us?"

Max slowly descended the cathedral steps, shoes clapping the worn granite. "I don't think so," he answered after a moment. "Thanks, really, but I think I'll just walk home—some other time, maybe."

"All right," Walter said, nodding amicably as Stephen waded into the traffic, beckoning a checker cab. "I'm in the book."

"Me too," Stephen said, yanking open the cab door, Chablis waiting diffidently behind him. "Take care, Max."

Max returned Chablis' wave and watched the taxicab vanish into the traffic, his hands in his trouser pockets as he turned back toward the cathedral, where Frank and Amelia DiGrassi were descending from the oaken door, Amelia reaching to adjust her veiled black hat against the rising wind as Frank protectively held her arm and helped her down the steps. Stepping forward, Max took a deep breath as the DiGrassis registered his presence and softened their expressions.

"Thank you, Max," Frank said heavily, his wife's gloved grip tenting the fabric of his dark overcoat as he extended his free arm. "Thank you for everything."

"I only did what I could," Max said gently, enfolding Frank's hand in both of his.

"Thank you, Max," Amelia whispered almost inaudibly, turning her pale face downward as she gripped her husband's arm, and Max reached to squeeze her trembling shoulder.

"There's somebody here to see you," Frank told him abruptly, releasing Amelia's arm and looking around, his gaze clearing as he reached to smooth his oiled black hair.

"What?" Max said, confused, looking between passersby at the near-deserted landscape of the street and then back at the DiGrassis as they stepped apart to reveal where Annabelle Taft stood alone on the sidewalk, wearing a black dress under her overcoat, the early evening light shining in her soft black hair as she raised her face to smile at him.

"Hello, Max Gantry," Annabelle said.

"Annabelle," Max finally managed to exhale as he stepped inadvertently toward her. "Annabelle Taft."

"I'm sorry I didn't find you beforehand," Annabelle told him, stepping primly forward, hair falling across her shoulders, earrings flashing. "I was a little bit late to this thing."

"That's—" Max swallowed as he spoke, and Annabelle watched him patiently, a lovely nervous movement of her eyebrows belying her composed gaze. "That's all right. I didn't know you were coming. I didn't know you were here."

"We'll be going home now, Max," Frank DiGrassi's voice toppled onto Max's ear, almost making him flinch. "Don't worry about us— She's been very anxious to see you and I know better than to get in her way."

"I'm sorry," Max said, turning back toward the DiGrassis. "Do you want me to come with you?"

"Oh, you've already been a saint," Amelia said quietly, smiling fondly at Max and leaning to kiss his cheek, releasing a wave of perfume. "We'll see you soon enough."

"Well, if you're sure," Max said, shaking Frank's hand again, and he nodded firmly at both DiGrassis as they stepped toward their waiting limousine before he turned back toward Annabelle, facing her for a moment before the cathedral steps until she awkwardly turned toward the nearby intersection and they began walking side by side.

"I didn't see you in the church," Max said after a moment, looking over at her as they crossed the avenue and noticing, as she gazed back at him, that the street had begun to darken into the indigo shadows that only show before the streetlights ignite, during the fleeting hour before true dusk.

"There were cameras," Annabelle explained. "I ran the gauntlet and spoke to Frank but I didn't want to make a spectacle of myself so I stayed by the baptistery. I saw *you.*" Annabelle smiled.

"Really?"

"Well, you're hard to miss," said Annabelle. "When we all sat down—I was watching but I wasn't *sure* it was you until you went up there. You didn't see me staring?"

"Didn't see a thing," Max said. "You believe me?"

The midtown cross street that they'd wandered onto had darkened like a canyon and Max and Annabelle walked around the awning-shadowed edge of a delicatessen's sidewalk flower table, its regimented rows of flowerpots wrapped in green and silver crumpled foil.

"It's good to see you," Max said hesitantly. "I'm— It's just so good to see you."

"God, I've got so much to tell you," Annabelle said, stepping closer to him and gazing straight ahead.

"I'm— I guess I'm supposed to ask about your career," Max said, putting his hands in his pockets. "Right?"

"Short topic," Annabelle said. "I'm set for a few years at least."

"Maybe you'll get to the top, right?" said Max, gazing at the sidewalk and then back at her. "I mean, there has to be a world's top model."

"I suppose there has to be," said Annabelle dismissively. "It's just a revenue question. You look beautiful, Max. I'm— You just look so good." Max turned his head as he heard the surprising hidden voltage of her voice, looking at her as they walked and stepping closer, and Annabelle put her arm in his as they kept walking. "Listen, did you know that woman that—the woman who left halfway through?"

"That was so strange," Max said, shaking his head. "Yeah, I met her right before, actually—she came up to me and said she was a friend of Douglas' and asked if I'd, you know, if he was here."

"Was her name Carol?" Annabelle asked, tightening her grip on his arm and reaching with her other hand toward the rough tweed of his lapel. "That's Carol?"

"I think so," Max said.

"Good," Annabelle said. "Douglas did the brave thing."

"I'm not going to ask," Max said, looking down at Annabelle as she smiled up at him in the pale overcast light.

"I— Listen, Max," Annabelle murmured, feigning breathlessness, turning her bright face toward his. "When you spoke—"

"Yes?" Max asked, looking back at her, their faces a few inches apart—Max heard the growing sounds of Park Avenue's traffic as he inhaled the aroma of Annabelle's hair.

"That thing you said about falling in love once," Annabelle asked, eyes flashing at him. "Did you mean it?"

"What part of it?"

"The love part," Annabelle said, very quietly, looking past Max's shoulder at the blue shadows across the quiet street.

"Yes," Max said. "Of course I meant it." They arrived onto Park Avenue and stood on the wide sidewalk surrounded by a vertical sea of bright windows that faced the evening sky. "But I said I didn't understand love and I meant that too."

"I'm not exactly sure I know how it works either," Annabelle said, stopping suddenly and hanging back and then reaching as Max turned to wrap her fingers lightly in the loose fabric of his overcoat, carelessly tugging at his lapels as she stepped backward. "Are you as nervous as I am?"

"*Oh,* yeah," Max said, looking easily away, staring down the receding distances of the darkening avenue as they both laughed and fell clumsily together, their arms around each other, Max feeling Annabelle's hair against his face and the warmth of her body against his, both of them laughing as he moved his hands tightly on her back.

"I missed you," said Annabelle, her voice muffled by Max's shoulder.

"I missed you so much," Max said, moving his hand to gently stroke the back of her head as she gripped him tightly. "During the summer, the summer afterwards, before school, I would— I used to look at the sky at night— I'd look at the Milky Way and I'd think about you and I was so sad."

"I was sad too," Annabelle murmured, her voice thickening.

"What's wrong, Annabelle?" Max whispered, feeling her body

beginning to tremble in his arms and turning his head so that his mouth brushed against her ear.

"Nothing's wrong," Annabelle whispered into Max's lapel, laughing self-consciously. "I'm shaking, for Christ's sake."

Max felt that he could barely breathe as he gently raised his arm and touched his fingers against the soft and warm surface of Annabelle's cheek and turned her face upward toward his, his eyes brimming, his breath catching as he felt Annabelle's hand slide up his coat and onto the back of his neck as her mouth opened and met his, and as they kissed Max caressed the curves of her face and moved his hands down the backs of her shoulders, his strong arms pulling her close to him as her eyelashes brushed the wet unshaven surface of his skin, and when the kiss ended and their heads drew slowly apart Max saw the stricken look on Annabelle's beautiful face and cried as he gently kissed her again, tenderly touching her and smiling as he cried.

"This is strange," Annabelle whispered, blinking in the soft light of dusk.

"I know," Max murmured.

"I always wanted to kiss you," Annabelle whispered, her shaking fingers moving under his lapel and brushing his chest.

"Me too," Max said, suddenly smiling and looking shyly down at the pavement.

"What?" Annabelle murmured, narrowing her eyes. "What's so funny?"

"Nothing. I know this joke," Max said, cradling her head against his shoulder and gazing at the vast avenue behind her. "It's about a guy who looks like whoever he's with."

"I haven't heard it," Annabelle said, squeezing her arms around him.

"Well, he goes up to another guy and immediately he looks just like him."

"Yeah?" Annabelle whispered, moving her head and gently biting his ear.

"And after he's done it, he says, How about that?" Max murmured, his eyes blurred, his mouth grazing against her forehead. "And the other guy says, What do you mean? So the first guy goes, Well, look— We're the same."

"Uh huh." Annabelle nodded as Max drew a shaking breath.

"So the other guy notices, and he says, that's great—but next time could we look like me rather than you?"

"There's another joke like that," Annabelle said, stroking a hand against Max's neck and jaw. "Two very sad people side by side not talking."

"Okay—"

"And then one of them suddenly says to the other one, I'm all alone in the world," Annabelle continued, her breath catching as Max looked down at her. "And the other one smiles and says, You too?"

"Stand in the sun with me," Max said quietly as they pulled together under the overcast November sky.

"I'll stand with you," Annabelle said, hugging him tightly.

Annabelle and Max stood with their arms around each other a block from the cathedral as dusk fell across the city, and many hours later, very early Tuesday morning, Douglas abruptly awoke in an unfamiliar bedroom, leaning to brush Carol's hair from her face before lifting the window to breathe the early wind from the river, and when the morning light shone over the rooftops Douglas was watching. Everyone else was still asleep but I was awake, ushering in another of those days when the minted air of winter has arrived and the parks are orange and green with the wet November leaves and the trampled grass. I'm still here.

THIRST

STEPHEN AMIDON

'A gifted and subtle piece of fiction' *The Guardian*

'*Thirst* is a brilliant novel and, true to its title, it leaves you crying for more. It is extremely gripping with a narrative fizzing with paradox and irony.' *Times Literary Supplement*

Daniel's alcoholic father Cal walked out on his family to dry out in the parched, ravaged landscape of Phoenix, Arizona. Now, thirteen years later, Daniel travels to the lunar wastelands of the American desert to unravel the mystery of his father's strange life on the margins of human existence.

'Humour and clarity characterise Amidon's writing which has never been tauter. His fraught, staccato prose maintains the momentum until the very last tension-saturated chapter. Couched in an impressive, intelligent thriller is an apocalyptic reminder of how 20th century life is encroaching on the natural world.' *Sunday Telegraph*

TOUCHSTONE
Fiction
ISBN: 0 671 71798 7
PRICE: £5.99

TONY AND SUSAN

AUSTIN WRIGHT

'Austin Wright's mesmerising novel... is absolutely irresistible' *The New York Times*

'*Tony and Susan* is marvellously written – the last thing you would expect in a story of blood and revenge' Saul Bellow

This startlingly brilliant novel is a gritty psychological thriller wrapped in a contemporary love story. Susan Morrow, a comfortable mother of three, receives the manuscript of a novel written by her first husband. He wants her to read it. Why? As she becomes engrossed in the chilling story of Tony Hastings, she realises that her life will never be the same again.

'Compelling... a harrowing exploration of the border between civilisation and barbarity, between justice and revenge' *The New York Times*

TOUCHSTONE
Fiction
ISBN: 0 671 71863 0
PRICE: £5.99

SHAMPOO PLANET

DOUGLAS COUPLAND

'A New Age J.D. Salinger on smart drugs' *Time Out*

'A major, authentic voice for a generation' *The Wall Street Journal*

Shampoo Planet tells the story of Tyler Johnson, a tree-hugging Reagan youth with a 'shampoo museum' in his bathroom. It chronicles his six-month journey from his home town of Lancaster, Washington, to Paris, an island in British Columbia, the Redwood Forests, Los Angeles, Hollywood, Seattle and finally back home. Along the way a delightful range of characters play a role in changing Tyler's life: his post-feminist girlfriend, a summer fling that comes back to haunt him, his sister Daisy, her dreadlocked boyfriend, Tyler's money-hoarding grandparents and his mother Jasmine, who offers her rootless son a much needed prescription for human connection.

'Nobody has a better finger on the pulse of the twenty-something generation, and not since the great writing days of Woody Allen has anyone been more hilarious or quotable' – *Cosmopolitan*

TOUCHSTONE
Fiction
ISBN: 0 671 71843 6
PRICE: £5.99